SQUIRE

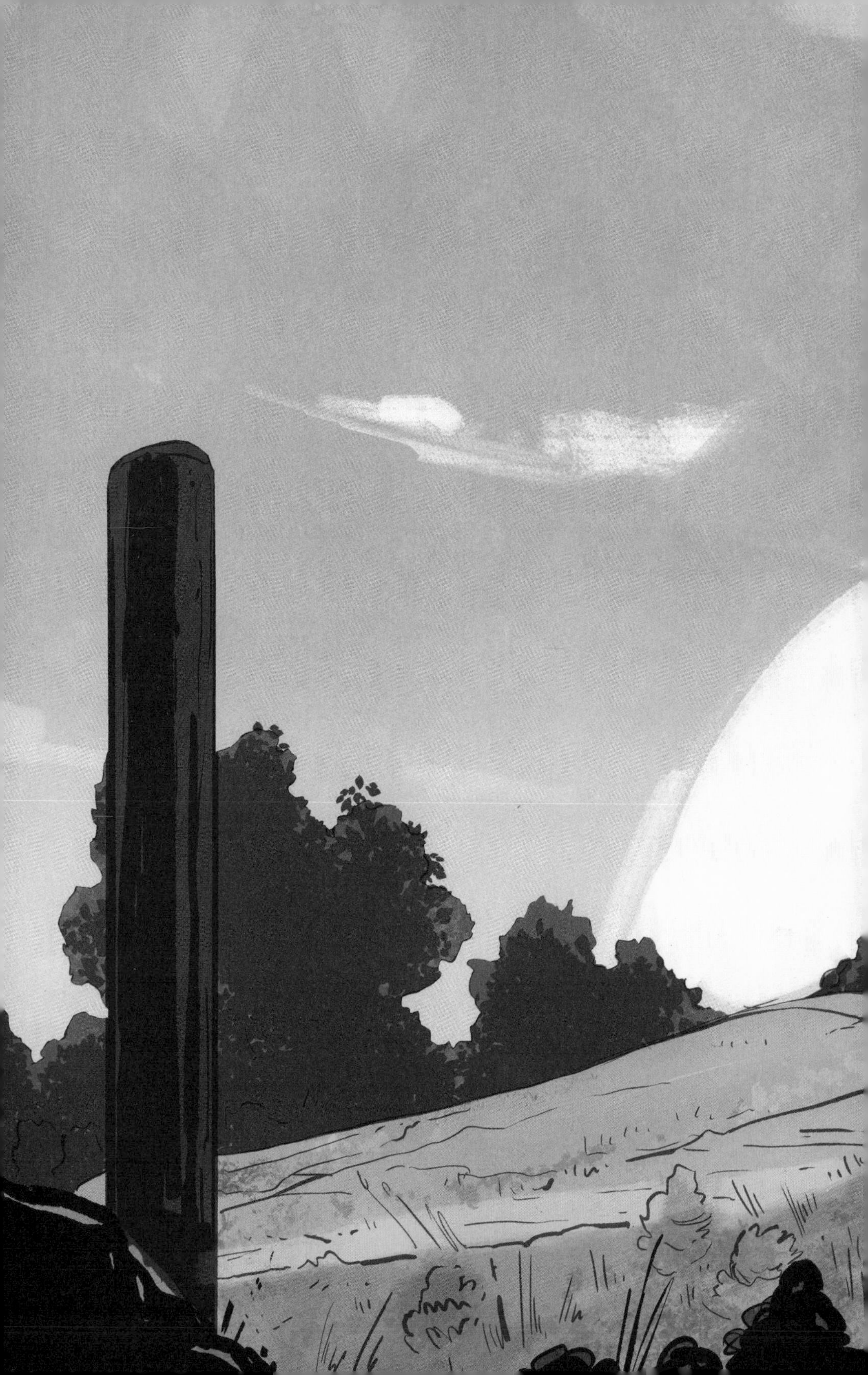

SQUIRE

SARA ALFAGEEH NADIA SHAMMAS

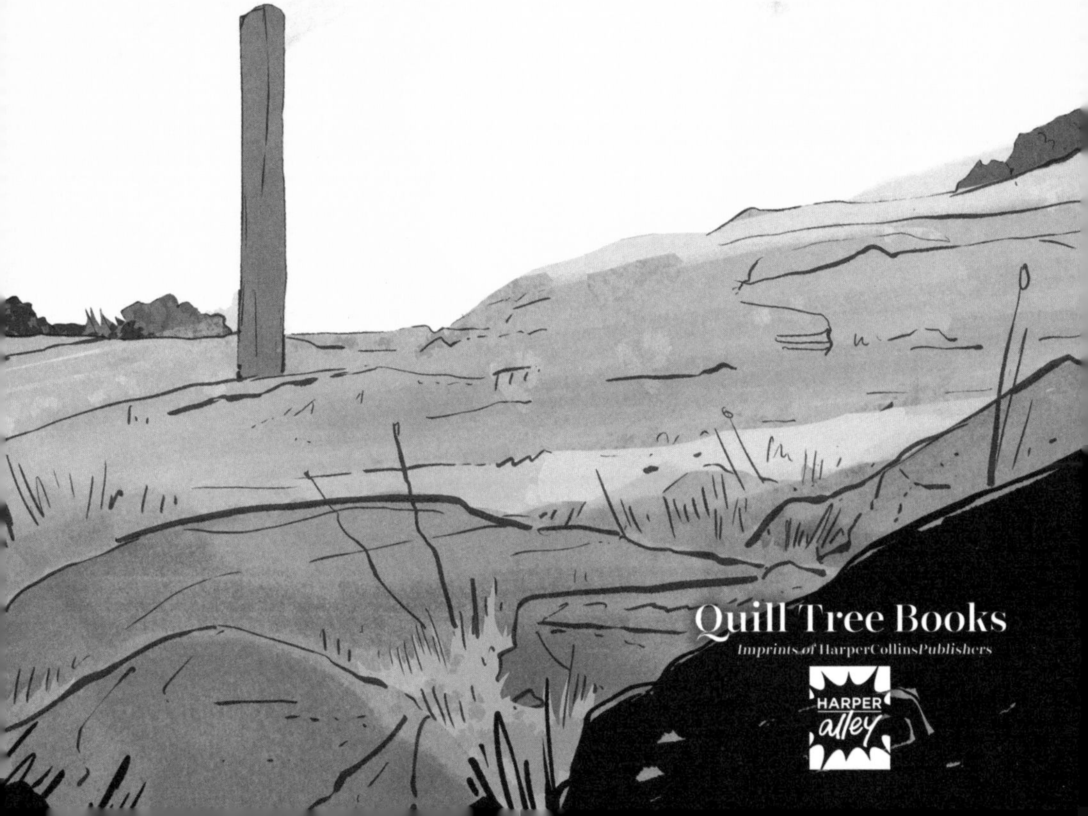

Quill Tree Books
Imprints of HarperCollinsPublishers
HARPER alley

Quill Tree Books and HarperAlley are imprints of HarperCollins Publishers.

Squire
Text copyright © 2022 by Nadia Shammas and Sara Alfageeh
Illustrations copyright © 2022 by Sara Alfageeh
All rights reserved. Manufactured in Italy.
For information address HarperCollins Children's Books, a division of HarperCollins
Publishers, 195 Broadway, New York, NY 10007.
www.harperalley.com

Library of Congress Control Number: 2021941642
ISBN 978-0-06-294584-6 (paperback)—ISBN 978-0-06-294585-3 (hardcover)

21 22 23 24 25 RTLO 10 9 8 7 6 5 4 3 2 1

First Edition

To Edward Said, for giving me the language to see myself clearly.
—N.S.

To ten-year-old Sara and long summers in Jordan.
—S.A.

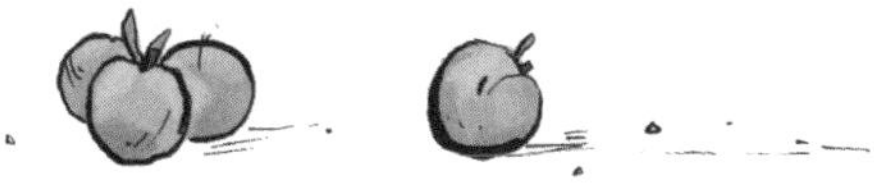

CHAPTER 1

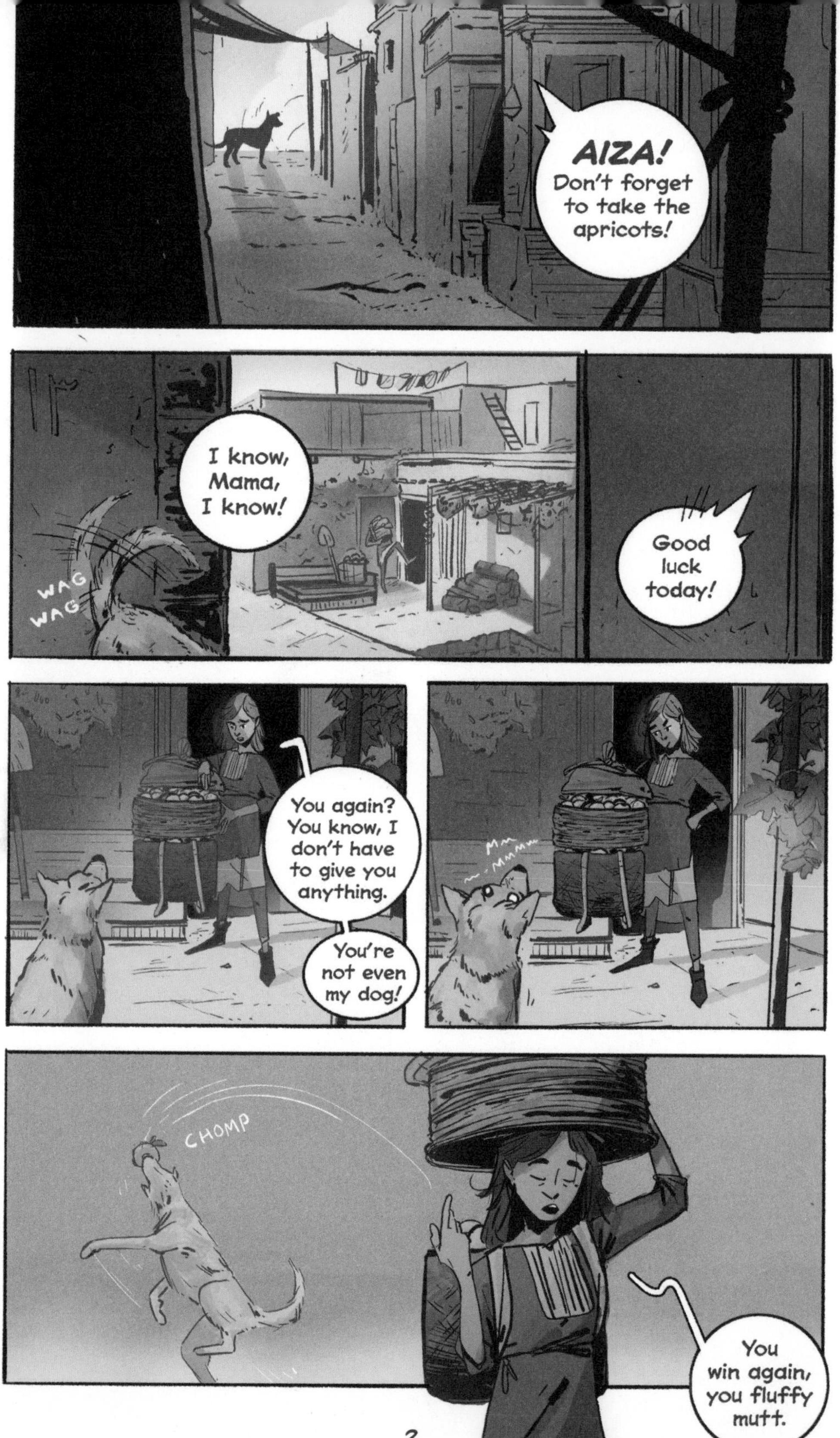
AIZA! Don't forget to take the apricots!
I know, Mama, I know!
WAG WAG
Good luck today!
You again? You know, I don't have to give you anything.
You're not even my dog!
Mm ~Mmm
CHOMP
You win again, you fluffy mutt.

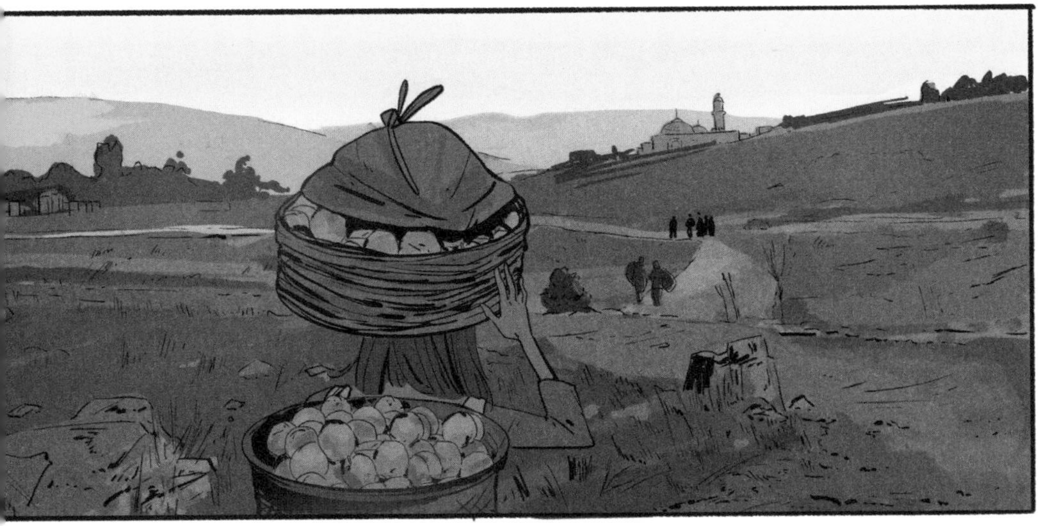

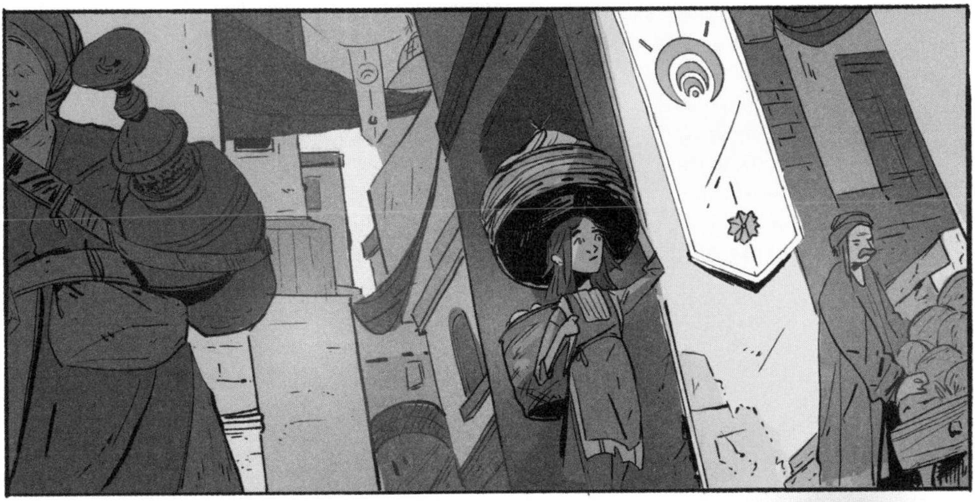

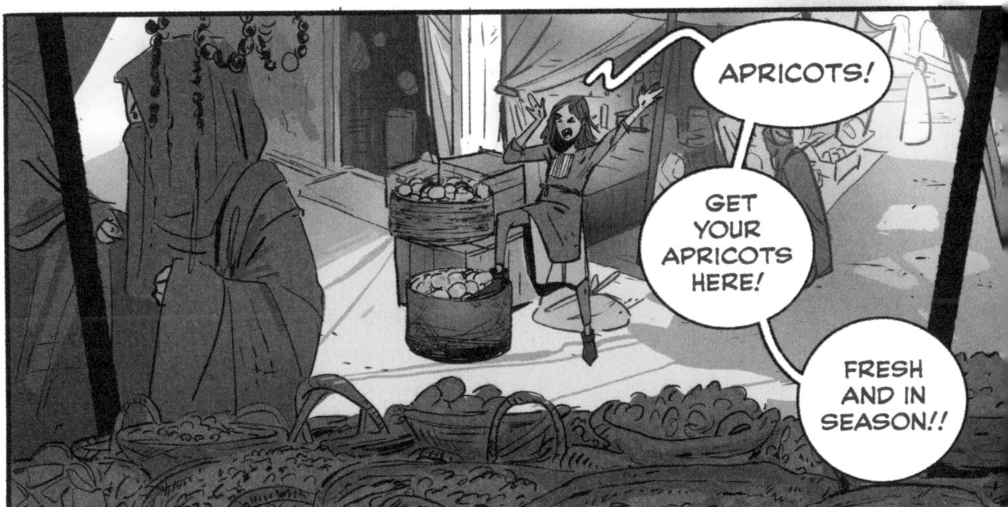
APRICOTS!
GET YOUR APRICOTS HERE!
FRESH AND IN SEASON!!

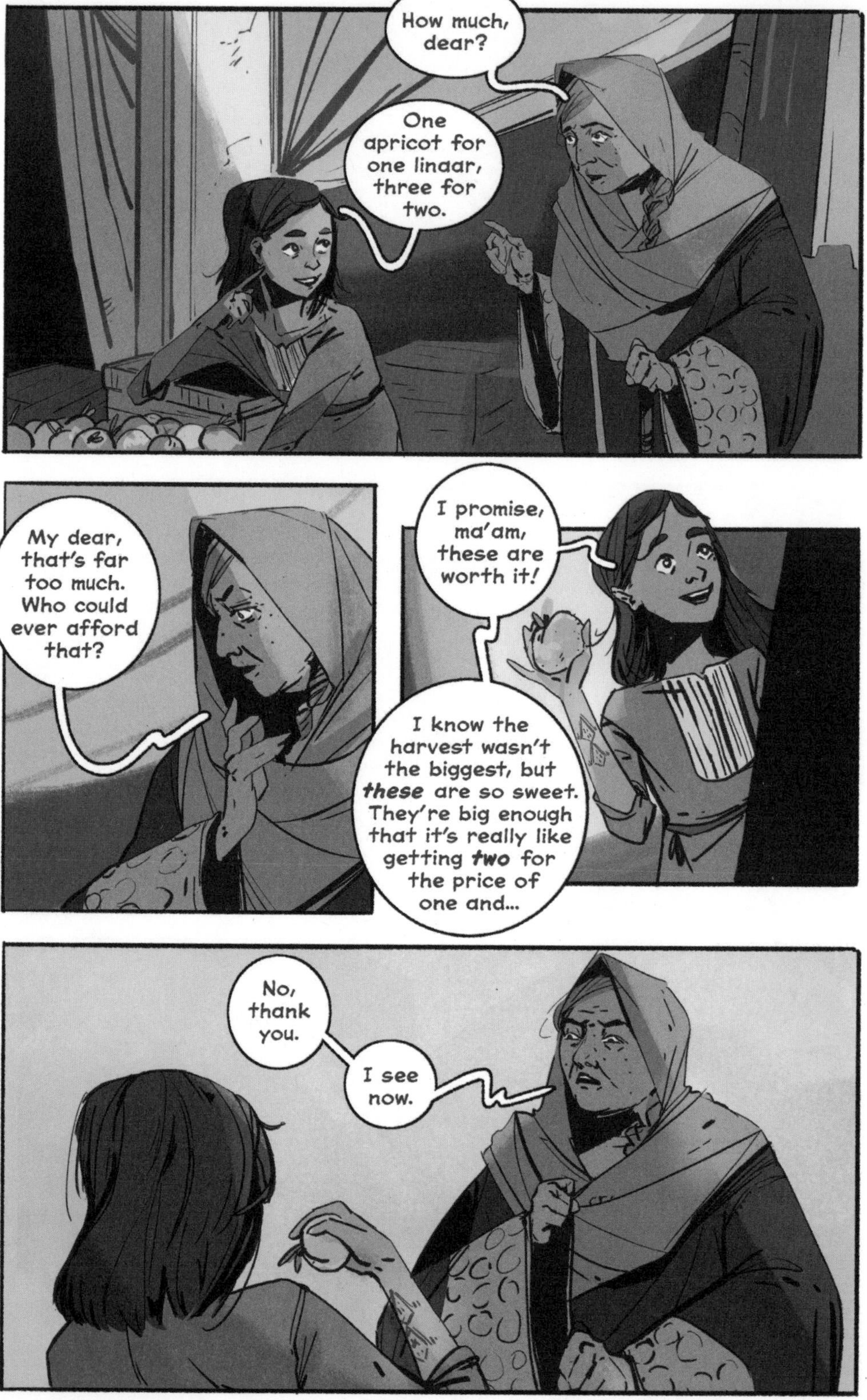
How much, dear?
One apricot for one linaar, three for two.
My dear, that's far too much. Who could ever afford that?
I promise, ma'am, these are worth it!
I know the harvest wasn't the biggest, but *these* are so sweet. They're big enough that it's really like getting *two* for the price of one and...
No, thank you.
I see now.

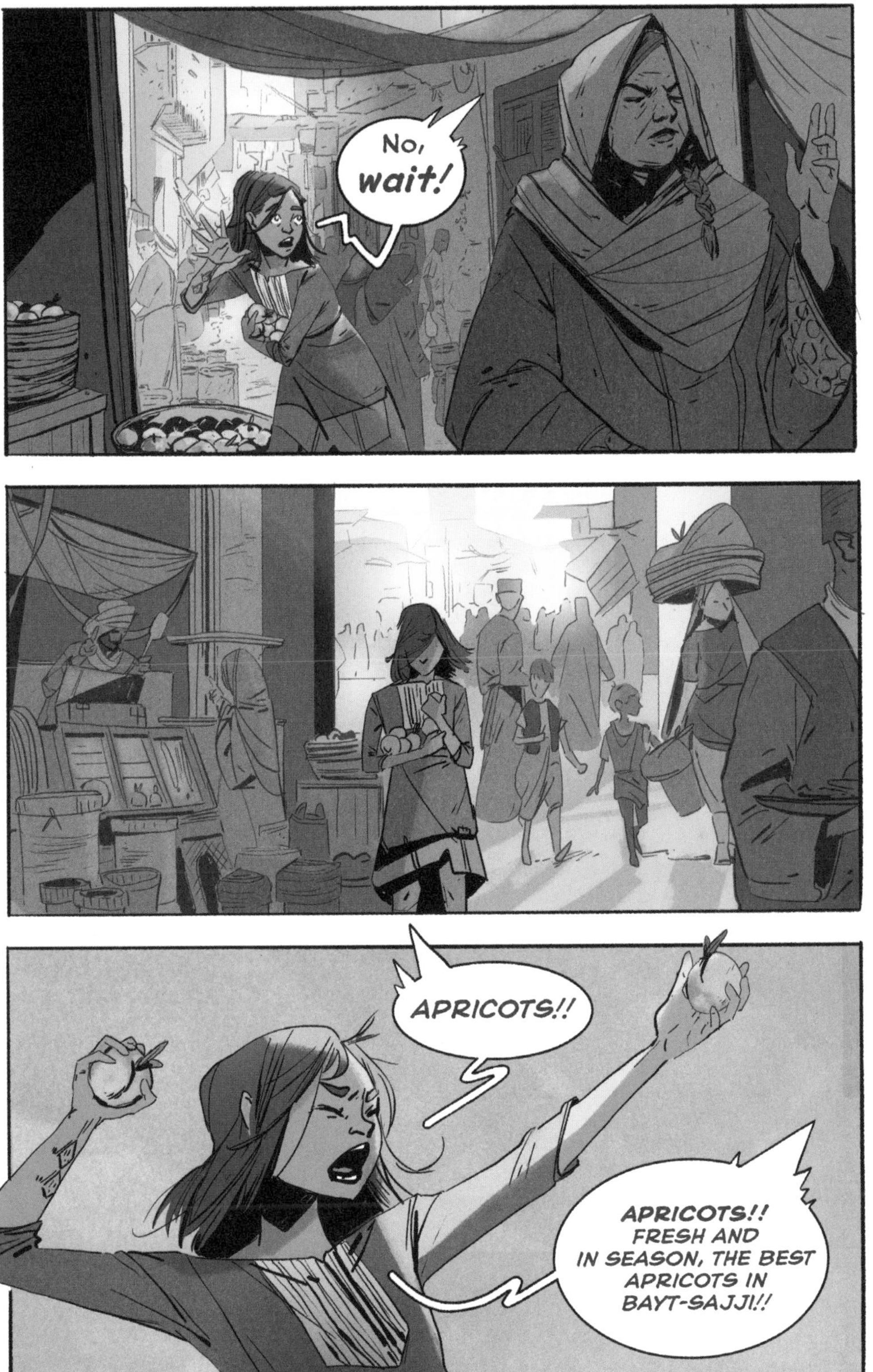
No, wait!
APRICOTS!!
APRICOTS!! FRESH AND IN SEASON, THE BEST APRICOTS IN BAYT-SAJJI!!

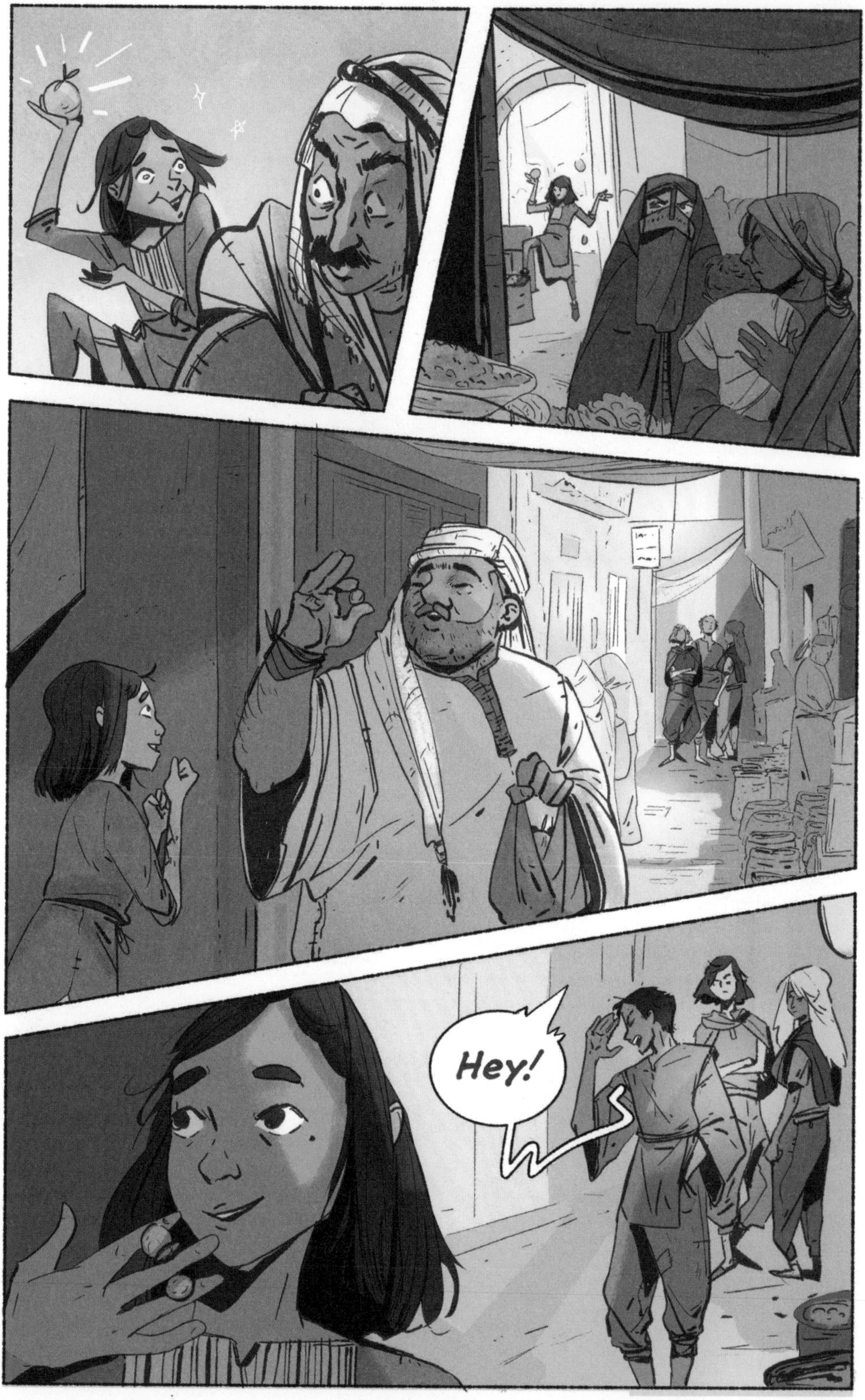
Hey!

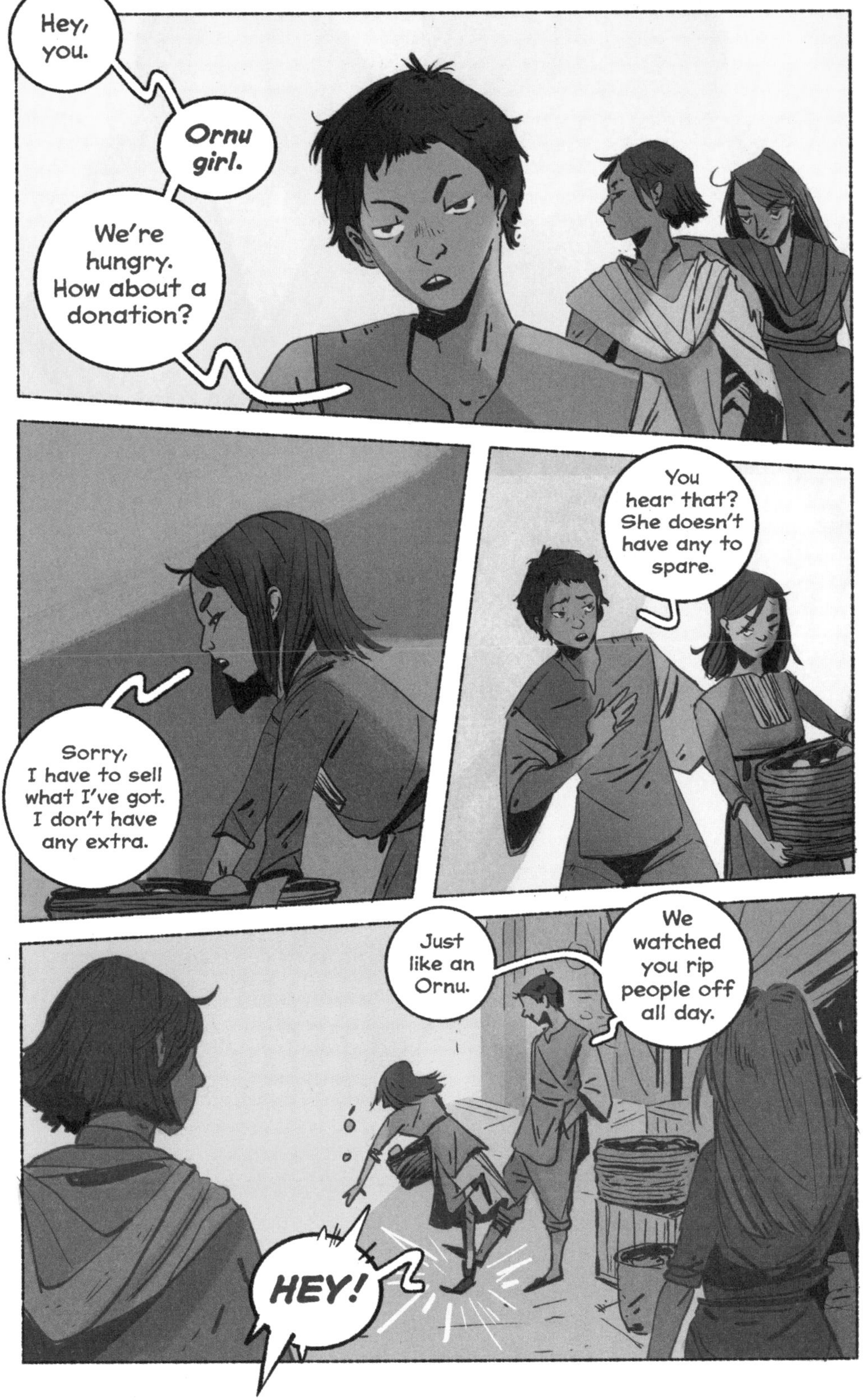
Hey, you.
Ornu girl.
We're hungry. How about a donation?
Sorry, I have to sell what I've got. I don't have any extra.
You hear that? She doesn't have any to spare.
Just like an Ornu.
We watched you rip people off all day.
HEY!

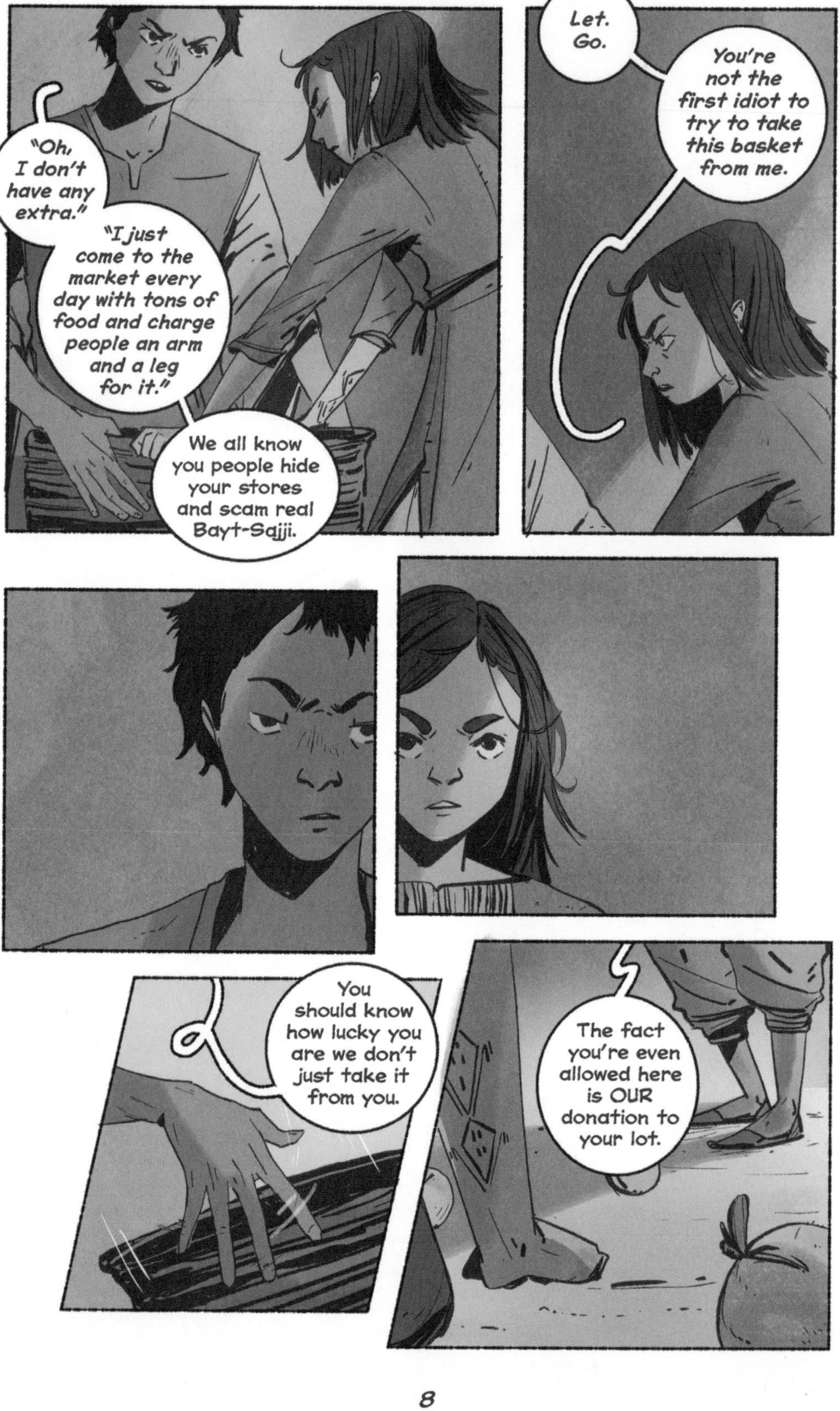
"Oh, I don't have any extra."
"I just come to the market every day with tons of food and charge people an arm and a leg for it."
We all know you people hide your stores and scam real Bayt-Sajji.
Let. Go.
You're not the first idiot to try to take this basket from me.
You should know how lucky you are we don't just take it from you.
The fact you're even allowed here is OUR donation to your lot.

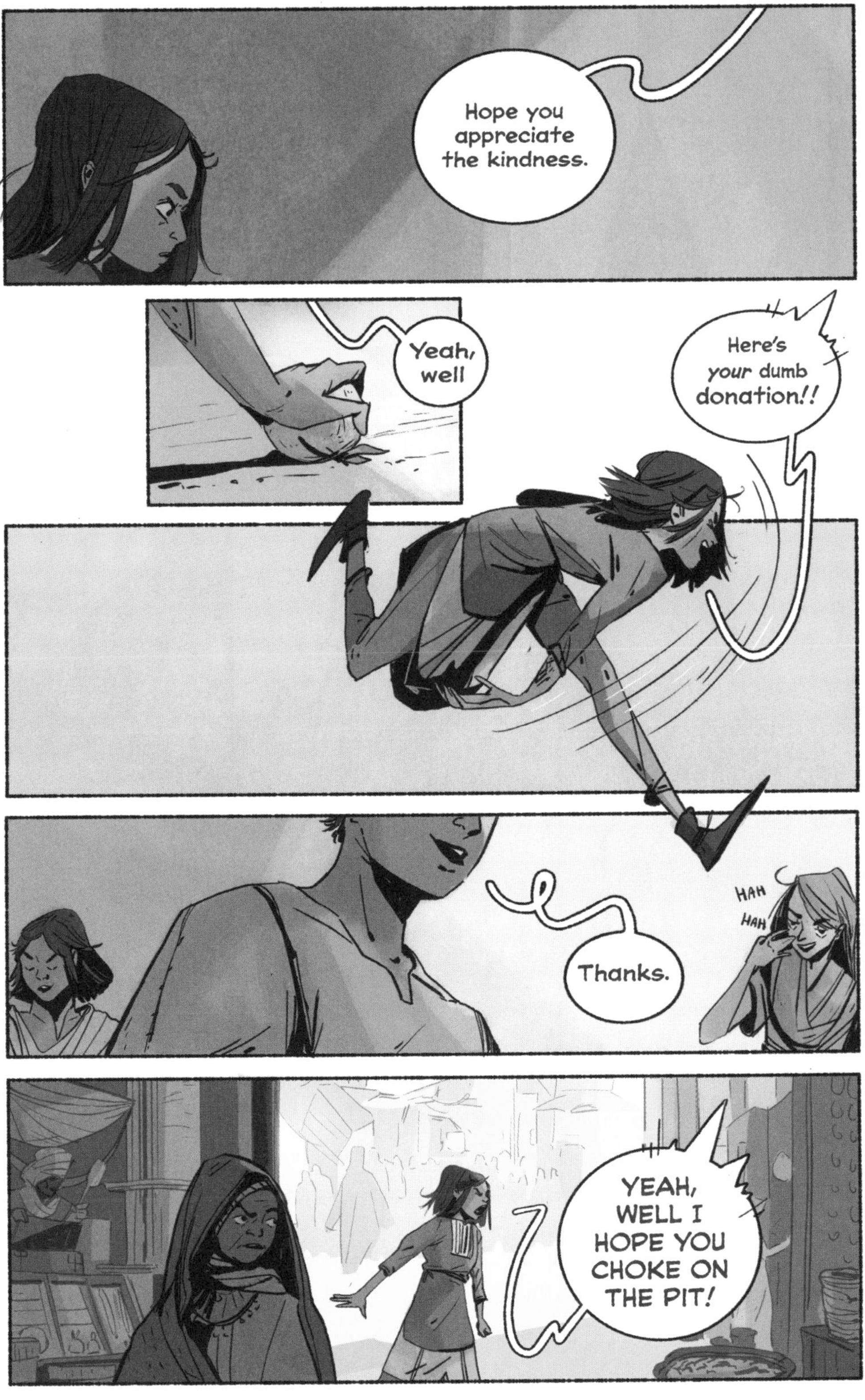
Hope you appreciate the kindness.
Yeah, well
Here's your dumb donation!!
Thanks.
HAH
HAH
YEAH, WELL I HOPE YOU CHOKE ON THE PIT!

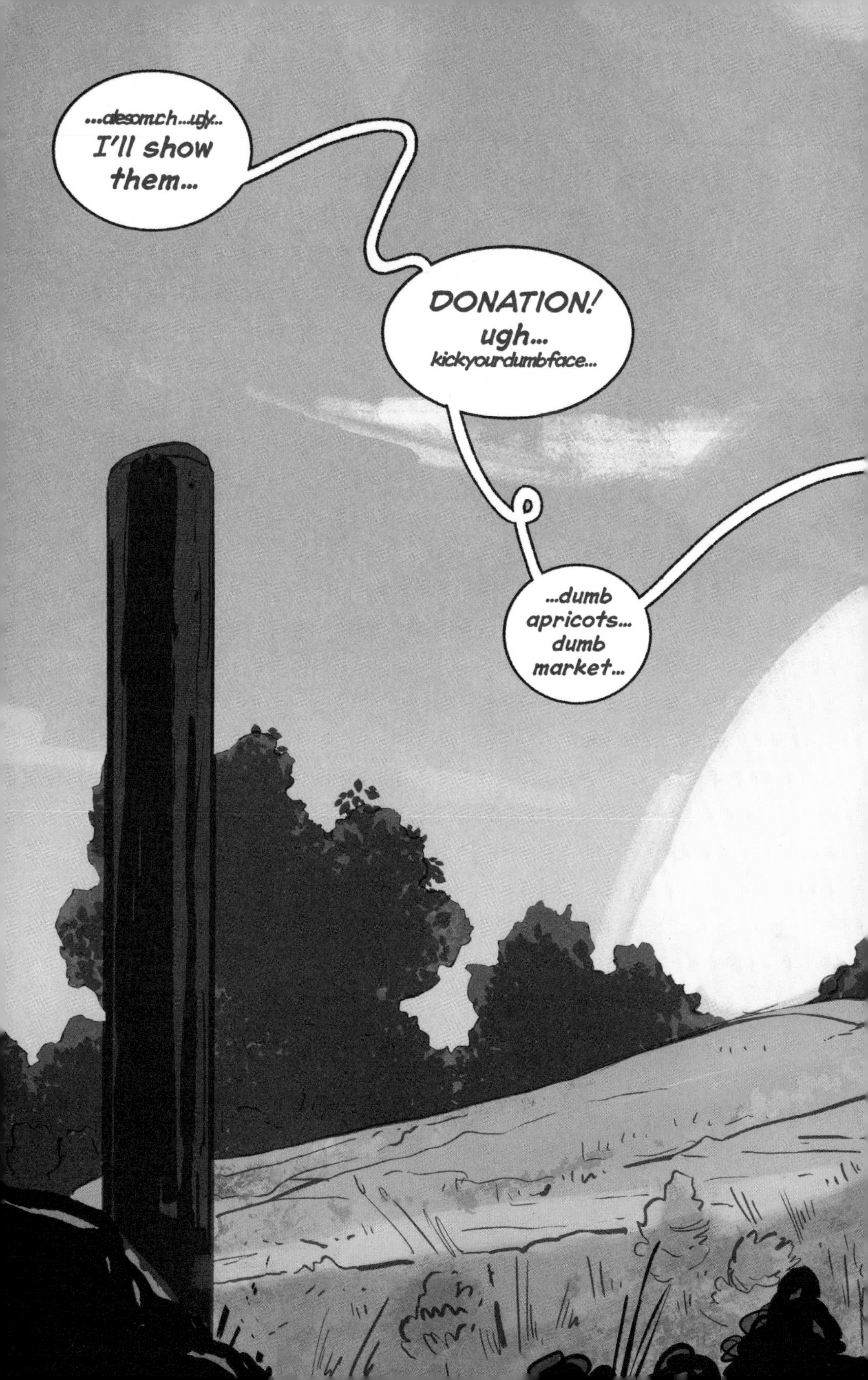

I'll show them...
DONATION! ugh... kickyourdumbface...
...dumb apricots... dumb market...

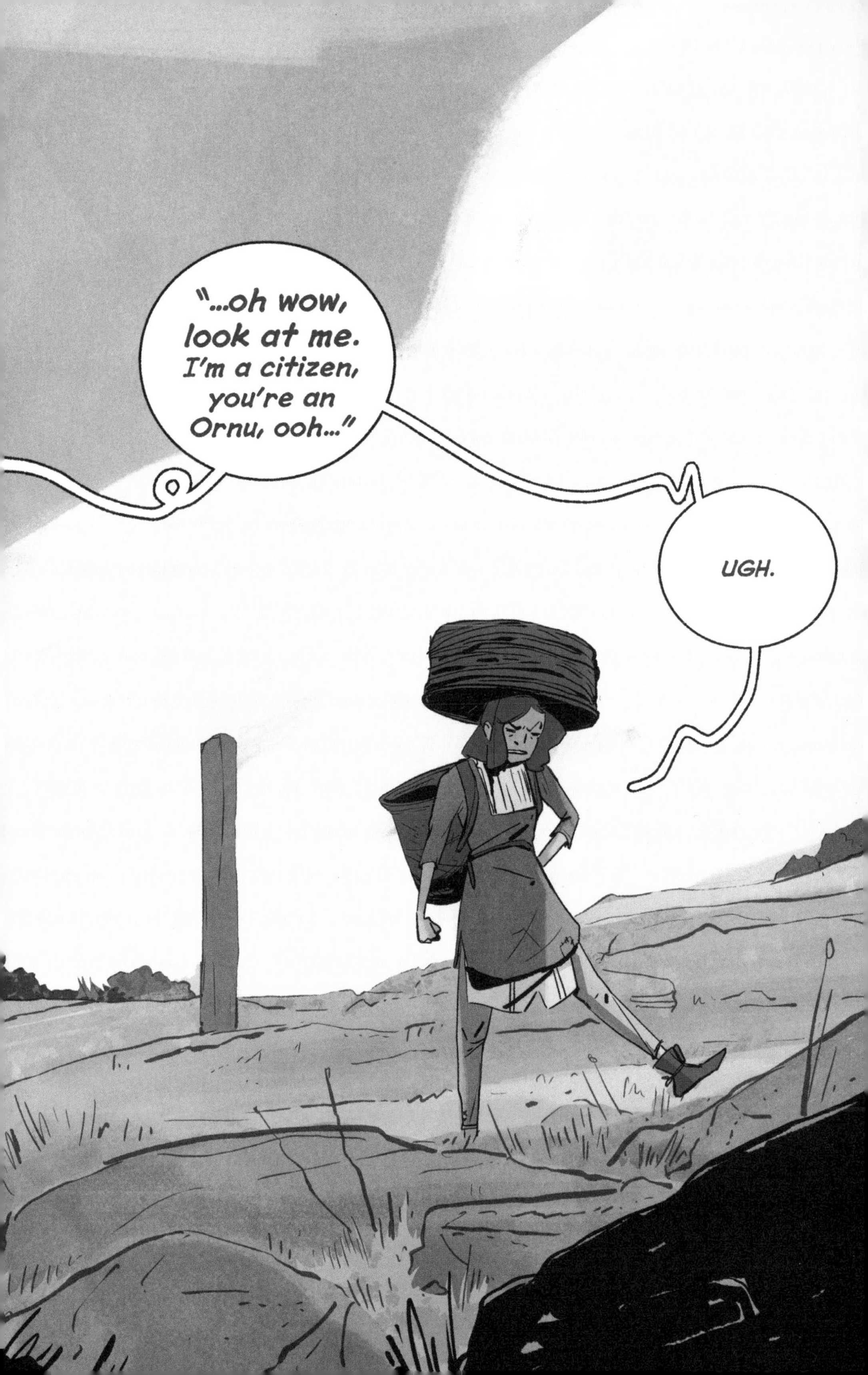
"...oh wow, look at me. I'm a citizen, you're an Ornu, ooh..."
UGH.

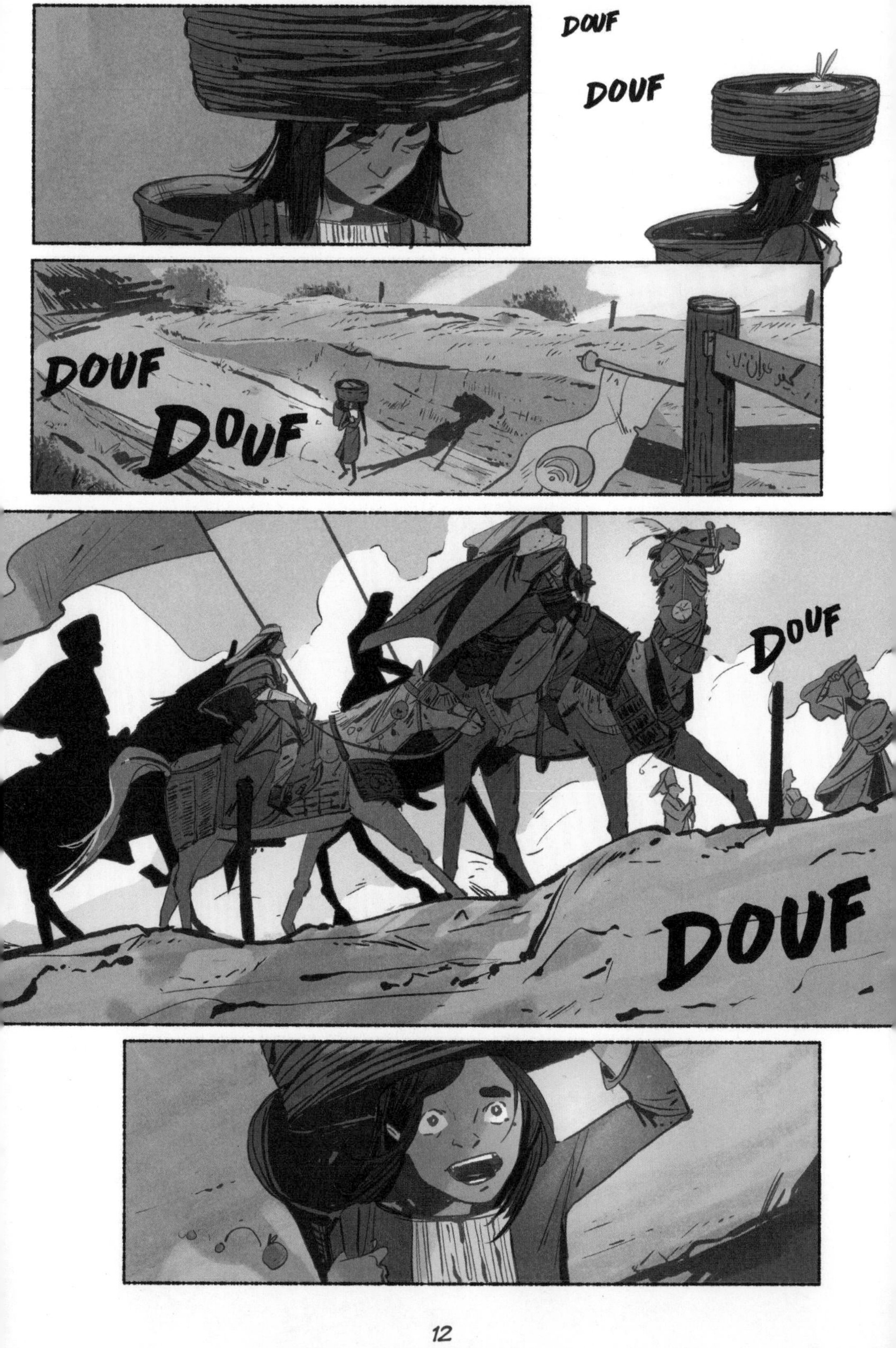
DOUF
DOUF
DOUF
DOUF
DOUF
DOUF

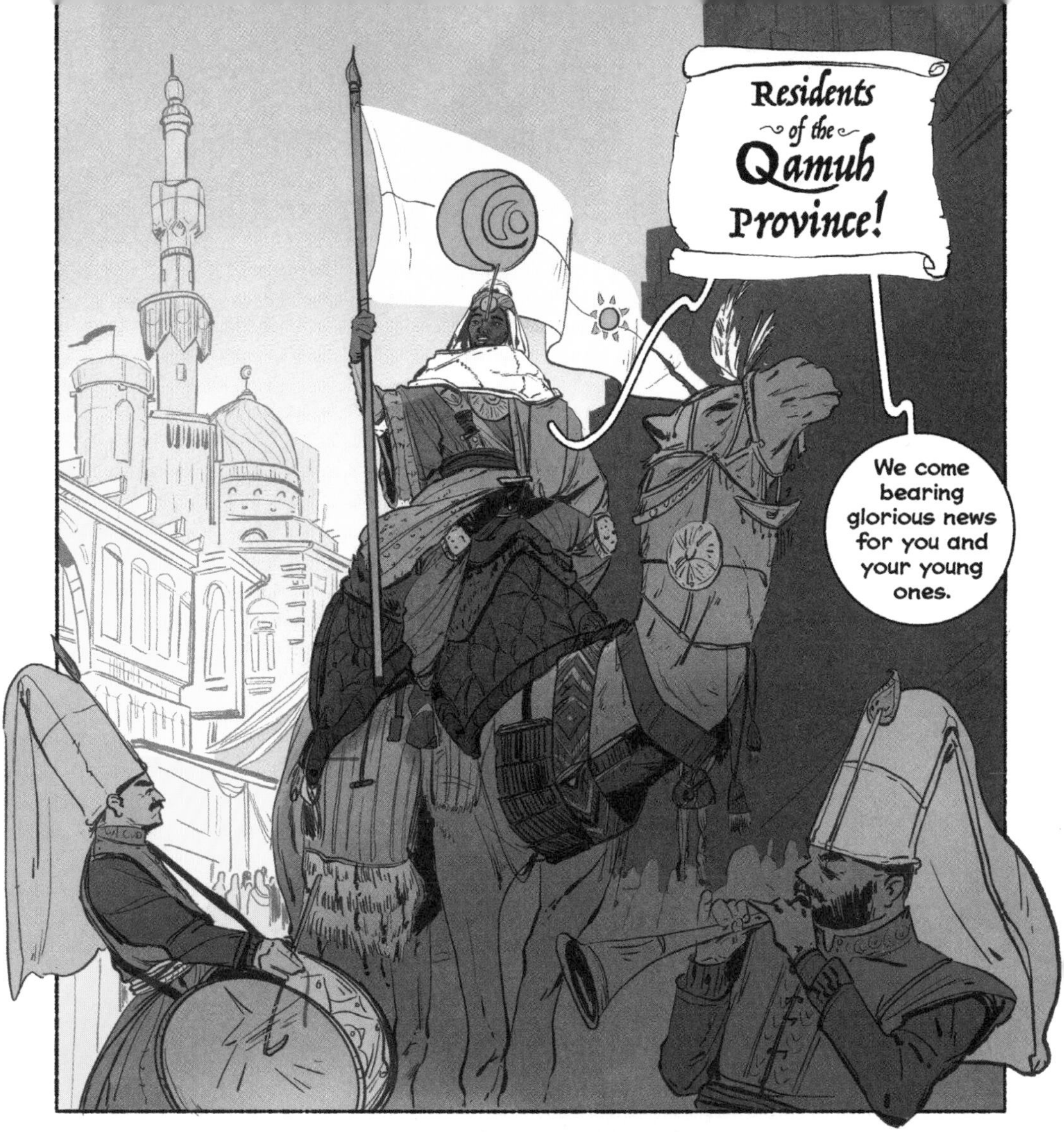
Residents of the Qamuh Province!
We come bearing glorious news for you and your young ones.

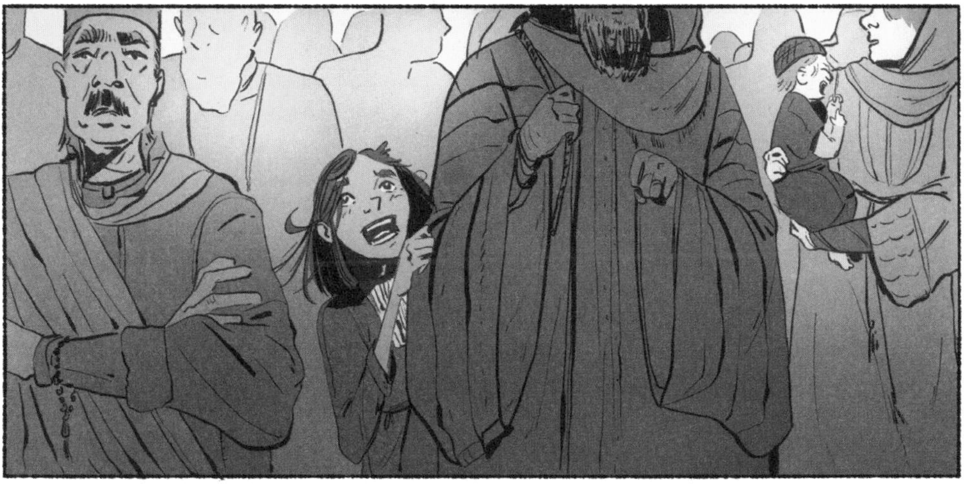

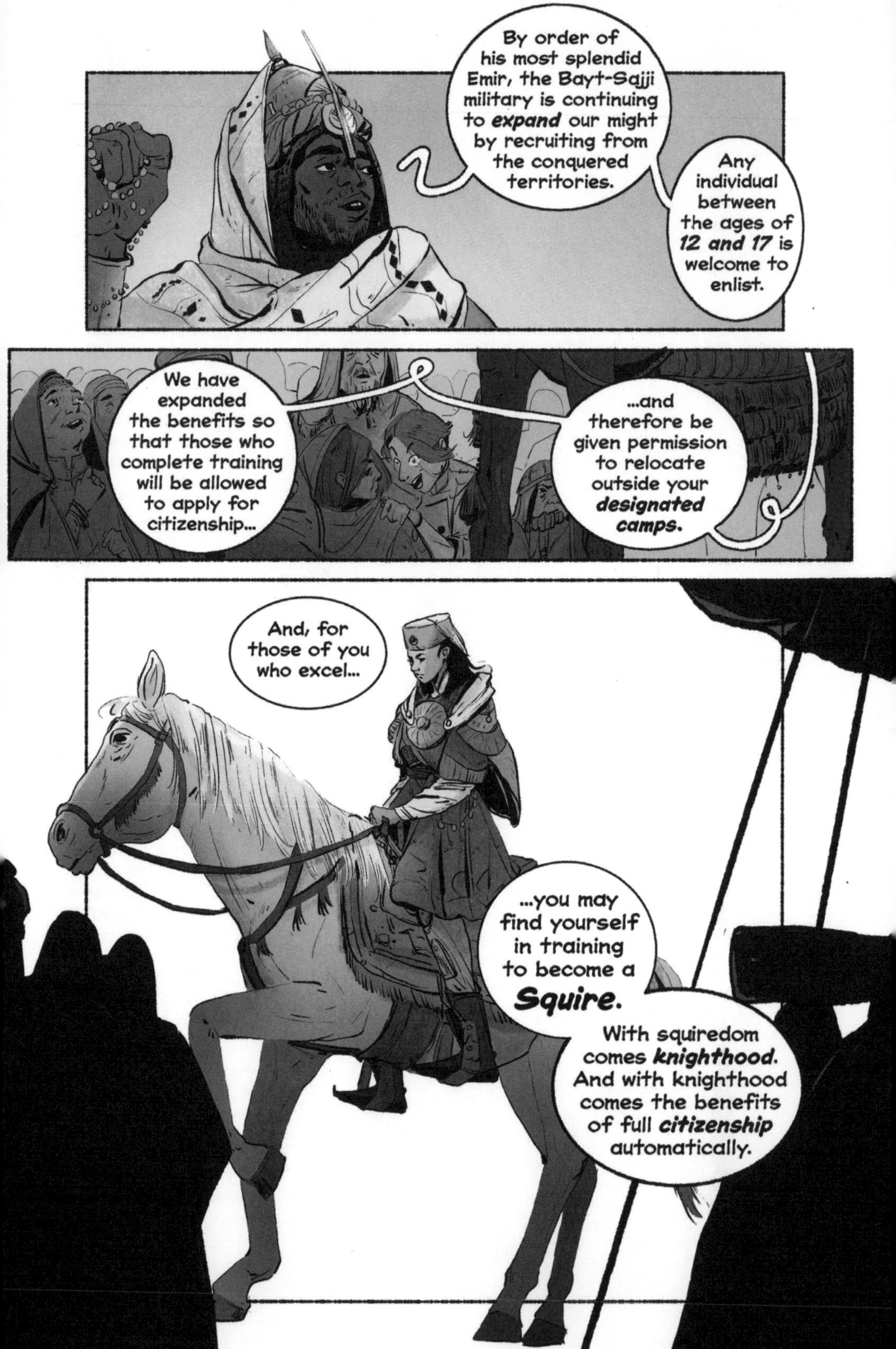

By order of his most splendid Emir, the Bayt-Sajji military is continuing to ***expand*** our might by recruiting from the conquered territories.
Any individual between the ages of ***12 and 17*** is welcome to enlist.
We have expanded the benefits so that those who complete training will be allowed to apply for citizenship...
...and therefore be given permission to relocate outside your ***designated camps.***
And, for those of you who excel...
...you may find yourself in training to become a **Squire.**
With squiredom comes ***knighthood.*** And with knighthood comes the benefits of full ***citizenship*** automatically.

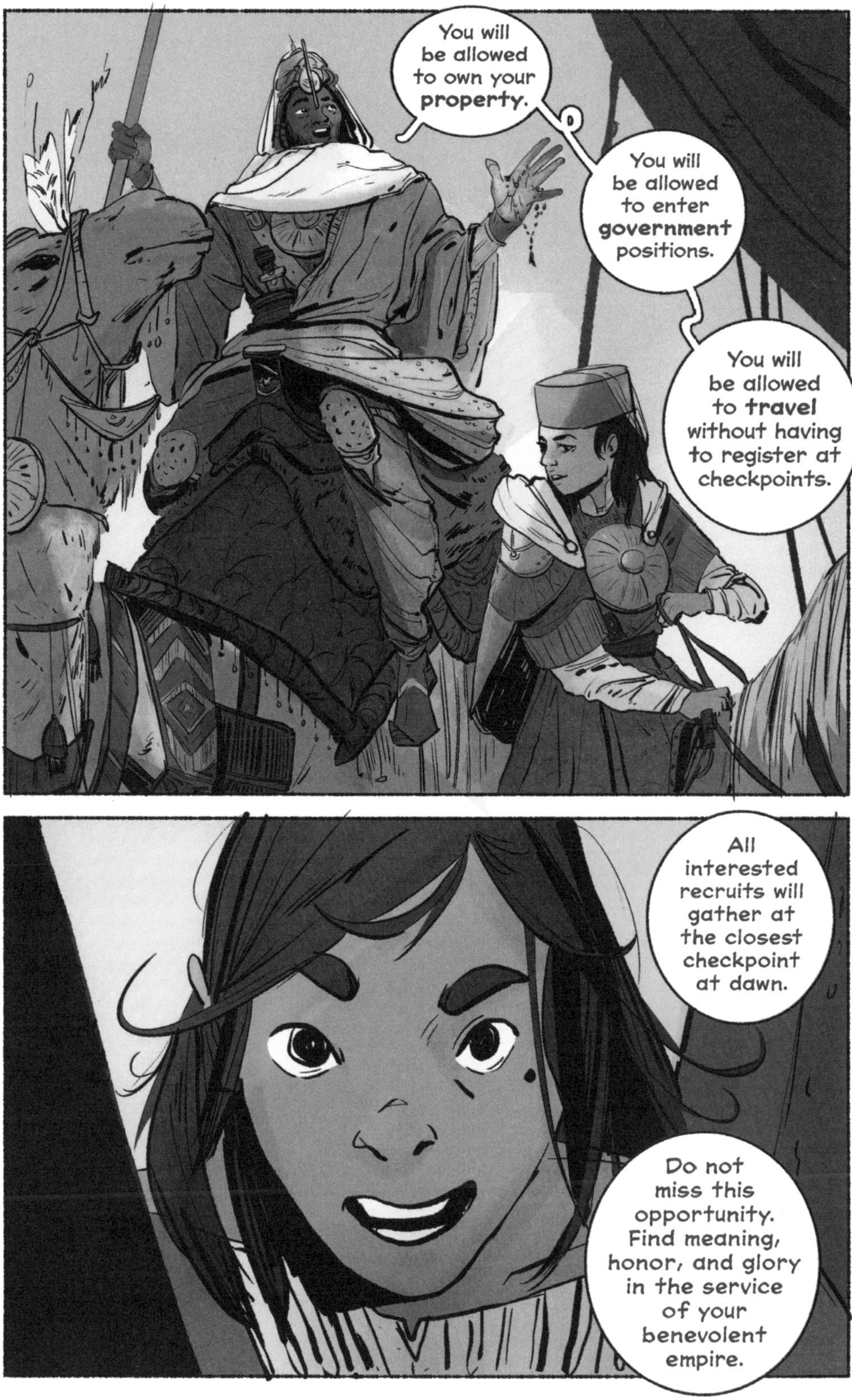
You will be allowed to own your **property**.
You will be allowed to enter **government** positions.
You will be allowed to **travel** without having to register at checkpoints.
All interested recruits will gather at the closest checkpoint at dawn.
Do not miss this opportunity. Find meaning, honor, and glory in the service of your benevolent empire.

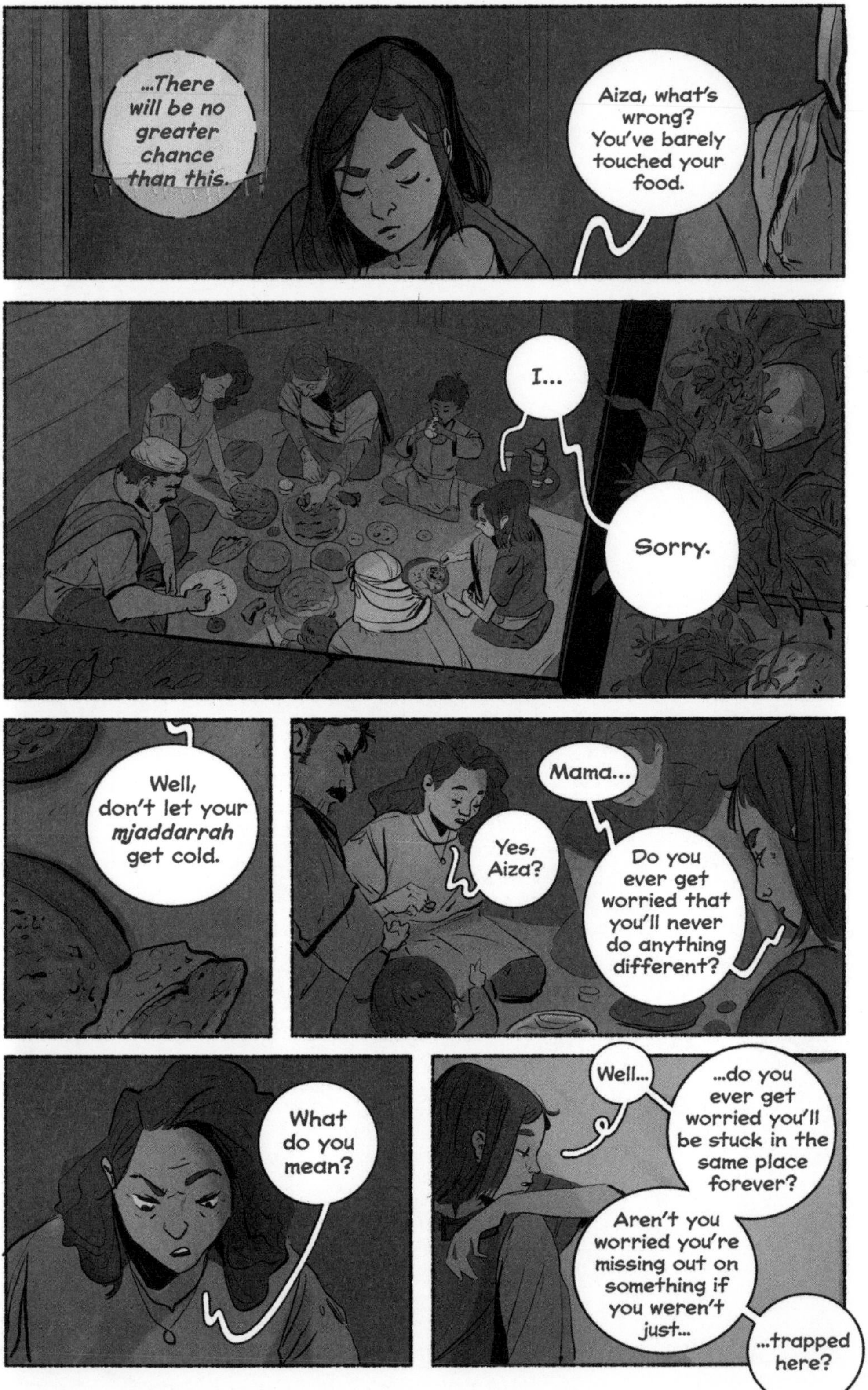
...There will be no greater chance than this.
Aiza, what's wrong? You've barely touched your food.
I...
Sorry.
Well, don't let your *mjaddarrah* get cold.
Mama...
Yes, Aiza?
Do you ever get worried that you'll never do anything different?
What do you mean?
Well...
...do you ever get worried you'll be stuck in the same place forever?
Aren't you worried you're missing out on something if you weren't just...
...trapped here?

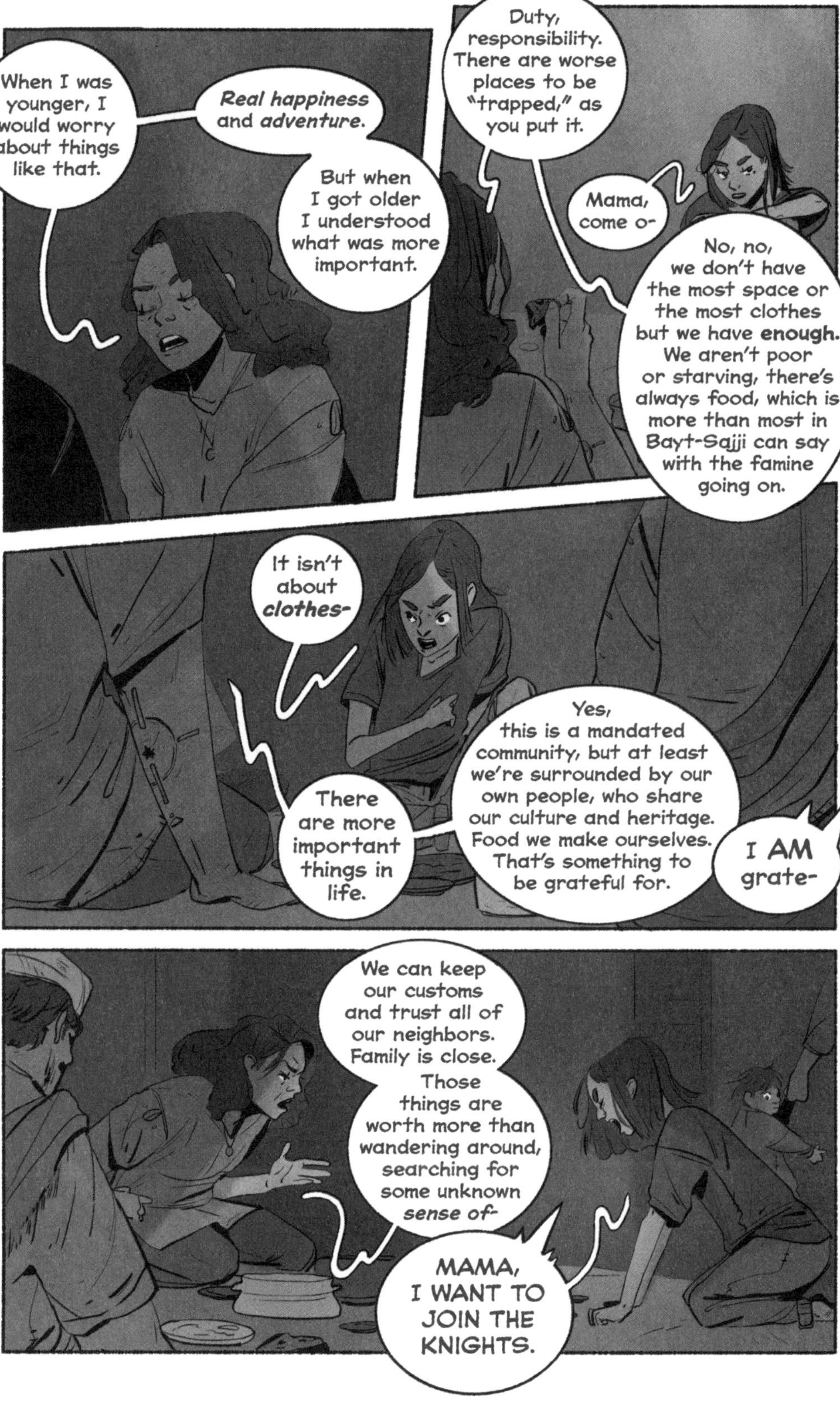
When I was younger, I would worry about things like that.
Real happiness and *adventure*.
But when I got older I understood what was more important.
Duty, responsibility. There are worse places to be "trapped," as you put it.
Mama, come o-
No, no, we don't have the most space or the most clothes but we have **enough.** We aren't poor or starving, there's always food, which is more than most in Bayt-Sajji can say with the famine going on.
It isn't about ***clothes-***
There are more important things in life.
Yes, this is a mandated community, but at least we're surrounded by our own people, who share our culture and heritage. Food we make ourselves. That's something to be grateful for.
I AM grate-
We can keep our customs and trust all of our neighbors. Family is close.
Those things are worth more than wandering around, searching for some unknown *sense of-*
MAMA, I WANT TO JOIN THE KNIGHTS.

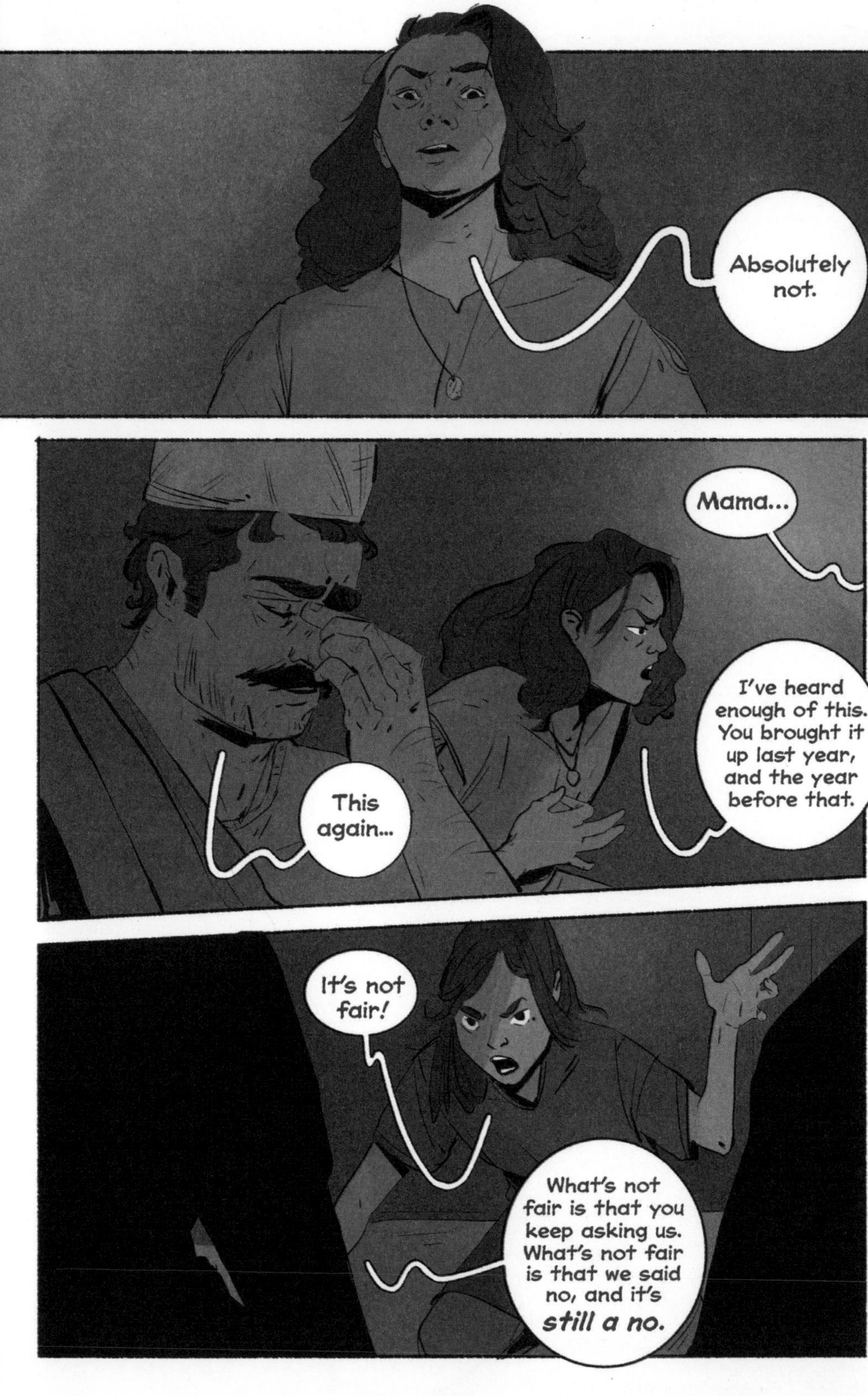
Absolutely not.
Mama...
I've heard enough of this. You brought it up last year, and the year before that.
This again...
It's not fair!
What's not fair is that you keep asking us. What's not fair is that we said no, and it's *still a no.*

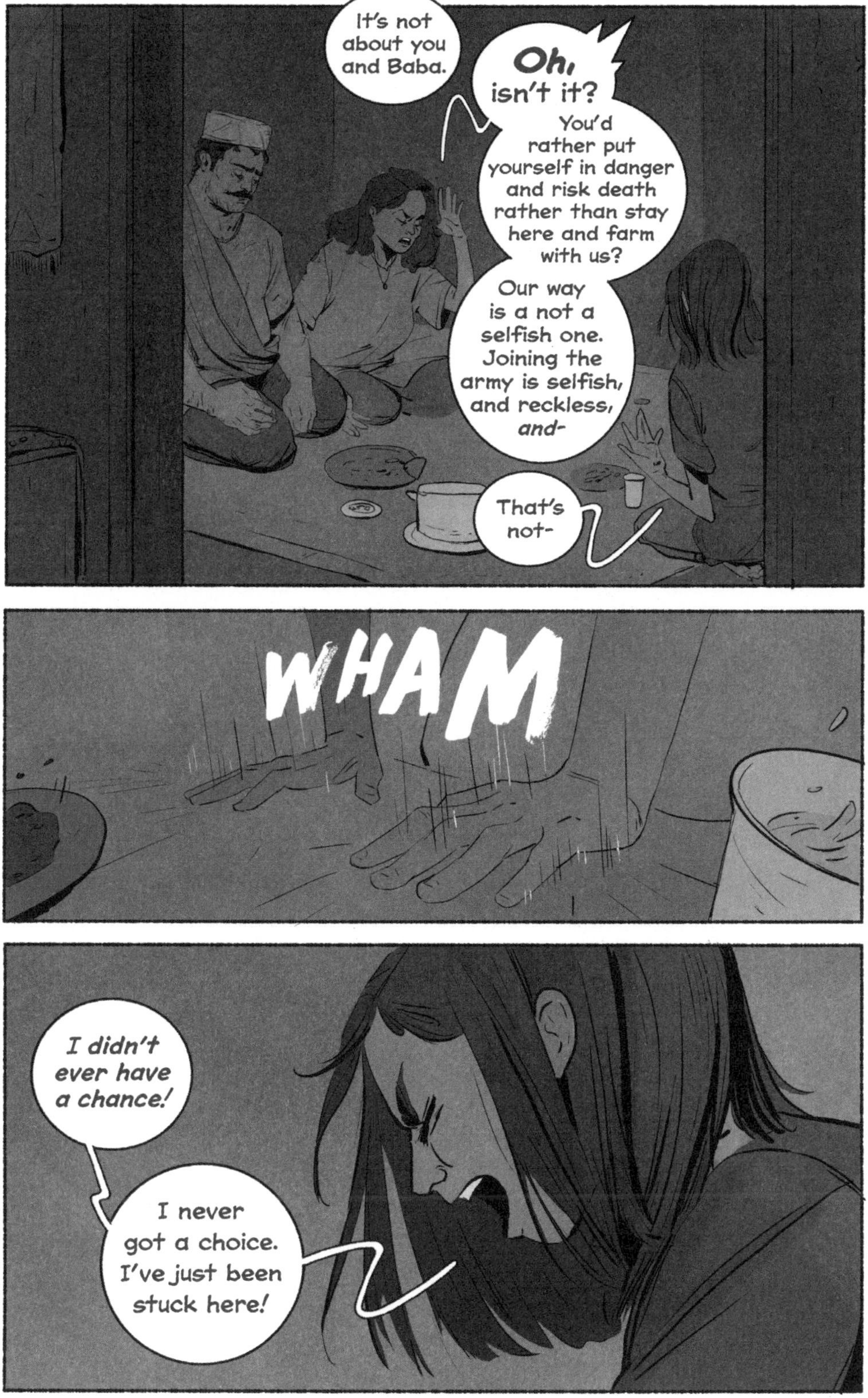
It's not about you and Baba.
Oh, isn't it?
You'd rather put yourself in danger and risk death rather than stay here and farm with us?
Our way is a not a selfish one. Joining the army is selfish, and reckless, *and-*
That's not-
WHAM
I didn't ever have a chance!
I never got a choice. I've just been stuck here!

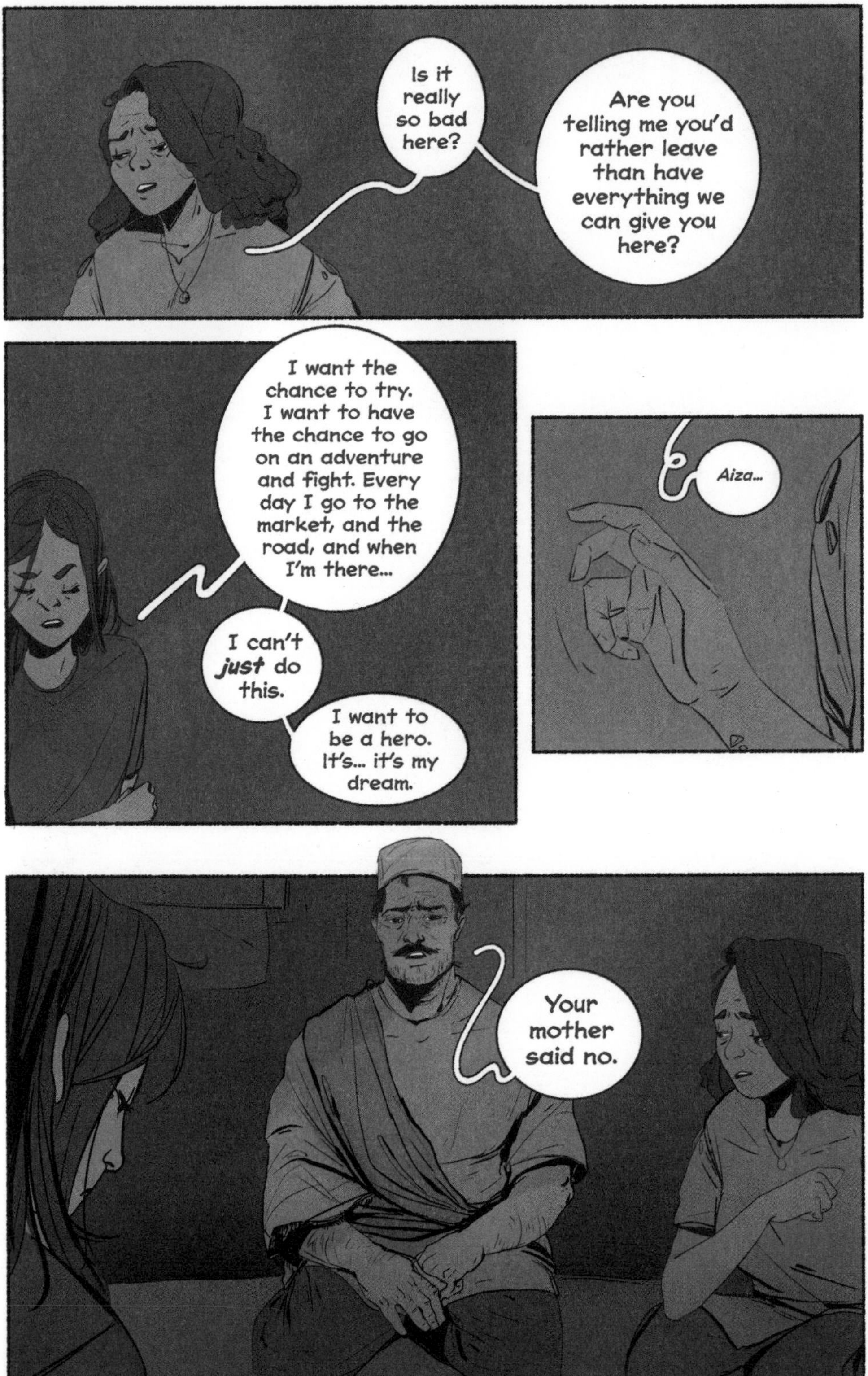
Is it really so bad here?
Are you telling me you'd rather leave than have everything we can give you here?
I want the chance to try. I want to have the chance to go on an adventure and fight. Every day I go to the market, and the road, and when I'm there...
I can't *just* do this.
I want to be a hero. It's... it's my dream.
Aiza...
Your mother said no.

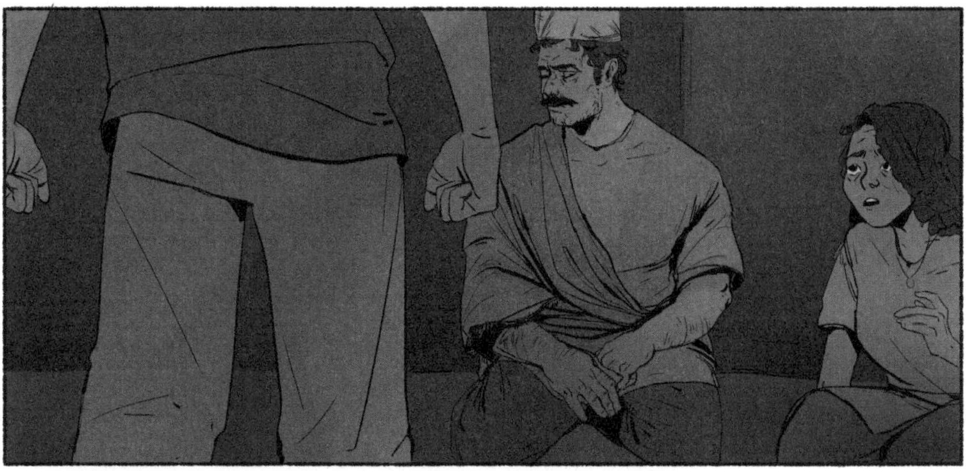

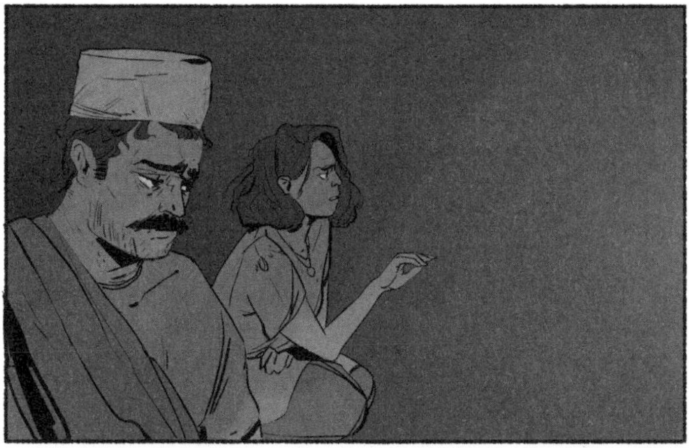

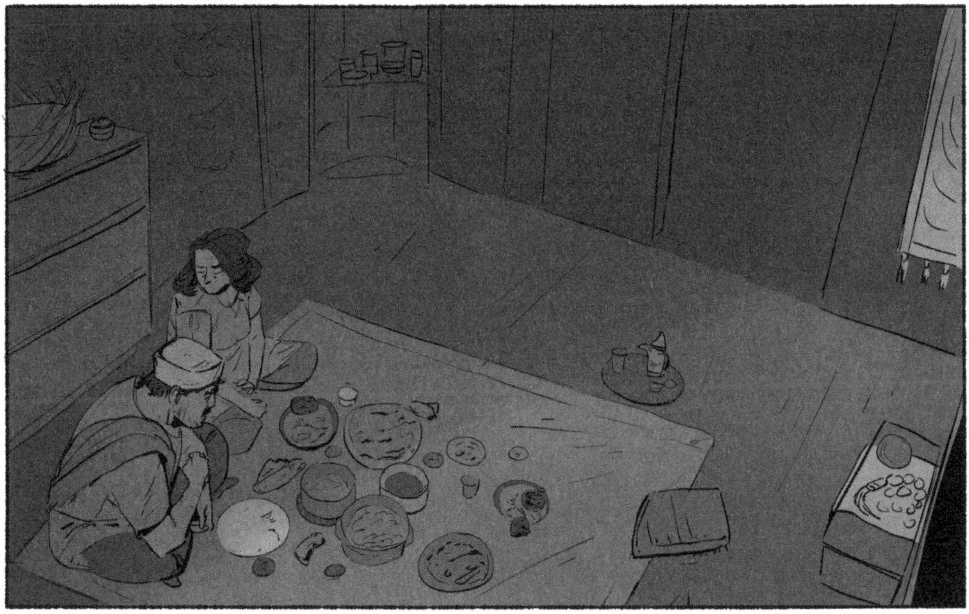

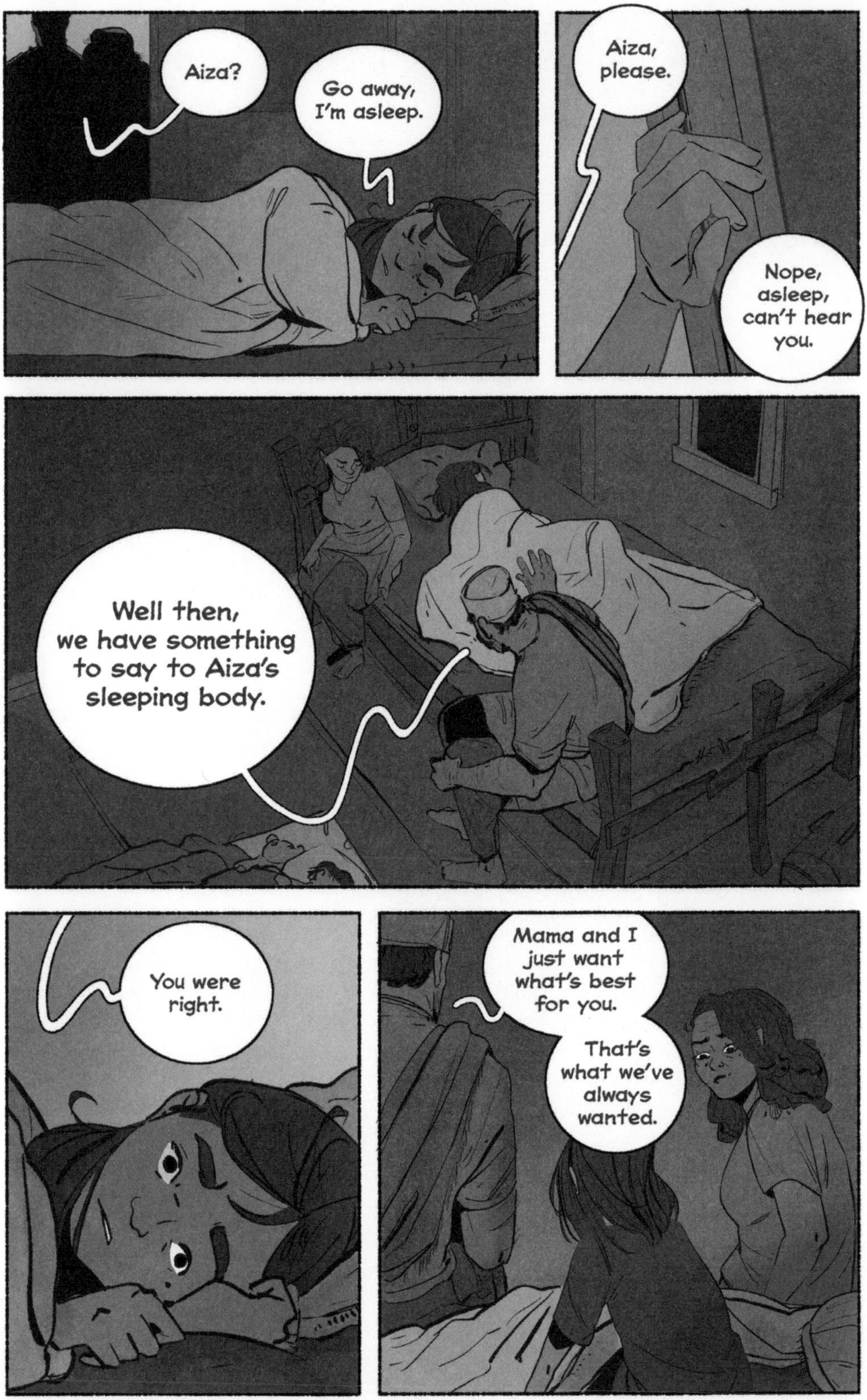
Aiza?
Go away, I'm asleep.
Aiza, please.
Nope, asleep, can't hear you.
Well then, we have something to say to Aiza's sleeping body.
You were right.
Mama and I just want what's best for you.
That's what we've always wanted.

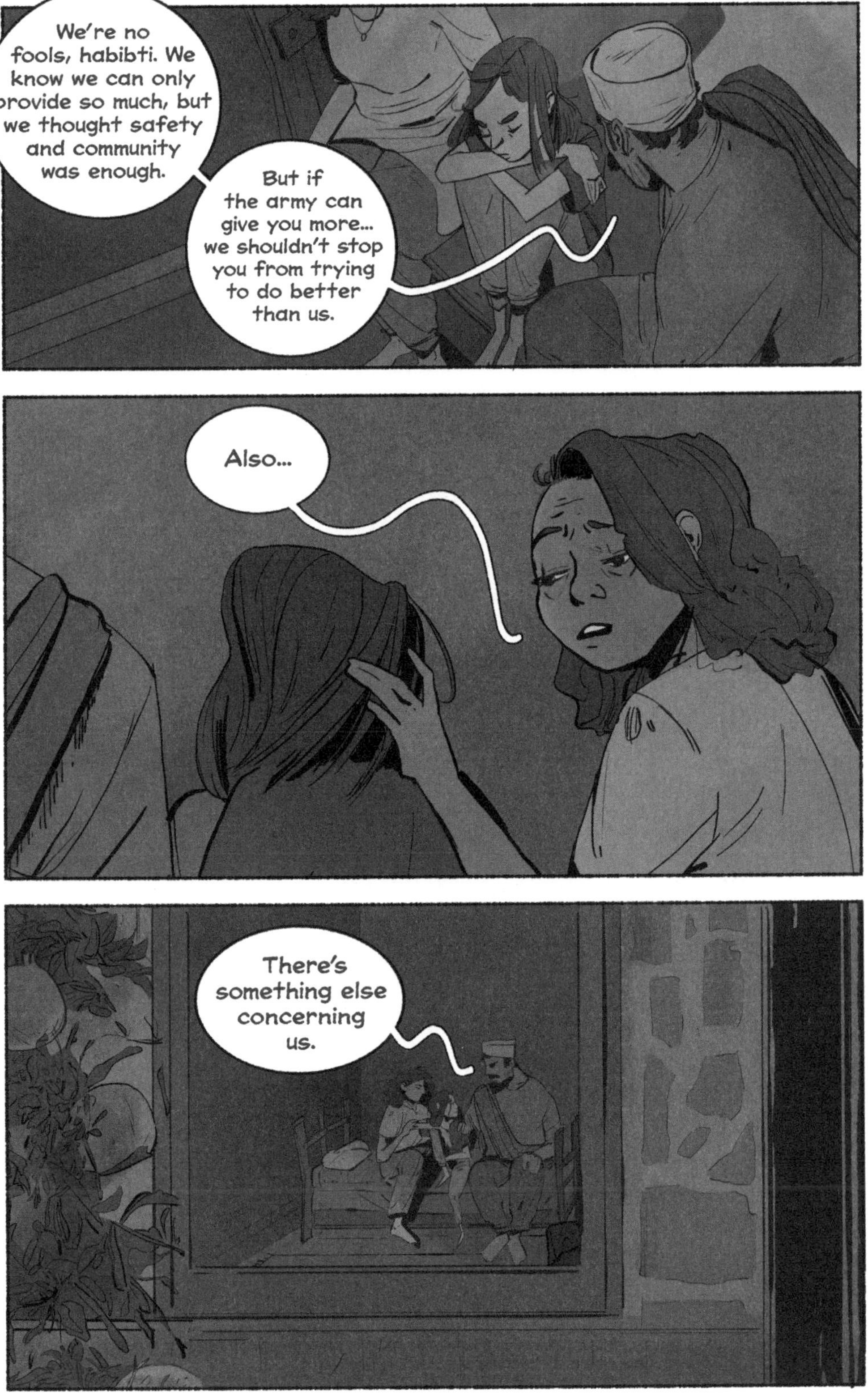
We're no fools, habibti. We know we can only provide so much, but we thought safety and community was enough.
But if the army can give you more... we shouldn't stop you from trying to do better than us.
Also...
There's something else concerning us.

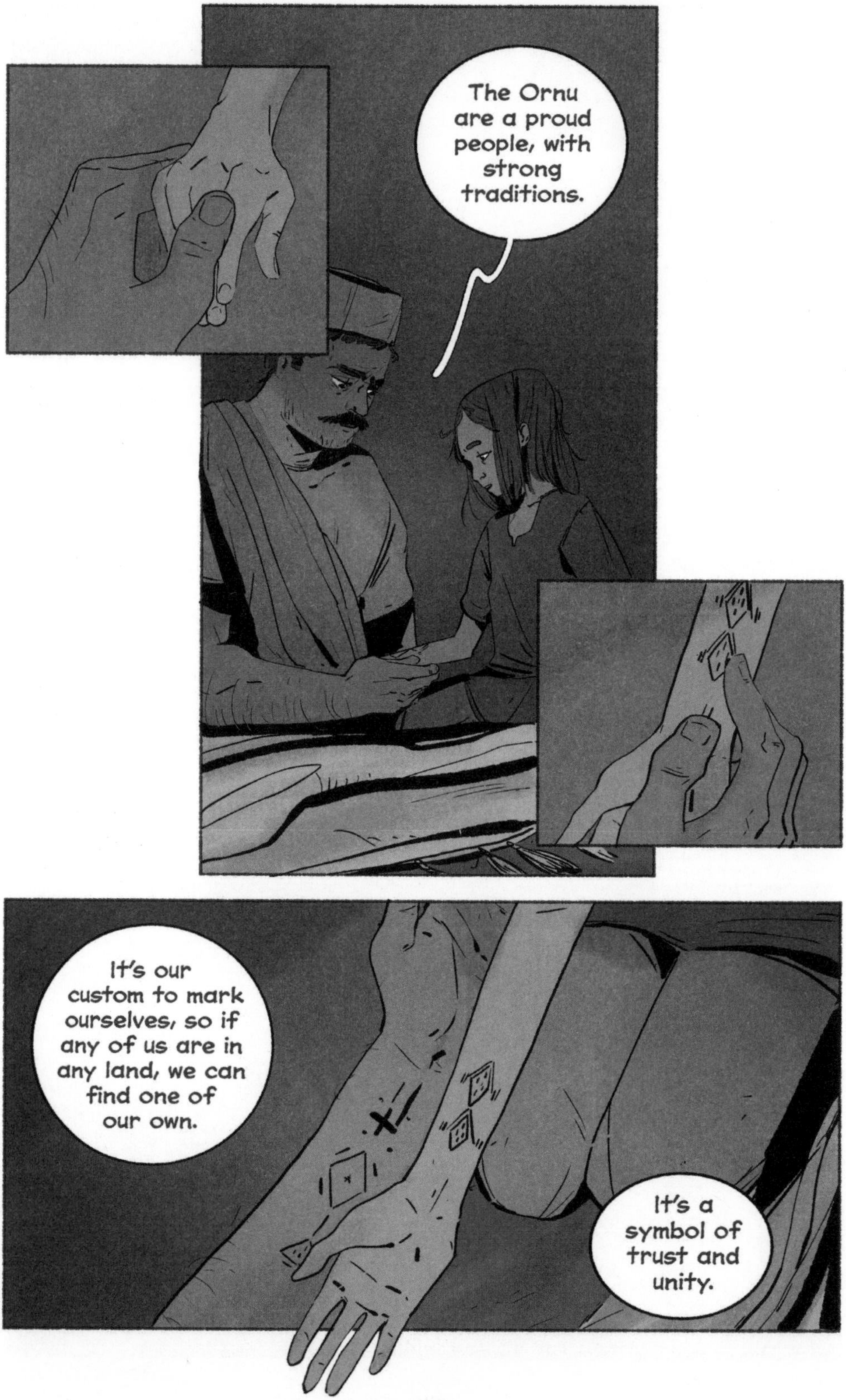
The Ornu are a proud people, with strong traditions.
It's our custom to mark ourselves, so if any of us are in any land, we can find one of our own.
It's a symbol of trust and unity.

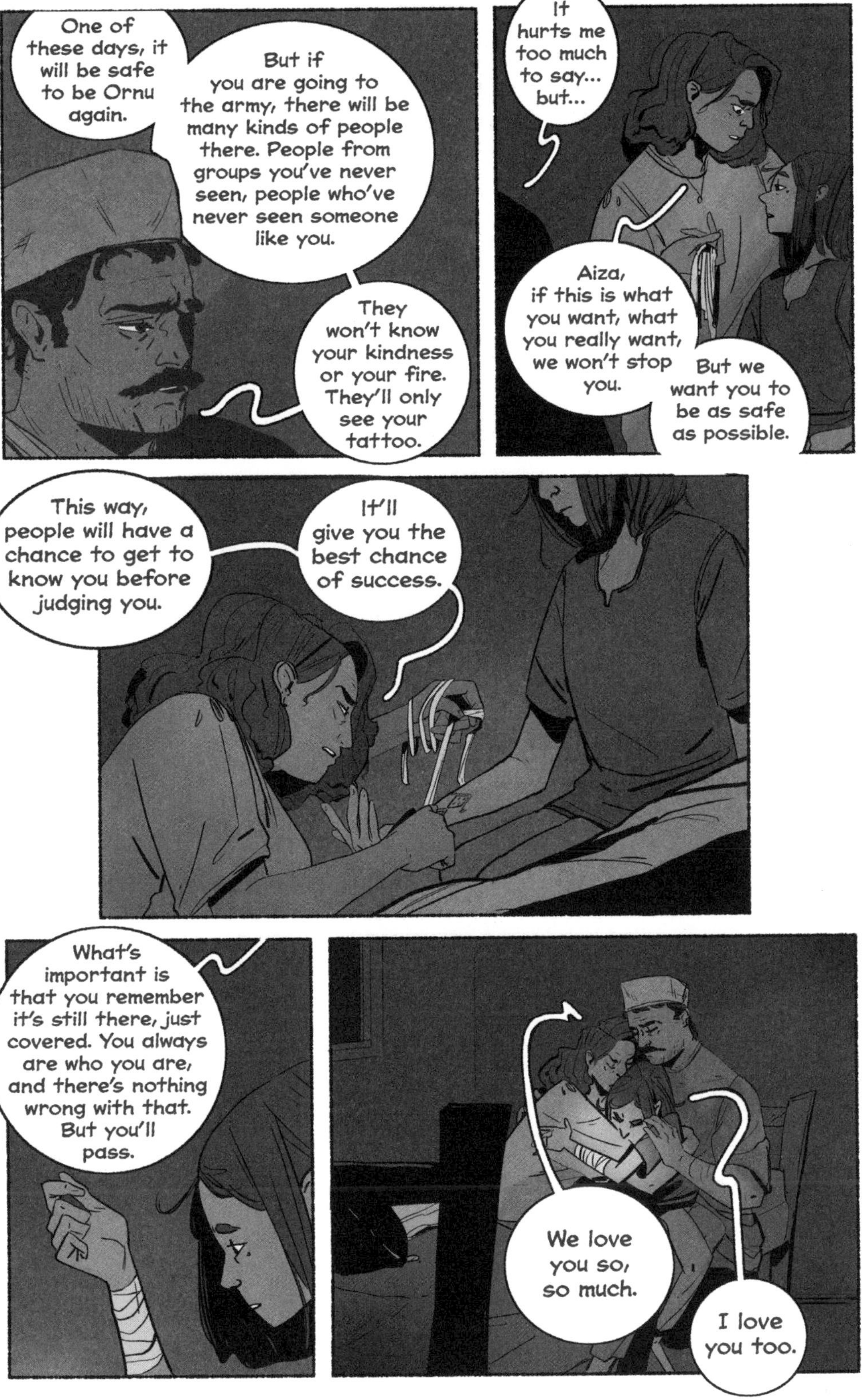
One of these days, it will be safe to be Ornu again.
But if you are going to the army, there will be many kinds of people there. People from groups you've never seen, people who've never seen someone like you.
They won't know your kindness or your fire. They'll only see your tattoo.
It hurts me too much to say... but...
Aiza, if this is what you want, what you really want, we won't stop you.
But we want you to be as safe as possible.
This way, people will have a chance to get to know you before judging you.
It'll give you the best chance of success.
What's important is that you remember it's still there, just covered. You always are who you are, and there's nothing wrong with that. But you'll pass.
We love you so, so much.
I love you too.

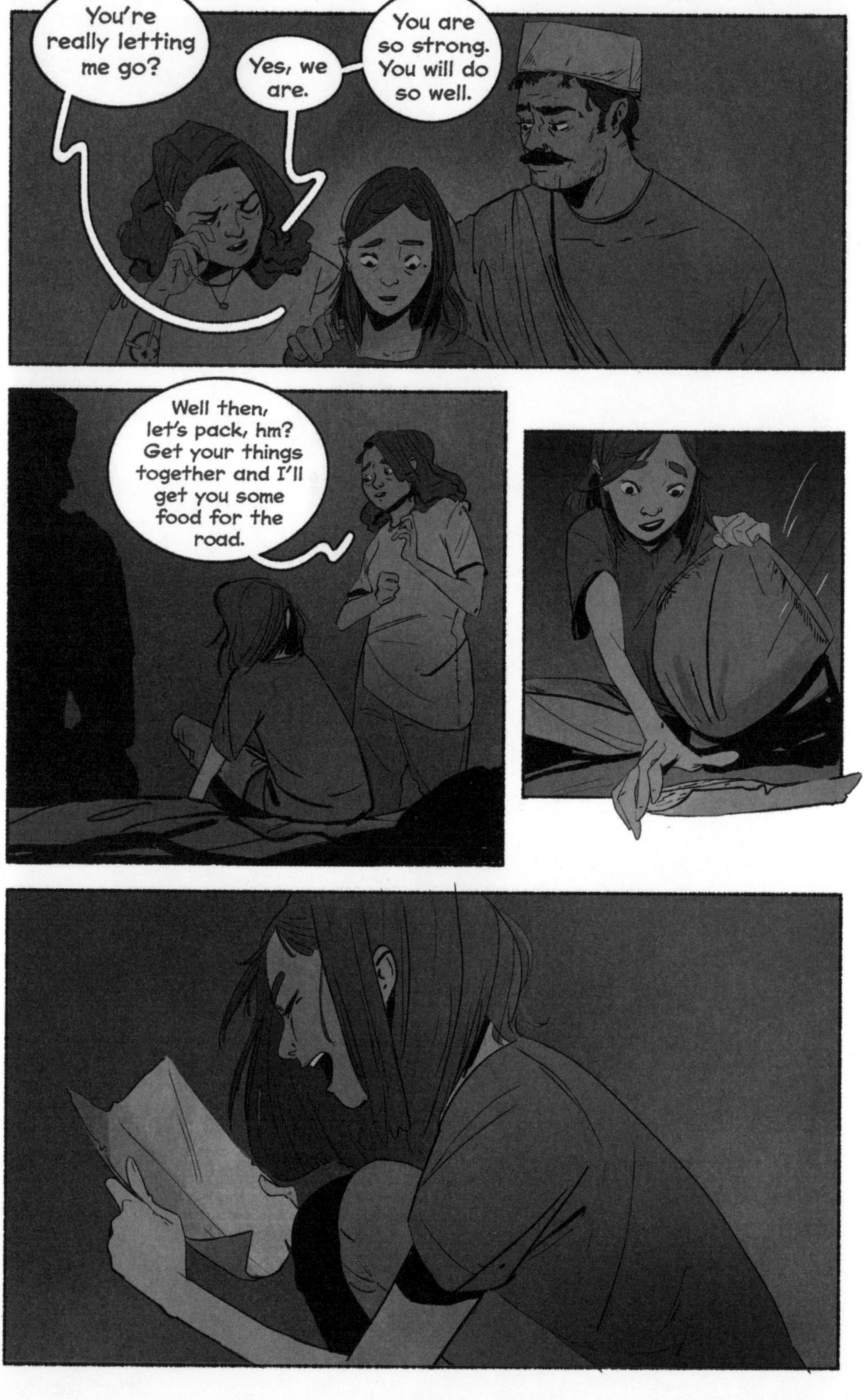
You're really letting me go?
Yes, we are.
You are so strong. You will do so well.
Well then, let's pack, hm? Get your things together and I'll get you some food for the road.

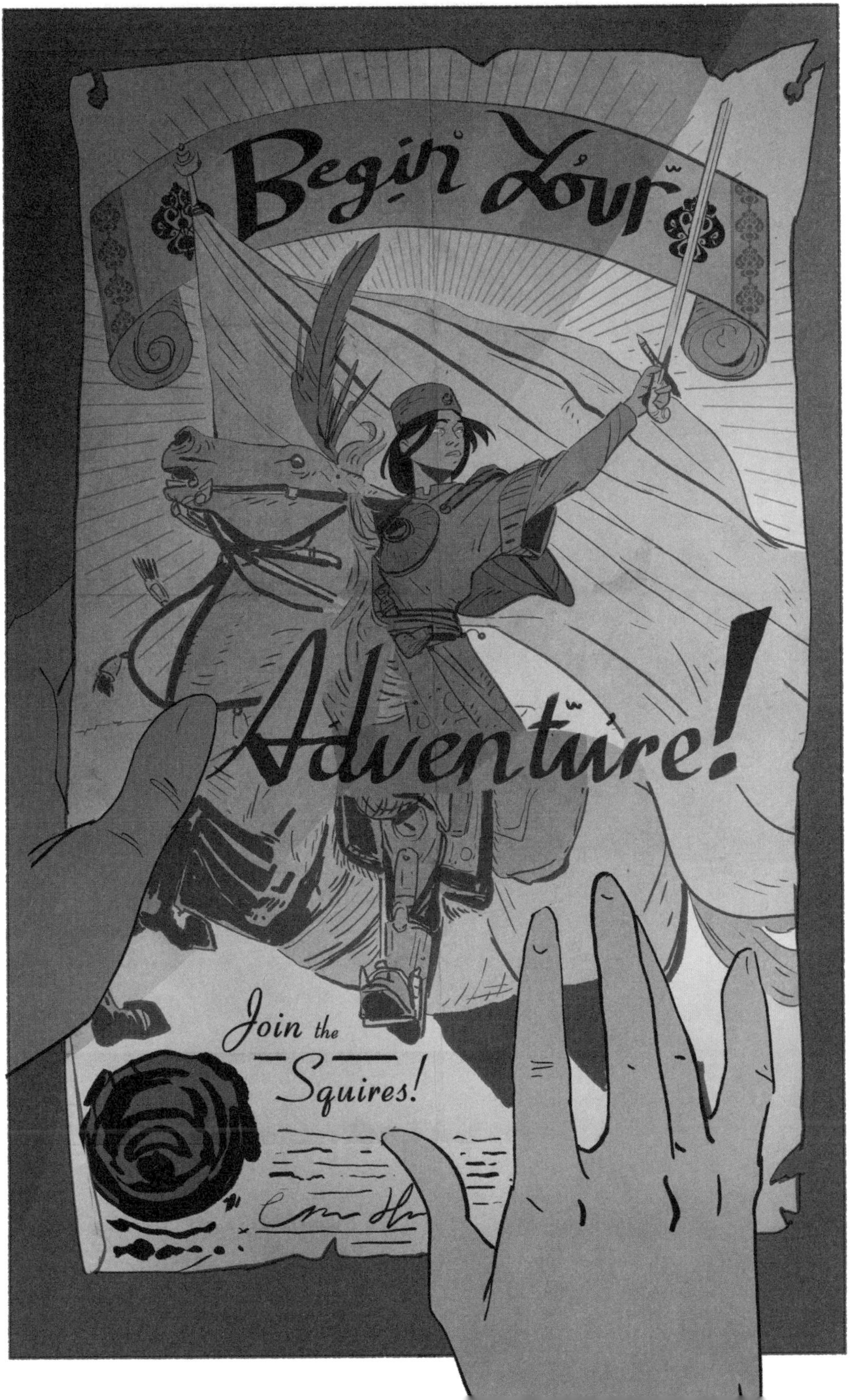
Begin Your
Adventure!
Join the
Squires!

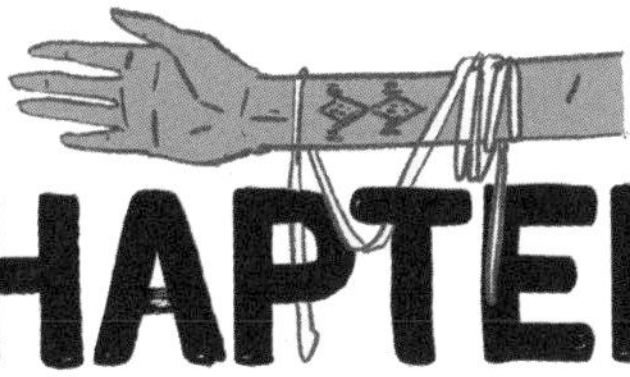

CHAPTER 2

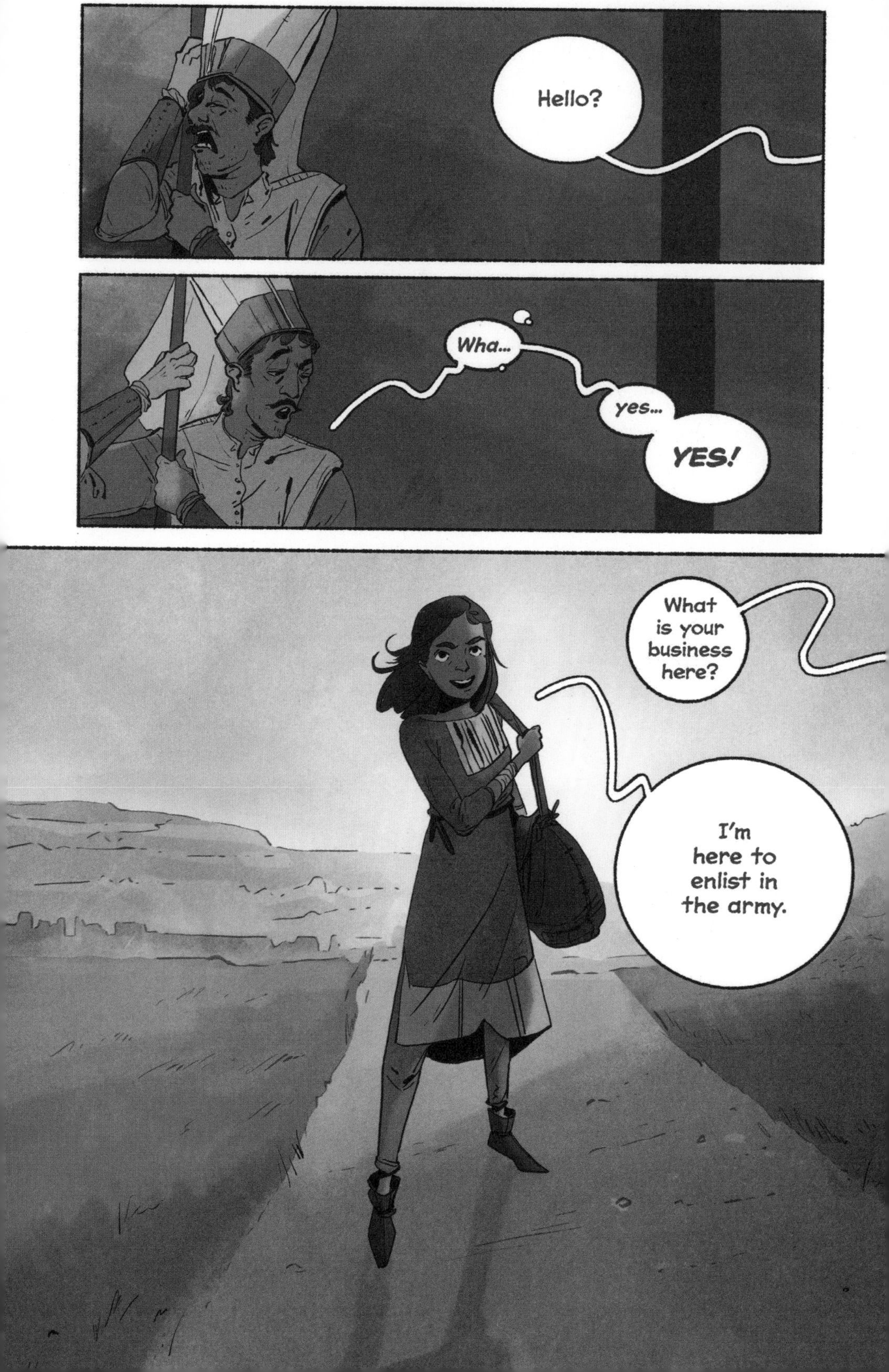
Hello?
Wha...
yes...
YES!
What is your business here?
I'm here to enlist in the army.

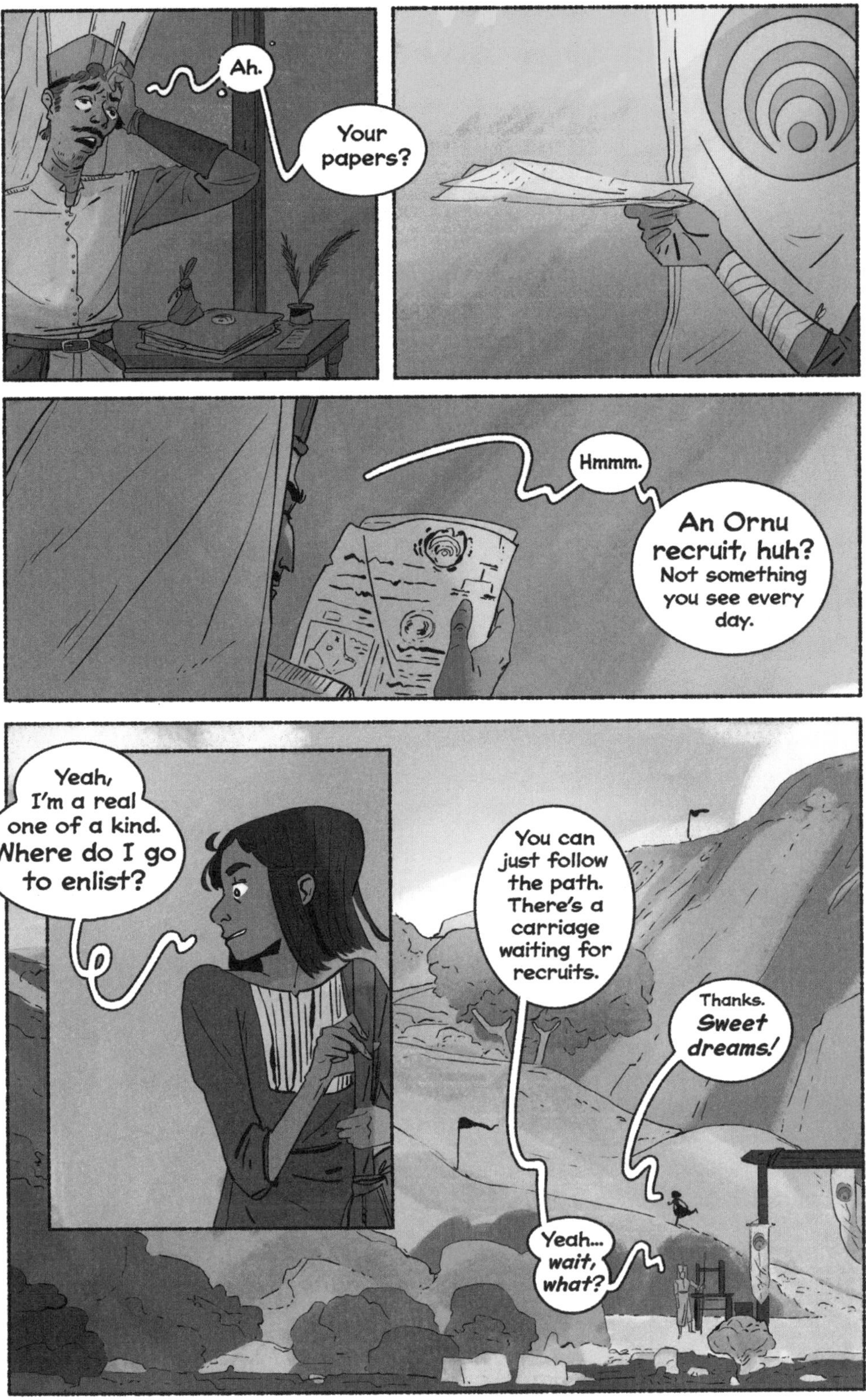
Ah.
Your papers?
Hmmm.
An Ornu recruit, huh? Not something you see every day.
Yeah, I'm a real one of a kind. Where do I go to enlist?
You can just follow the path. There's a carriage waiting for recruits.
Thanks. *Sweet dreams!*
Yeah... *wait, what?*

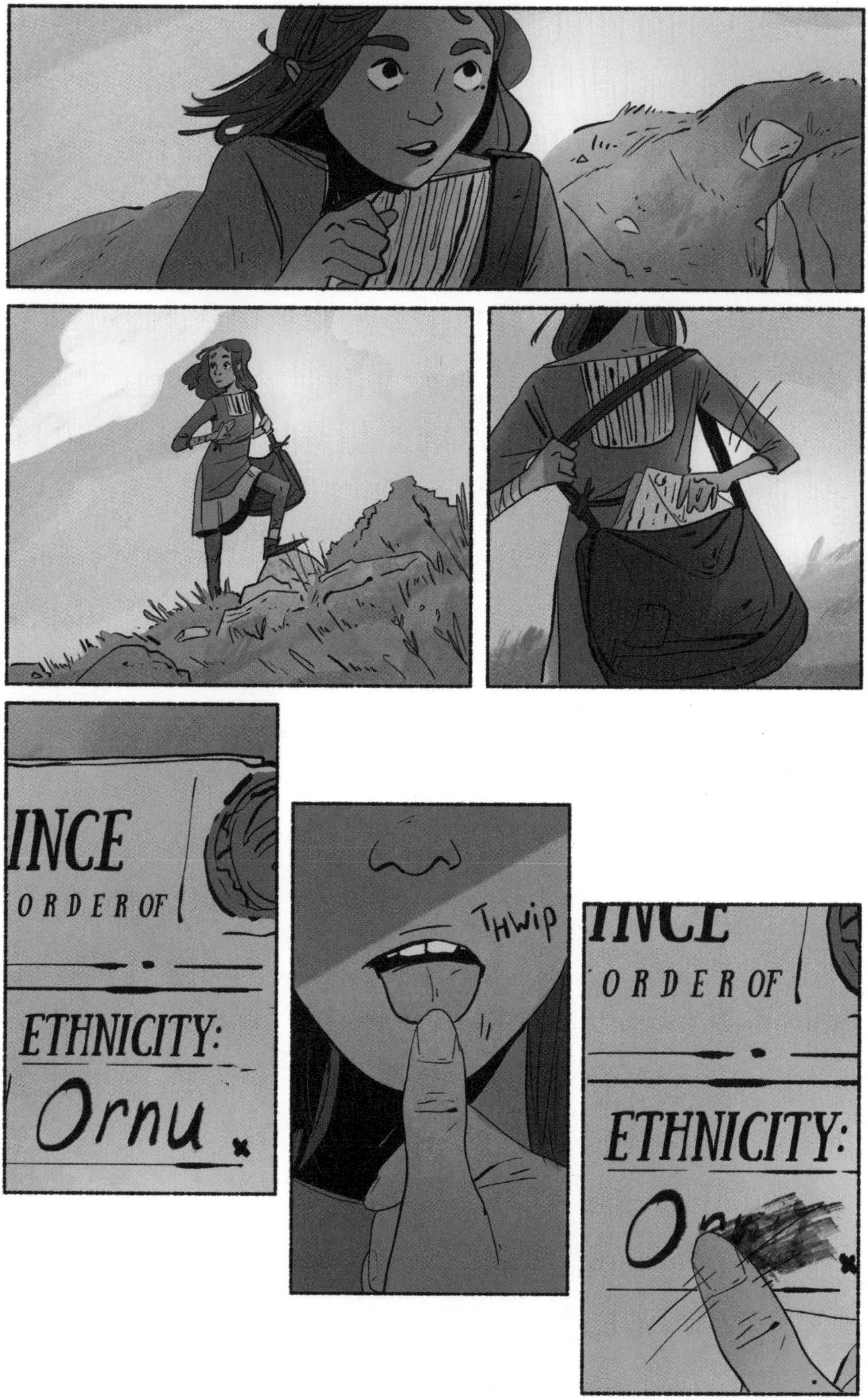
INCE
ORDER OF
ETHNICITY:
Ornu
THWip
INCE
ORDER OF
ETHNICITY:

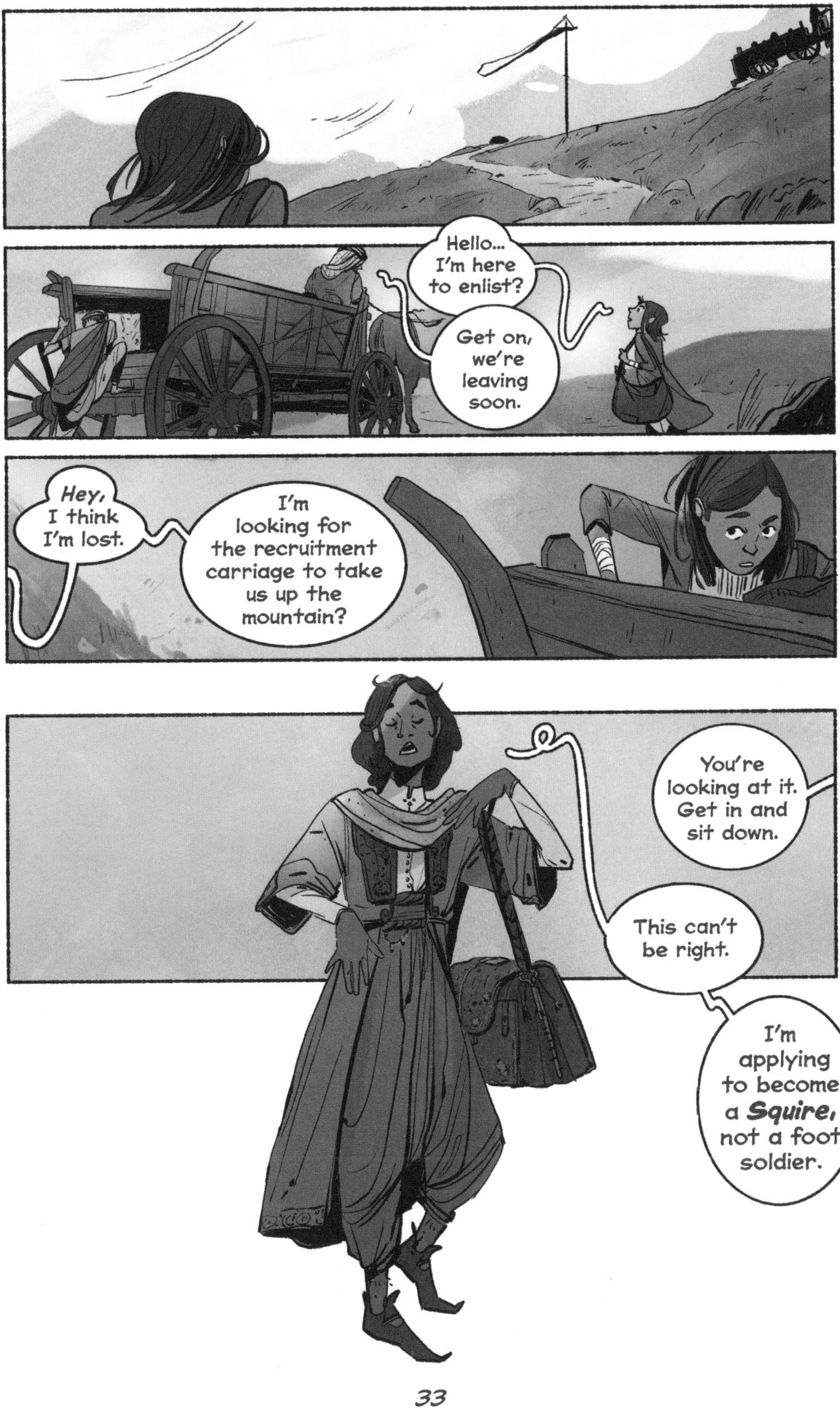
Hello... I'm here to enlist?
Get on, we're leaving soon.
Hey, I think I'm lost.
I'm looking for the recruitment carriage to take us up the mountain?
You're looking at it. Get in and sit down.
This can't be right.
I'm applying to become a ***Squire,*** not a foot soldier.

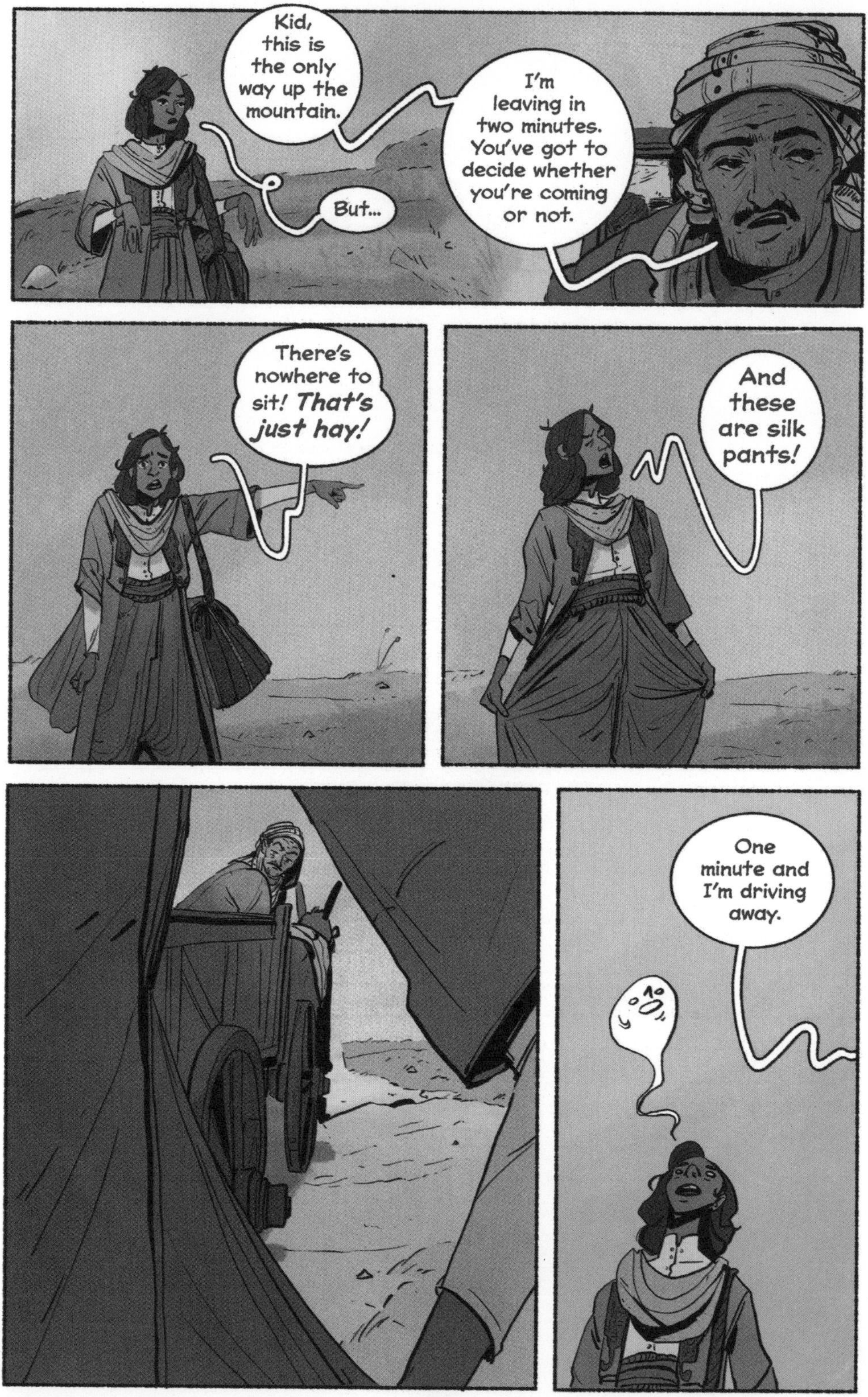
Kid, this is the only way up the mountain.
But...
I'm leaving in two minutes. You've got to decide whether you're coming or not.
There's nowhere to sit! That's just hay!
And these are silk pants!
One minute and I'm driving away.

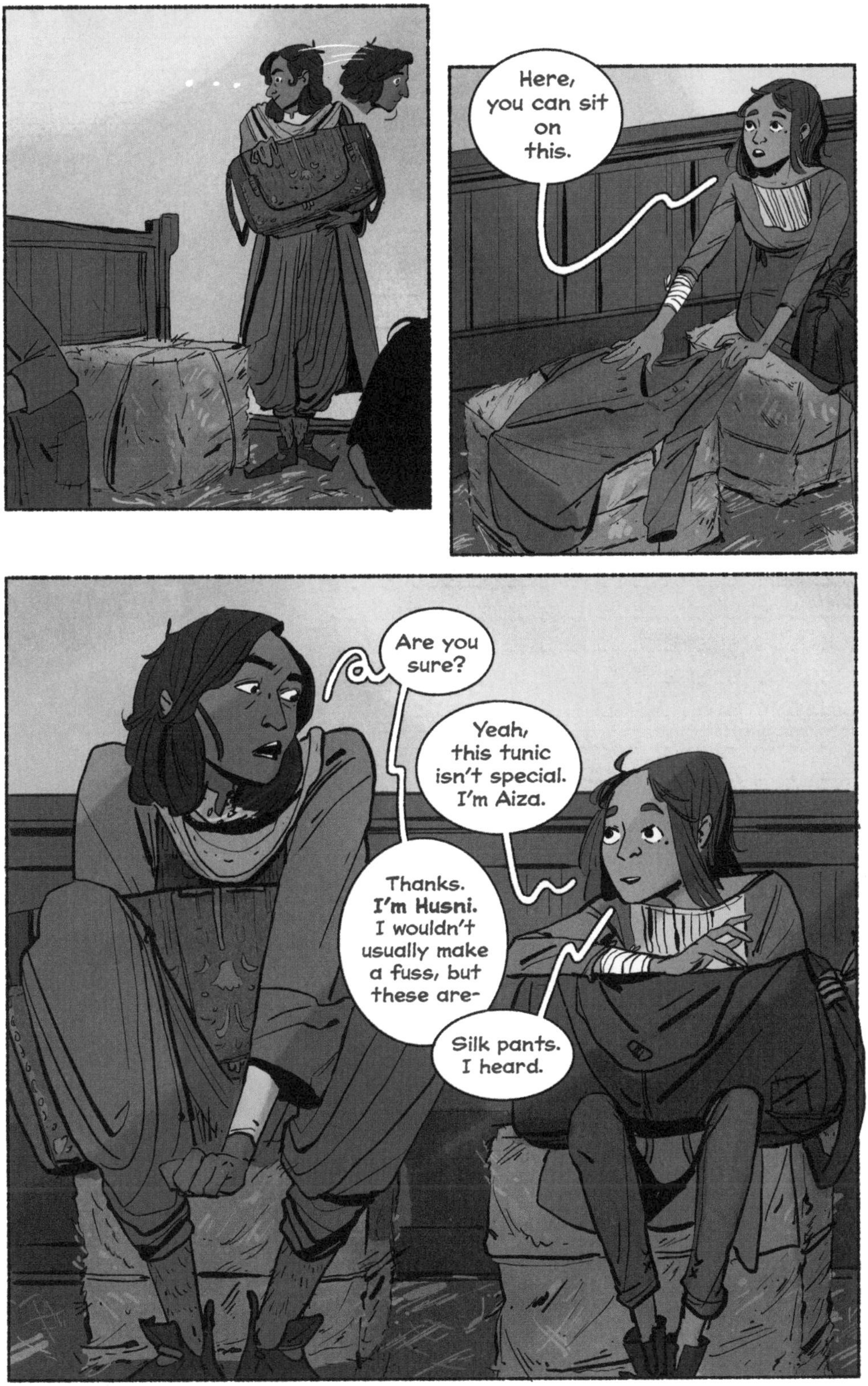
Here, you can sit on this.
Are you sure?
Yeah, this tunic isn't special. I'm Aiza.
Thanks. **I'm Husni.** I wouldn't usually make a fuss, but these are-
Silk pants. I heard.

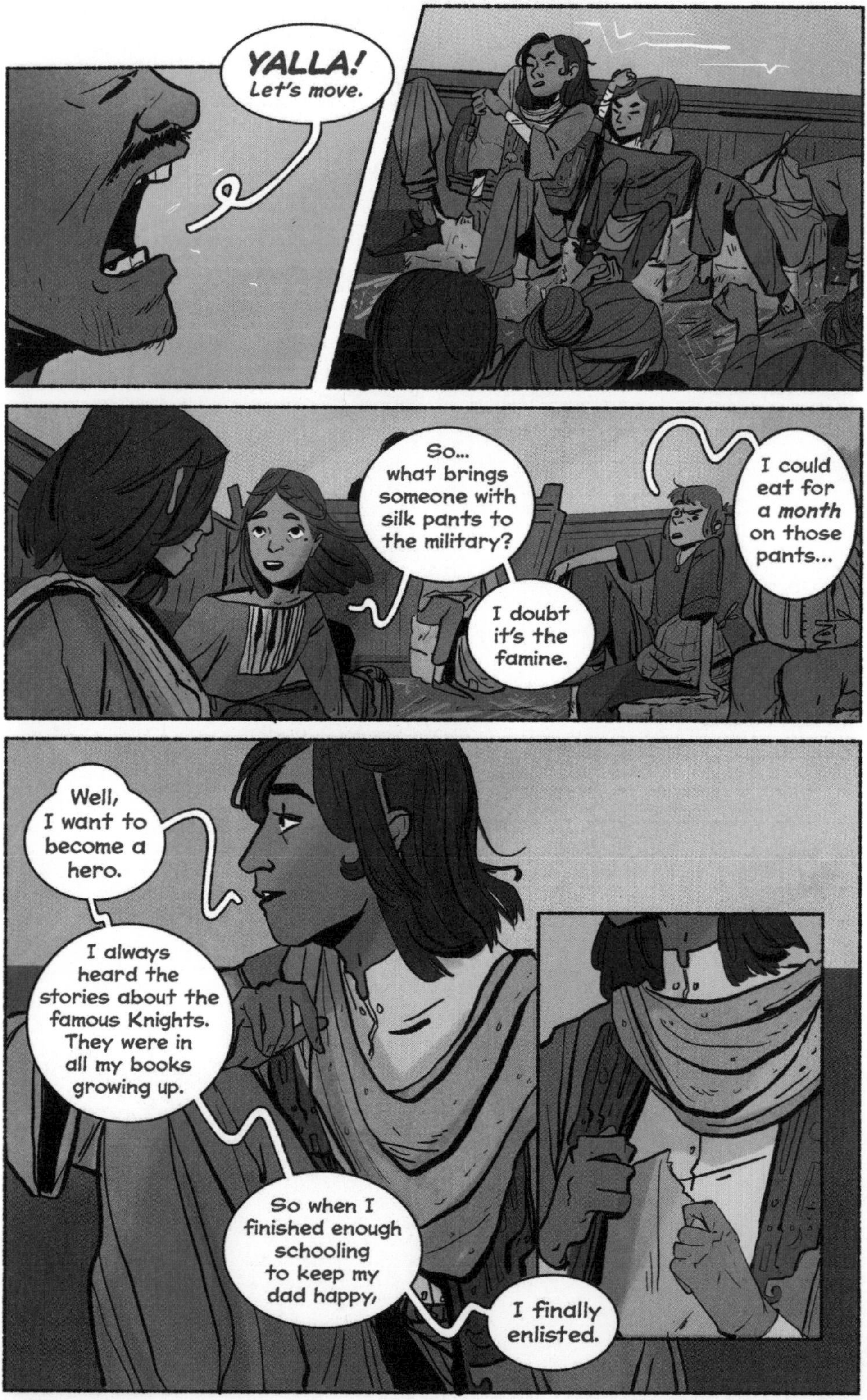
YALLA! Let's move.
So... what brings someone with silk pants to the military?
I doubt it's the famine.
I could eat for a *month* on those pants...
Well, I want to become a hero.
I always heard the stories about the famous Knights. They were in all my books growing up.
So when I finished enough schooling to keep my dad happy,
I finally enlisted.

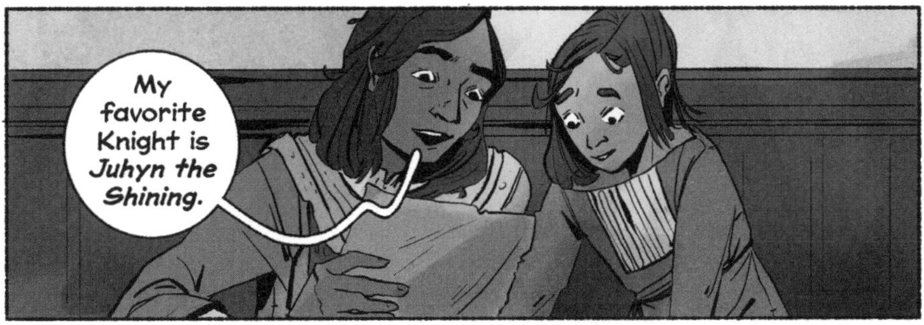
My favorite Knight is *Juhyn the Shining.*

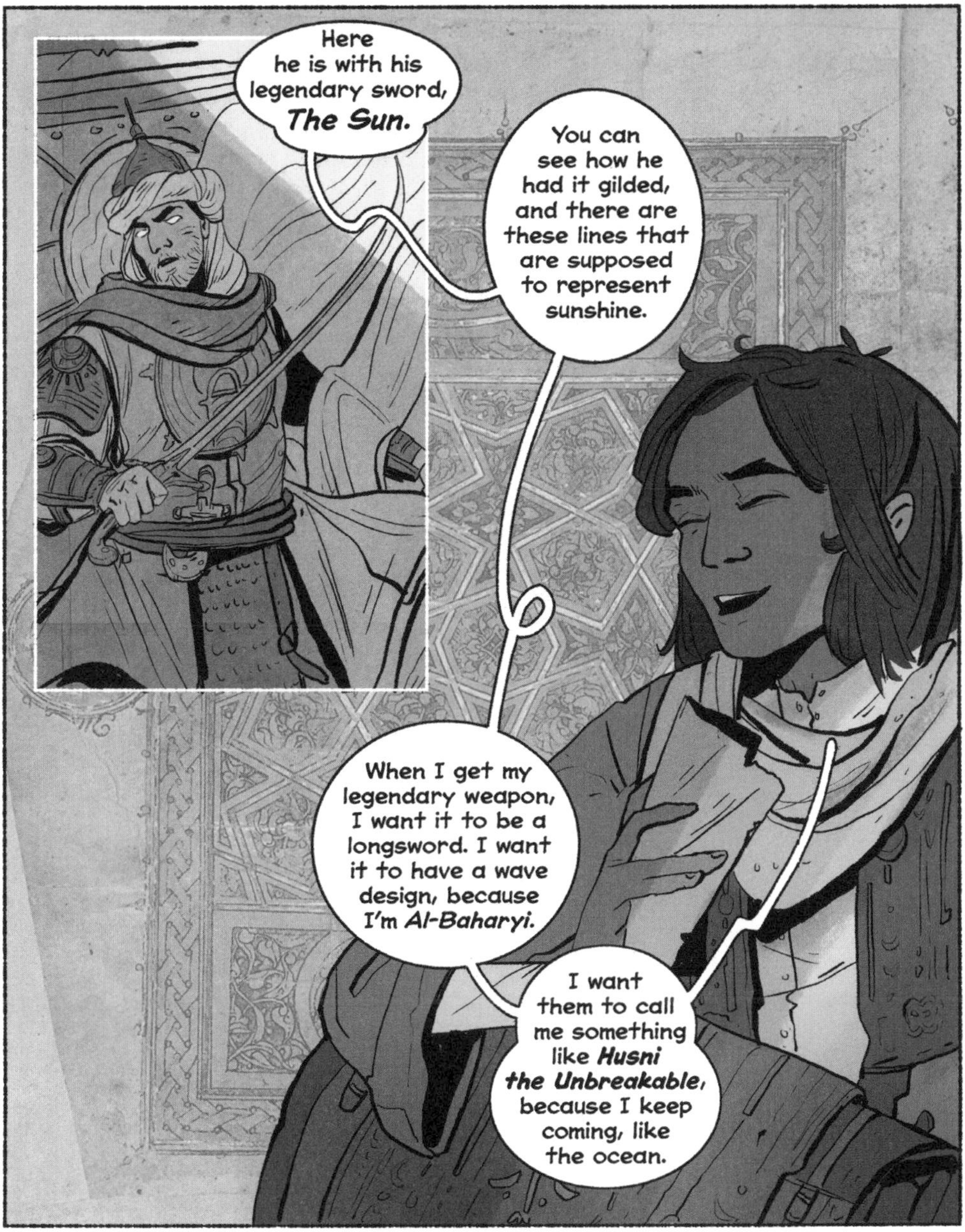
Here he is with his legendary sword, ***The Sun.***
You can see how he had it gilded, and there are these lines that are supposed to represent sunshine.
When I get my legendary weapon, I want it to be a longsword. I want it to have a wave design, because I'm *Al-Baharyi.*
I want them to call me something like ***Husni the Unbreakable***, because I keep coming, like the ocean.

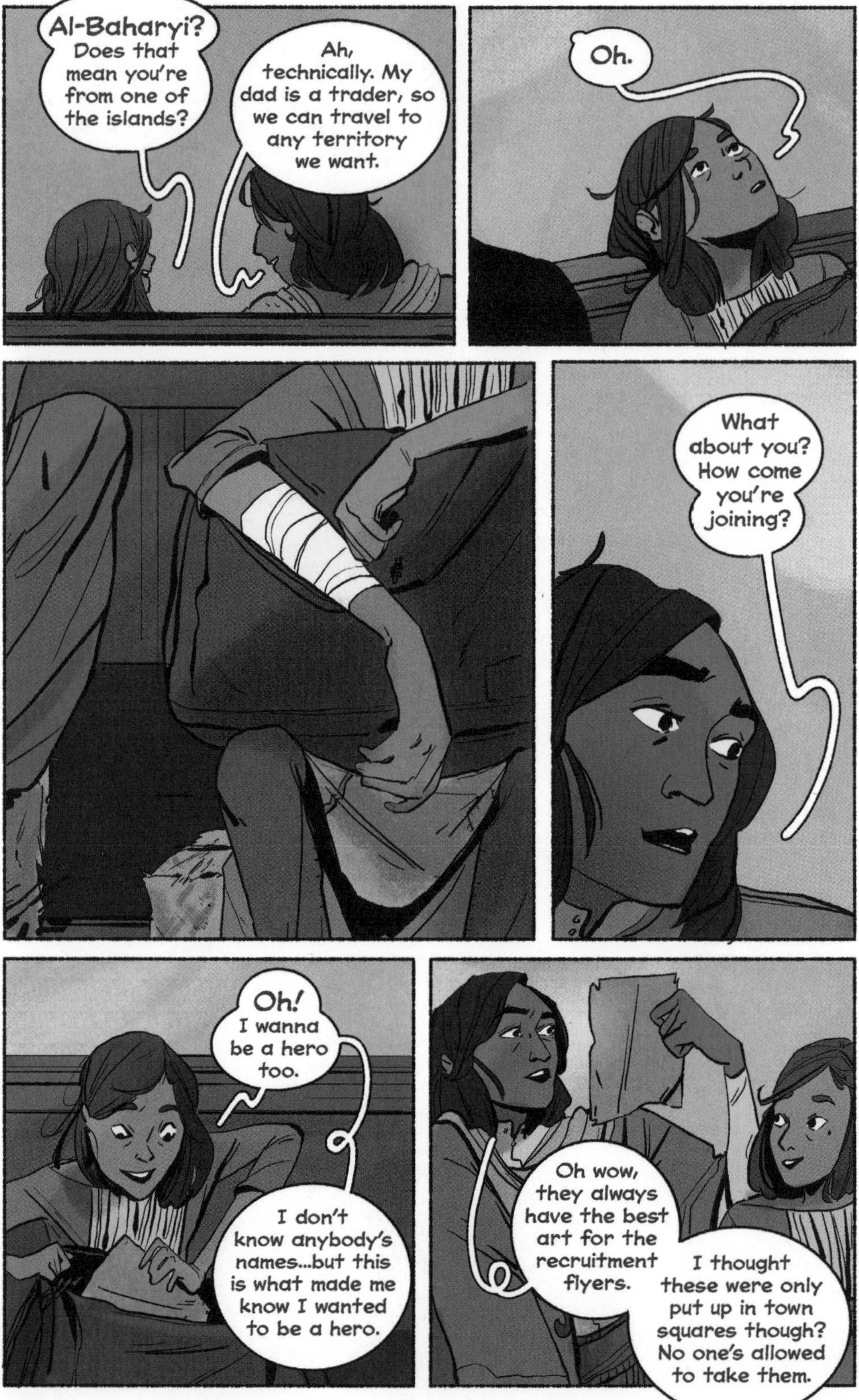
Al-Baharyi? Does that mean you're from one of the islands?
Ah, technically. My dad is a trader, so we can travel to any territory we want.
Oh.
What about you? How come you're joining?
Oh! I wanna be a hero too.
I don't know anybody's names...but this is what made me know I wanted to be a hero.
Oh wow, they always have the best art for the recruitment flyers.
I thought these were only put up in town squares though? No one's allowed to take them.

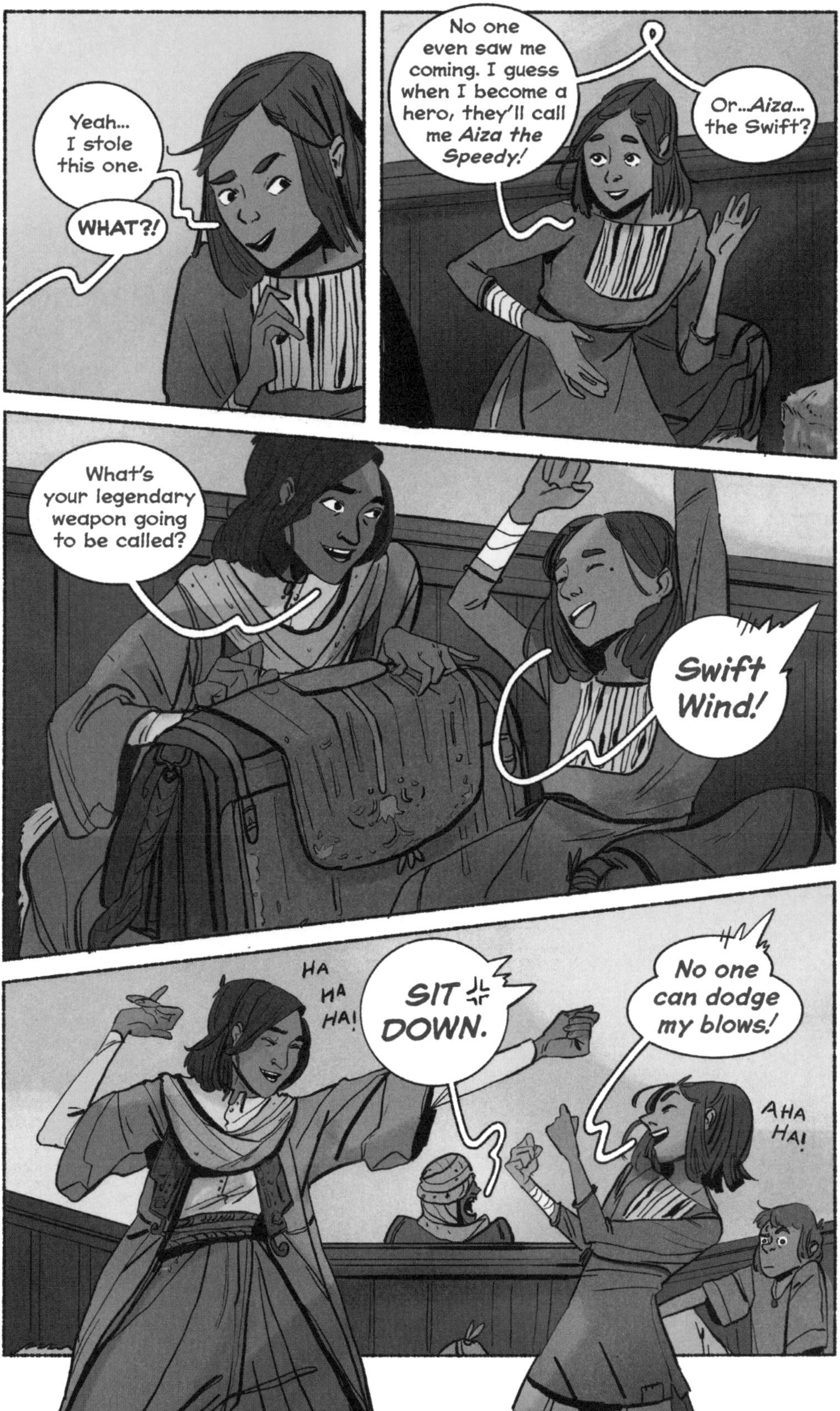
Yeah... I stole this one.
WHAT?!
No one even saw me coming. I guess when I become a hero, they'll call me *Aiza the Speedy!*
Or...*Aiza*... the Swift?
What's your legendary weapon going to be called?
Swift Wind!
HA HA HA!
SIT DOWN.
No one can dodge my blows!
AHA HA!

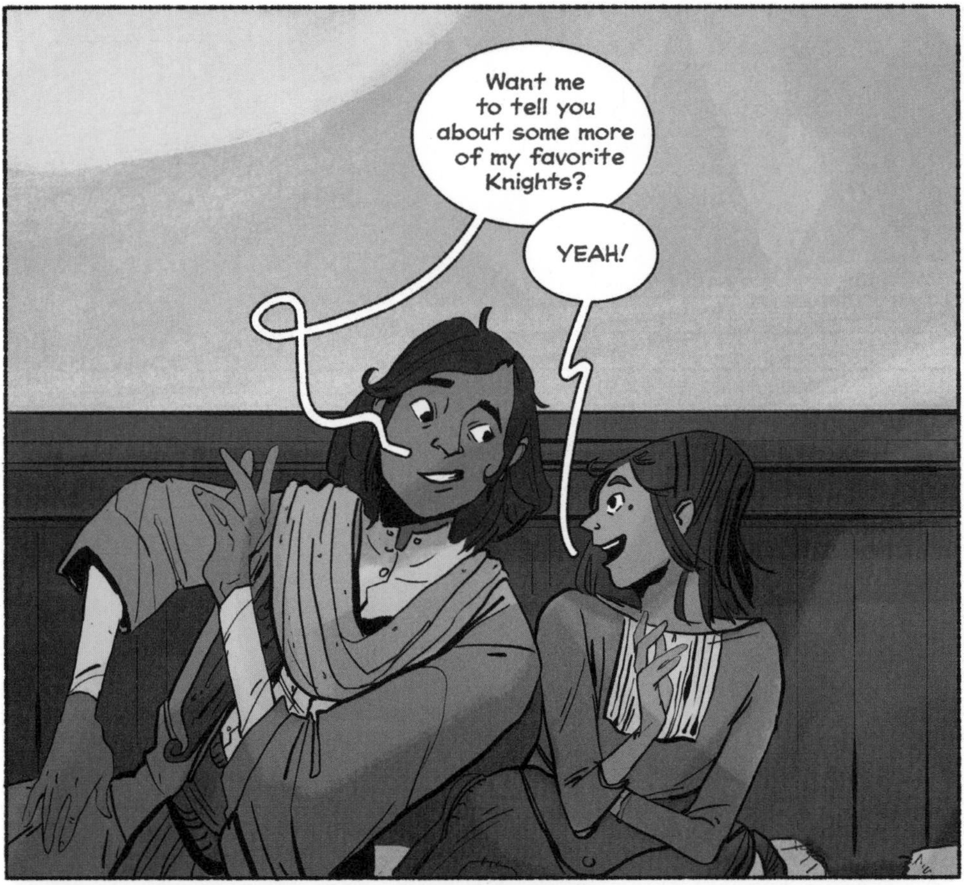
Want me to tell you about some more of my favorite Knights?
YEAH!
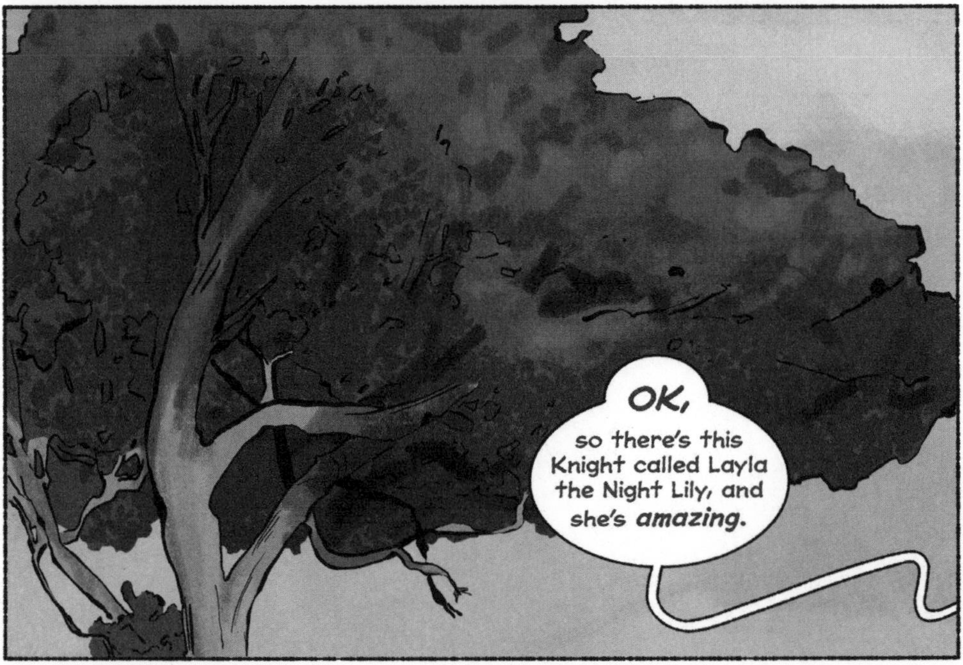
OK, so there's this Knight called Layla the Night Lily, and she's *amazing*.

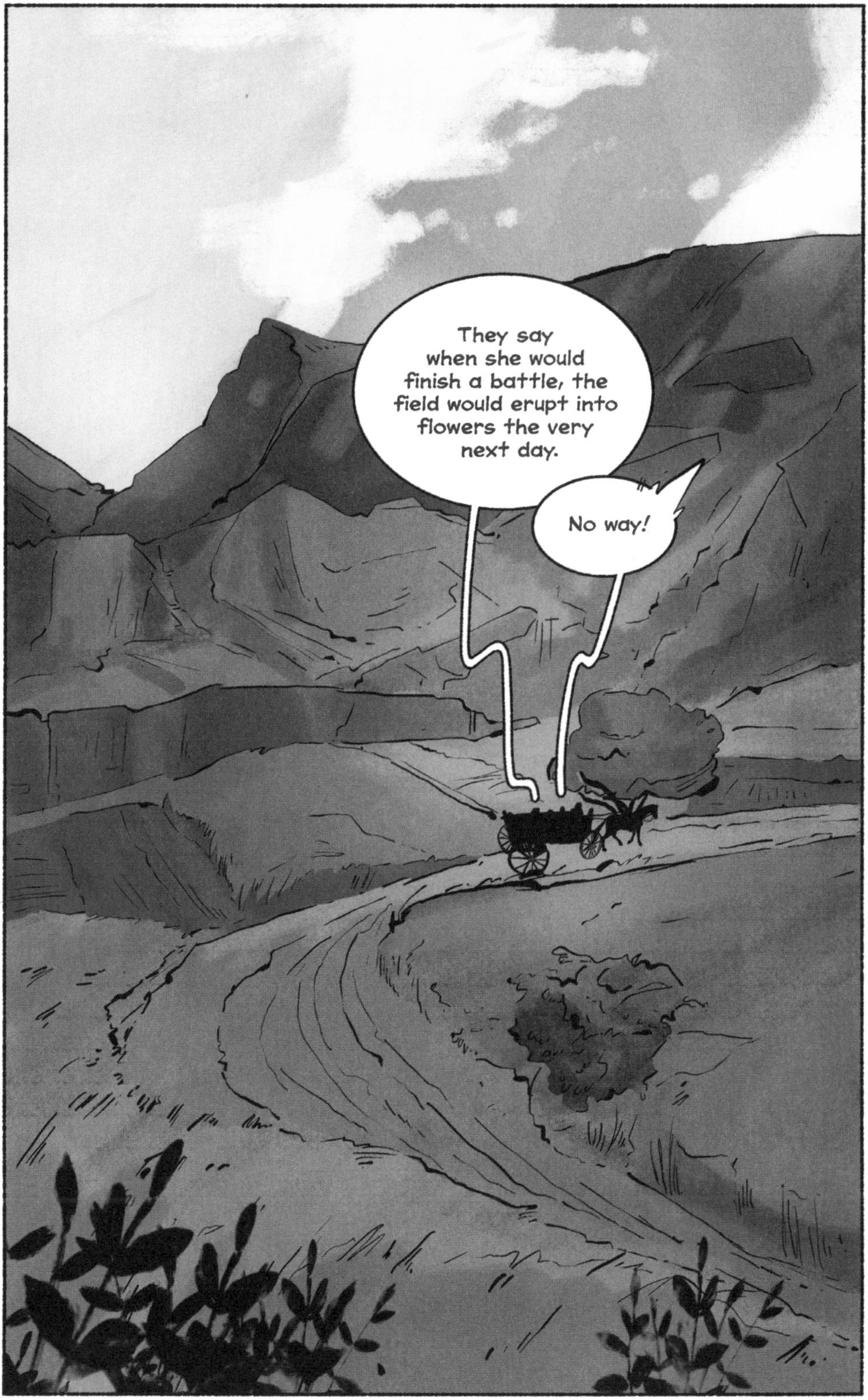
They say when she would finish a battle, the field would erupt into flowers the very next day.
No way!

CHAPTER 3

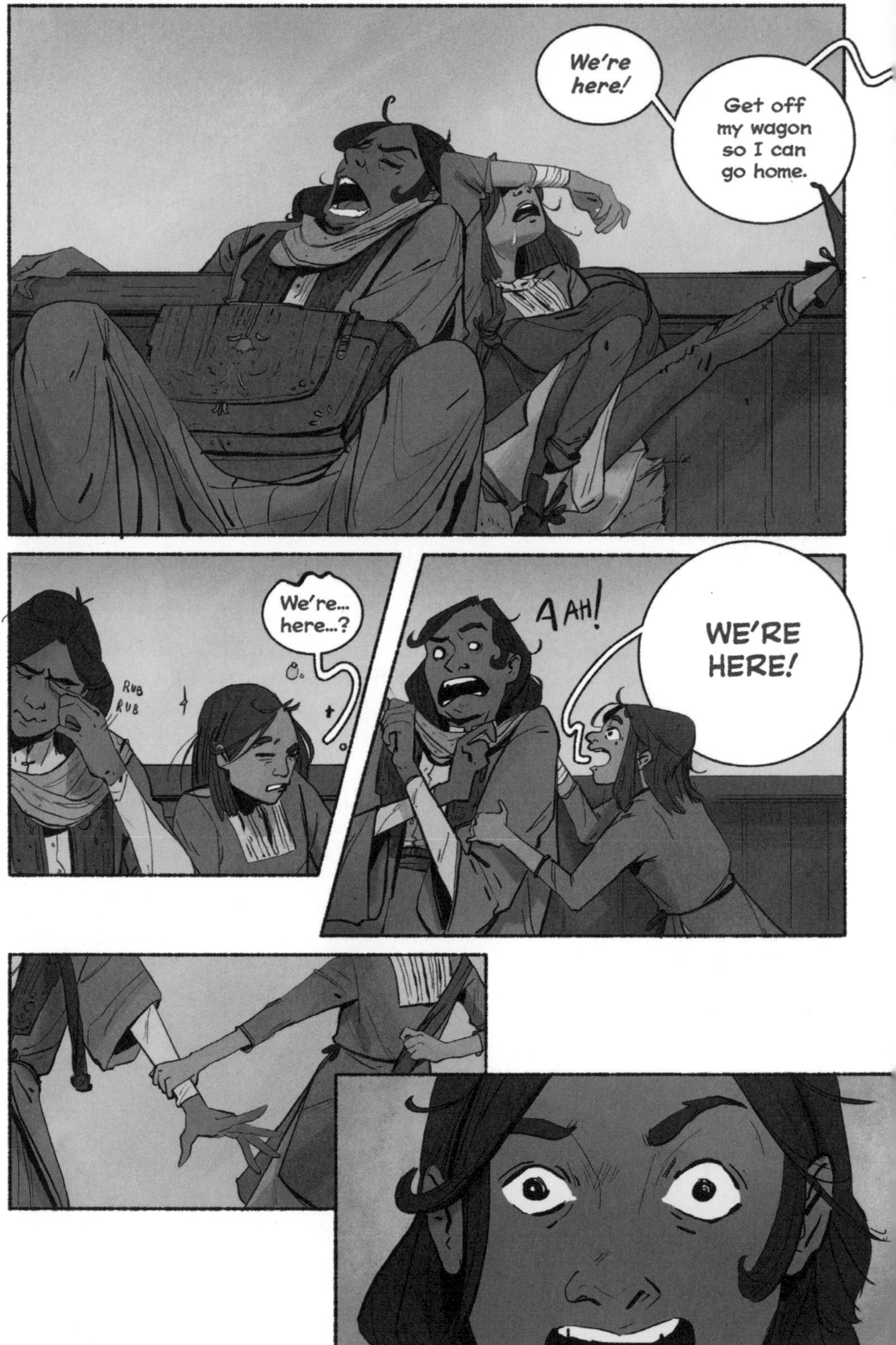
We're here!
Get off my wagon so I can go home.
We're... here...?
RUB RUB
AAH!
WE'RE HERE!

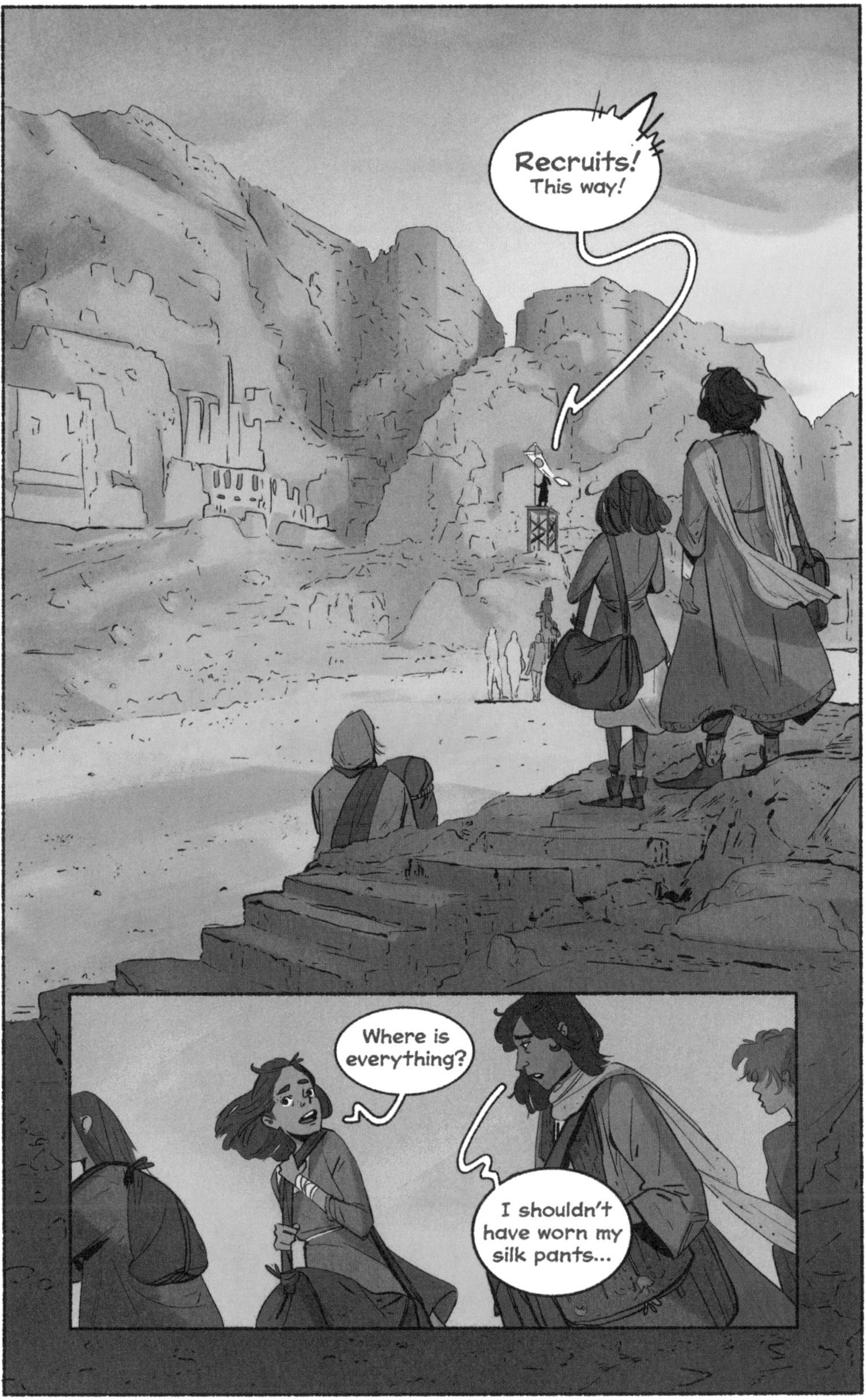
Recruits! This way!
Where is everything?
I shouldn't have worn my silk pants...

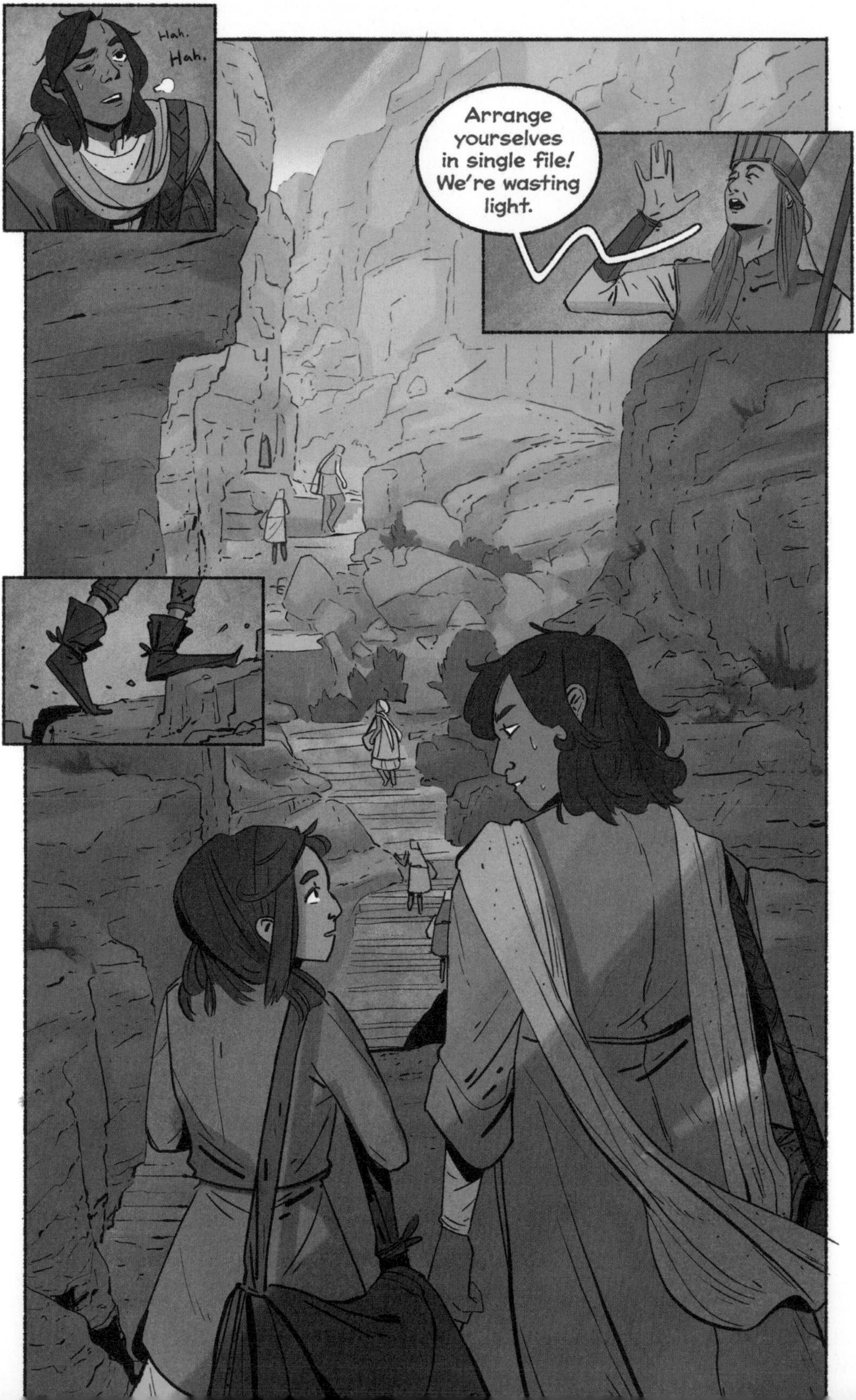
Hah.
Hah.
Arrange yourselves in single file! We're wasting light.

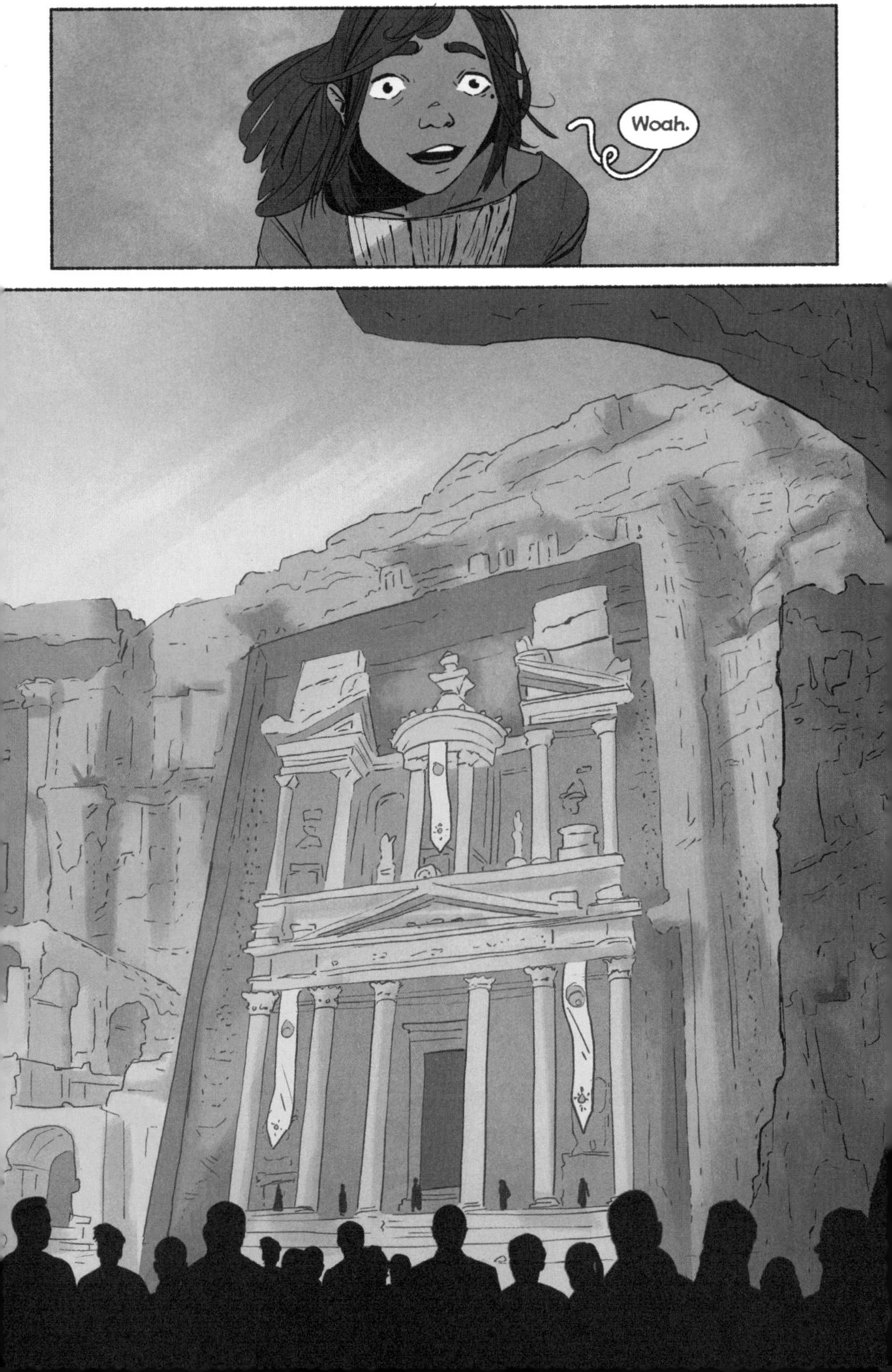
Woah.

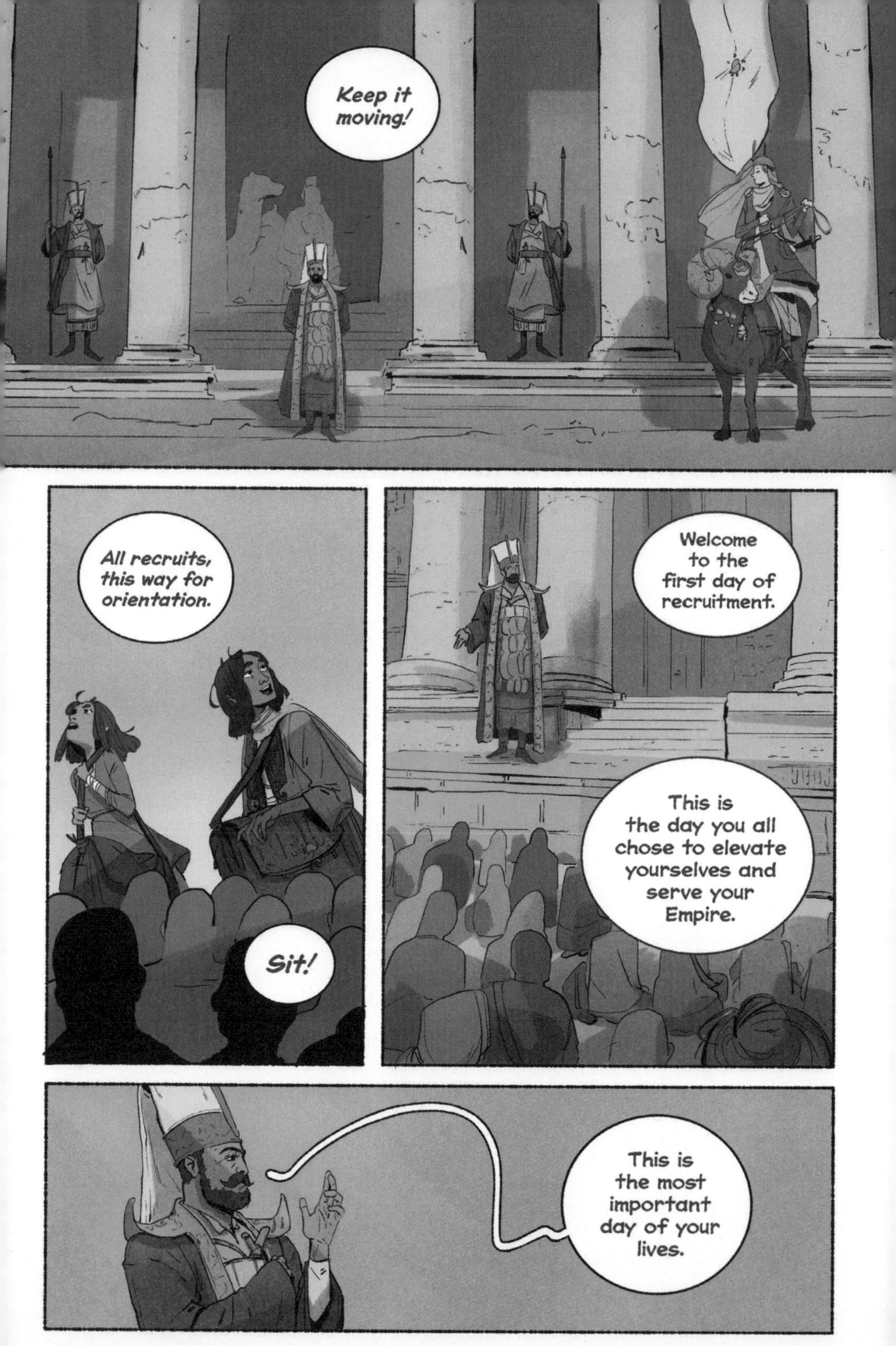
Keep it moving!
All recruits, this way for orientation.
Sit!
Welcome to the first day of recruitment.
This is the day you all chose to elevate yourselves and serve your Empire.
This is the most important day of your lives.

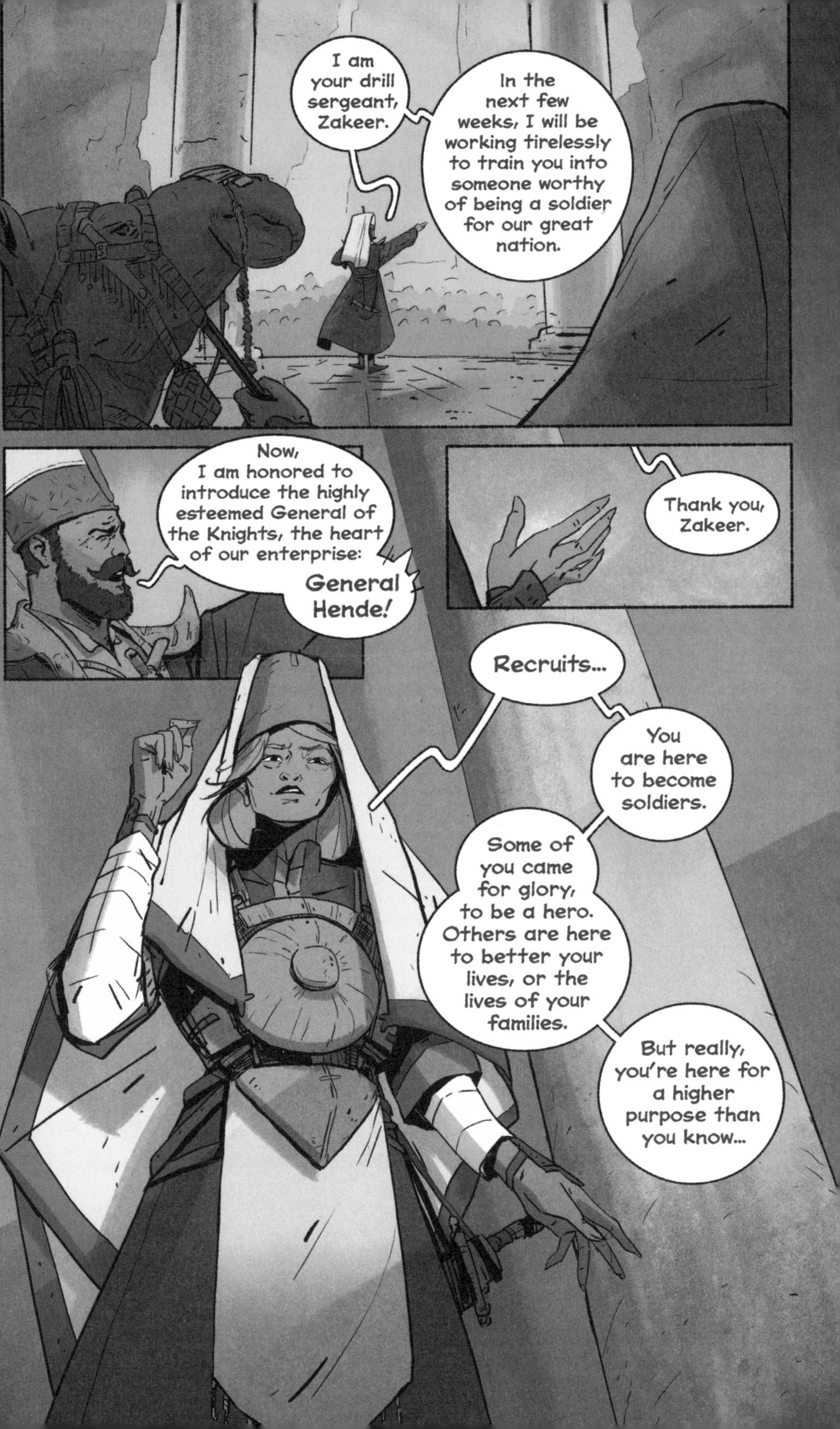
I am your drill sergeant, Zakeer.
In the next few weeks, I will be working tirelessly to train you into someone worthy of being a soldier for our great nation.
Now, I am honored to introduce the highly esteemed General of the Knights, the heart of our enterprise:
General Hende!
Thank you, Zakeer.
Recruits...
You are here to become soldiers.
Some of you came for glory, to be a hero. Others are here to better your lives, or the lives of your families.
But really, you're here for a higher purpose than you know...

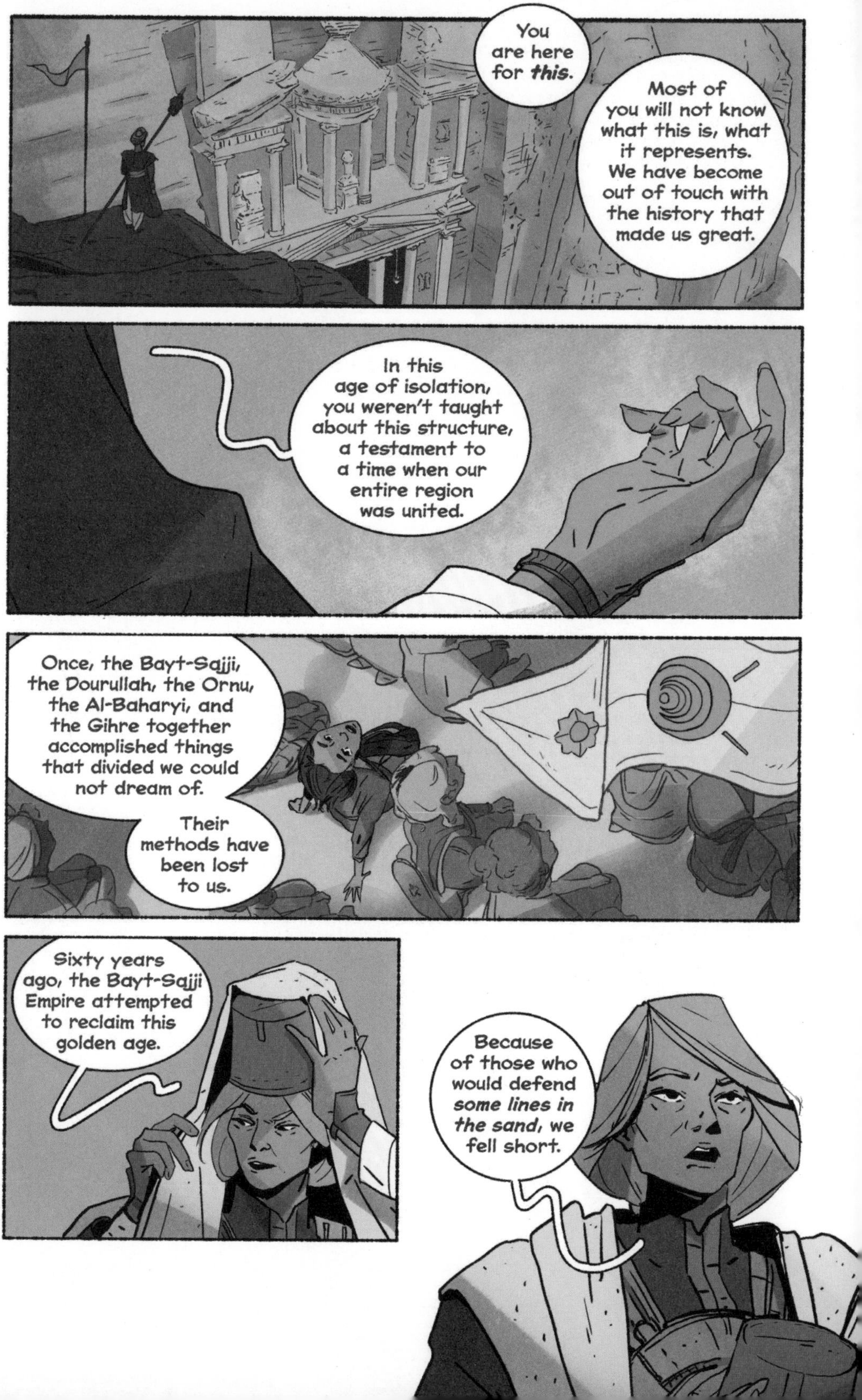

You are here for *this*.
Most of you will not know what this is, what it represents. We have become out of touch with the history that made us great.
In this age of isolation, you weren't taught about this structure, a testament to a time when our entire region was united.
Once, the Bayt-Sajji, the Dourullah, the Ornu, the Al-Baharyi, and the Gihre together accomplished things that divided we could not dream of.
Their methods have been lost to us.
Sixty years ago, the Bayt-Sajji Empire attempted to reclaim this golden age.
Because of those who would defend *some lines in the sand*, we fell short.

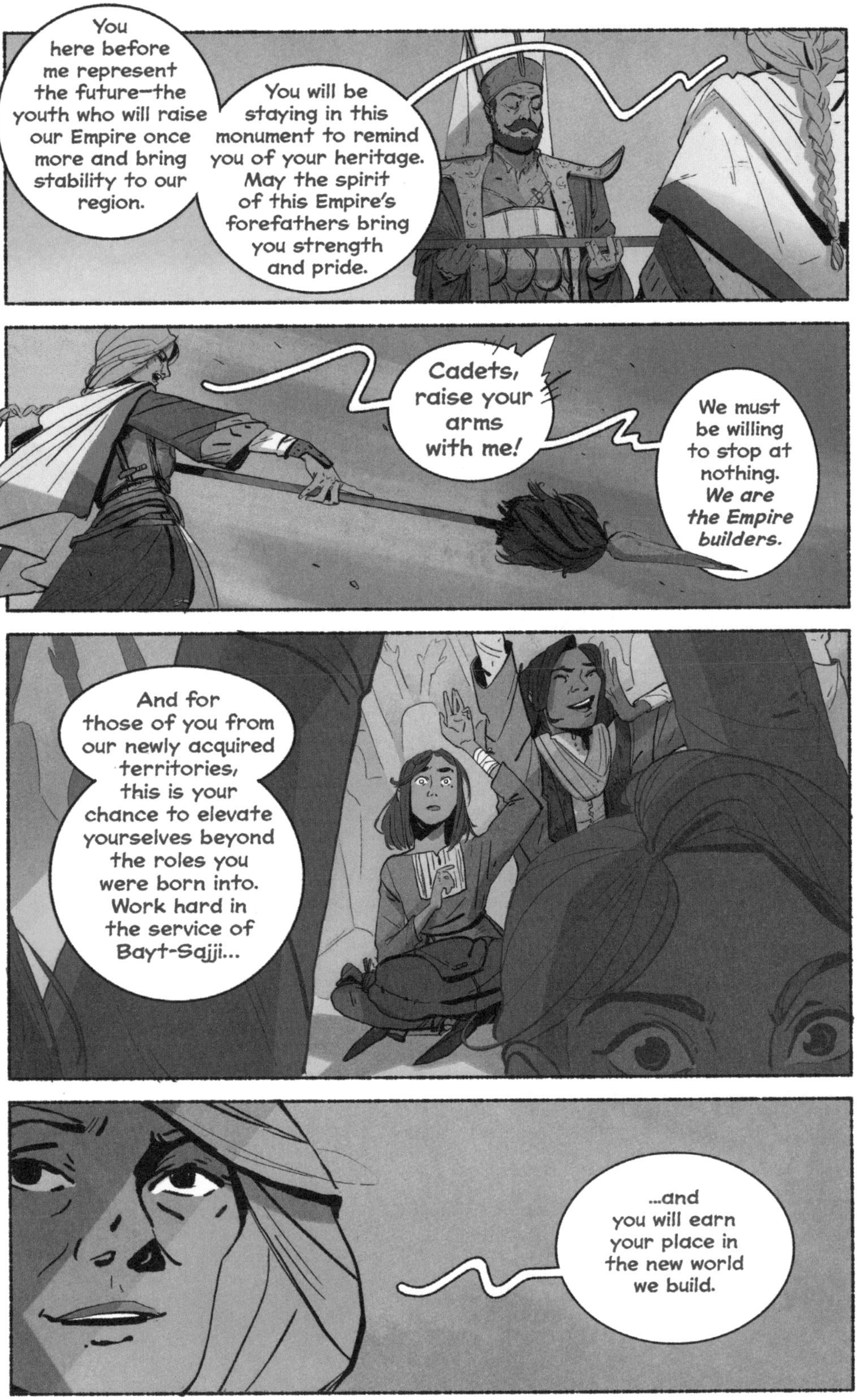
You here before me represent the future—the youth who will raise our Empire once more and bring stability to our region.
You will be staying in this monument to remind you of your heritage. May the spirit of this Empire's forefathers bring you strength and pride.
Cadets, raise your arms with me!
We must be willing to stop at nothing. *We are the Empire builders.*
And for those of you from our newly acquired territories, this is your chance to elevate yourselves beyond the roles you were born into. Work hard in the service of Bayt-Sajji...
...and you will earn your place in the new world we build.

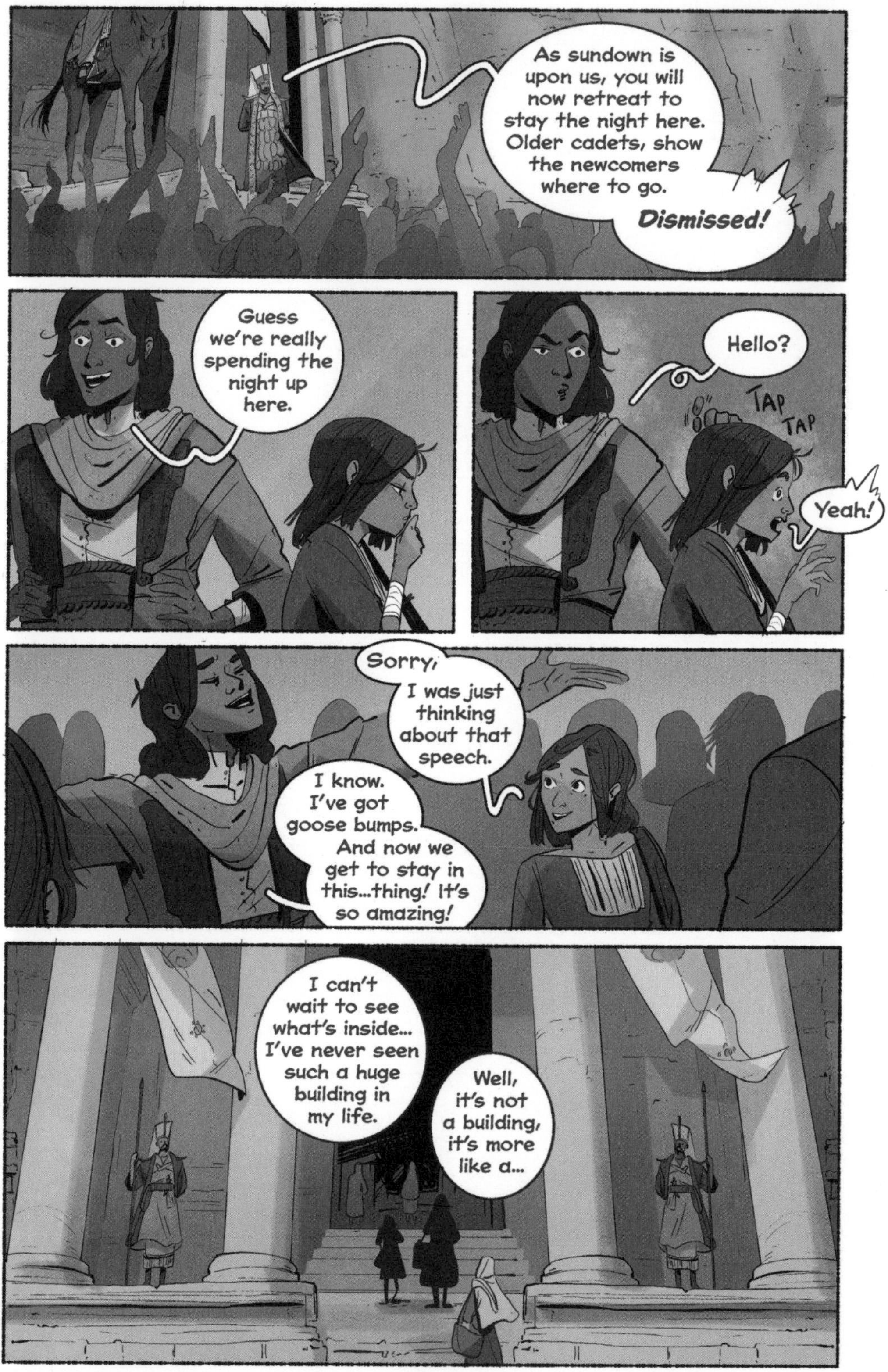
As sundown is upon us, you will now retreat to stay the night here. Older cadets, show the newcomers where to go.
Dismissed!
Guess we're really spending the night up here.
Hello?
TAP TAP
Yeah!
Sorry,
I was just thinking about that speech.
I know. I've got goose bumps.
And now we get to stay in this...thing! It's so amazing!
I can't wait to see what's inside... I've never seen such a huge building in my life.
Well, it's not a building, it's more like a...

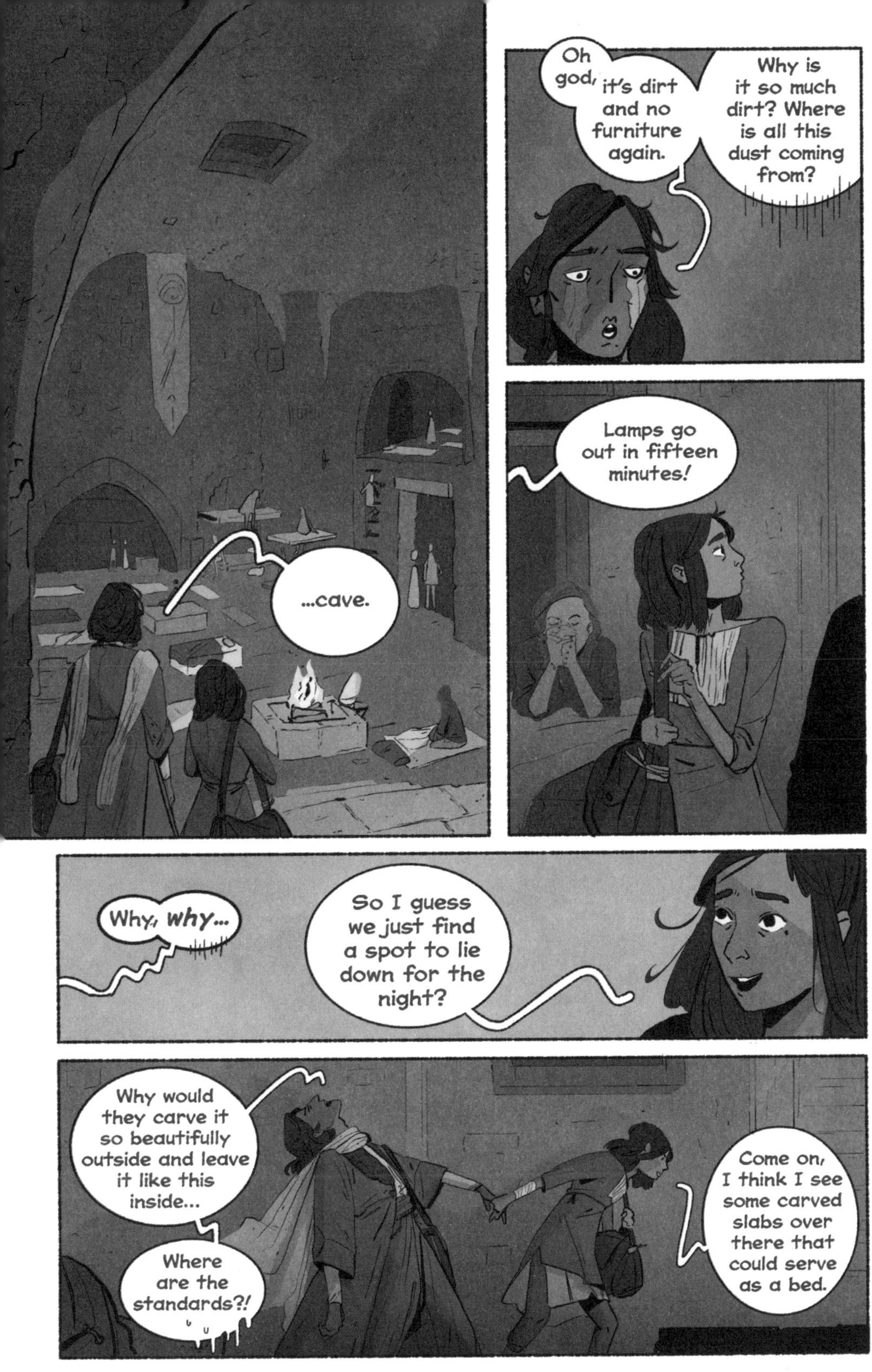
...cave.
Oh god, it's dirt and no furniture again.
Why is it so much dirt? Where is all this dust coming from?
Lamps go out in fifteen minutes!
Why, why...
So I guess we just find a spot to lie down for the night?
Why would they carve it so beautifully outside and leave it like this inside...
Where are the standards?!
Come on, I think I see some carved slabs over there that could serve as a bed.

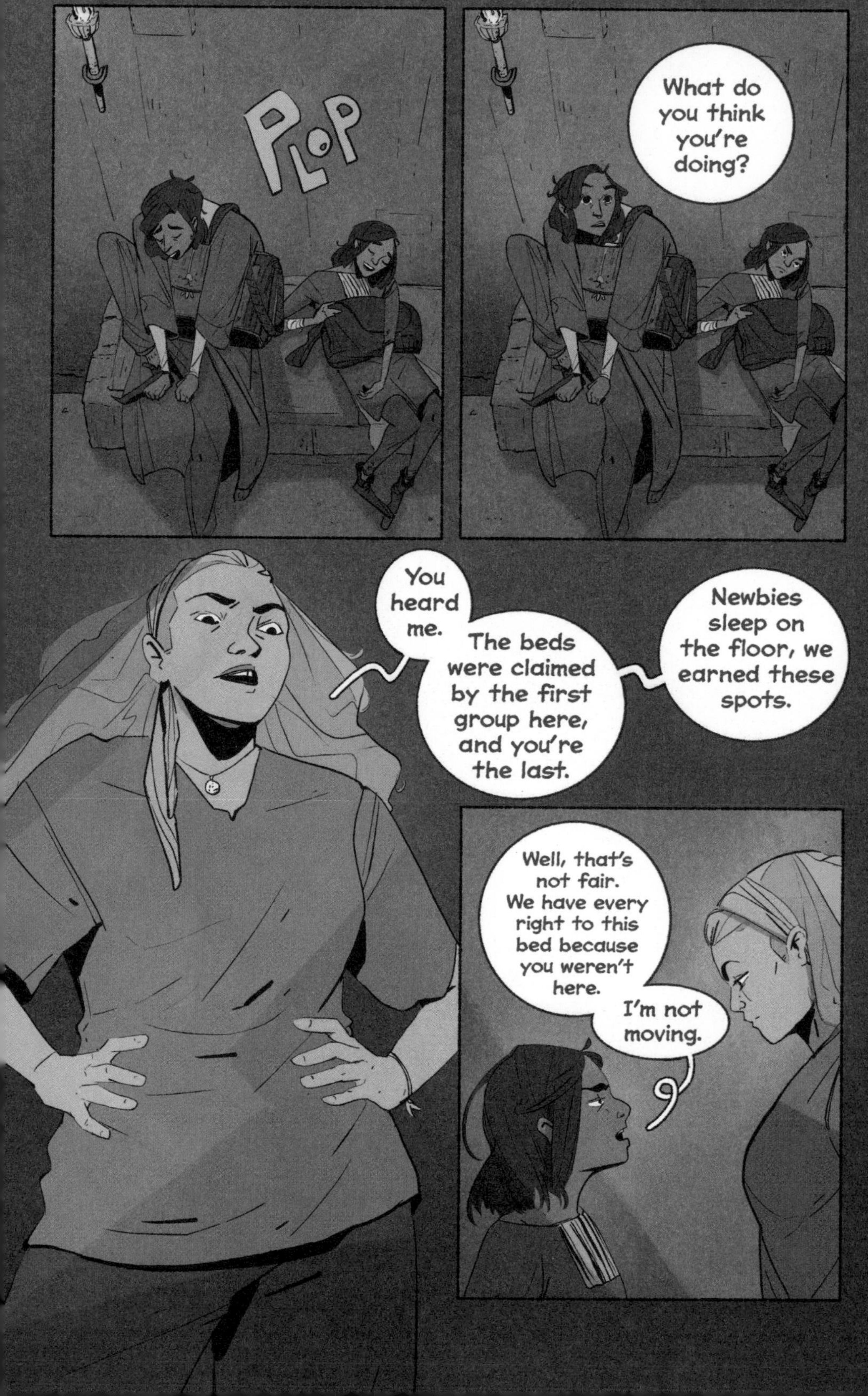
PLOP
What do you think you're doing?
You heard me.
The beds were claimed by the first group here, and you're the last.
Newbies sleep on the floor, we earned these spots.
Well, that's not fair. We have every right to this bed because you weren't here.
I'm not moving.

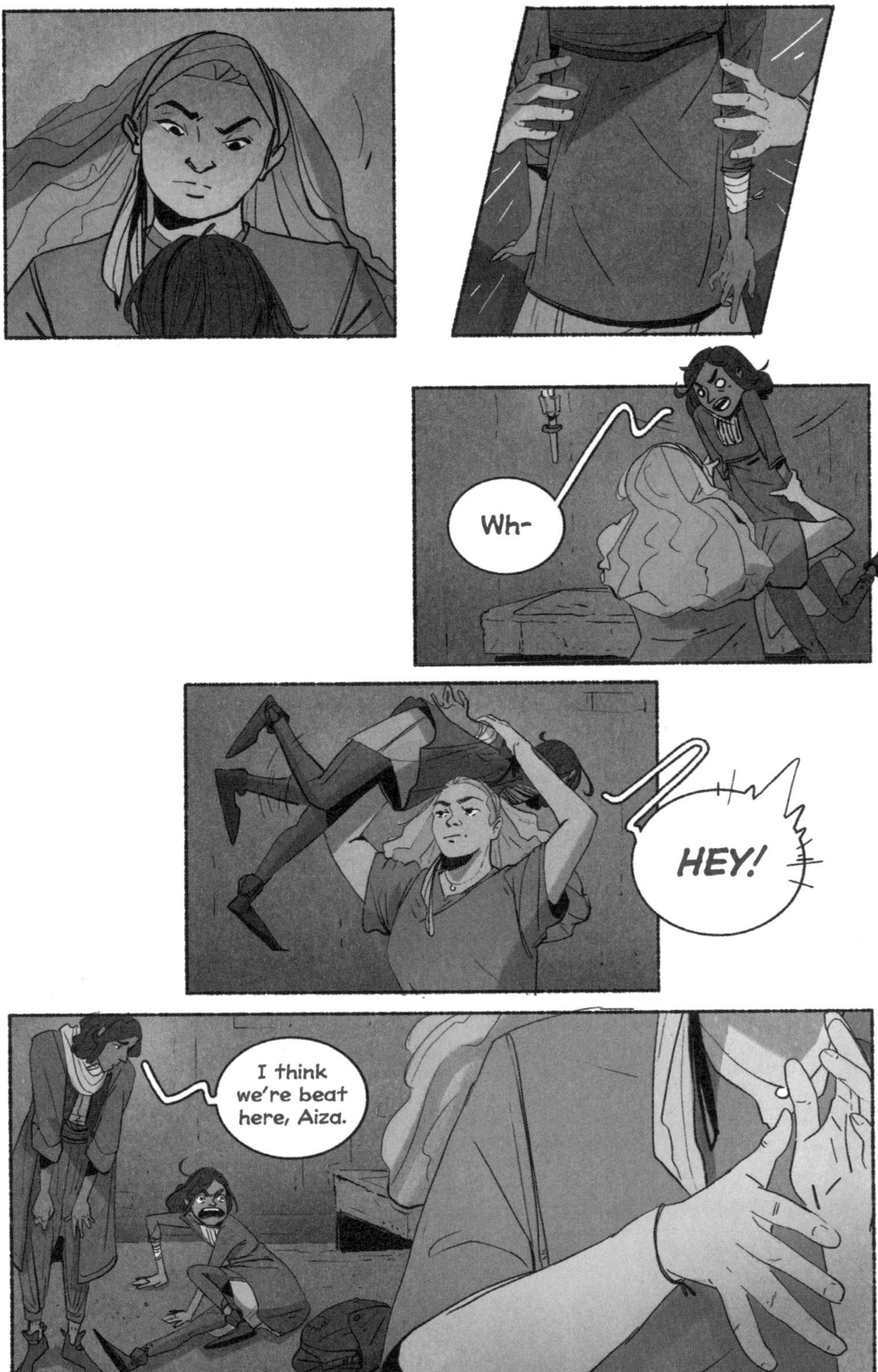
Wh-
HEY!
I think we're beat here, Aiza.

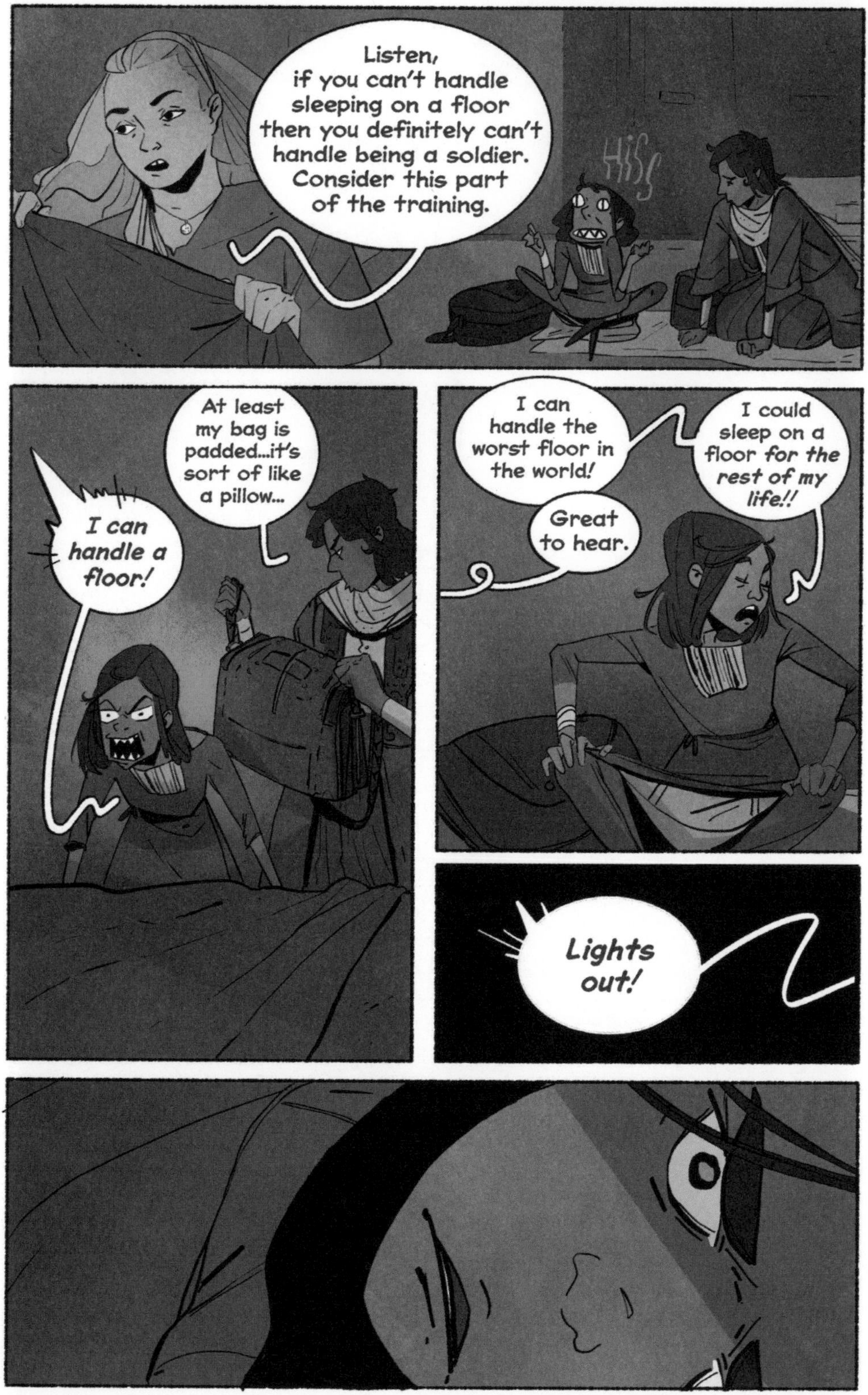
Listen, if you can't handle sleeping on a floor then you definitely can't handle being a soldier. Consider this part of the training.
HISS
At least my bag is padded...it's sort of like a pillow...
I can handle a floor!
I can handle the worst floor in the world!
I could sleep on a floor for the rest of my life!!
Great to hear.
Lights out!

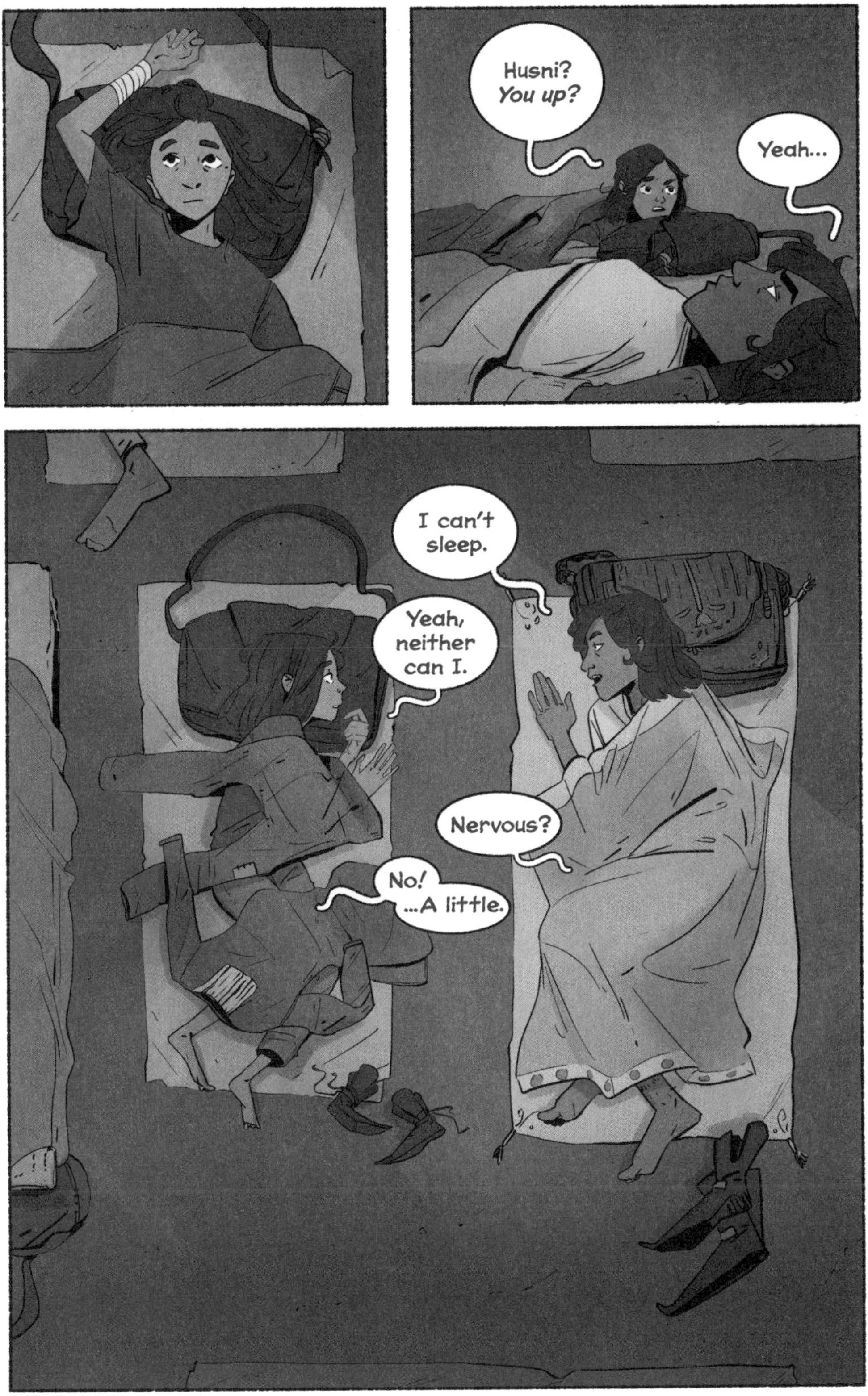
Husni? You up?
Yeah...
I can't sleep.
Yeah, neither can I.
Nervous?
No! ...A little.

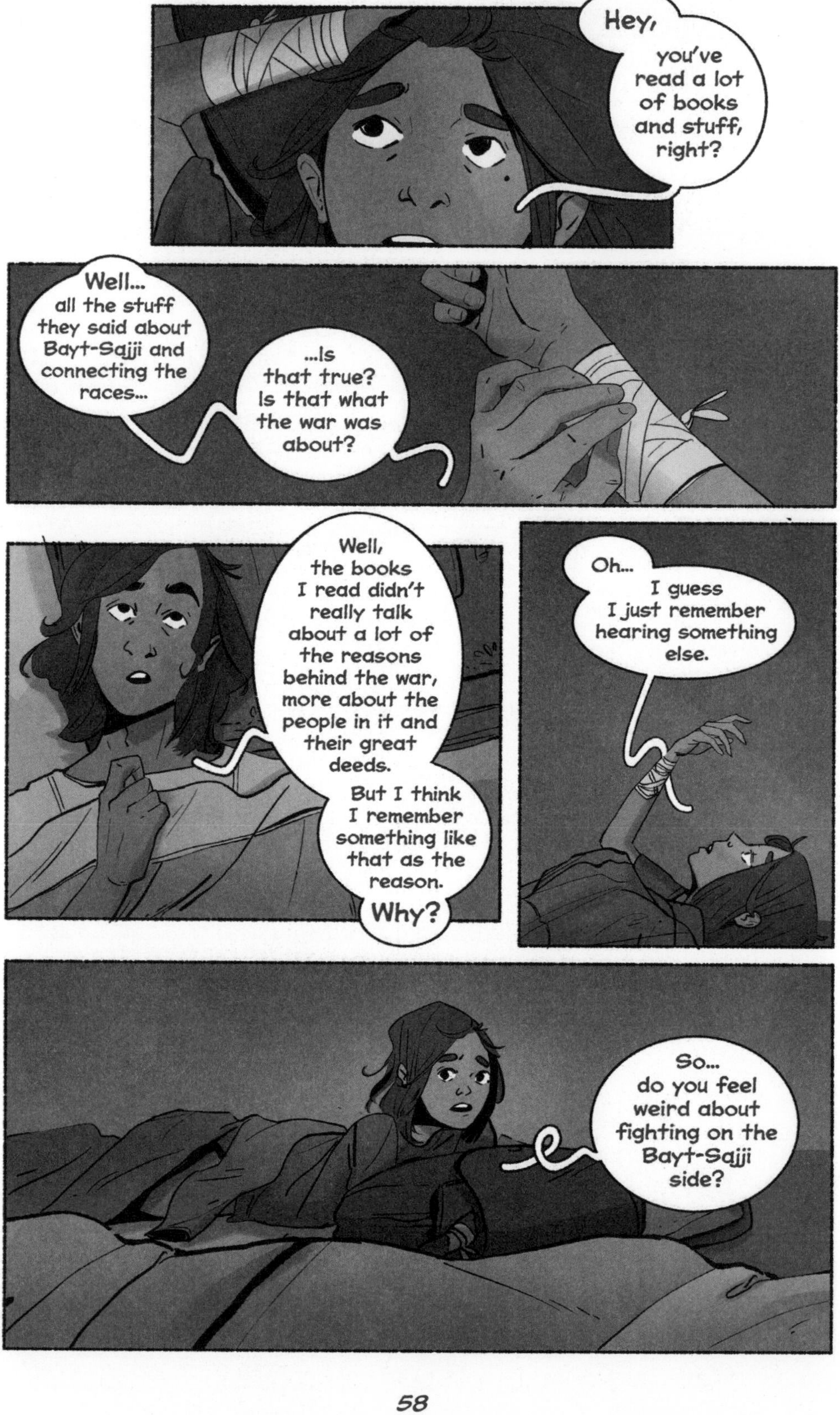
Hey, you've read a lot of books and stuff, right?
Well... all the stuff they said about Bayt-Sajji and connecting the races...
...Is that true? Is that what the war was about?
Well, the books I read didn't really talk about a lot of the reasons behind the war, more about the people in it and their great deeds.
But I think I remember something like that as the reason.
Why?
Oh... I guess I just remember hearing something else.
So... do you feel weird about fighting on the Bayt-Sajji side?

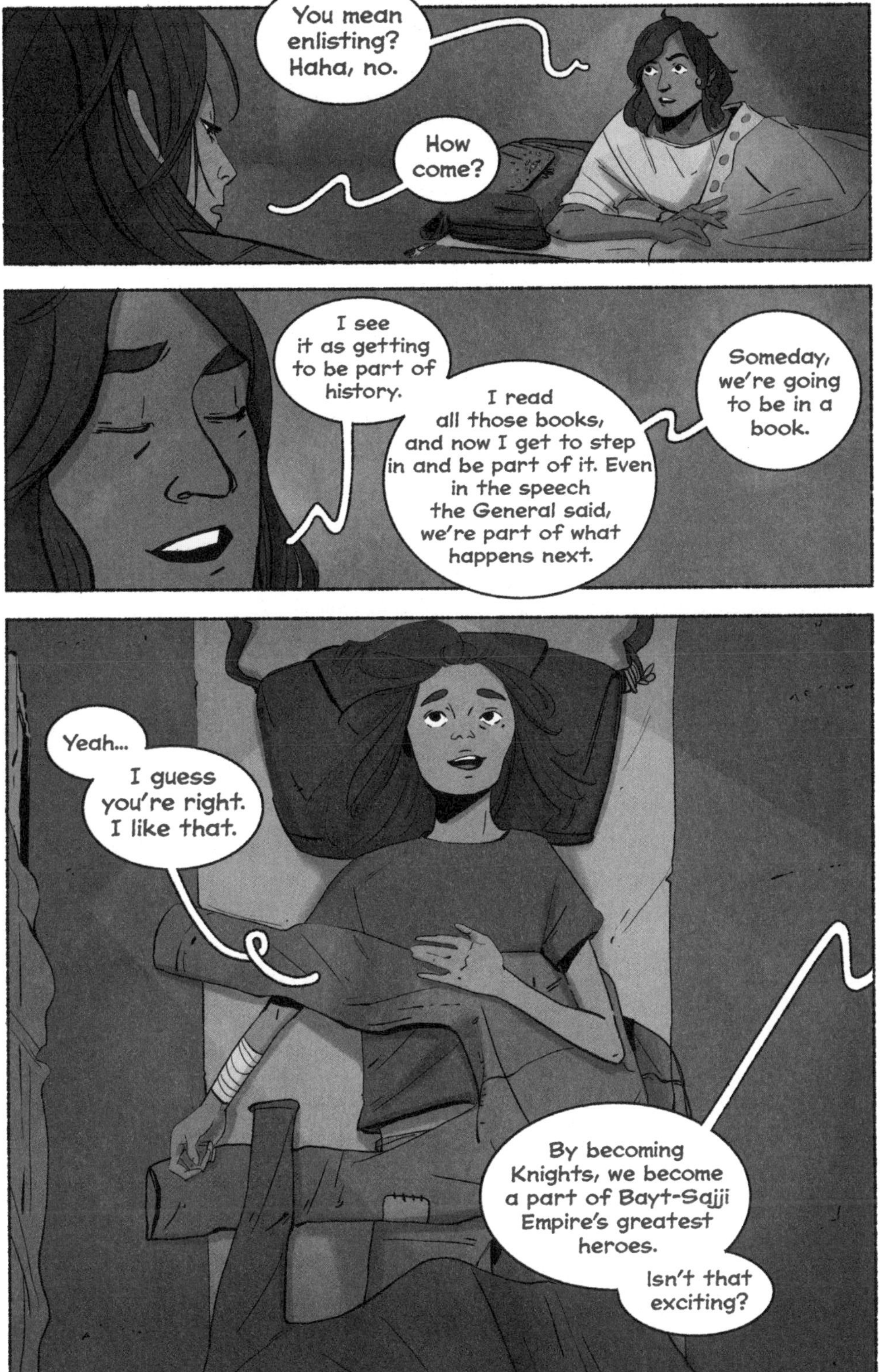
You mean enlisting? Haha, no.
How come?
I see it as getting to be part of history.
I read all those books, and now I get to step in and be part of it. Even in the speech the General said, we're part of what happens next.
Someday, we're going to be in a book.
Yeah...
I guess you're right. I like that.
By becoming Knights, we become a part of Bayt-Sajji Empire's greatest heroes.
Isn't that exciting?

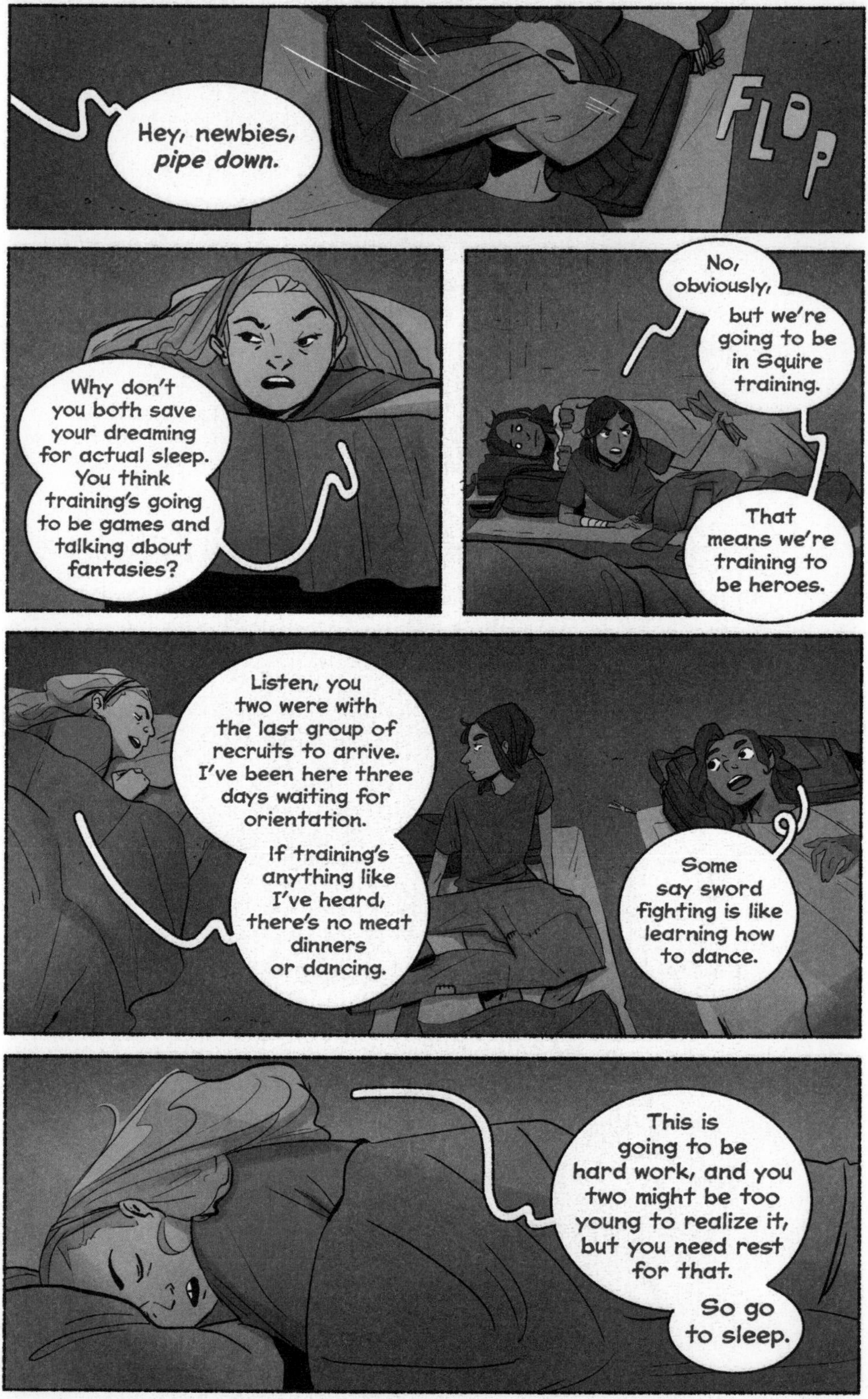

Hey, newbies, *pipe down.*
FLOP
Why don't you both save your dreaming for actual sleep. You think training's going to be games and talking about fantasies?
No, obviously,
but we're going to be in Squire training.
That means we're training to be heroes.
Listen, you two were with the last group of recruits to arrive. I've been here three days waiting for orientation.
If training's anything like I've heard, there's no meat dinners or dancing.
Some say sword fighting is like learning how to dance.
This is going to be hard work, and you two might be too young to realize it, but you need rest for that.
So go to sleep.

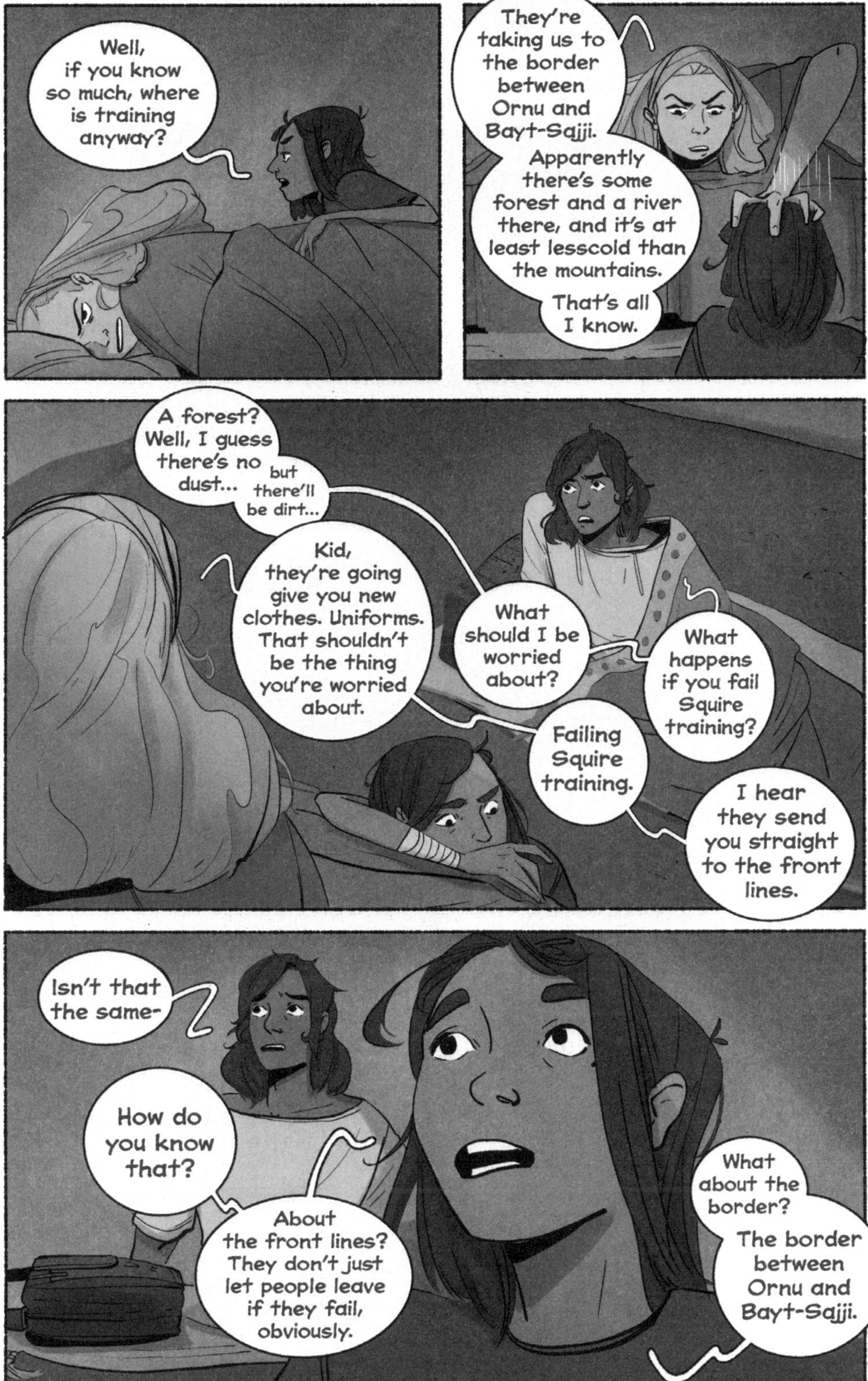
Well, if you know so much, where is training anyway?
They're taking us to the border between Ornu and Bayt-Sajji.
Apparently there's some forest and a river there, and it's at least lesscold than the mountains.
That's all I know.
A forest? Well, I guess there's no dust...
but there'll be dirt...
Kid, they're going give you new clothes. Uniforms. That shouldn't be the thing you're worried about.
What should I be worried about?
Failing Squire training.
What happens if you fail Squire training?
I hear they send you straight to the front lines.
Isn't that the same-
How do you know that?
About the front lines? They don't just let people leave if they fail, obviously.
What about the border?
The border between Ornu and Bayt-Sajji.

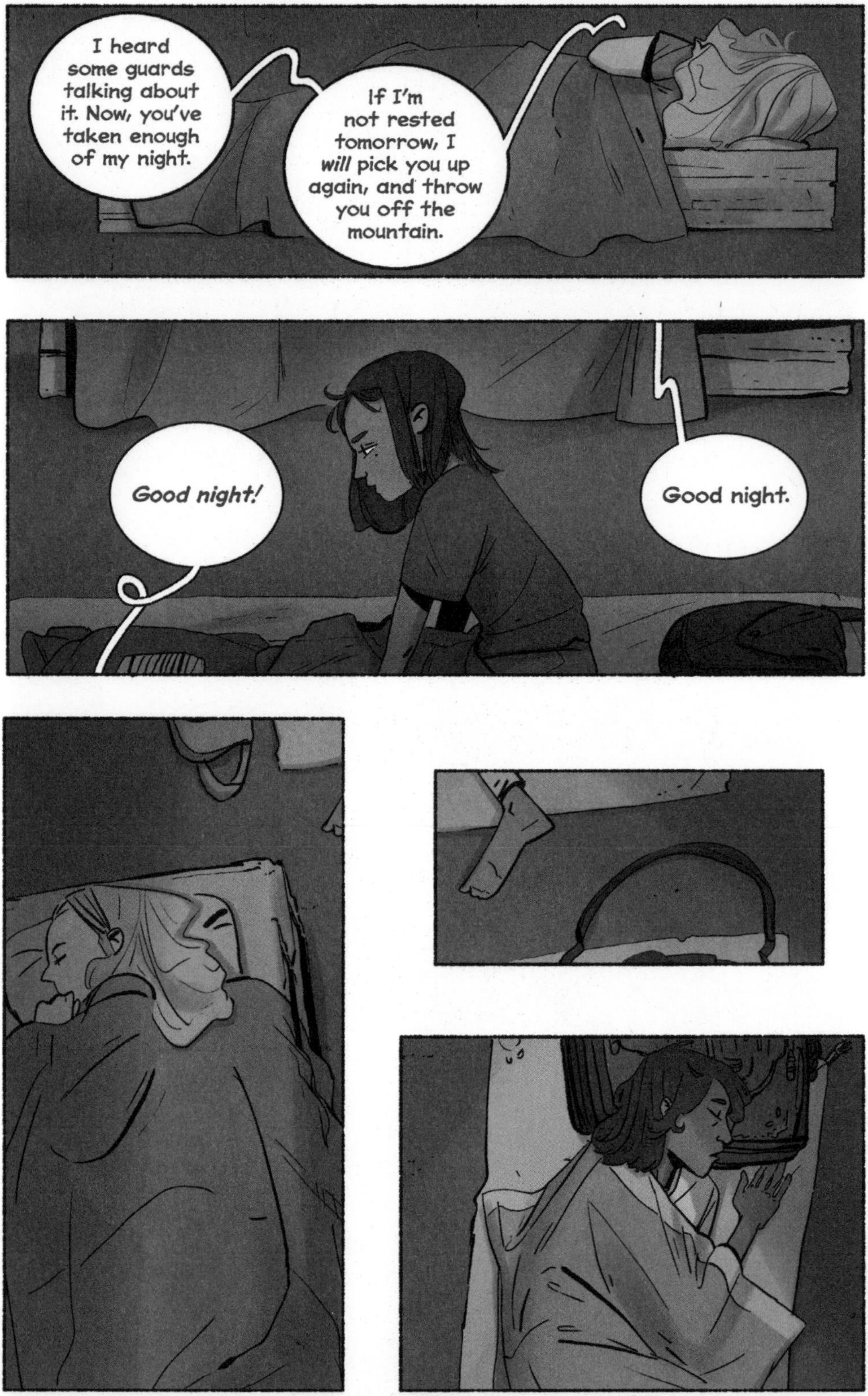
I heard some guards talking about it. Now, you've taken enough of my night.
If I'm not rested tomorrow, I *will* pick you up again, and throw you off the mountain.
Good night!
Good night.

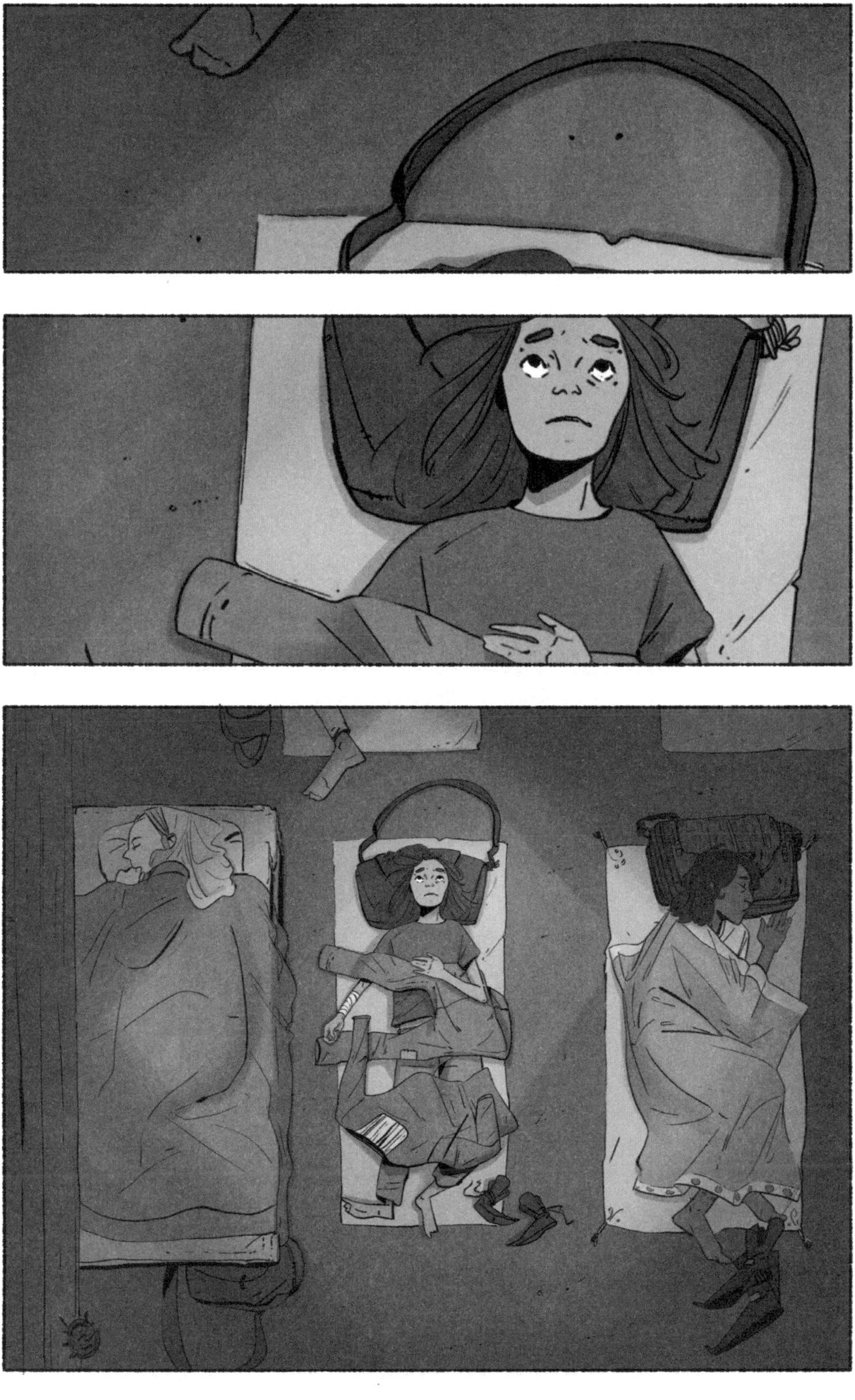

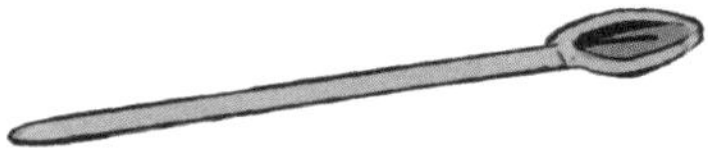

CHAPTER 4

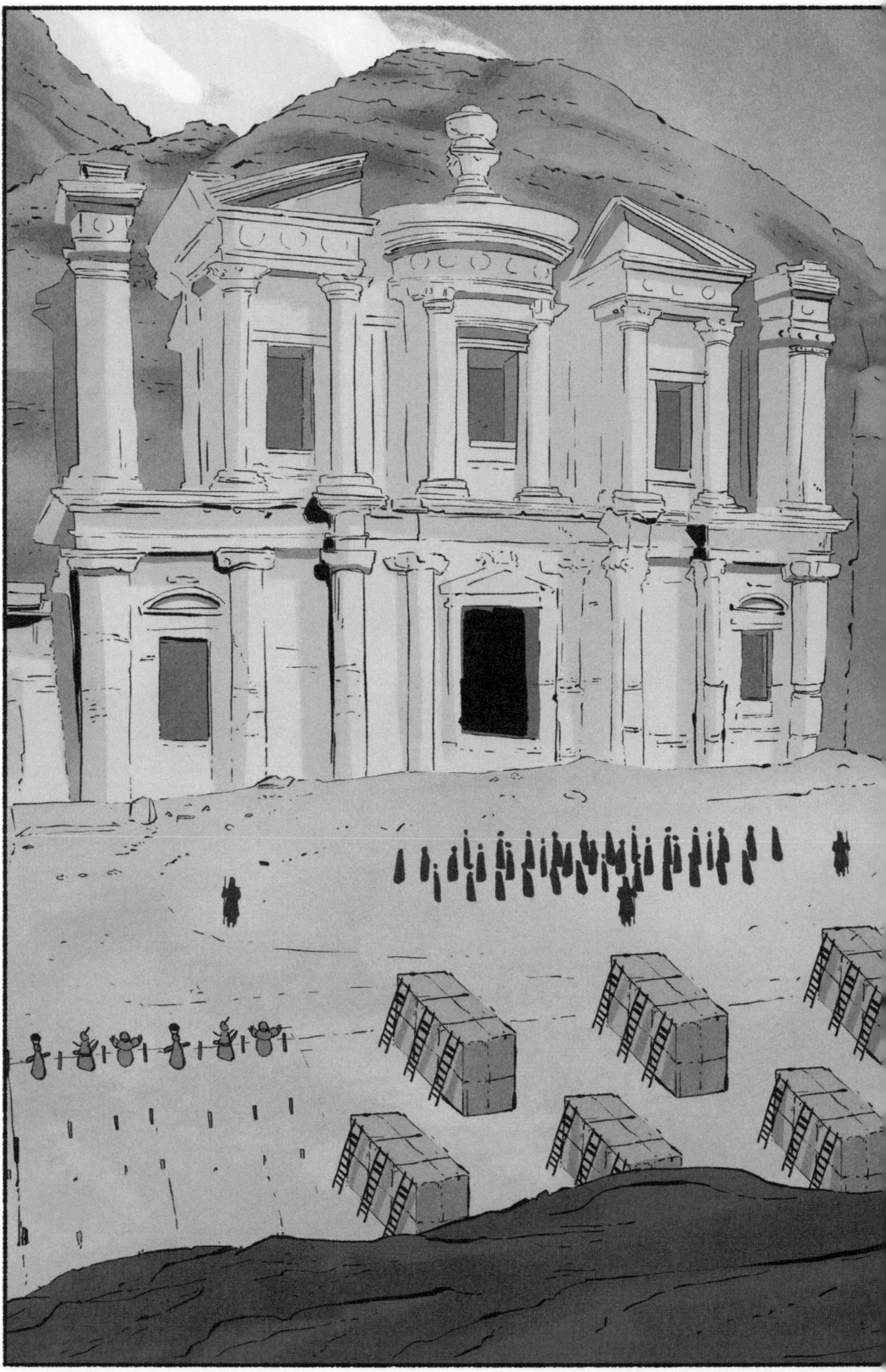

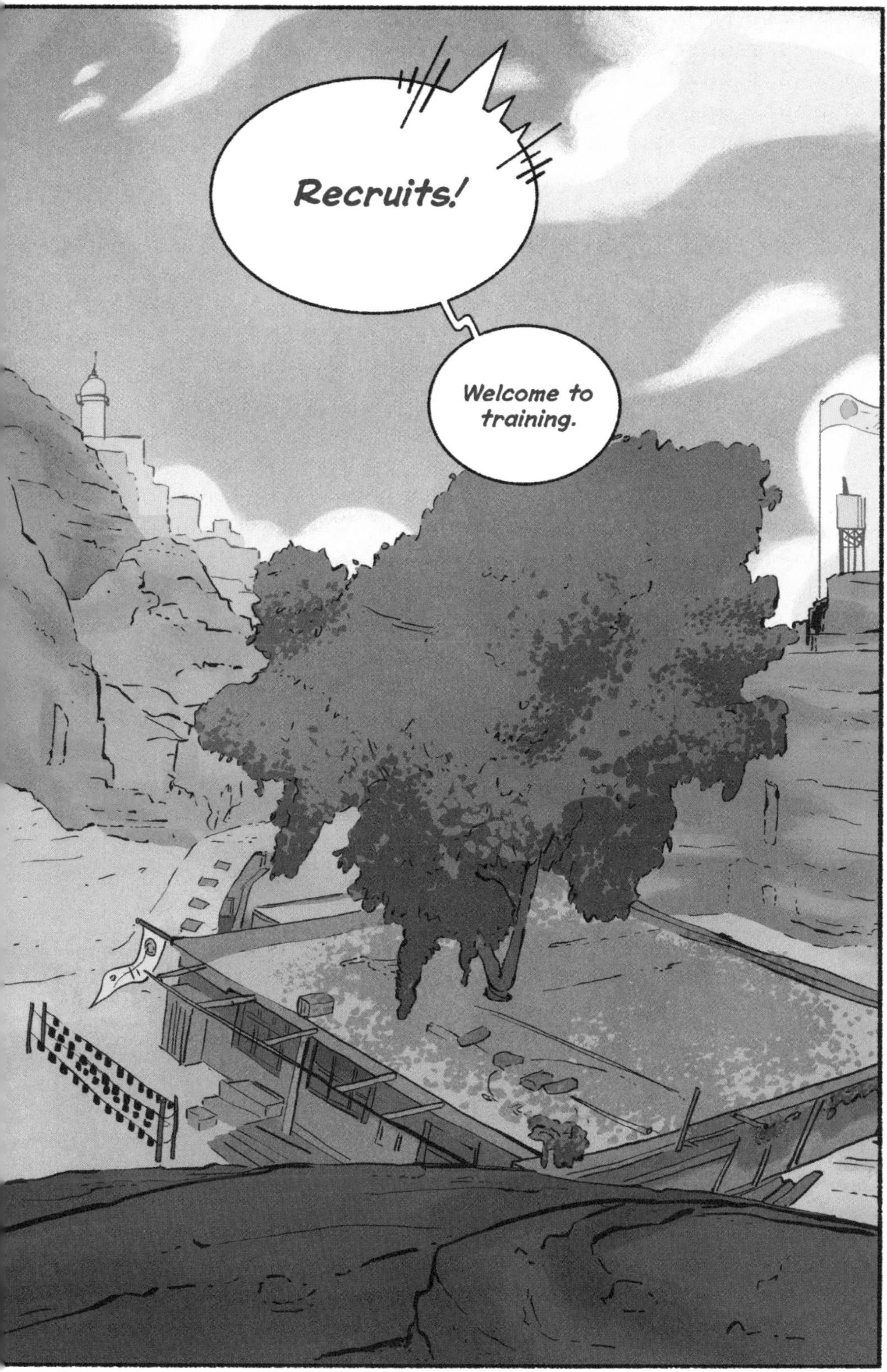
Recruits!
Welcome to training.

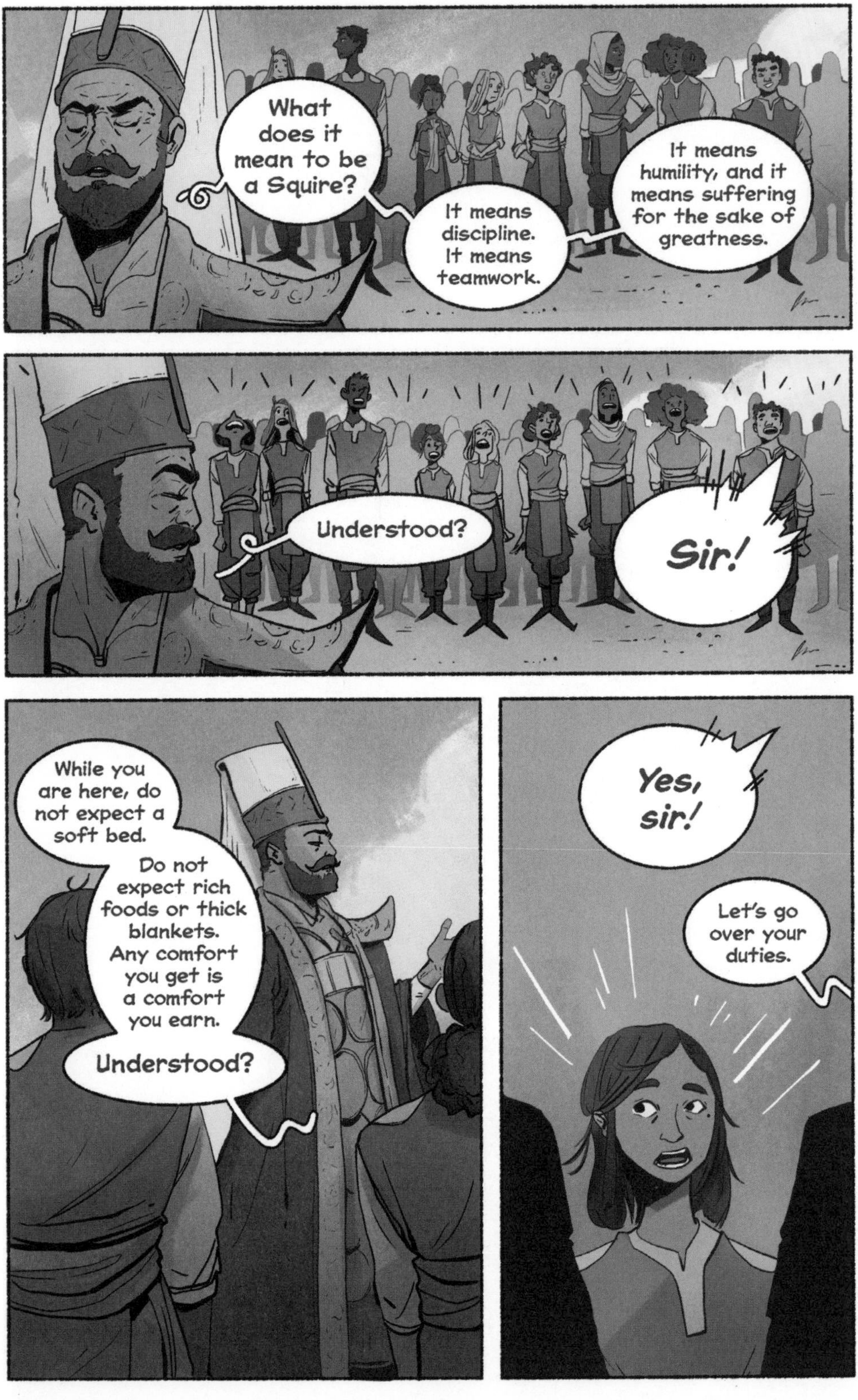
What does it mean to be a Squire?
It means discipline. It means teamwork.
It means humility, and it means suffering for the sake of greatness.
Understood?
Sir!
While you are here, do not expect a soft bed.
Do not expect rich foods or thick blankets. Any comfort you get is a comfort you earn.
Understood?
Yes, sir!
Let's go over your duties.

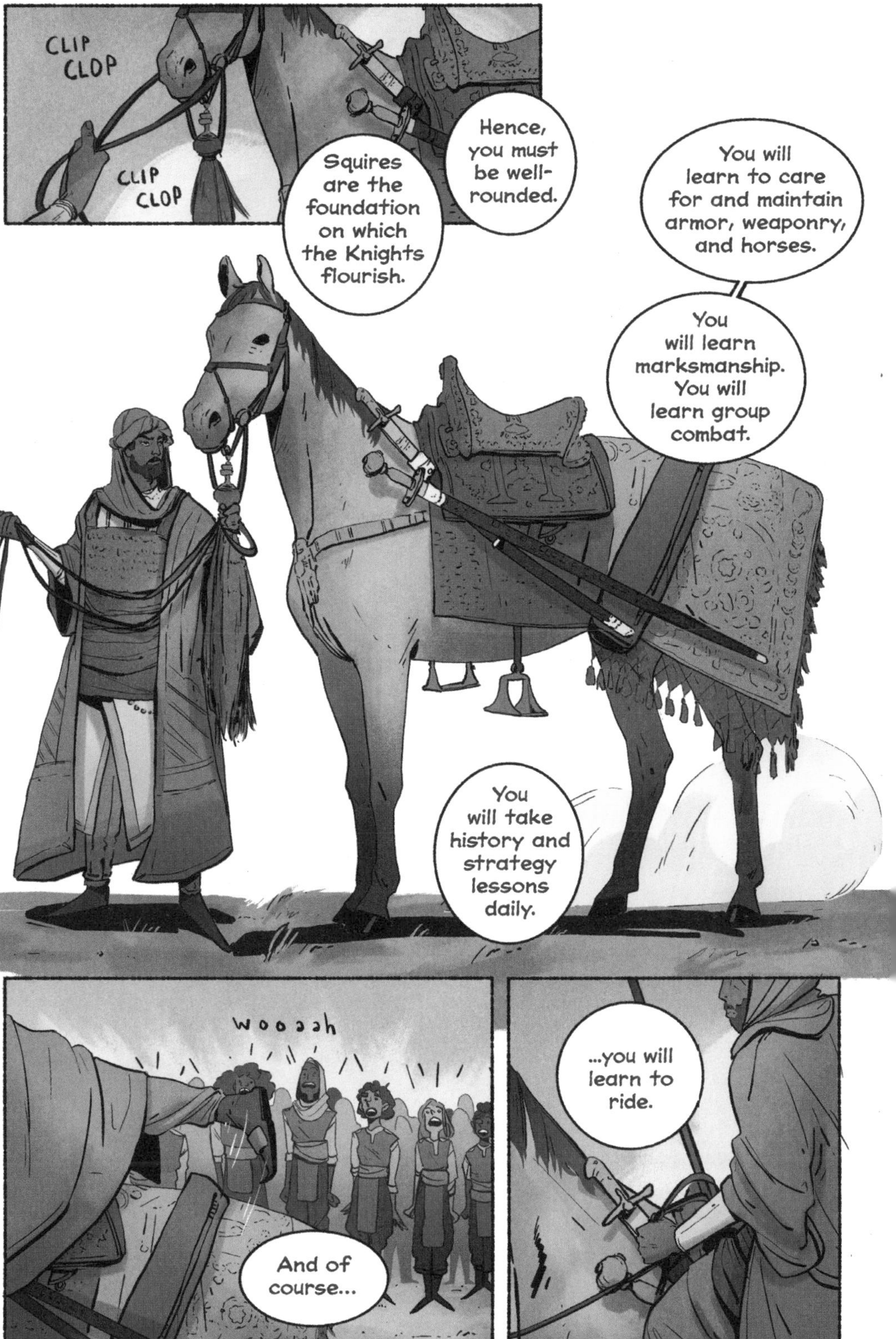
CLIP CLOP
CLIP CLOP
Squires are the foundation on which the Knights flourish.
Hence, you must be well-rounded.
You will learn to care for and maintain armor, weaponry, and horses.
You will learn marksmanship. You will learn group combat.
You will take history and strategy lessons daily.
woooah
And of course...
...you will learn to ride.

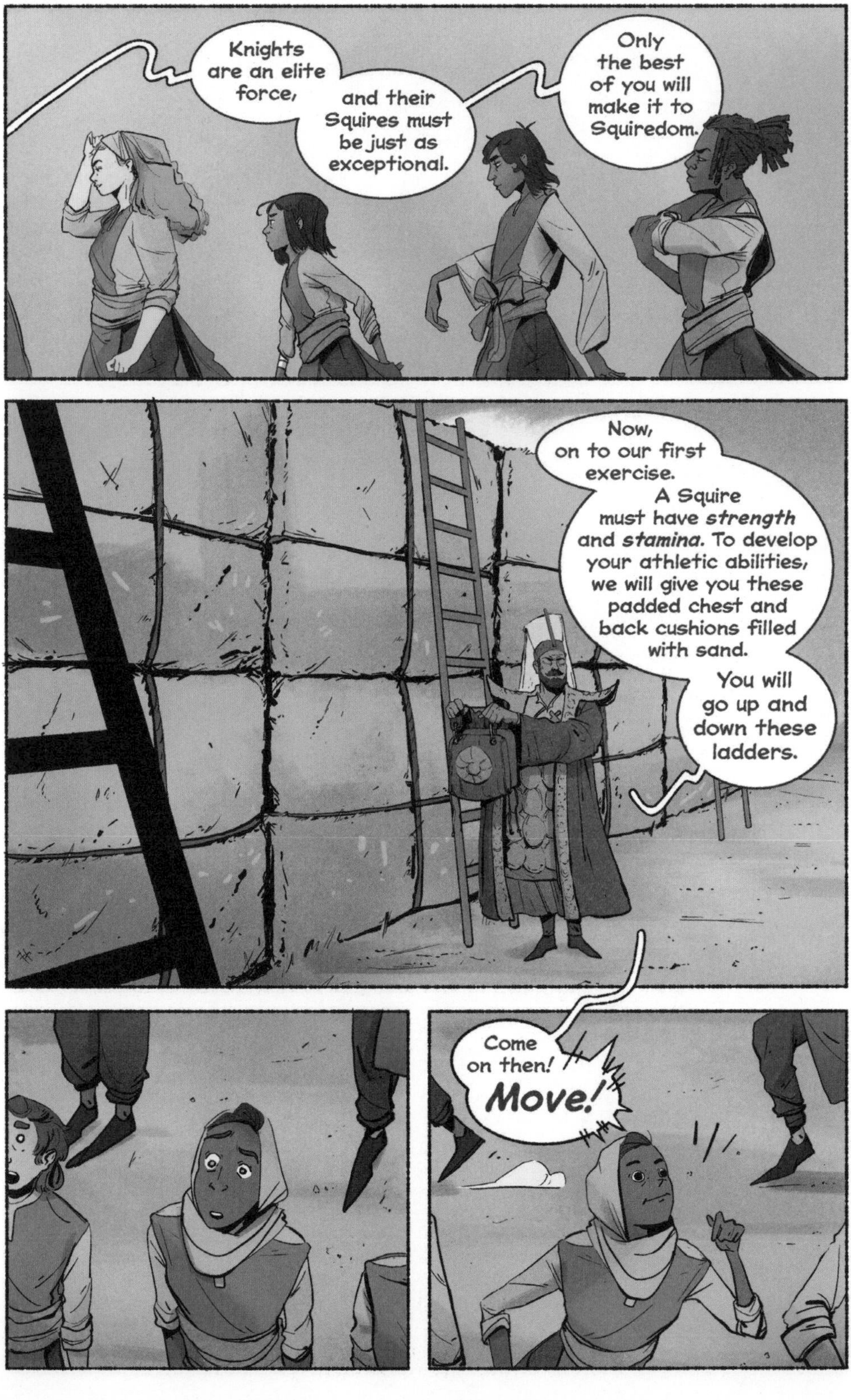

Knights are an elite force,
and their Squires must be just as exceptional.
Only the best of you will make it to Squiredom.
Now, on to our first exercise.
A Squire must have *strength* and *stamina*. To develop your athletic abilities, we will give you these padded chest and back cushions filled with sand.
You will go up and down these ladders.
Come on then!
Move!

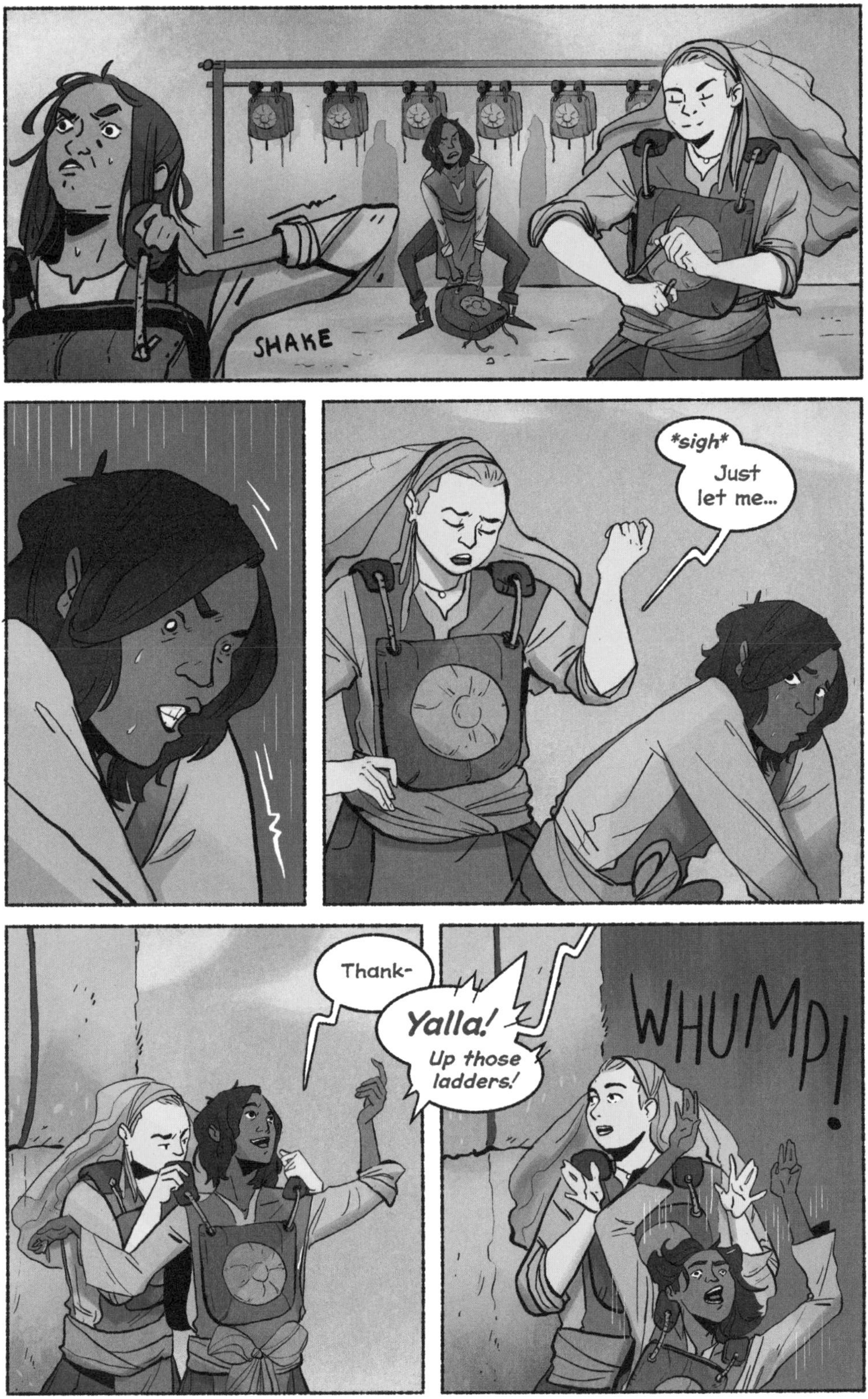
SHAKE
sigh
Just let me...
Thank-
Yalla!
Up those ladders!
WHUMP!

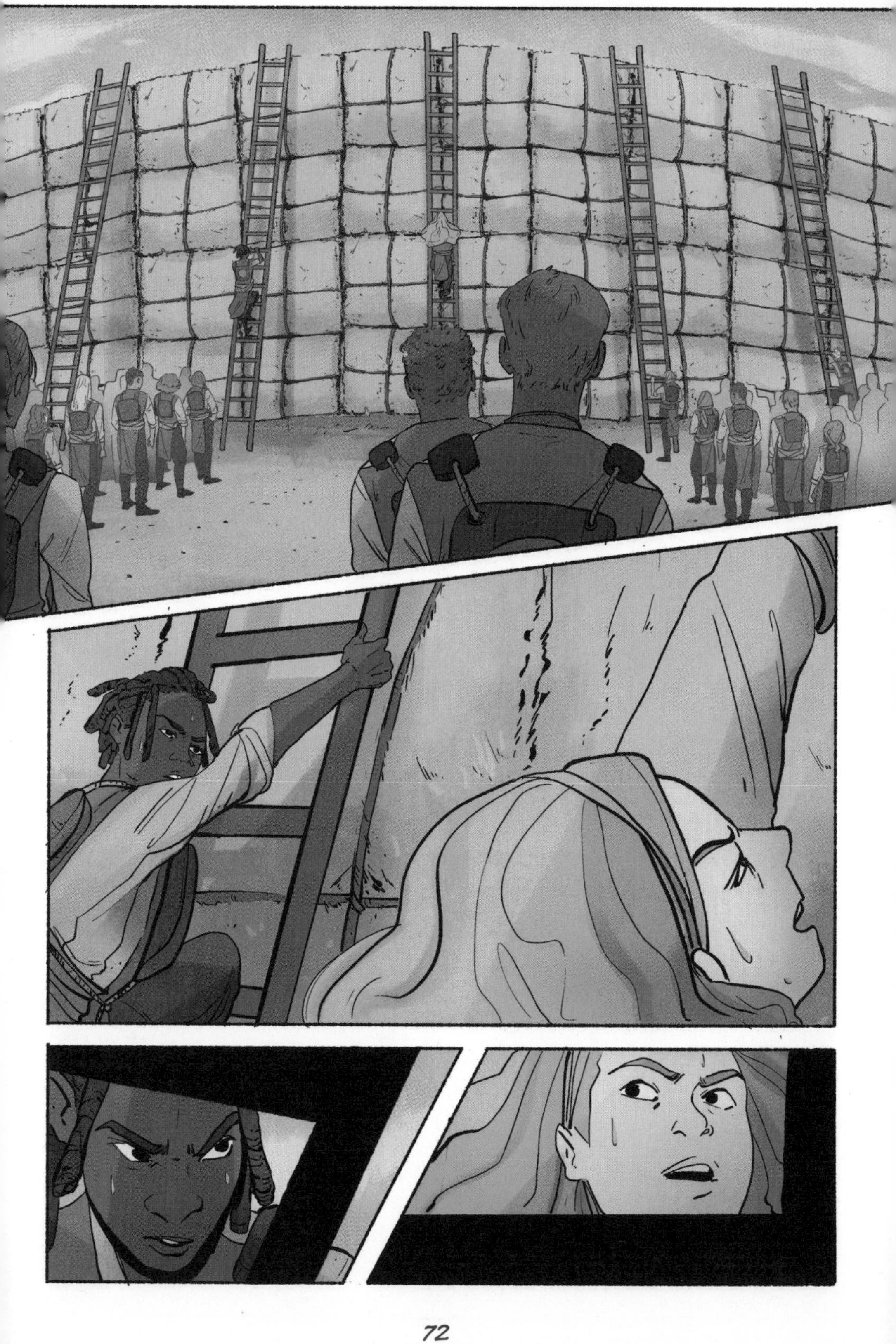

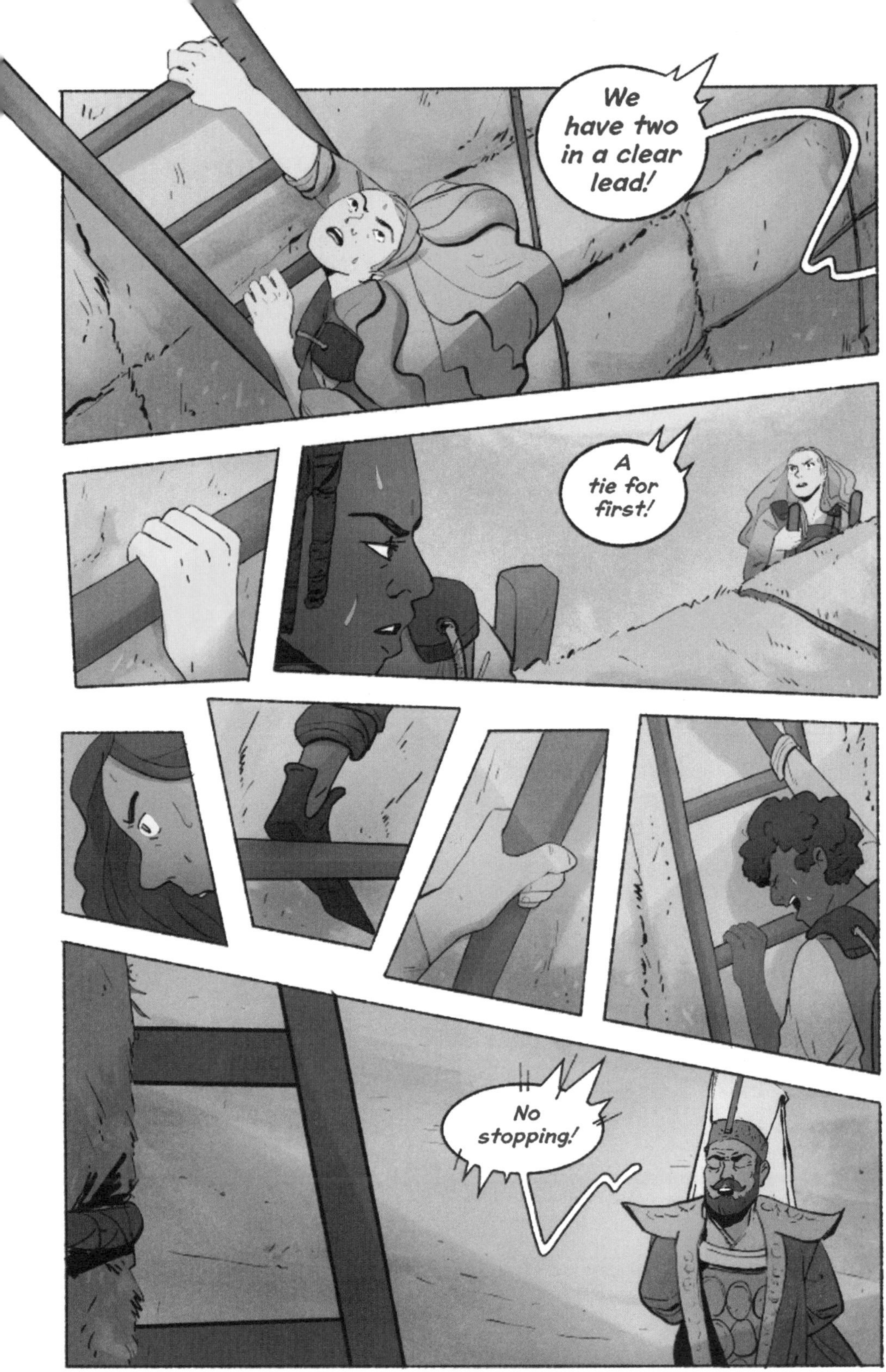
We have two in a clear lead!
A tie for first!
No stopping!

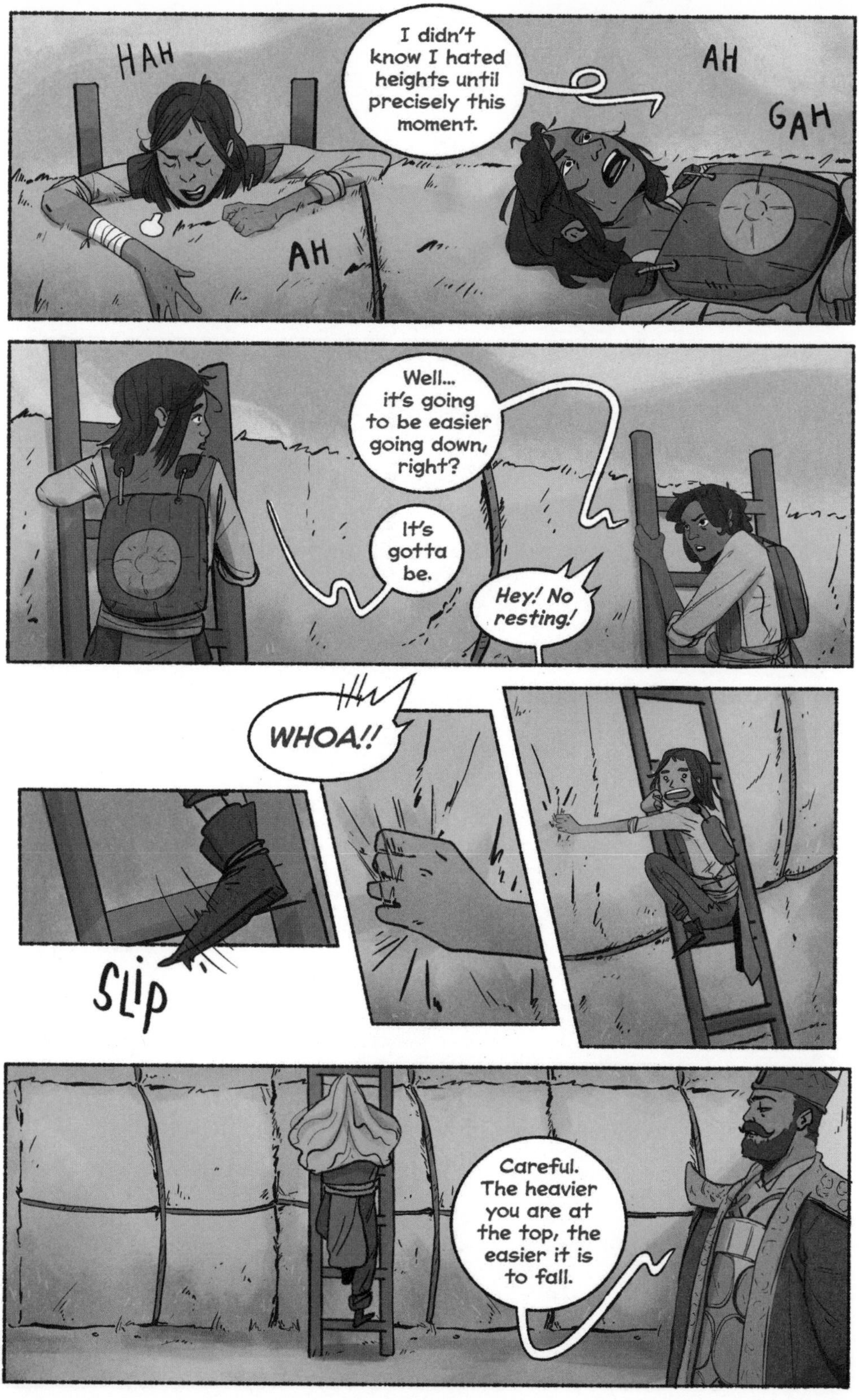
HAH
I didn't know I hated heights until precisely this moment.
AH
GAH
AH
Well... it's going to be easier going down, right?
It's gotta be.
Hey! No resting!
WHOA!!
SLIP
Careful. The heavier you are at the top, the easier it is to fall.

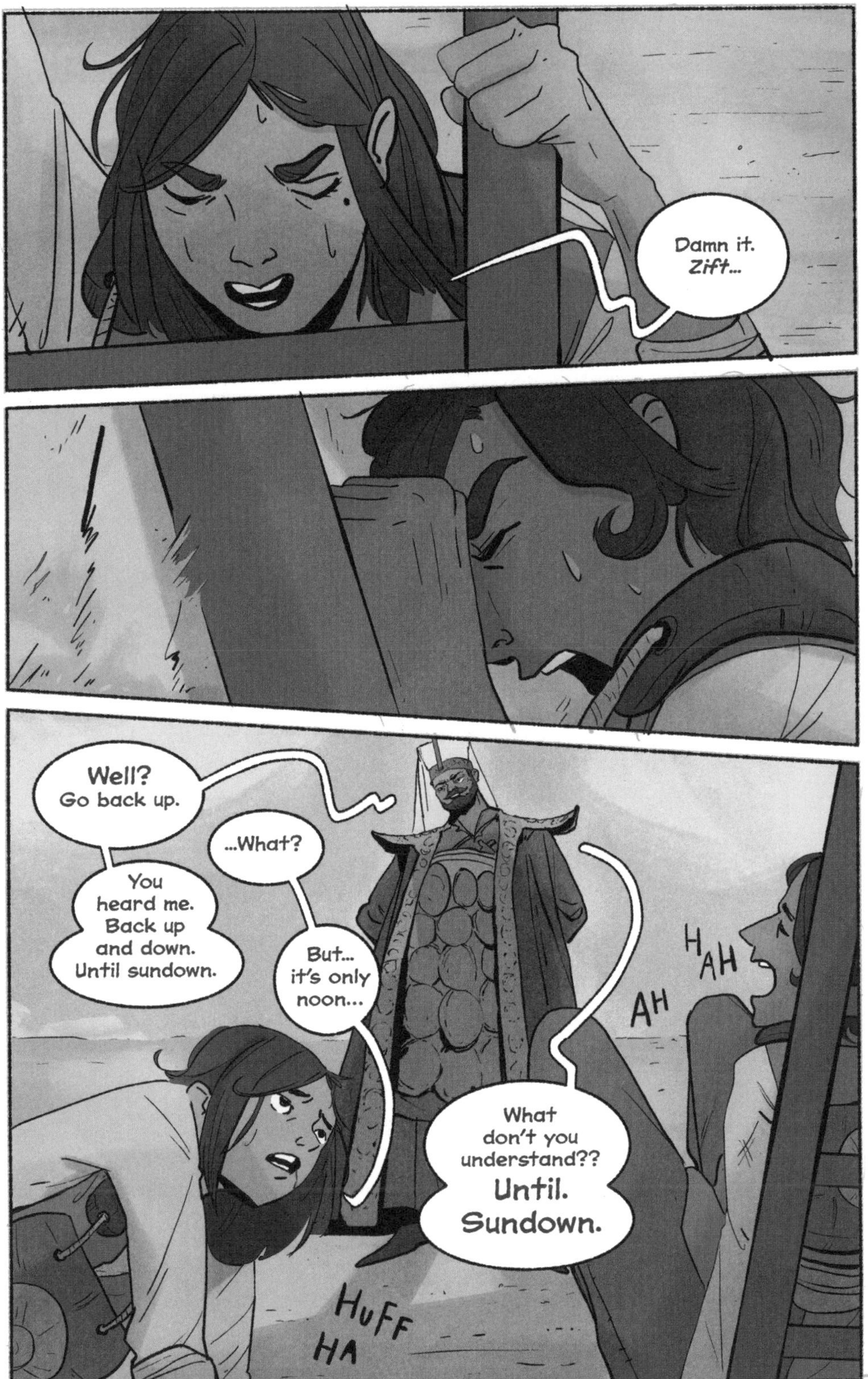
Damn it.
Zift...
Well?
Go back up.
...What?
You heard me. Back up and down. Until sundown.
But... it's only noon...
HAH
AH
What don't you understand?? Until. Sundown.
HUFF
HA

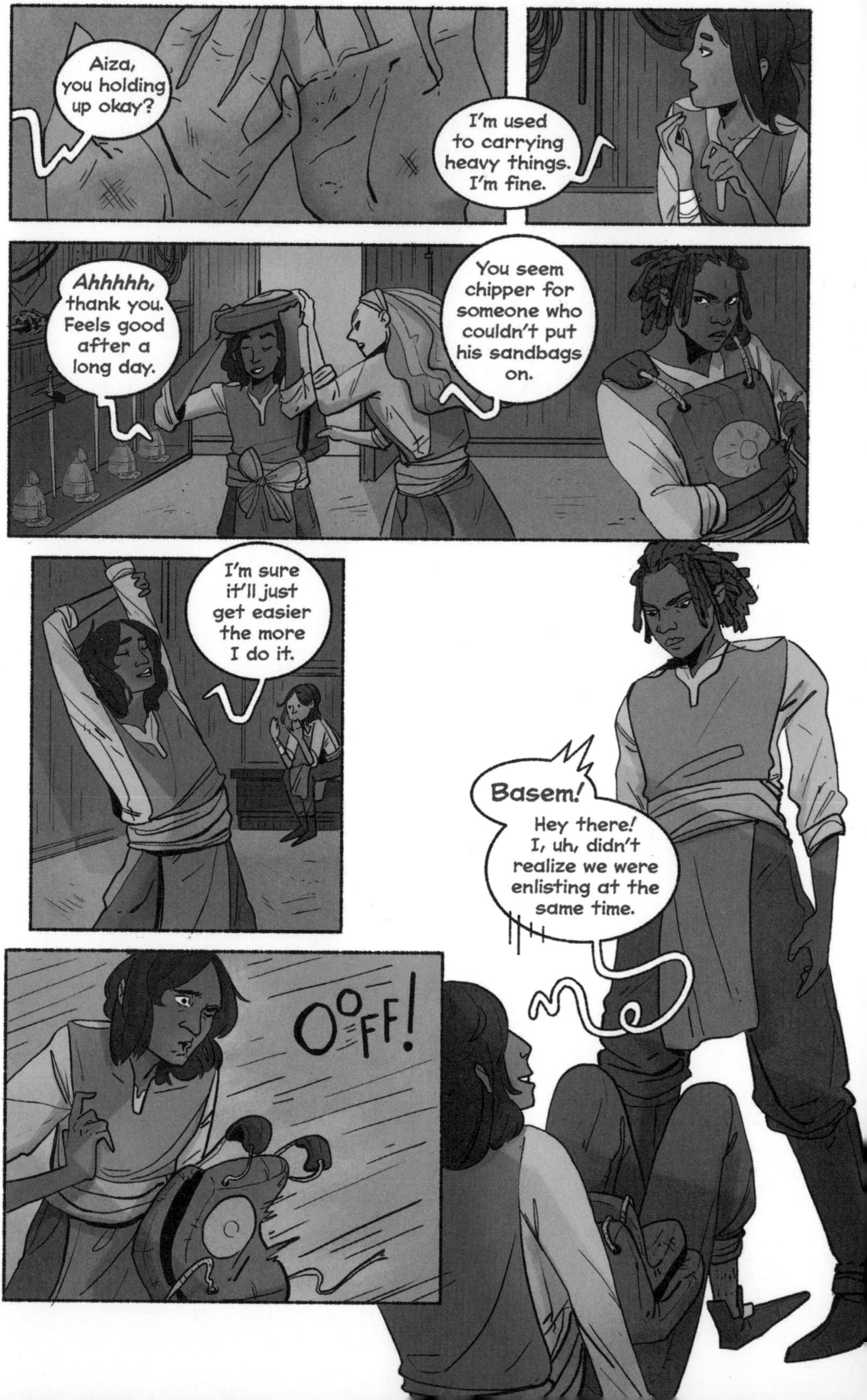
Aiza, you holding up okay?
I'm used to carrying heavy things. I'm fine.
Ahhhhh, thank you. Feels good after a long day.
You seem chipper for someone who couldn't put his sandbags on.
I'm sure it'll just get easier the more I do it.
OOFF!
Basem!
Hey there! I, uh, didn't realize we were enlisting at the same time.

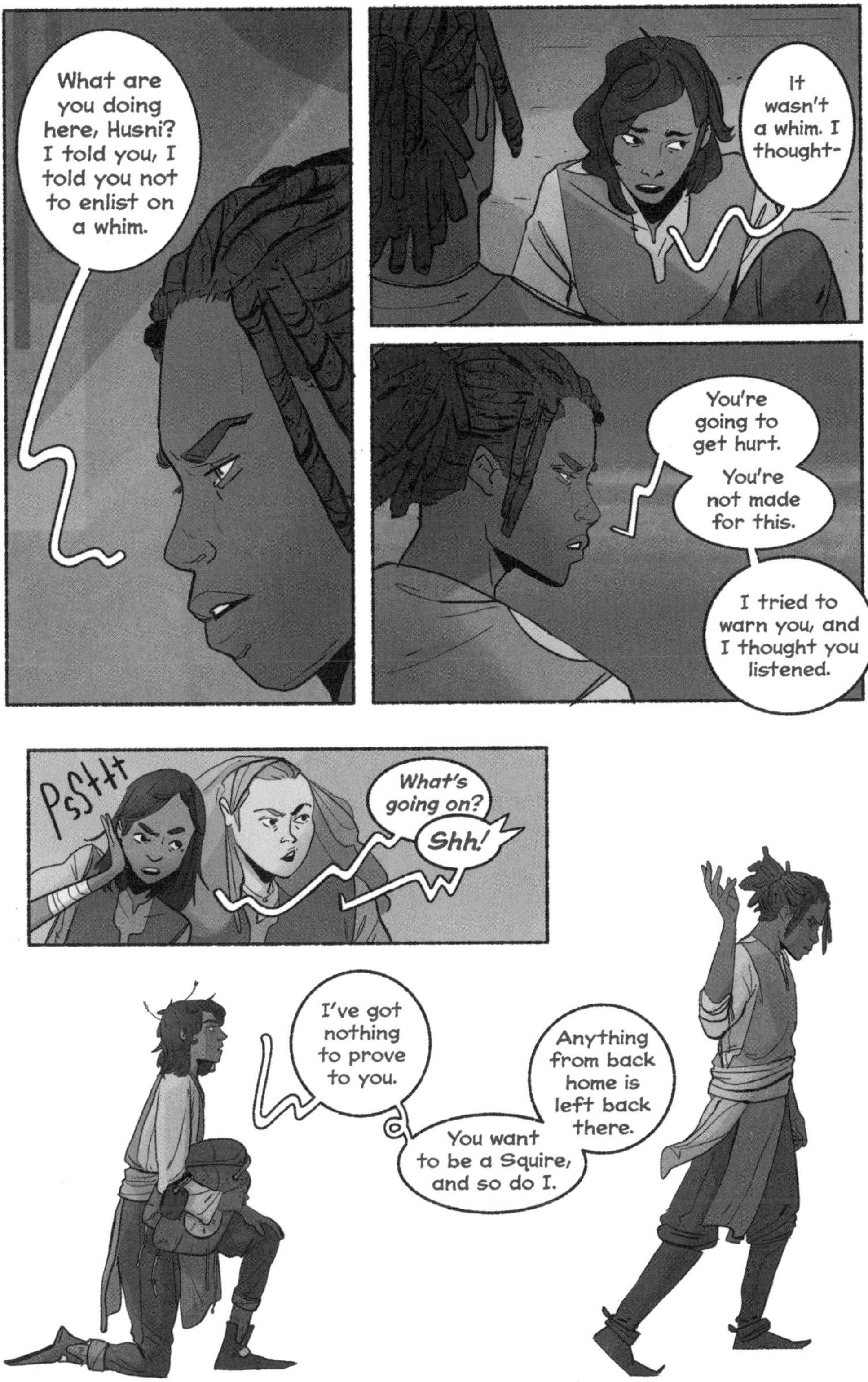
What are you doing here, Husni? I told you, I told you not to enlist on a whim.
It wasn't a whim. I thought-
You're going to get hurt.
You're not made for this.
I tried to warn you, and I thought you listened.
PsSttt
What's going on?
Shh!
I've got nothing to prove to you.
You want to be a Squire, and so do I.
Anything from back home is left back there.

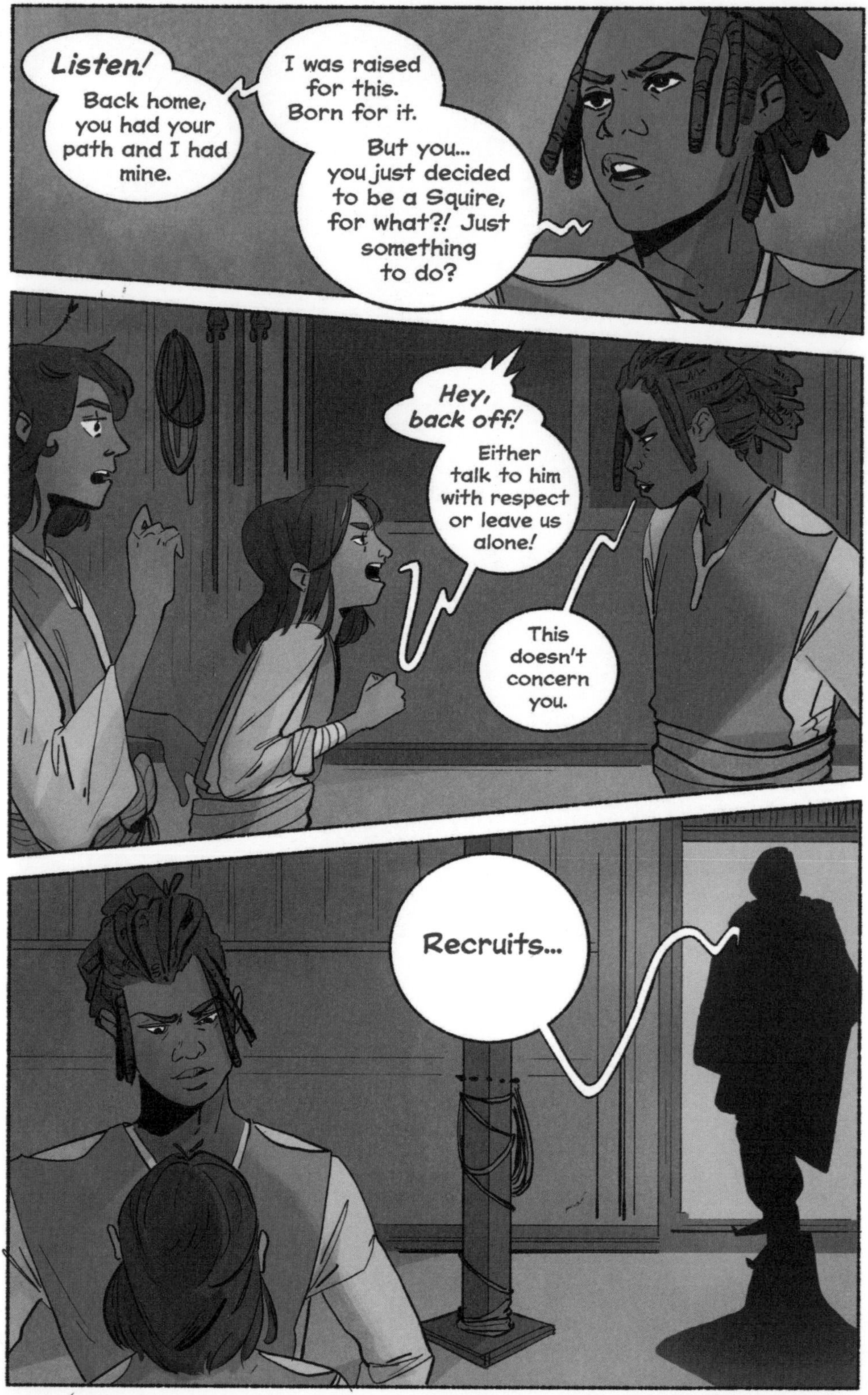
Listen! Back home, you had your path and I had mine.
I was raised for this. Born for it.
But you... you just decided to be a Squire, for what?! Just something to do?
Hey, back off! Either talk to him with respect or leave us alone!
This doesn't concern you.
Recruits...

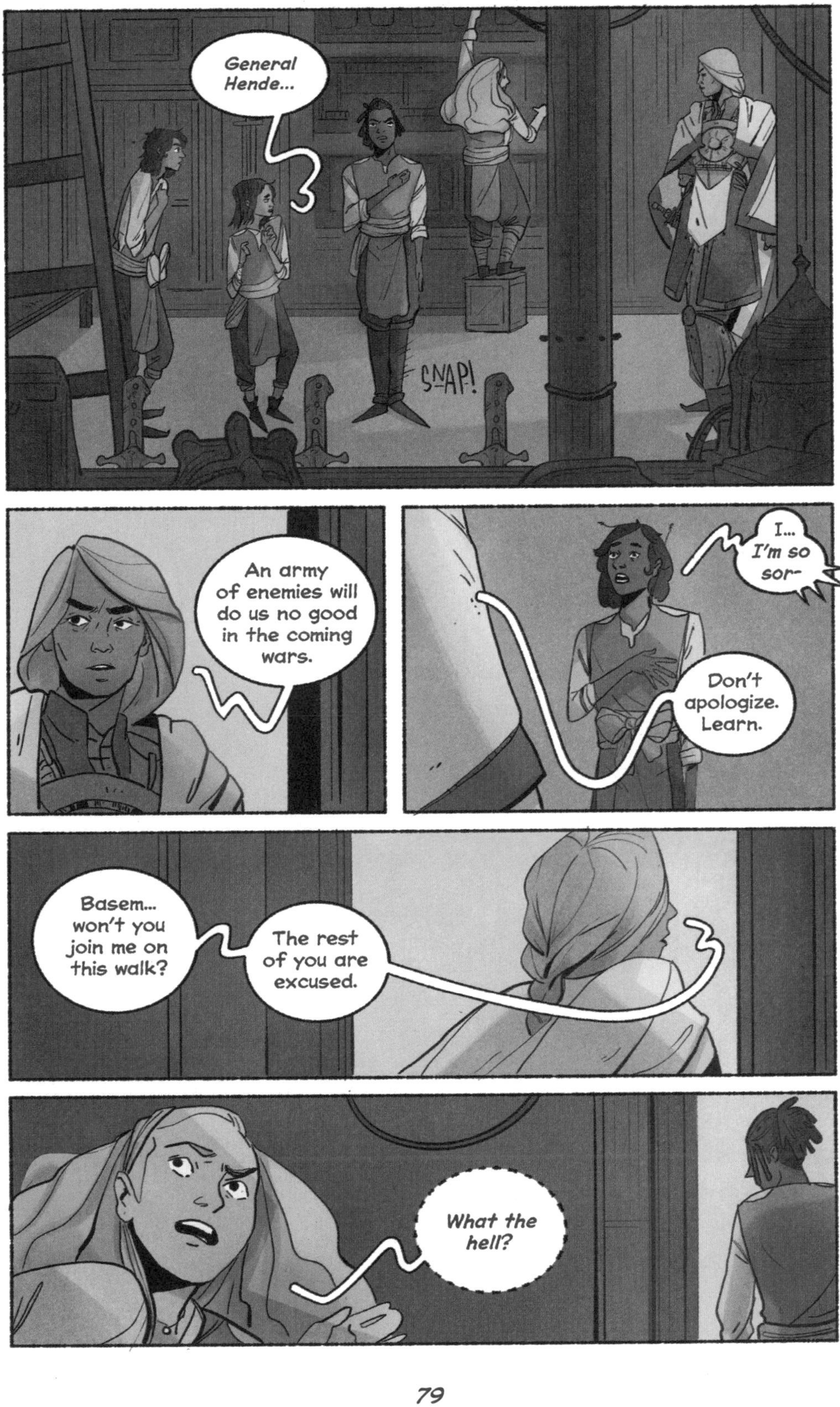
General Hende...
SNAP!
An army of enemies will do us no good in the coming wars.
I... I'm so sor-
Don't apologize. Learn.
Basem... won't you join me on this walk?
The rest of you are excused.
What the hell?

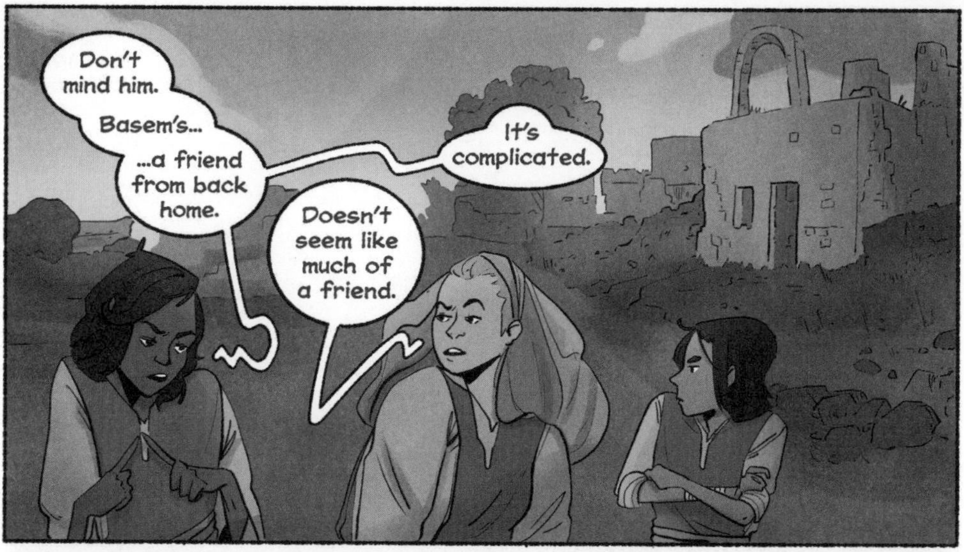
Don't mind him.
Basem's...
...a friend from back home.
It's complicated.
Doesn't seem like much of a friend.

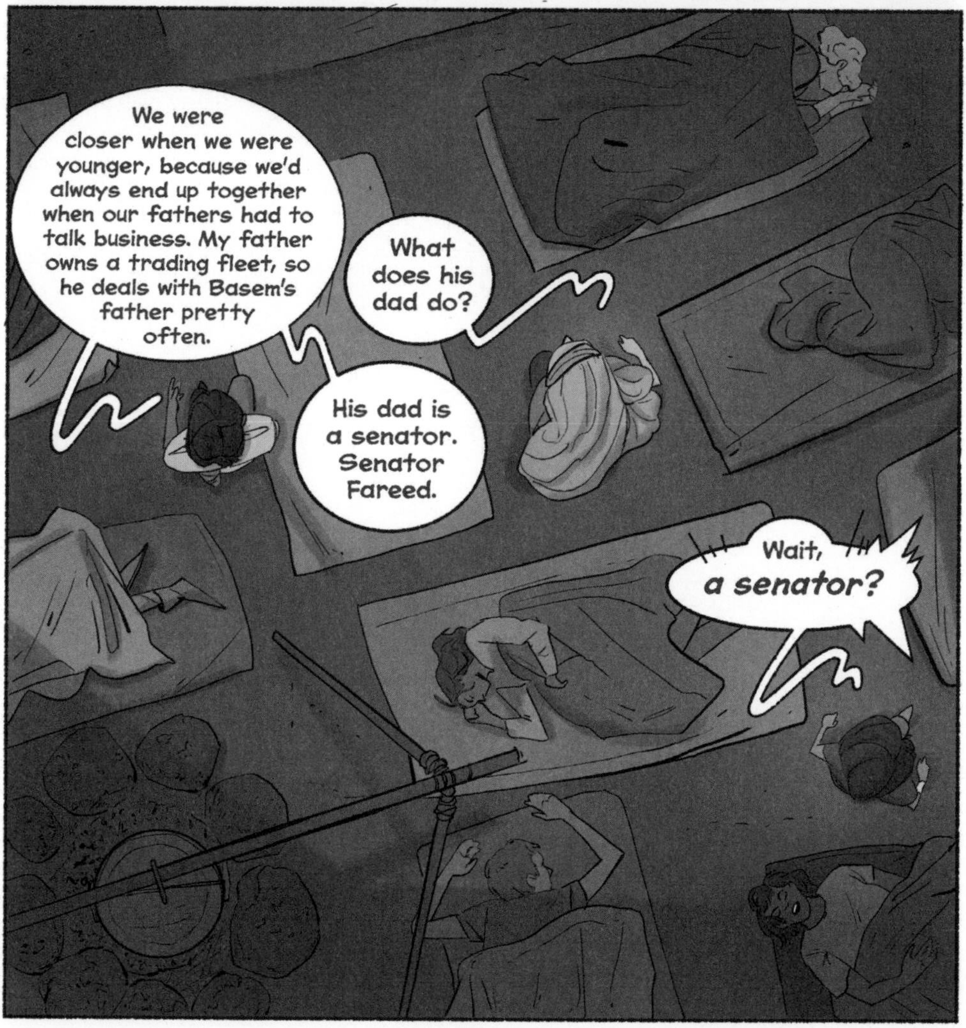
We were closer when we were younger, because we'd always end up together when our fathers had to talk business. My father owns a trading fleet, so he deals with Basem's father pretty often.
What does his dad do?
His dad is a senator. Senator Fareed.
Wait, *a senator?*

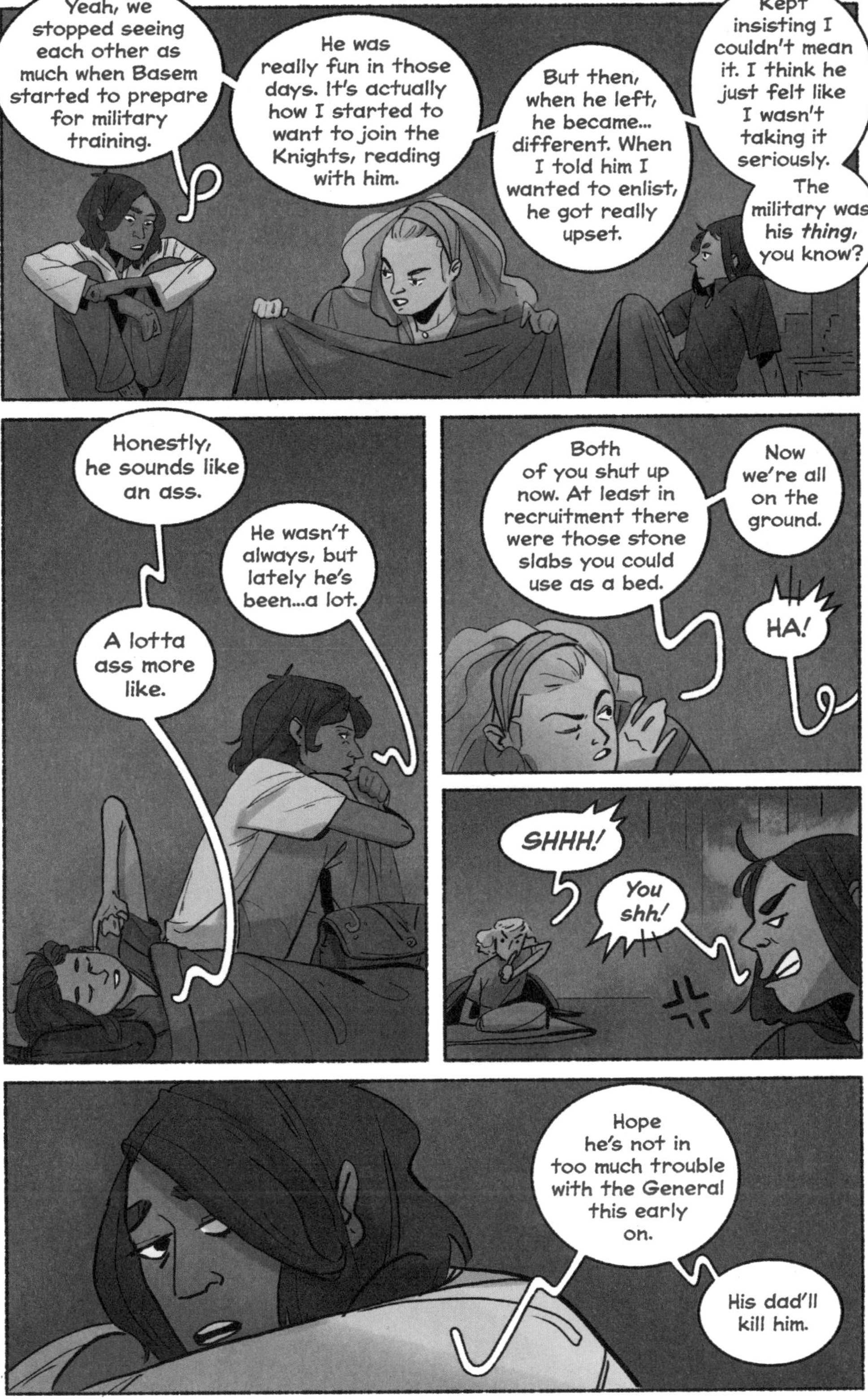
Yeah, we stopped seeing each other as much when Basem started to prepare for military training.
He was really fun in those days. It's actually how I started to want to join the Knights, reading with him.
But then, when he left, he became... different. When I told him I wanted to enlist, he got really upset.
Kept insisting I couldn't mean it. I think he just felt like I wasn't taking it seriously.
The military was his *thing,* you know?
Honestly, he sounds like an ass.
He wasn't always, but lately he's been...a lot.
A lotta ass more like.
Both of you shut up now. At least in recruitment there were those stone slabs you could use as a bed.
Now we're all on the ground.
HA!
SHHH!
You shh!
Hope he's not in too much trouble with the General this early on.
His dad'll kill him.

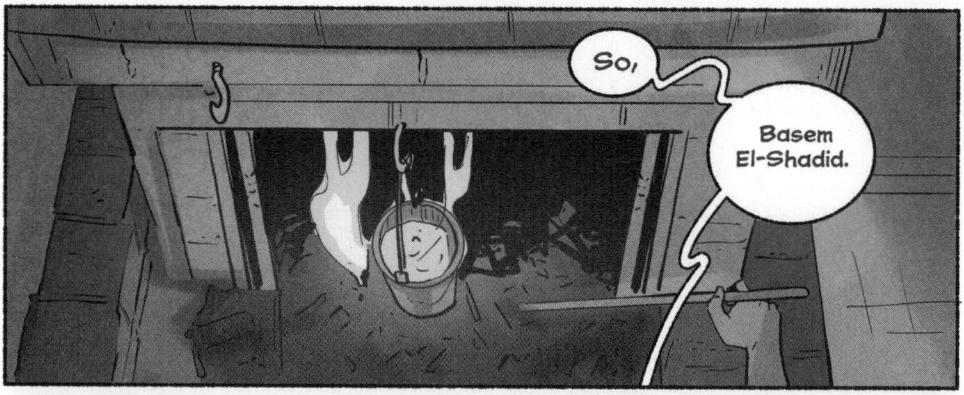
So,
Basem El-Shadid.

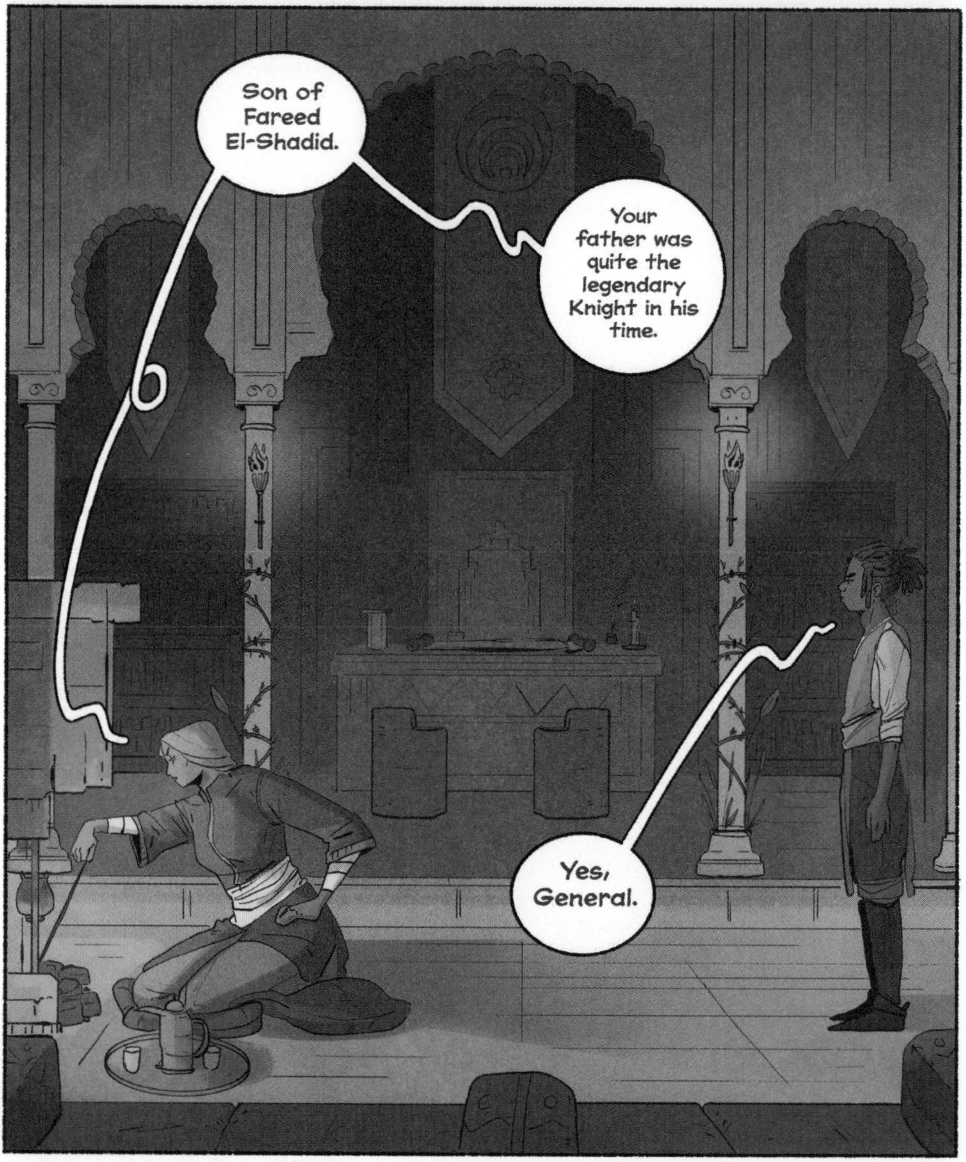
Son of Fareed El-Shadid.
Your father was quite the legendary Knight in his time.
Yes, General.

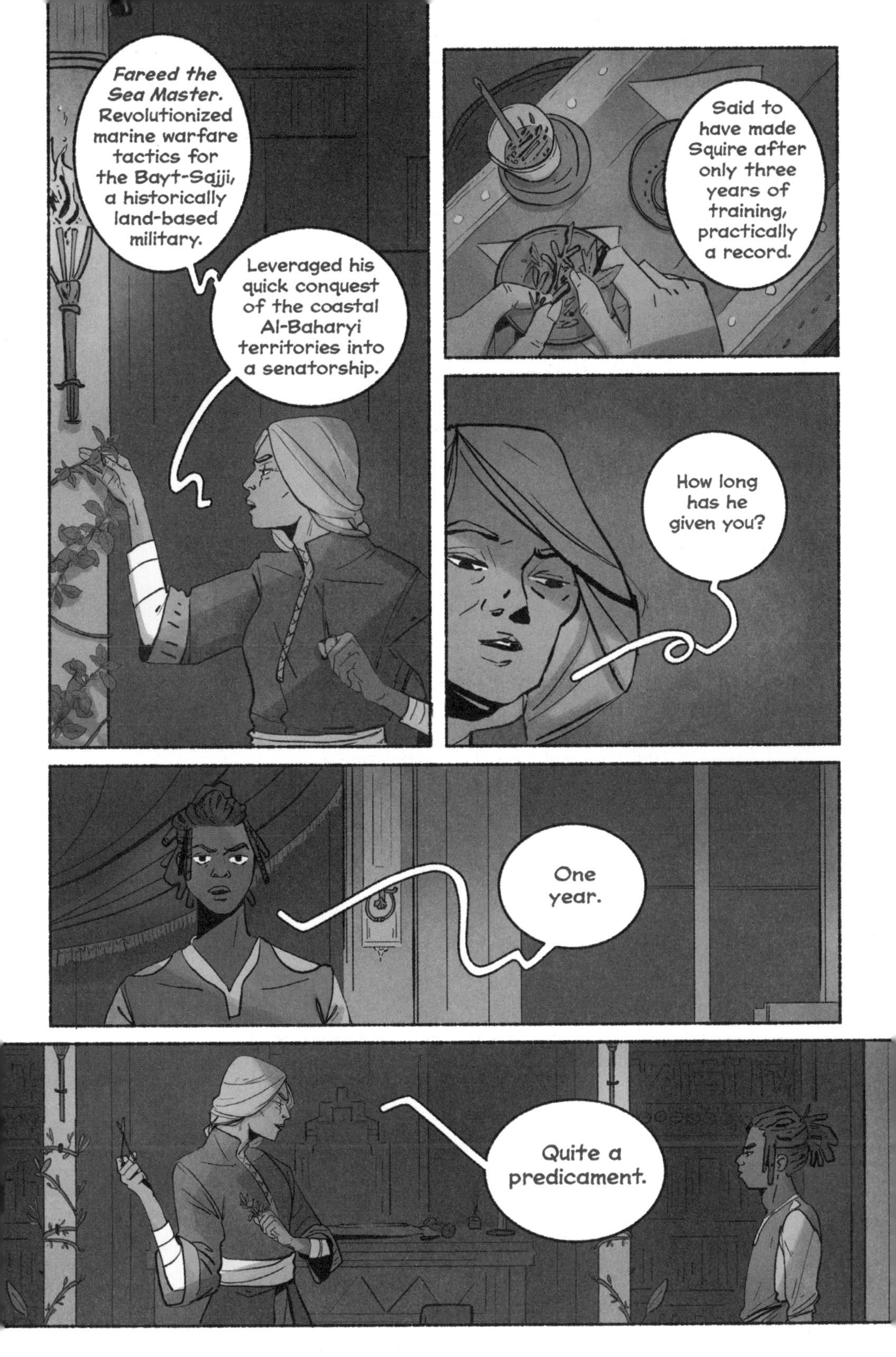
Fareed the Sea Master. Revolutionized marine warfare tactics for the Bayt-Sajji, a historically land-based military.
Leveraged his quick conquest of the coastal Al-Baharyi territories into a senatorship.
Said to have made Squire after only three years of training, practically a record.
How long has he given you?
One year.
Quite a predicament.

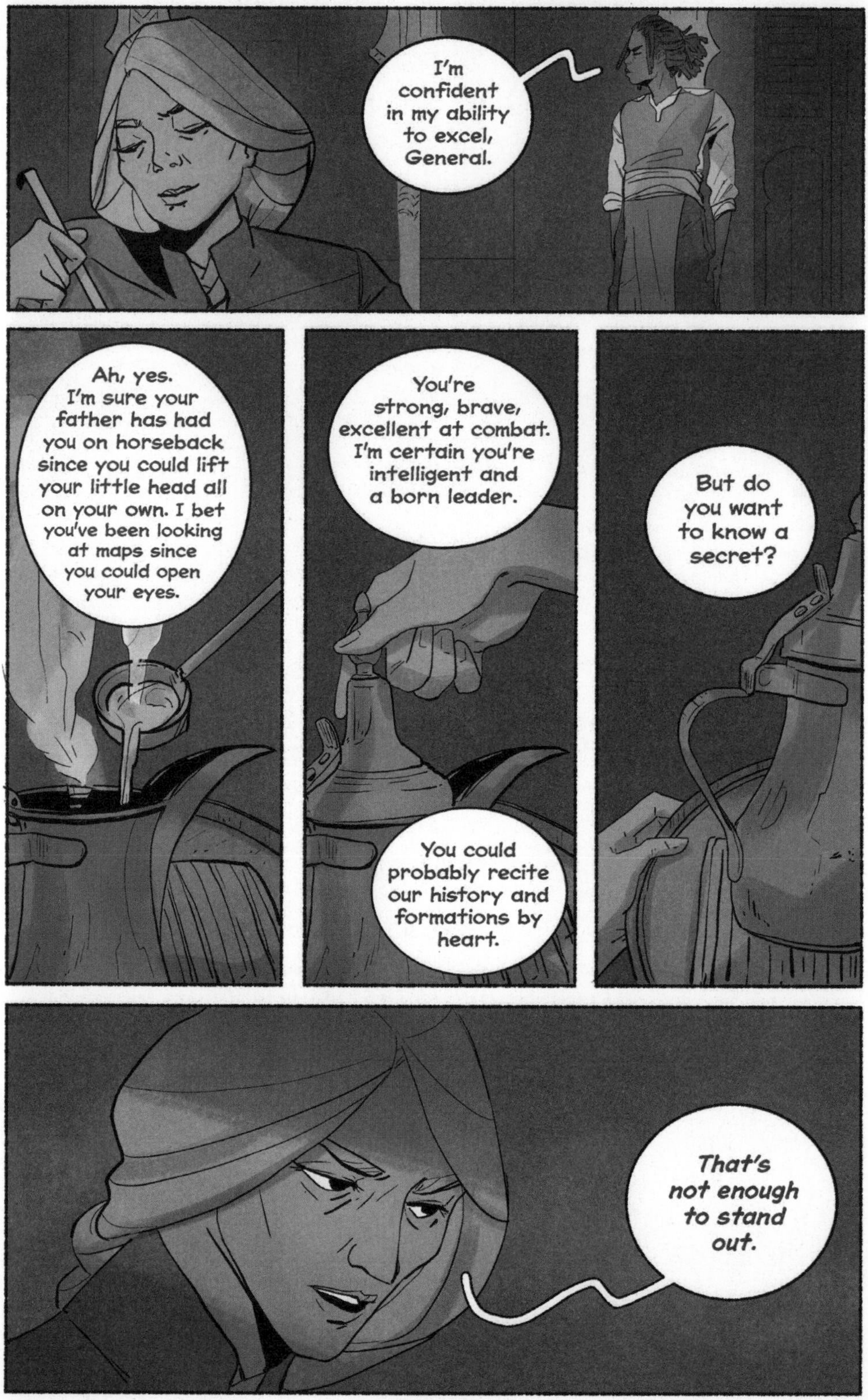

I'm confident in my ability to excel, General.
Ah, yes. I'm sure your father has had you on horseback since you could lift your little head all on your own. I bet you've been looking at maps since you could open your eyes.
You're strong, brave, excellent at combat. I'm certain you're intelligent and a born leader.
You could probably recite our history and formations by heart.
But do you want to know a secret?
That's not enough to stand out.

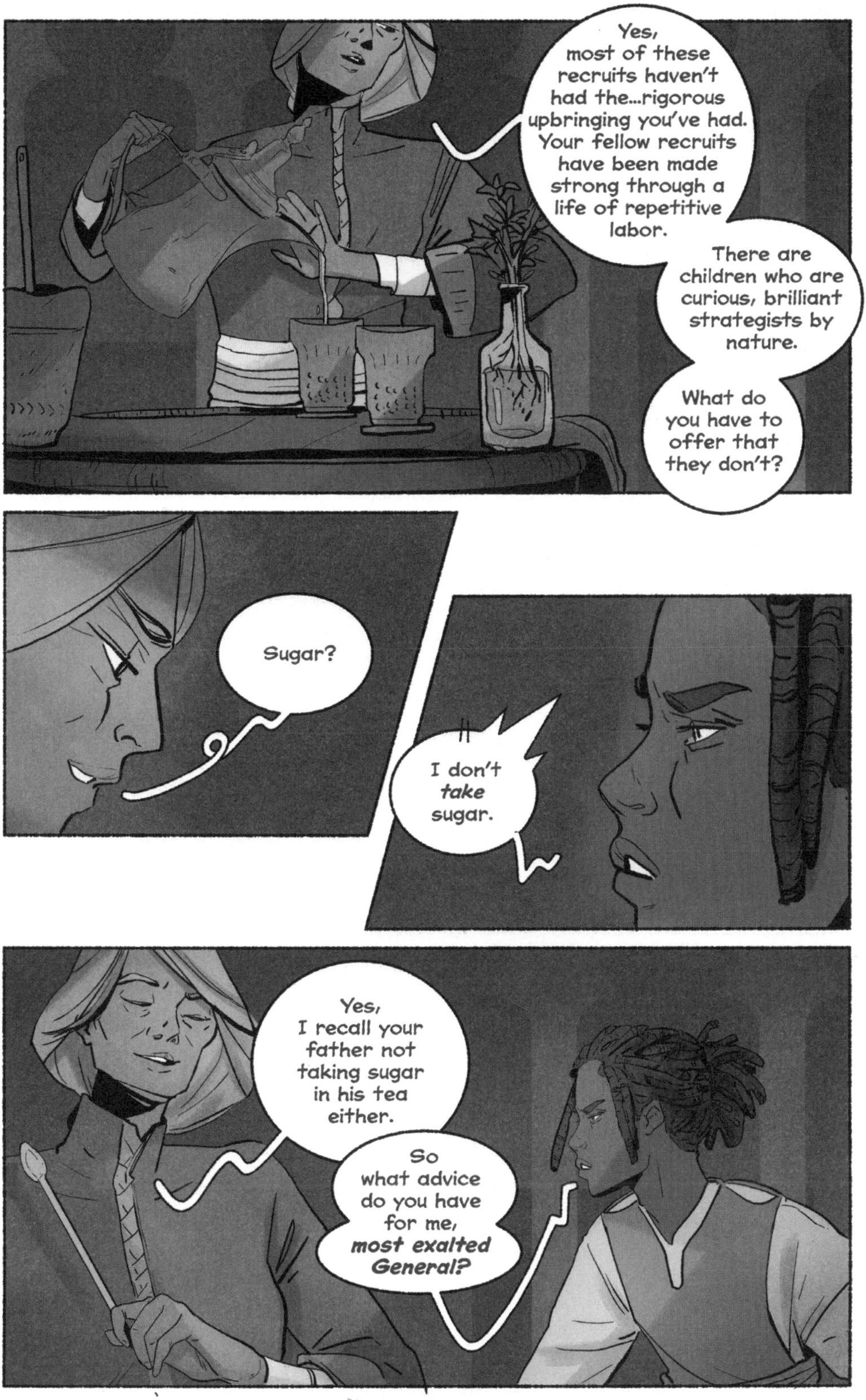
Yes, most of these recruits haven't had the...rigorous upbringing you've had. Your fellow recruits have been made strong through a life of repetitive labor.
There are children who are curious, brilliant strategists by nature.
What do you have to offer that they don't?
Sugar?
I don't *take* sugar.
Yes, I recall your father not taking sugar in his tea either.
So what advice do you have for me, ***most exalted General?***

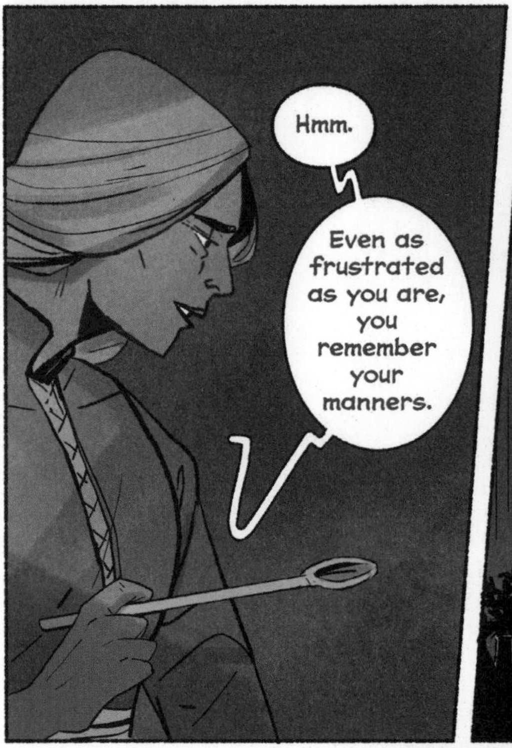
Hmm.
Even as frustrated as you are, you remember your manners.

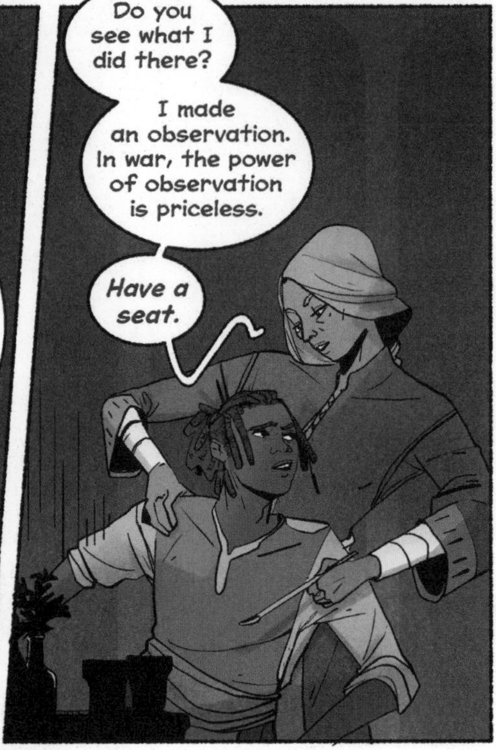
Do you see what I did there?
I made an observation. In war, the power of observation is priceless.
Have a seat.

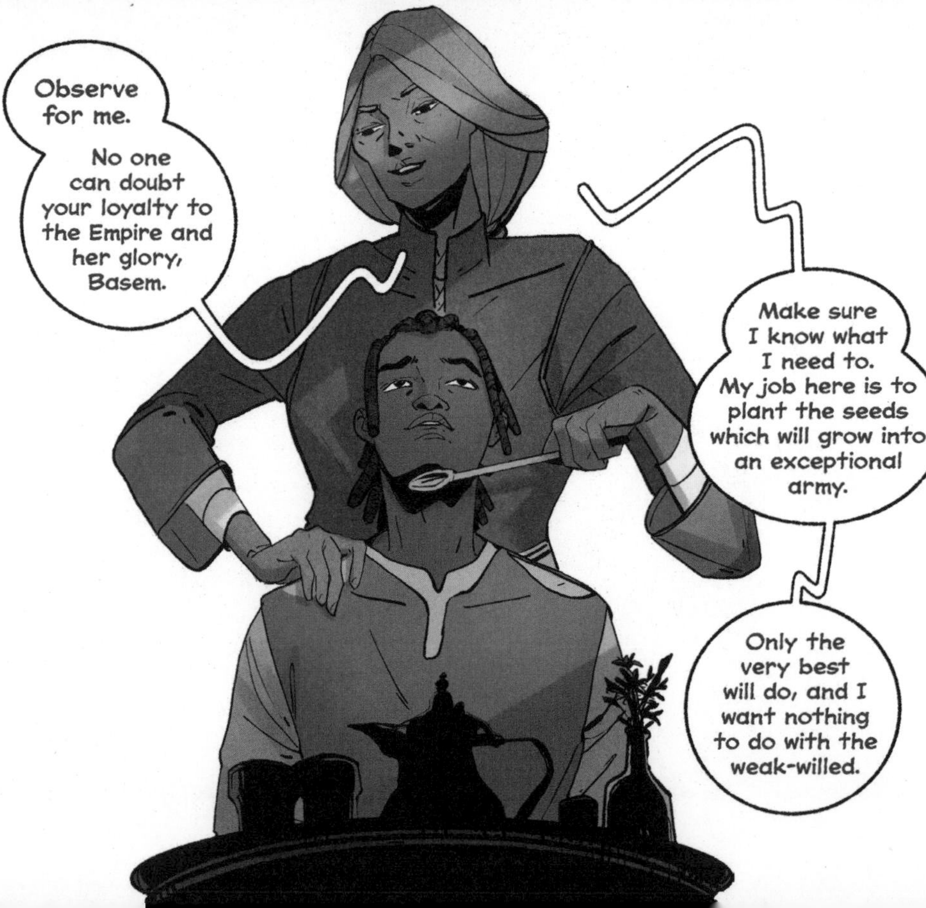
Observe for me.
No one can doubt your loyalty to the Empire and her glory, Basem.
Make sure I know what I need to. My job here is to plant the seeds which will grow into an exceptional army.
Only the very best will do, and I want nothing to do with the weak-willed.

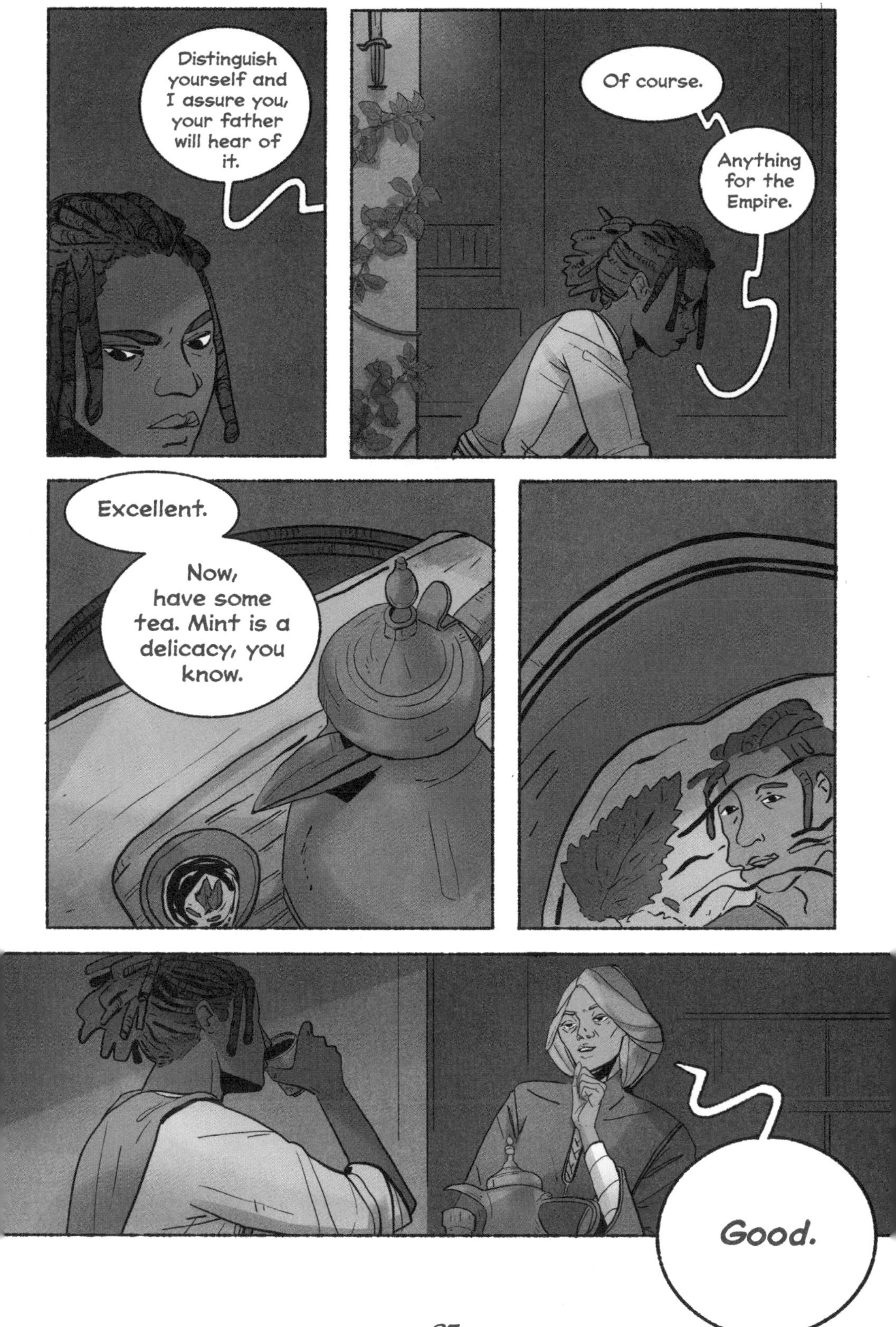
Distinguish yourself and I assure you, your father will hear of it.
Of course.
Anything for the Empire.
Excellent.
Now, have some tea. Mint is a delicacy, you know.
Good.

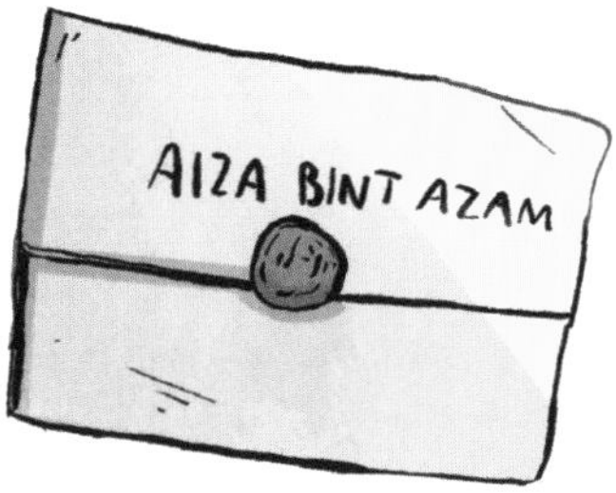
AIZA BINT AZAM

CHAPTER 5

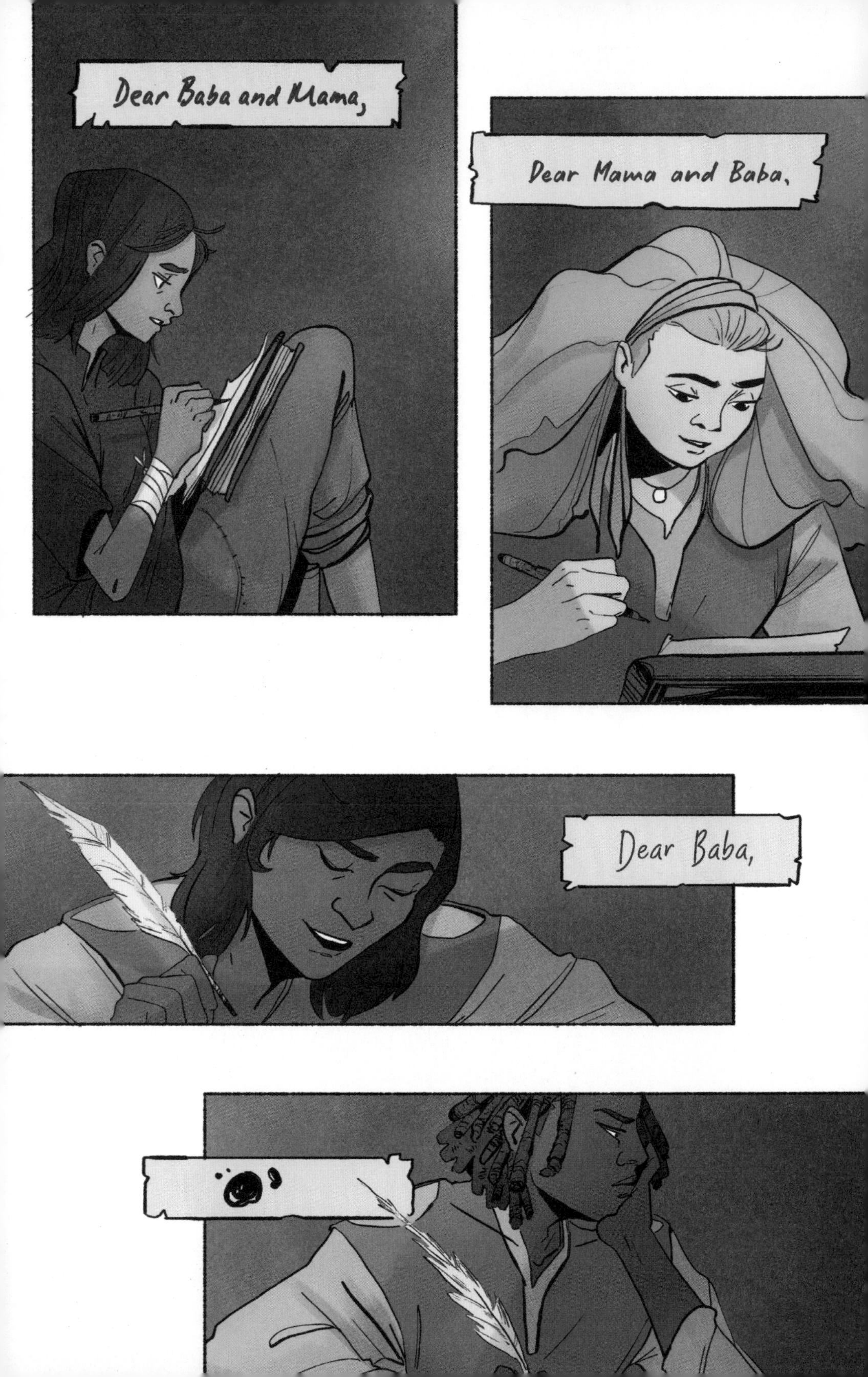
Dear Baba and Mama,
Dear Mama and Baba,
Dear Baba,

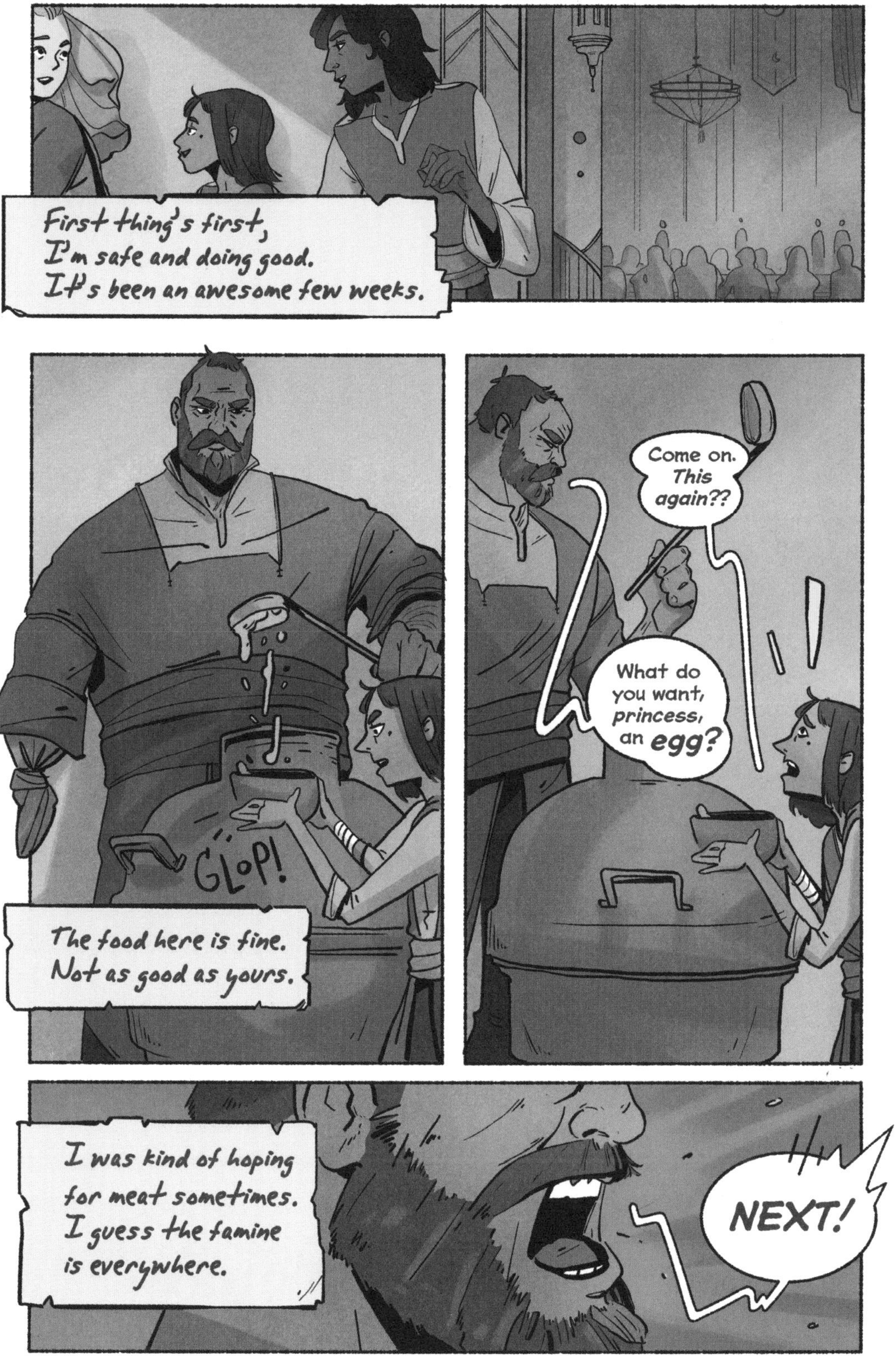
First thing's first,
I'm safe and doing good.
It's been an awesome few weeks.
GLOP!
The food here is fine.
Not as good as yours.
Come on. This again??
What do you want, princess, an egg?
I was kind of hoping for meat sometimes. I guess the famine is everywhere.
NEXT!

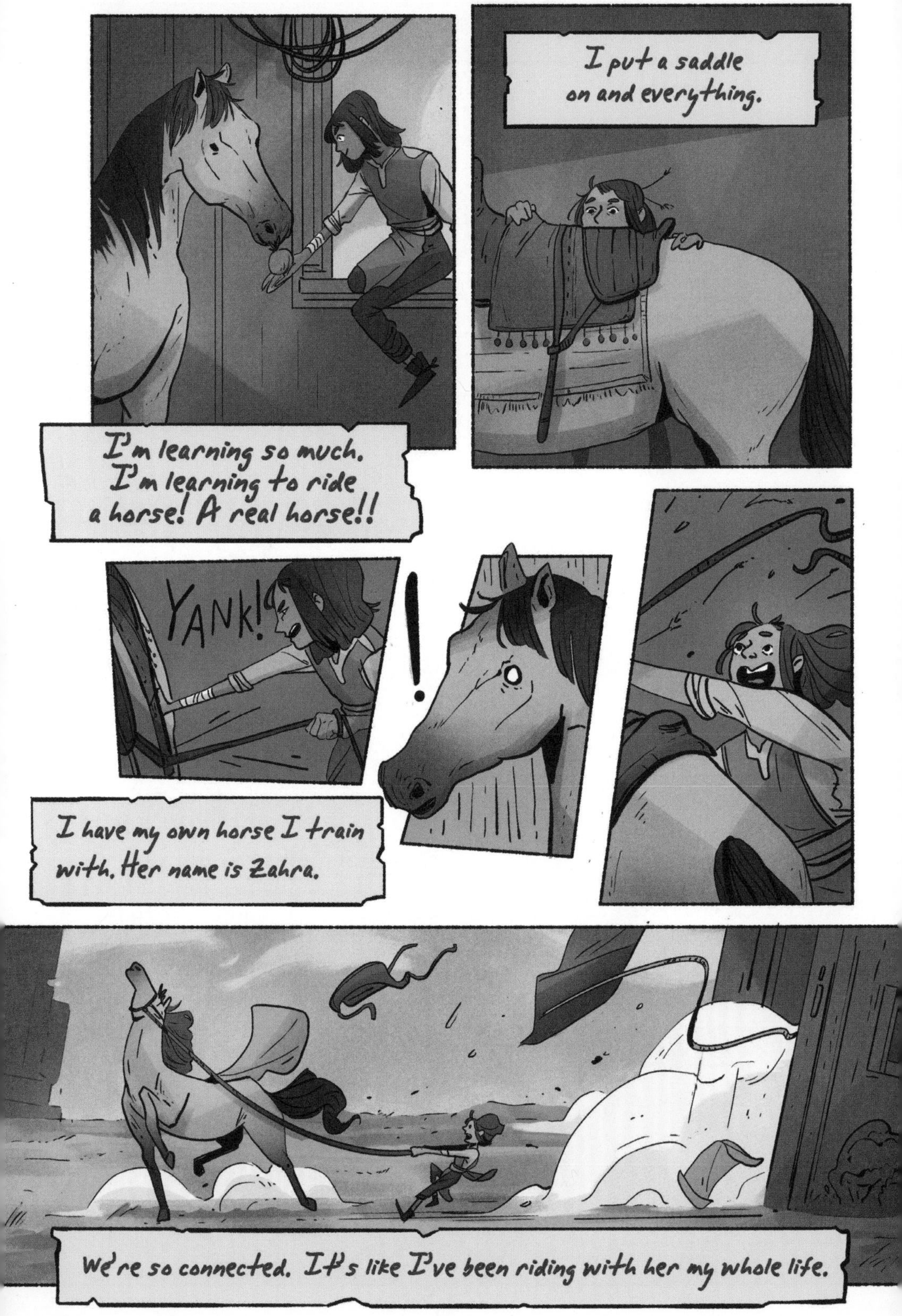
I put a saddle on and everything.
I'm learning so much. I'm learning to ride a horse! A real horse!!
YANK!
!
I have my own horse I train with. Her name is Zahra.
We're so connected. It's like I've been riding with her my whole life.

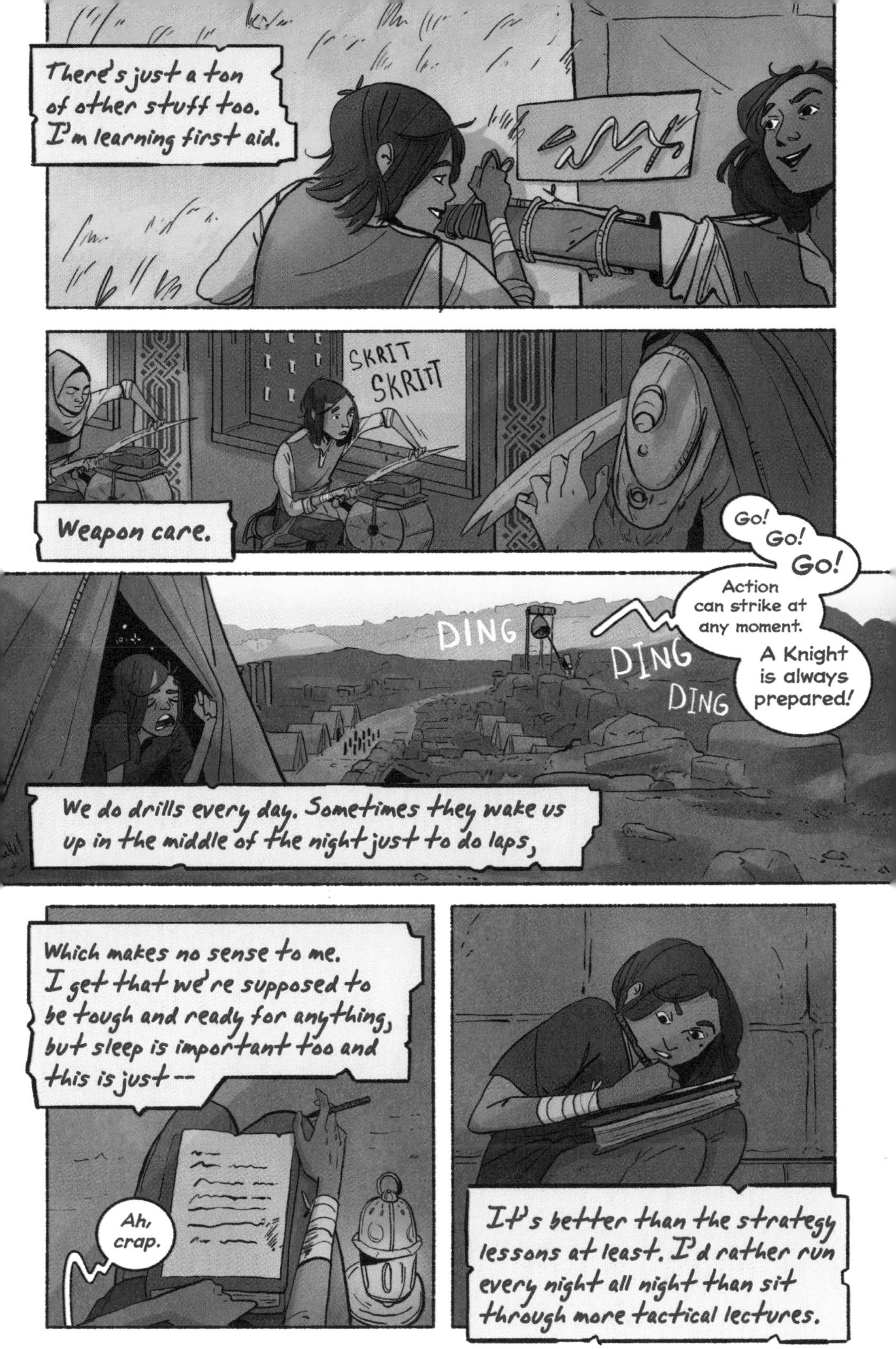
There's just a ton of other stuff too. I'm learning first aid.
SKRIT SKRIT
Weapon care.
Go! Go! Go!
Action can strike at any moment.
A Knight is always prepared!
DING DING DING
We do drills every day. Sometimes they wake us up in the middle of the night just to do laps,
Which makes no sense to me. I get that we're supposed to be tough and ready for anything, but sleep is important too and this is just--
Ah, crap.
It's better than the strategy lessons at least. I'd rather run every night all night than sit through more tactical lectures.

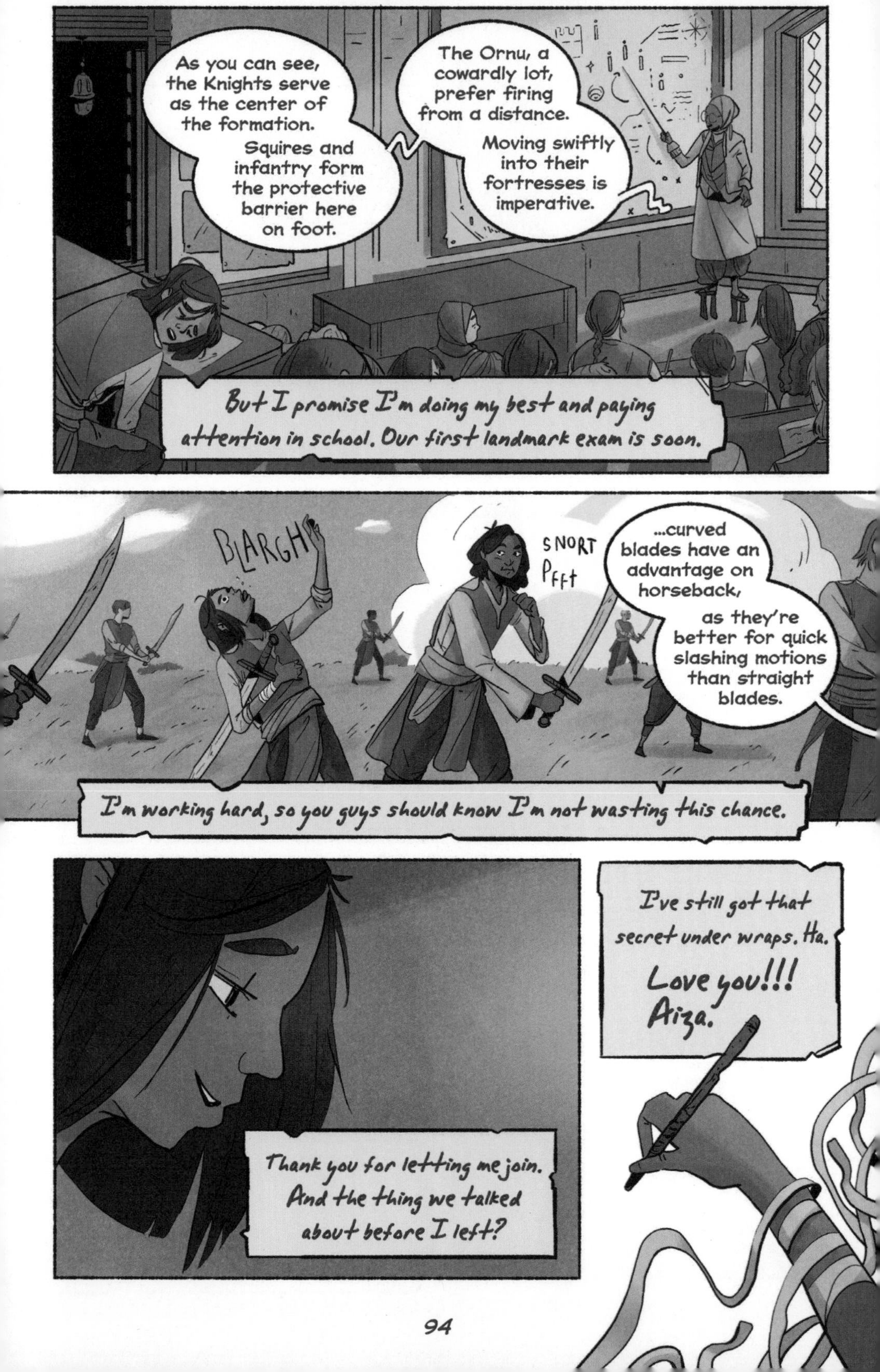
As you can see, the Knights serve as the center of the formation.
Squires and infantry form the protective barrier here on foot.
The Ornu, a cowardly lot, prefer firing from a distance.
Moving swiftly into their fortresses is imperative.
But I promise I'm doing my best and paying attention in school. Our first landmark exam is soon.
BLARGH
SNORT
Pfft
...curved blades have an advantage on horseback,
as they're better for quick slashing motions than straight blades.
I'm working hard, so you guys should know I'm not wasting this chance.
Thank you for letting me join. And the thing we talked about before I left?
I've still got that secret under wraps. Ha.
Love you!!! Aiza.

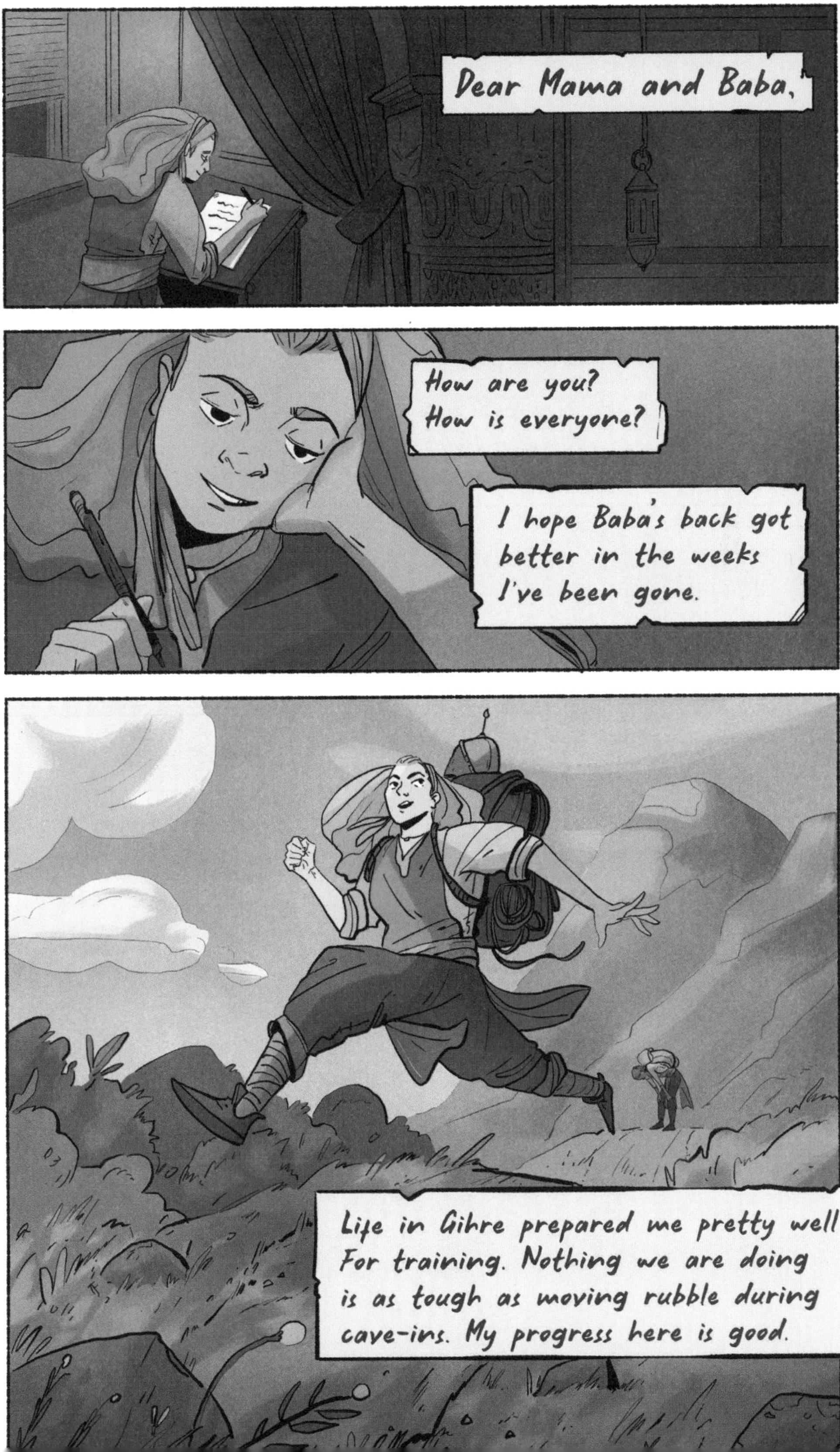
Dear Mama and Baba,
How are you?
How is everyone?
I hope Baba's back got better in the weeks I've been gone.
Life in Gihre prepared me pretty well For training. Nothing we are doing is as tough as moving rubble during cave-ins. My progress here is good.

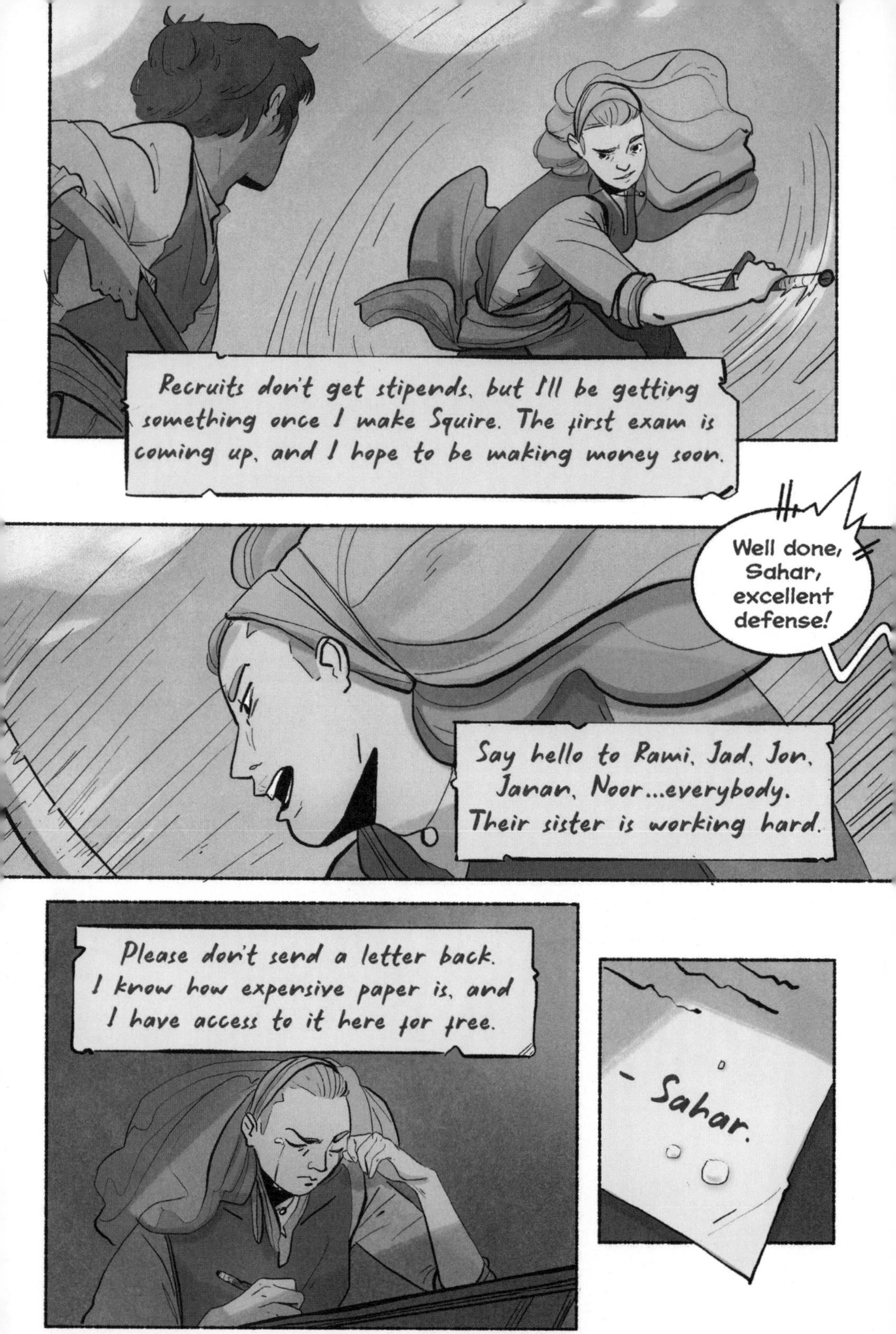
Recruits don't get stipends, but I'll be getting something once I make Squire. The first exam is coming up, and I hope to be making money soon.
Well done, Sahar, excellent defense!
Say hello to Rami, Jad, Jon, Janan, Noor...everybody. Their sister is working hard.
Please don't send a letter back. I know how expensive paper is, and I have access to it here for free.
- Sahar.

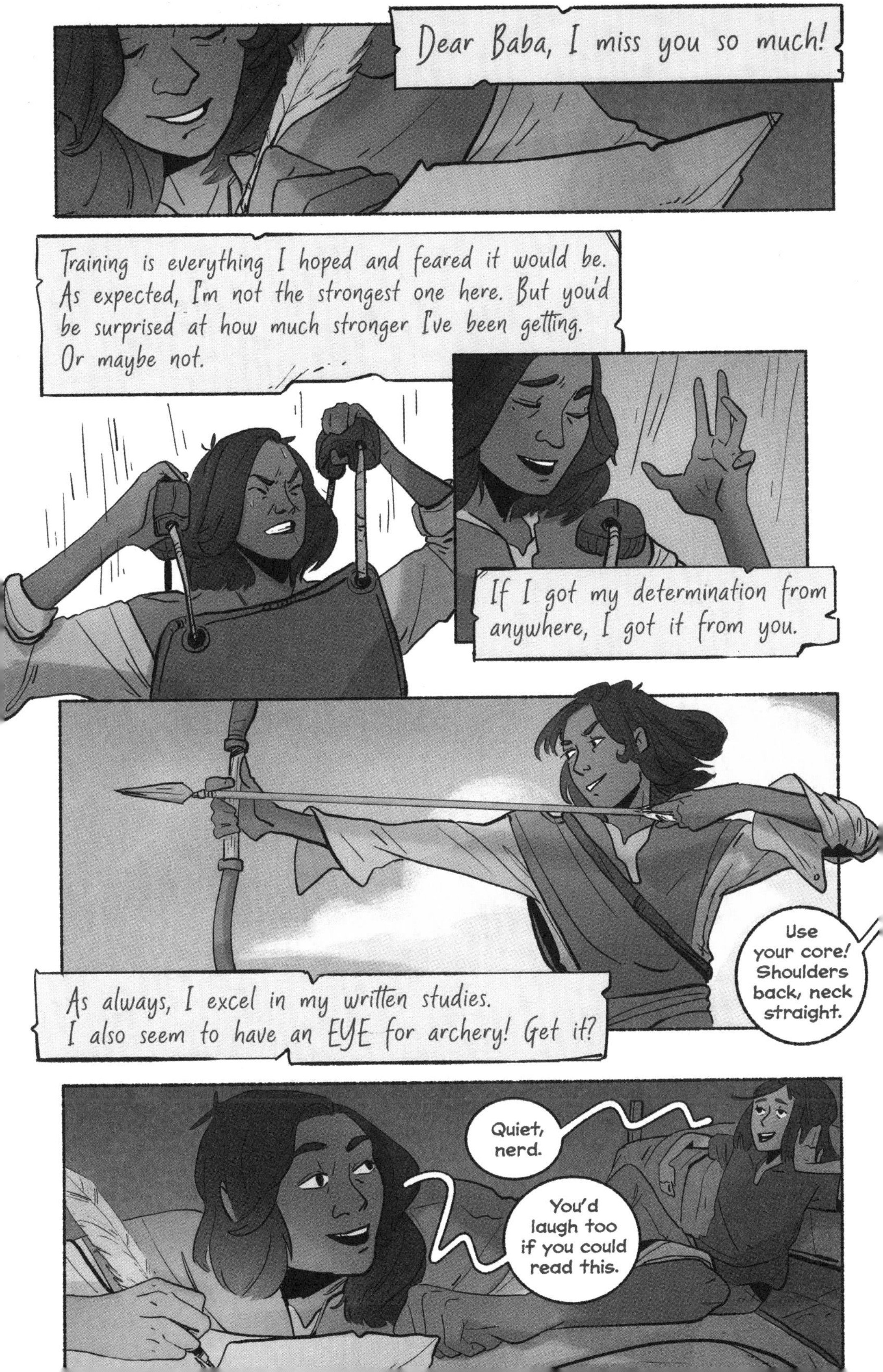
Dear Baba, I miss you so much!
Training is everything I hoped and feared it would be. As expected, I'm not the strongest one here. But you'd be surprised at how much stronger I've been getting. Or maybe not.
If I got my determination from anywhere, I got it from you.
As always, I excel in my written studies. I also seem to have an EYE for archery! Get it?
Use your core! Shoulders back, neck straight.
Quiet, nerd.
You'd laugh too if you could read this.

Oh, and Basem's here!
It was nice to see him.

Although, not so sure he
was so happy to see me.

py to see me.

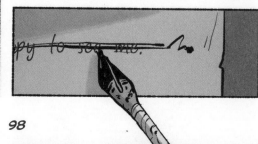

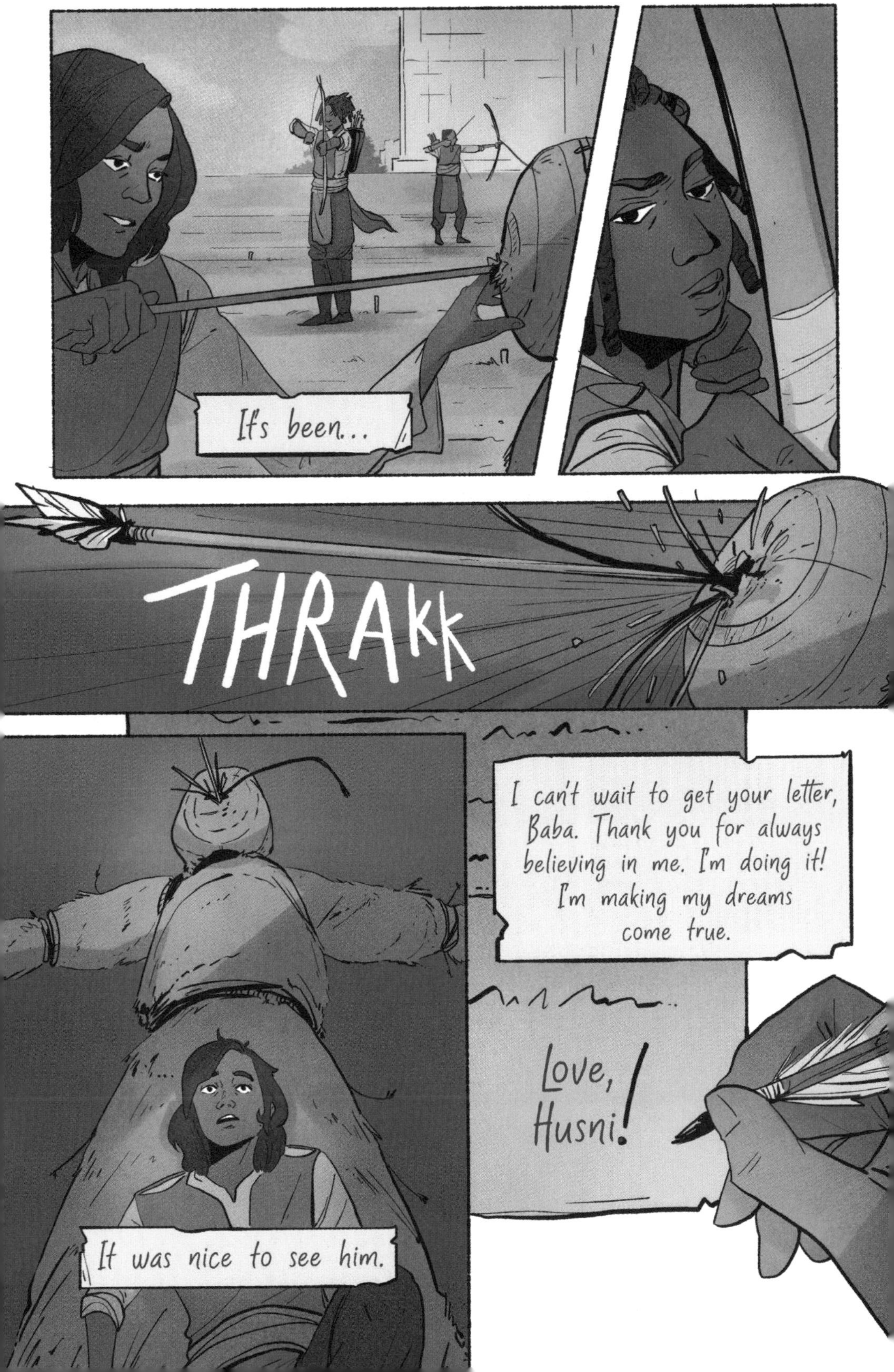
It's been...
THRAKK
I can't wait to get your letter, Baba. Thank you for always believing in me. I'm doing it! I'm making my dreams come true.
Love, Husni!
It was nice to see him.

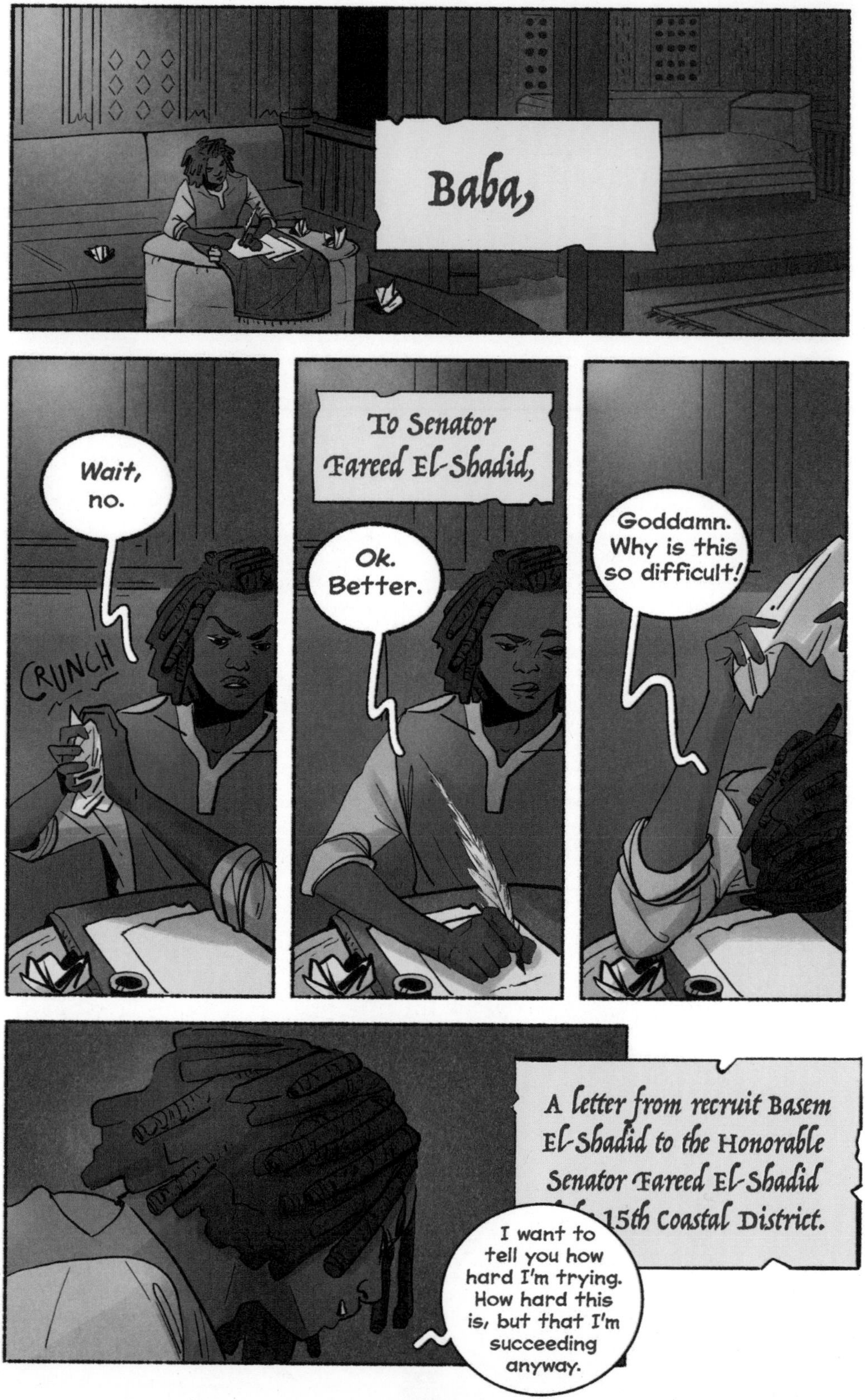
Baba,
Wait, no.
CRUNCH
To Senator Fareed El-Shadid,
Ok. Better.
Goddamn. Why is this so difficult!
A letter from recruit Basem El-Shadid to the Honorable Senator Fareed El-Shadid
15th Coastal District.
I want to tell you how hard I'm trying. How hard this is, but that I'm succeeding anyway.

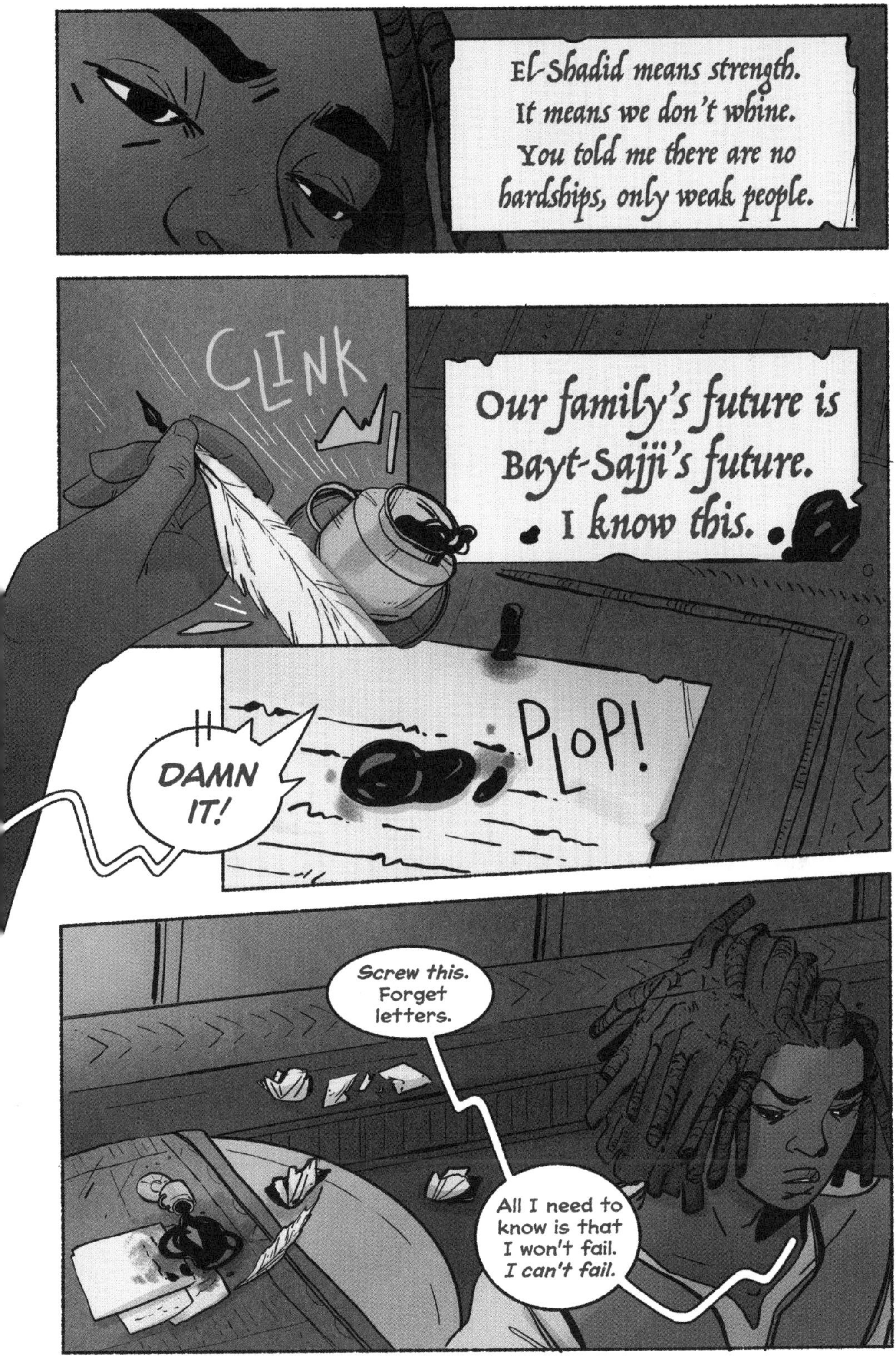
El-Shadid means strength. It means we don't whine. You told me there are no hardships, only weak people.
CLINK
Our family's future is Bayt-Sajji's future. I know this.
PLOP!
DAMN IT!
Screw this. Forget letters.
All I need to know is that I won't fail. I can't fail.

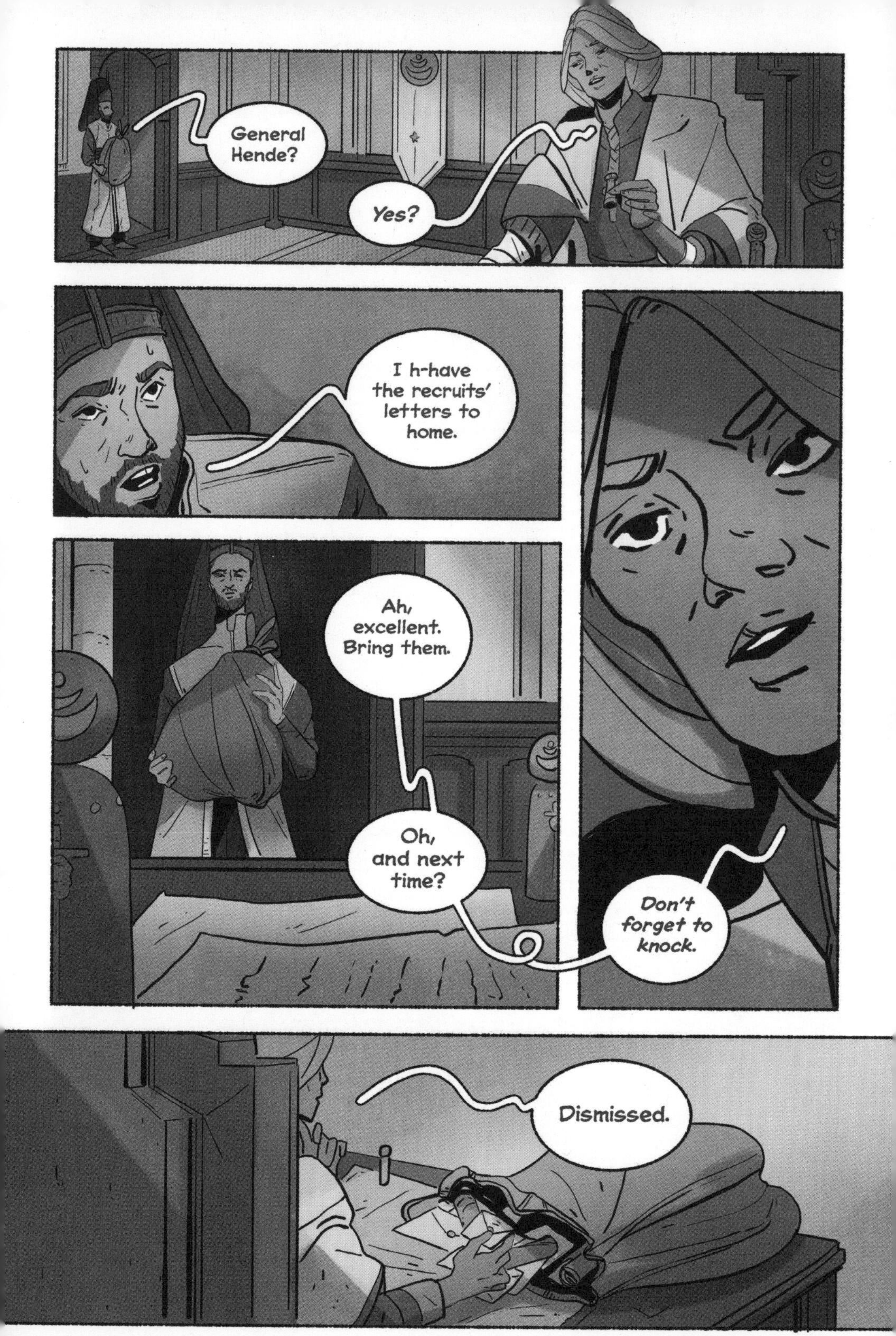
General Hende?
Yes?
I h-have the recruits' letters to home.
Ah, excellent. Bring them.
Oh, and next time?
Don't forget to knock.
Dismissed.

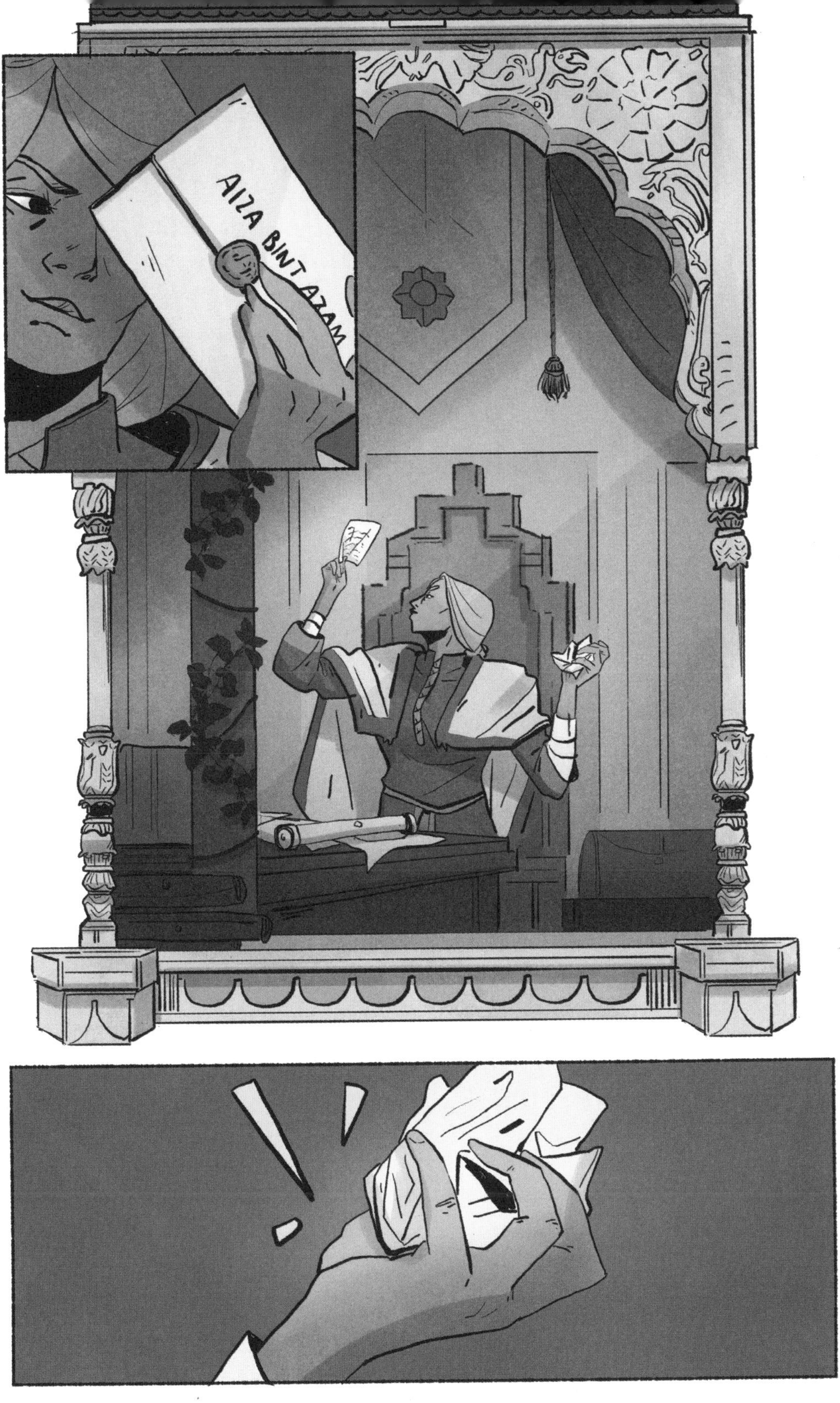
AIZA BINT AZAM

CHAPTER 6

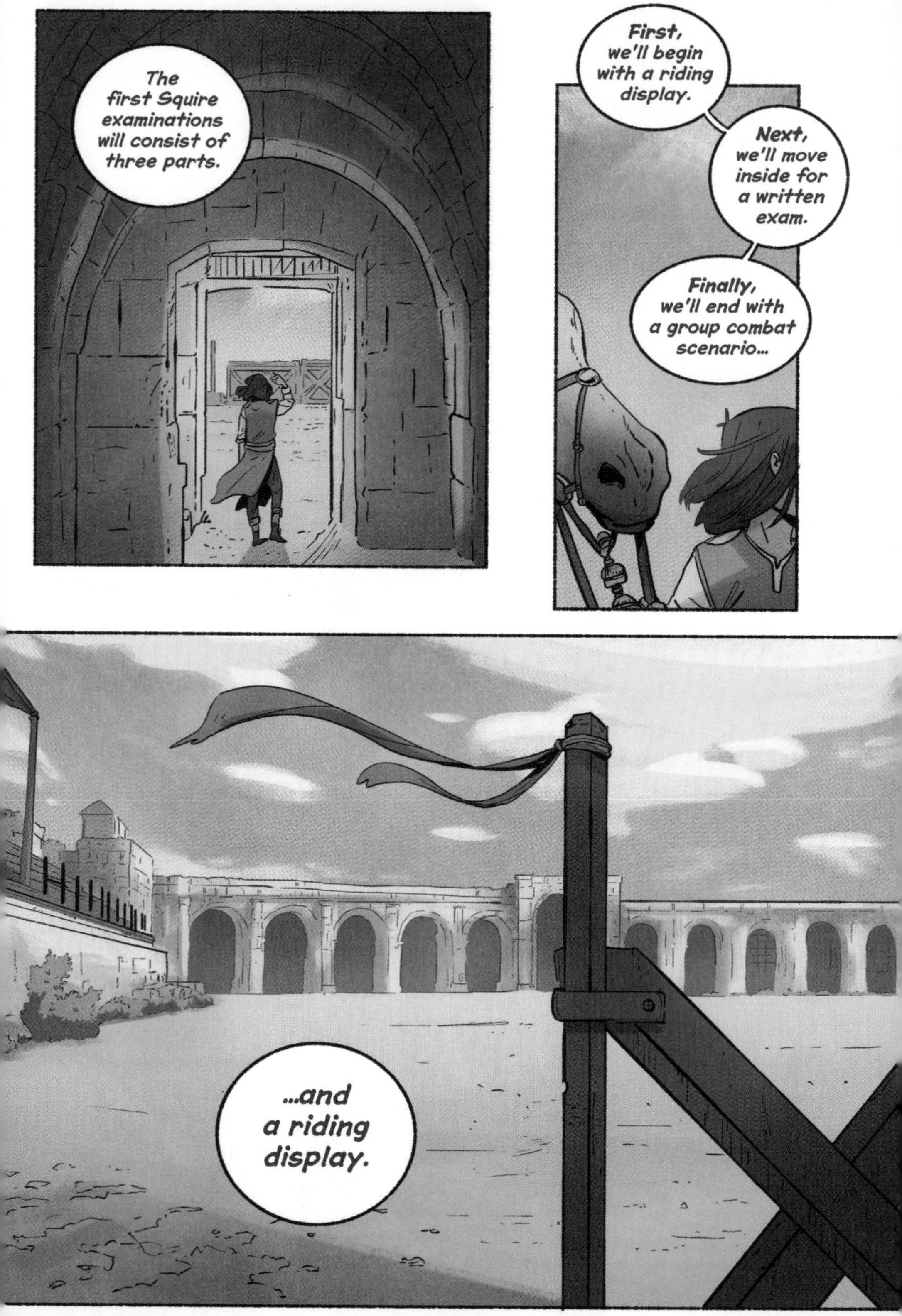
The first Squire examinations will consist of three parts.
First, we'll begin with a riding display.
Next, we'll move inside for a written exam.
Finally, we'll end with a group combat scenario...
...and a riding display.

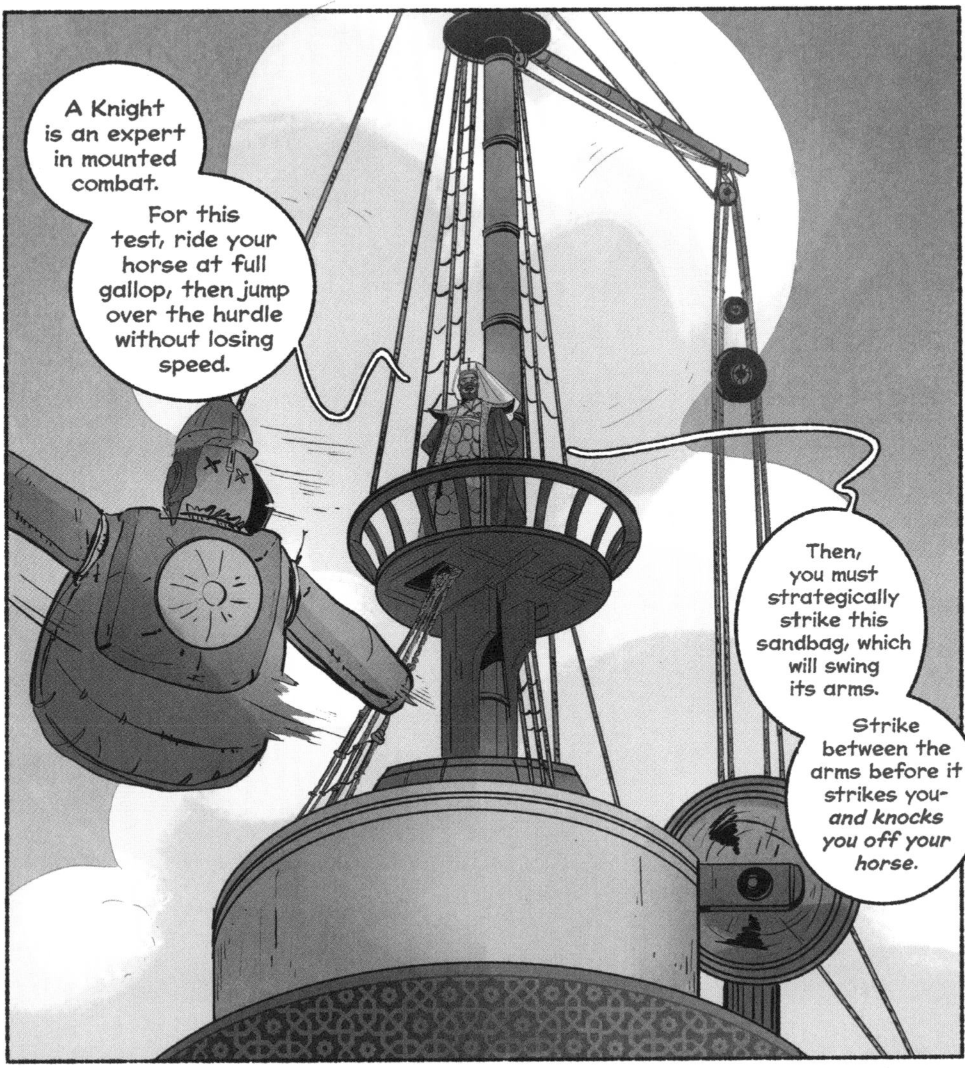
A Knight is an expert in mounted combat.
For this test, ride your horse at full gallop, then jump over the hurdle without losing speed.
Then, you must strategically strike this sandbag, which will swing its arms.
Strike between the arms before it strikes you- *and knocks you off your horse.*

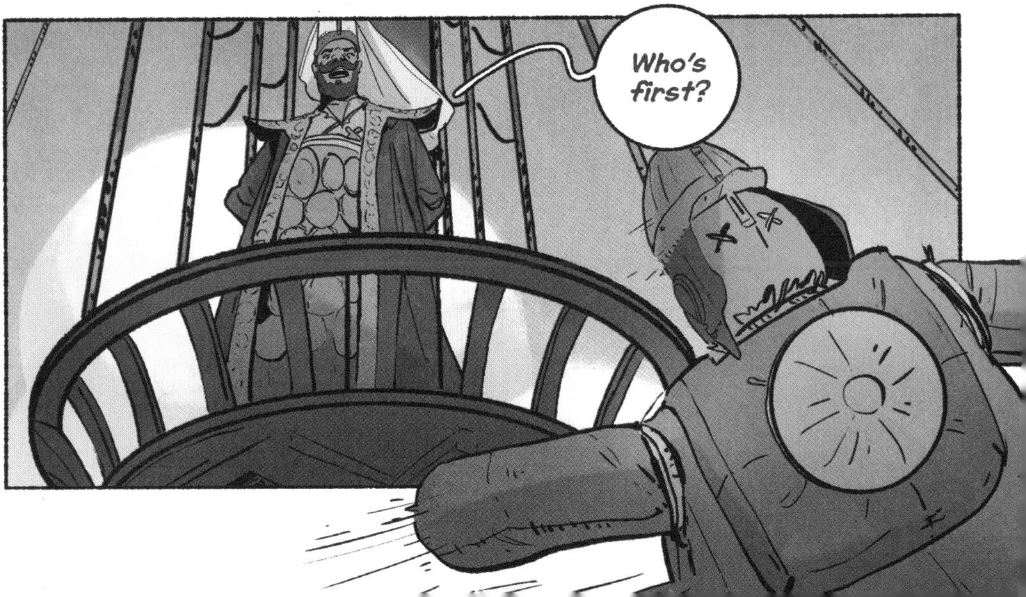
Who's first?

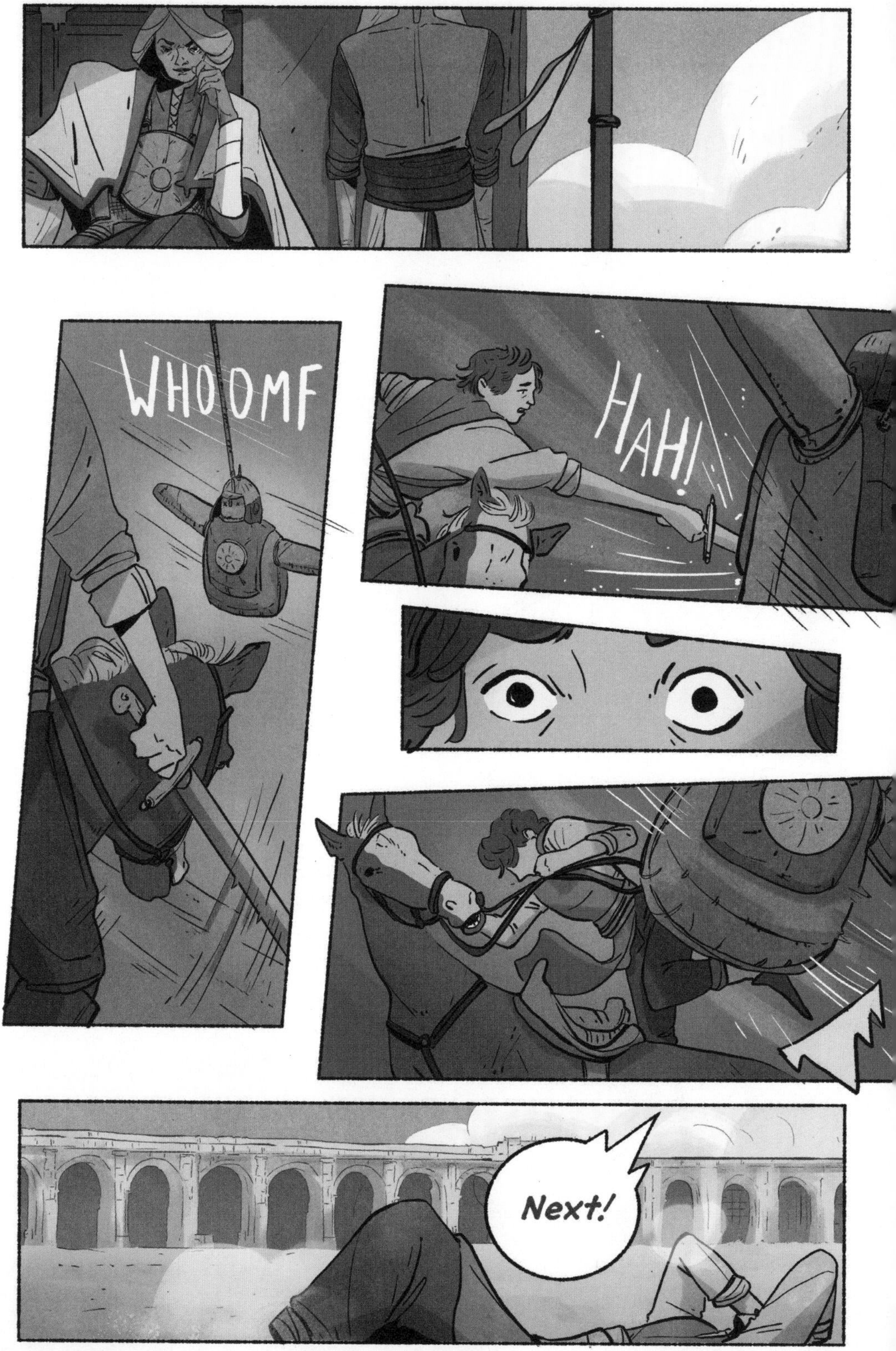
WHOOMF
HAH!
Next!

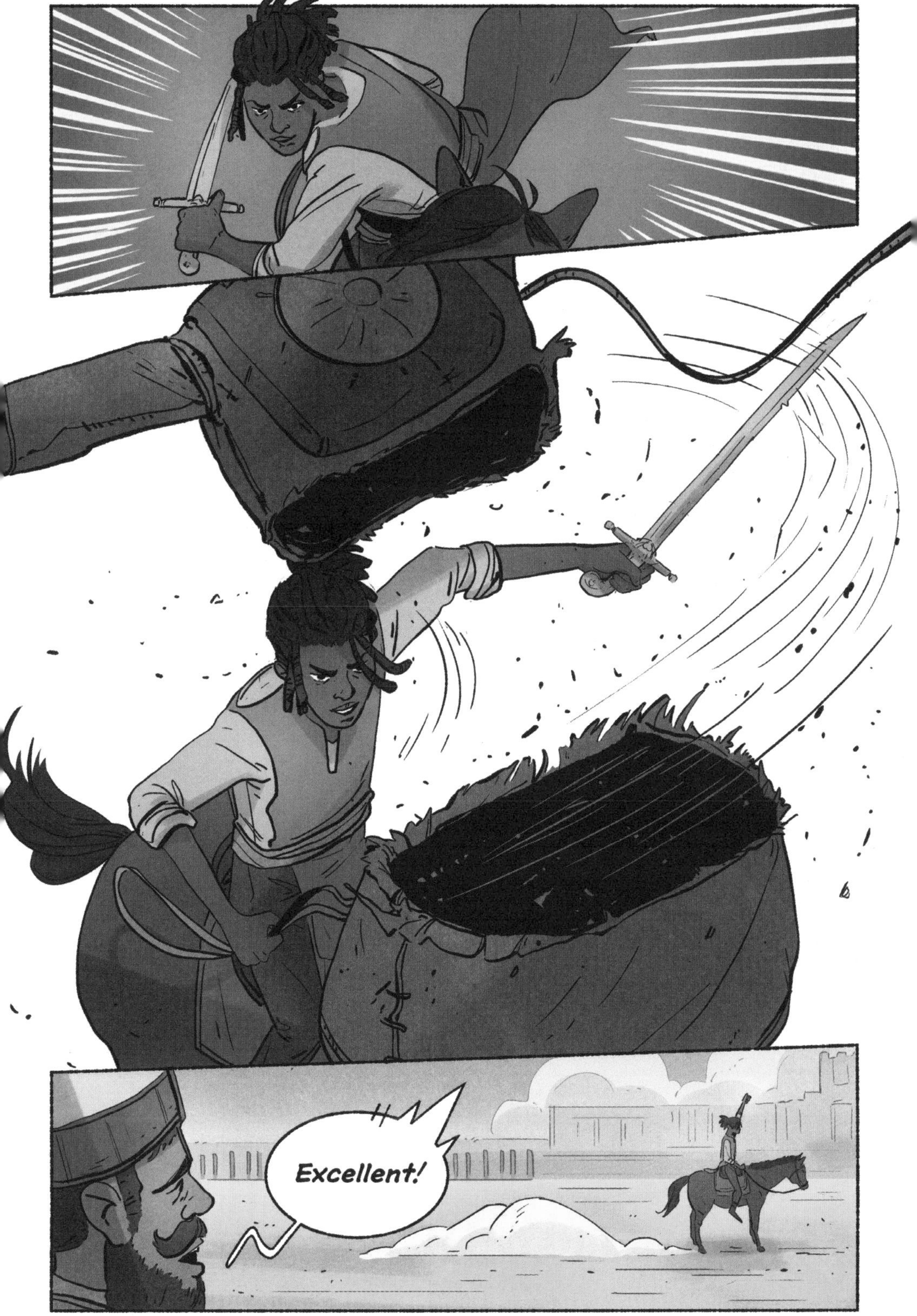
Excellent!

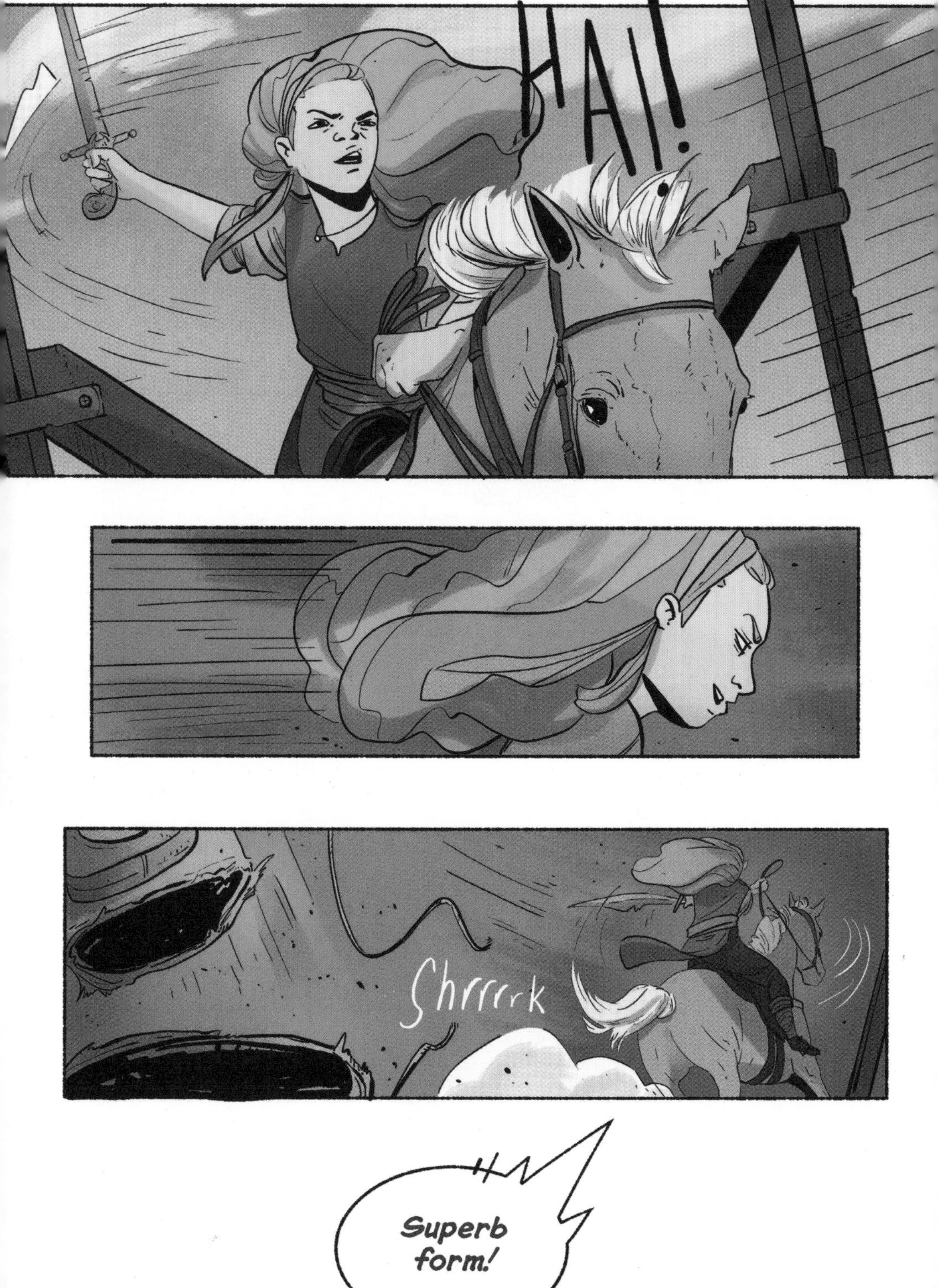
HAI!
Shrrrrk
Superb form!

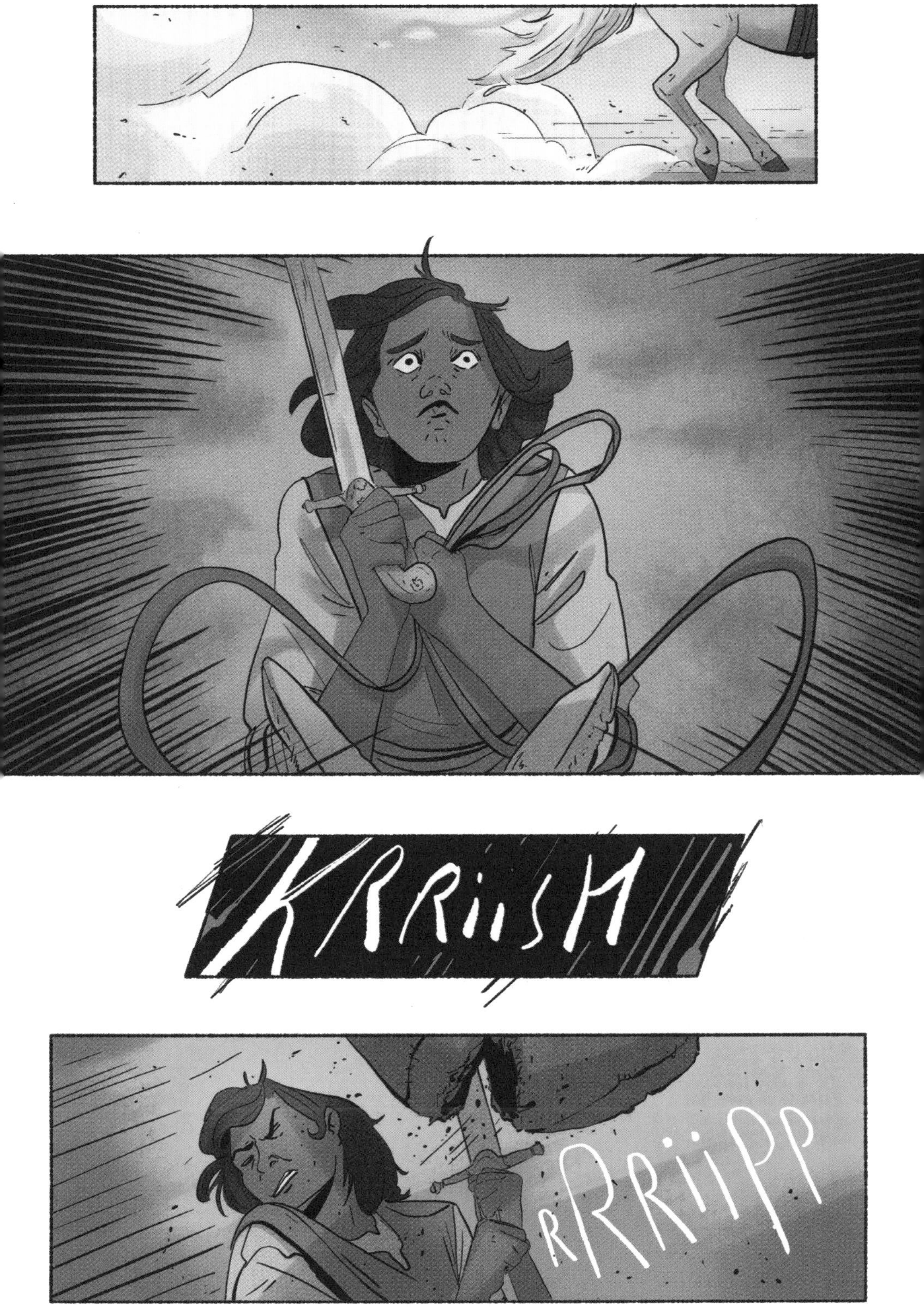
KRRiiSM
rRRiiPP

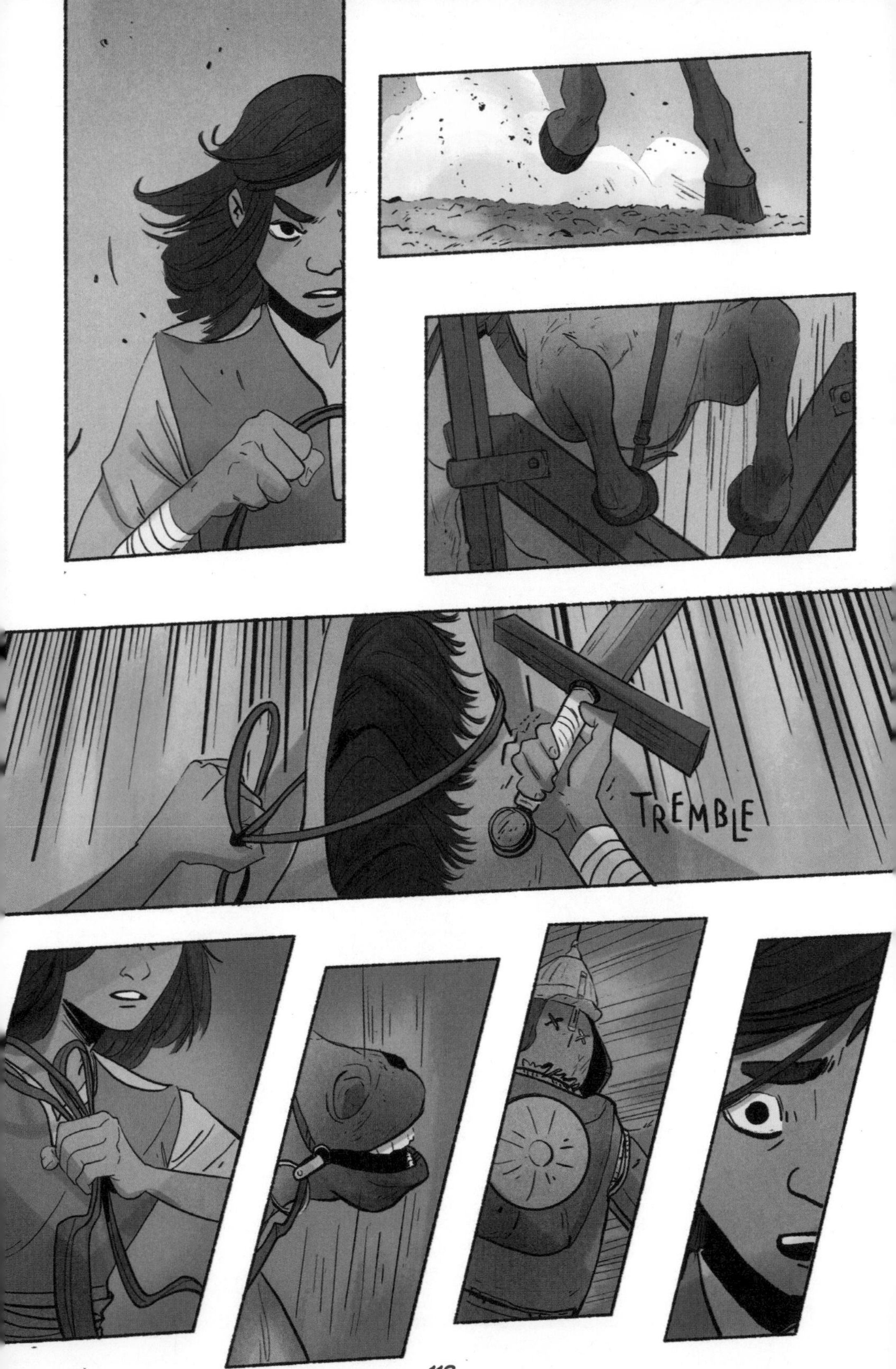
TREMBLE

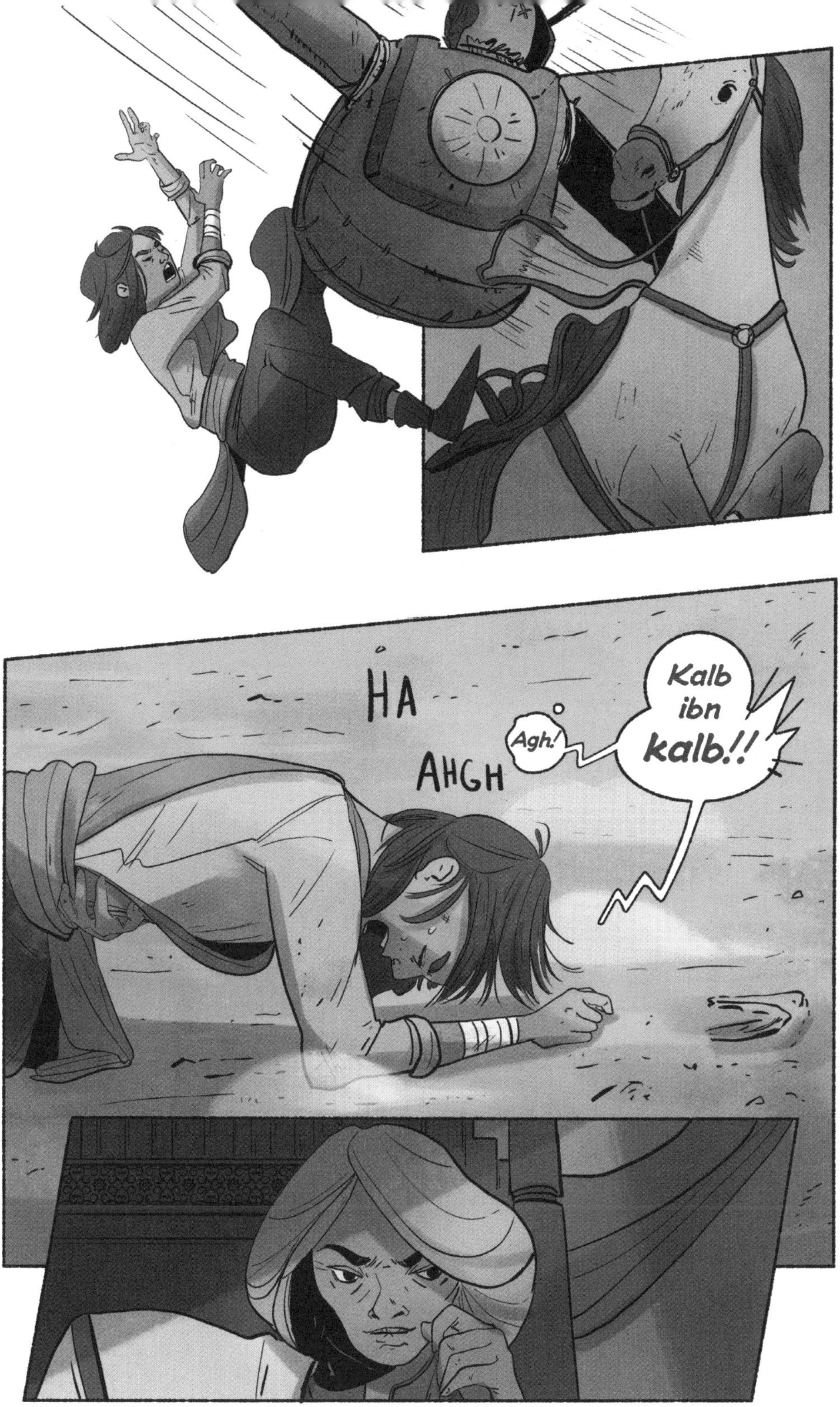
HA
AHGH
Agh!
Kalb ibn kalb!!

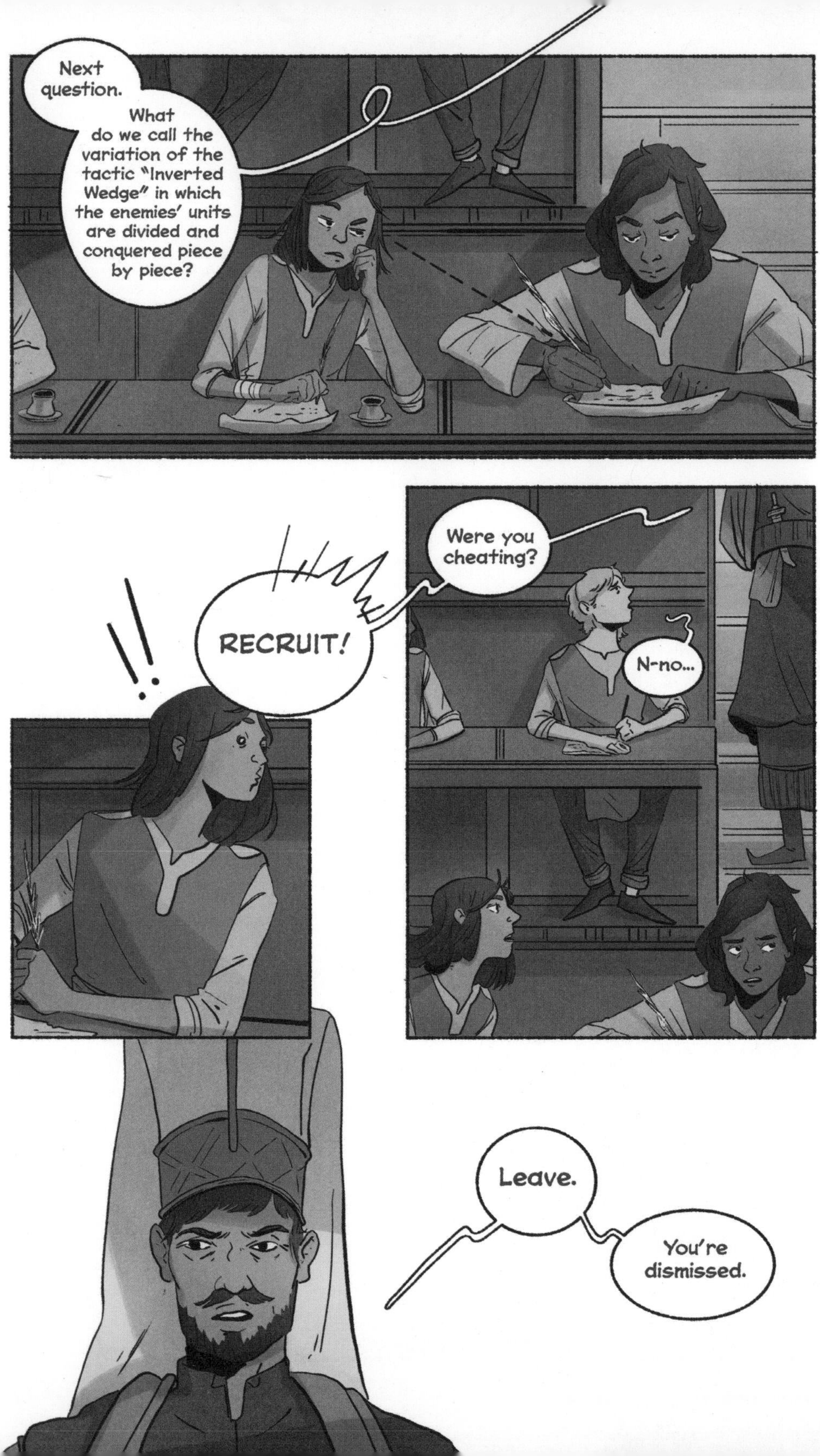
Next question.
What do we call the variation of the tactic "Inverted Wedge" in which the enemies' units are divided and conquered piece by piece?
RECRUIT!
Were you cheating?
N-no...
Leave.
You're dismissed.

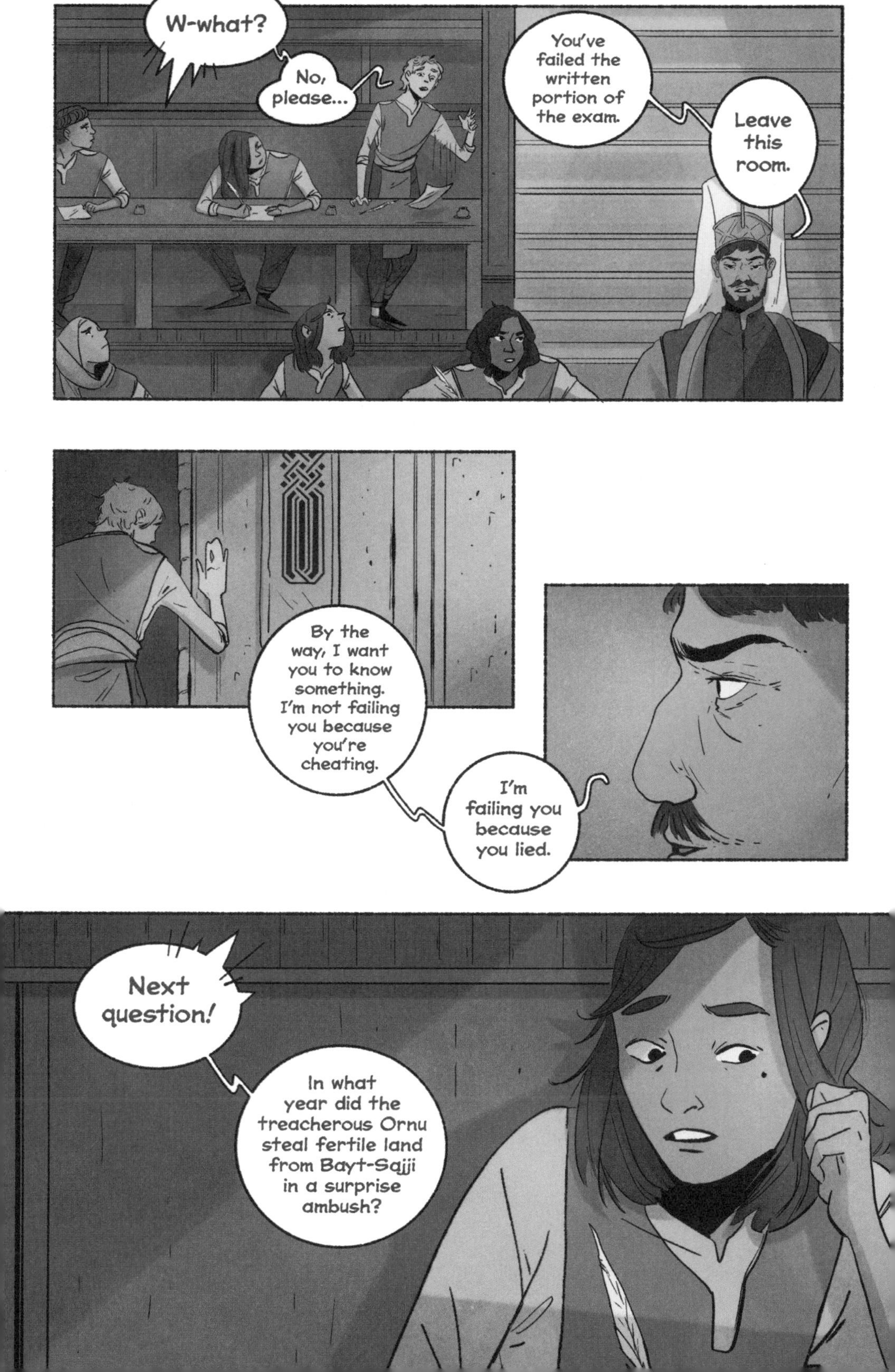
W-what?
No, please...
You've failed the written portion of the exam.
Leave this room.
By the way, I want you to know something. I'm not failing you because you're cheating.
I'm failing you because you lied.
Next question!
In what year did the treacherous Ornu steal fertile land from Bayt-Sajji in a surprise ambush?

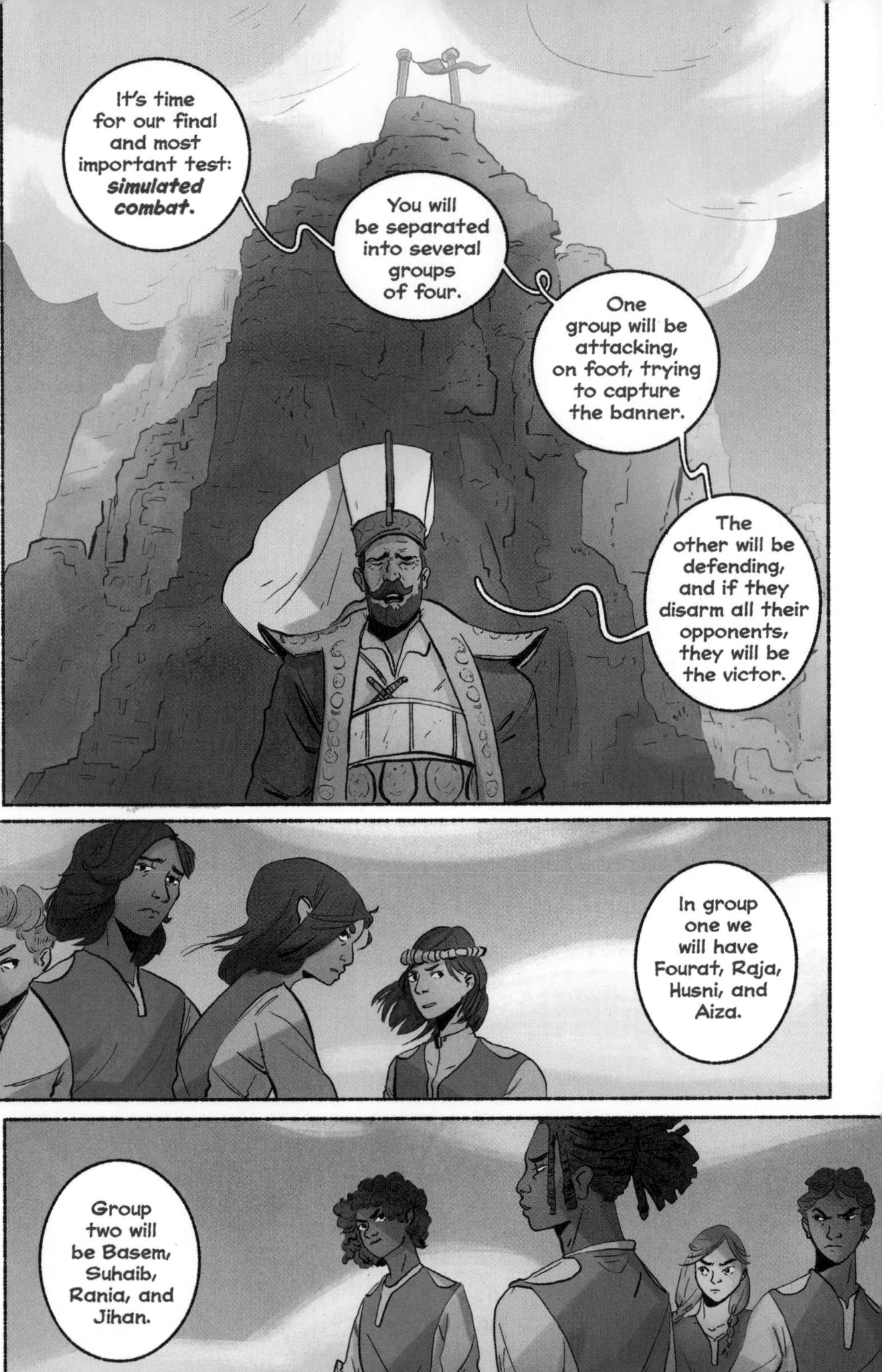
It's time for our final and most important test: ***simulated combat.***
You will be separated into several groups of four.
One group will be attacking, on foot, trying to capture the banner.
The other will be defending, and if they disarm all their opponents, they will be the victor.
In group one we will have Fourat, Raja, Husni, and Aiza.
Group two will be Basem, Suhaib, Rania, and Jihan.

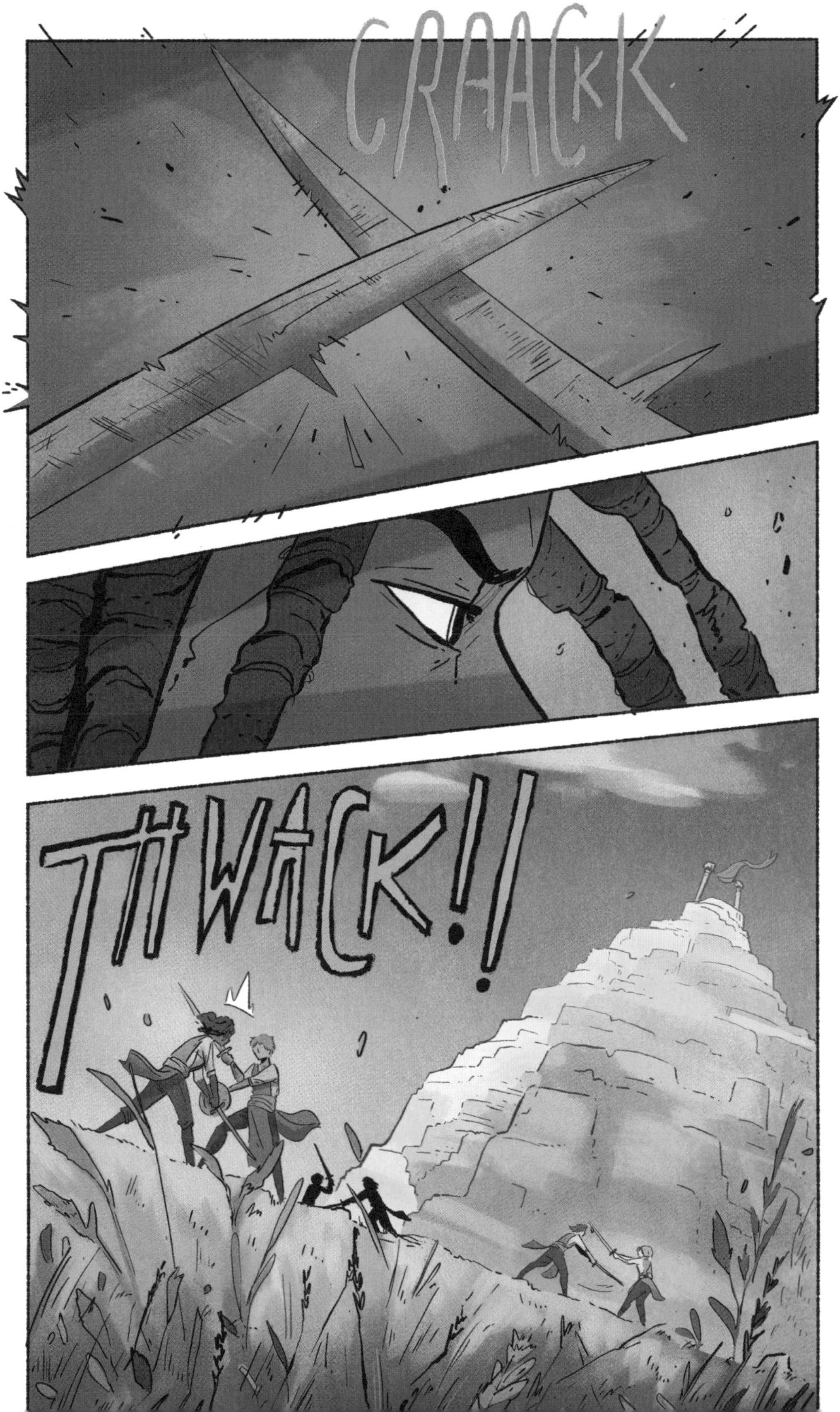
CRAACKK
THWACK!!

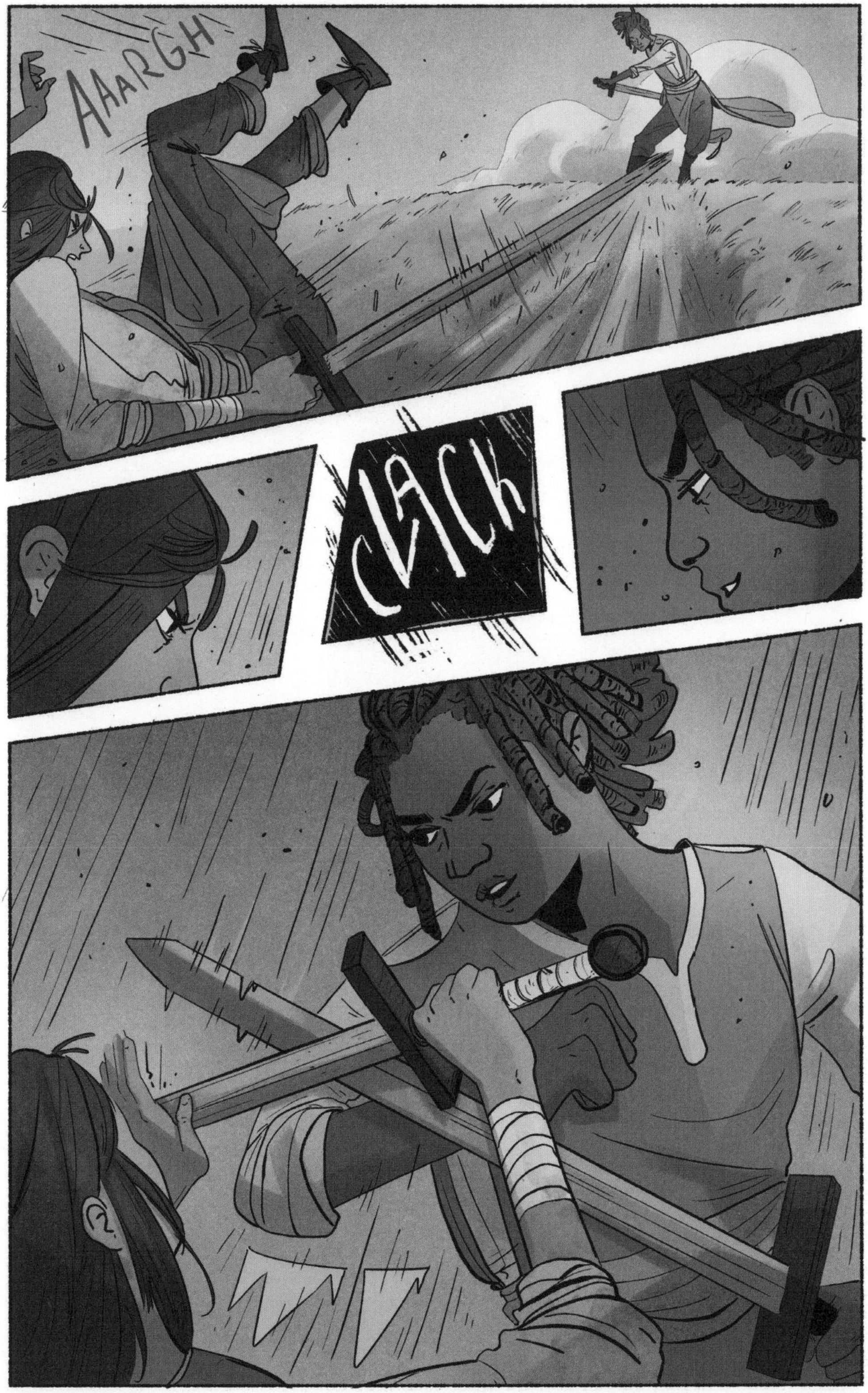
AAARGH
CLACK

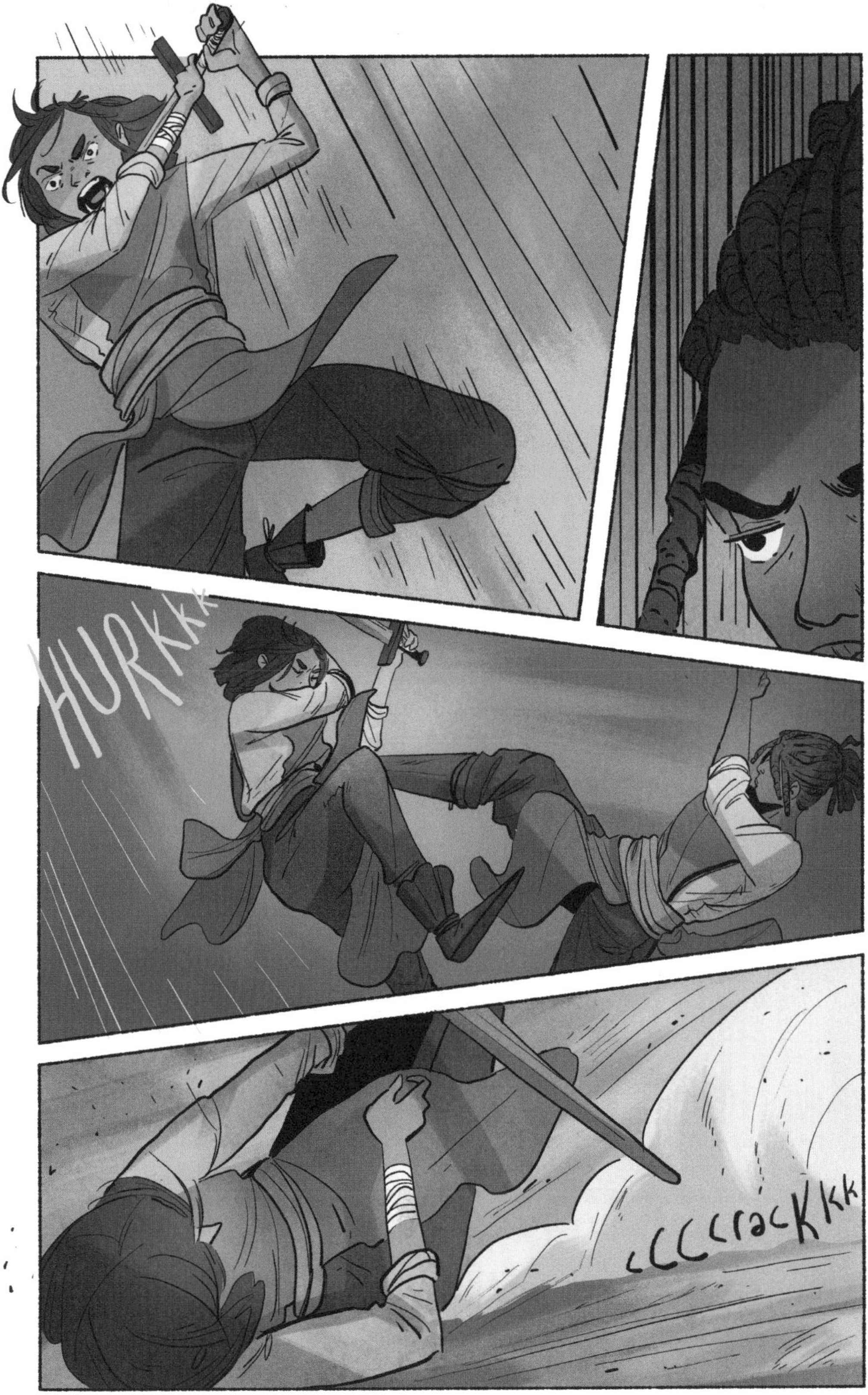
HURKKK
CCCCracKkk

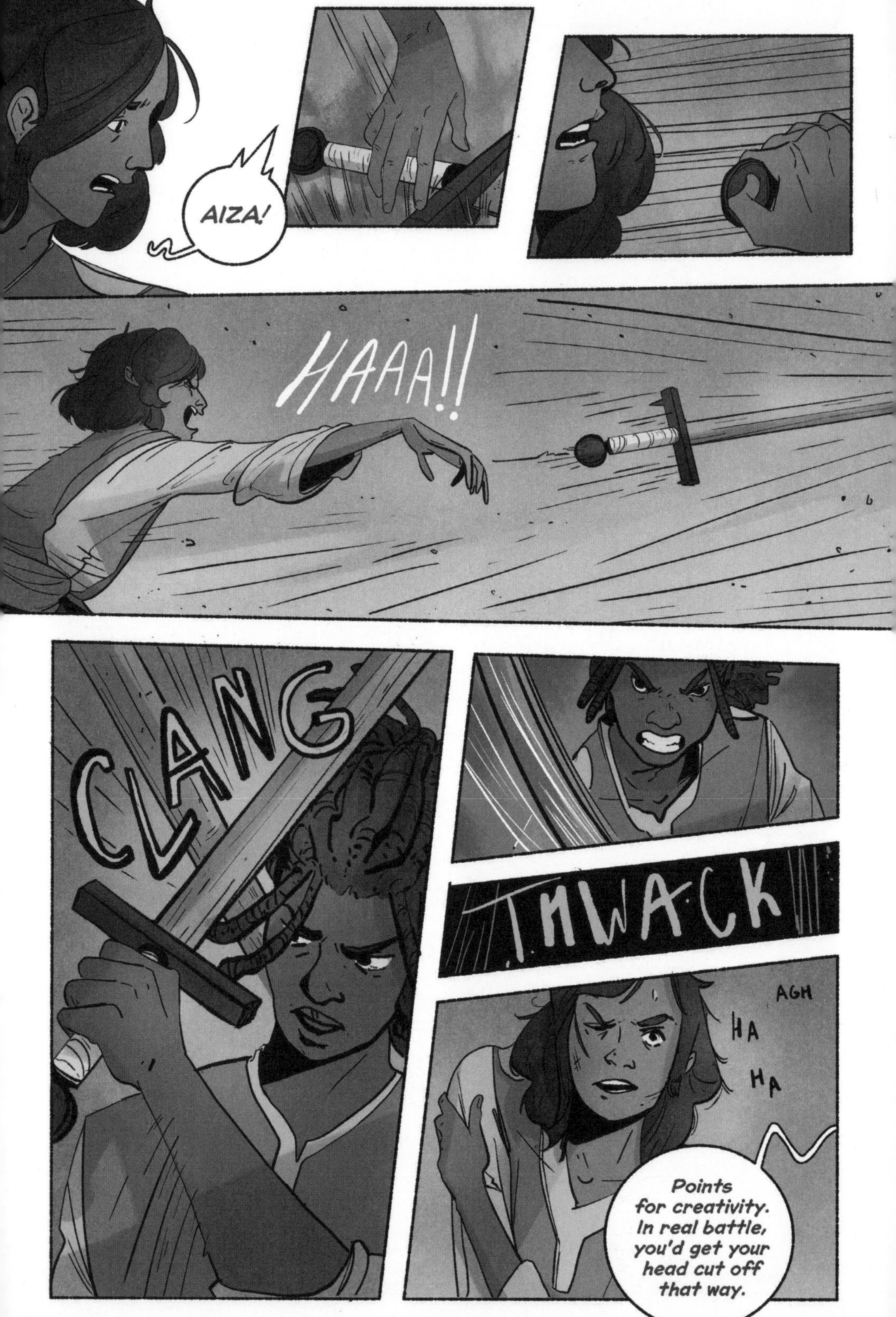
AIZA!
HAAA!!
CLANG
THWACK
AGH
HA
HA
Points for creativity. In real battle, you'd get your head cut off that way.

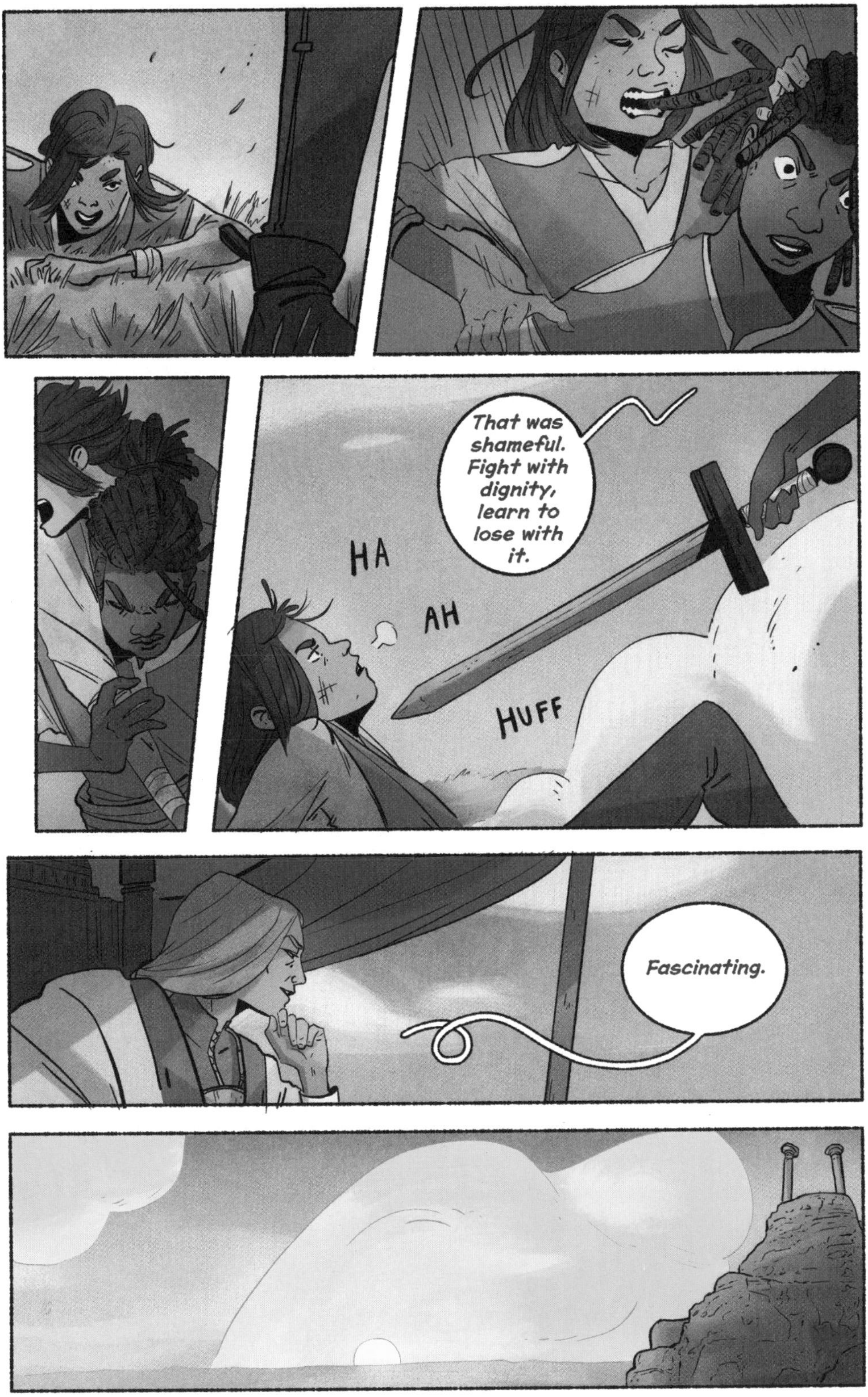
That was shameful. Fight with dignity, learn to lose with it.
HA
AH
HUFF
Fascinating.

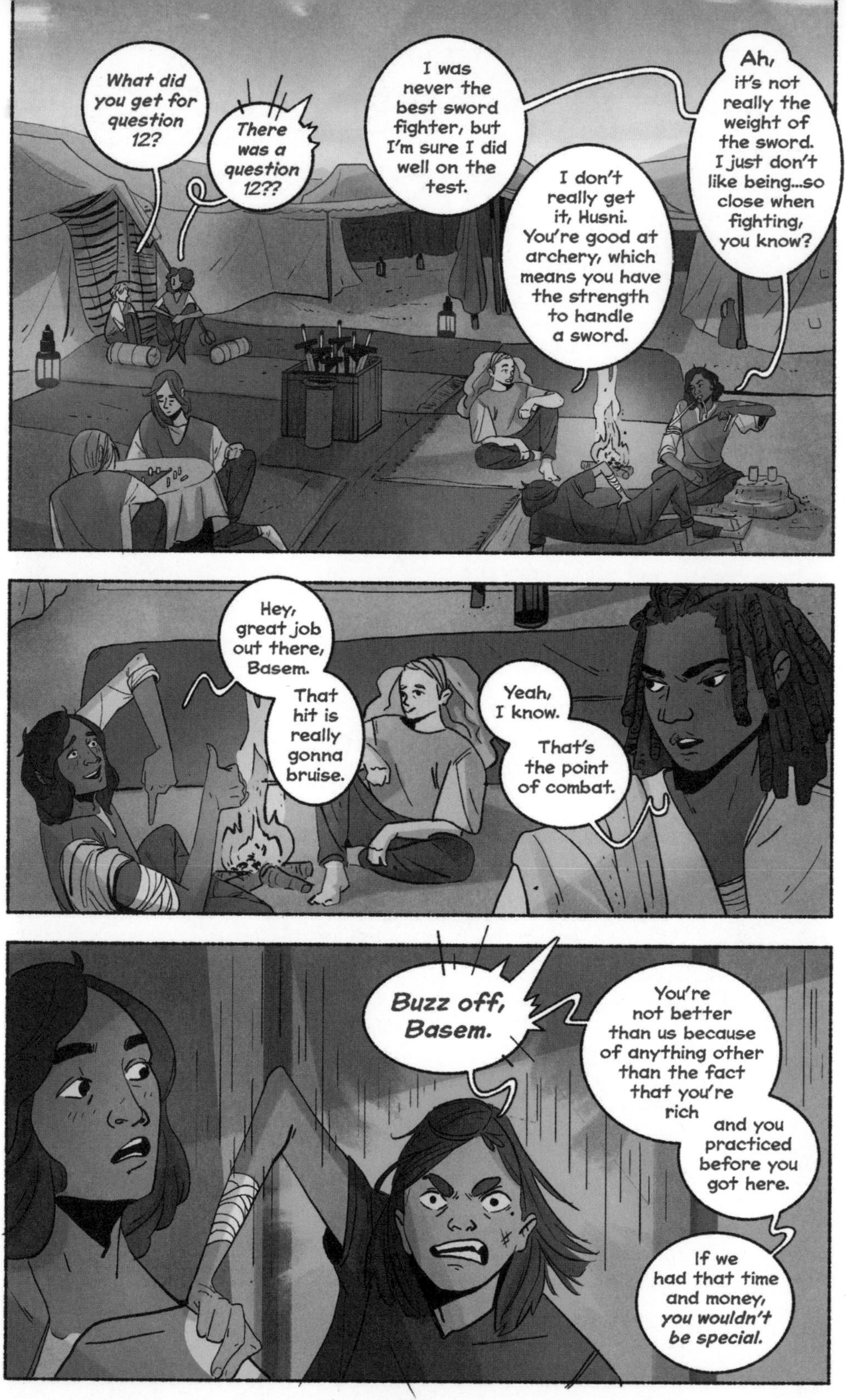

What did you get for question 12?
There was a question 12??
I was never the best sword fighter, but I'm sure I did well on the test.
I don't really get it, Husni. You're good at archery, which means you have the strength to handle a sword.
Ah, it's not really the weight of the sword. I just don't like being...so close when fighting, you know?
Hey, great job out there, Basem.
That hit is really gonna bruise.
Yeah, I know.
That's the point of combat.
Buzz off, Basem.
You're not better than us because of anything other than the fact that you're rich
and you practiced before you got here.
If we had that time and money, you wouldn't be special.

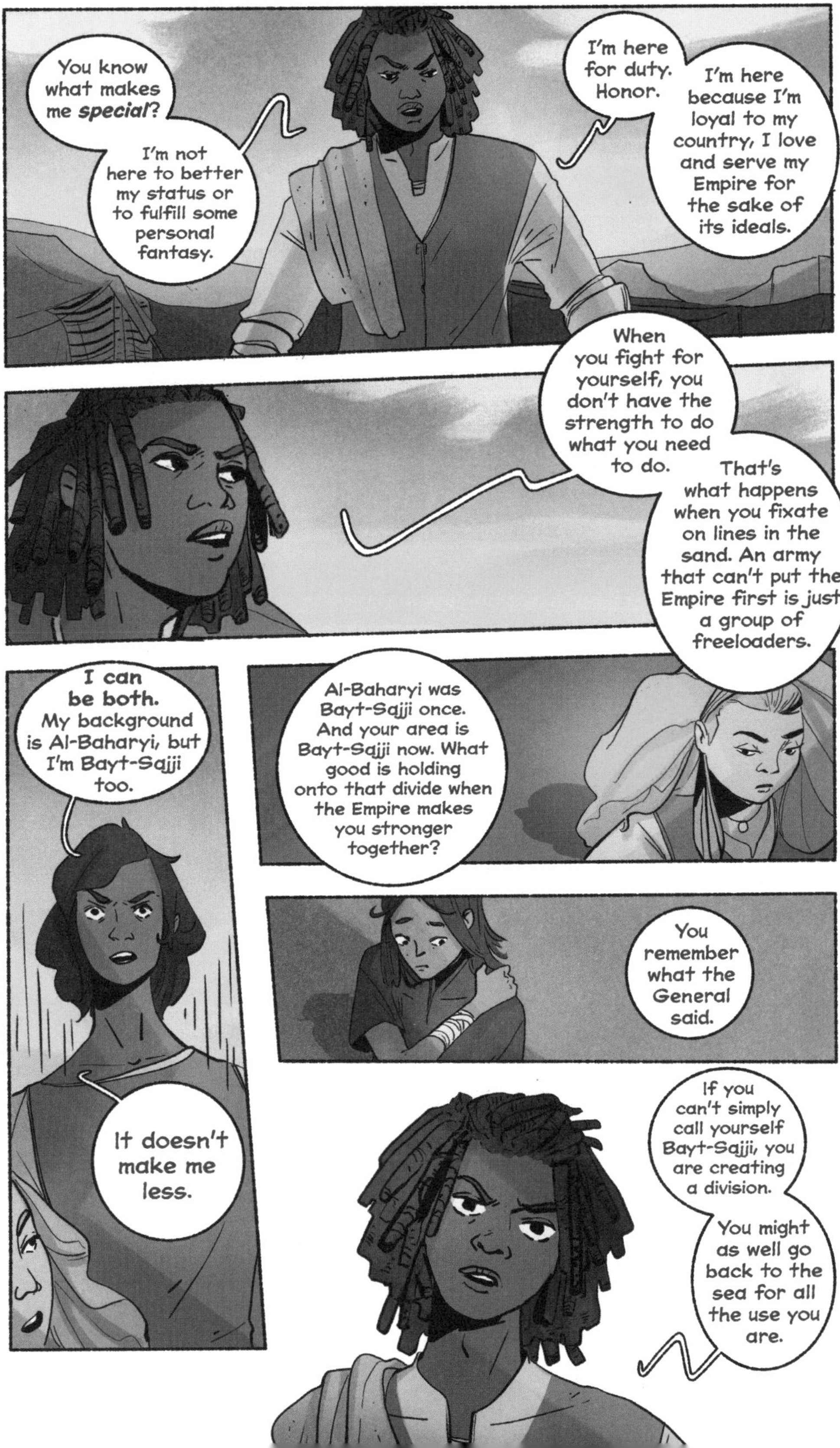
You know what makes me *special*?
I'm not here to better my status or to fulfill some personal fantasy.
I'm here for duty. Honor.
I'm here because I'm loyal to my country, I love and serve my Empire for the sake of its ideals.
When you fight for yourself, you don't have the strength to do what you need to do.
That's what happens when you fixate on lines in the sand. An army that can't put the Empire first is just a group of freeloaders.
I can be both. My background is Al-Baharyi, but I'm Bayt-Sajji too.
It doesn't make me less.
Al-Baharyi was Bayt-Sajji once. And your area is Bayt-Sajji now. What good is holding onto that divide when the Empire makes you stronger together?
You remember what the General said.
If you can't simply call yourself Bayt-Sajji, you are creating a division.
You might as well go back to the sea for all the use you are.

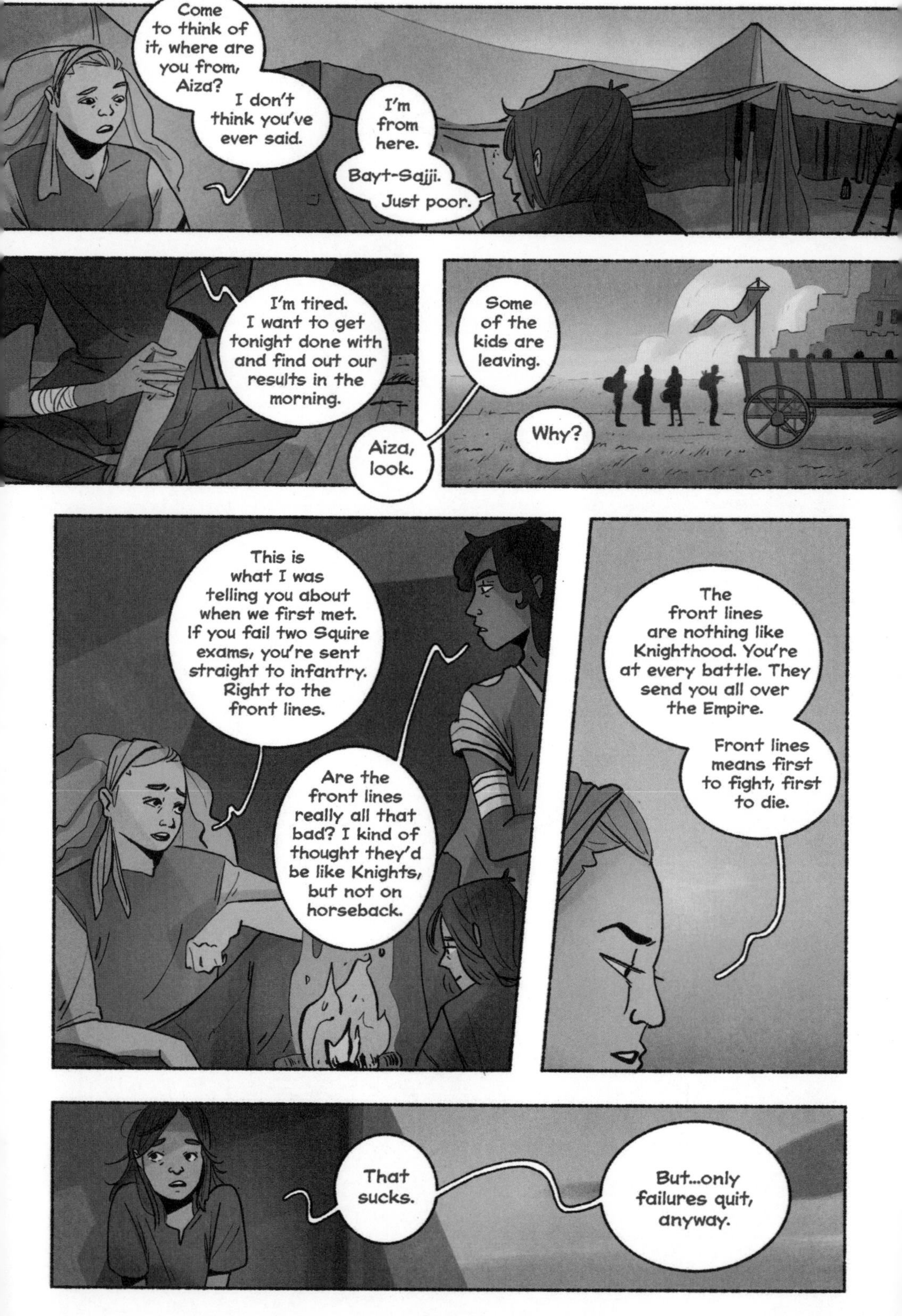
Come to think of it, where are you from, Aiza?
I don't think you've ever said.
I'm from here.
Bayt-Sajji.
Just poor.
I'm tired. I want to get tonight done with and find out our results in the morning.
Some of the kids are leaving.
Aiza, look.
Why?
This is what I was telling you about when we first met. If you fail two Squire exams, you're sent straight to infantry. Right to the front lines.
Are the front lines really all that bad? I kind of thought they'd be like Knights, but not on horseback.
The front lines are nothing like Knighthood. You're at every battle. They send you all over the Empire.
Front lines means first to fight, first to die.
That sucks.
But...only failures quit, anyway.

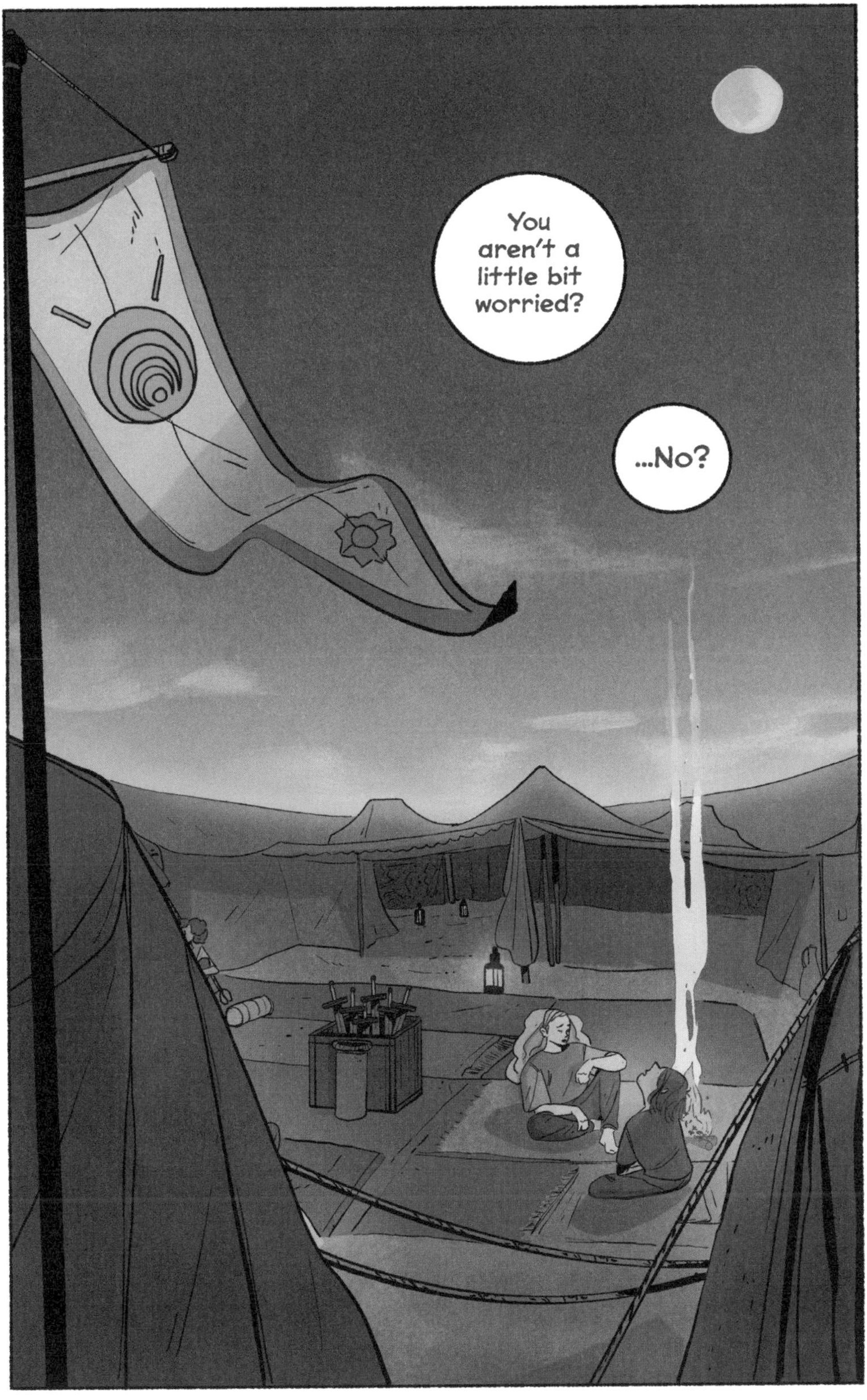
You aren't a little bit worried?
...No?

CHAPTER 7

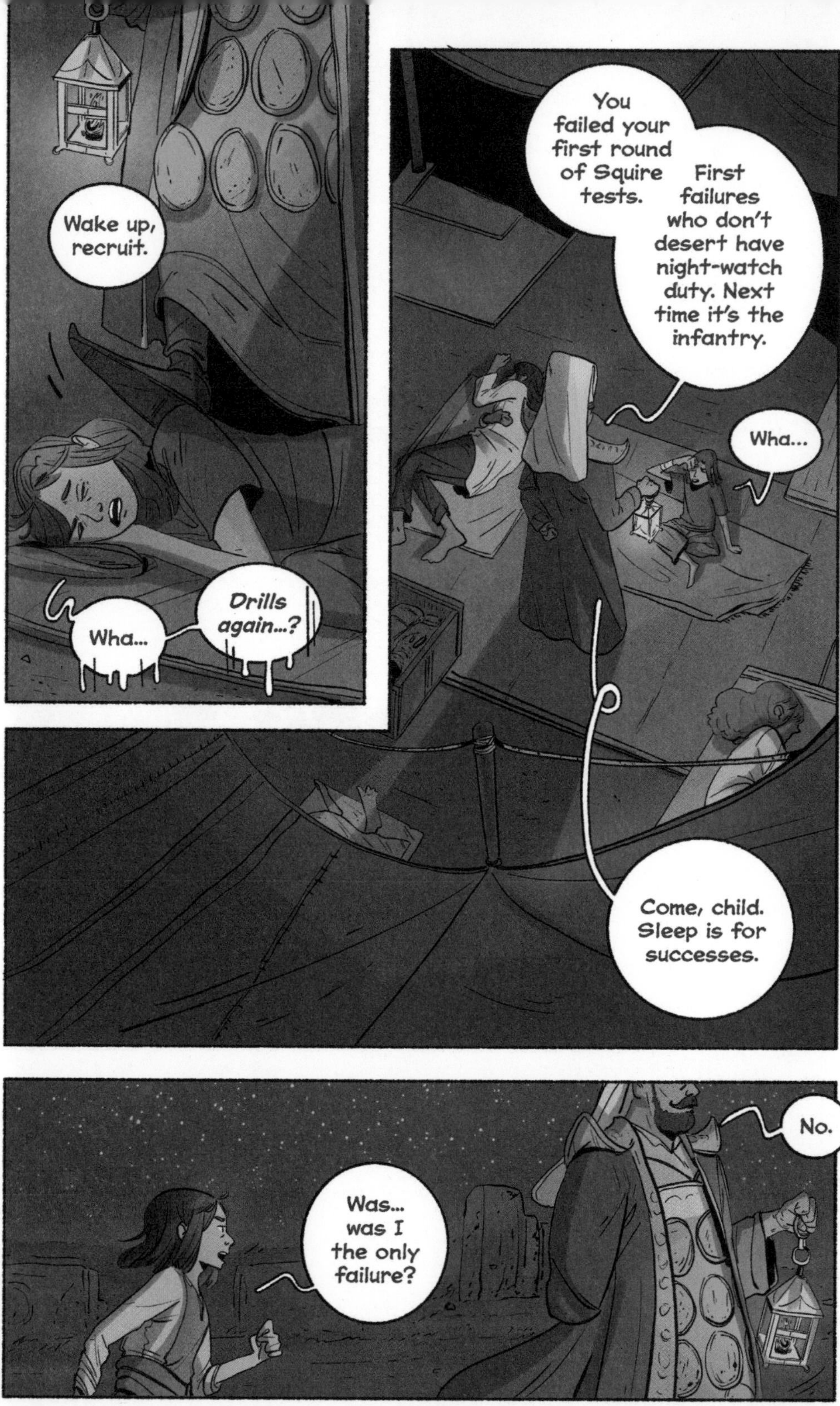
Wake up, recruit.
Wha...
Drills again...?
You failed your first round of Squire tests.
First failures who don't desert have night-watch duty. Next time it's the infantry.
Wha...
Come, child. Sleep is for successes.
No.
Was... was I the only failure?

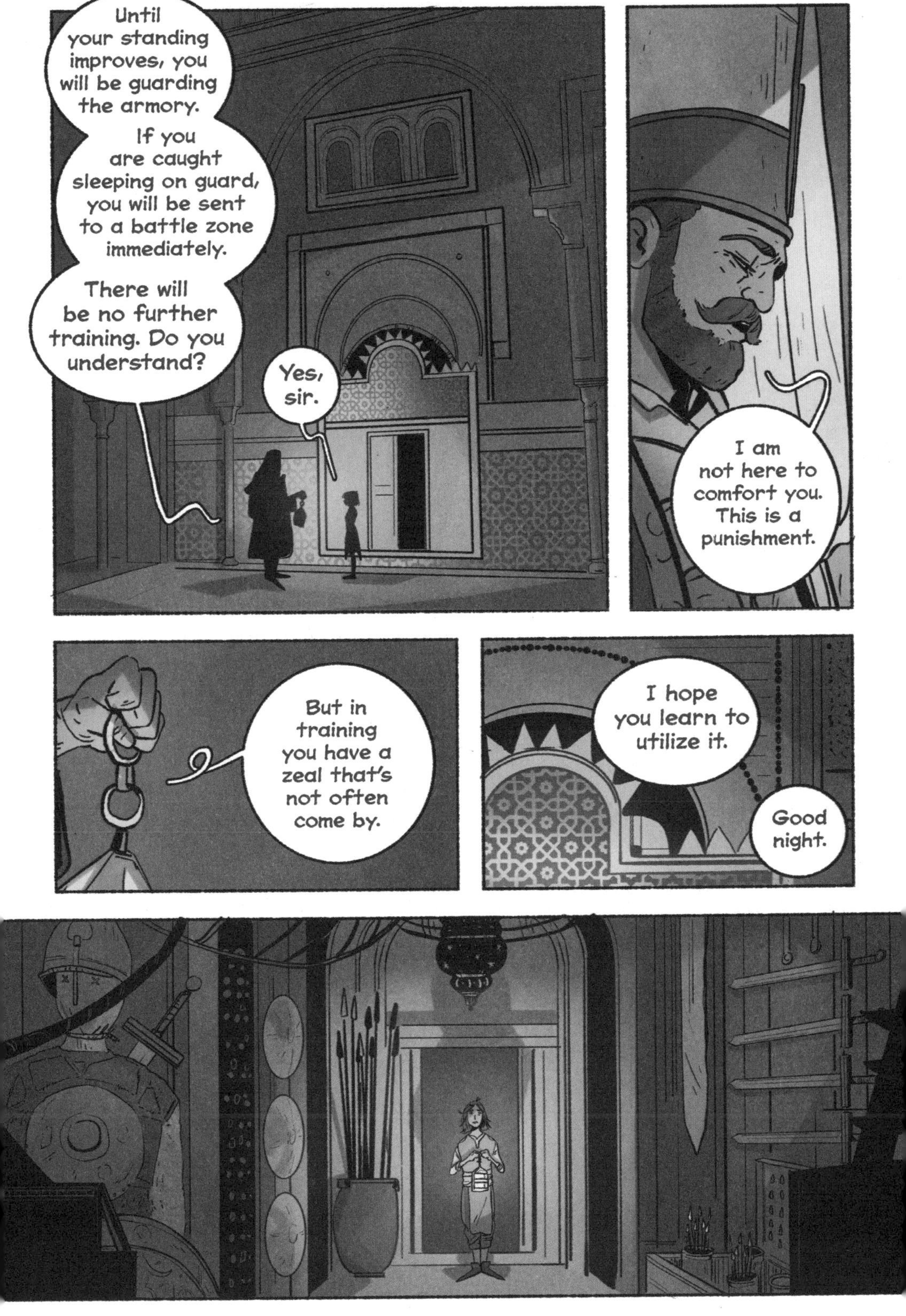
Until your standing improves, you will be guarding the armory.
If you are caught sleeping on guard, you will be sent to a battle zone immediately.
There will be no further training. Do you understand?
Yes, sir.
I am not here to comfort you. This is a punishment.
But in training you have a zeal that's not often come by.
I hope you learn to utilize it.
Good night.

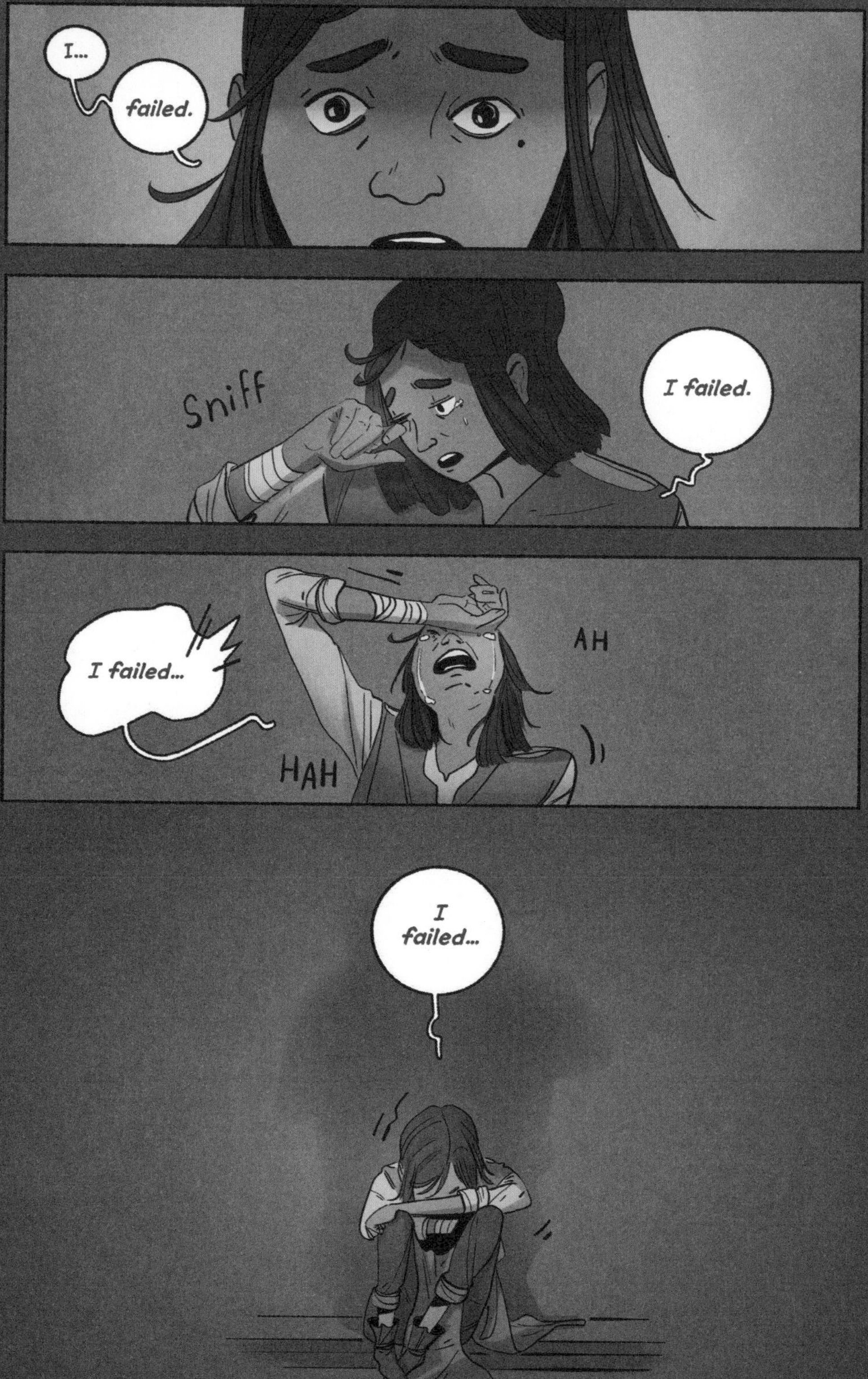
I...
failed.
Sniff
I failed.
I failed...
AH
HAH
I failed...

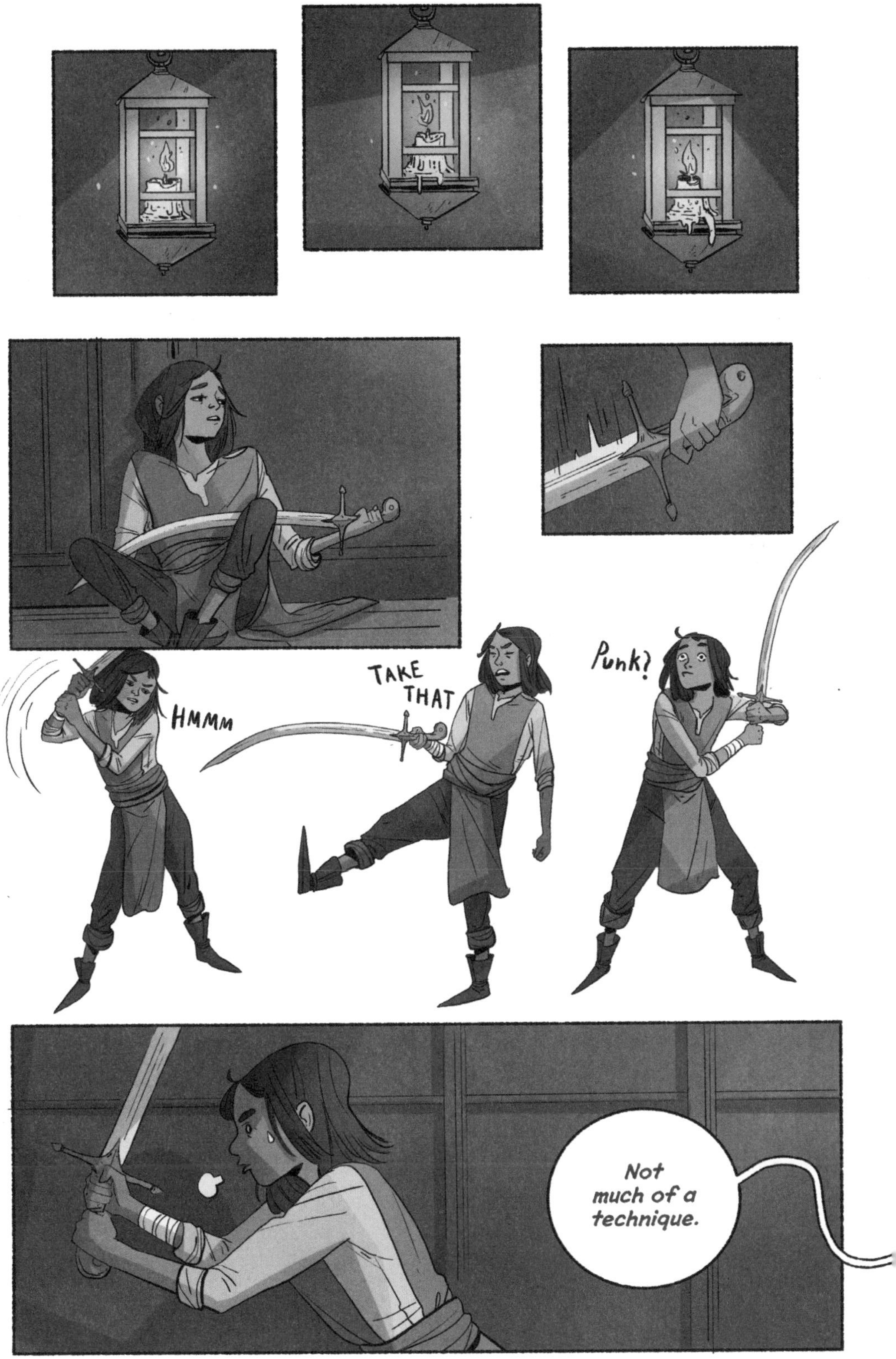
HMMM
TAKE THAT
Punk?
Not much of a technique.

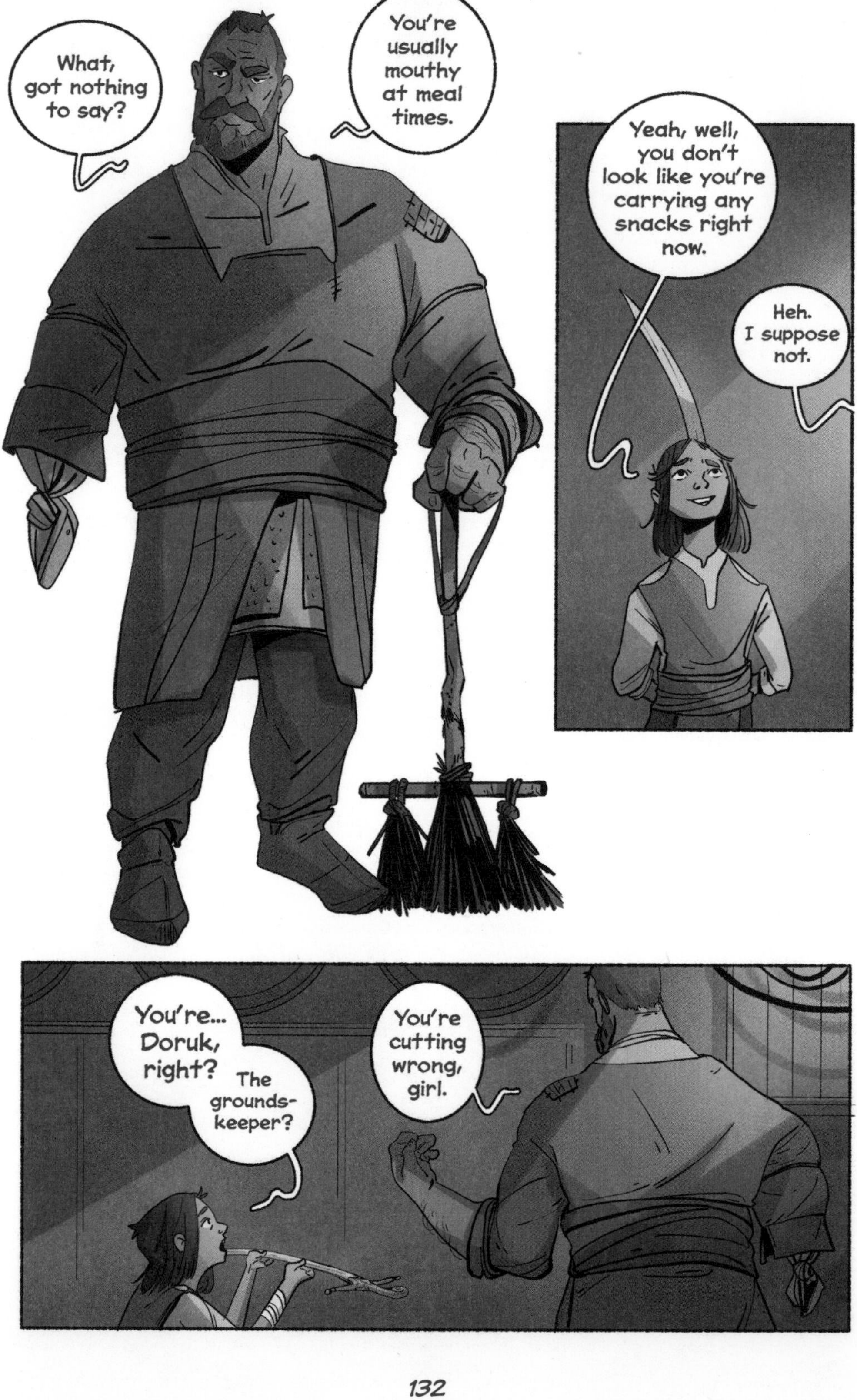
What, got nothing to say?
You're usually mouthy at meal times.
Yeah, well, you don't look like you're carrying any snacks right now.
Heh. I suppose not.
You're... Doruk, right?
The grounds-keeper?
You're cutting wrong, girl.

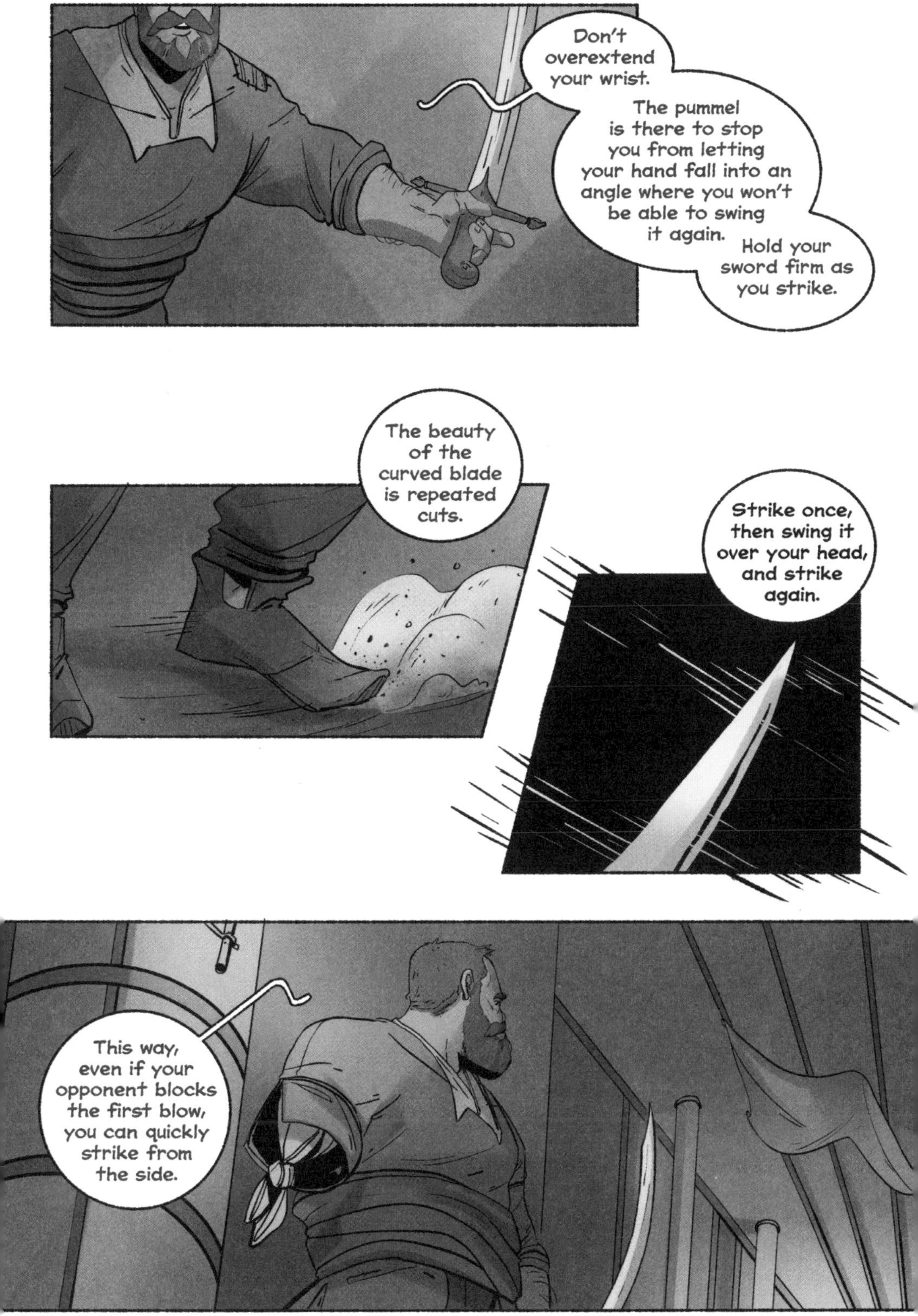
Don't overextend your wrist.
The pummel is there to stop you from letting your hand fall into an angle where you won't be able to swing it again.
Hold your sword firm as you strike.
The beauty of the curved blade is repeated cuts.
Strike once, then swing it over your head, and strike again.
This way, even if your opponent blocks the first blow, you can quickly strike from the side.

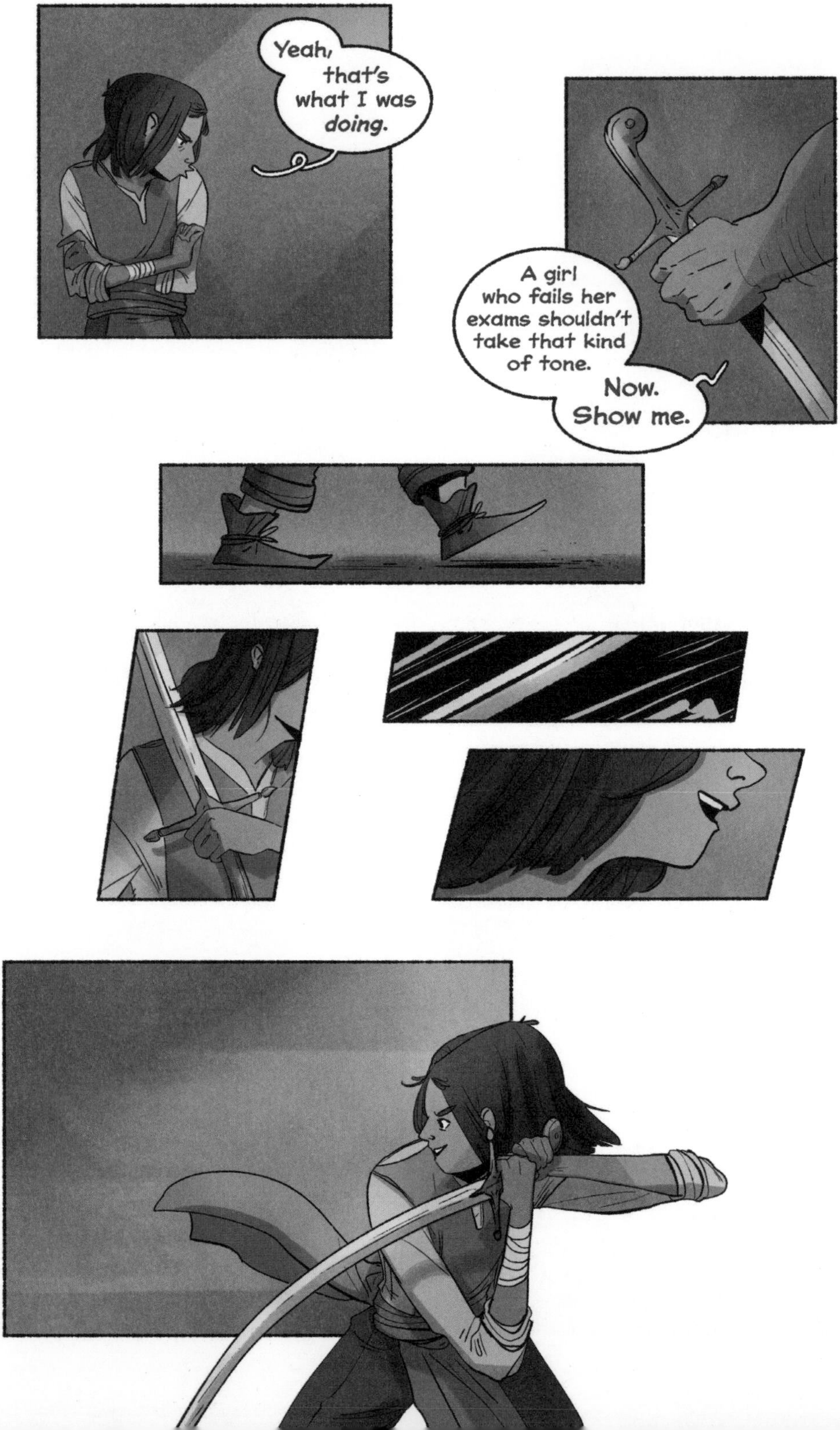

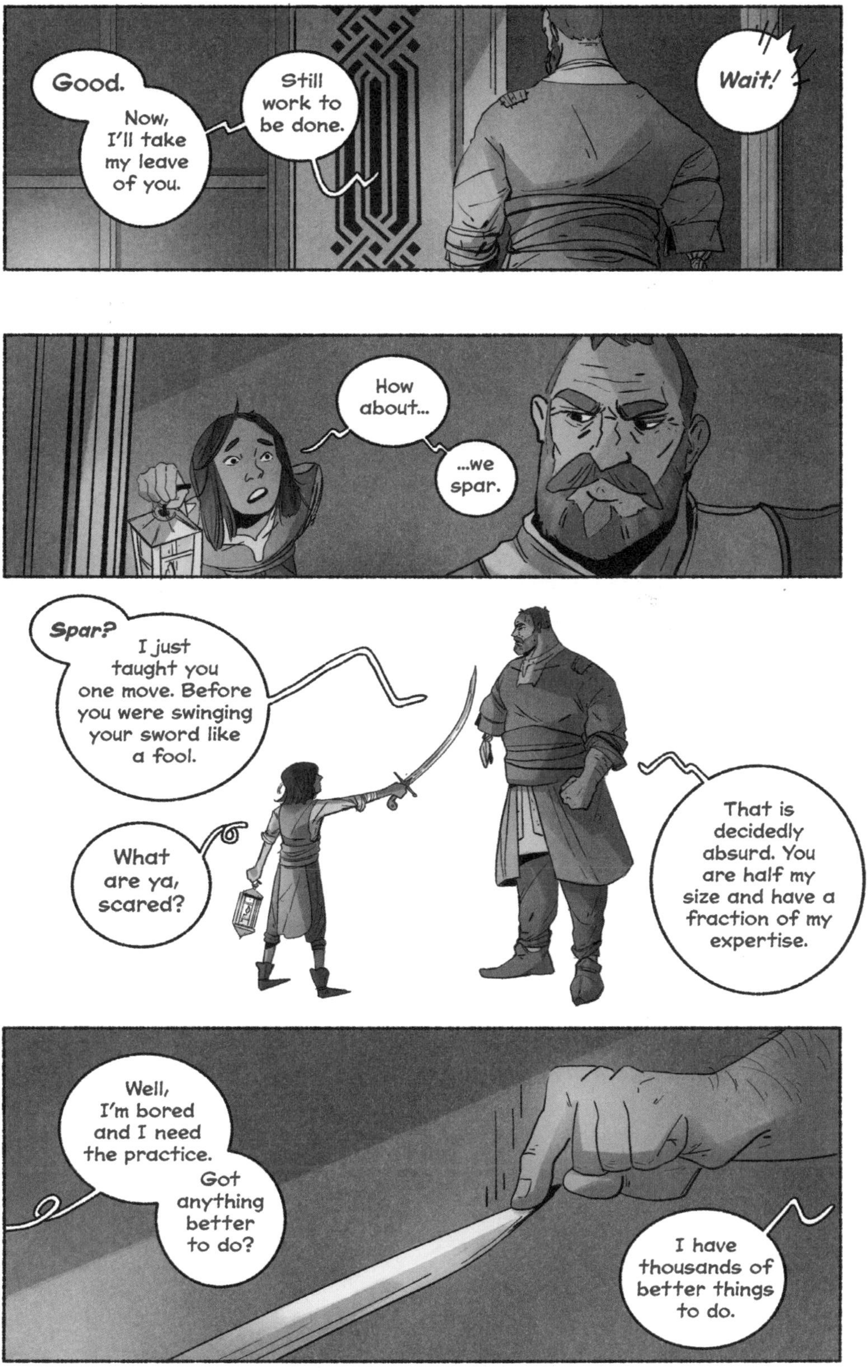
Good.
Now, I'll take my leave of you.
Still work to be done.
Wait!
How about...
...we spar.
Spar? I just taught you one move. Before you were swinging your sword like a fool.
What are ya, scared?
That is decidedly absurd. You are half my size and have a fraction of my expertise.
Well, I'm bored and I need the practice.
Got anything better to do?
I have thousands of better things to do.

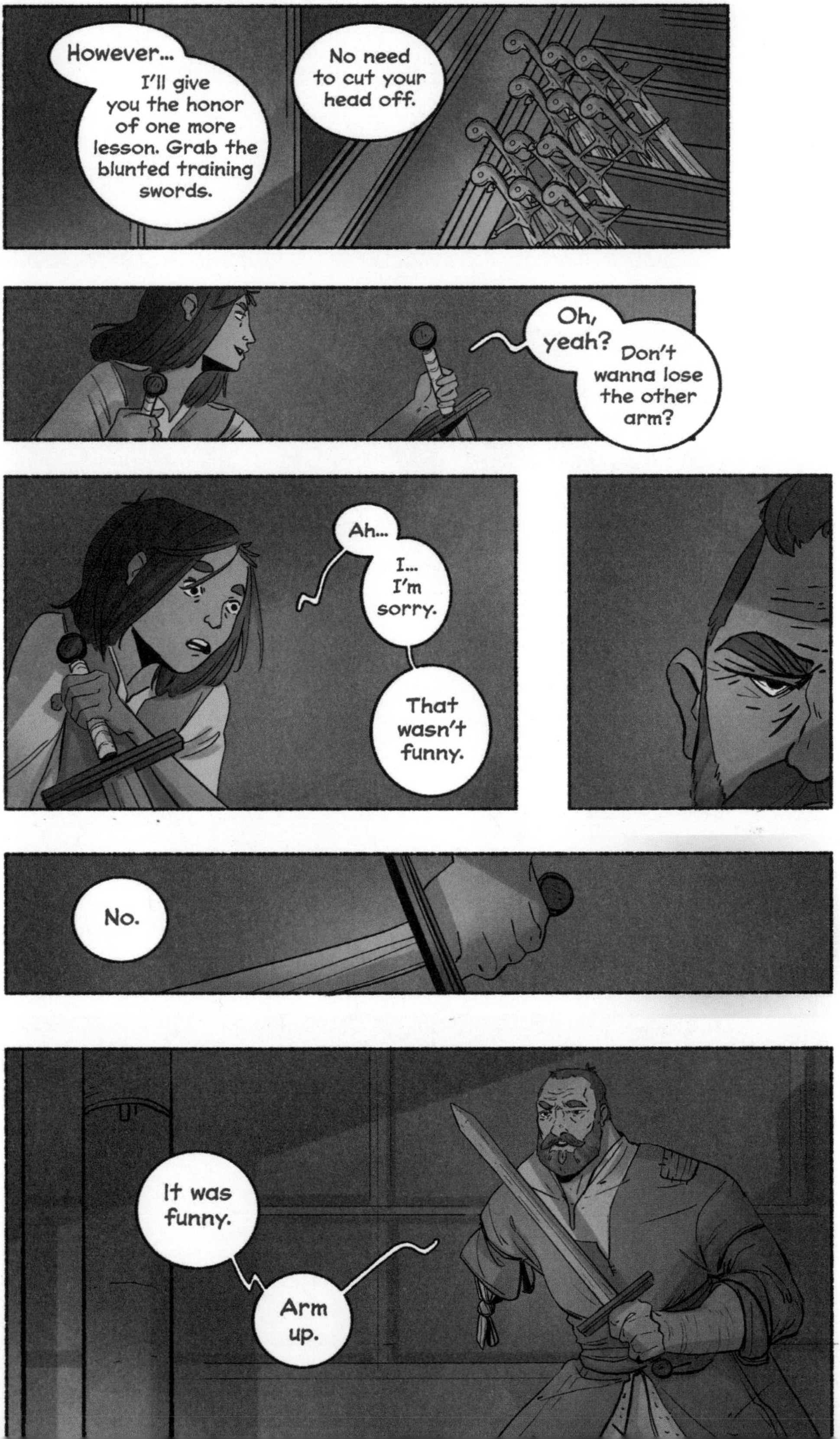
However...
I'll give you the honor of one more lesson. Grab the blunted training swords.
No need to cut your head off.
Oh, yeah?
Don't wanna lose the other arm?
Ah...
I... I'm sorry.
That wasn't funny.
No.
It was funny.
Arm up.

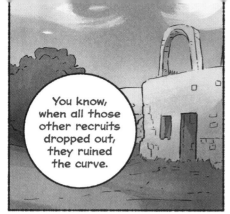

You know, when all those other recruits dropped out, they ruined the curve.

The only reason I didn't fail was the written portion of the exams.

When the bottom drops out it brings everyone in the middle closer to the bottom.

NEXT!

GLOROP

You know, statistics are really fascinating actually...

Give it a rest, Husni!

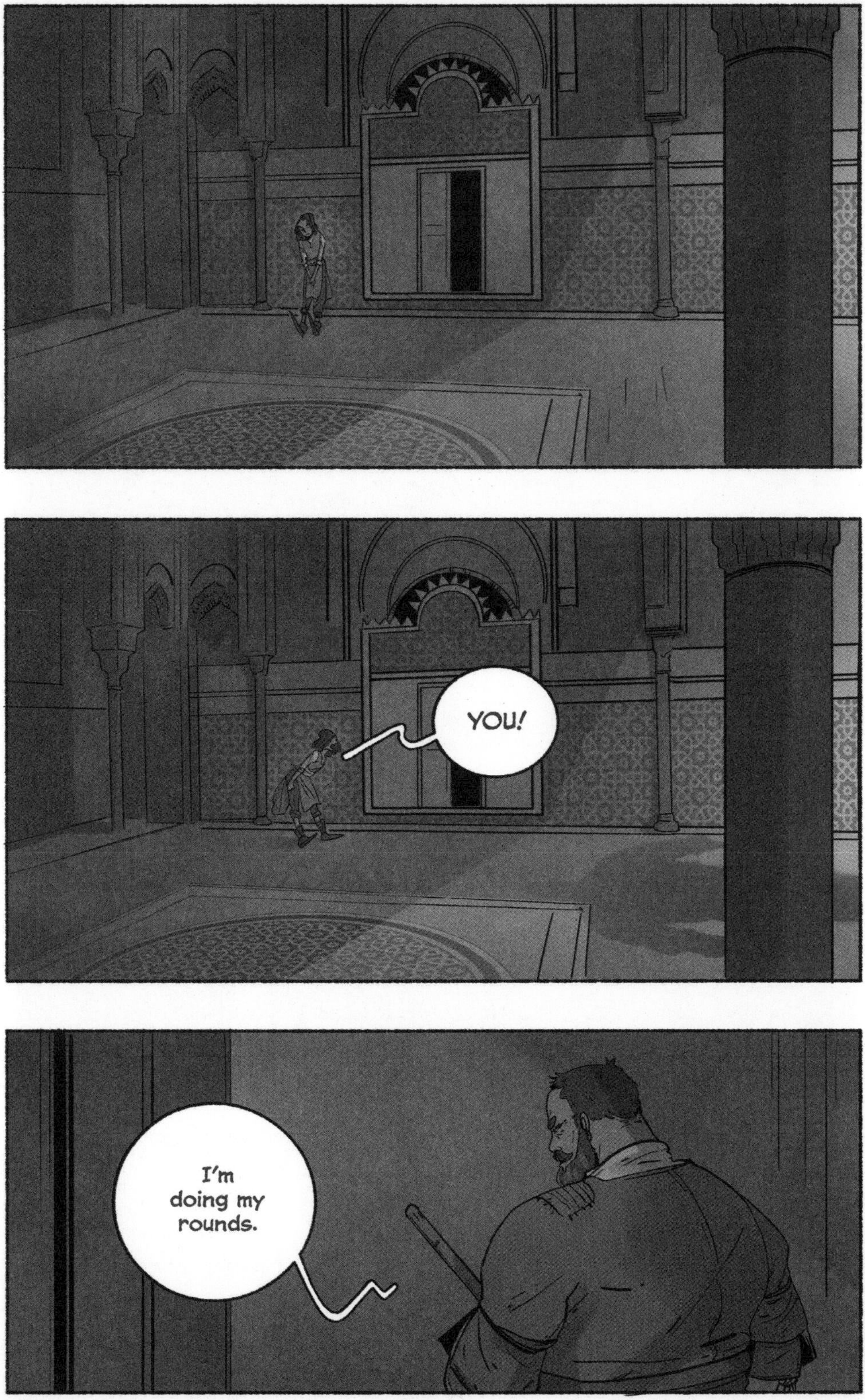
YOU!
I'm doing my rounds.

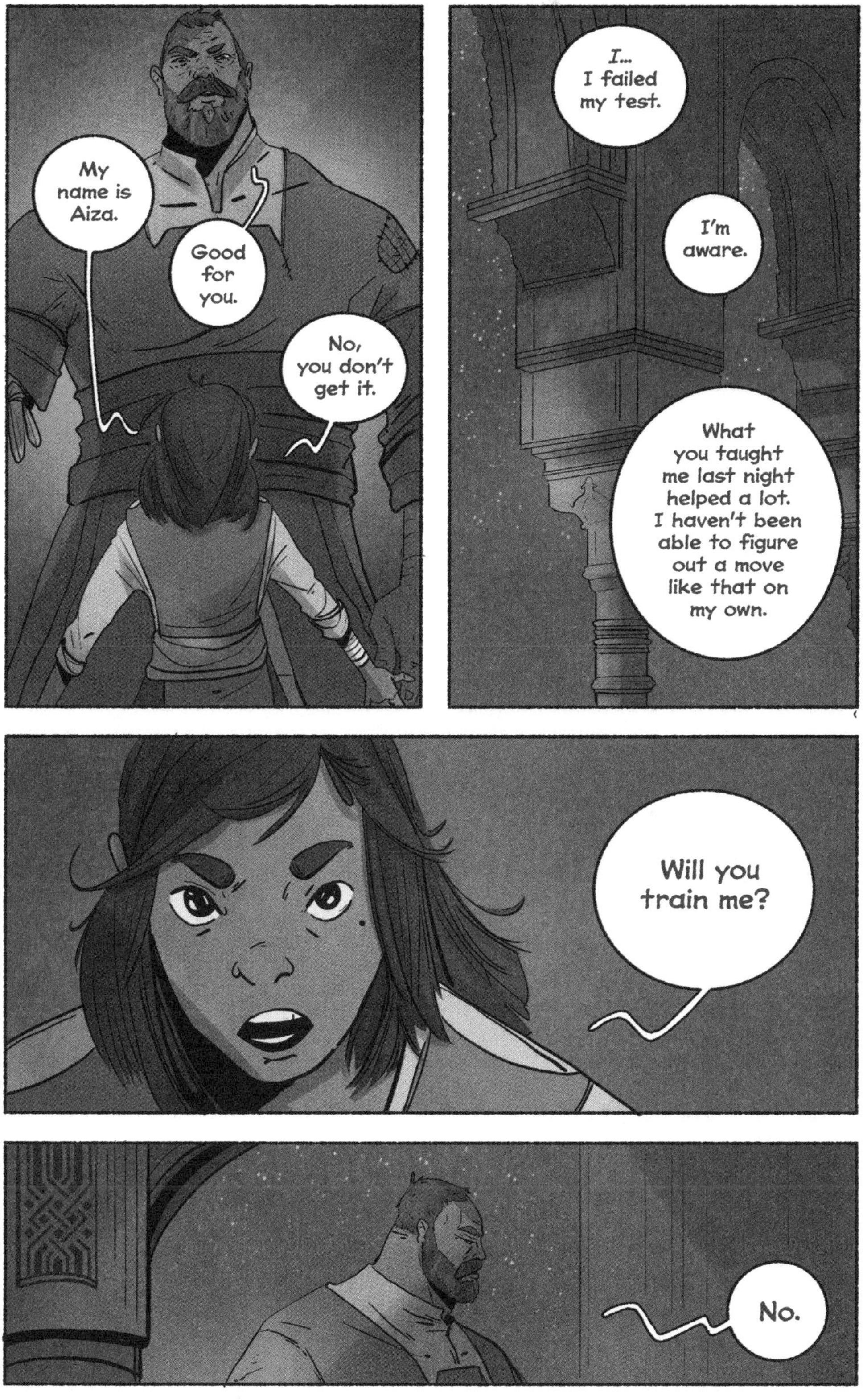
My name is Aiza.
Good for you.
No, you don't get it.
I... I failed my test.
I'm aware.
What you taught me last night helped a lot. I haven't been able to figure out a move like that on my own.
Will you train me?
No.

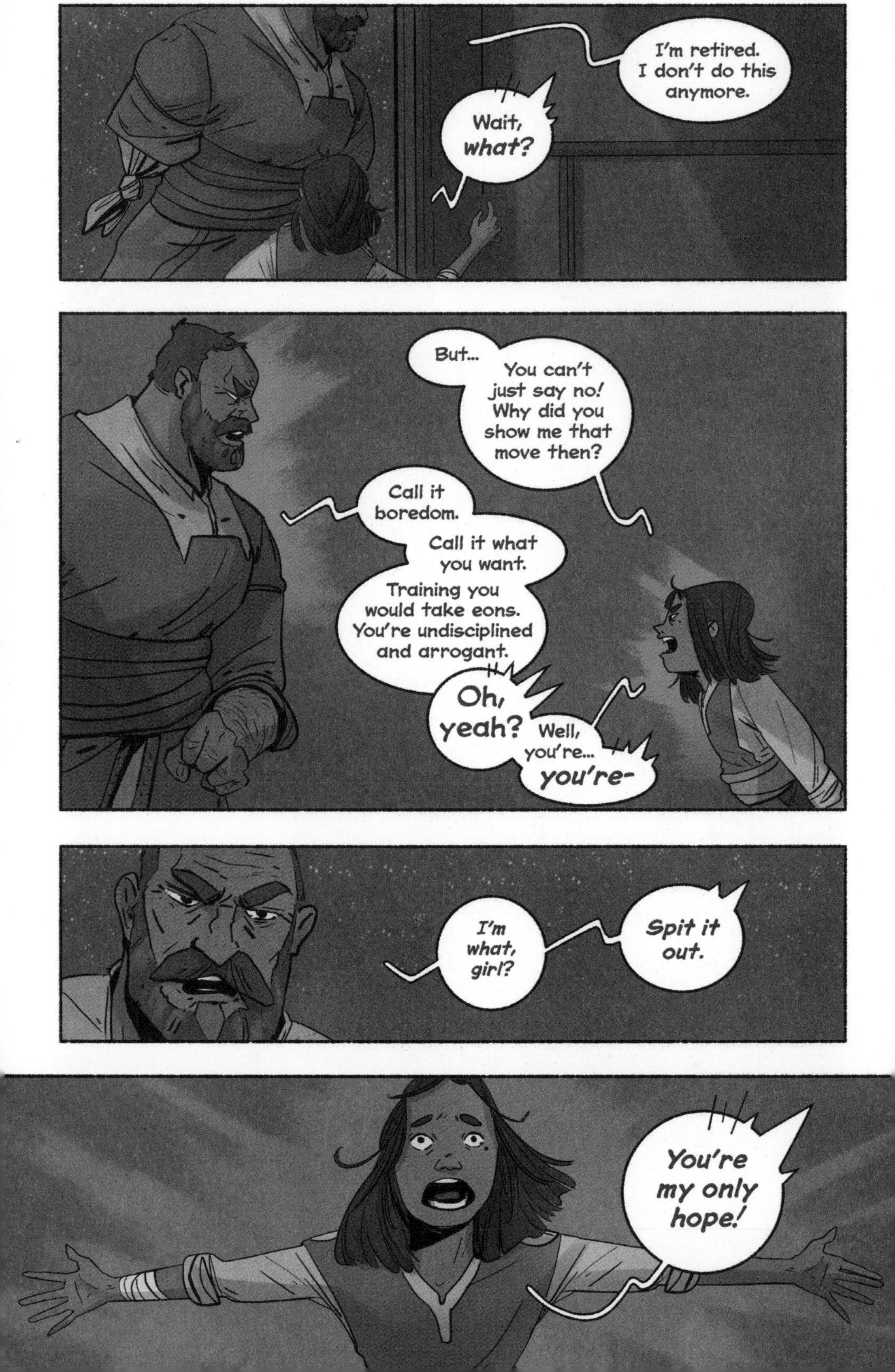
I'm retired. I don't do this anymore.
Wait, *what?*
But...
You can't just say no! Why did you show me that move then?
Call it boredom.
Call it what you want.
Training you would take eons. You're undisciplined and arrogant.
Oh, yeah?
Well, you're... *you're-*
I'm what, girl?
Spit it out.
You're my only hope!

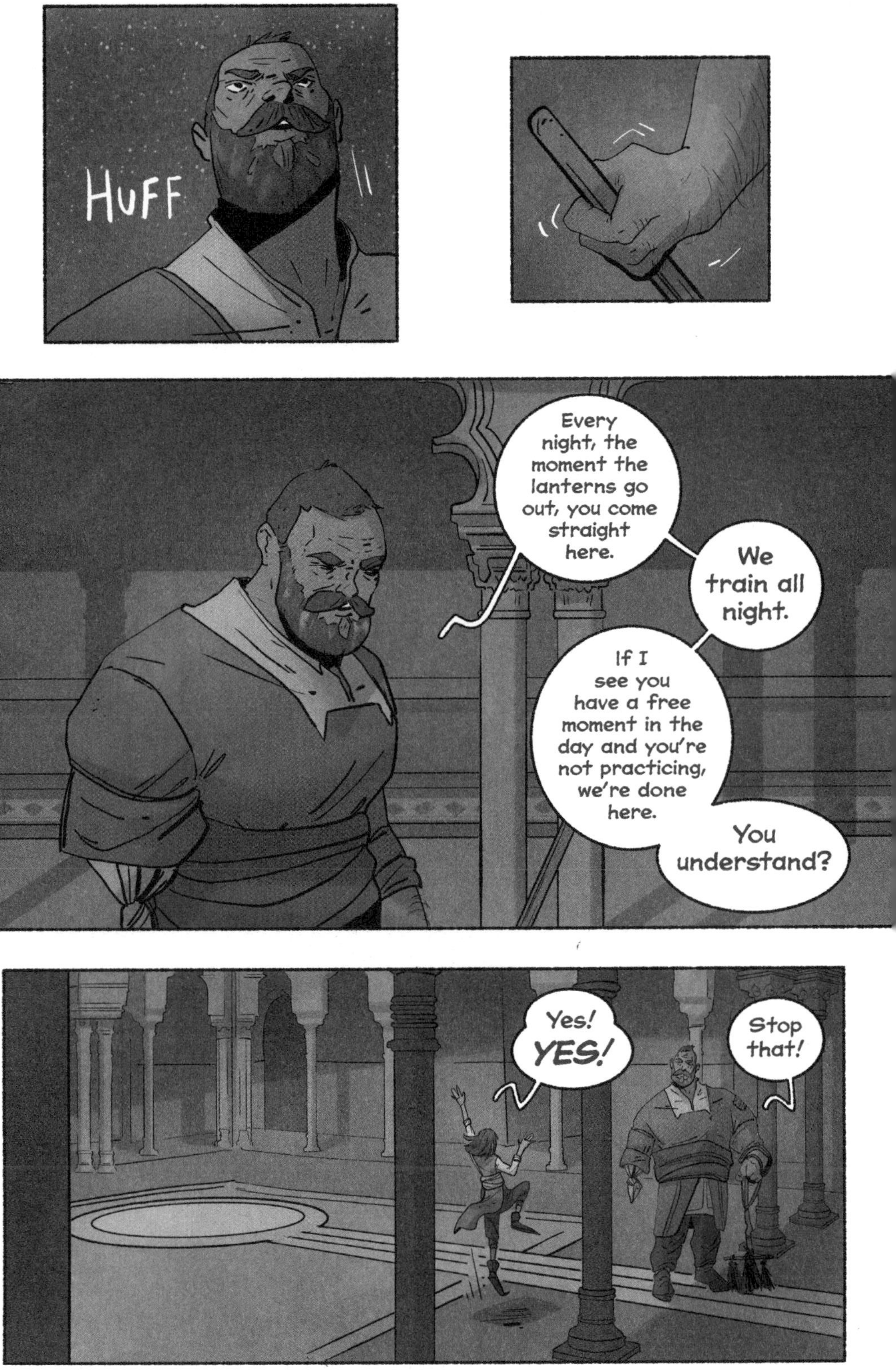
HUFF
Every night, the moment the lanterns go out, you come straight here.
We train all night.
If I see you have a free moment in the day and you're not practicing, we're done here.
You understand?
Yes! YES!
Stop that!

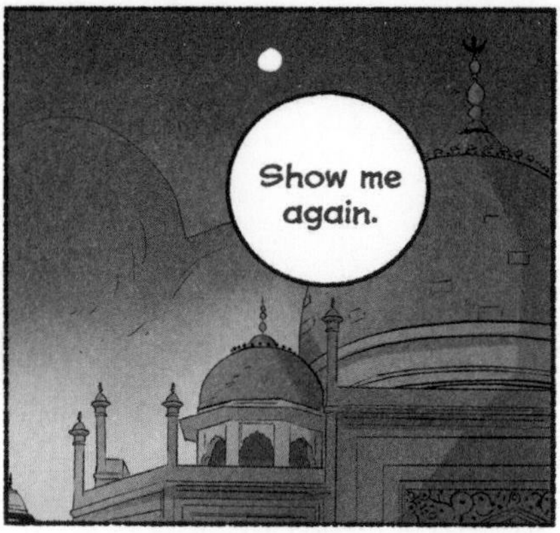
Show me again.

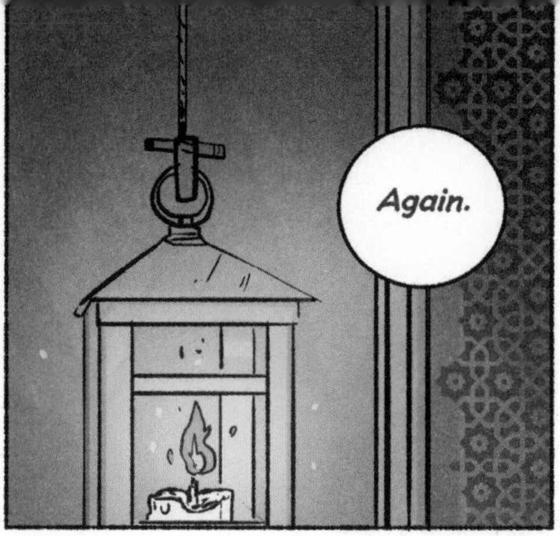
Again.

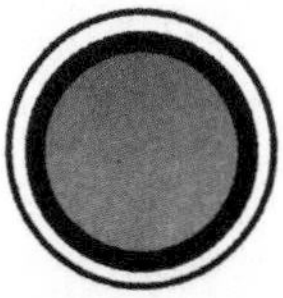

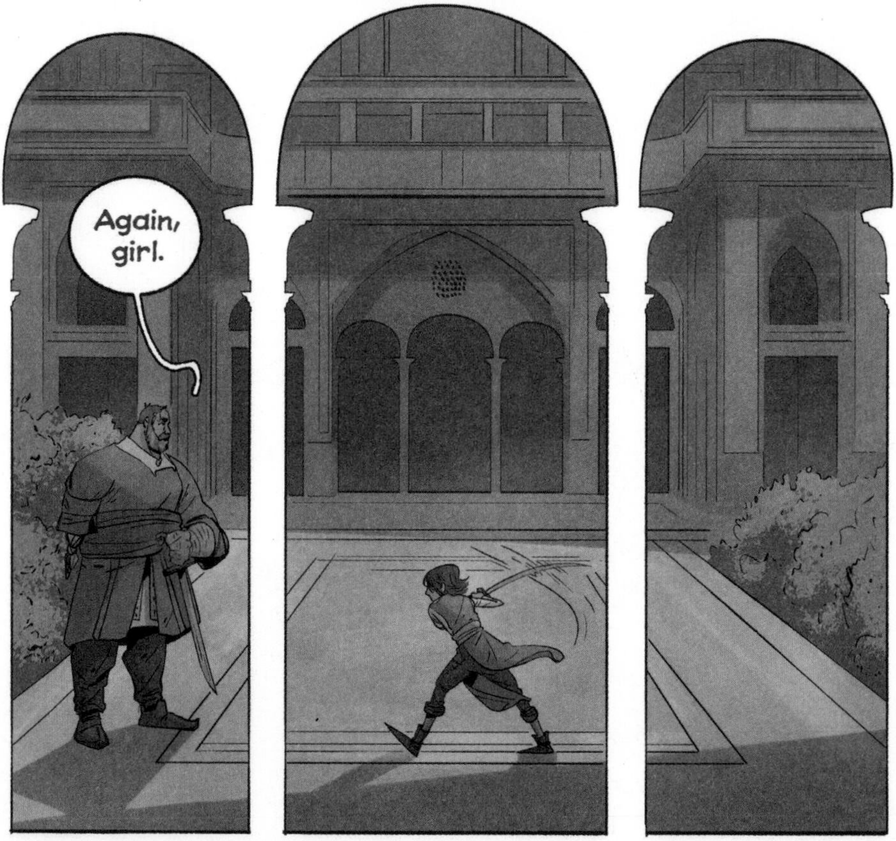
Again, girl.

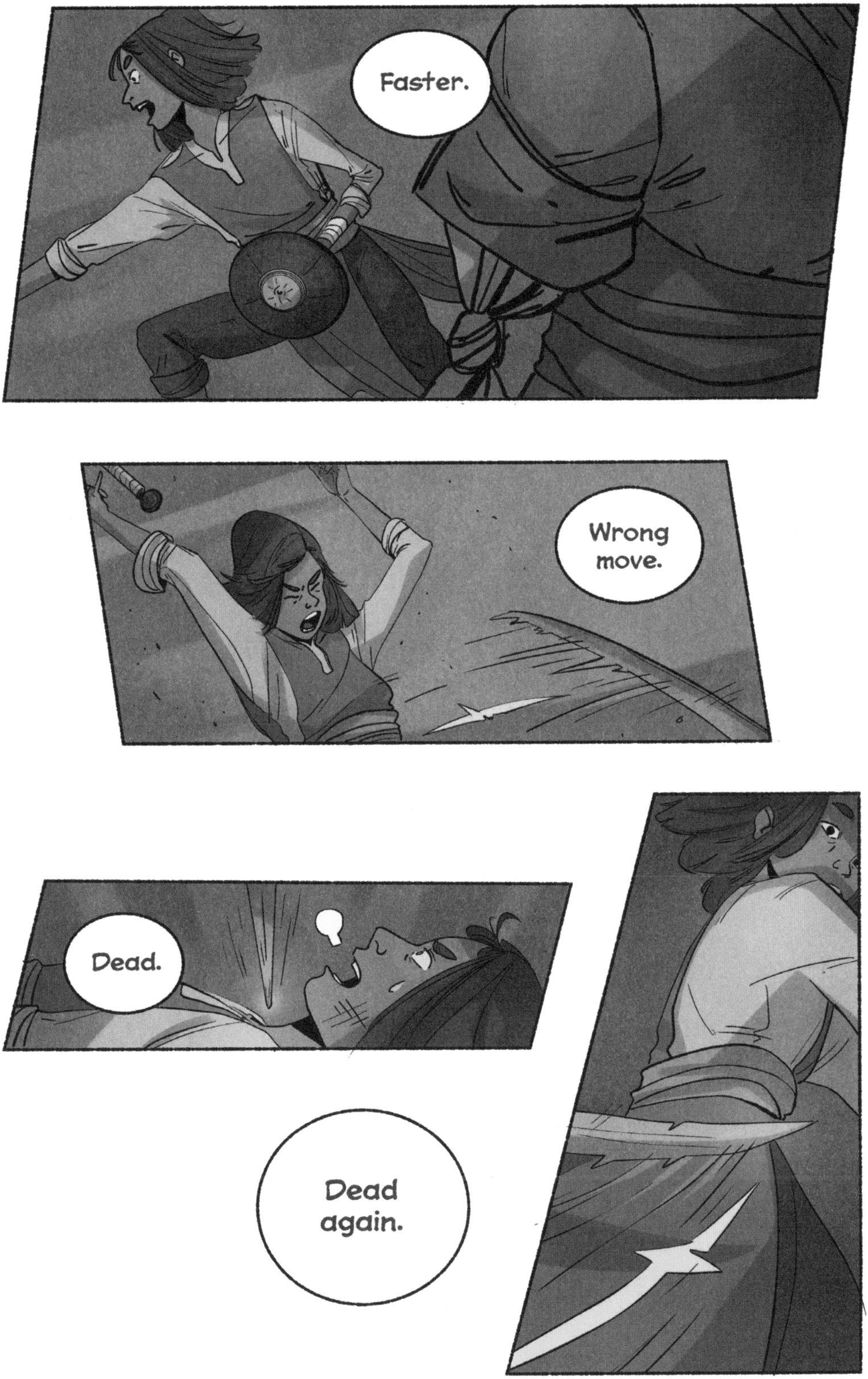
Faster.
Wrong move.
Dead.
Dead again.

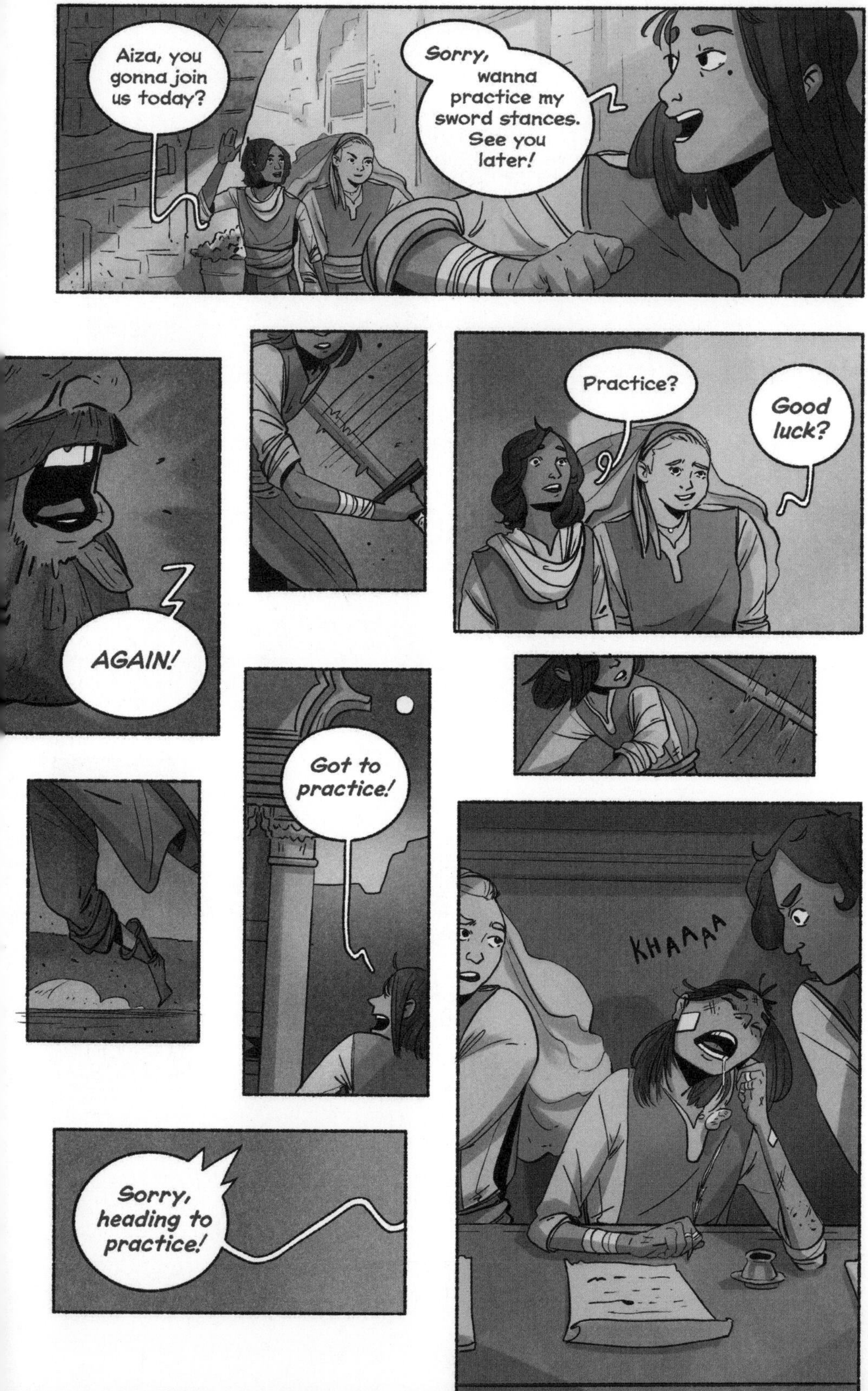
Aiza, you gonna join us today?
Sorry, wanna practice my sword stances. See you later!
AGAIN!
Practice?
Good luck?
Got to practice!
Sorry, heading to practice!
KHAAAA

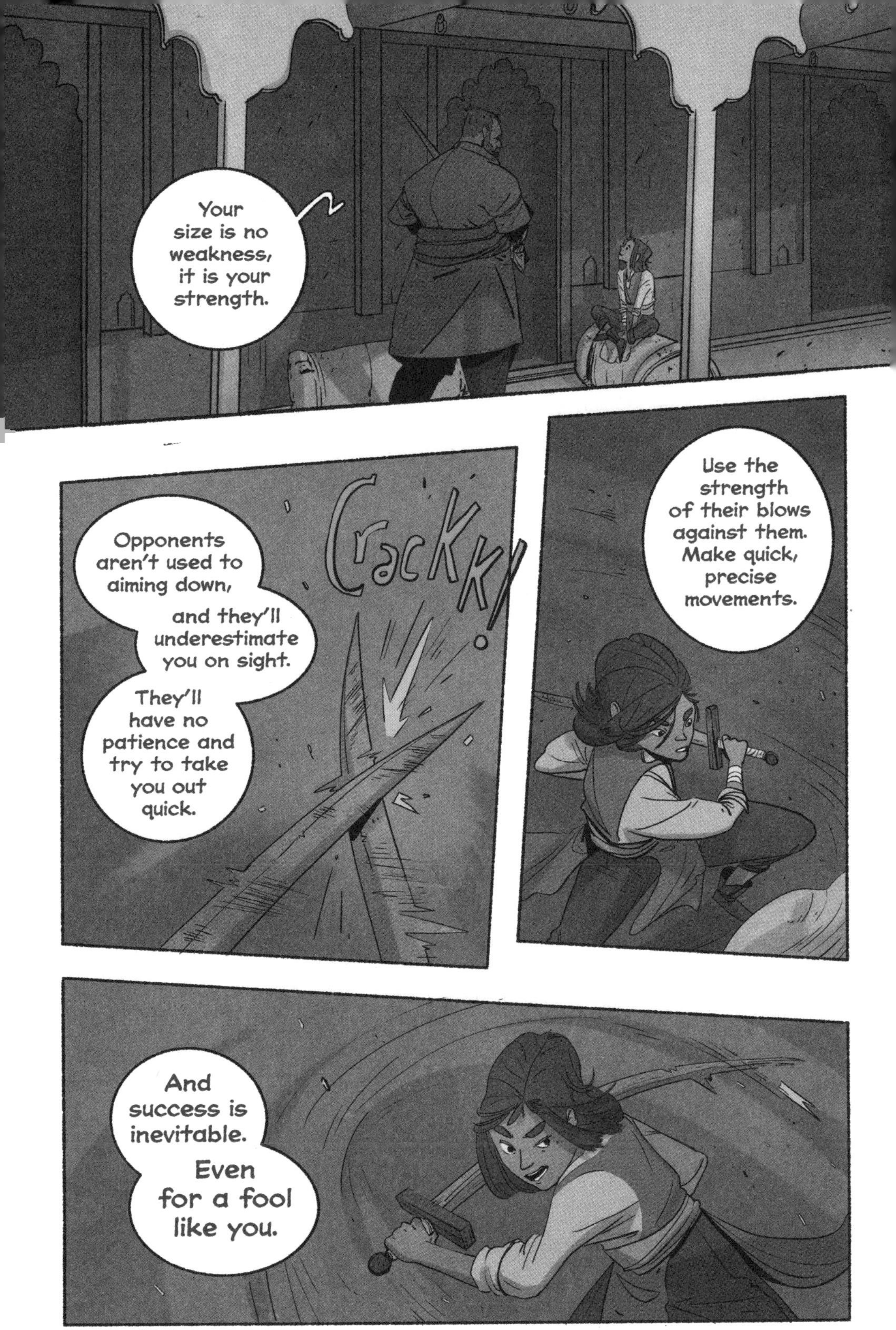
Your size is no weakness, it is your strength.
Opponents aren't used to aiming down,
and they'll underestimate you on sight.
They'll have no patience and try to take you out quick.
CracKK!
Use the strength of their blows against them. Make quick, precise movements.
And success is inevitable.
Even for a fool like you.

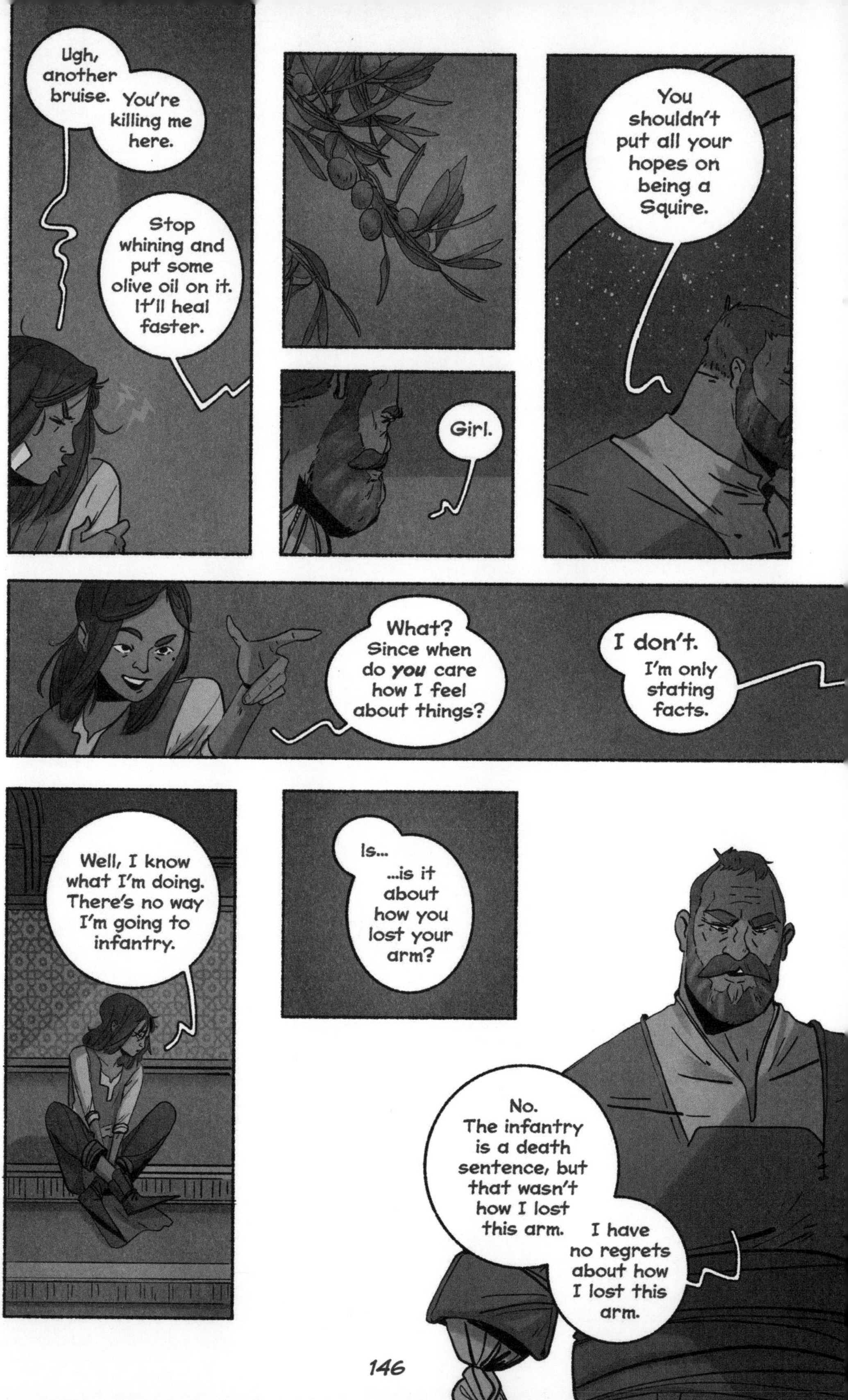

Ugh, another bruise. You're killing me here.
Stop whining and put some olive oil on it. It'll heal faster.
Girl.
You shouldn't put all your hopes on being a Squire.
What? Since when do *you* care how I feel about things?
I don't.
I'm only stating facts.
Well, I know what I'm doing. There's no way I'm going to infantry.
Is...
...is it about how you lost your arm?
No. The infantry is a death sentence, but that wasn't how I lost this arm.
I have no regrets about how I lost this arm.

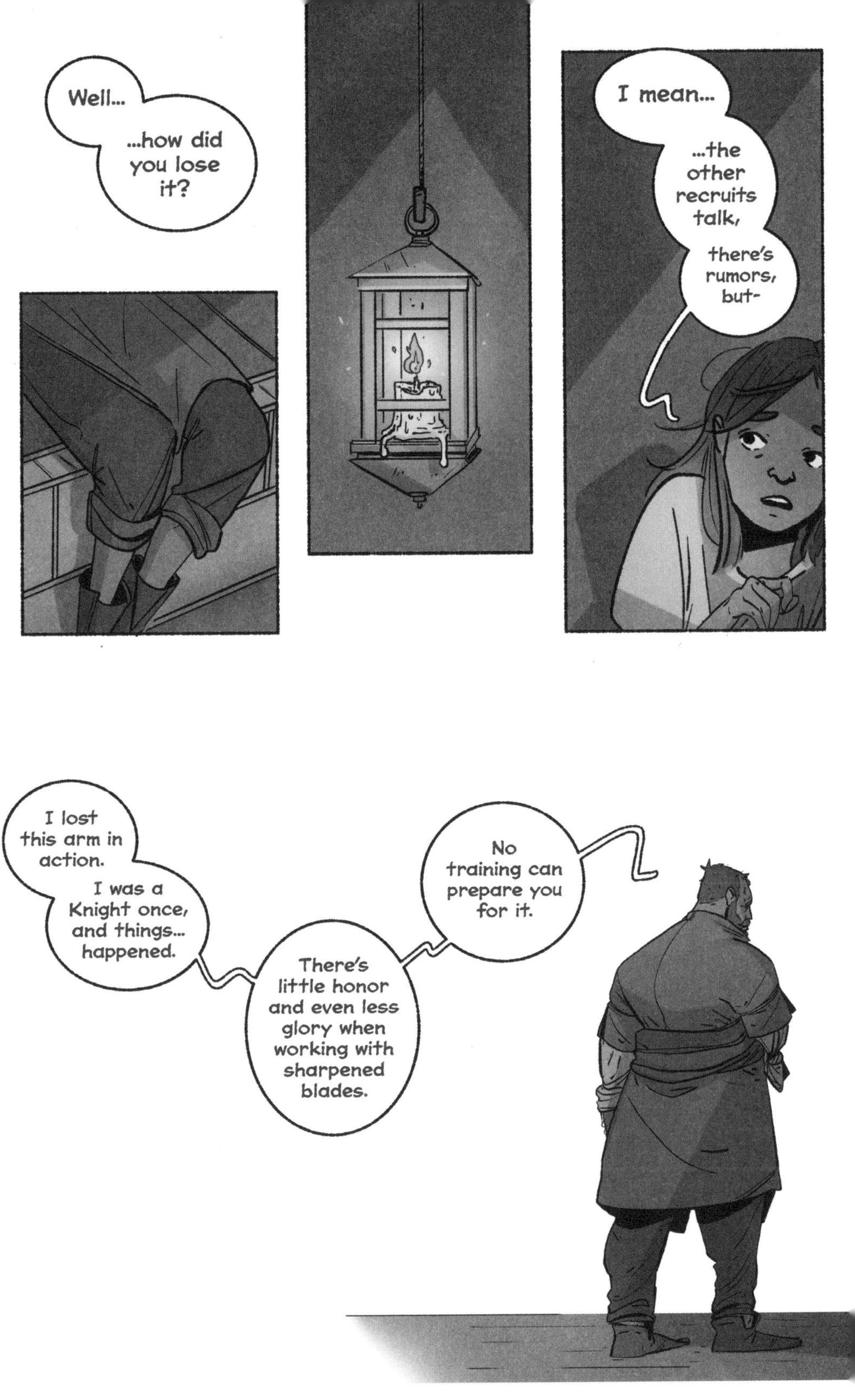
Well...
...how did you lose it?
I mean...
...the other recruits talk,
there's rumors, but-
I lost this arm in action.
I was a Knight once, and things... happened.
There's little honor and even less glory when working with sharpened blades.
No training can prepare you for it.

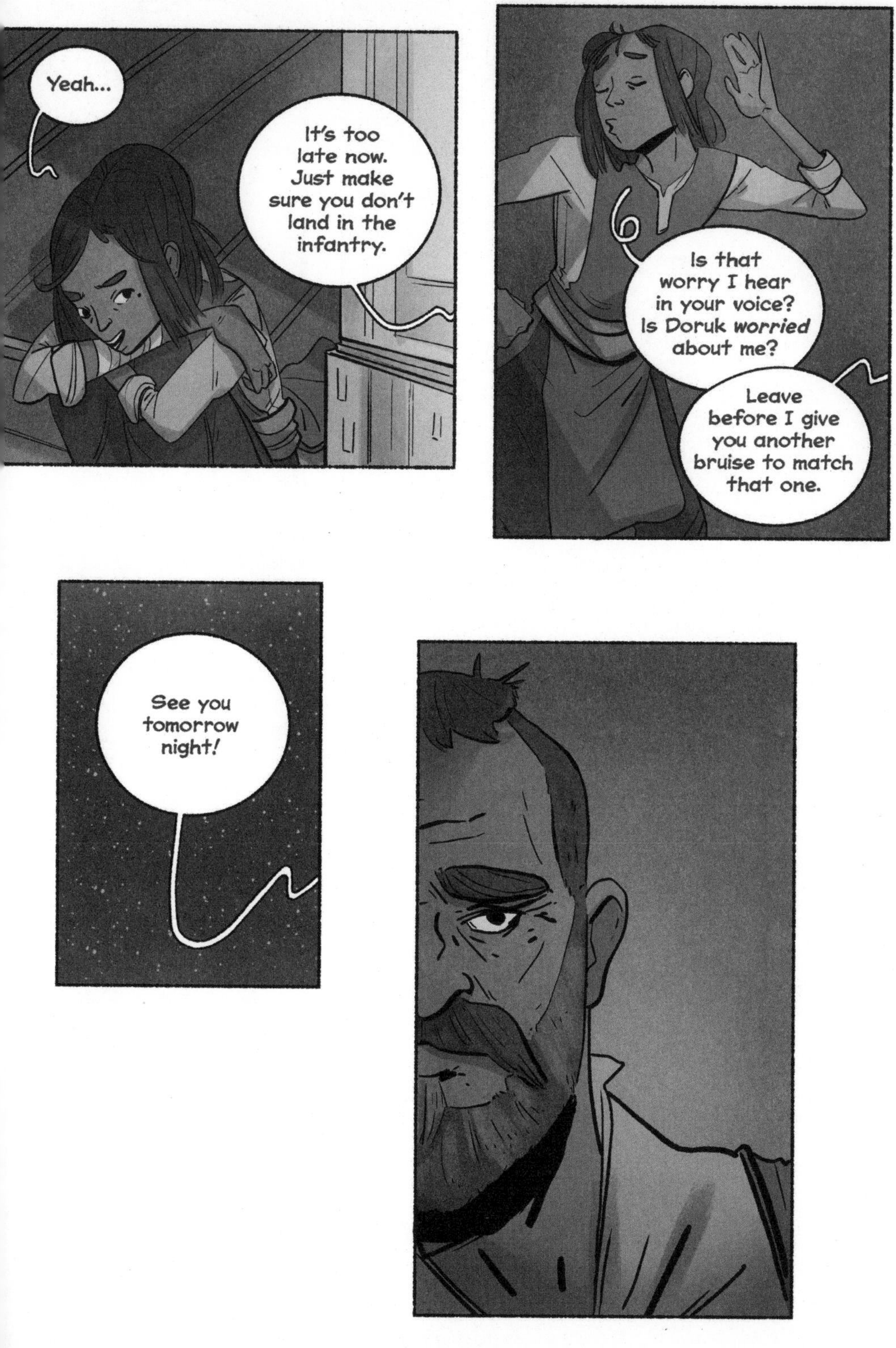
Yeah...
It's too late now. Just make sure you don't land in the infantry.
Is that worry I hear in your voice? Is Doruk *worried* about me?
Leave before I give you another bruise to match that one.
See you tomorrow night!

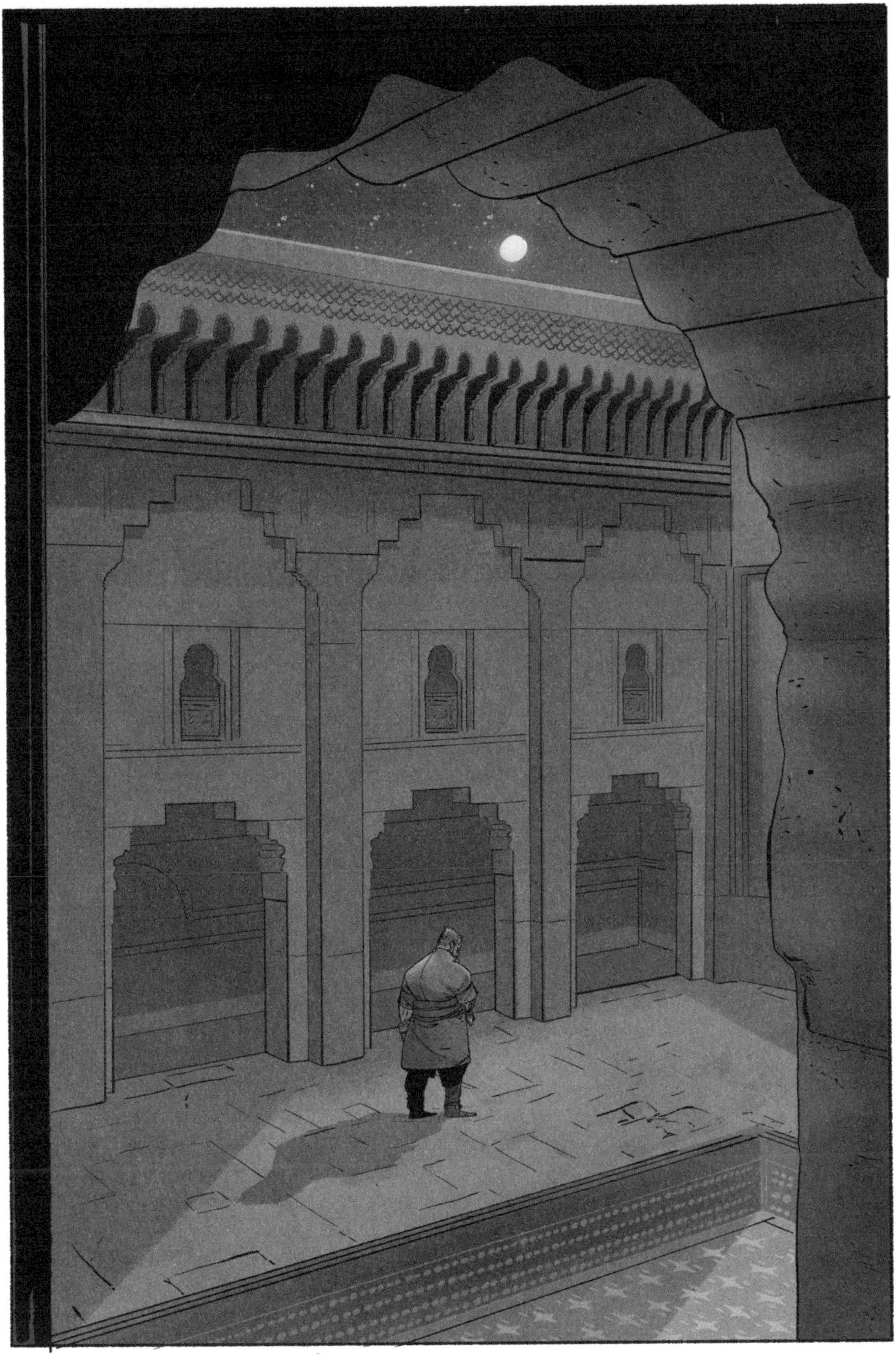

CHAPTER 8

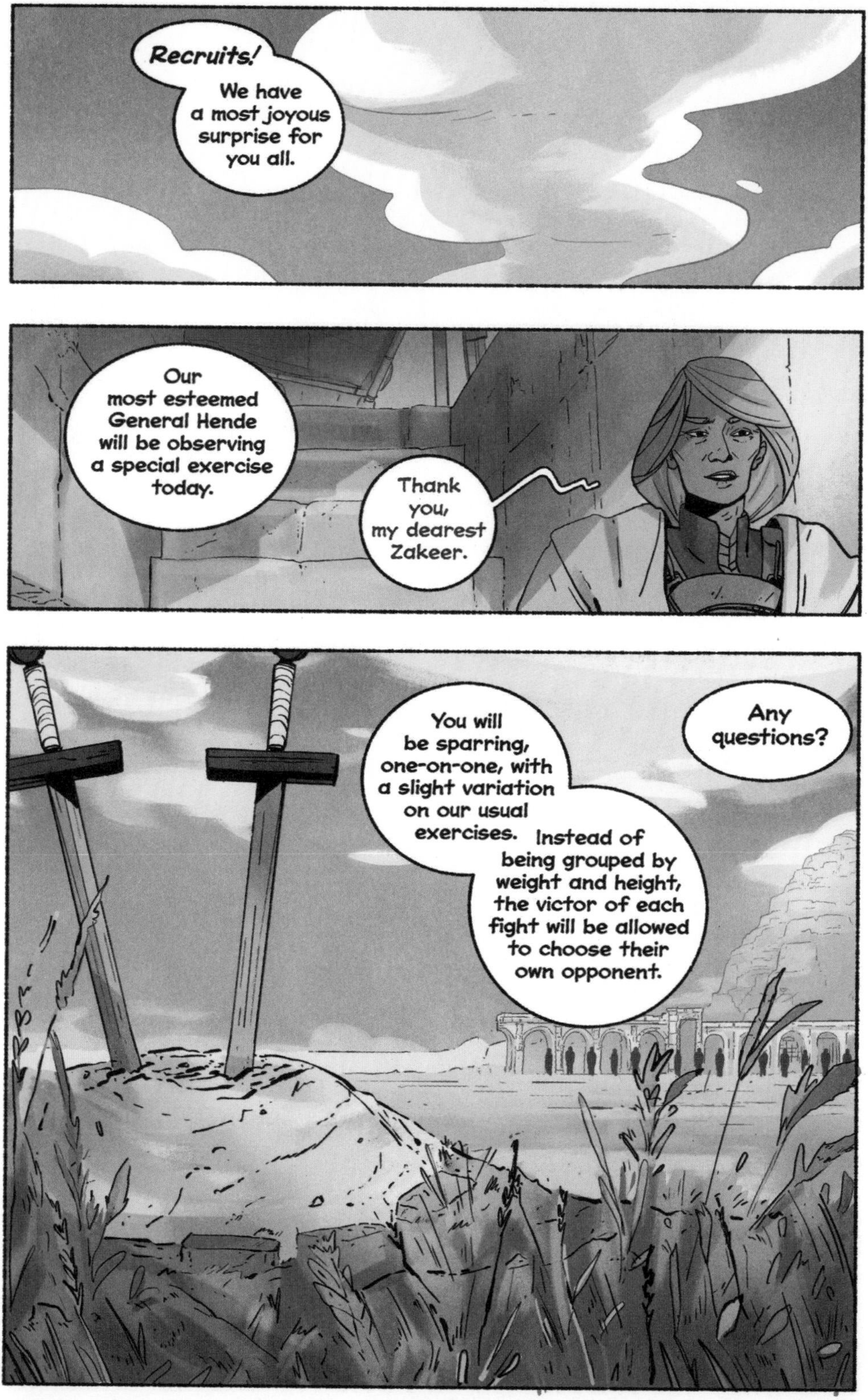
Recruits!
We have a most joyous surprise for you all.
Our most esteemed General Hende will be observing a special exercise today.
Thank you, my dearest Zakeer.
You will be sparring, one-on-one, with a slight variation on our usual exercises.
Instead of being grouped by weight and height, the victor of each fight will be allowed to choose their own opponent.
Any questions?

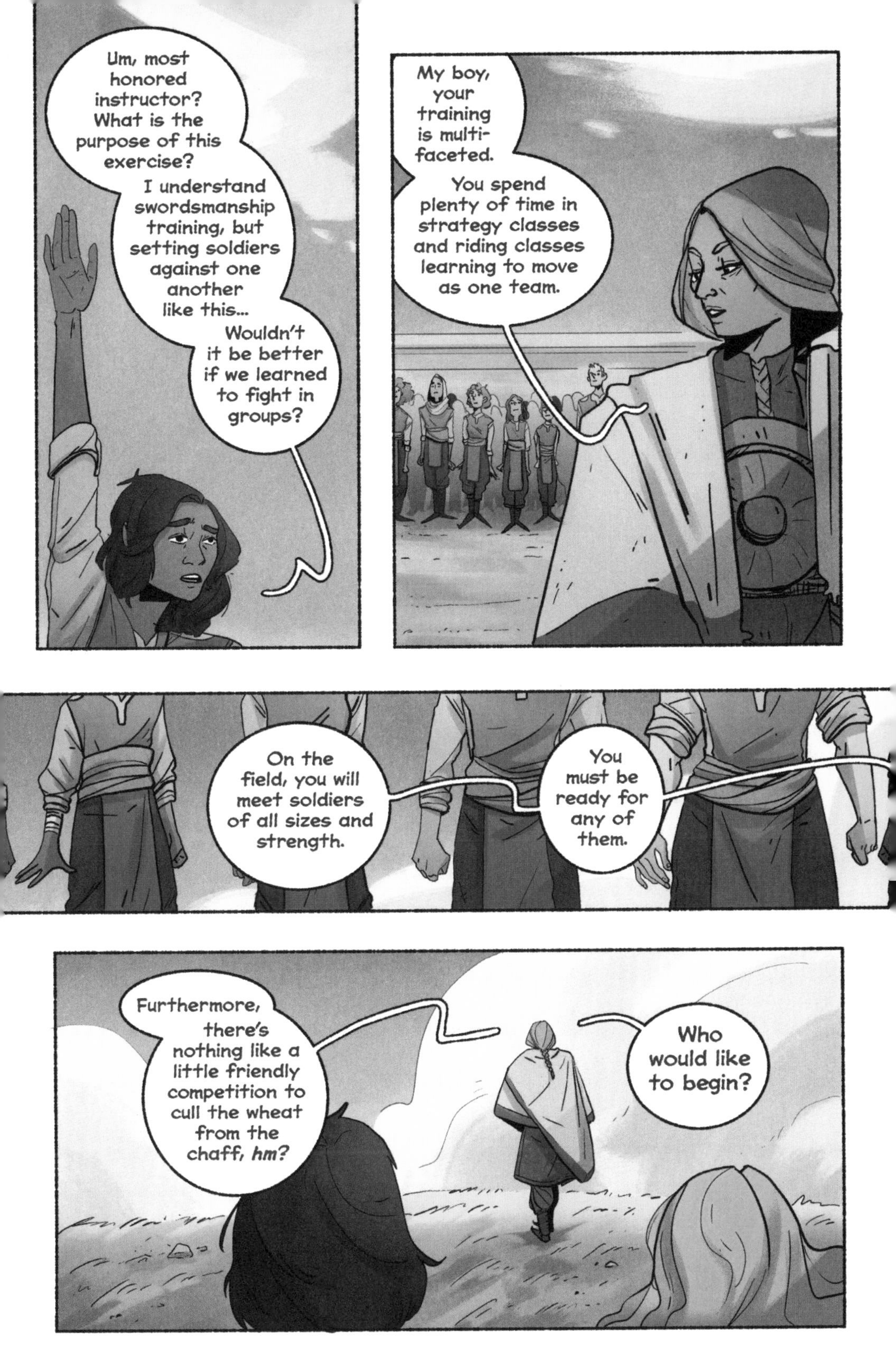
Um, most honored instructor? What is the purpose of this exercise?
I understand swordsmanship training, but setting soldiers against one another like this...
Wouldn't it be better if we learned to fight in groups?
My boy, your training is multi-faceted.
You spend plenty of time in strategy classes and riding classes learning to move as one team.
On the field, you will meet soldiers of all sizes and strength.
You must be ready for any of them.
Furthermore, there's nothing like a little friendly competition to cull the wheat from the chaff, *hm*?
Who would like to begin?

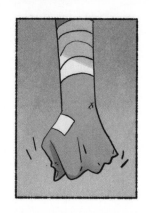

I'll be first.

Aiza, who do you choose as your opponent?

Basem.

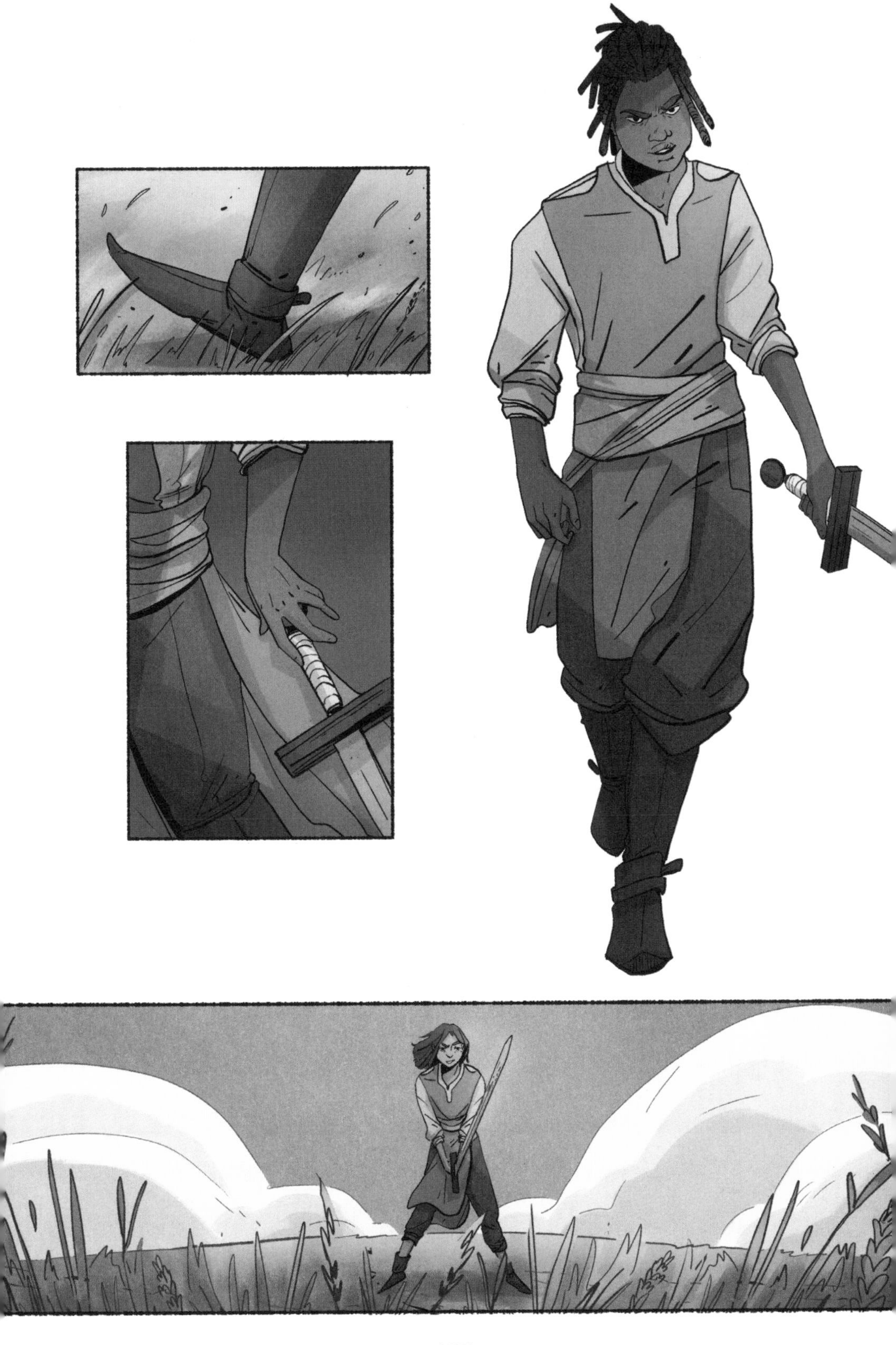

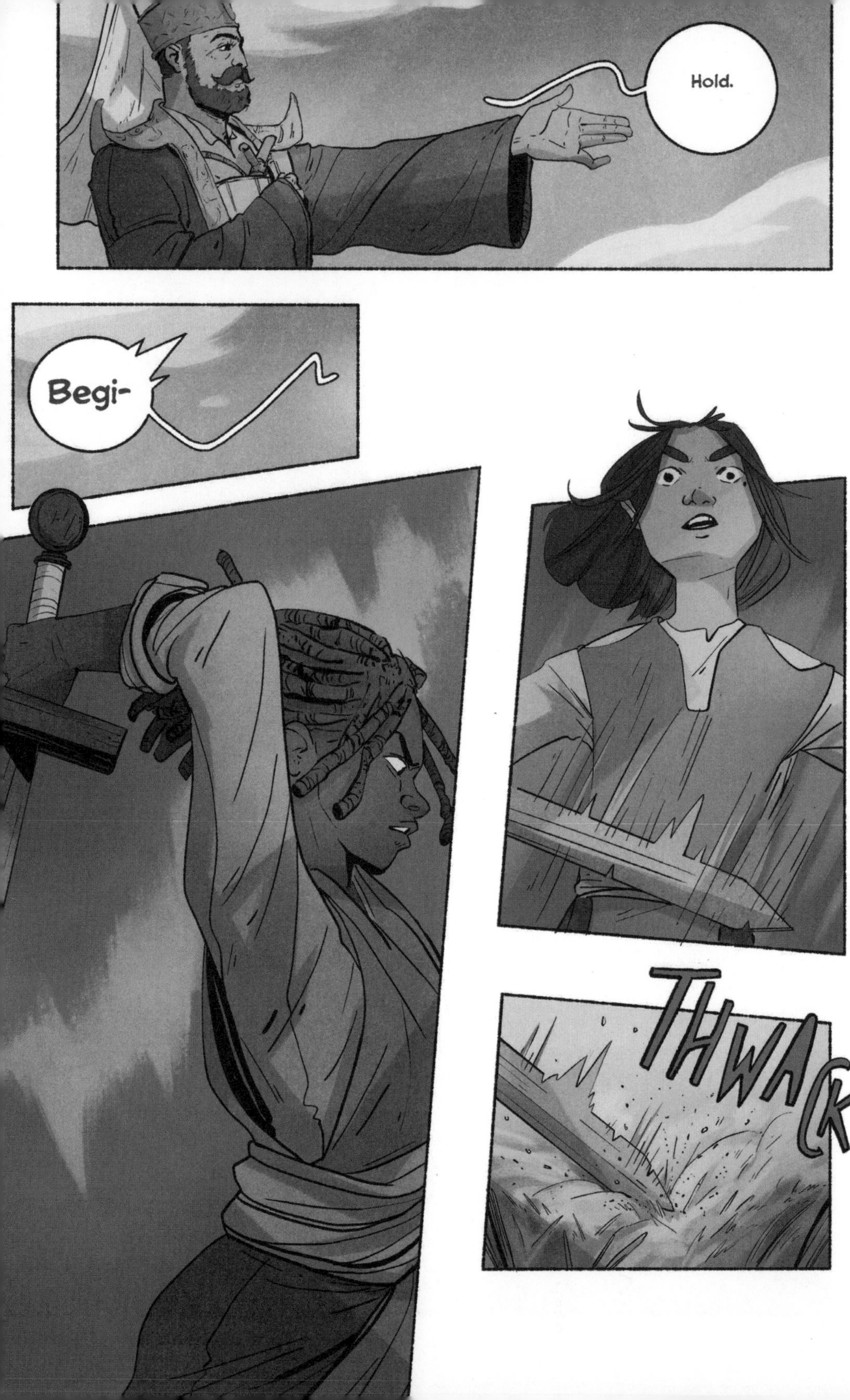
Hold.
Begi-
THWACK

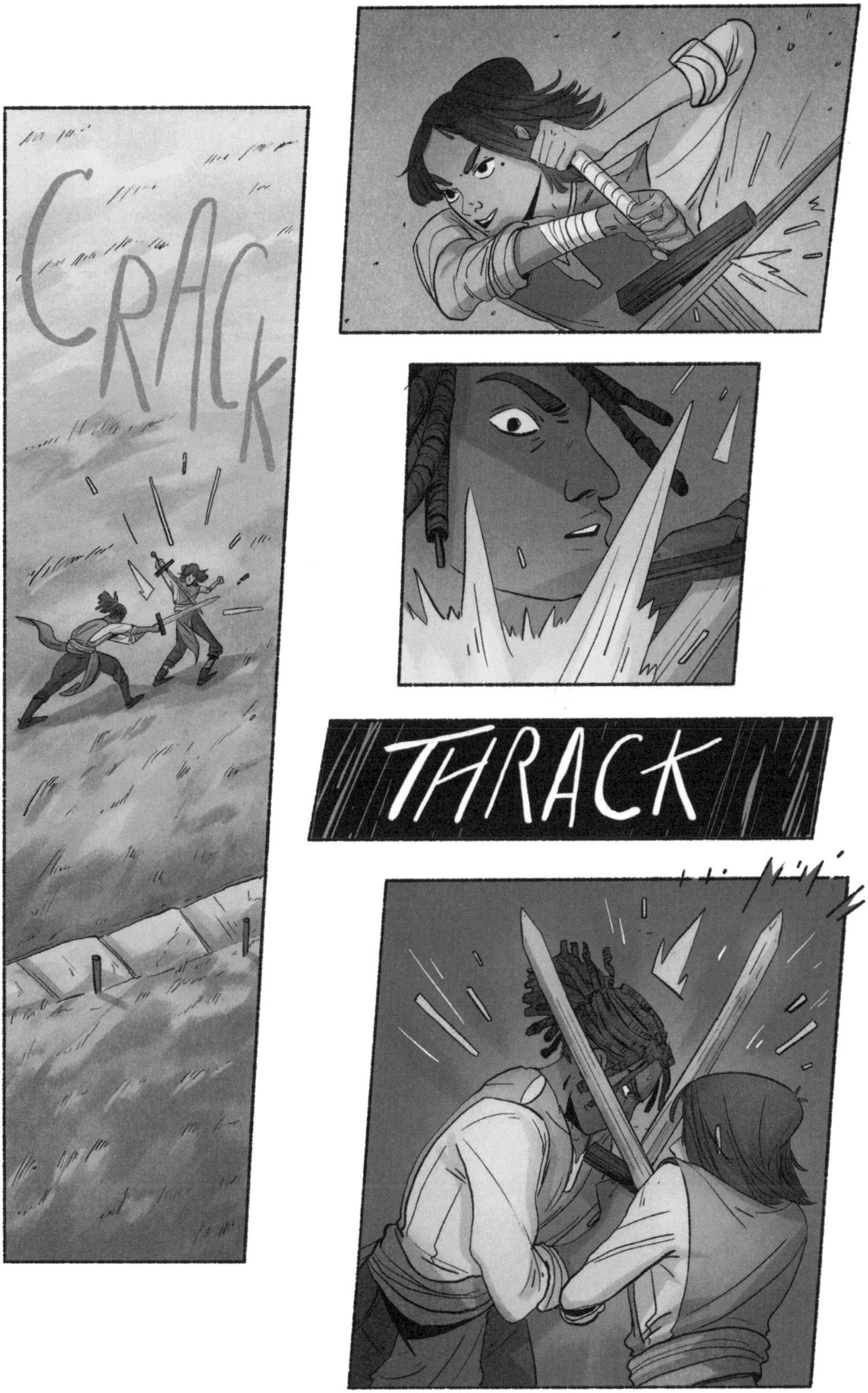
CRACK
THRACK

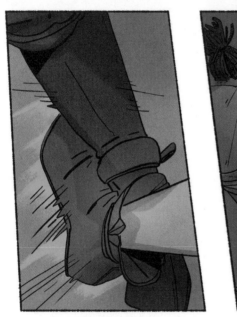

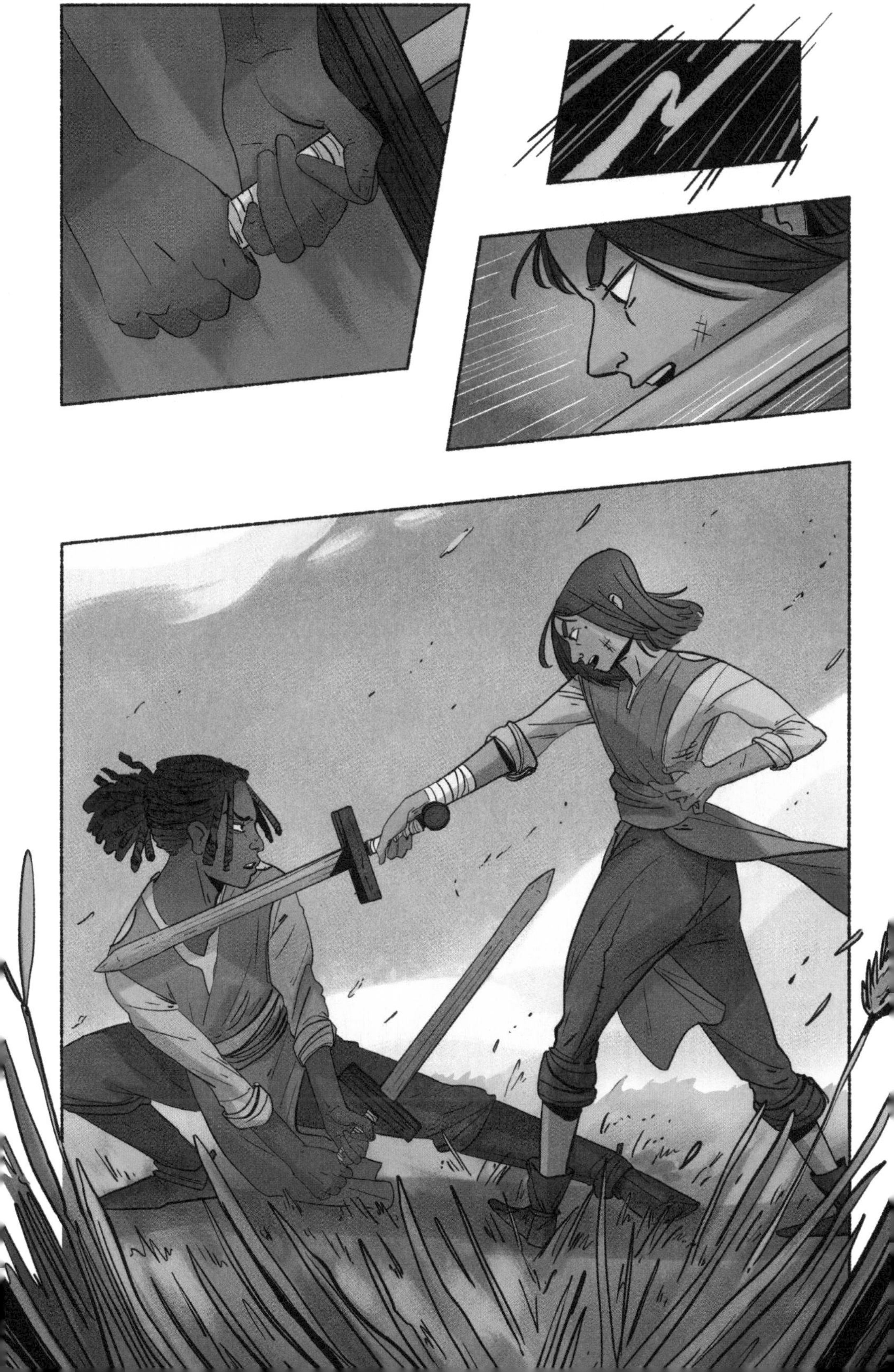

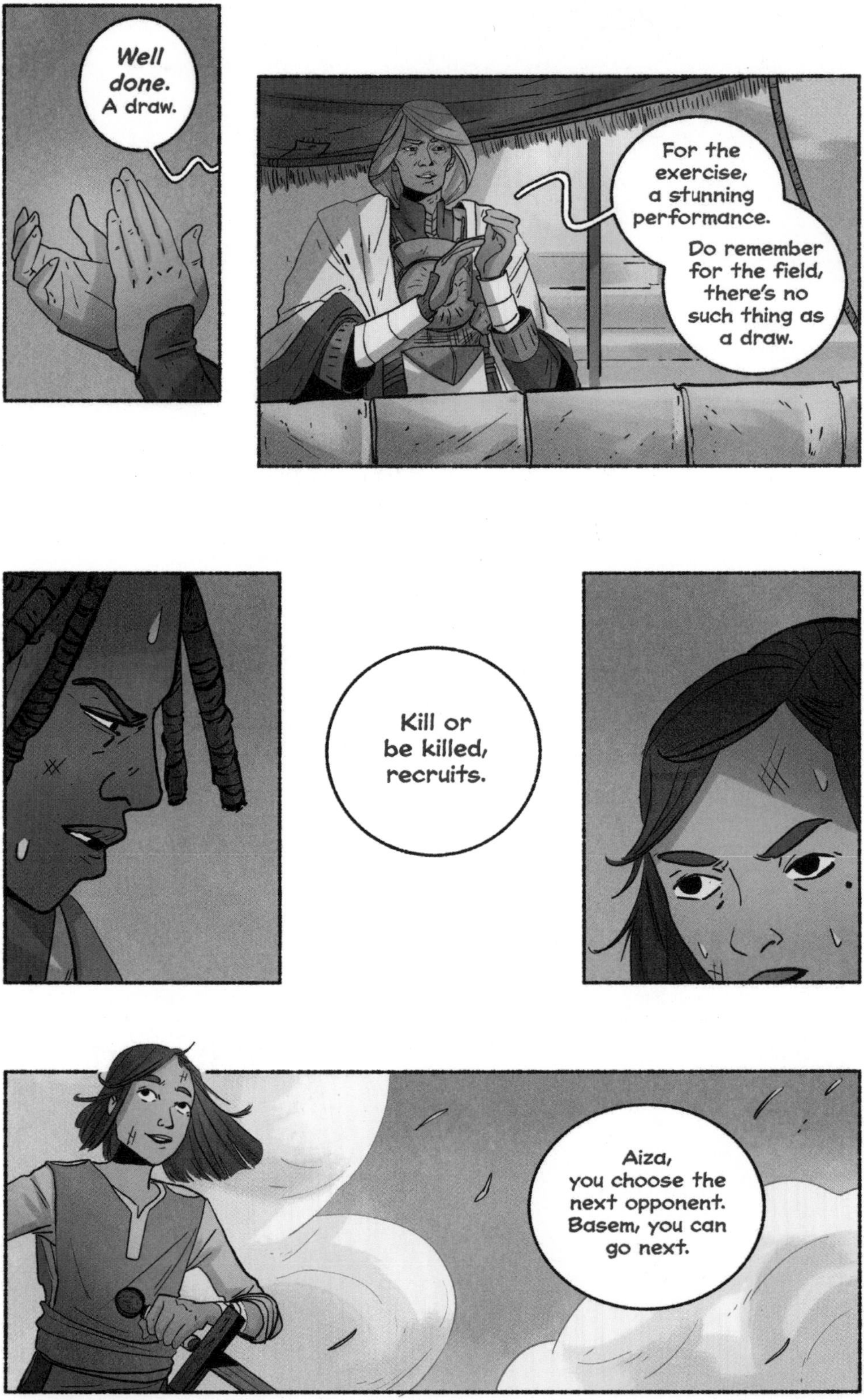
Well done. A draw.
For the exercise, a stunning performance.
Do remember for the field, there's no such thing as a draw.
Kill or be killed, recruits.
Aiza, you choose the next opponent. Basem, you can go next.

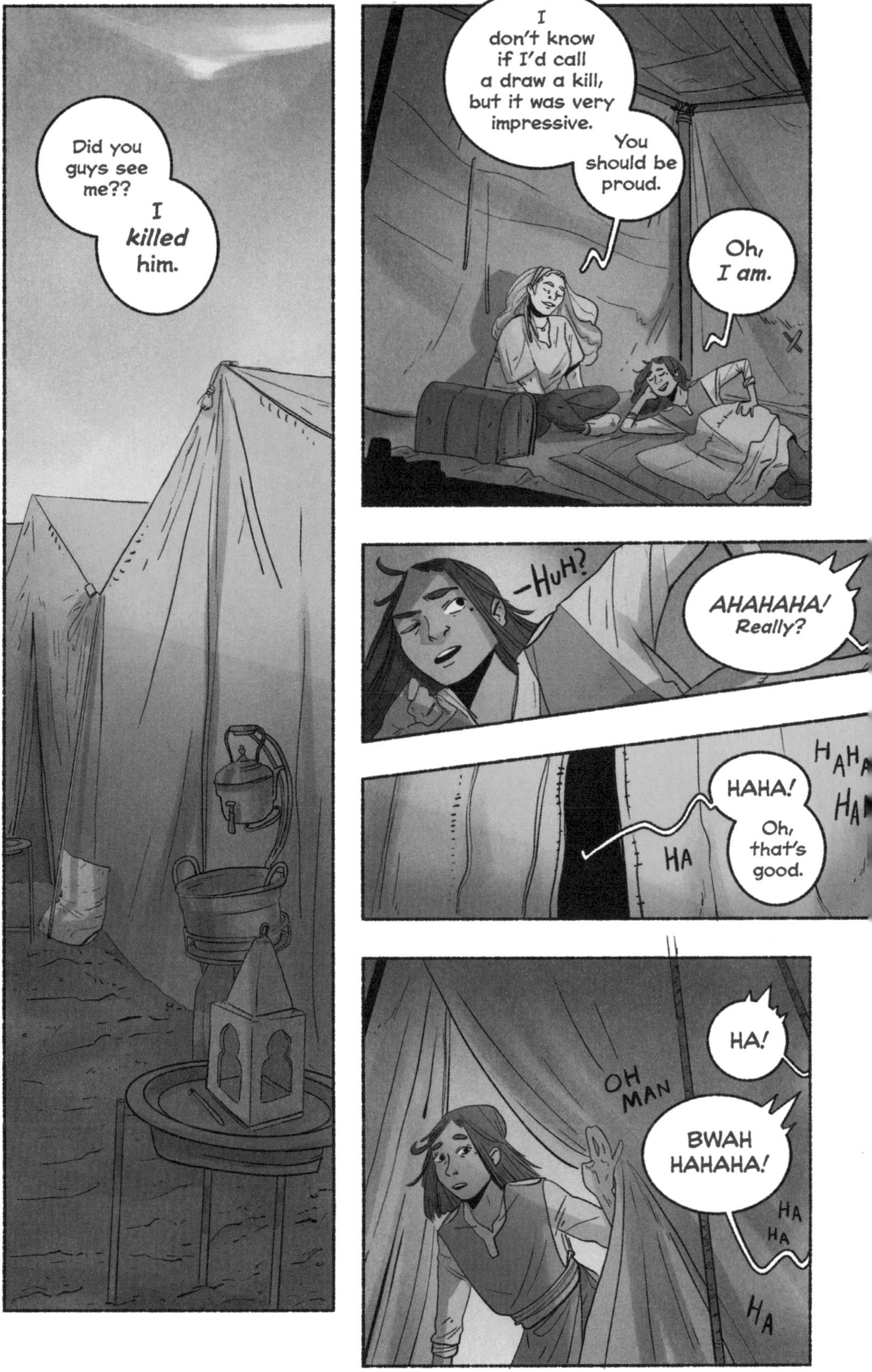

Did you guys see me??
I killed him.
I don't know if I'd call a draw a kill, but it was very impressive.
You should be proud.
Oh, I am.
-HuH?
AHAHAHA! Really?
HAHA!
Oh, that's good.
HA
HAHA
HA
HA!
OH MAN
BWAH HAHAHA!
HA HA
HA

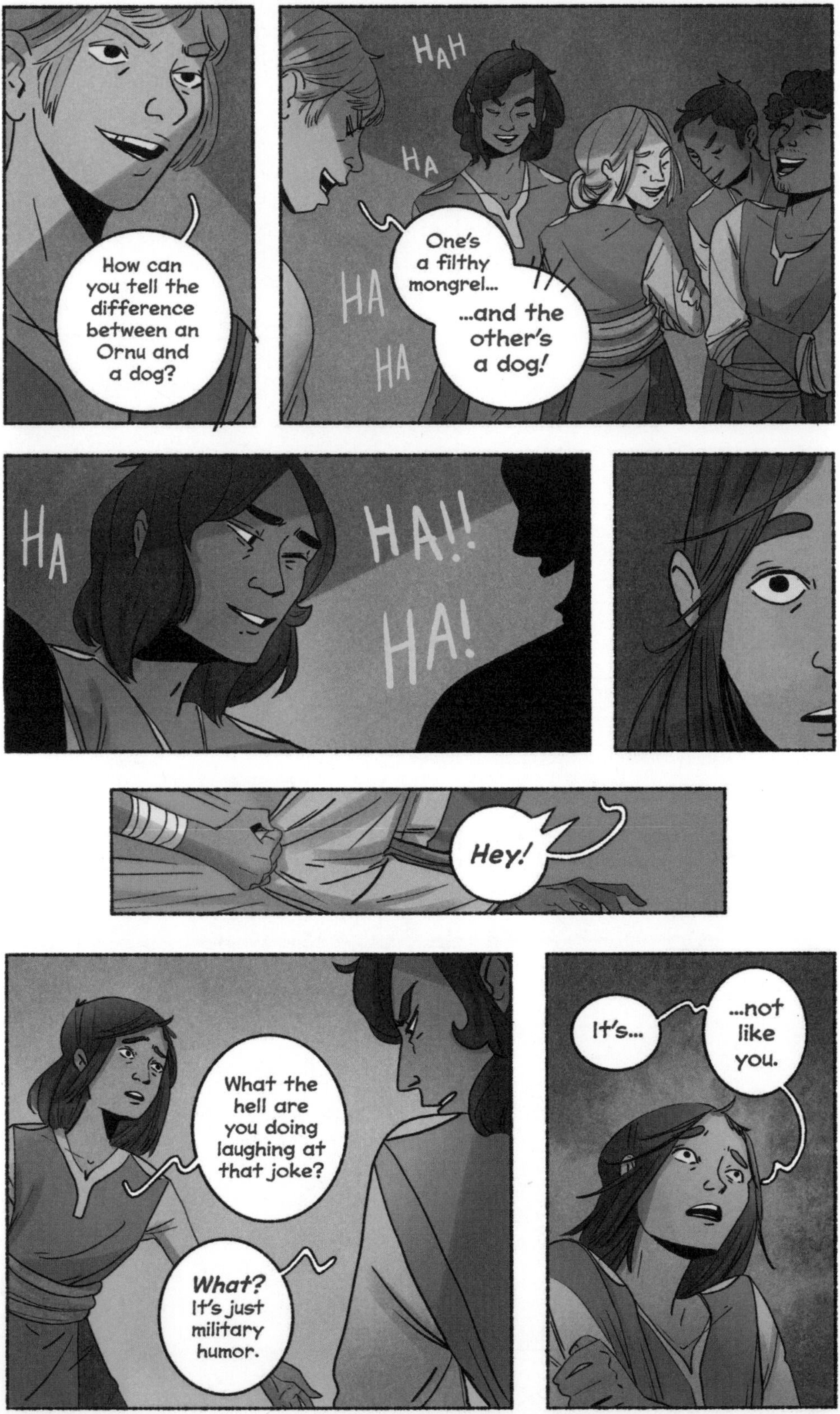
How can you tell the difference between an Ornu and a dog?
HAH
HA
HA
HA
One's a filthy mongrel...
...and the other's a dog!
HA
HA!!
HA!
Hey!
What the hell are you doing laughing at that joke?
What? It's just military humor.
It's...
...not like you.

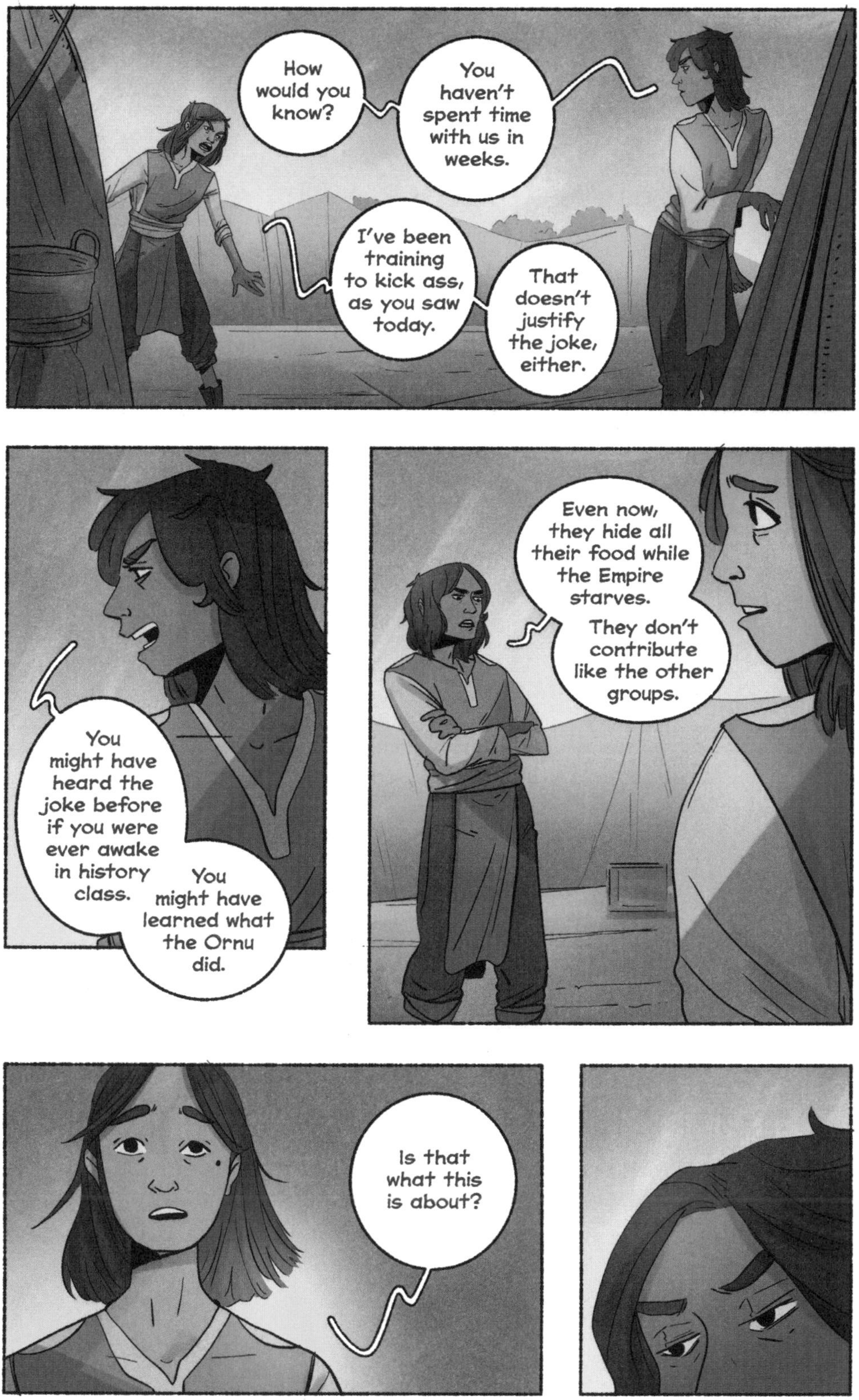
How would you know?
You haven't spent time with us in weeks.
I've been training to kick ass, as you saw today.
That doesn't justify the joke, either.
You might have heard the joke before if you were ever awake in history class.
You might have learned what the Ornu did.
Even now, they hide all their food while the Empire starves.
They don't contribute like the other groups.
Is that what this is about?

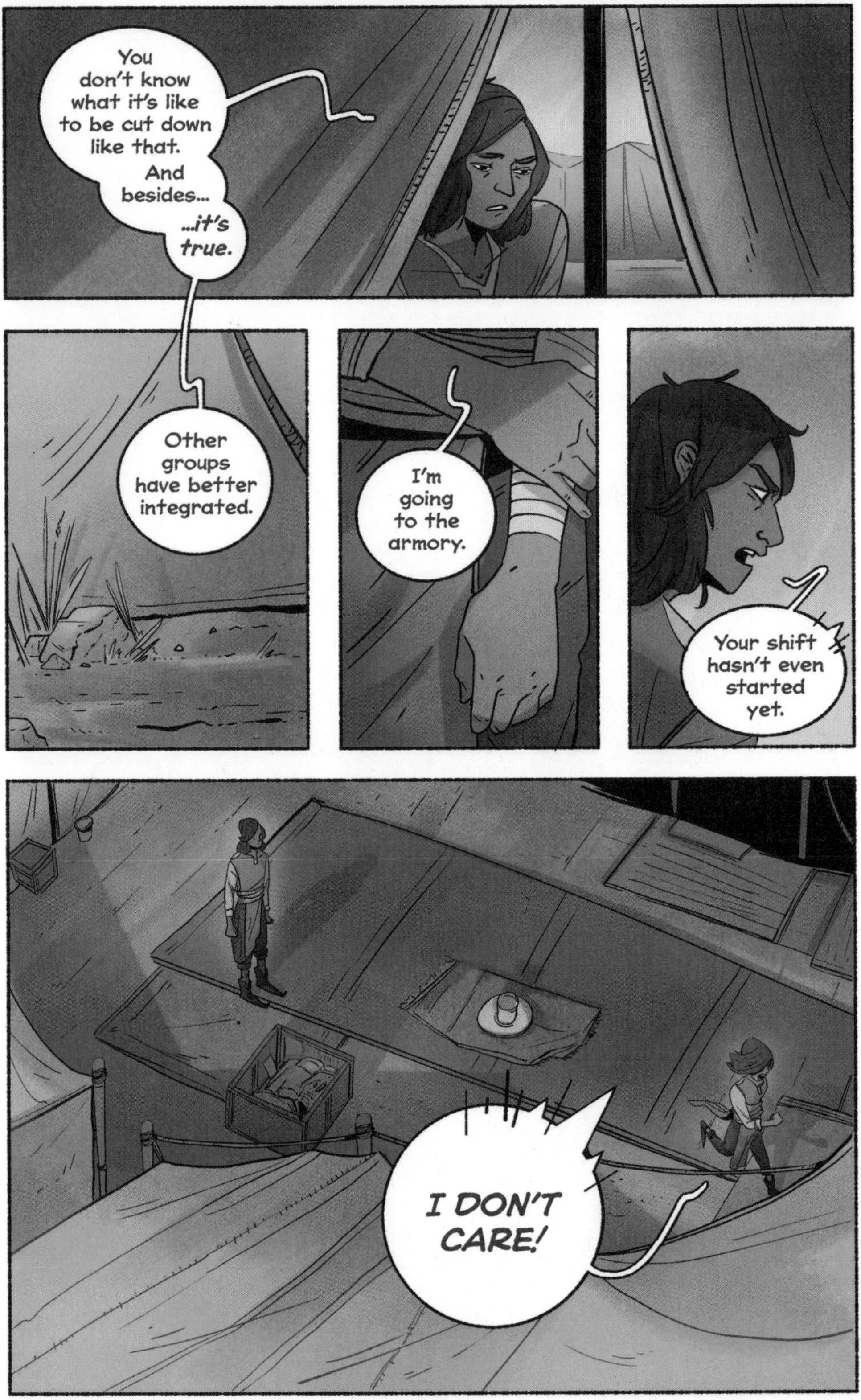
You don't know what it's like to be cut down like that.
And besides...
...it's true.
Other groups have better integrated.
I'm going to the armory.
Your shift hasn't even started yet.
I DON'T CARE!

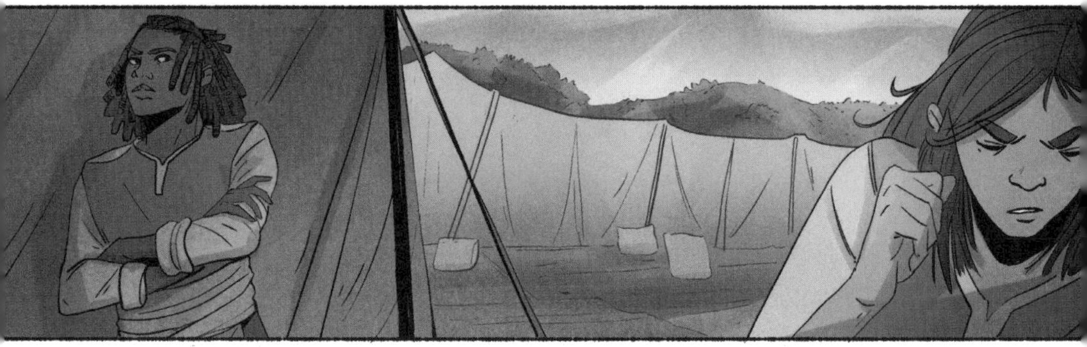

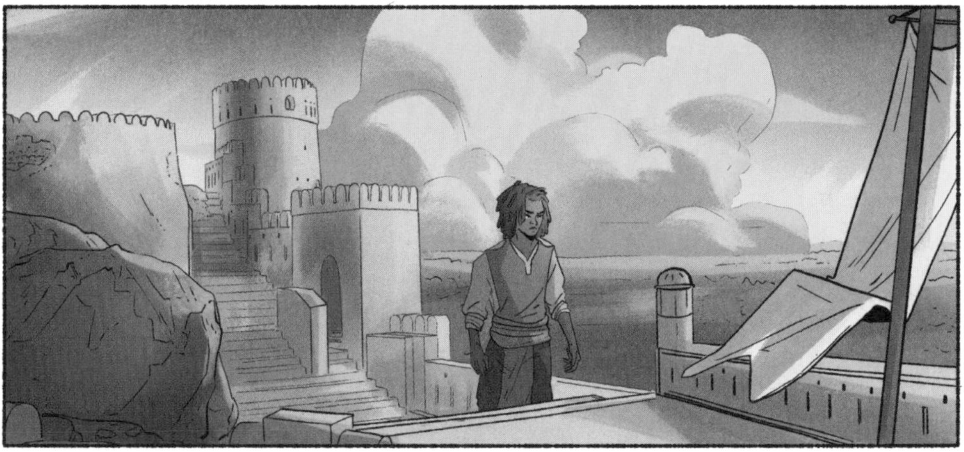

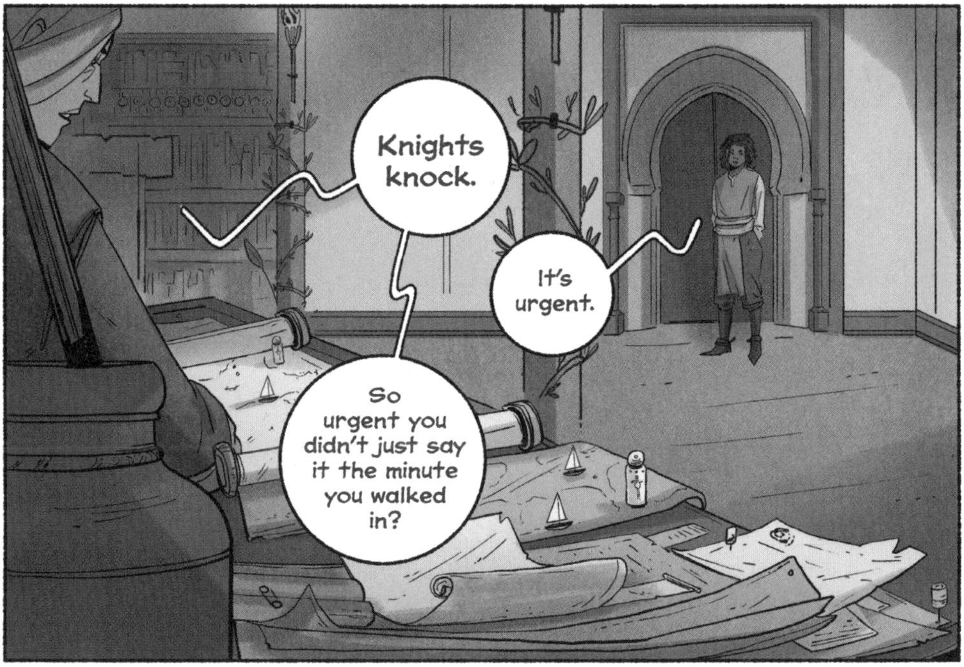
Knights knock.
It's urgent.
So urgent you didn't just say it the minute you walked in?

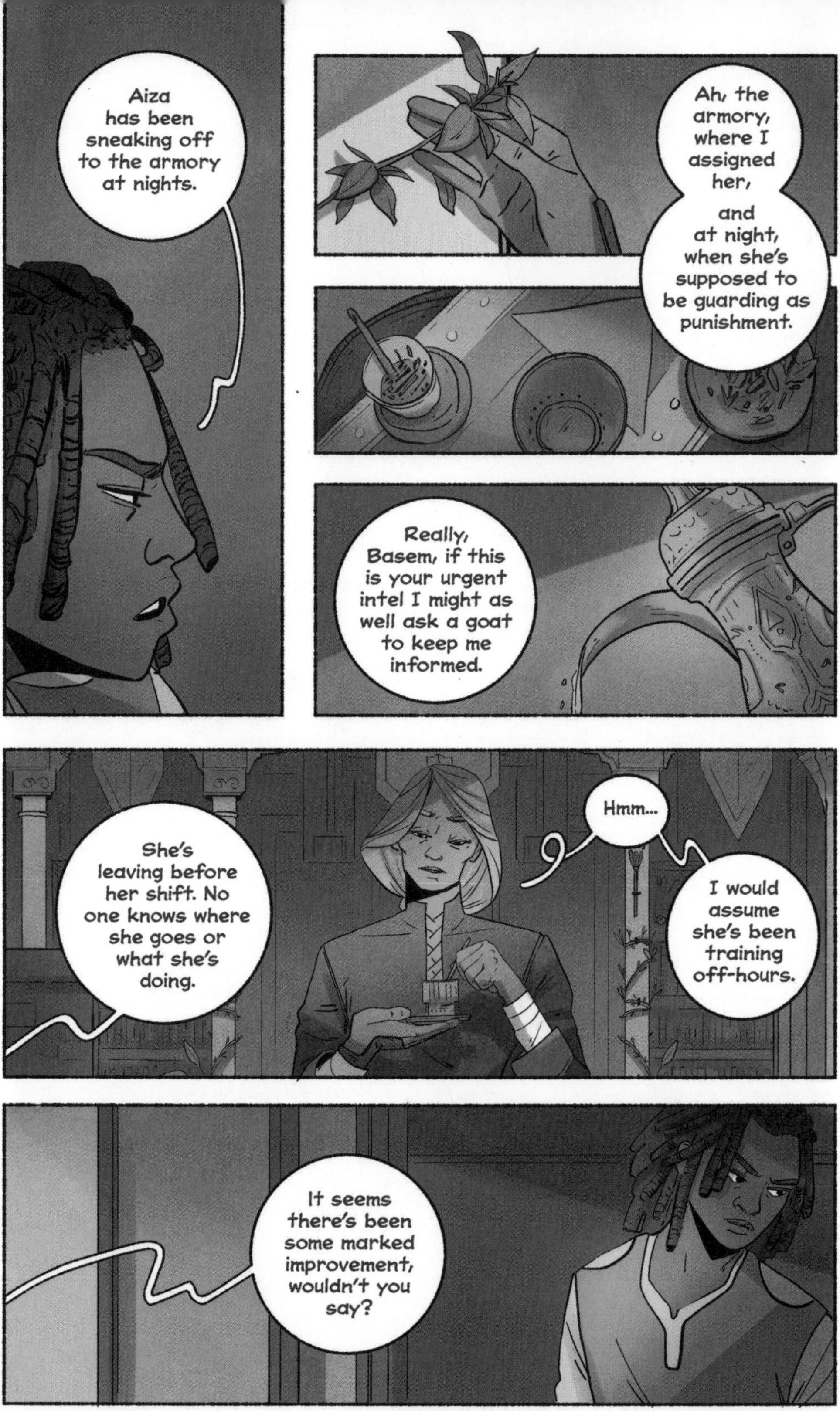

Aiza has been sneaking off to the armory at nights.
Ah, the armory, where I assigned her,
and at night, when she's supposed to be guarding as punishment.
Really, Basem, if this is your urgent intel I might as well ask a goat to keep me informed.
She's leaving before her shift. No one knows where she goes or what she's doing.
Hmm...
I would assume she's been training off-hours.
It seems there's been some marked improvement, wouldn't you say?

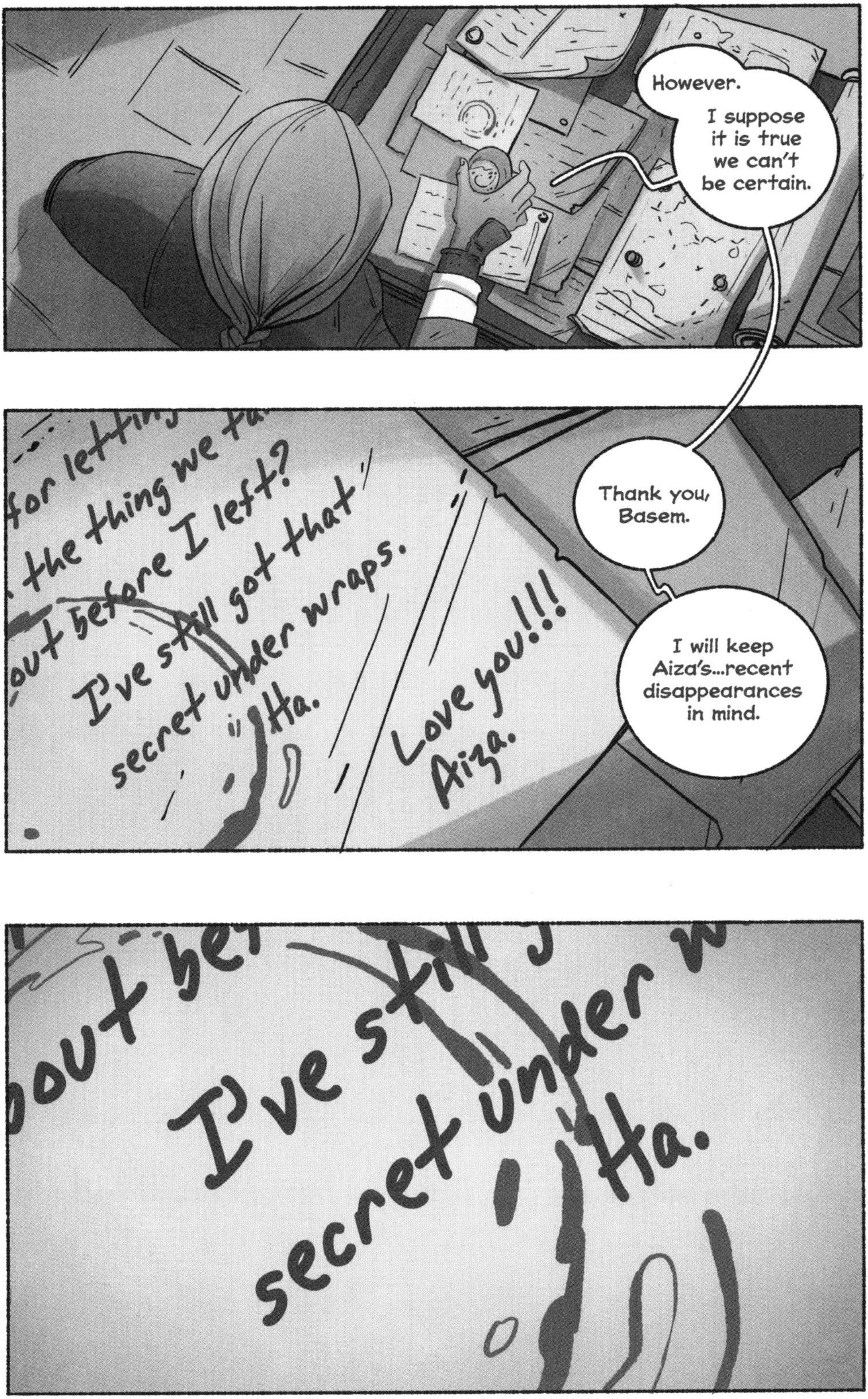
However.
I suppose it is true we can't be certain.
the thing we
before I left?
I've still got that
secret under wraps.
Ha.
Love you!!!
Aiza.
Thank you, Basem.
I will keep Aiza's...recent disappearances in mind.
I've
secret under
Ha.

YAWN

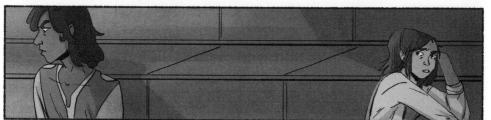

Oh, come on, you two.

Ah, recruits.

I'm sure you're wondering why I asked six of you, specifically, to meet me at so early an hour.

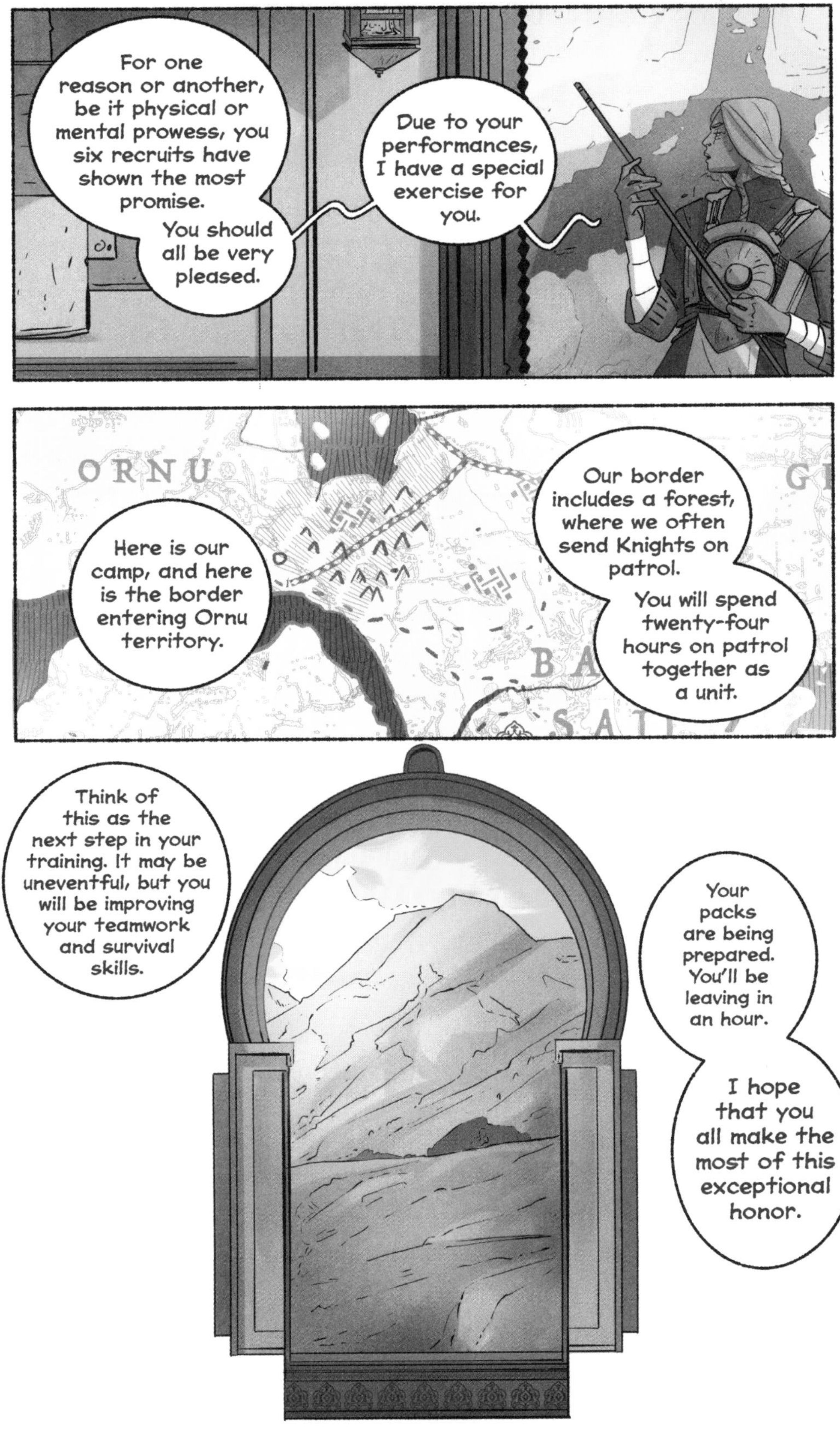
For one reason or another, be it physical or mental prowess, you six recruits have shown the most promise.
You should all be very pleased.
Due to your performances, I have a special exercise for you.
ORNU
Here is our camp, and here is the border entering Ornu territory.
Our border includes a forest, where we often send Knights on patrol.
You will spend twenty-four hours on patrol together as a unit.
Think of this as the next step in your training. It may be uneventful, but you will be improving your teamwork and survival skills.
Your packs are being prepared. You'll be leaving in an hour.
I hope that you all make the most of this exceptional honor.

CHAPTER 9

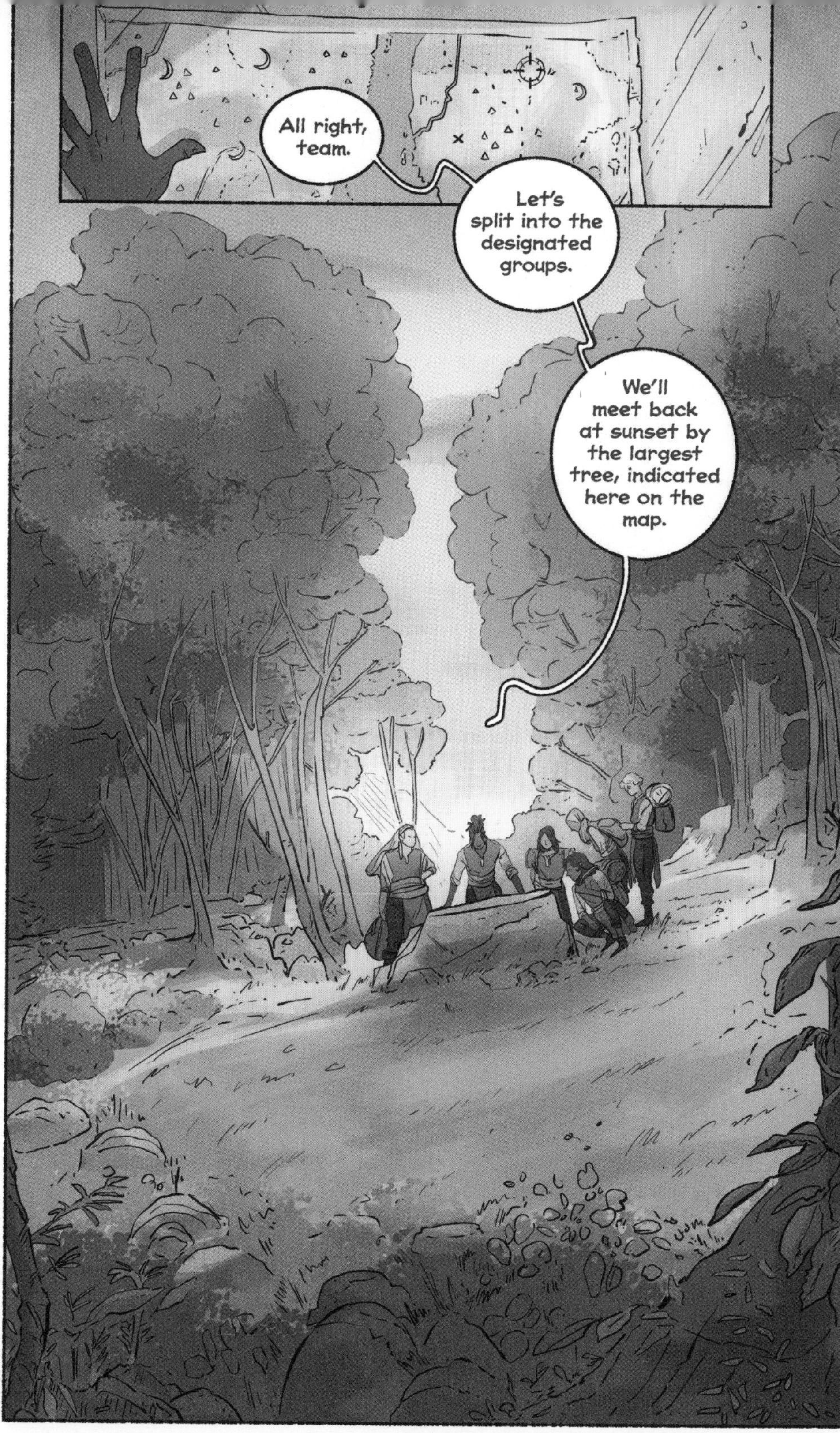
All right, team.
Let's split into the designated groups.
We'll meet back at sunset by the largest tree, indicated here on the map.

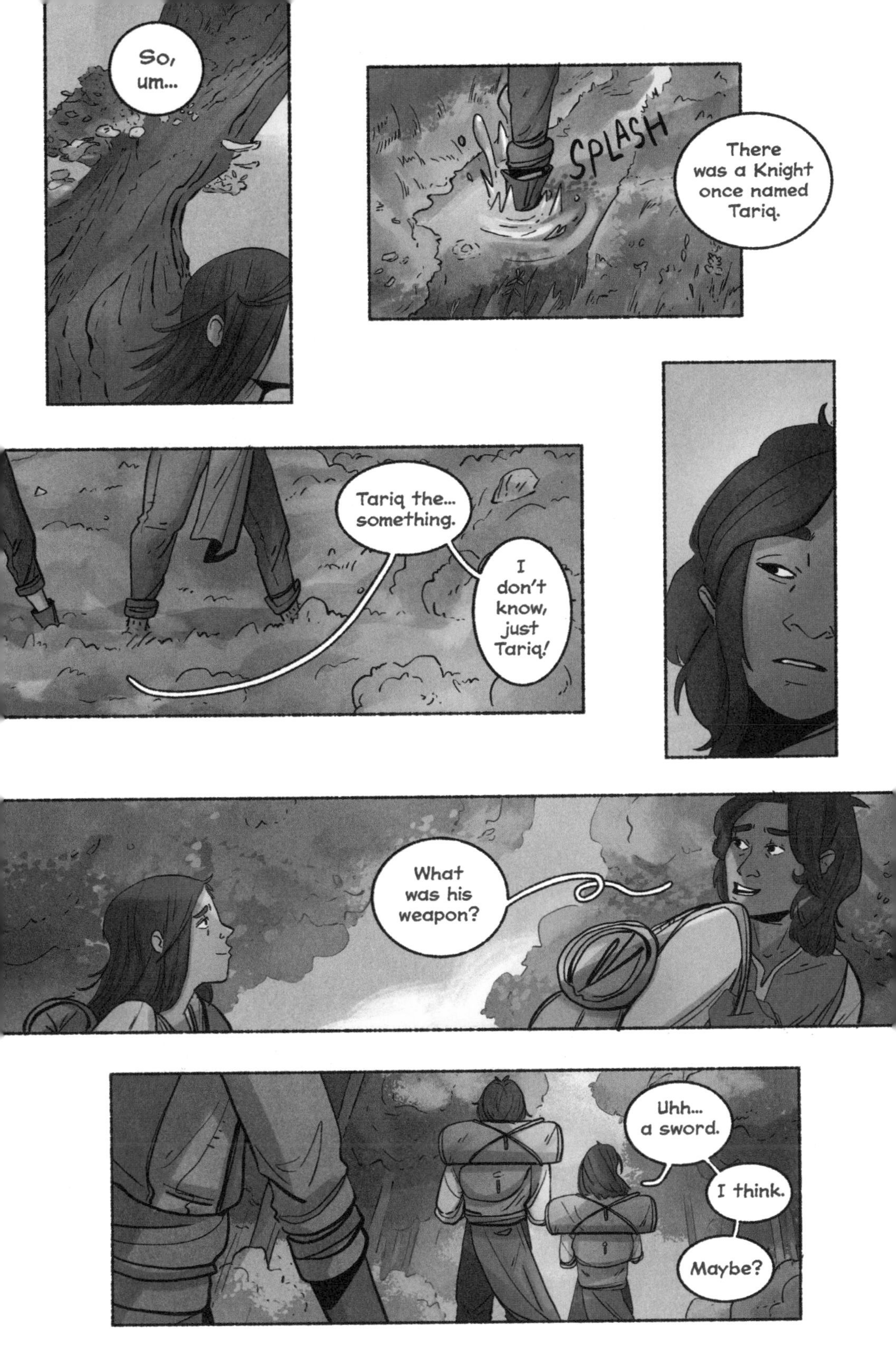
So, um...
SPLASH
There was a Knight once named Tariq.
Tariq the... something.
I don't know, just Tariq!
What was his weapon?
Uhh... a sword.
I think.
Maybe?

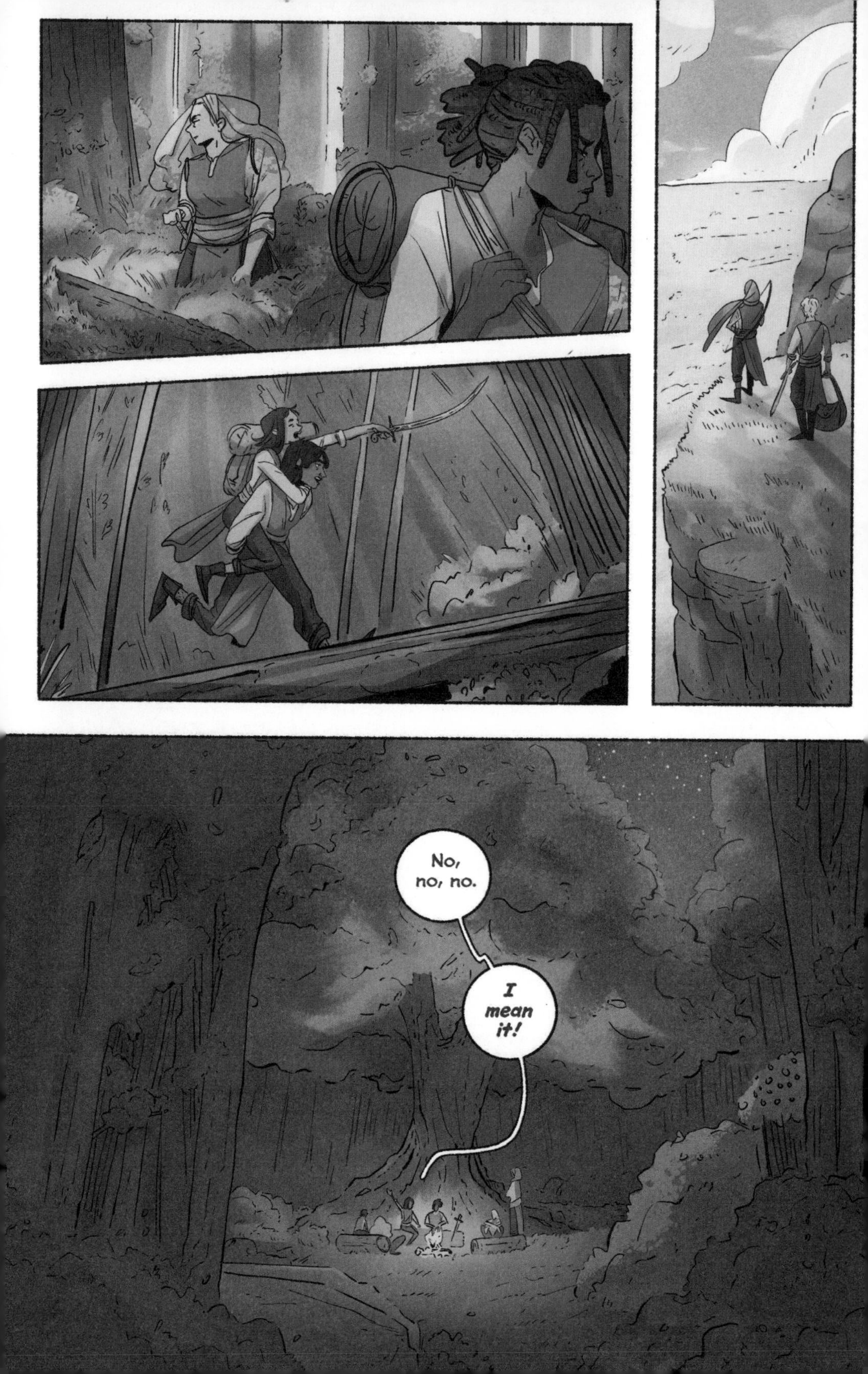
No, no, no.
I mean it!

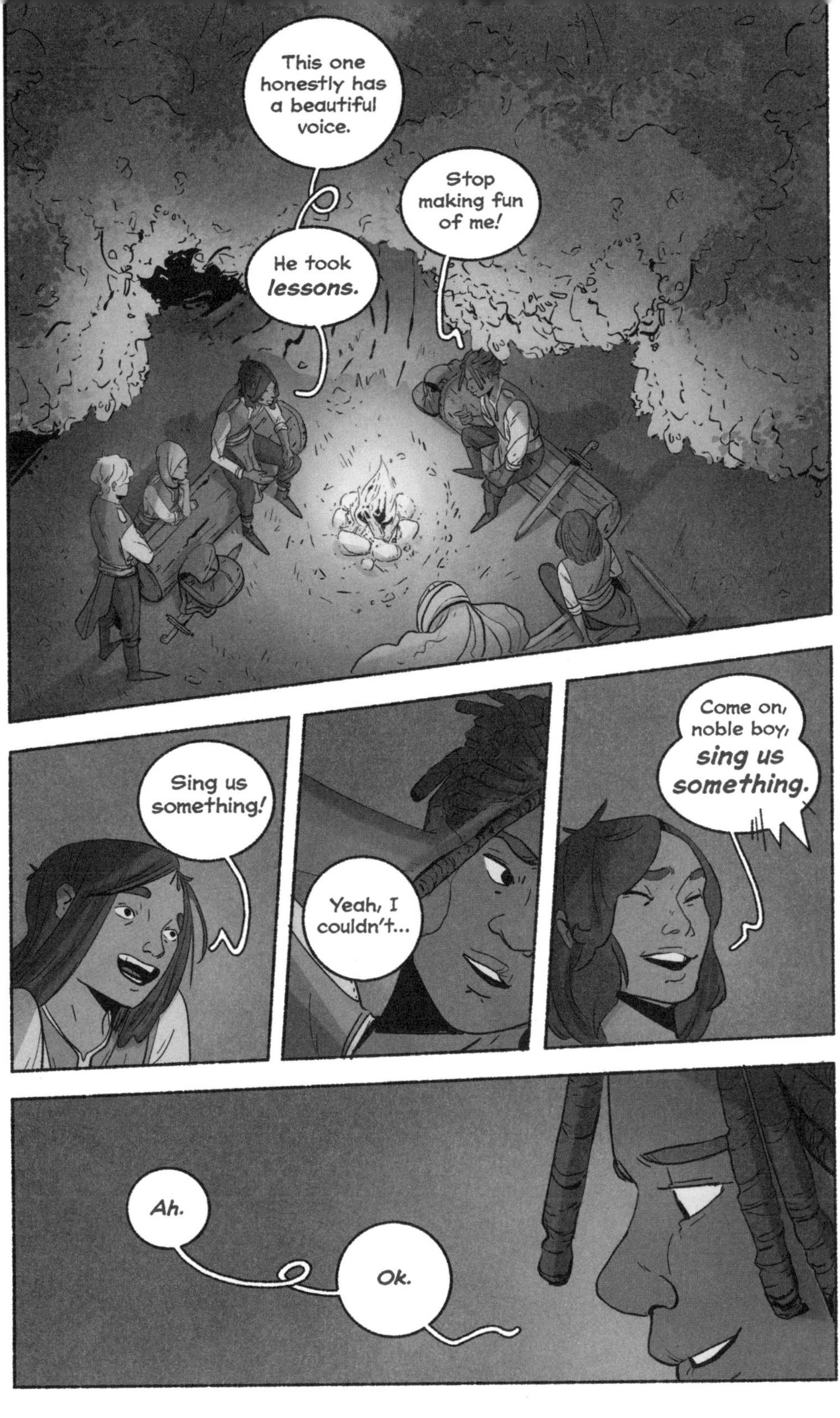
This one honestly has a beautiful voice.
He took *lessons.*
Stop making fun of me!
Sing us something!
Yeah, I couldn't...
Come on, noble boy, **sing us something.**
Ah.
Ok.

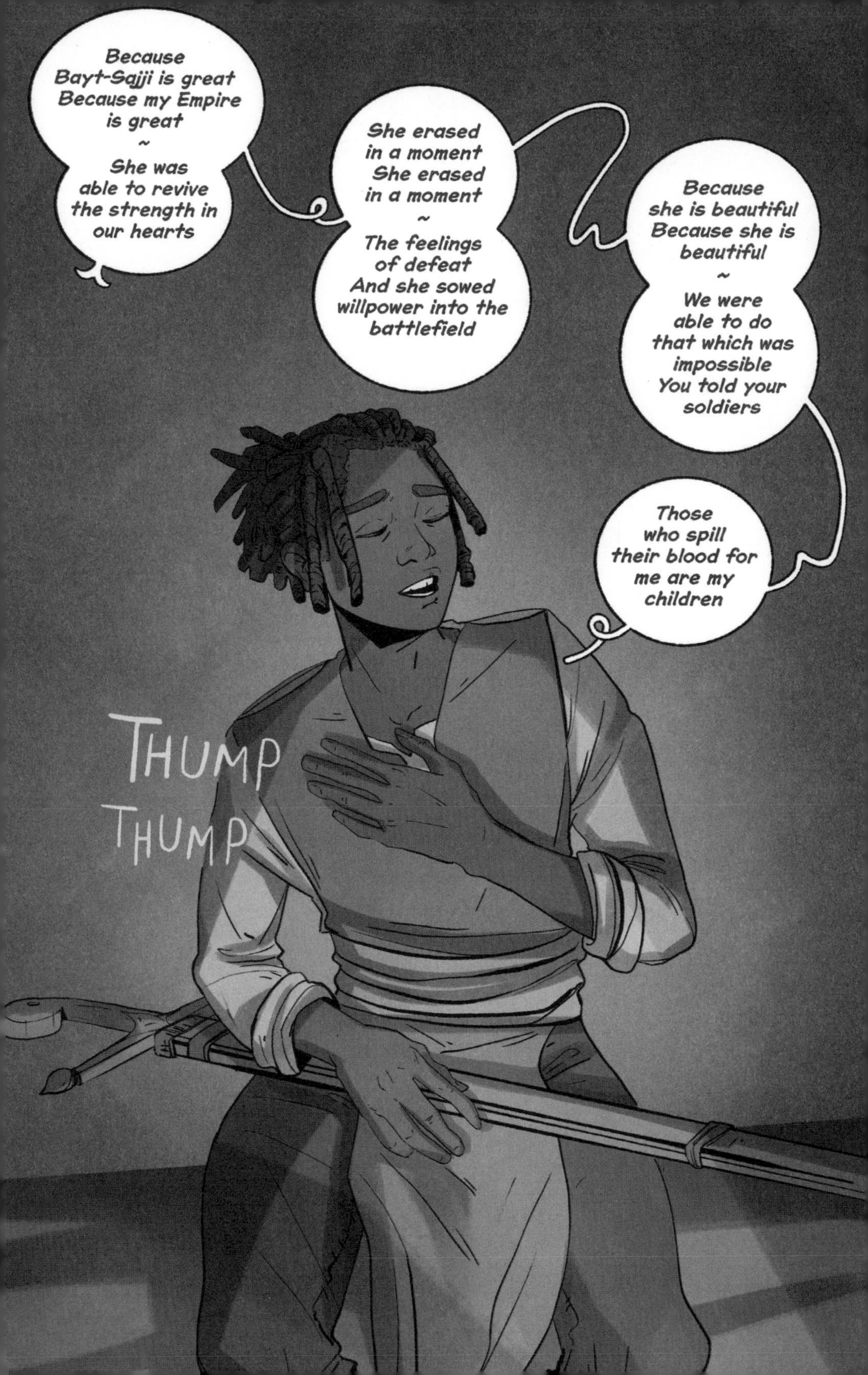
Because Bayt-Sajji is great Because my Empire is great ~ She was able to revive the strength in our hearts
She erased in a moment She erased in a moment ~ The feelings of defeat And she sowed willpower into the battlefield
Because she is beautiful Because she is beautiful ~ We were able to do that which was impossible You told your soldiers
Those who spill their blood for me are my children
THUMP THUMP

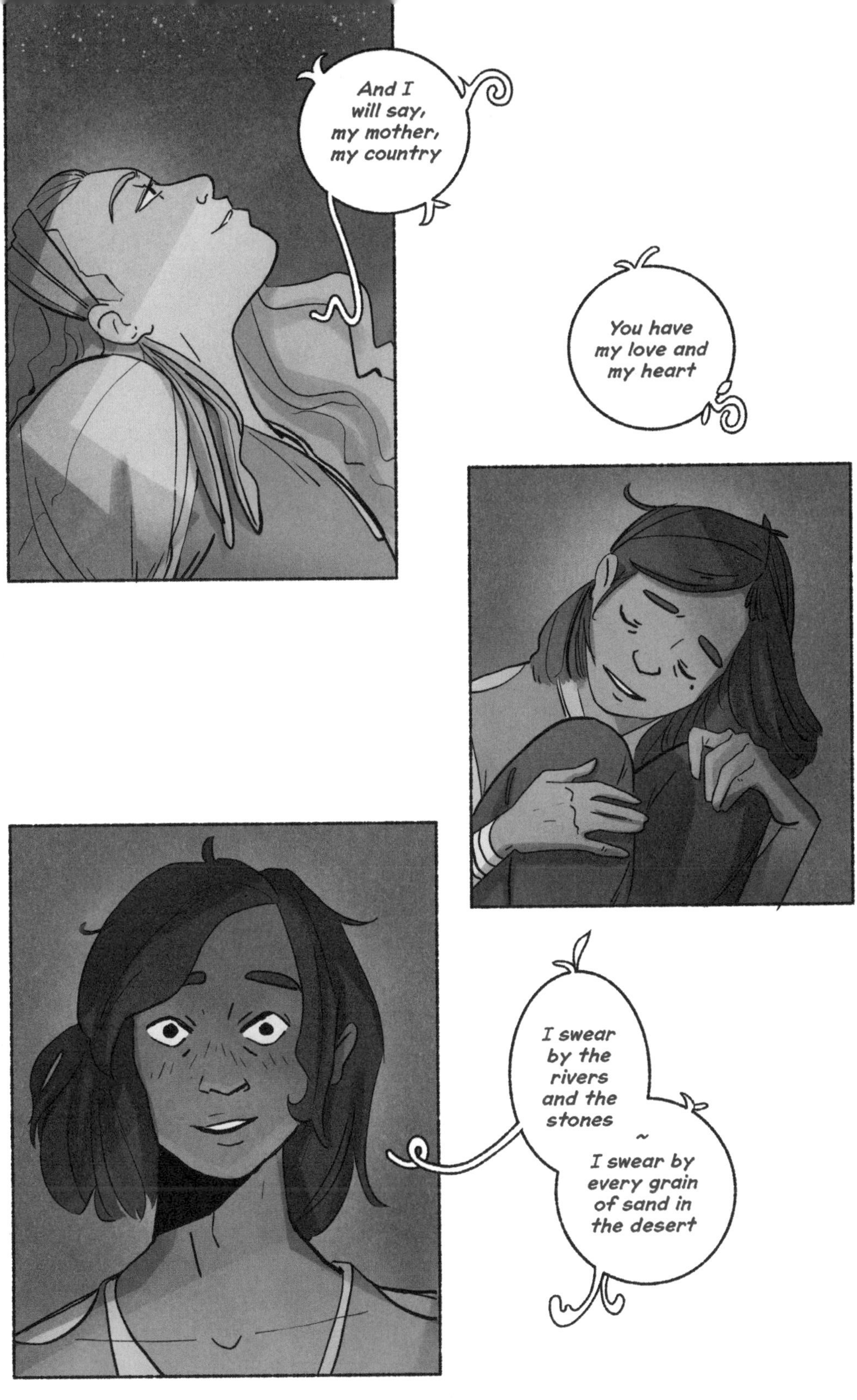
And I will say, my mother, my country
You have my love and my heart
I swear by the rivers and the stones
~
I swear by every grain of sand in the desert

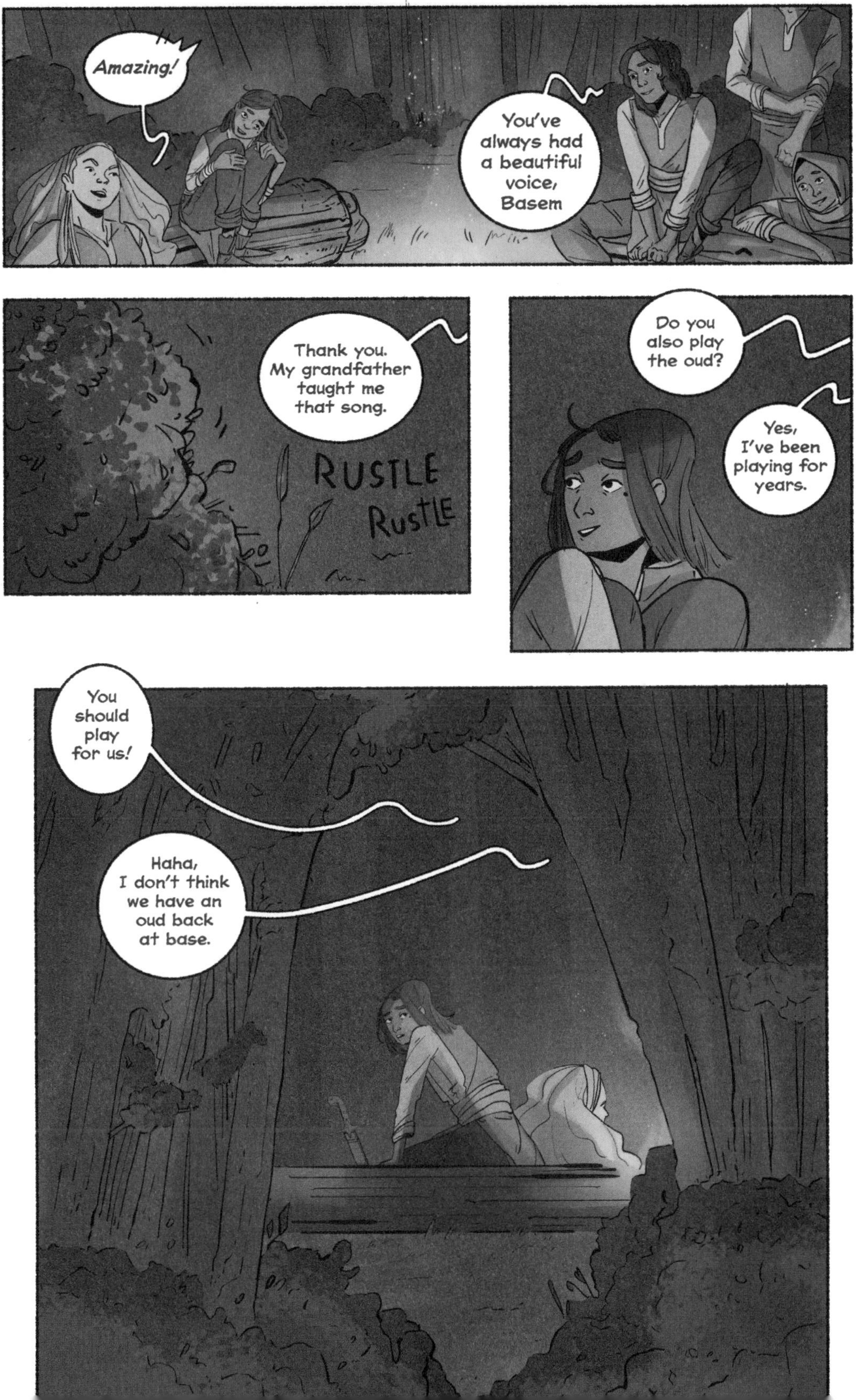
Amazing!
You've always had a beautiful voice, Basem
Thank you. My grandfather taught me that song.
RUSTLE
RUSTLE
Do you also play the oud?
Yes, I've been playing for years.
You should play for us!
Haha, I don't think we have an oud back at base.

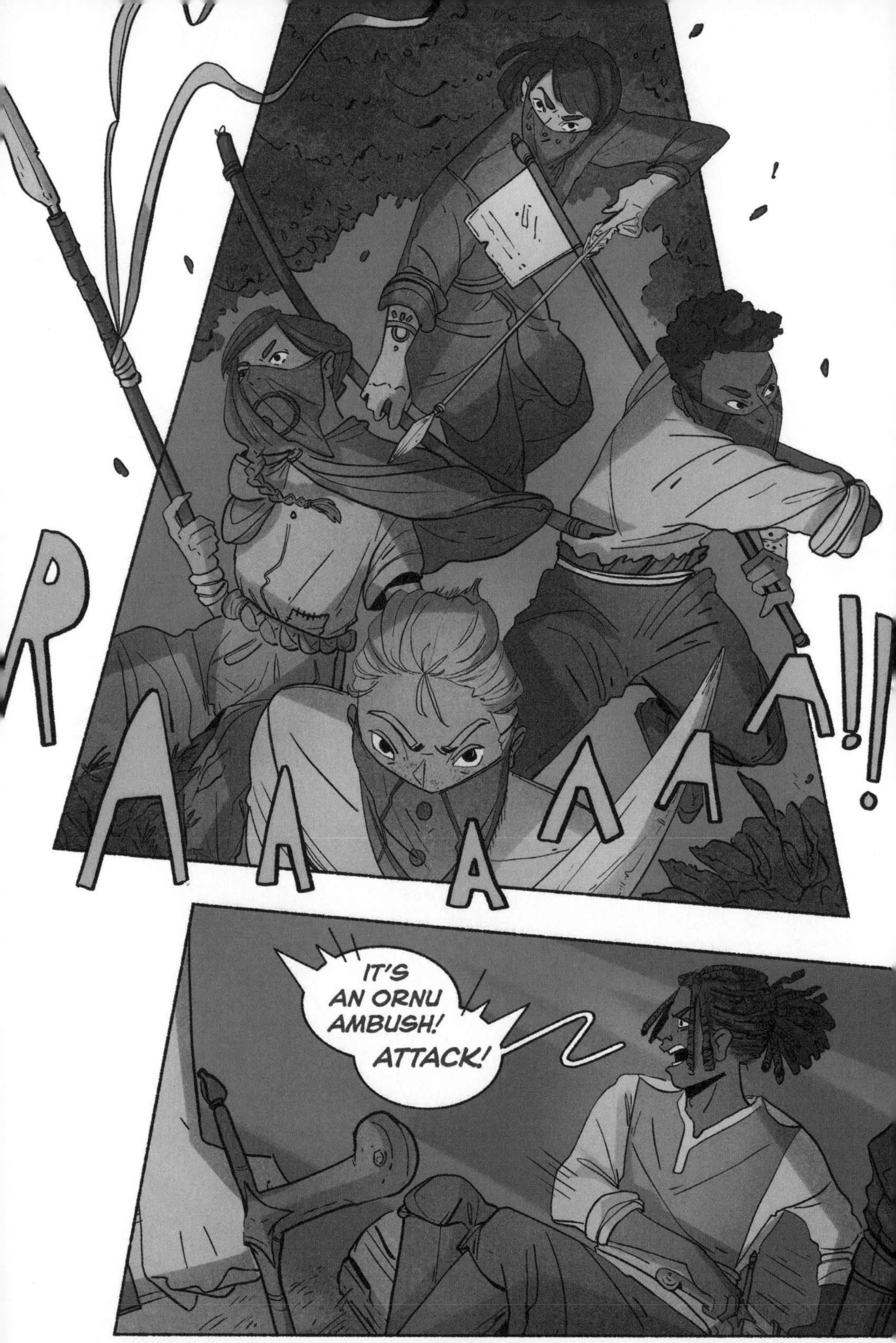
RAAAAAA!!!
IT'S AN ORNU AMBUSH! ATTACK!

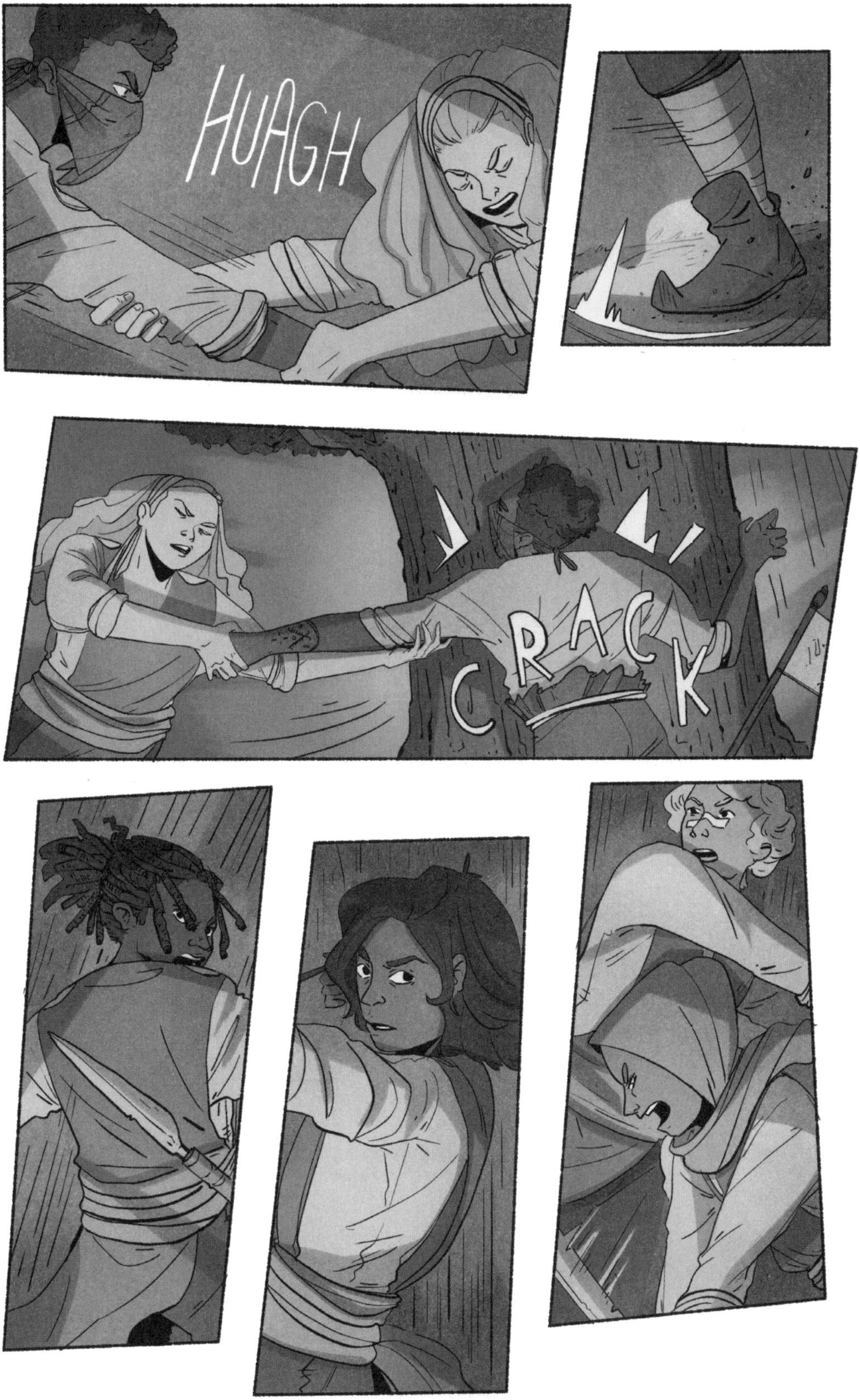
HUAGH
CRACK

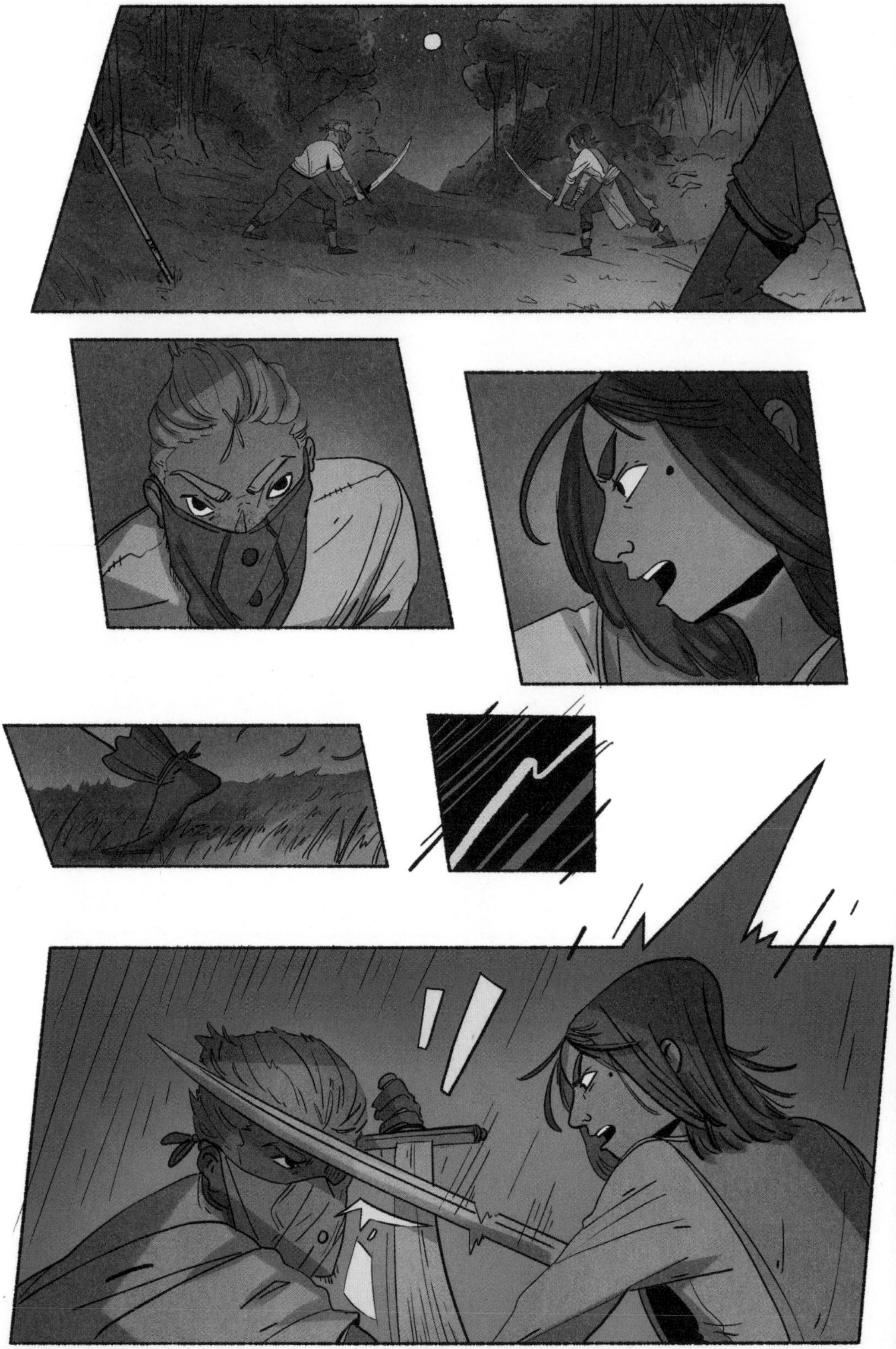

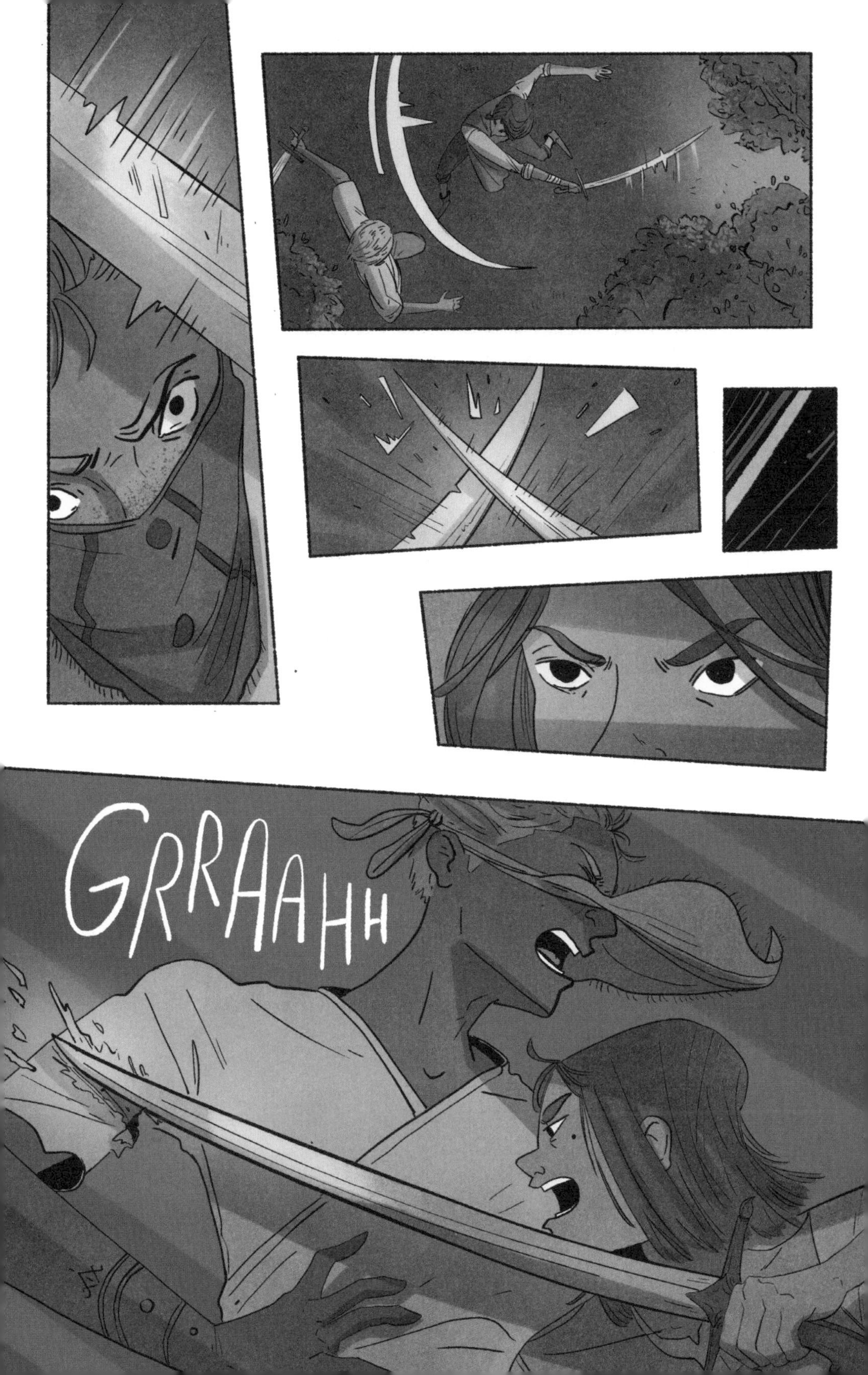
GRRAAHH

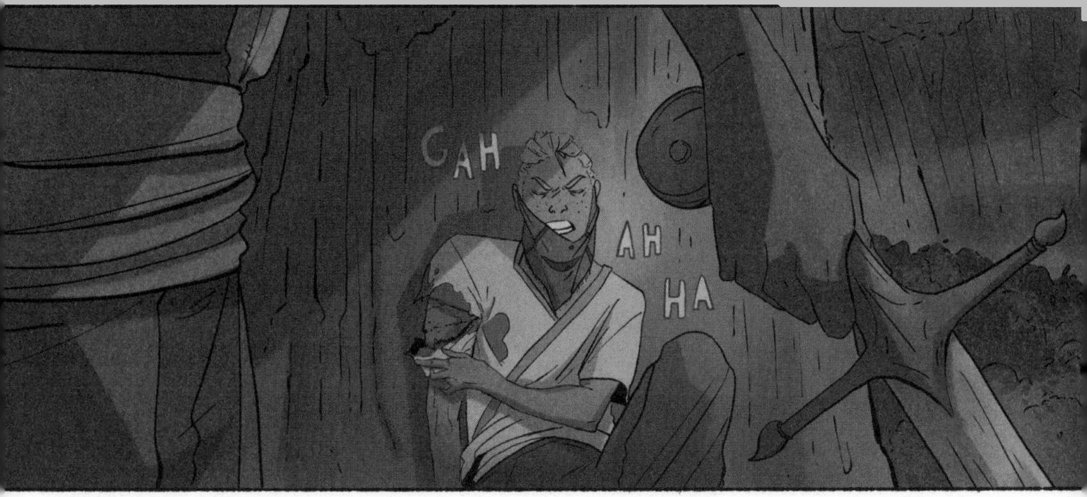
GAH
AH
HA

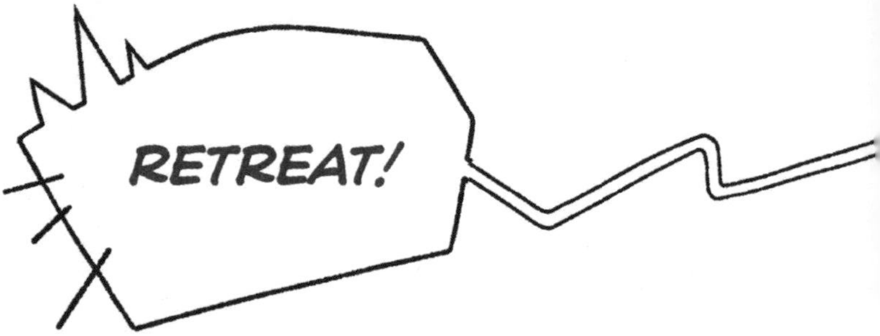
RETREAT!

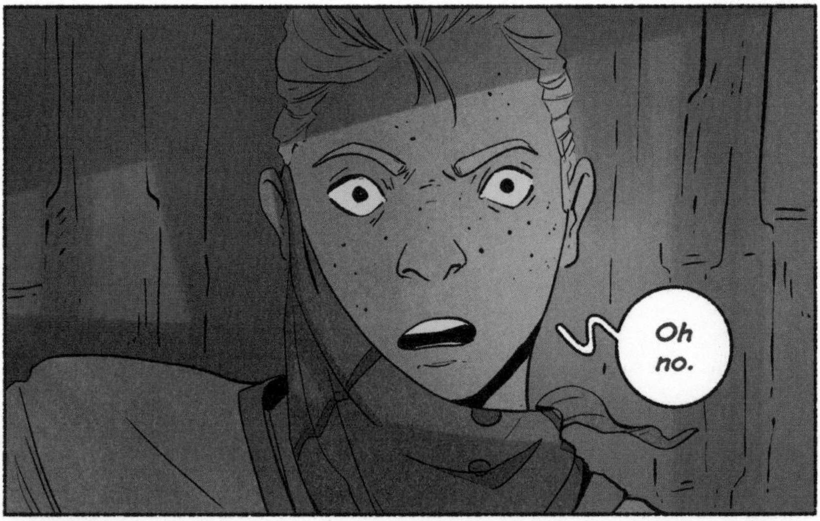
Oh no.

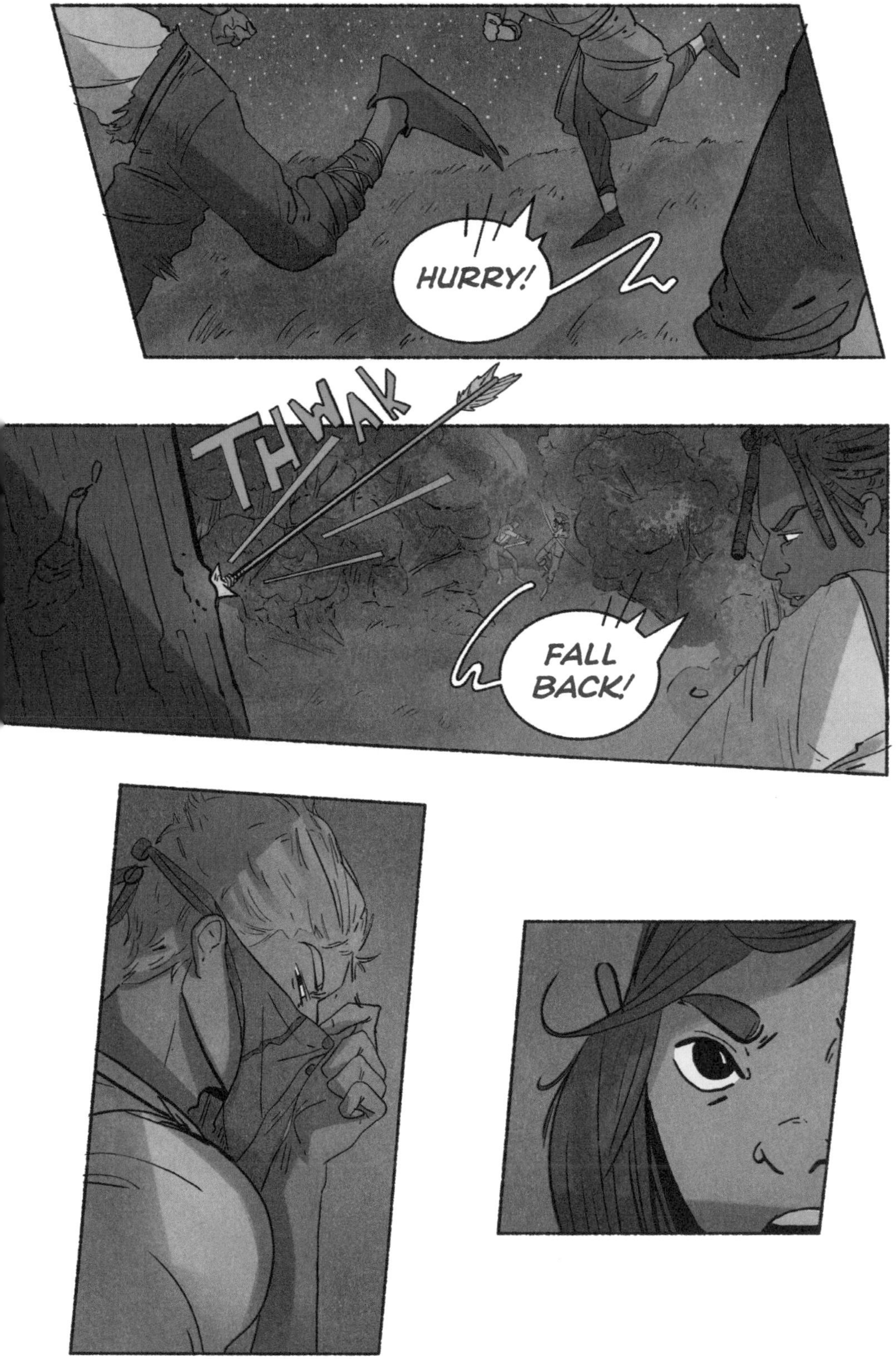
HURRY!
THWAK
FALL BACK!

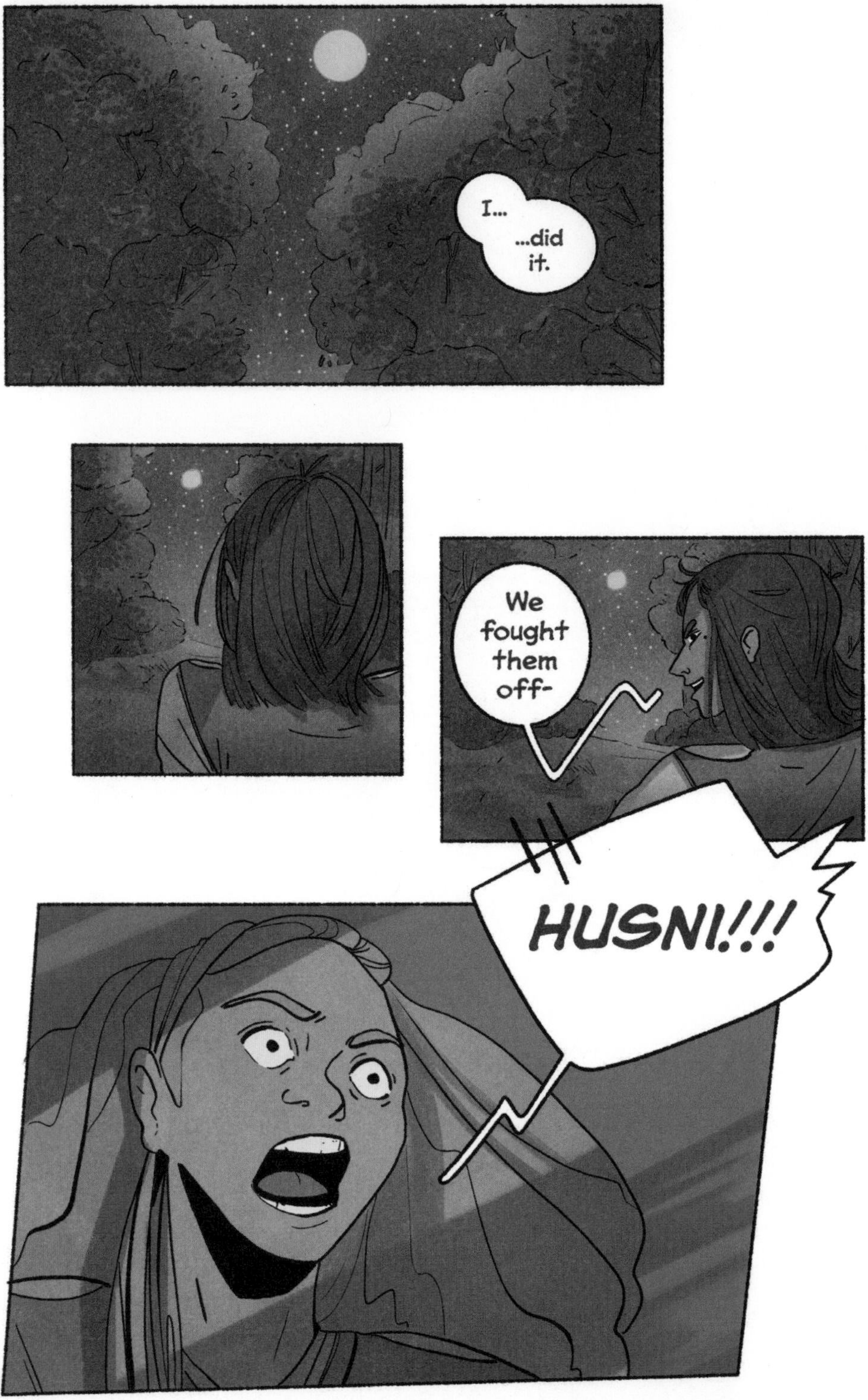
I...
...did it.
We fought them off-
HUSNI!!!

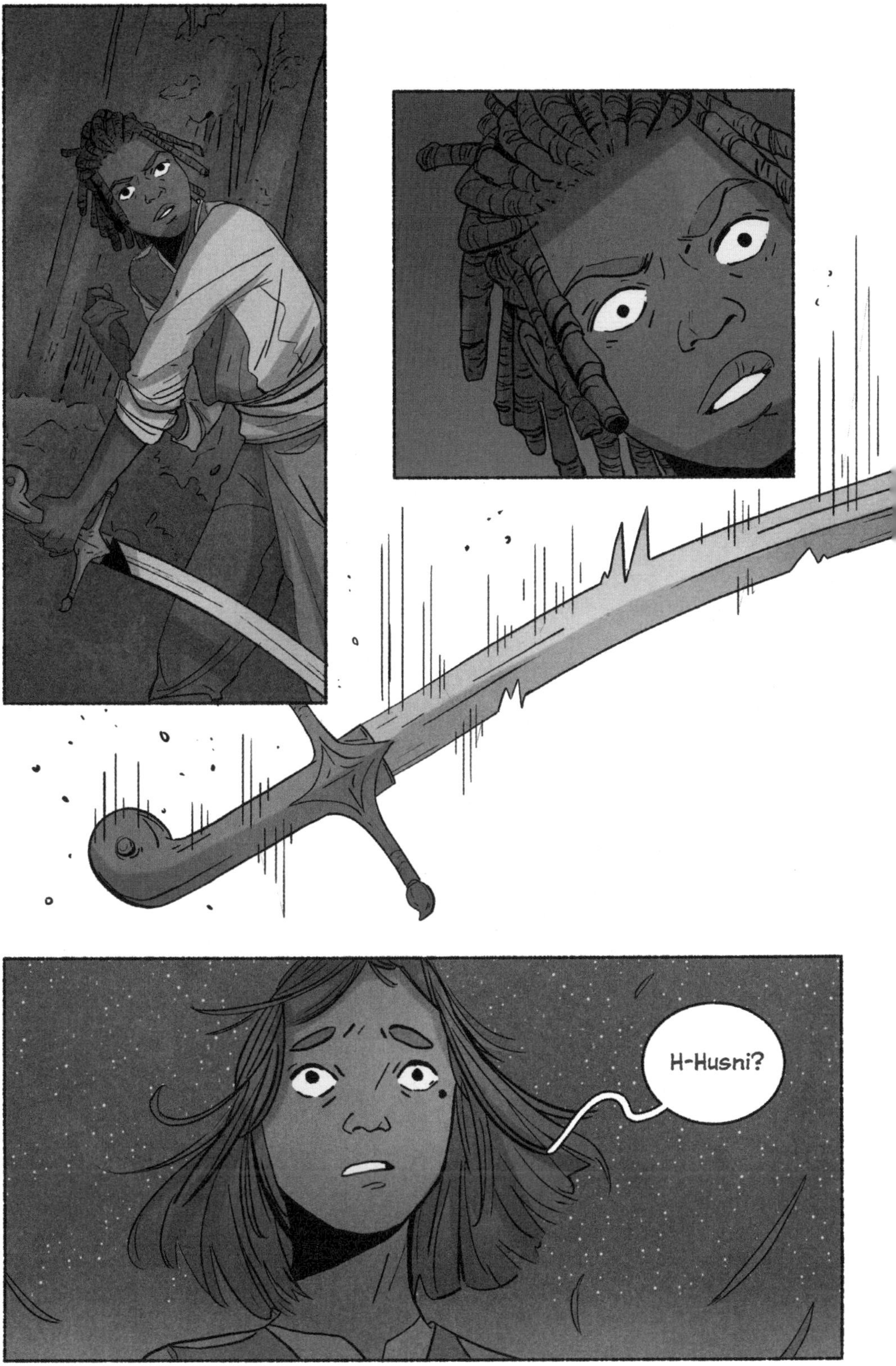
H-Husni?

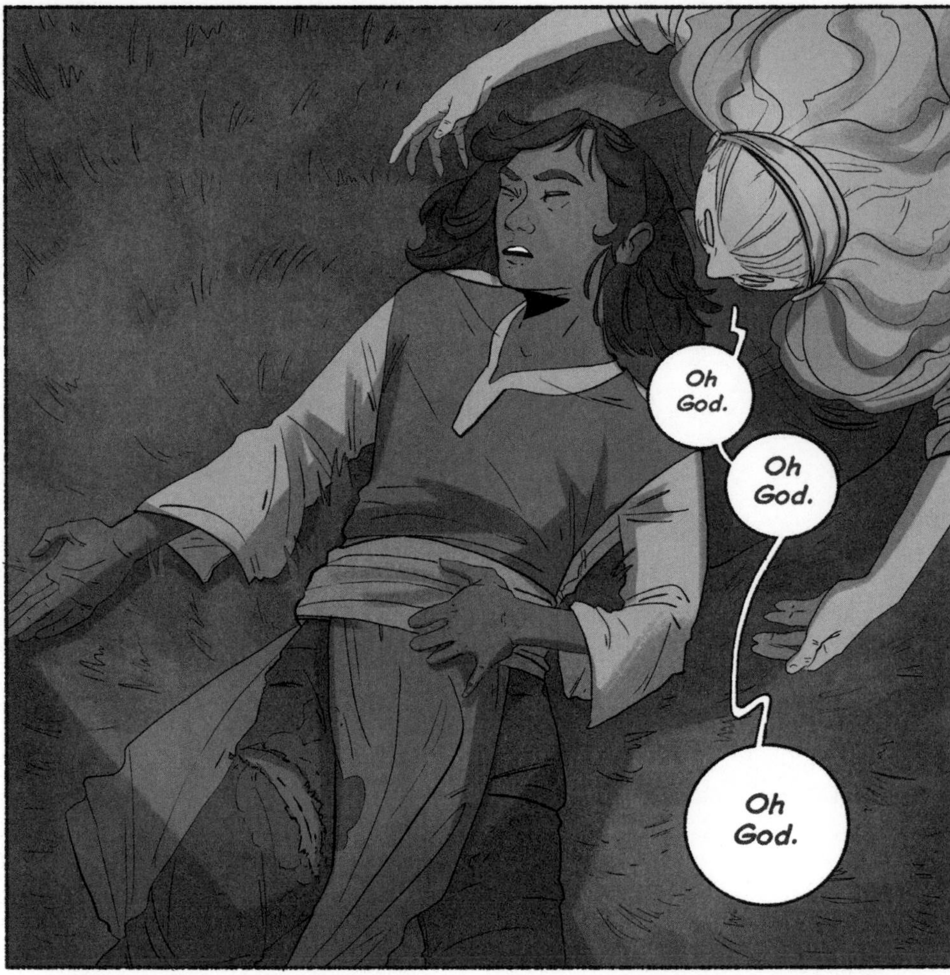
Oh God.
Oh God.
Oh God.

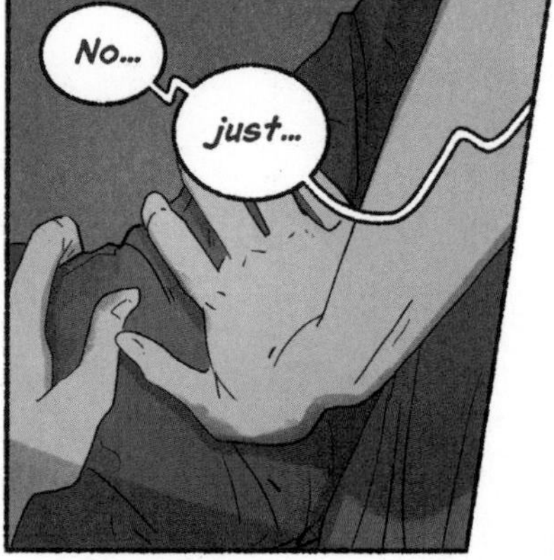
No...
just...

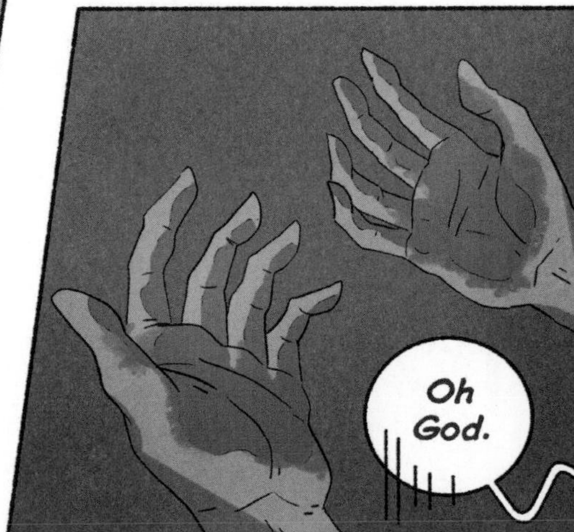
Oh God.

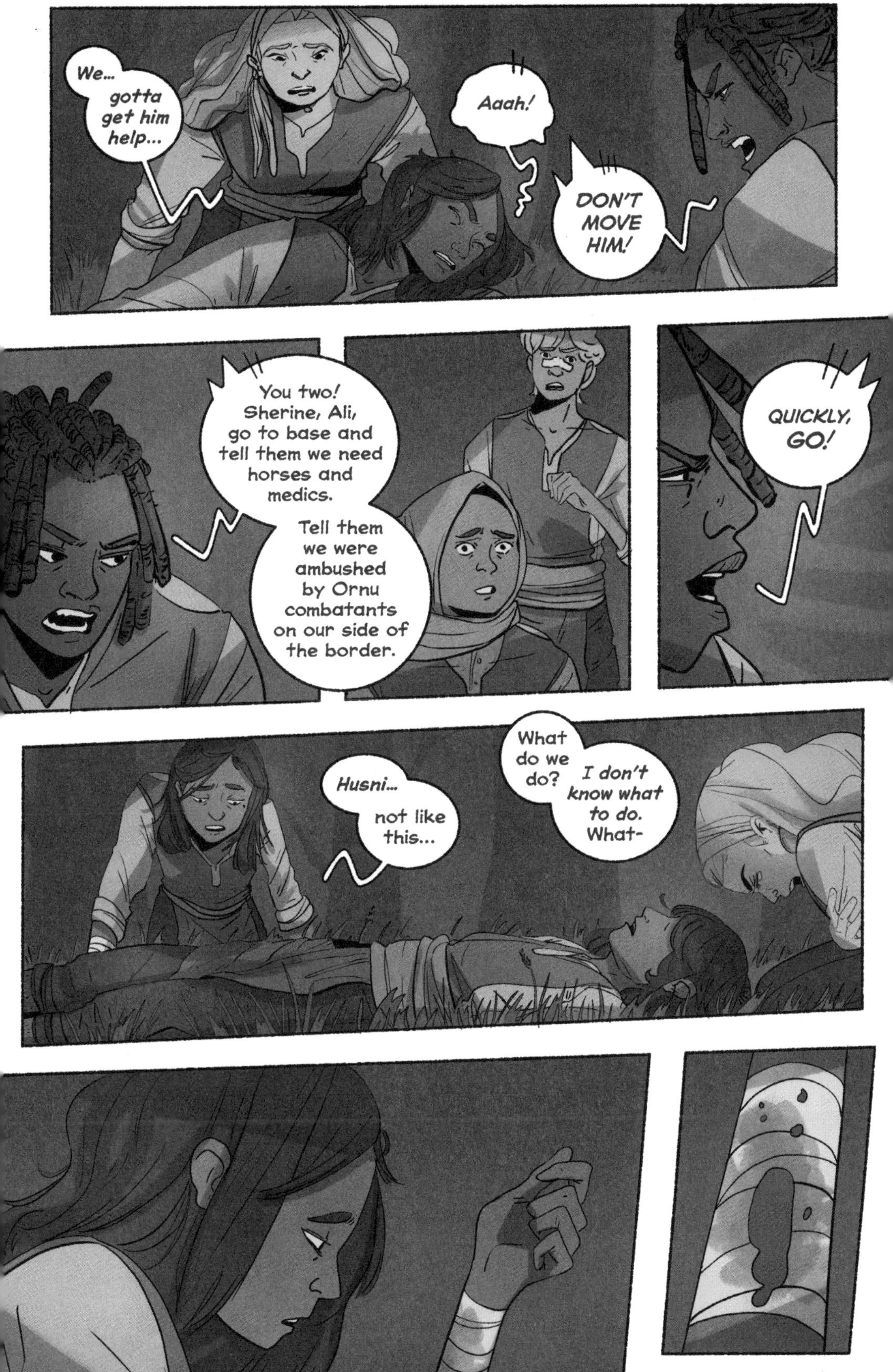
We... gotta get him help...
Aaah!
DON'T MOVE HIM!
You two! Sherine, Ali, go to base and tell them we need horses and medics.
Tell them we were ambushed by Ornu combatants on our side of the border.
QUICKLY, GO!
Husni... not like this...
What do we do?
I don't know what to do. What-

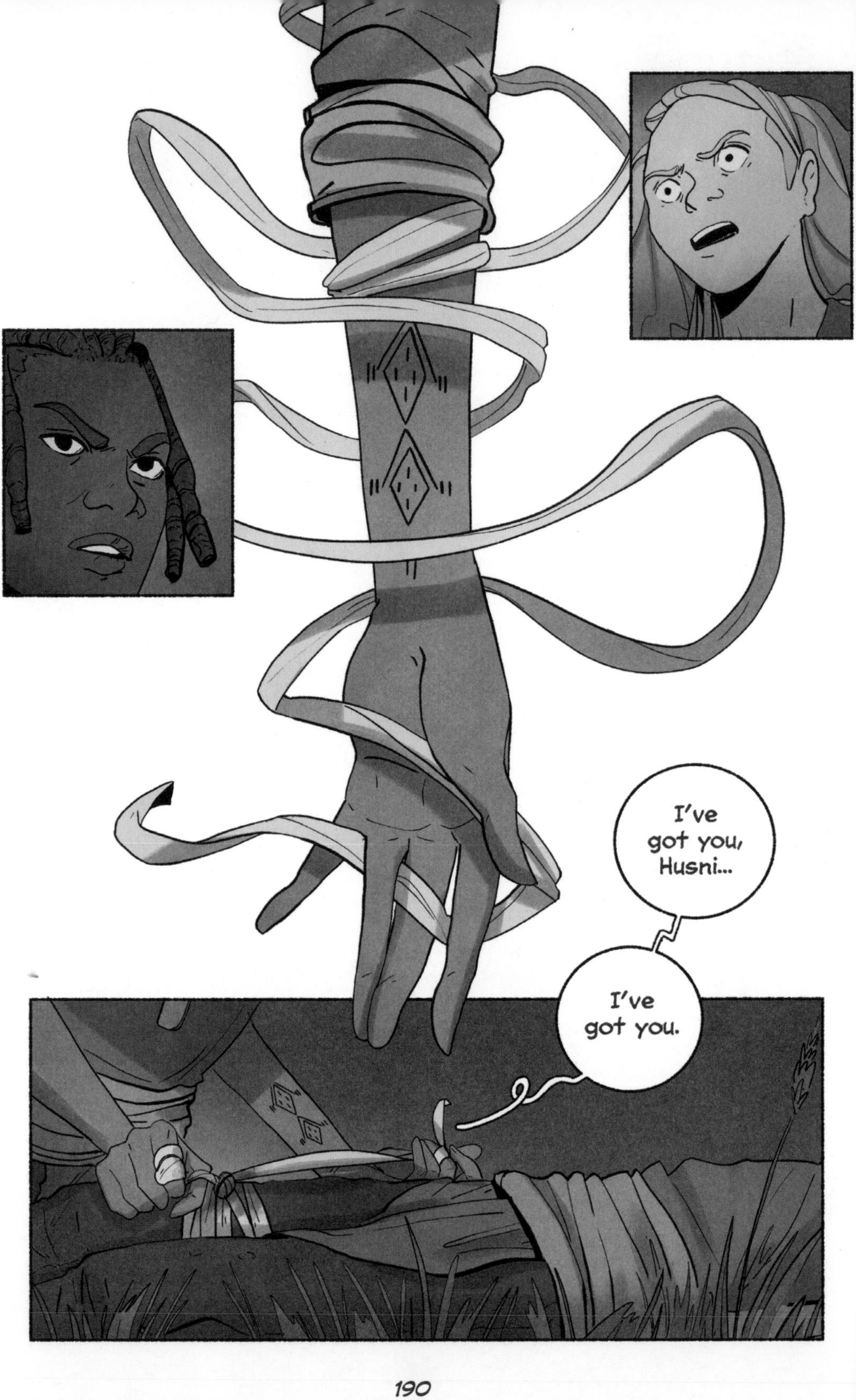
I've got you, Husni...
I've got you.

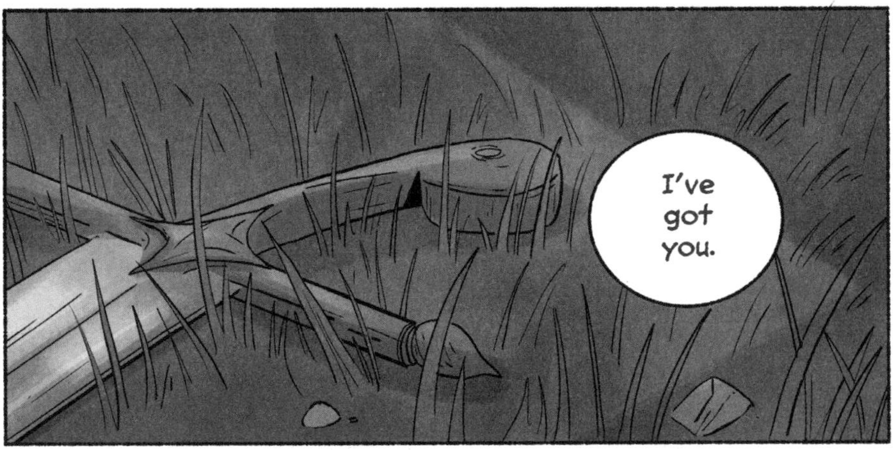
I've got you.

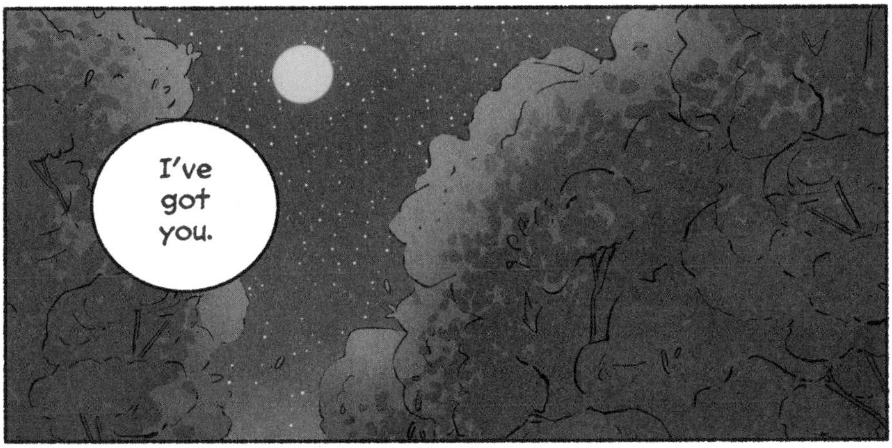
I've got you.

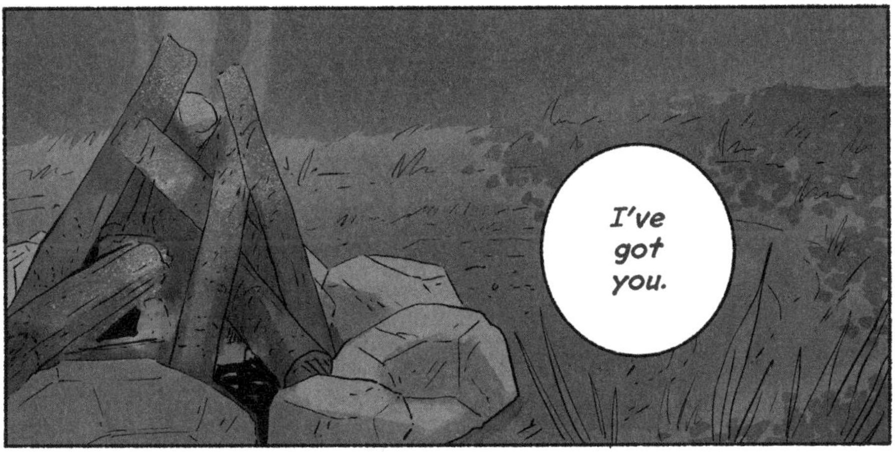
I've got you.

CHAPTER 10

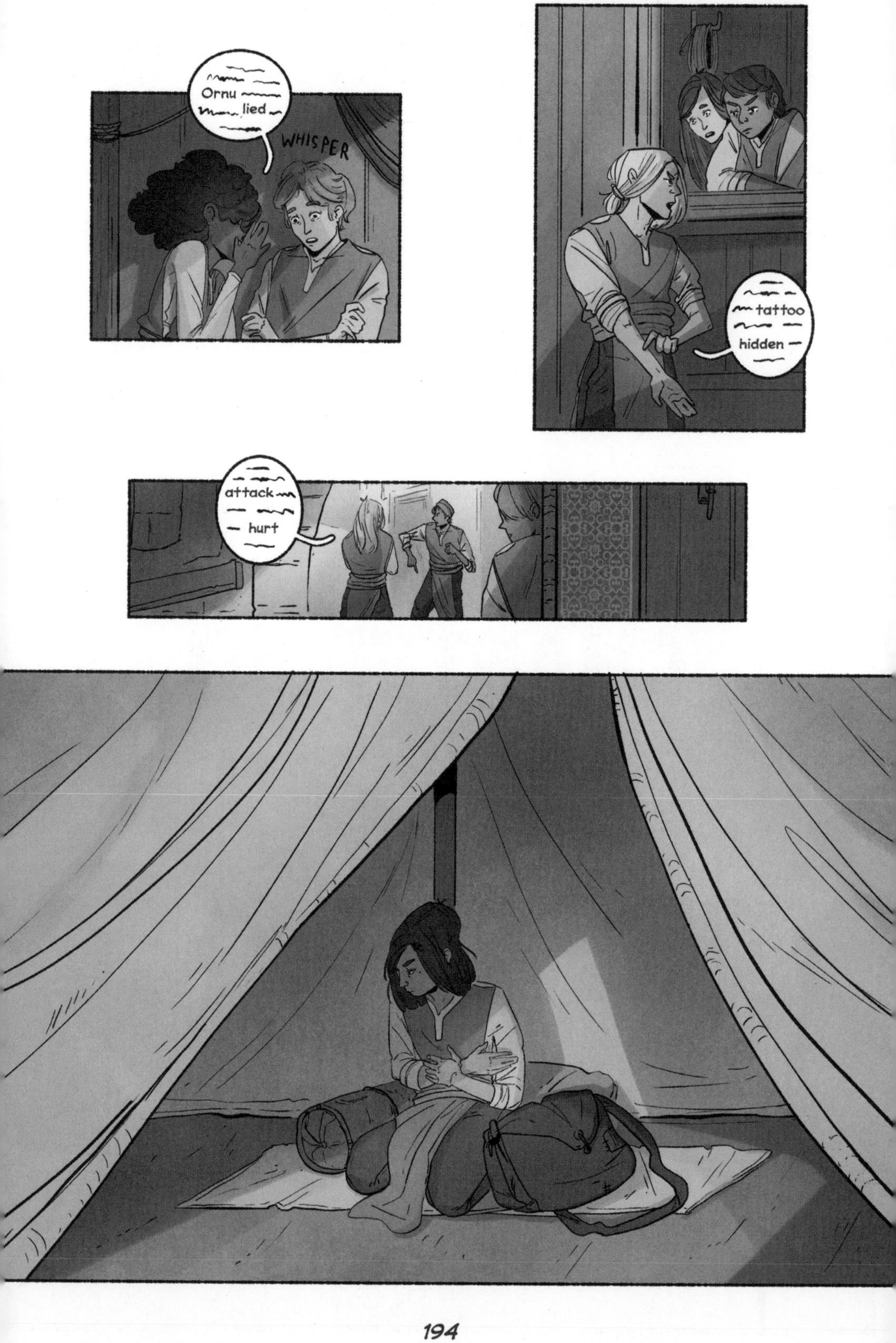
Ornu lied
WHISPER
tattoo hidden
attack hurt

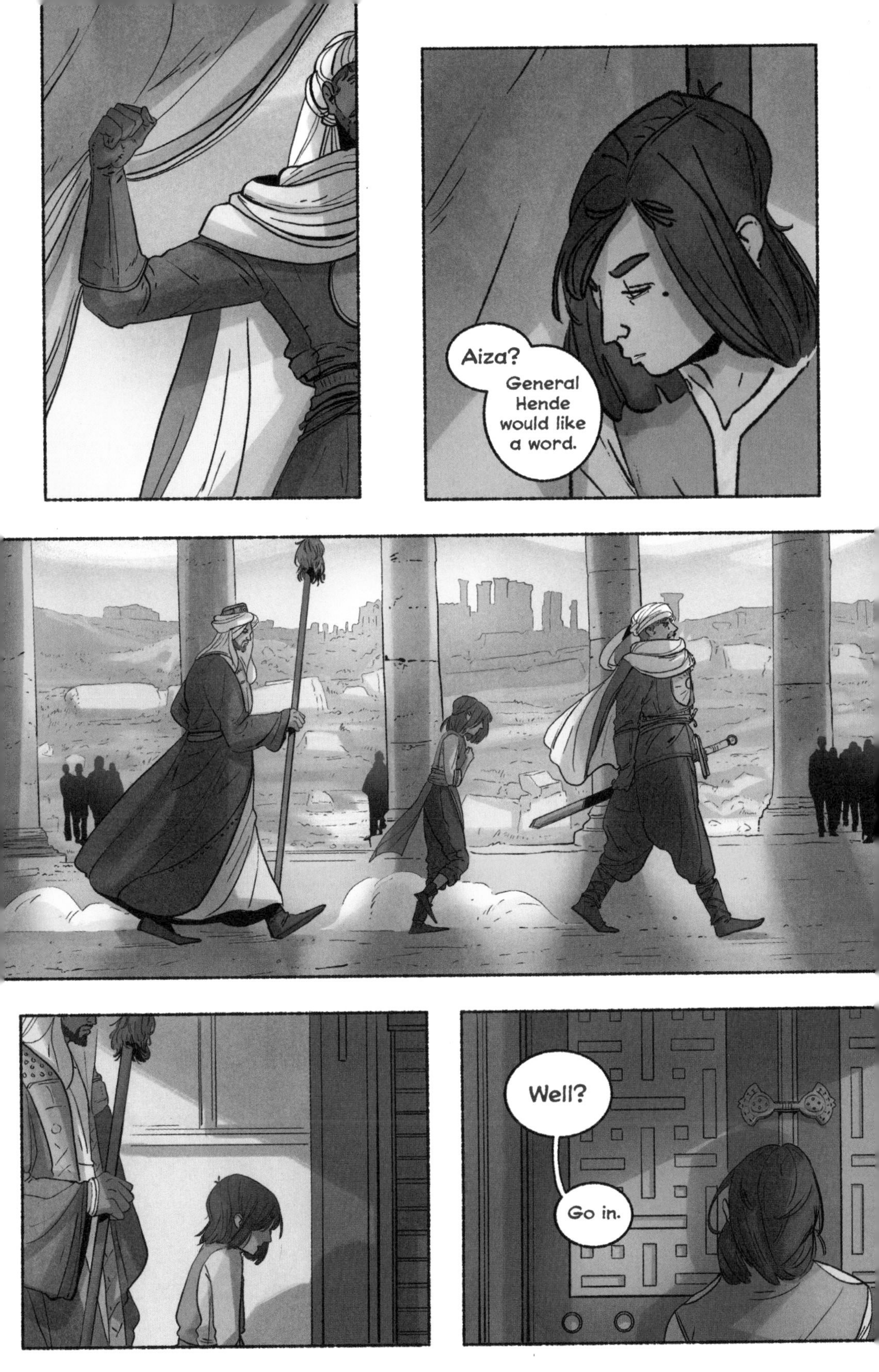
Aiza?
General Hende would like a word.
Well?
Go in.

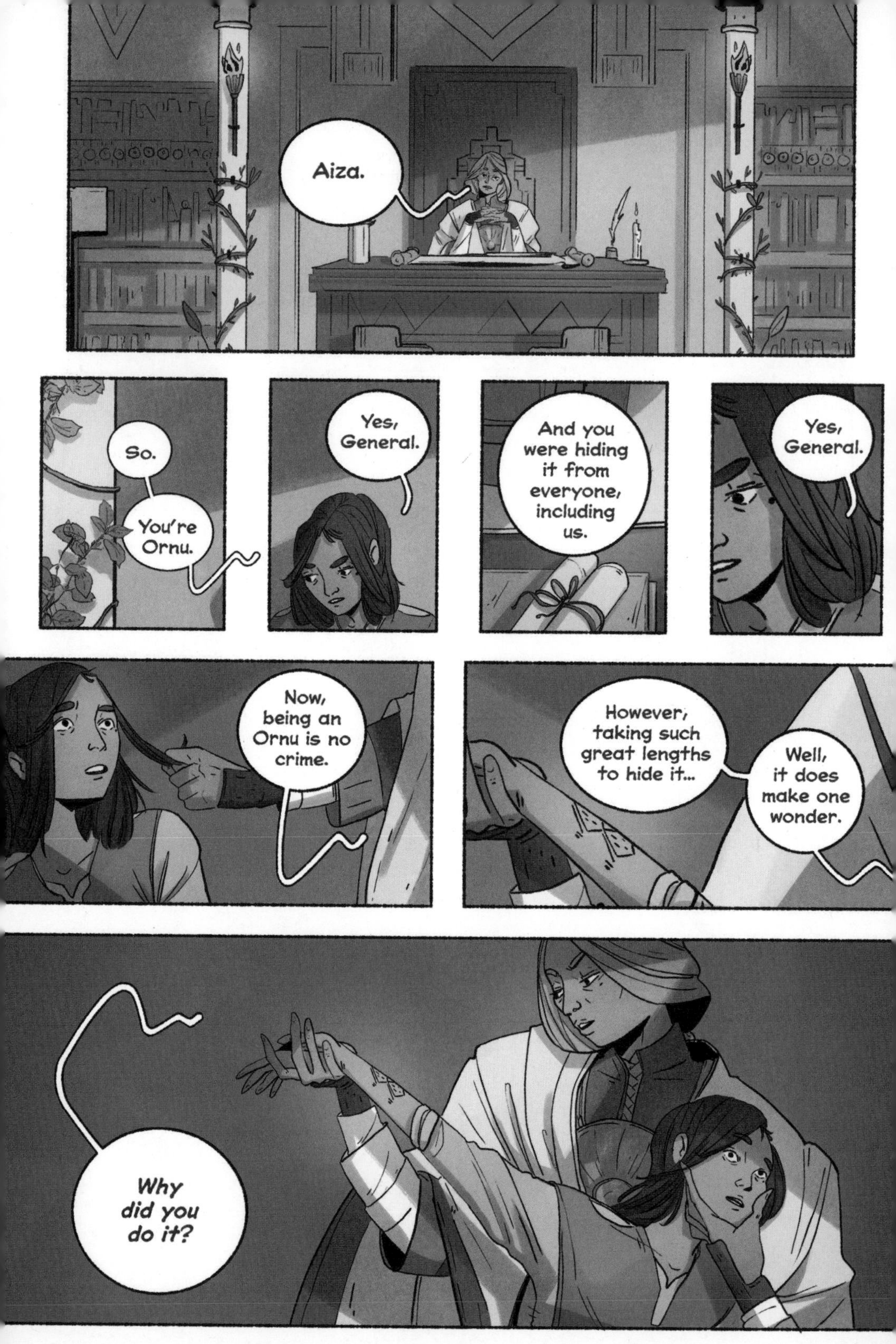

Aiza.
So.
You're Ornu.
Yes, General.
And you were hiding it from everyone, including us.
Yes, General.
Now, being an Ornu is no crime.
However, taking such great lengths to hide it...
Well, it does make one wonder.
Why did you do it?

I...

I made a promise.

I thought... I thought it was the right thing to do.

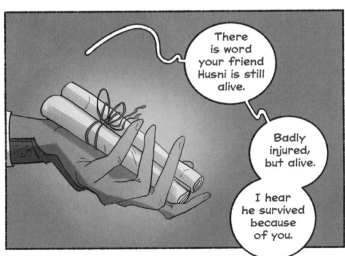

There is word your friend Husni is still alive.

Badly injured, but alive.

I hear he survived because of you.

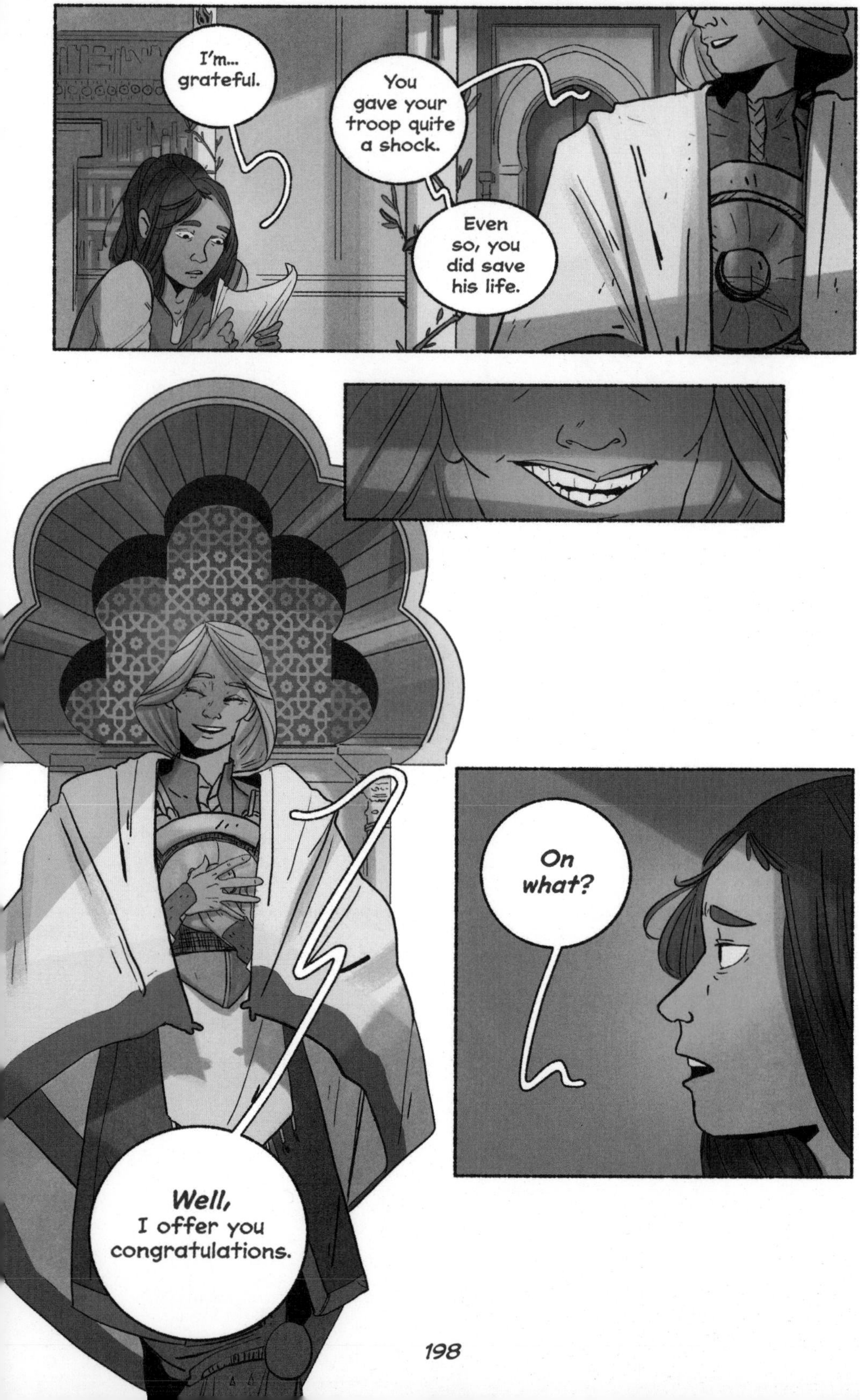
I'm... grateful.
You gave your troop quite a shock.
Even so, you did save his life.
On what?
Well, I offer you congratulations.

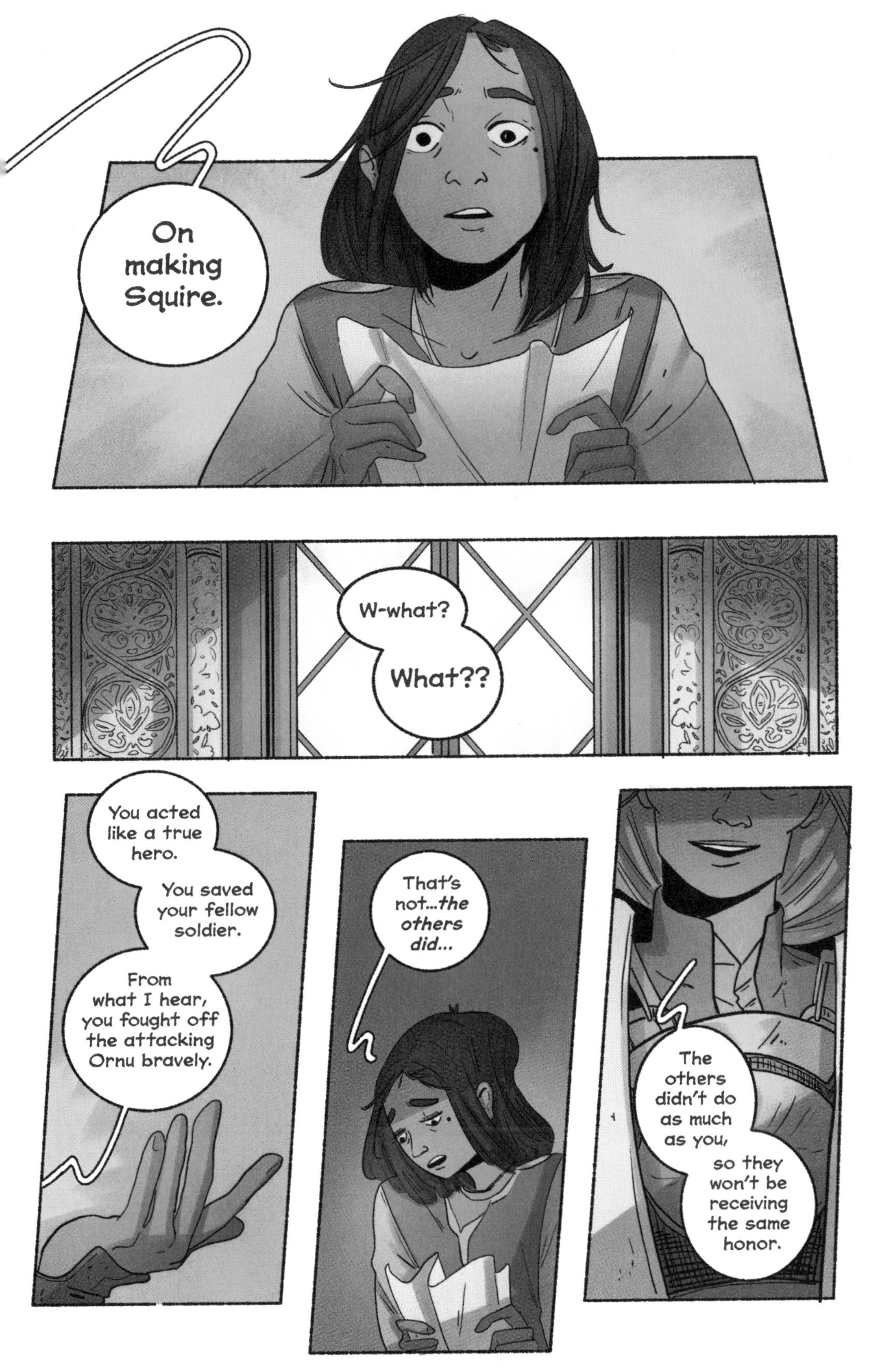

On making Squire.
W-what?
What??
You acted like a true hero.
You saved your fellow soldier.
From what I hear, you fought off the attacking Ornu bravely.
That's not...*the others did*...
The others didn't do as much as you,
so they won't be receiving the same honor.

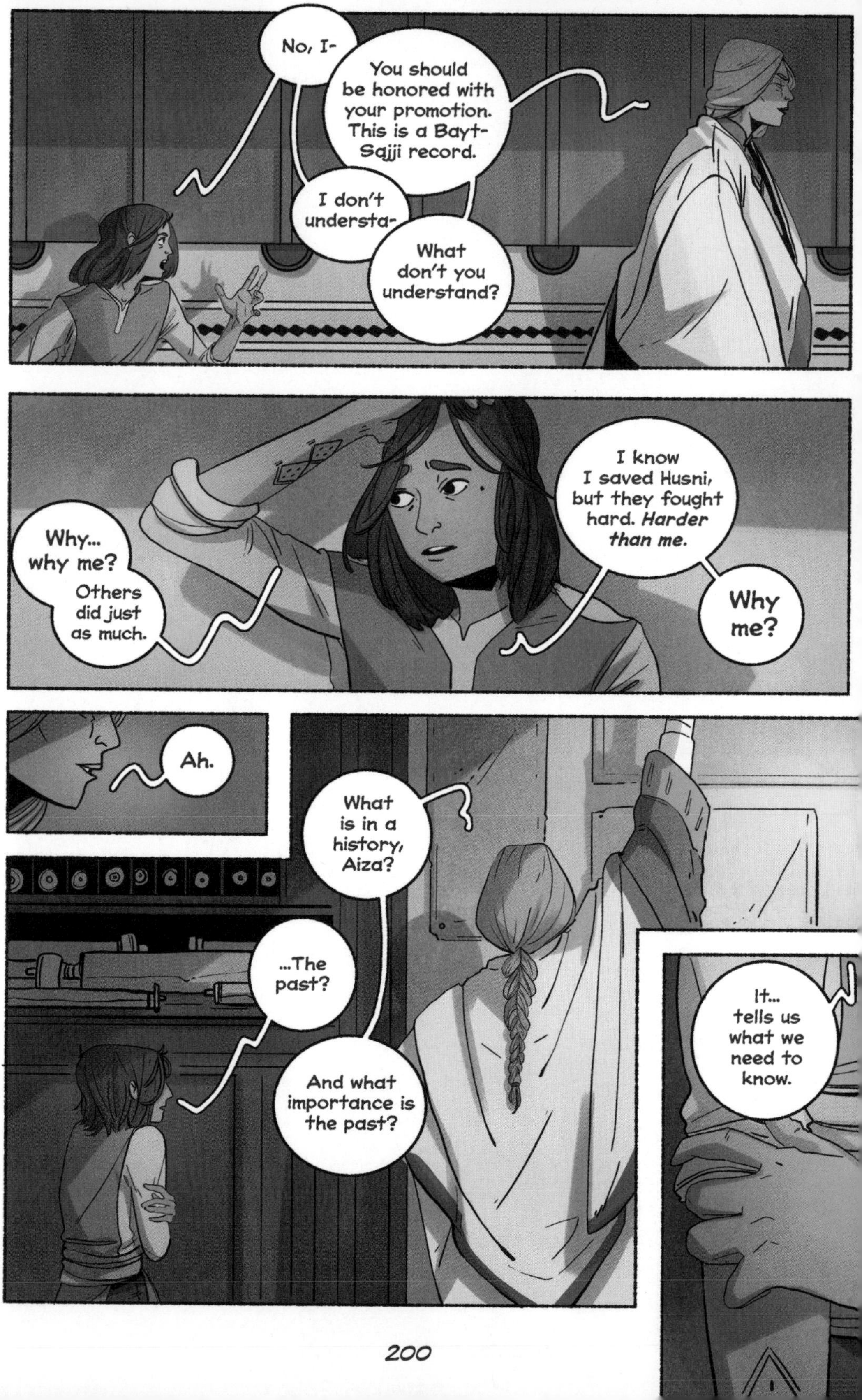
No, I-
You should be honored with your promotion. This is a Bayt-Sajji record.
I don't understa-
What don't you understand?
Why... why me?
Others did just as much.
I know I saved Husni, but they fought hard. *Harder than me.*
Why me?
Ah.
What is in a history, Aiza?
...The past?
And what importance is the past?
It... tells us what we need to know.

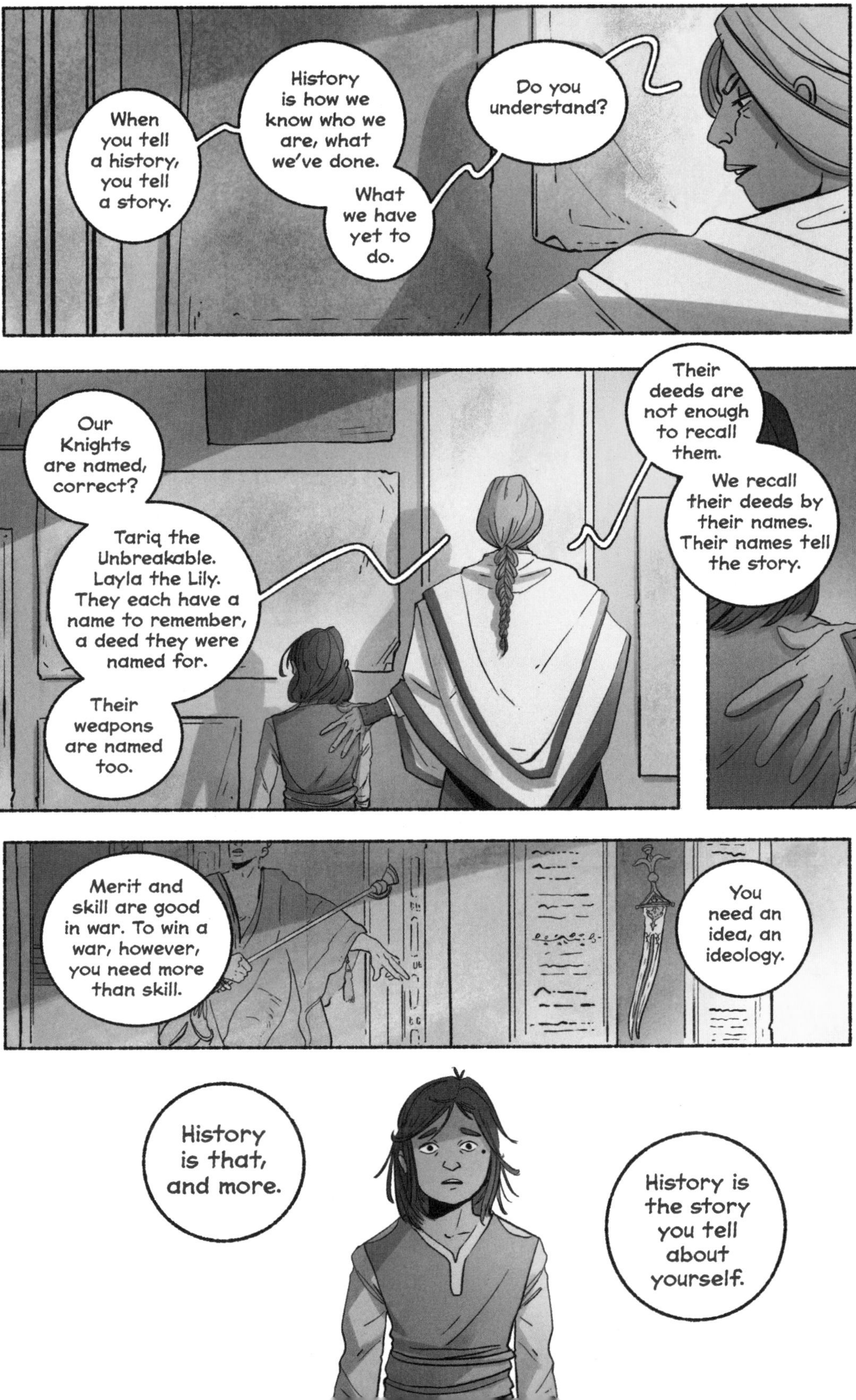
When you tell a history, you tell a story.
History is how we know who we are, what we've done.
What we have yet to do.
Do you understand?
Our Knights are named, correct?
Tariq the Unbreakable. Layla the Lily. They each have a name to remember, a deed they were named for.
Their weapons are named too.
Their deeds are not enough to recall them.
We recall their deeds by their names. Their names tell the story.
Merit and skill are good in war. To win a war, however, you need more than skill.
You need an idea, an ideology.
History is that, and more.
History is the story you tell about yourself.

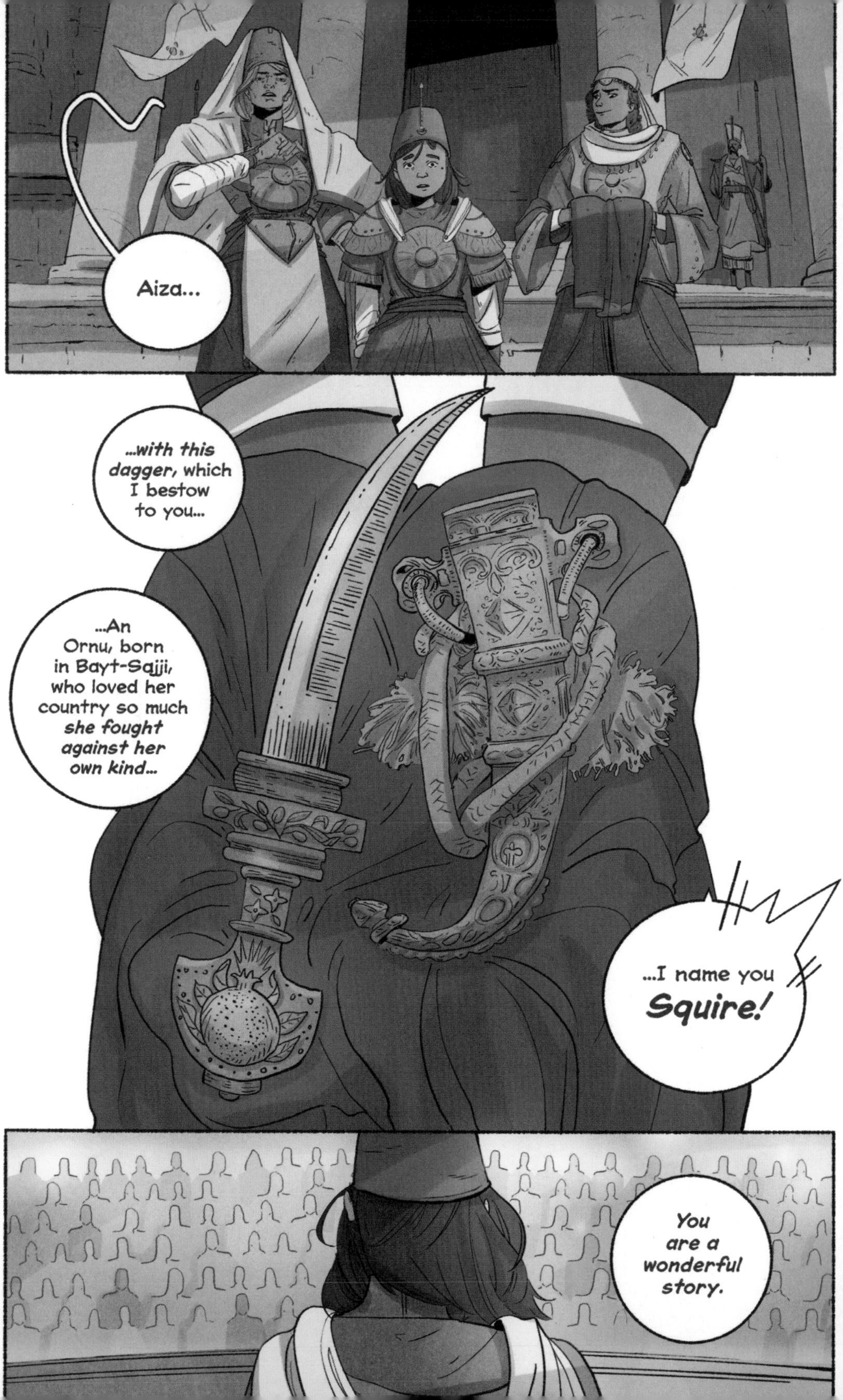
Aiza...
...with this dagger, which I bestow to you...
...An Ornu, born in Bayt-Sajji, who loved her country so much she fought against her own kind...
...I name you Squire!
You are a wonderful story.

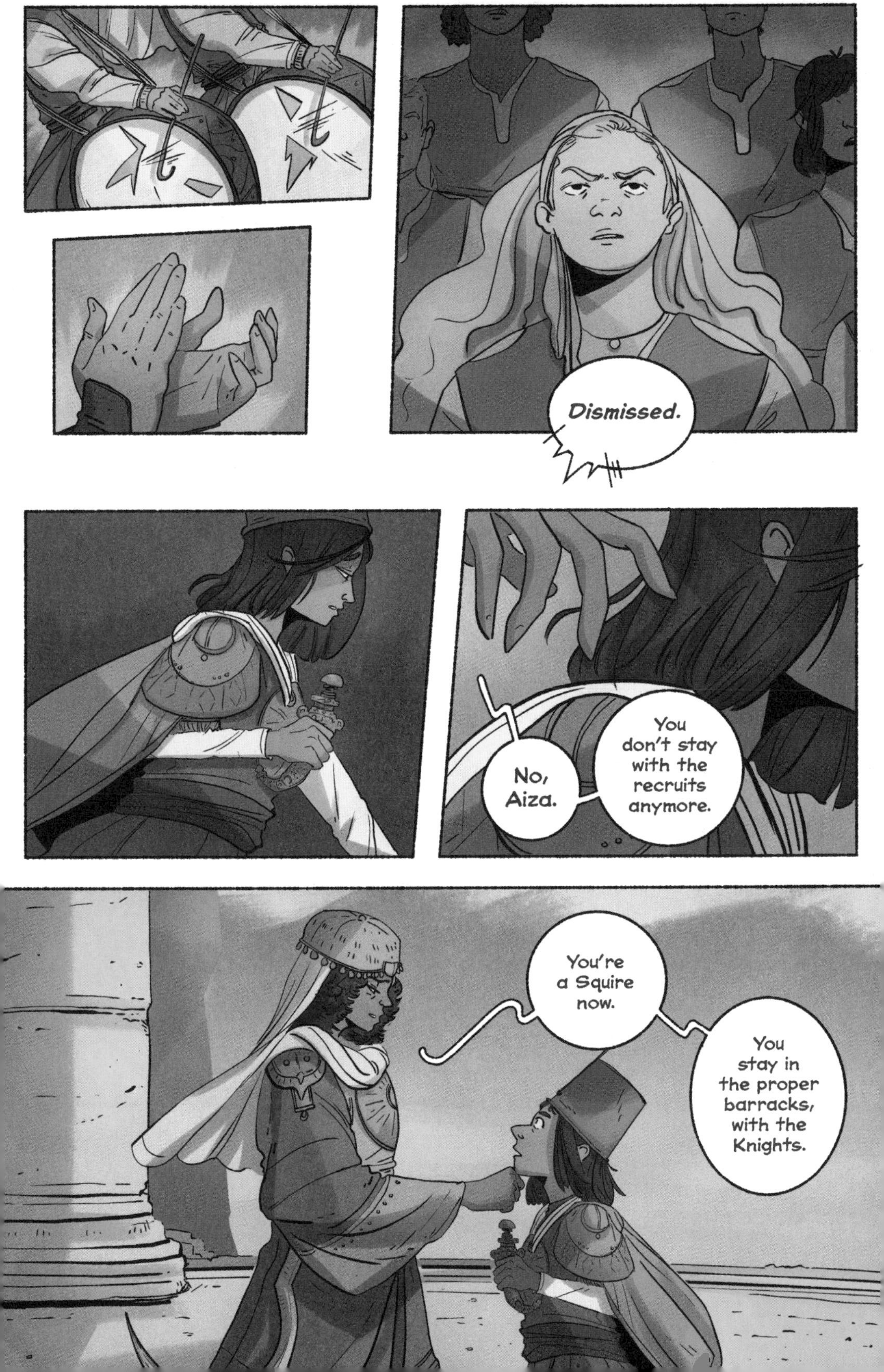
Dismissed.
No, Aiza.
You don't stay with the recruits anymore.
You're a Squire now.
You stay in the proper barracks, with the Knights.

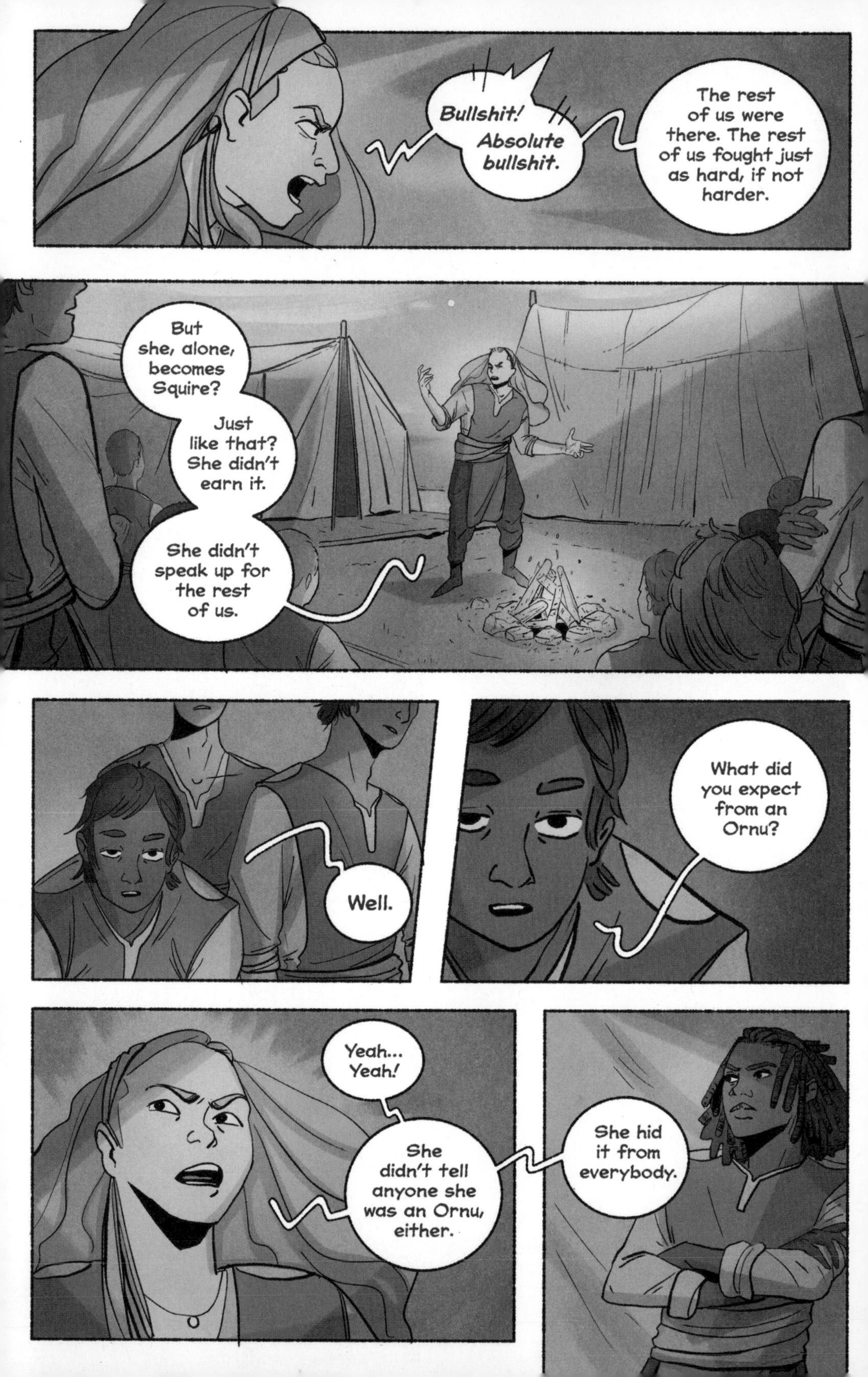
Bullshit! Absolute bullshit.
The rest of us were there. The rest of us fought just as hard, if not harder.
But she, alone, becomes Squire?
Just like that? She didn't earn it.
She didn't speak up for the rest of us.
Well.
What did you expect from an Ornu?
Yeah... Yeah!
She didn't tell anyone she was an Ornu, either.
She hid it from everybody.

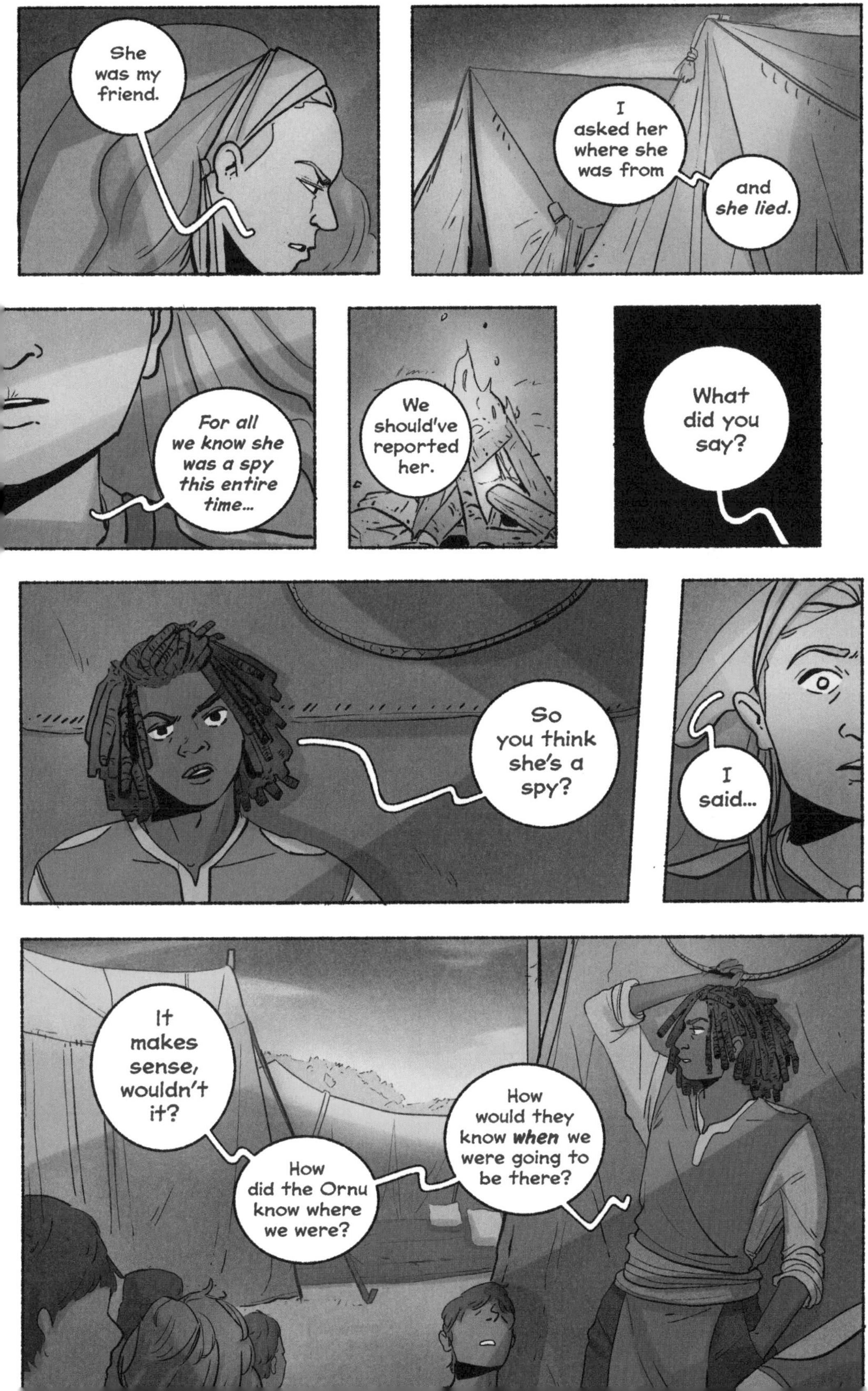

She was my friend.
I asked her where she was from
and *she lied.*
For all we know she was a spy this entire time...
We should've reported her.
What did you say?
So you think she's a spy?
I said...
It makes sense, wouldn't it?
How did the Ornu know where we were?
How would they know ***when*** we were going to be there?

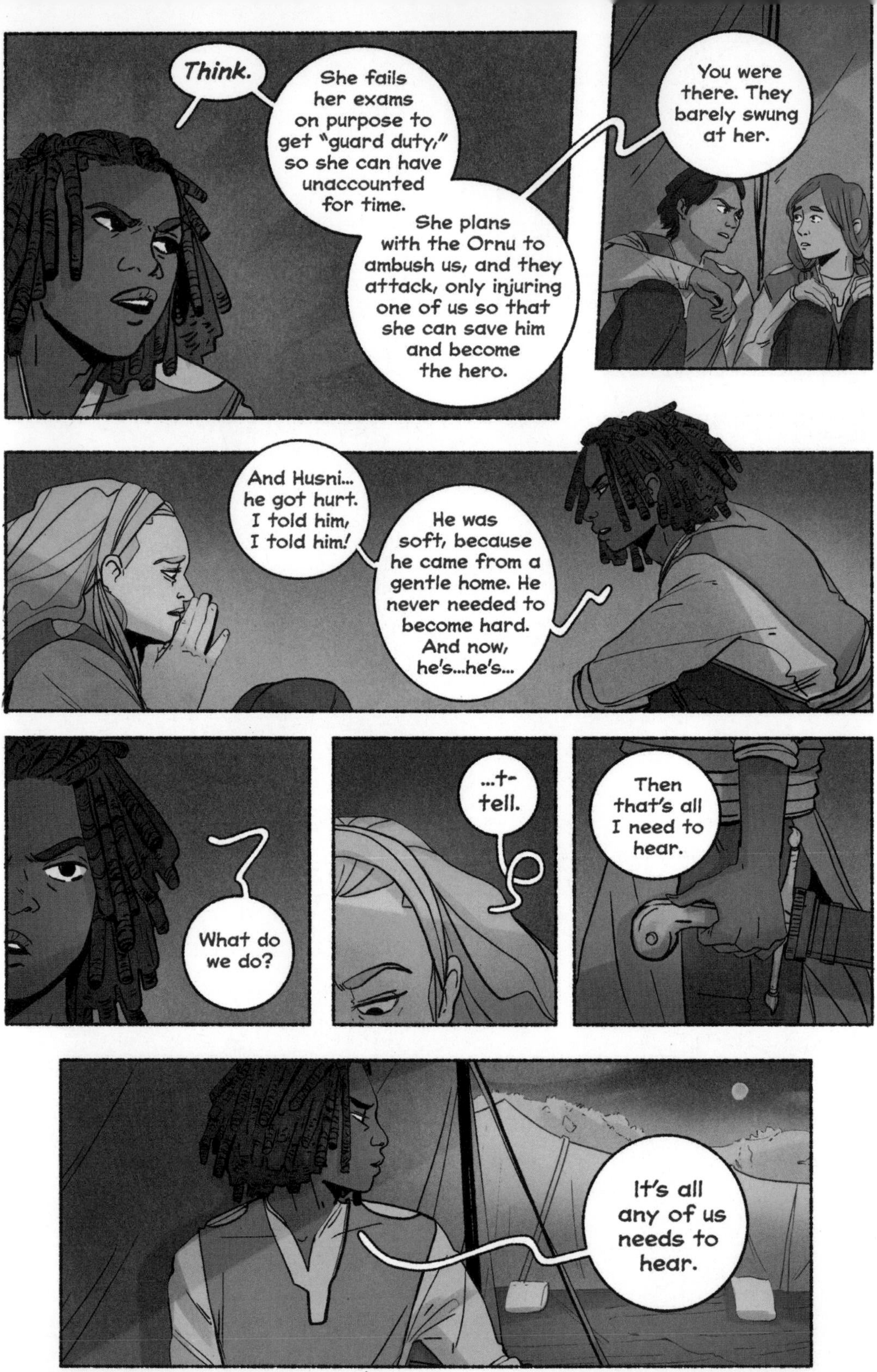
Think.
She fails her exams on purpose to get "guard duty," so she can have unaccounted for time.
She plans with the Ornu to ambush us, and they attack, only injuring one of us so that she can save him and become the hero.
You were there. They barely swung at her.
And Husni... he got hurt. I told him, I told him!
He was soft, because he came from a gentle home. He never needed to become hard. And now, he's...he's...
What do we do?
...t-tell.
Then that's all I need to hear.
It's all any of us needs to hear.

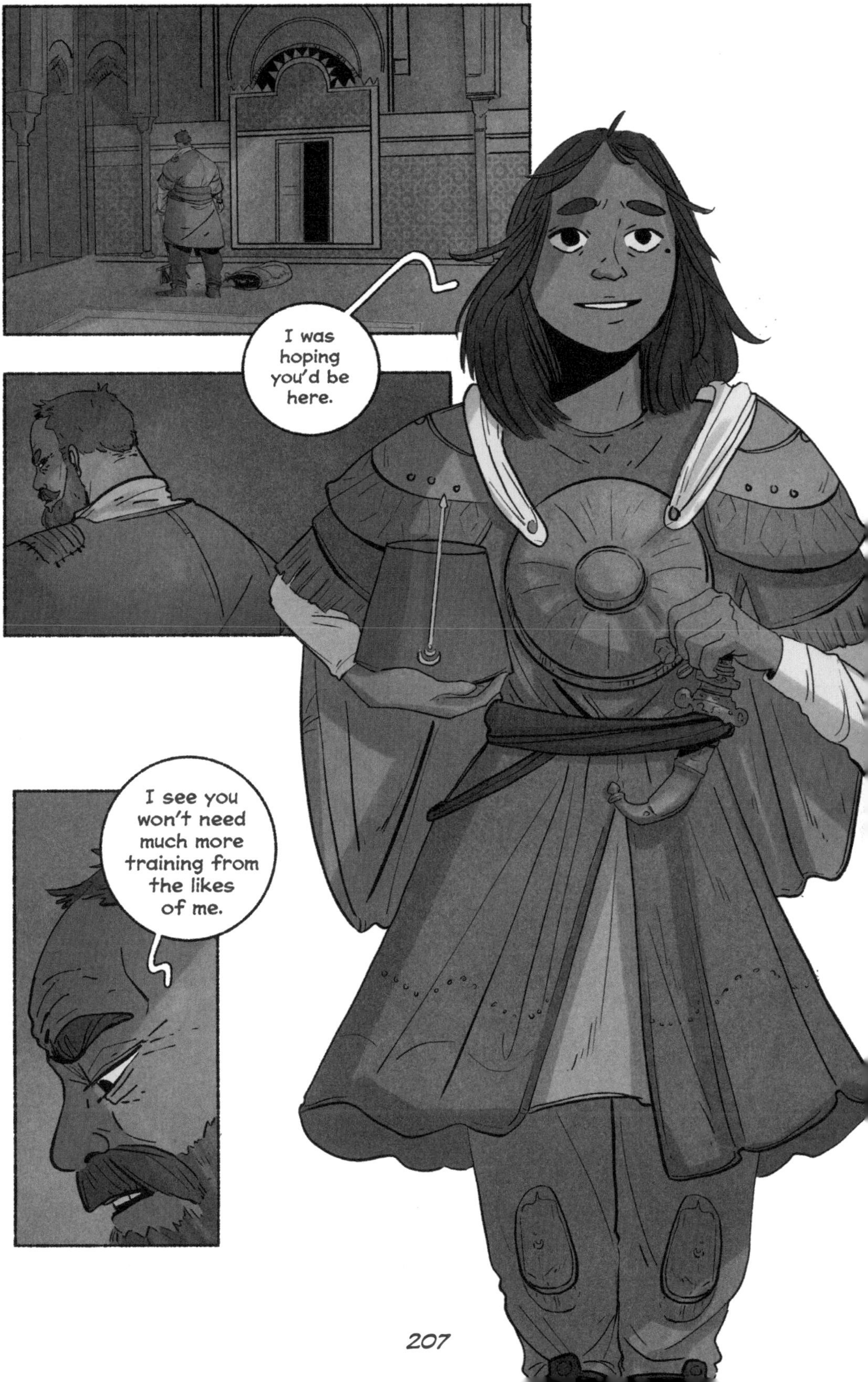
I was hoping you'd be here.
I see you won't need much more training from the likes of me.

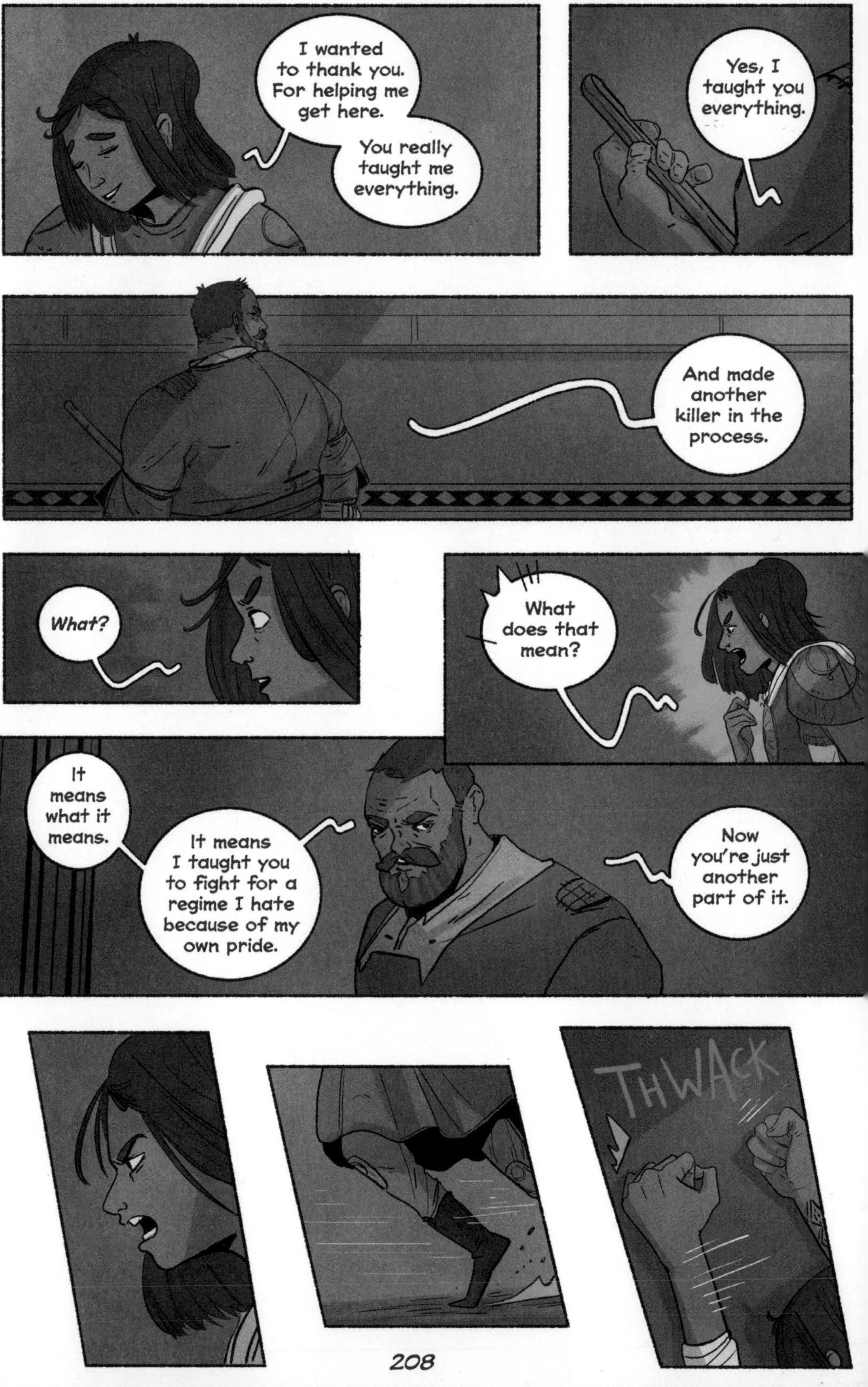
I wanted to thank you. For helping me get here.
You really taught me everything.
Yes, I taught you everything.
And made another killer in the process.
What?
What does that mean?
It means what it means.
It means I taught you to fight for a regime I hate because of my own pride.
Now you're just another part of it.
THWACK

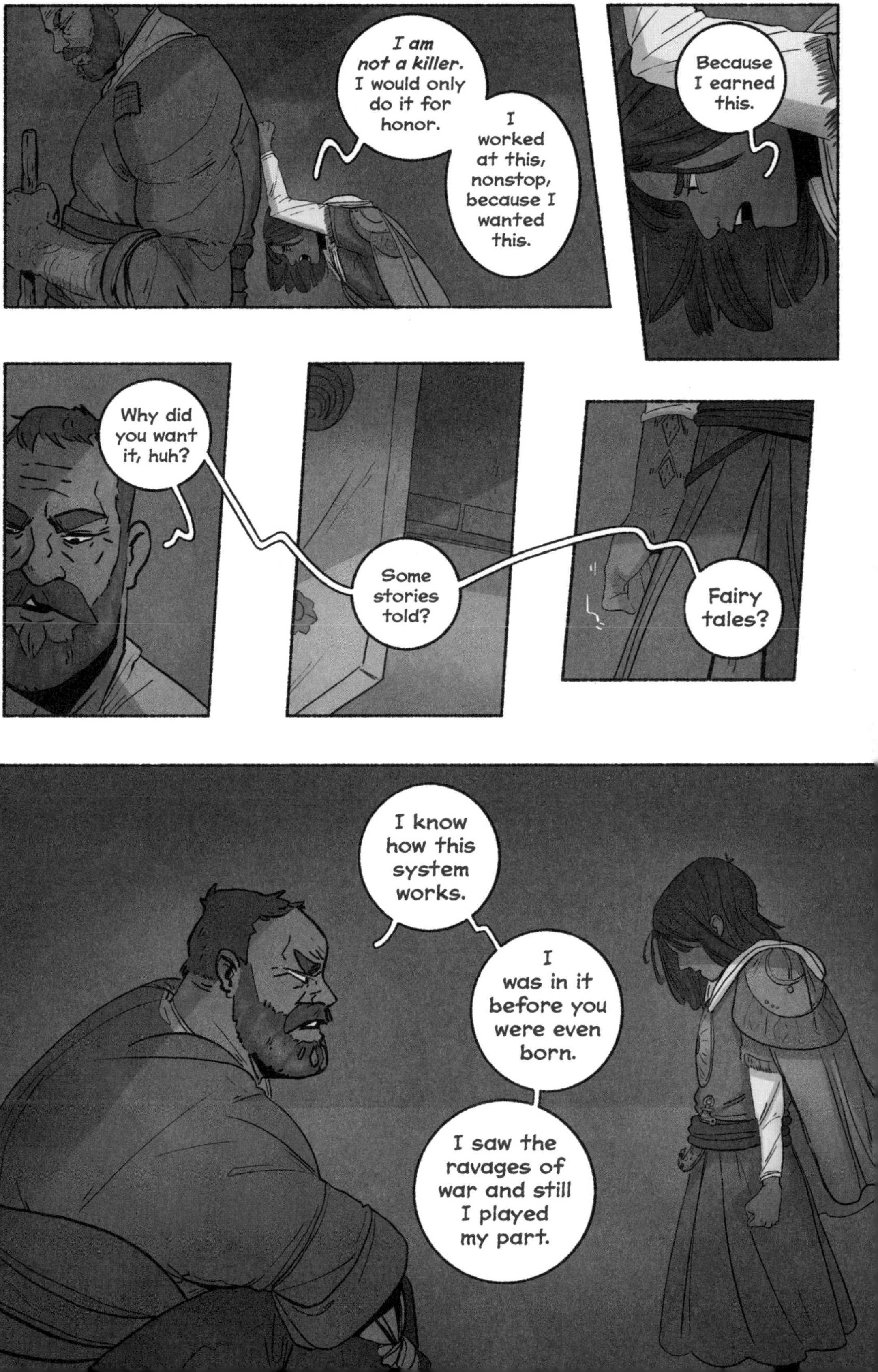

I am not a killer. I would only do it for honor.
I worked at this, nonstop, because I wanted this.
Because I earned this.
Why did you want it, huh?
Some stories told?
Fairy tales?
I know how this system works.
I was in it before you were even born.
I saw the ravages of war and still I played my part.

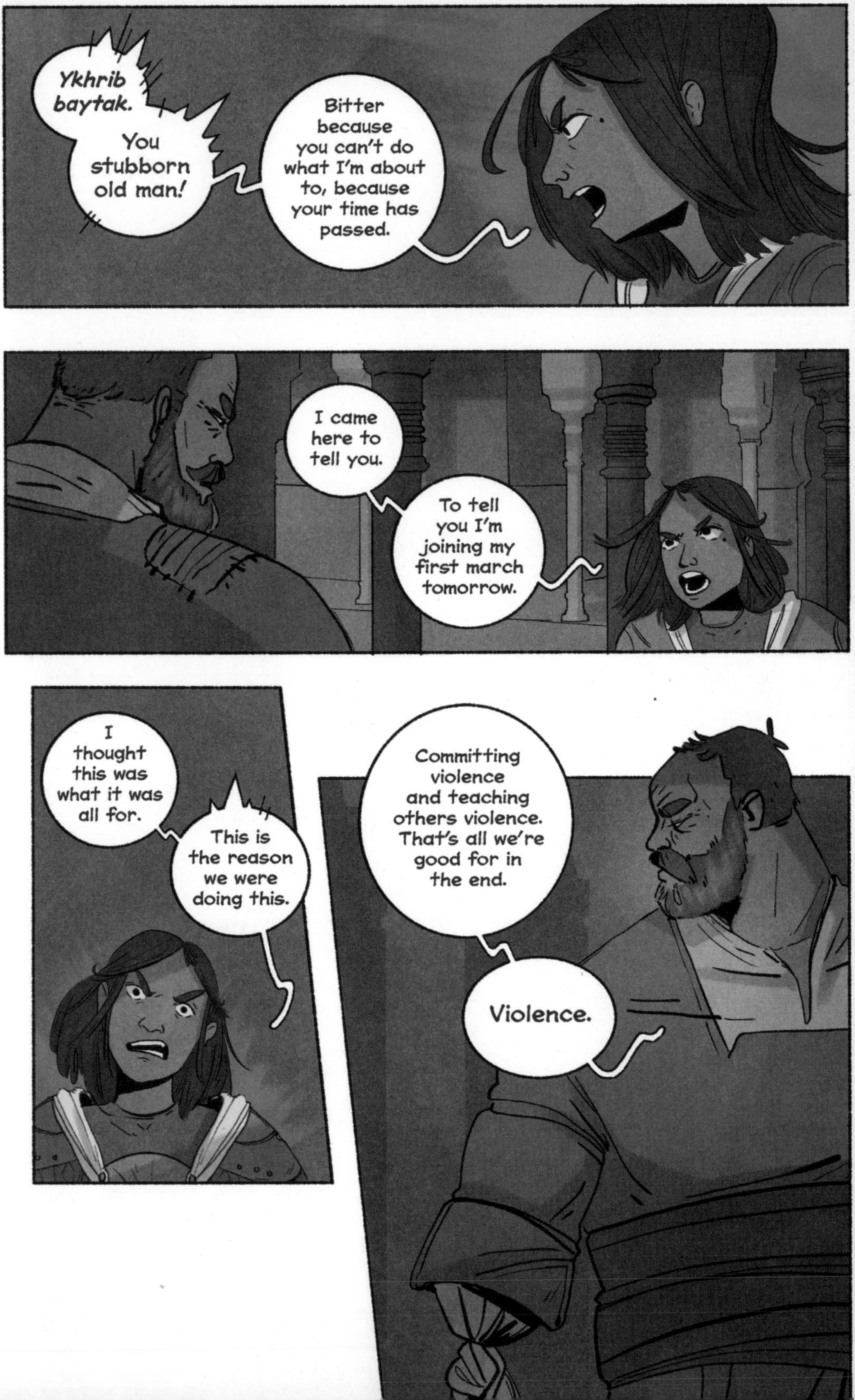

Ykhrib baytak.
You stubborn old man!
Bitter because you can't do what I'm about to, because your time has passed.
I came here to tell you.
To tell you I'm joining my first march tomorrow.
I thought this was what it was all for.
This is the reason we were doing this.
Committing violence and teaching others violence. That's all we're good for in the end.
Violence.

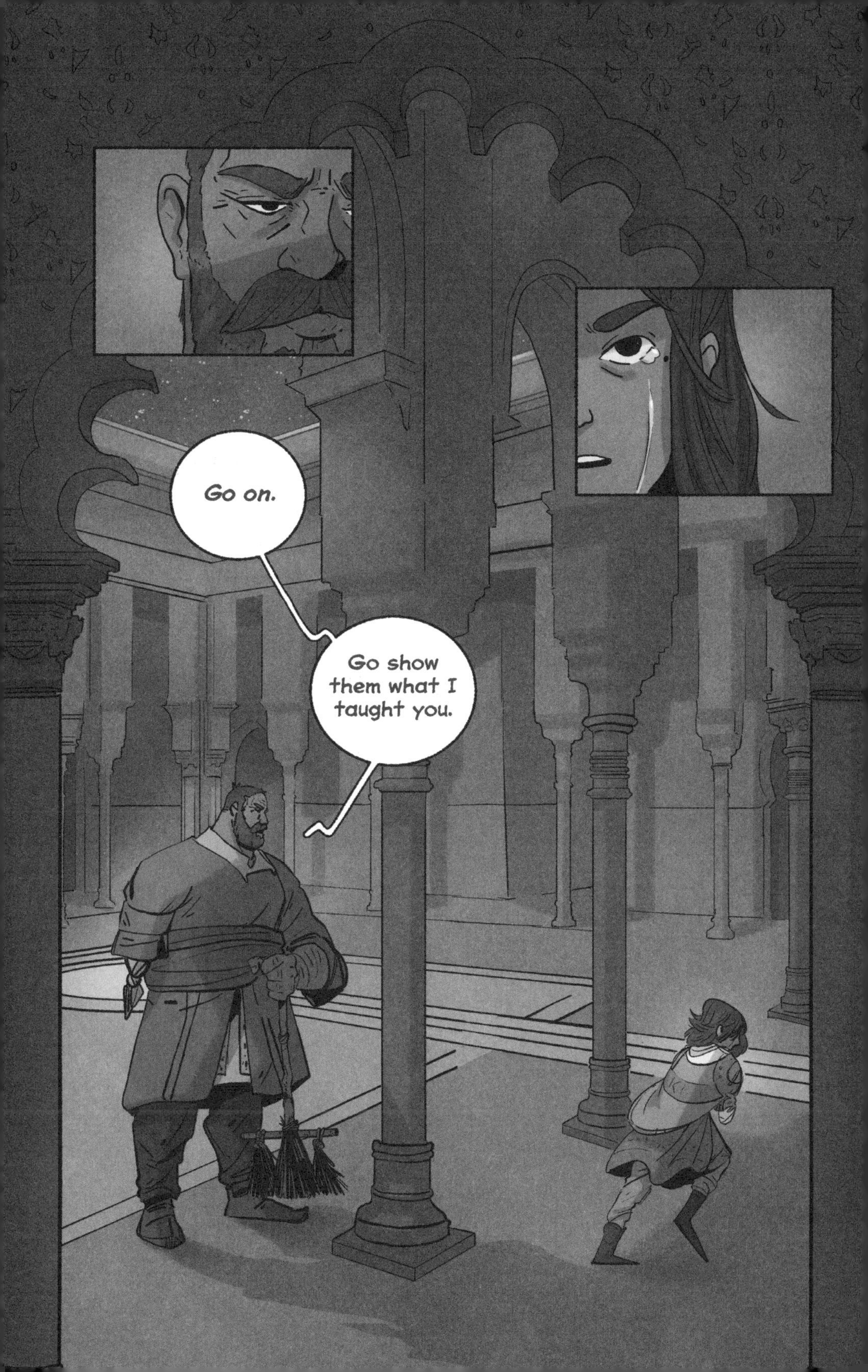
Go on.
Go show them what I taught you.

CHAPTER 11

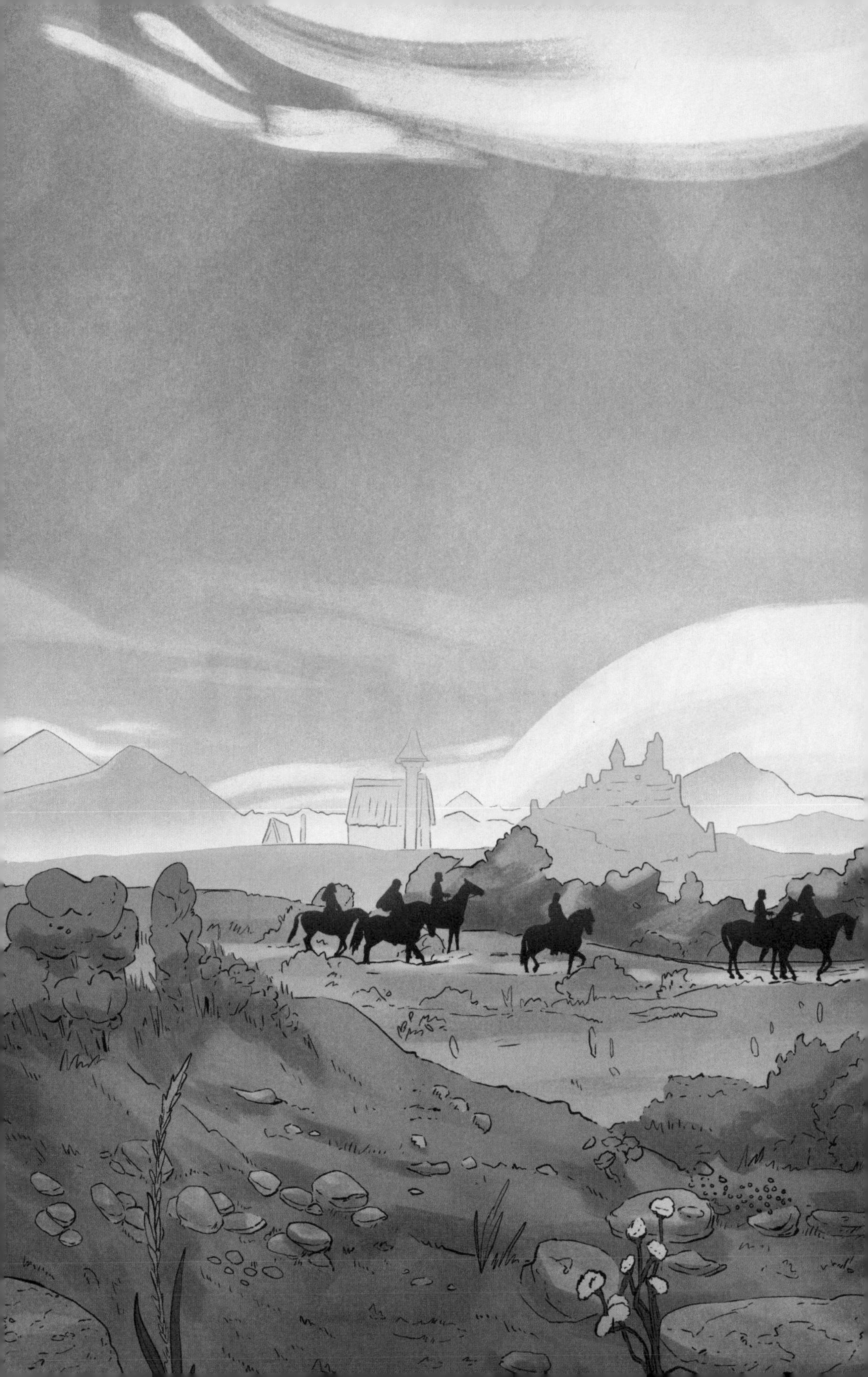

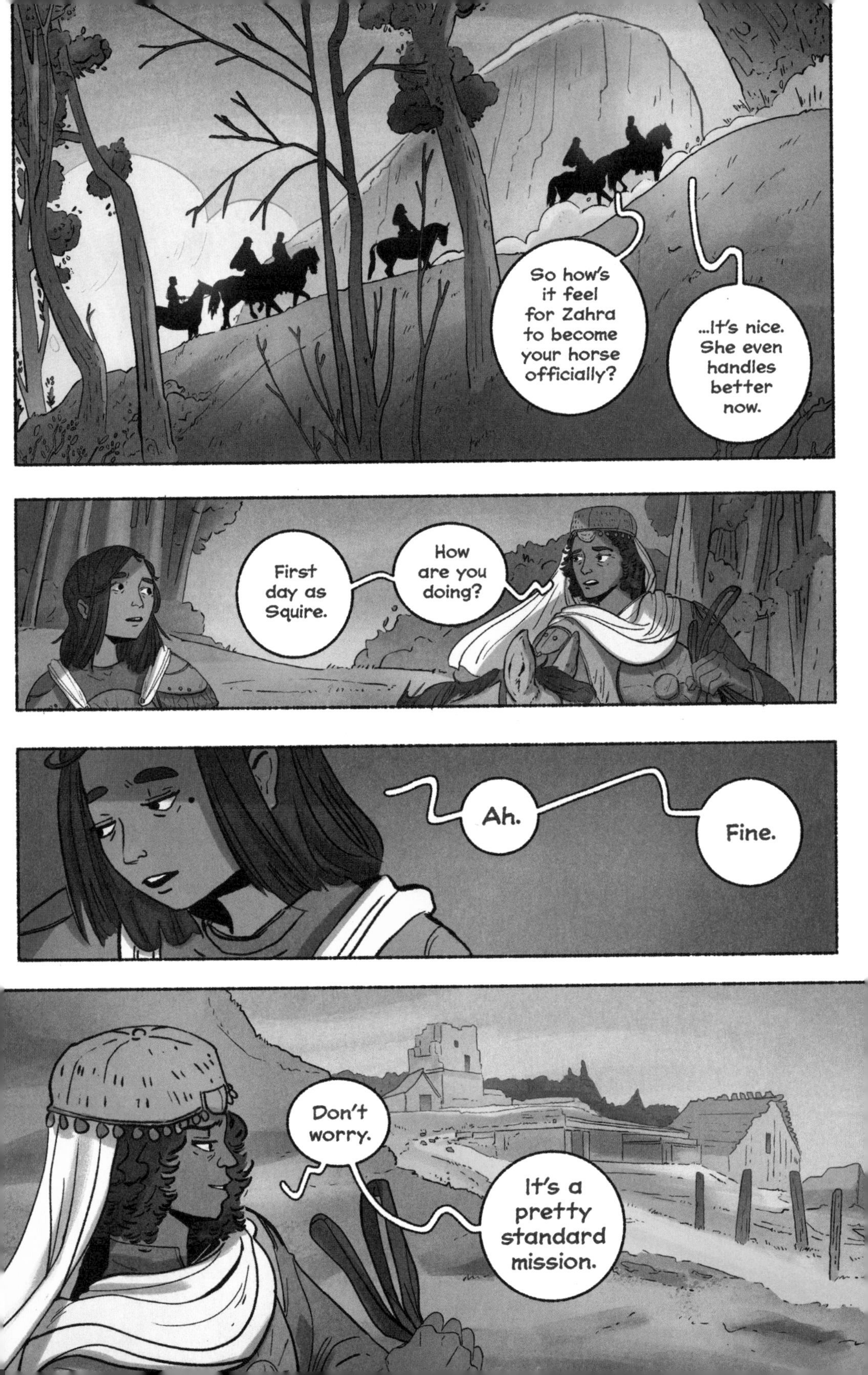

So how's it feel for Zahra to become your horse officially?
...It's nice. She even handles better now.
First day as Squire.
How are you doing?
Ah.
Fine.
Don't worry.
It's a pretty standard mission.

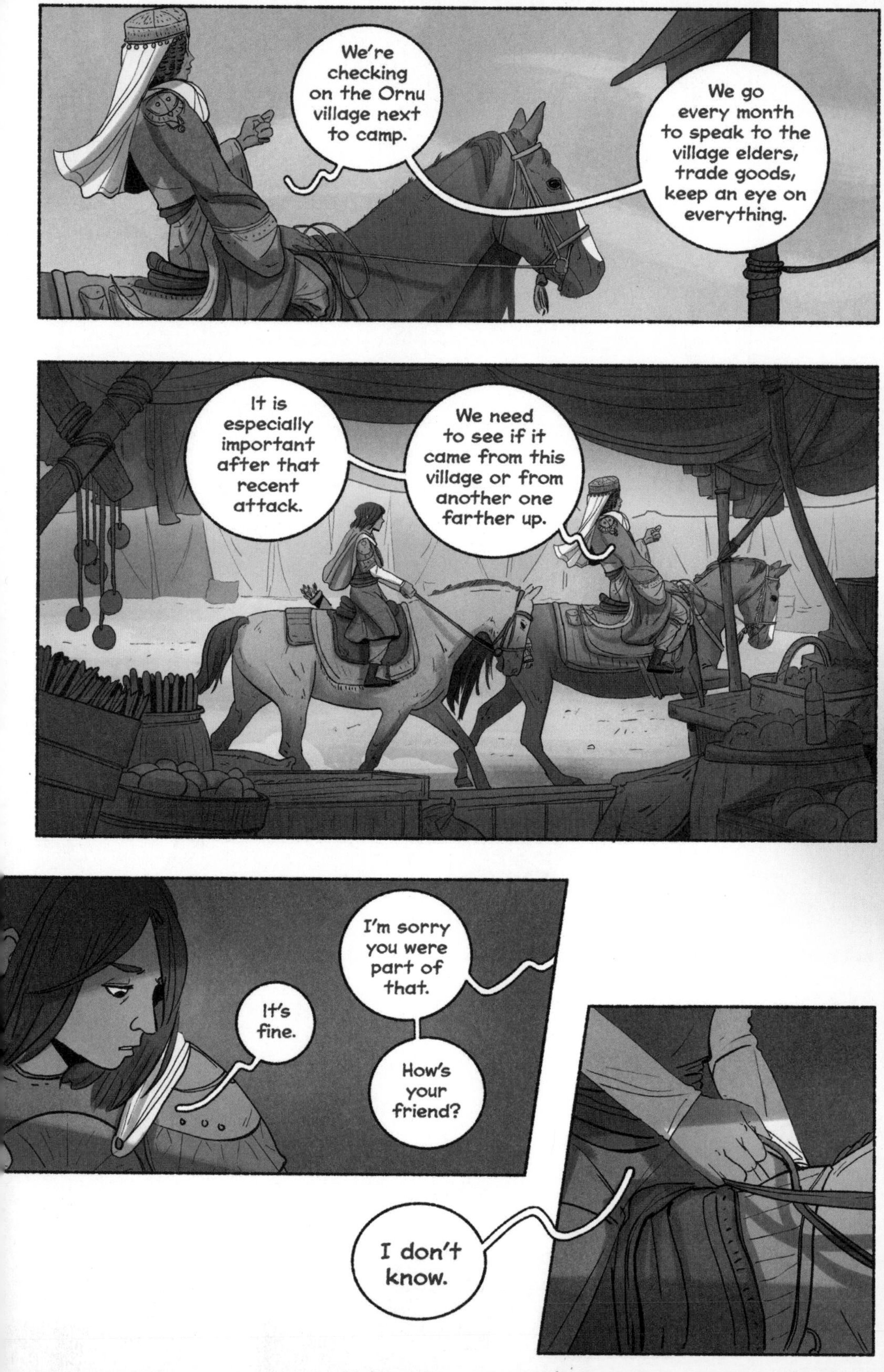
We're checking on the Ornu village next to camp.
We go every month to speak to the village elders, trade goods, keep an eye on everything.
It is especially important after that recent attack.
We need to see if it came from this village or from another one farther up.
I'm sorry you were part of that.
It's fine.
How's your friend?
I don't know.

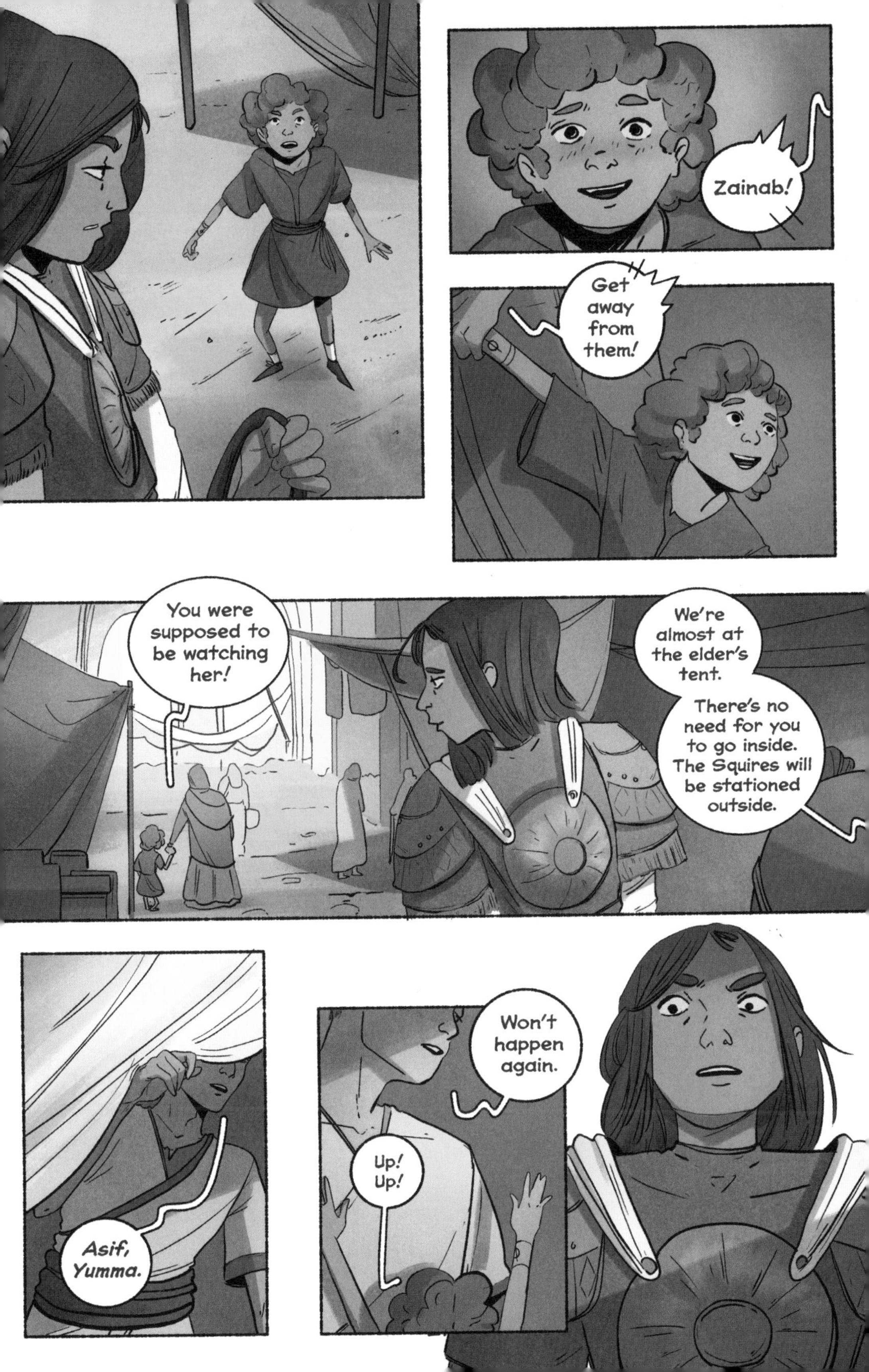
Zainab!
Get away from them!
You were supposed to be watching her!
We're almost at the elder's tent.
There's no need for you to go inside. The Squires will be stationed outside.
Asif, Yumma.
Won't happen again.
Up! Up!

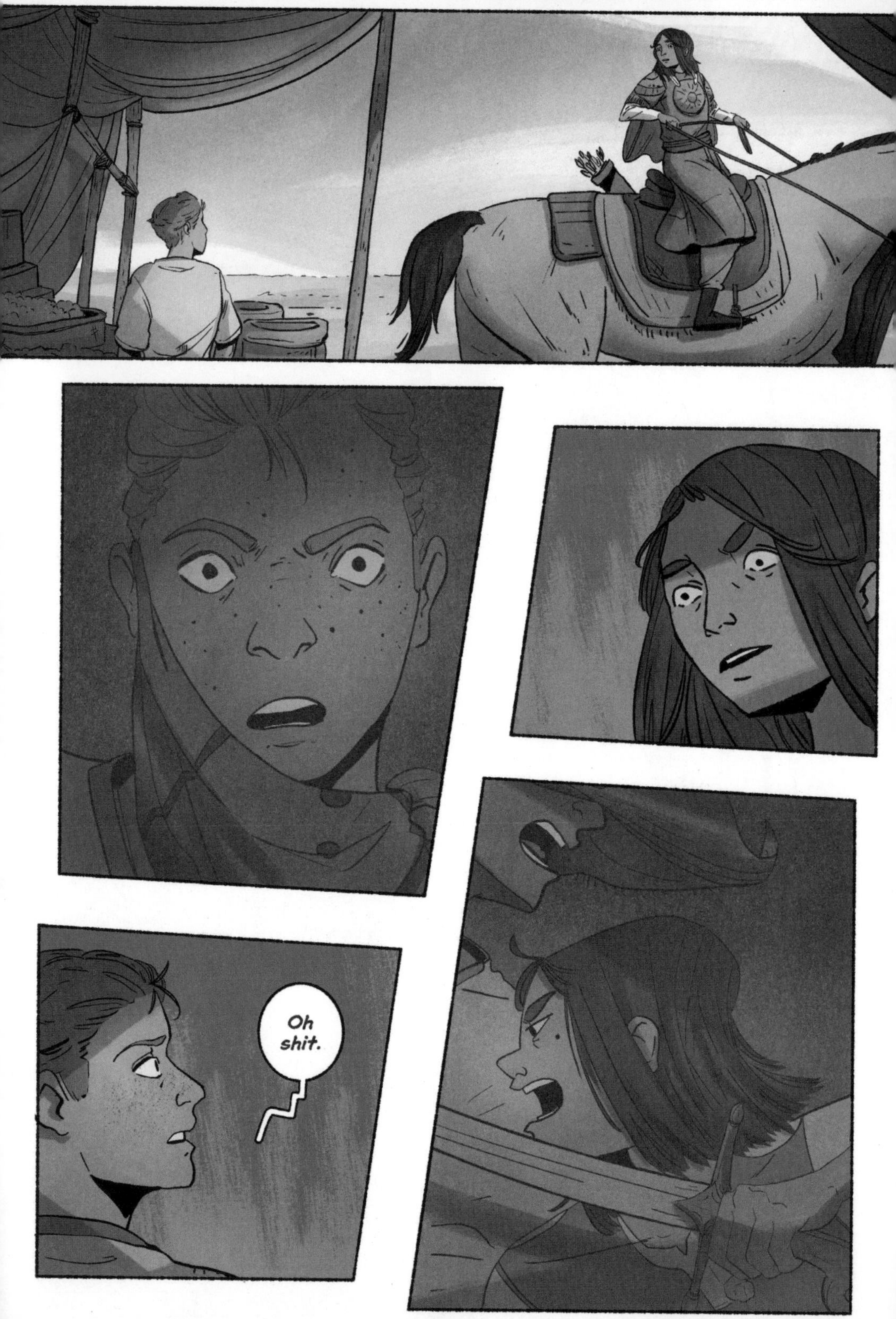
Oh shit.

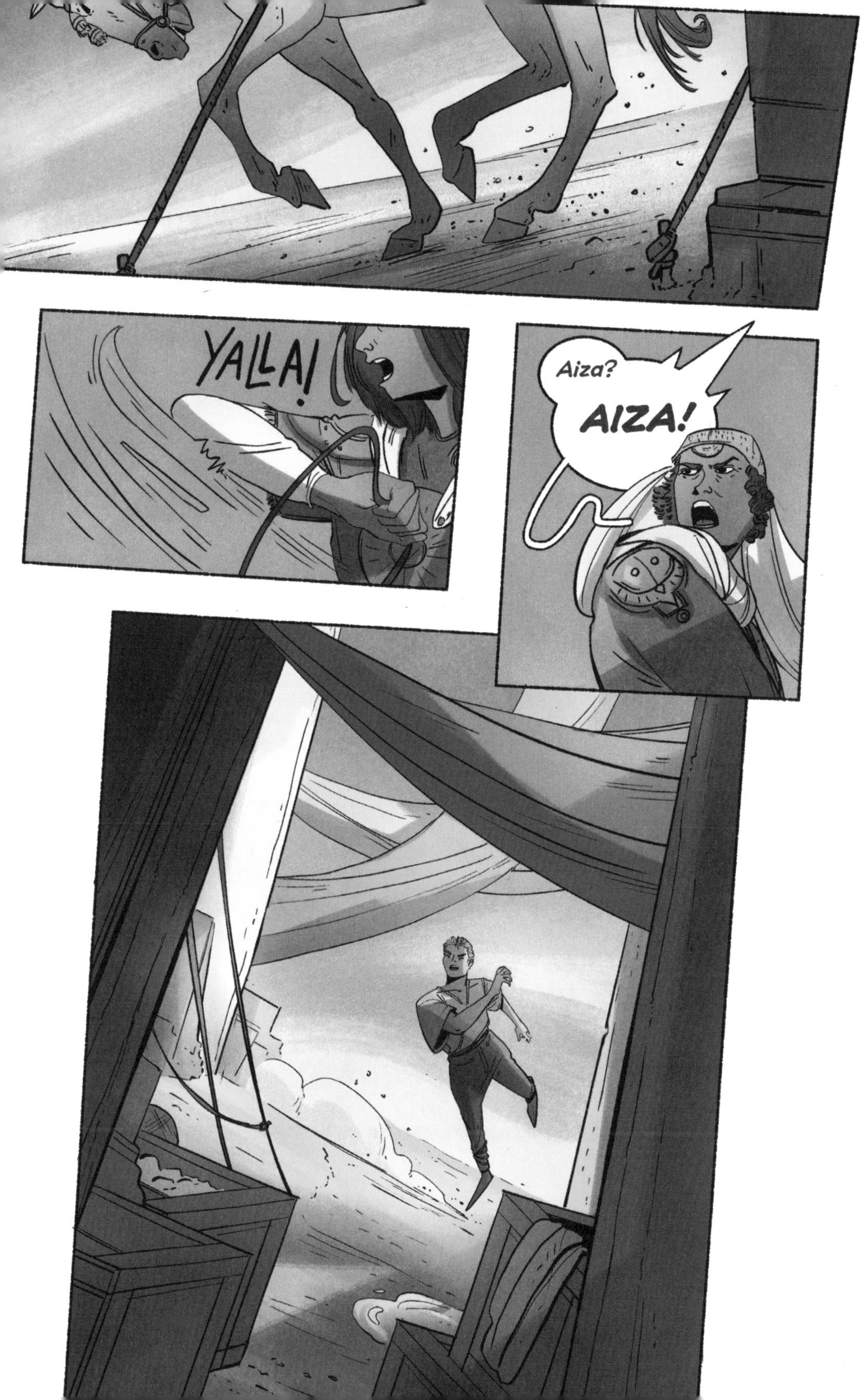
YALLA!
Aiza?
AIZA!

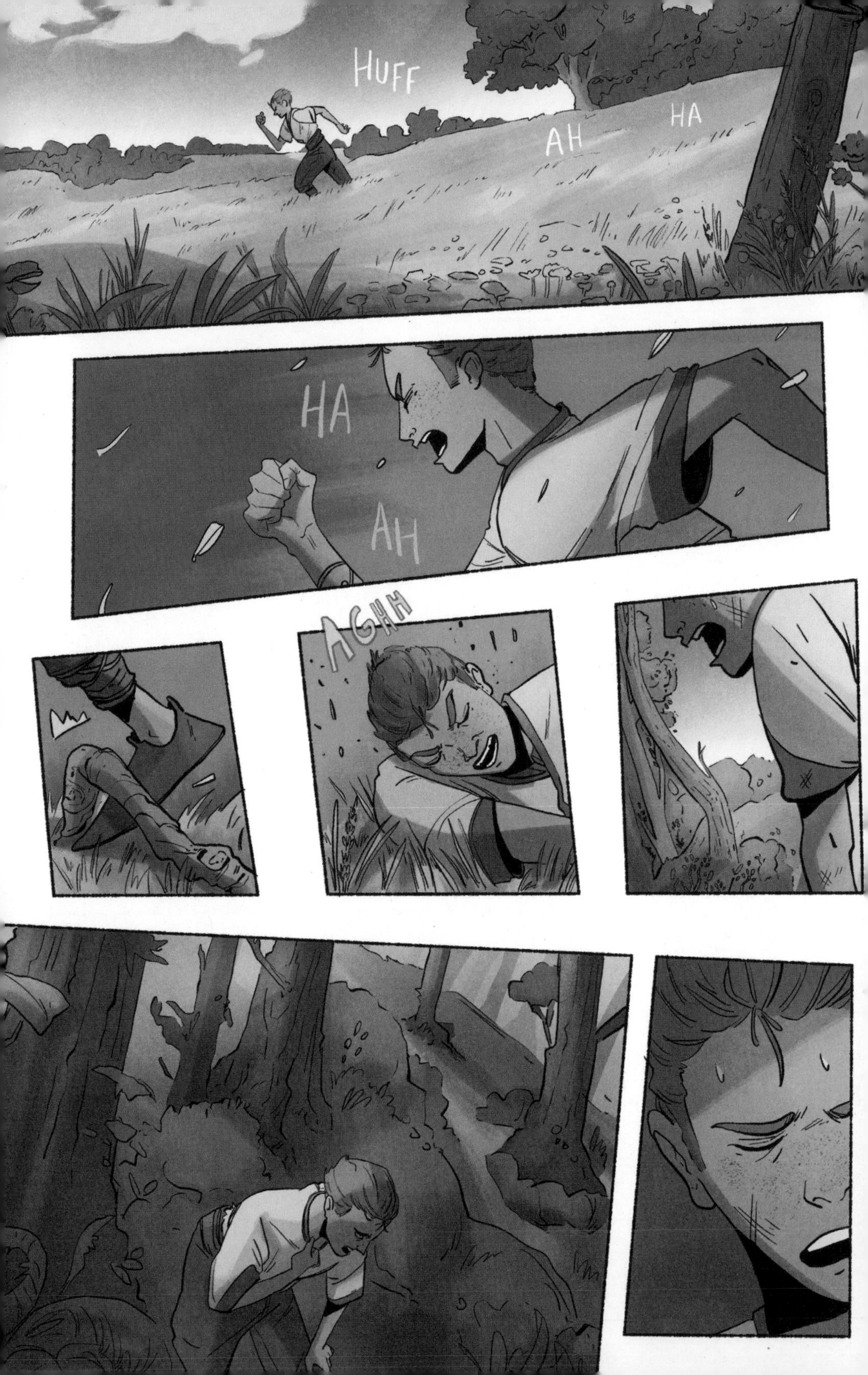
HUFF
AH
HA
HA
AH
AGHH

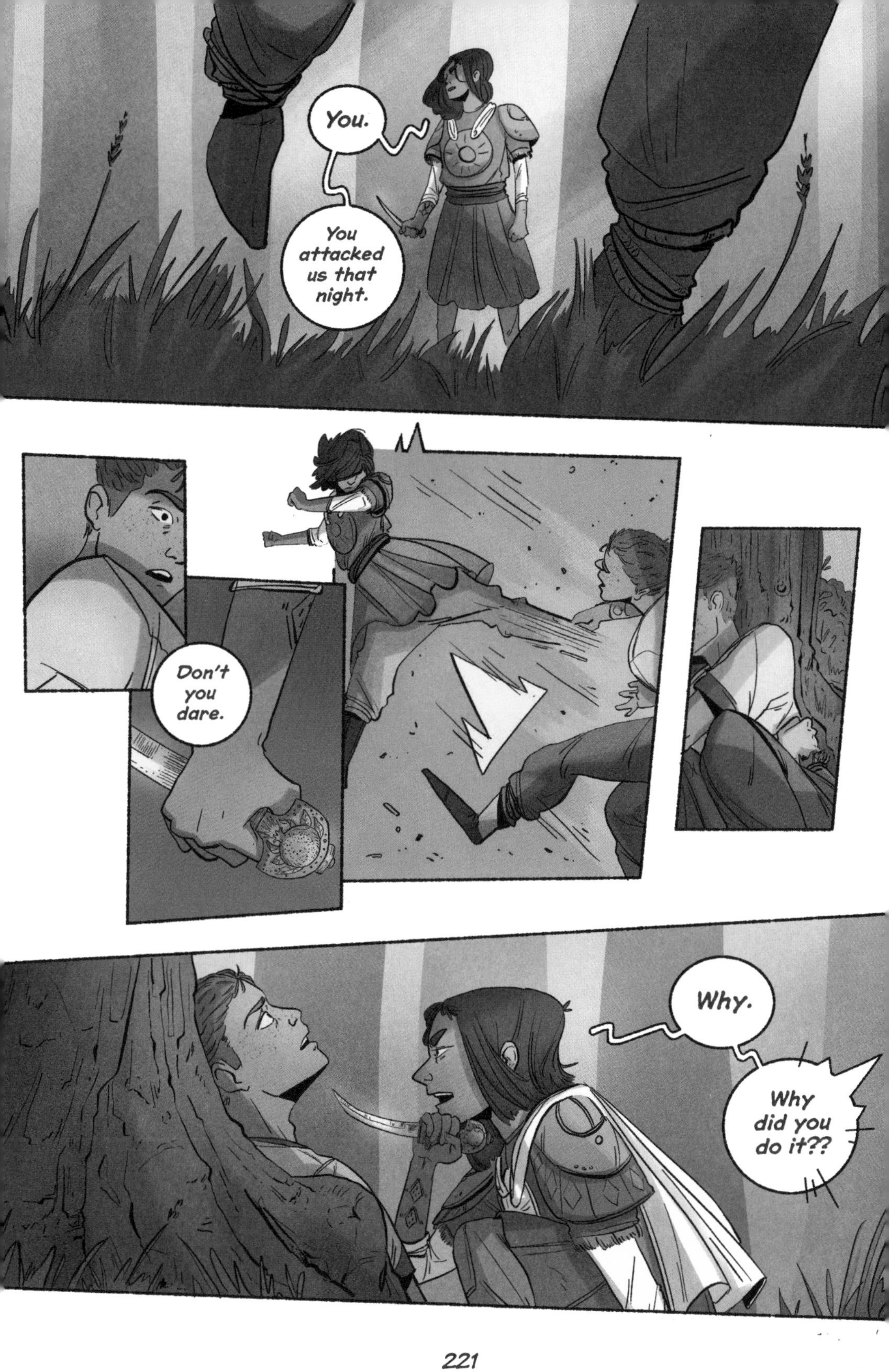
You.
You attacked us that night.
Don't you dare.
Why.
Why did you do it??

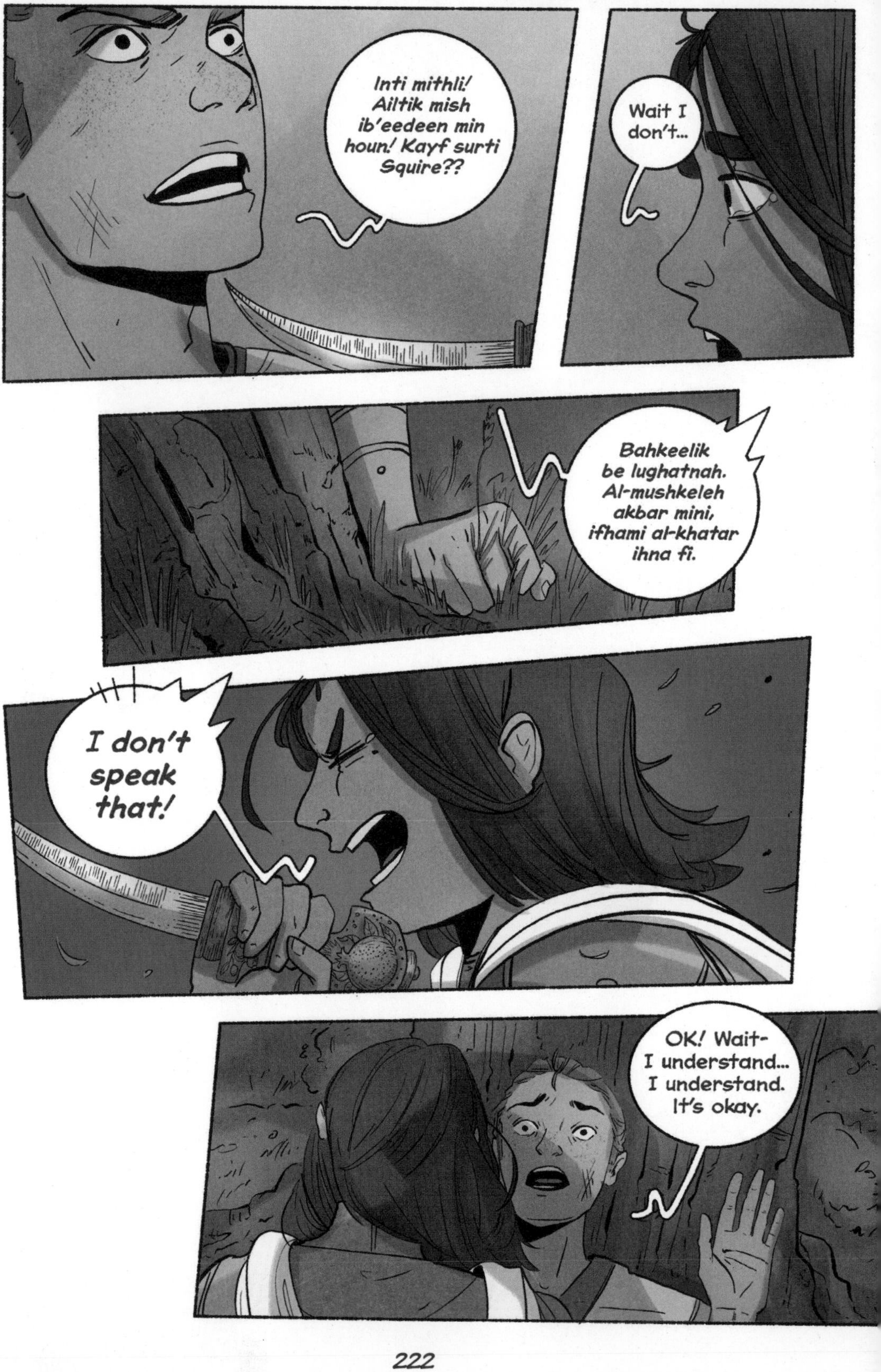
Inti mithli! Ailtik mish ib'eedeen min houn! Kayf surti Squire??
Wait I don't...
Bahkeelik be lughatnah. Al-mushkeleh akbar mini, ifhami al-khatar ihna fi.
I don't speak that!
OK! Wait- I understand... I understand. It's okay.

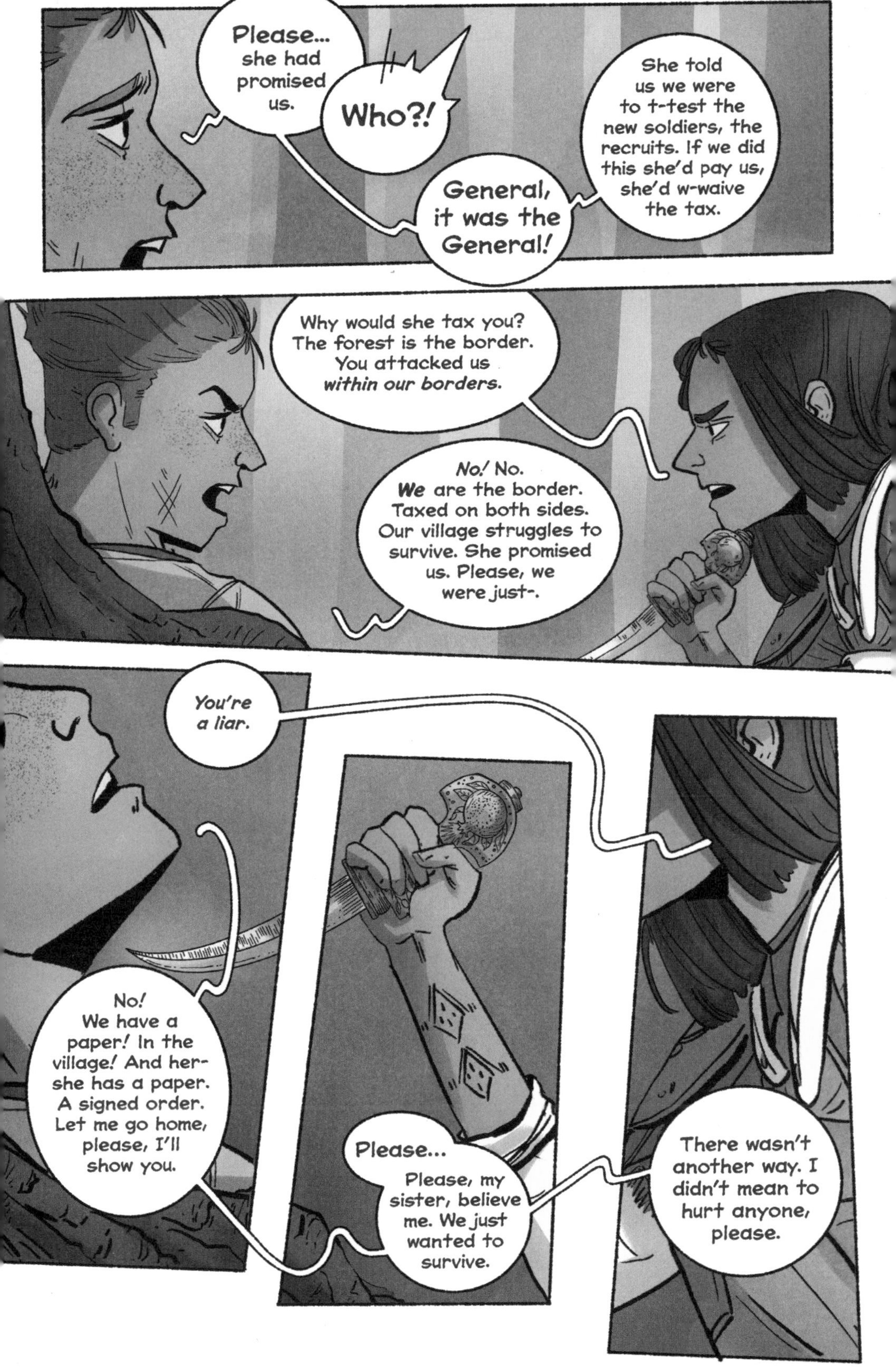
Please... she had promised us.
Who?!
General, it was the General!
She told us we were to t-test the new soldiers, the recruits. If we did this she'd pay us, she'd w-waive the tax.
Why would she tax you? The forest is the border. You attacked us *within our borders.*
No! No. **We** are the border. Taxed on both sides. Our village struggles to survive. She promised us. Please, we were just-.
You're a liar.
No! We have a paper! In the village! And her- she has a paper. A signed order. Let me go home, please, I'll show you.
Please...
Please, my sister, believe me. We just wanted to survive.
There wasn't another way. I didn't mean to hurt anyone, please.

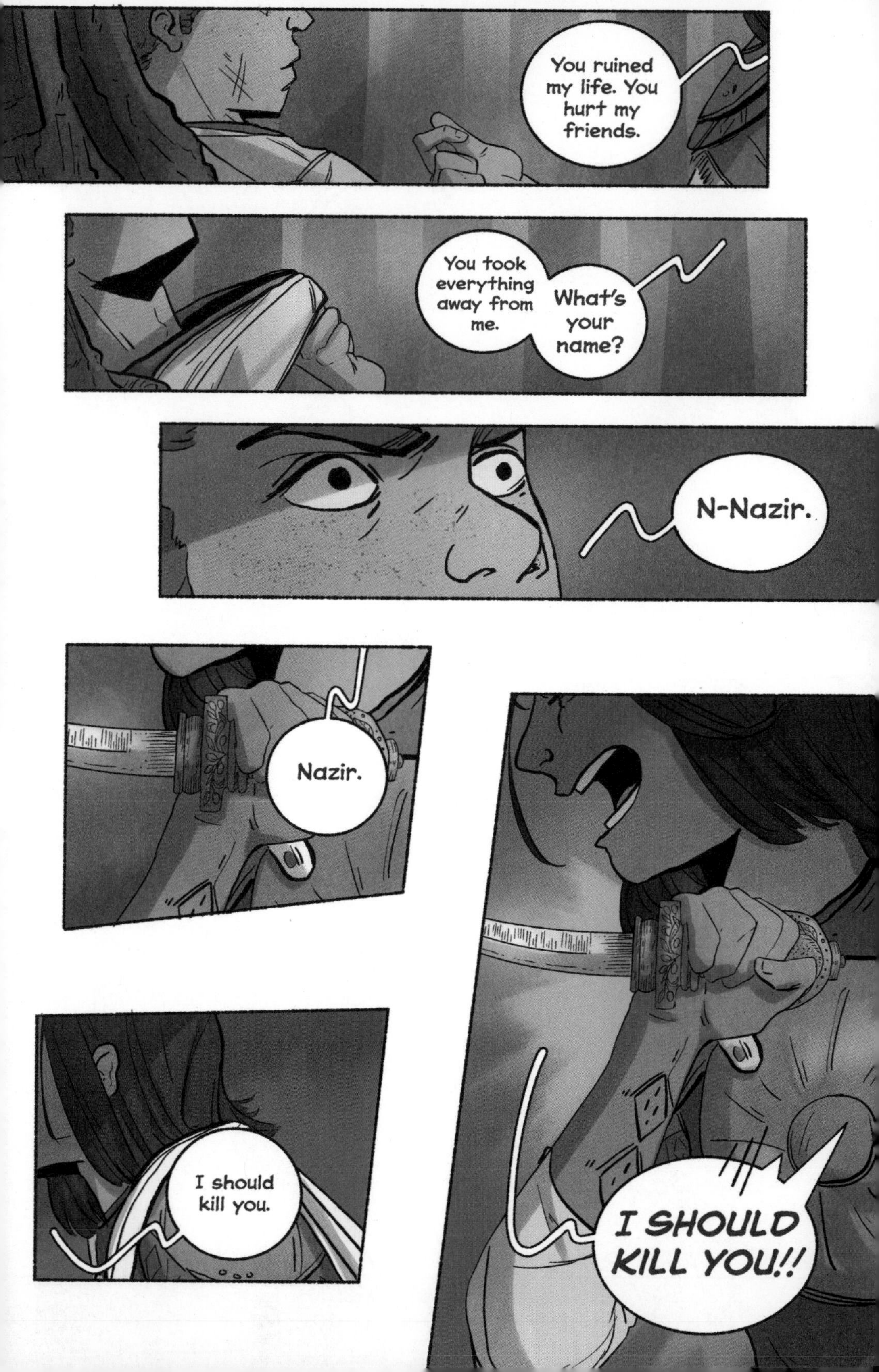
You ruined my life. You hurt my friends.
You took everything away from me.
What's your name?
N-Nazir.
Nazir.
I should kill you.
I SHOULD KILL YOU!!

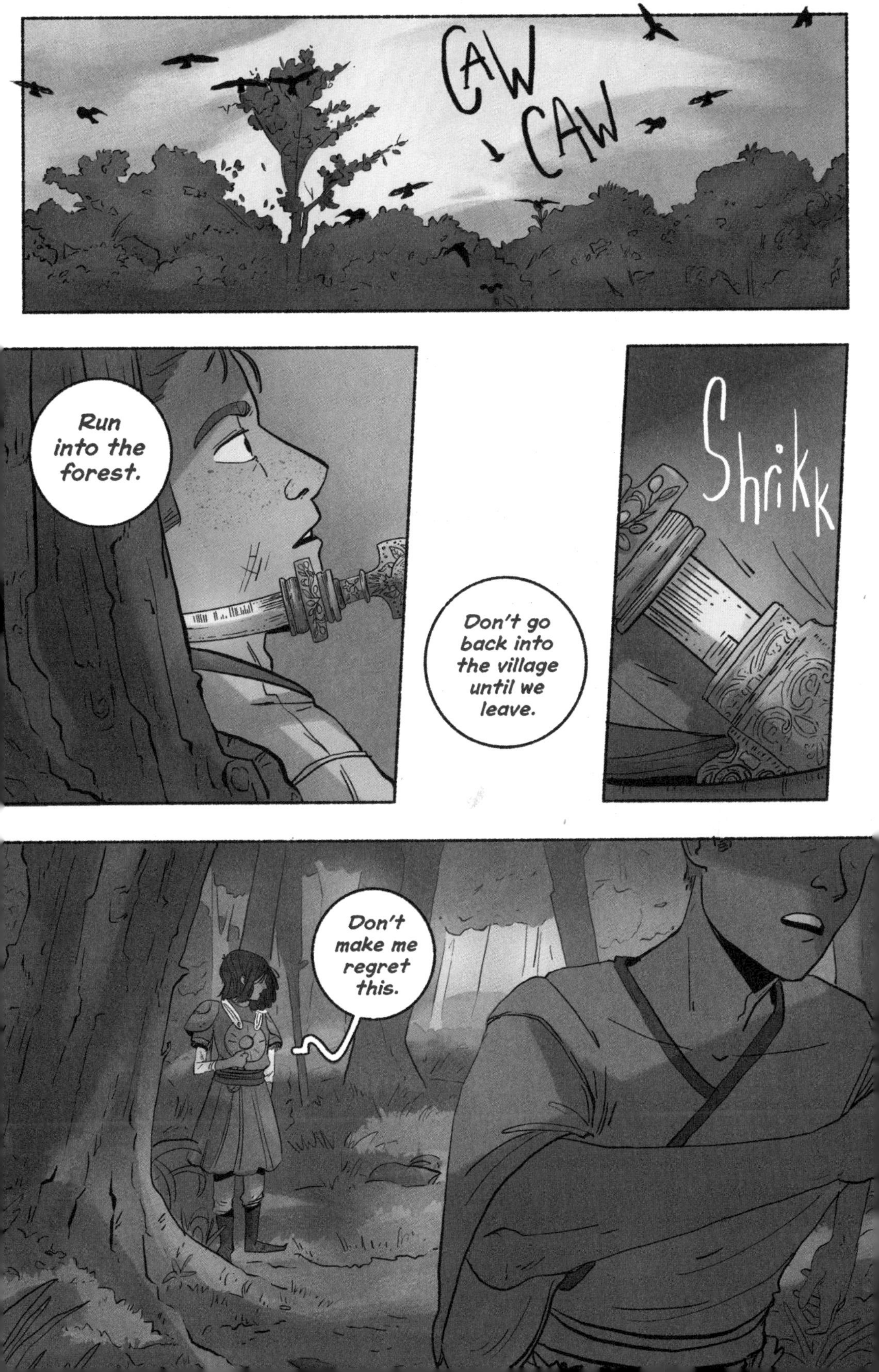
CAW
CAW
Run into the forest.
Shrikk
Don't go back into the village until we leave.
Don't make me regret this.

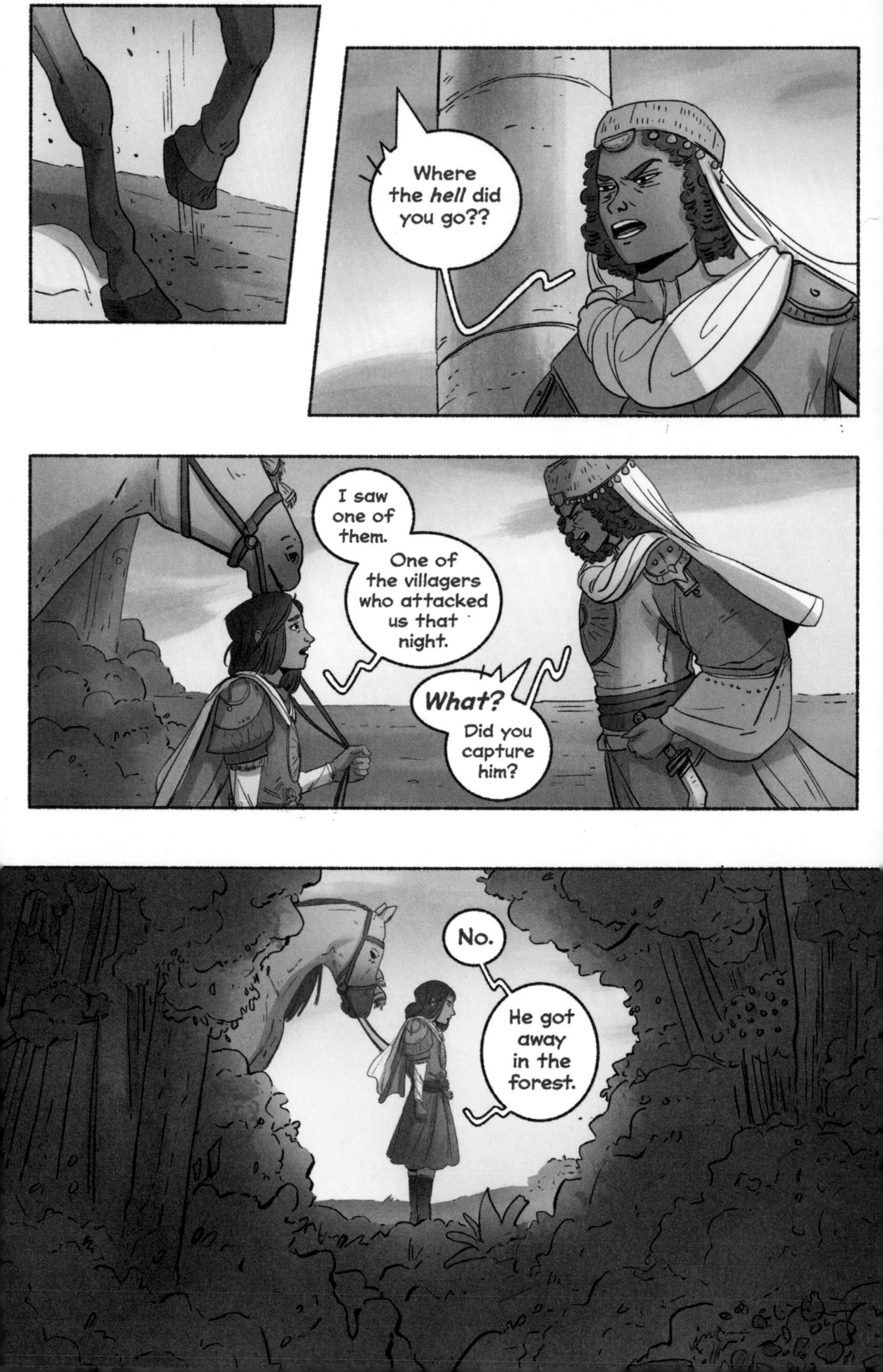
Where the *hell* did you go??
I saw one of them.
One of the villagers who attacked us that night.
What?
Did you capture him?
No.
He got away in the forest.

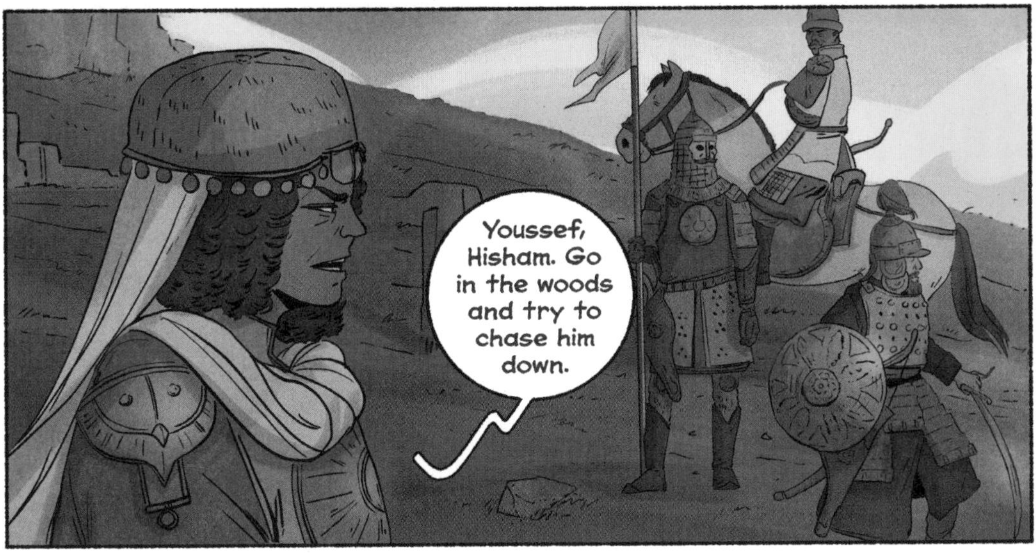
Youssef, Hisham. Go in the woods and try to chase him down.

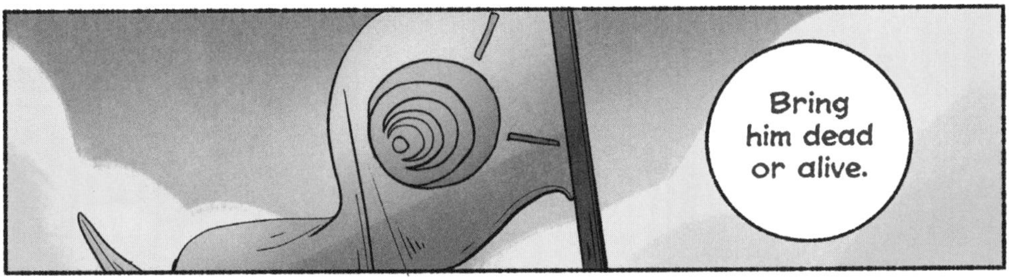
Bring him dead or alive.

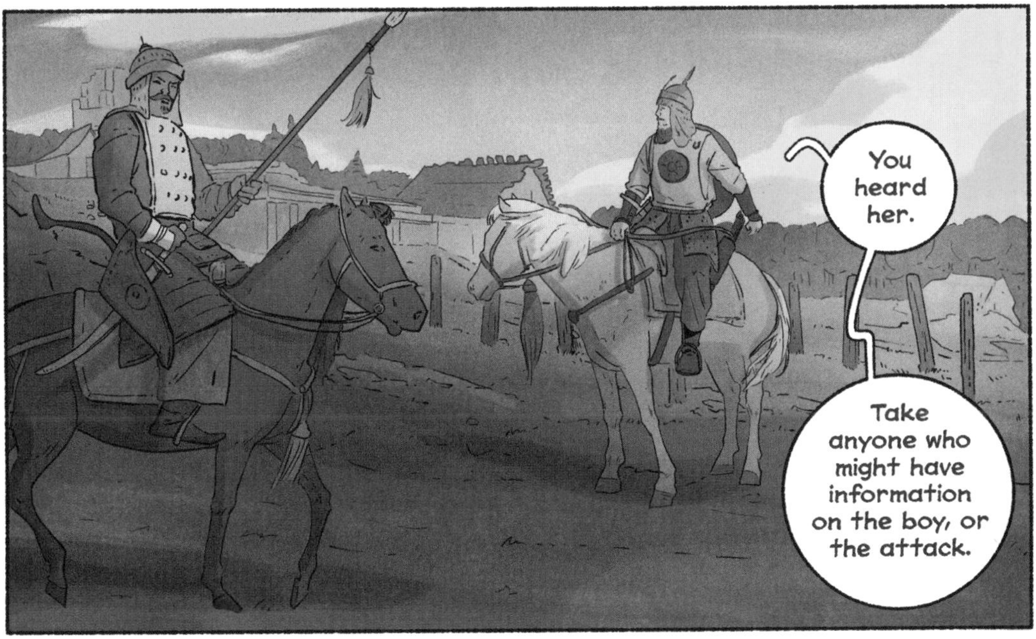
You heard her.
Take anyone who might have information on the boy, or the attack.

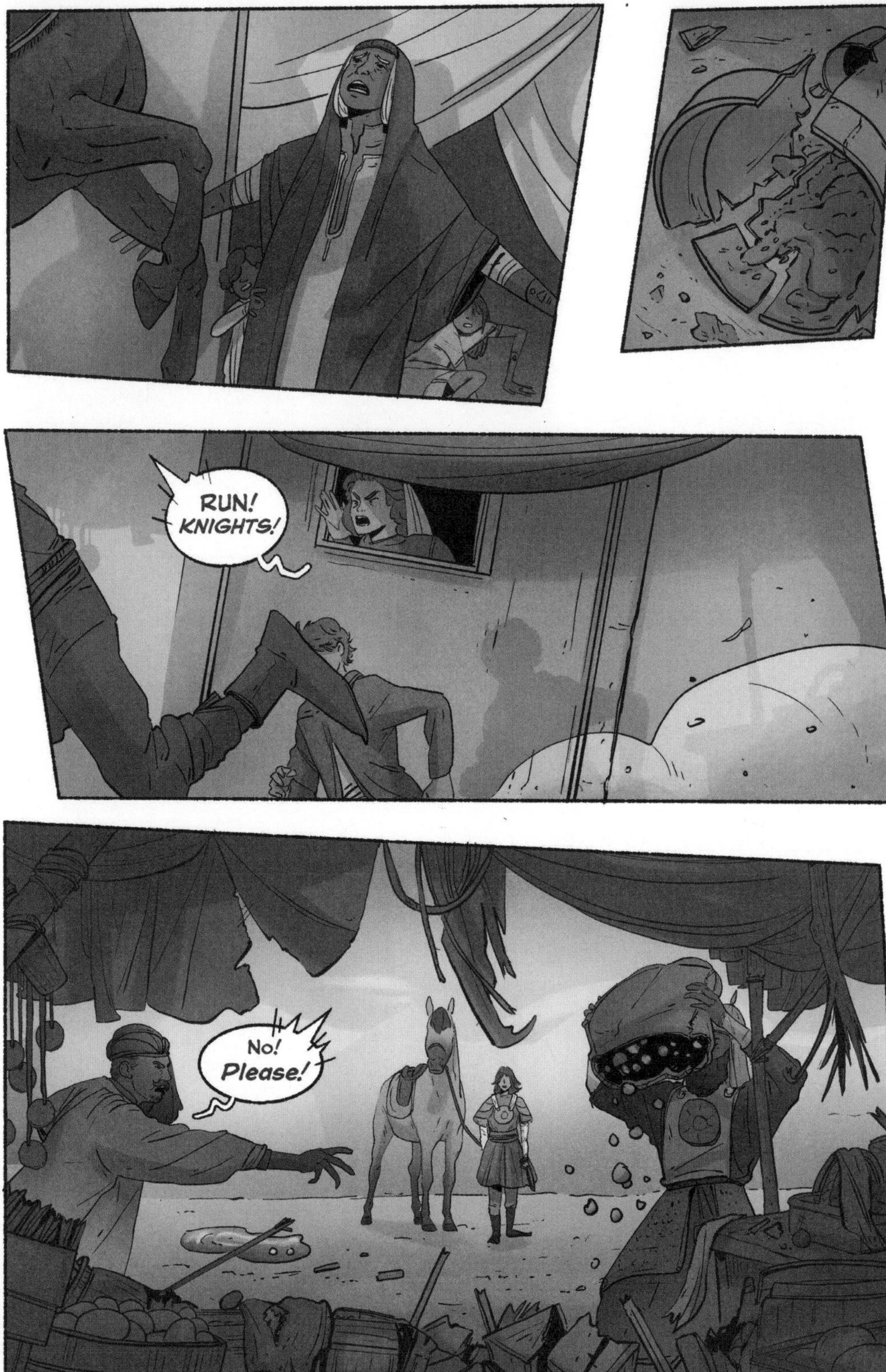
RUN! KNIGHTS!
No! Please!

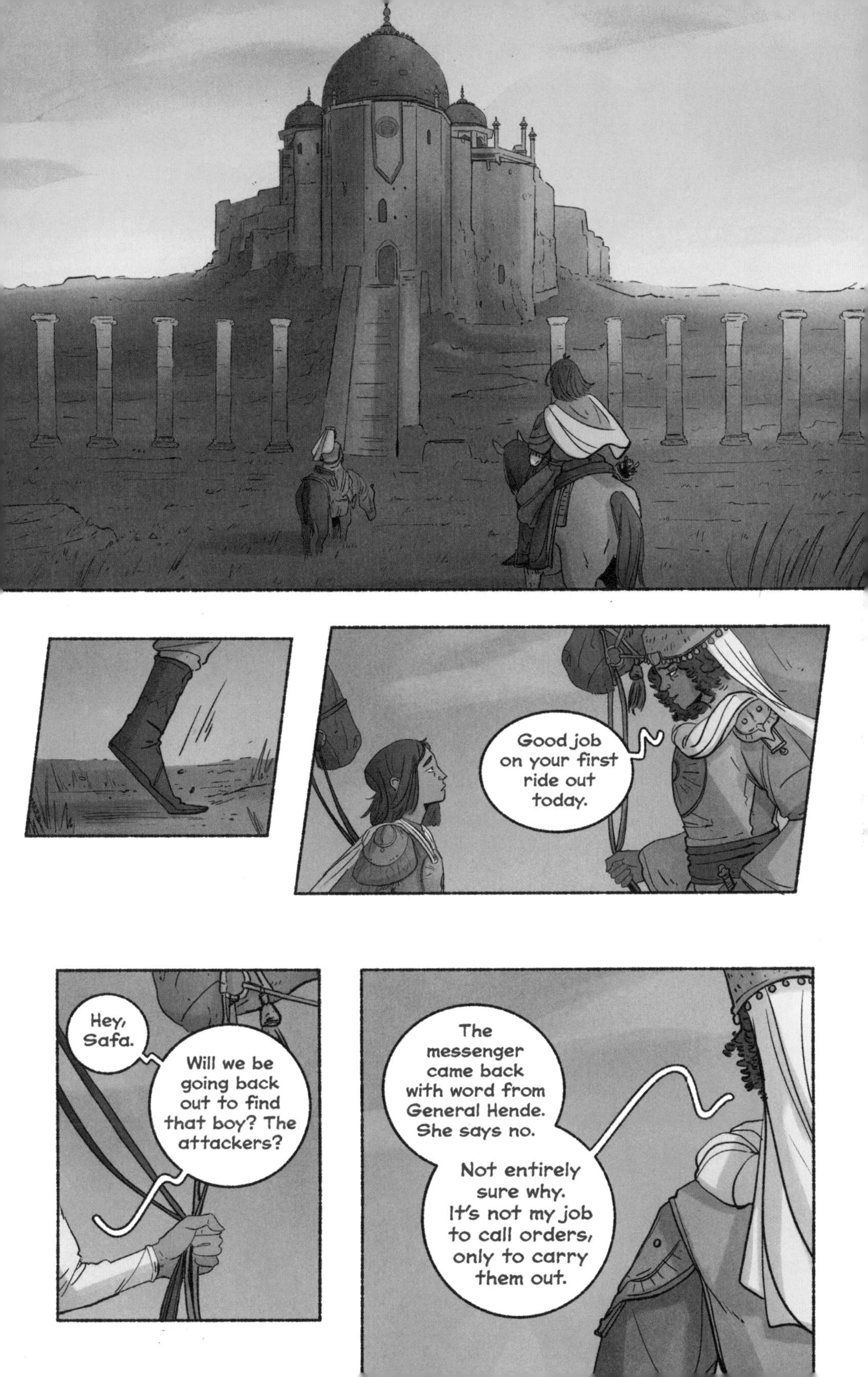
Good job on your first ride out today.
Hey, Safa.
Will we be going back out to find that boy? The attackers?
The messenger came back with word from General Hende. She says no.
Not entirely sure why. It's not my job to call orders, only to carry them out.

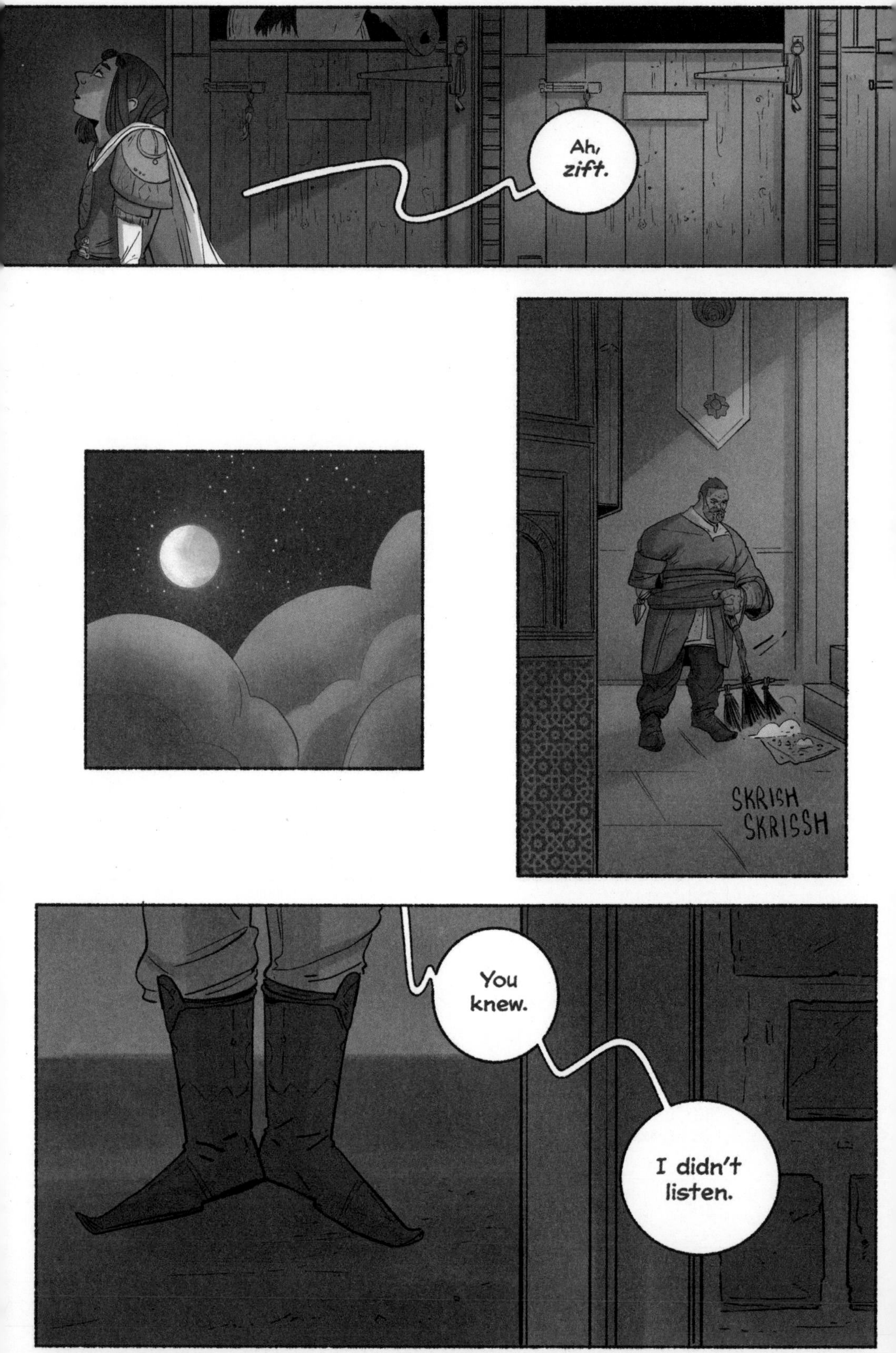
Ah, zift.
SKRISH SKRISSH
You knew.
I didn't listen.

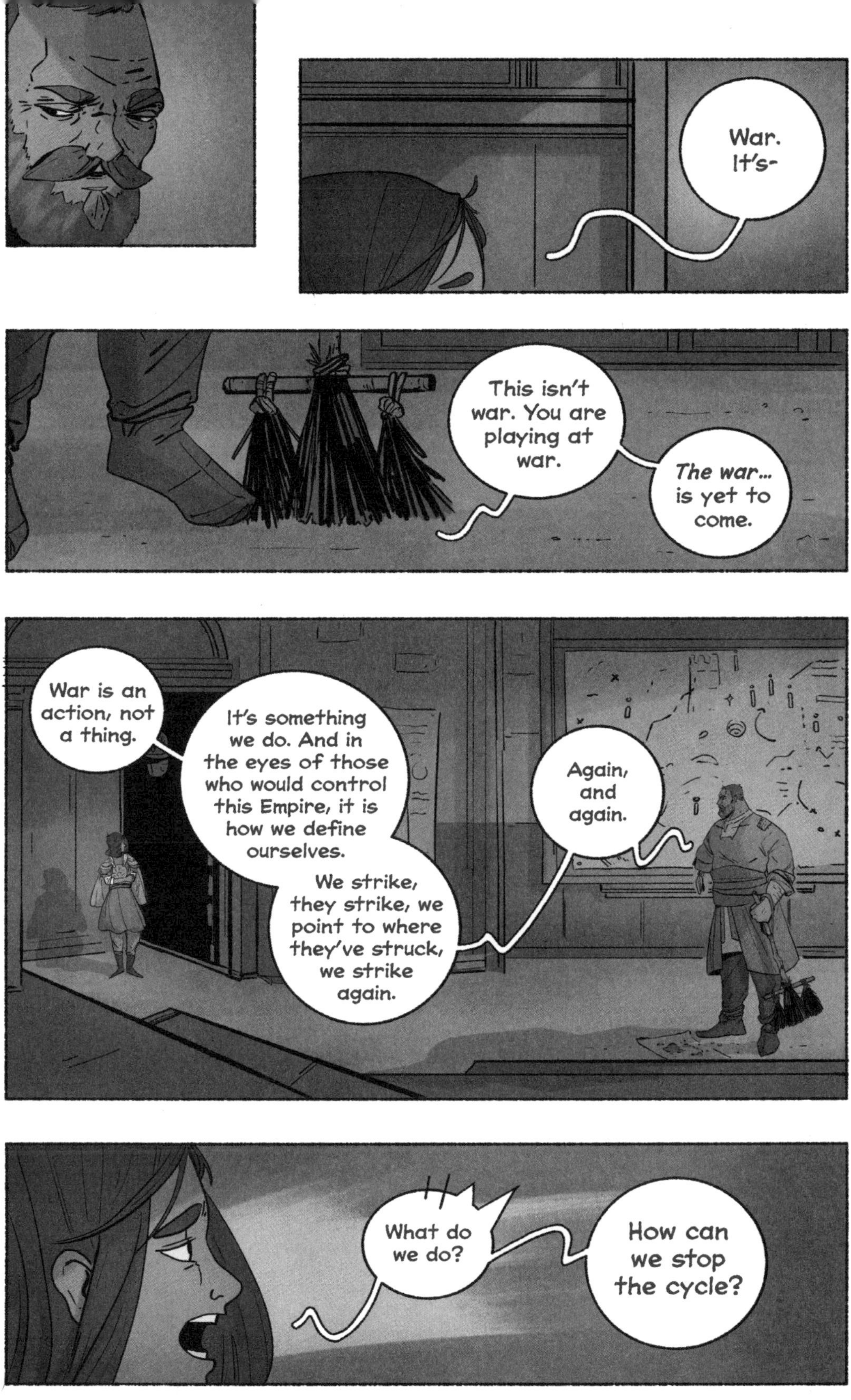
War. It's-
This isn't war. You are playing at war.
The war... is yet to come.
War is an action, not a thing.
It's something we do. And in the eyes of those who would control this Empire, it is how we define ourselves.
We strike, they strike, we point to where they've struck, we strike again.
Again, and again.
What do we do?
How can we stop the cycle?

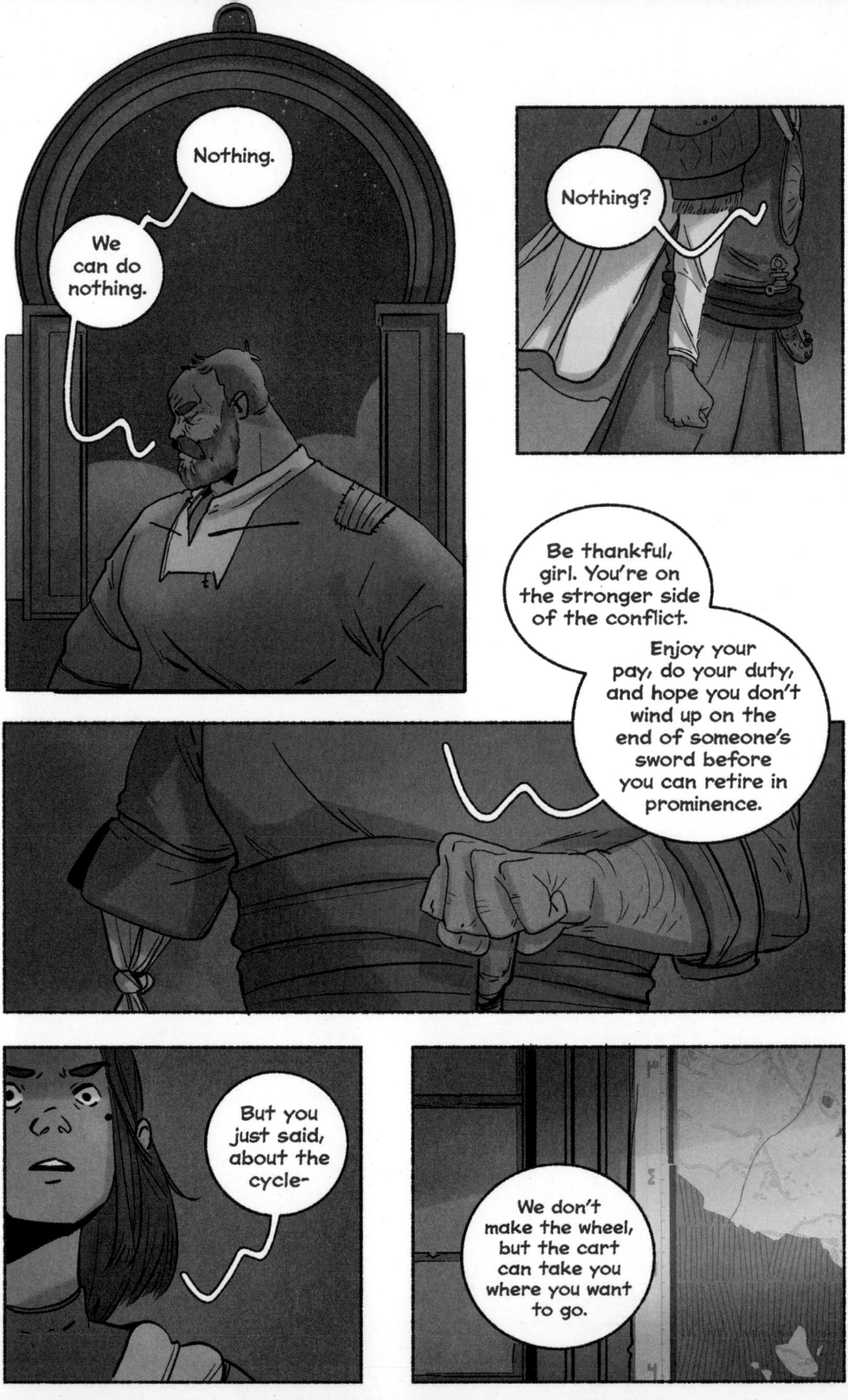
Nothing.
We can do nothing.
Nothing?
Be thankful, girl. You're on the stronger side of the conflict.
Enjoy your pay, do your duty, and hope you don't wind up on the end of someone's sword before you can retire in prominence.
But you just said, about the cycle-
We don't make the wheel, but the cart can take you where you want to go.

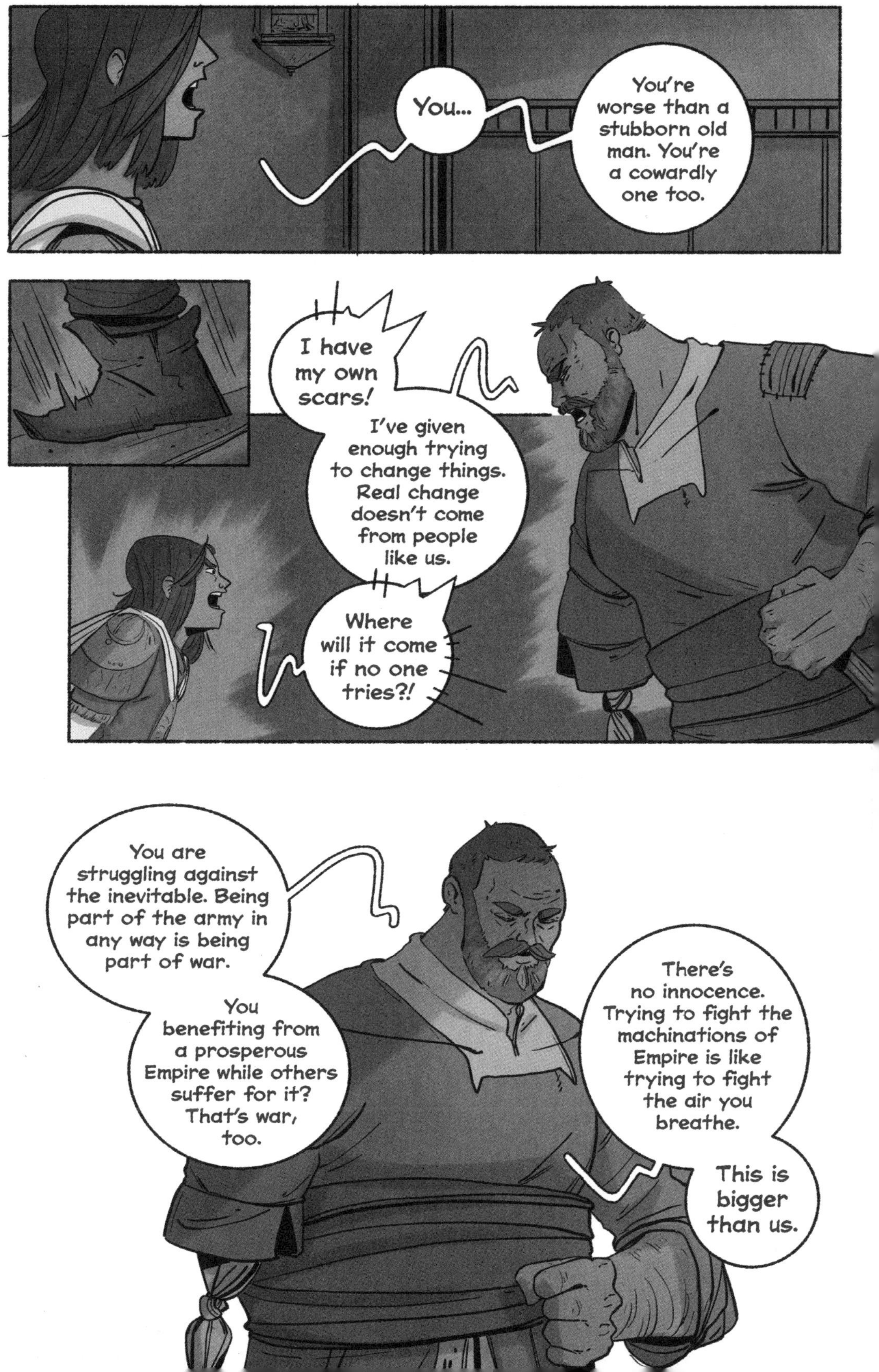
You...
You're worse than a stubborn old man. You're a cowardly one too.
I have my own scars!
I've given enough trying to change things. Real change doesn't come from people like us.
Where will it come if no one tries?!
You are struggling against the inevitable. Being part of the army in any way is being part of war.
You benefiting from a prosperous Empire while others suffer for it? That's war, too.
There's no innocence. Trying to fight the machinations of Empire is like trying to fight the air you breathe.
This is bigger than us.

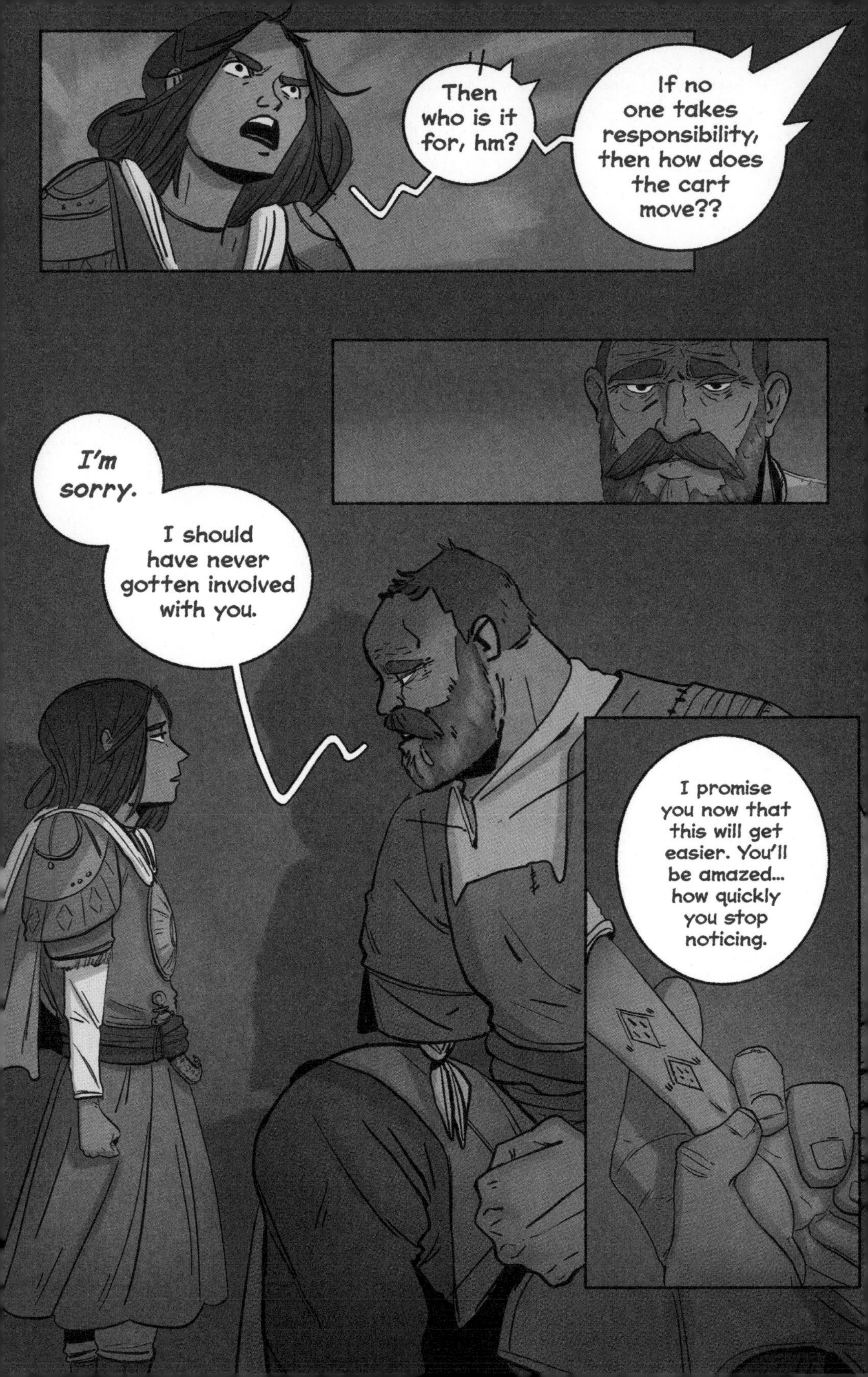

Then who is it for, hm?
If no one takes responsibility, then how does the cart move??
I'm sorry.
I should have never gotten involved with you.
I promise you now that this will get easier. You'll be amazed... how quickly you stop noticing.

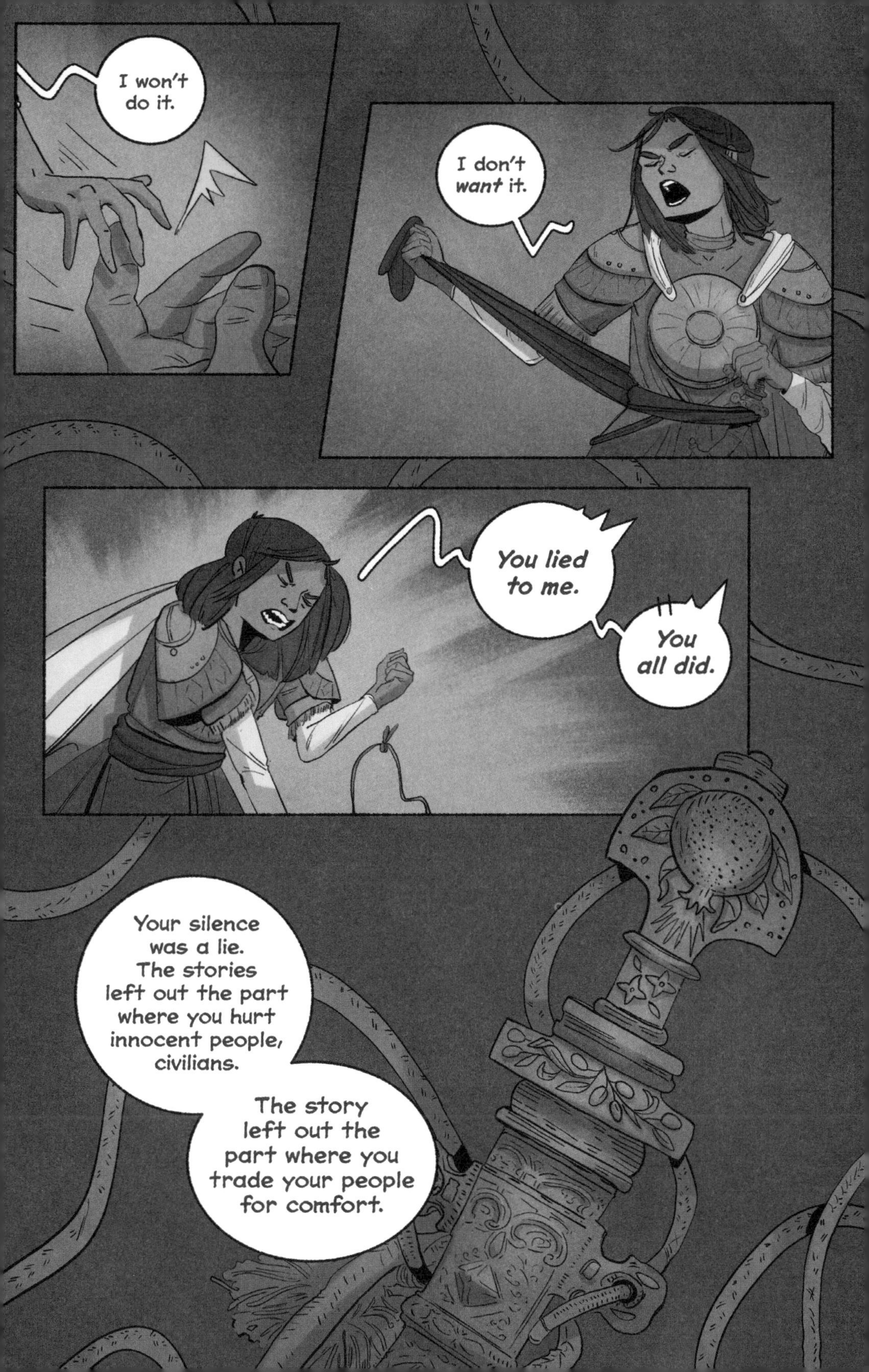
I won't do it.
I don't *want* it.
You lied to me.
You all did.
Your silence was a lie. The stories left out the part where you hurt innocent people, civilians.
The story left out the part where you trade your people for comfort.

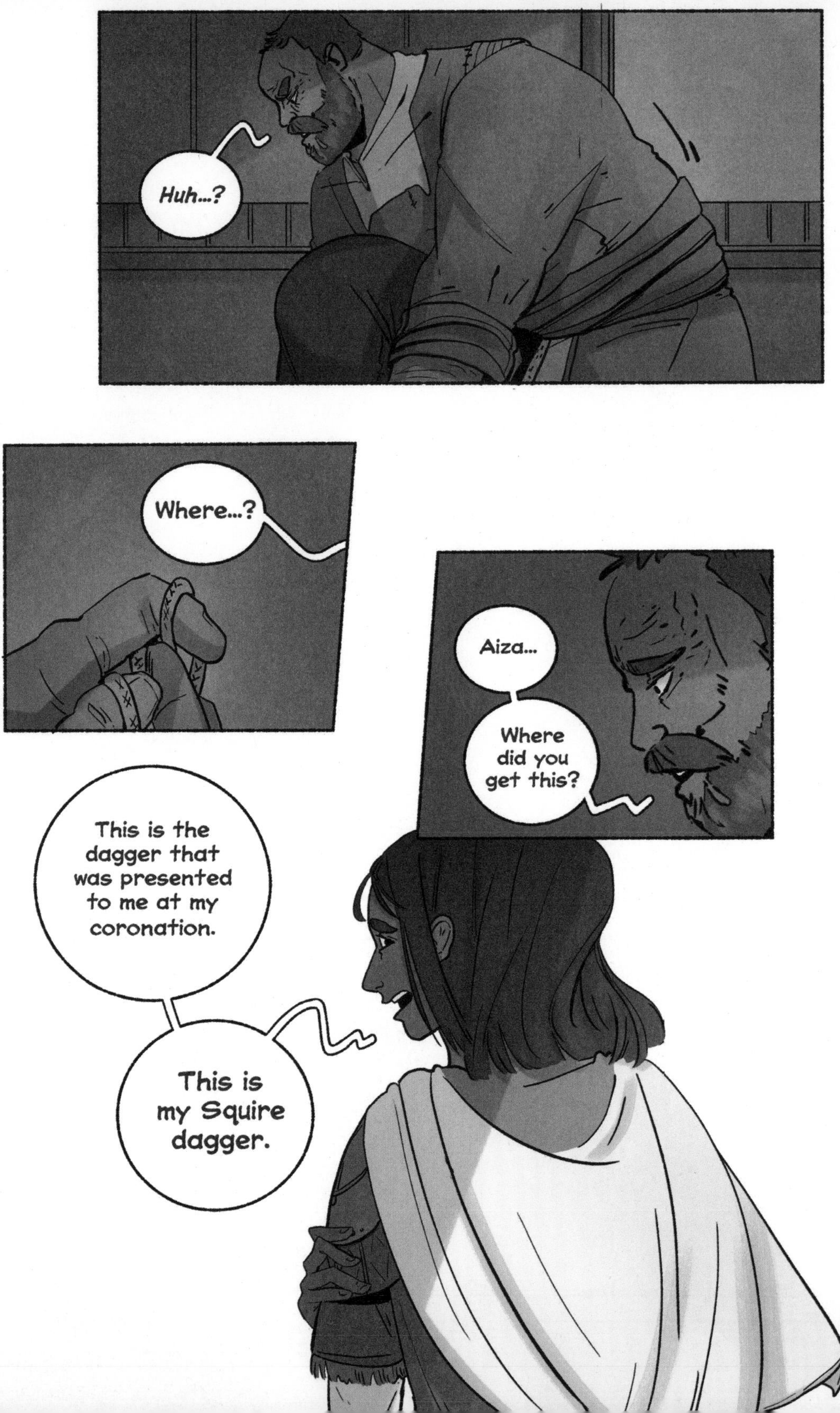
Huh...?
Where...?
Aiza...
Where did you get this?
This is the dagger that was presented to me at my coronation.
This is my Squire dagger.

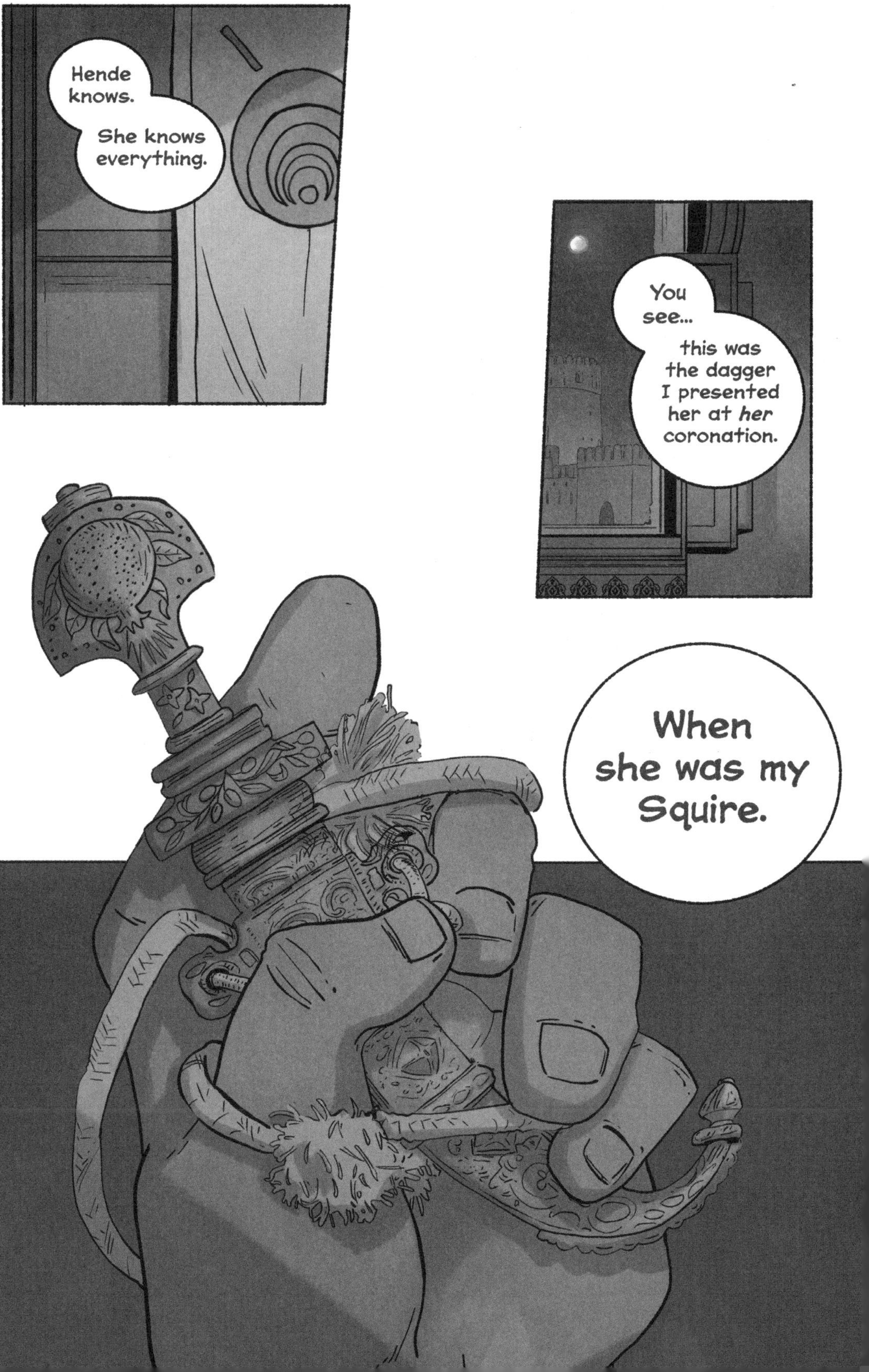
Hende knows.
She knows everything.
You see...
this was the dagger I presented her at *her* coronation.
When she was my Squire.

CHAPTER 12

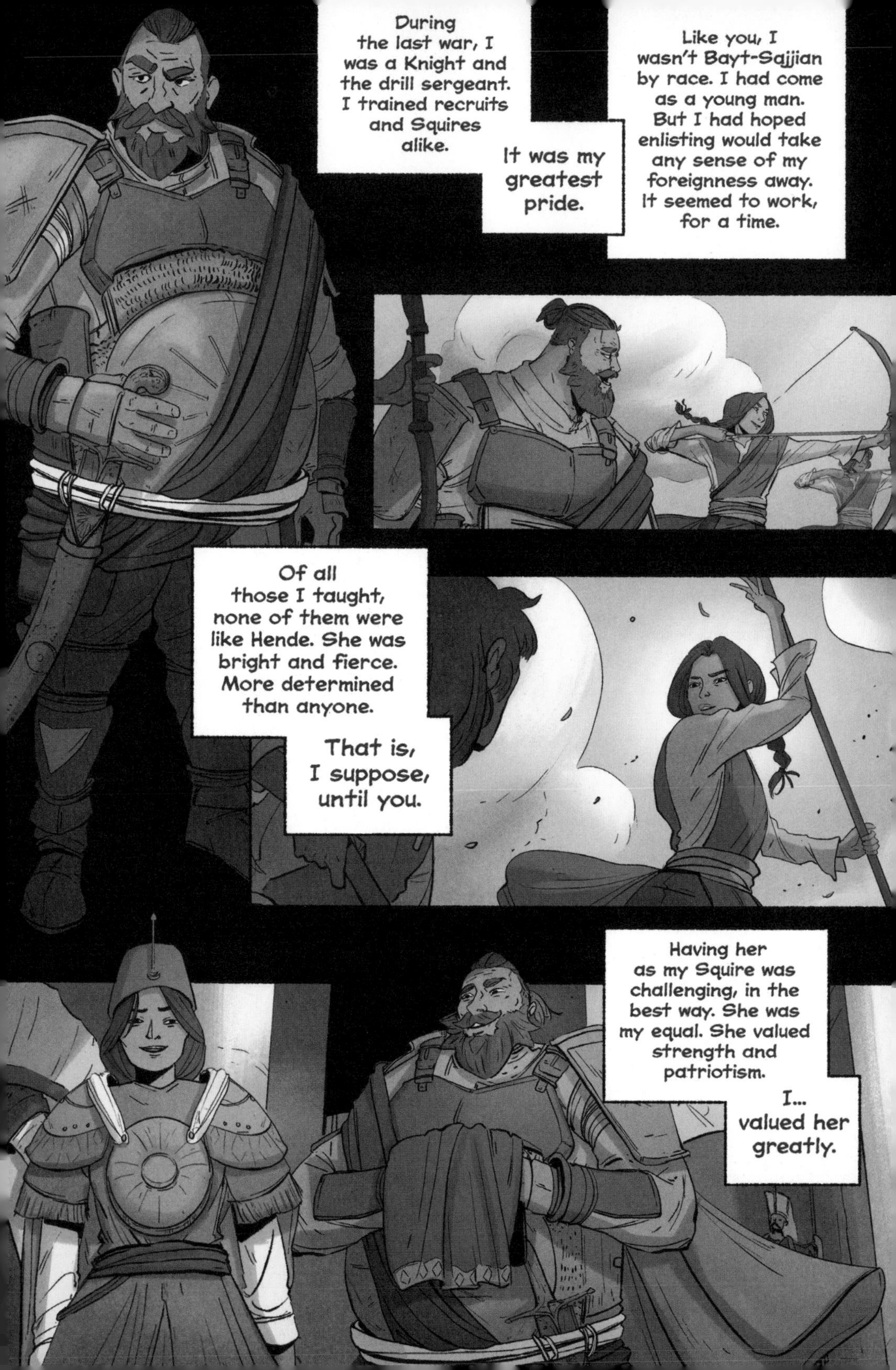
During the last war, I was a Knight and the drill sergeant. I trained recruits and Squires alike.
It was my greatest pride.
Like you, I wasn't Bayt-Sajjian by race. I had come as a young man. But I had hoped enlisting would take any sense of my foreignness away. It seemed to work, for a time.
Of all those I taught, none of them were like Hende. She was bright and fierce. More determined than anyone.
That is, I suppose, until you.
Having her as my Squire was challenging, in the best way. She was my equal. She valued strength and patriotism.
I... valued her greatly.

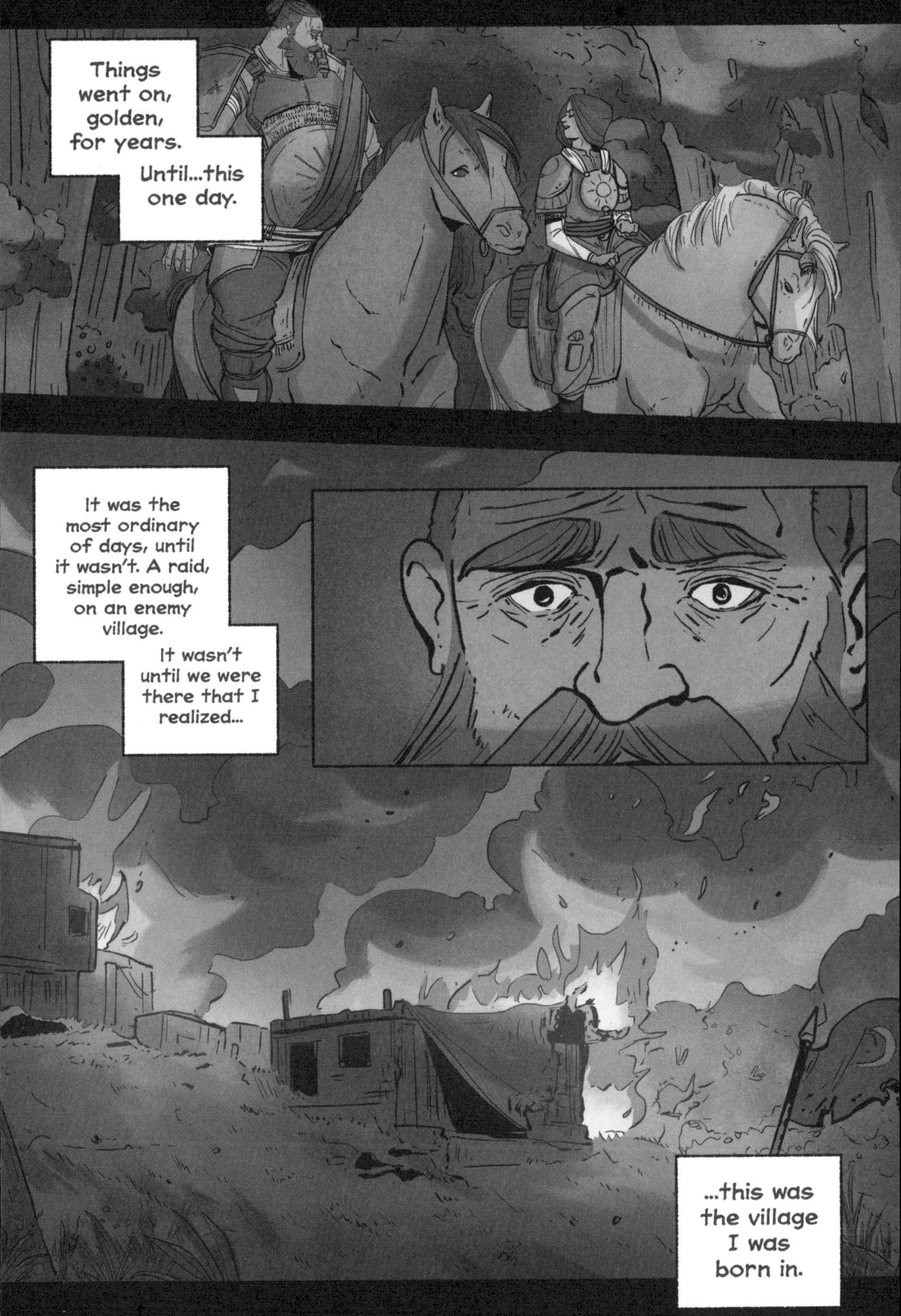
Things went on, golden, for years.
Until...this one day.
It was the most ordinary of days, until it wasn't. A raid, simple enough, on an enemy village.
It wasn't until we were there that I realized...
...this was the village I was born in.

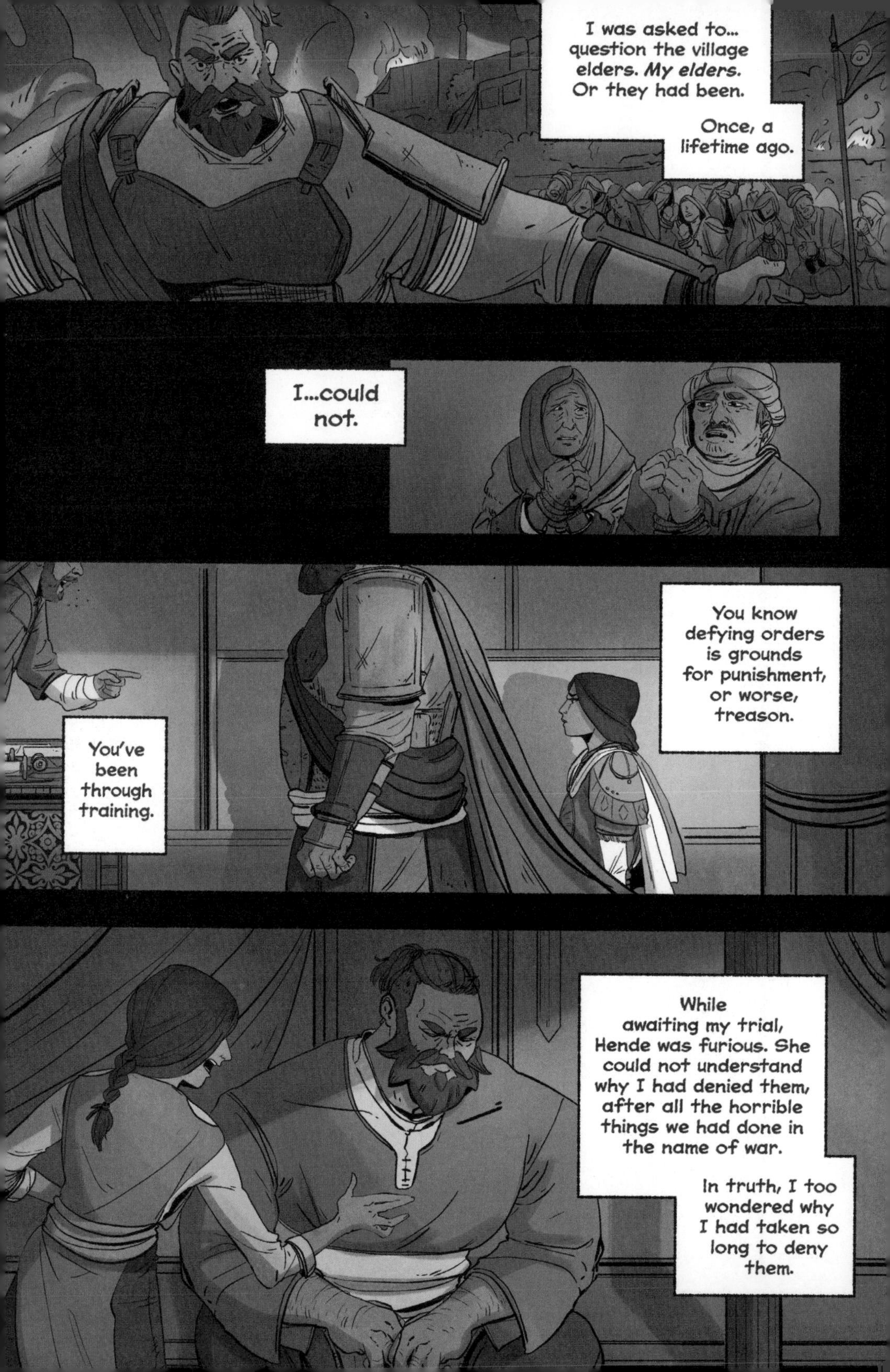
I was asked to... question the village elders. *My elders.* Or they had been.
Once, a lifetime ago.
I...could not.
You've been through training.
You know defying orders is grounds for punishment, or worse, treason.
While awaiting my trial, Hende was furious. She could not understand why I had denied them, after all the horrible things we had done in the name of war.
In truth, I too wondered why I had taken so long to deny them.

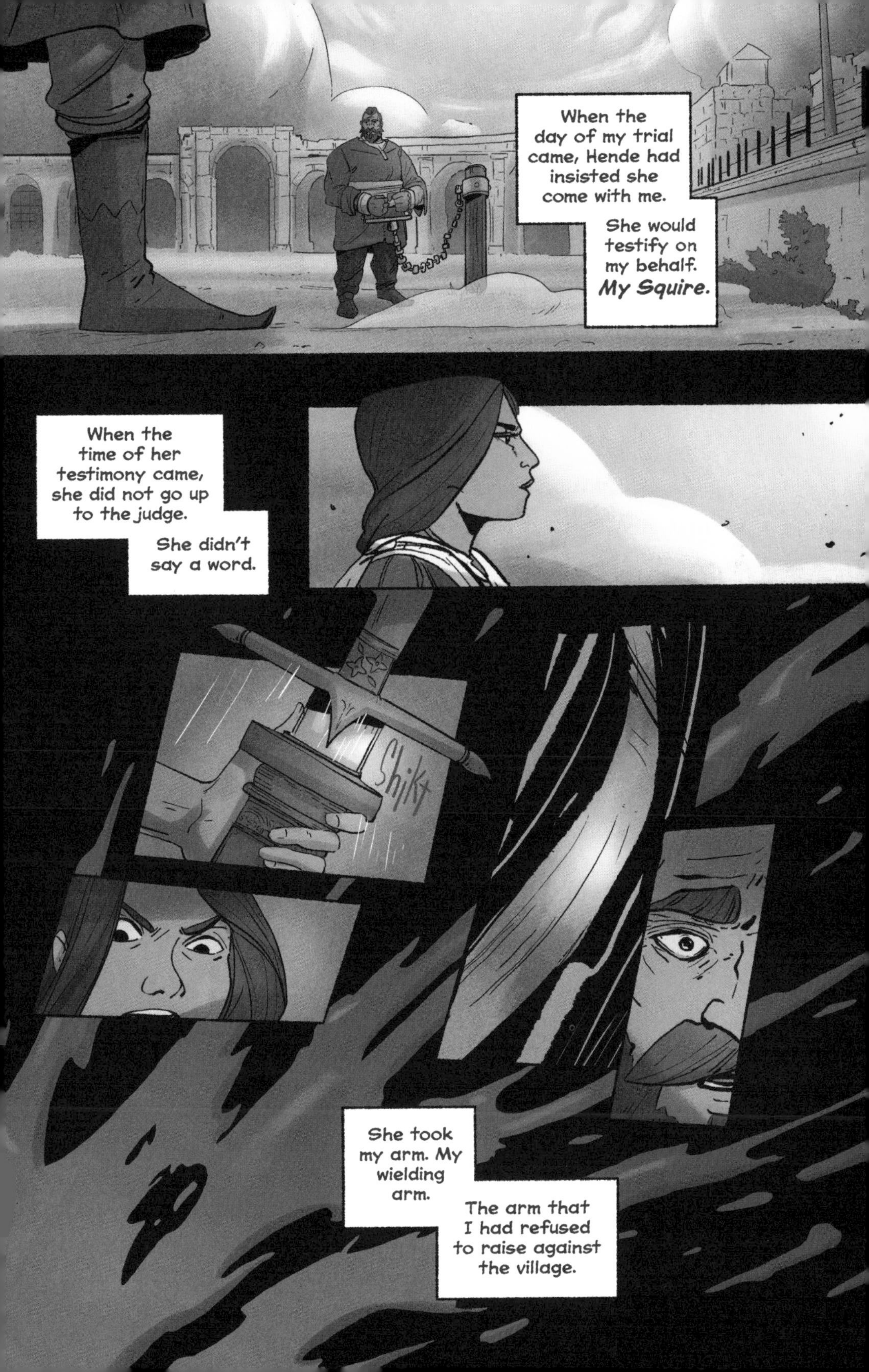
When the day of my trial came, Hende had insisted she come with me.
She would testify on my behalf. *My Squire.*
When the time of her testimony came, she did not go up to the judge.
She didn't say a word.
Shikt
She took my arm. My wielding arm.
The arm that I had refused to raise against the village.

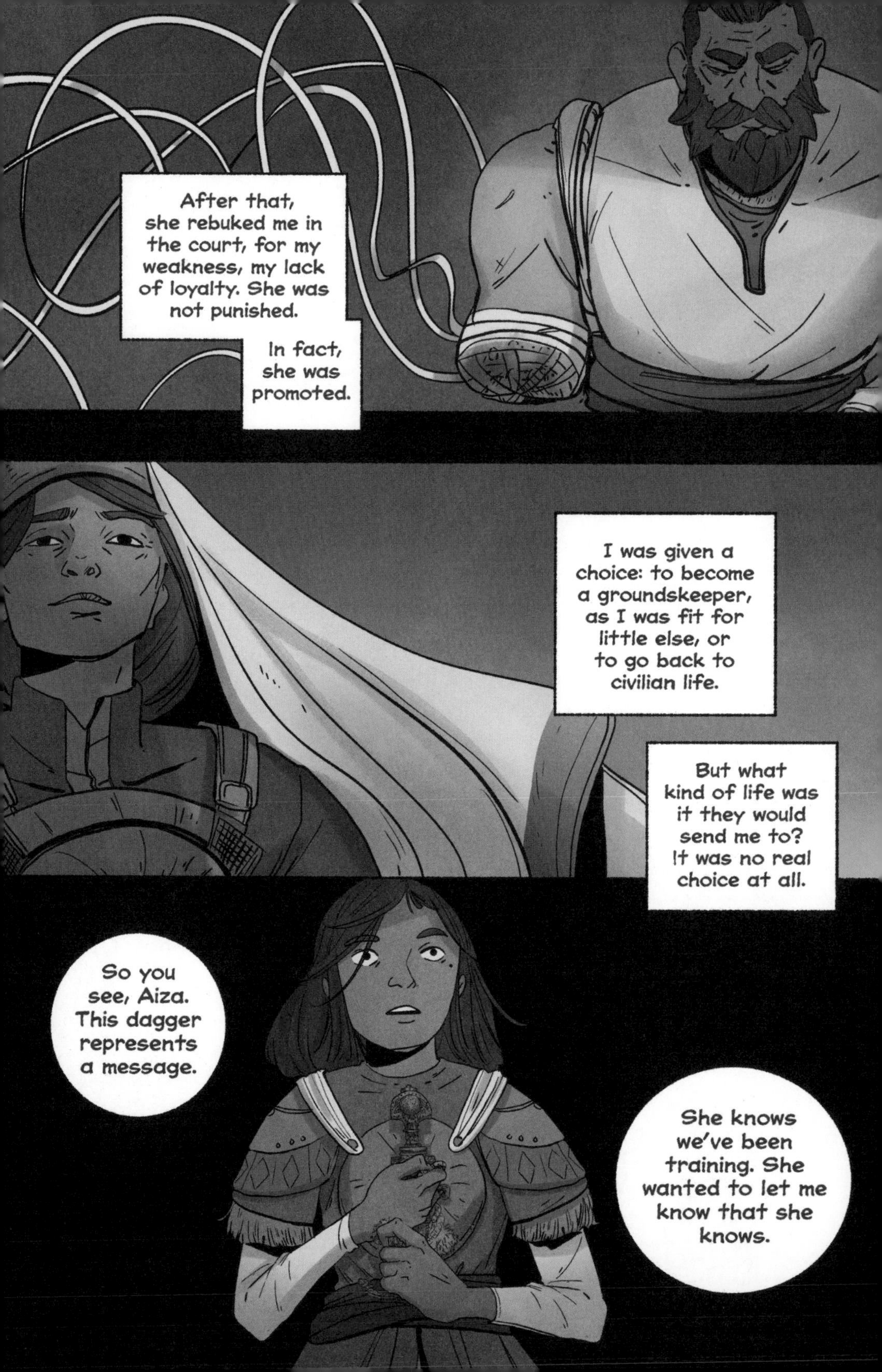
After that, she rebuked me in the court, for my weakness, my lack of loyalty. She was not punished.
In fact, she was promoted.
I was given a choice: to become a groundskeeper, as I was fit for little else, or to go back to civilian life.
But what kind of life was it they would send me to? It was no real choice at all.
So you see, Aiza. This dagger represents a message.
She knows we've been training. She wanted to let me know that she knows.

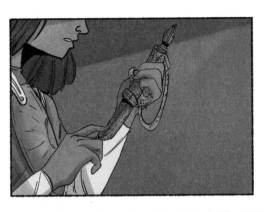

We have to stop her.

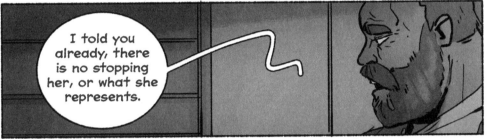

I told you already, there is no stopping her, or what she represents.

You're wrong. Don't you see? We're in a war of our own. The war for *truth*.

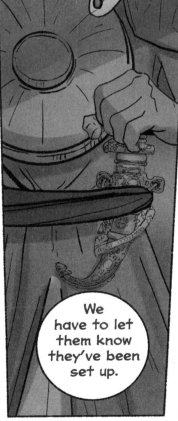

We have to let them know they've been set up.

And why would they believe you?

Because we're going to get them proof.

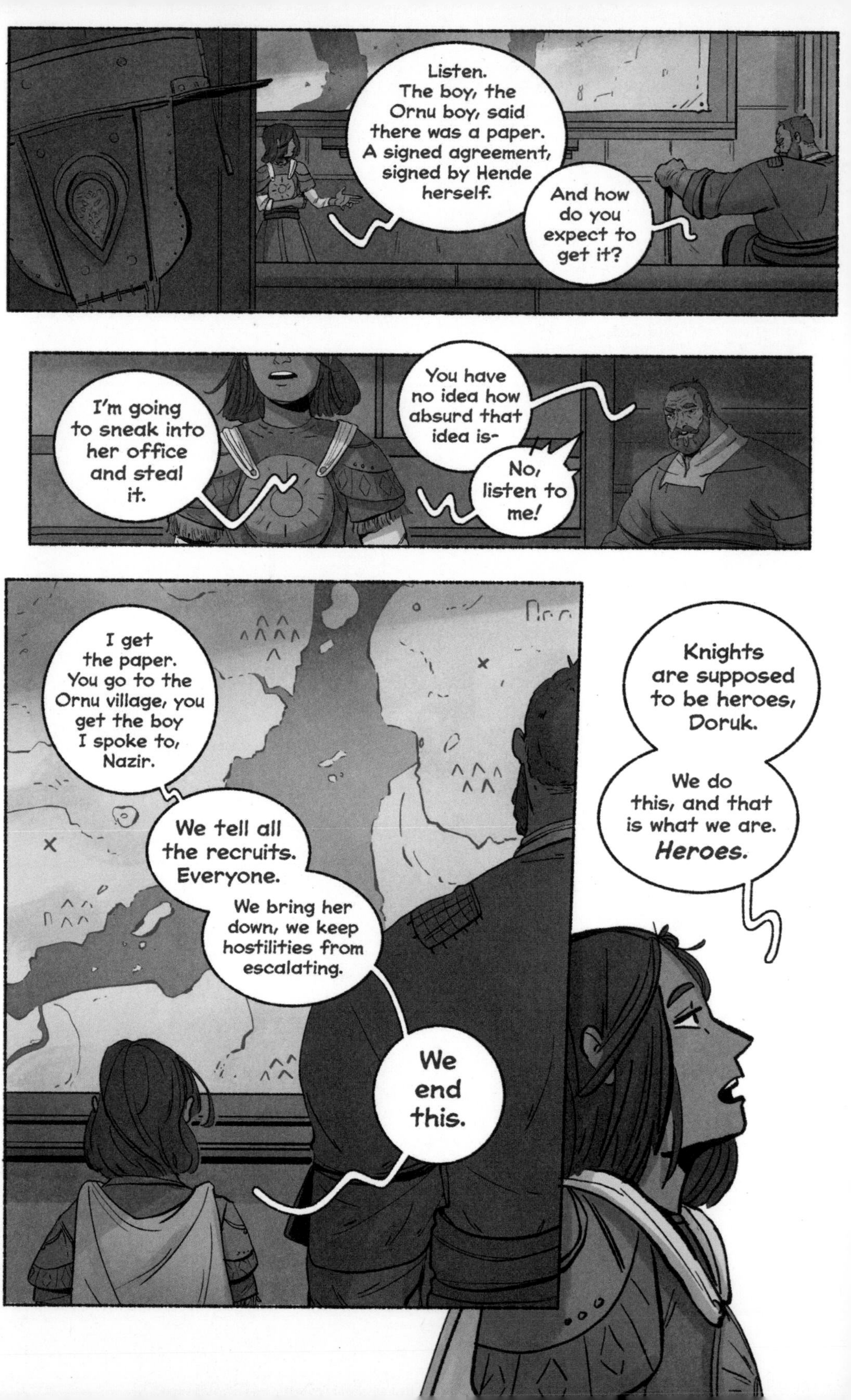

Listen. The boy, the Ornu boy, said there was a paper. A signed agreement, signed by Hende herself.
And how do you expect to get it?
I'm going to sneak into her office and steal it.
You have no idea how absurd that idea is-
No, listen to me!
I get the paper. You go to the Ornu village, you get the boy I spoke to, Nazir.
We tell all the recruits. Everyone.
We bring her down, we keep hostilities from escalating.
We end this.
Knights are supposed to be heroes, Doruk.
We do this, and that is what we are. *Heroes.*

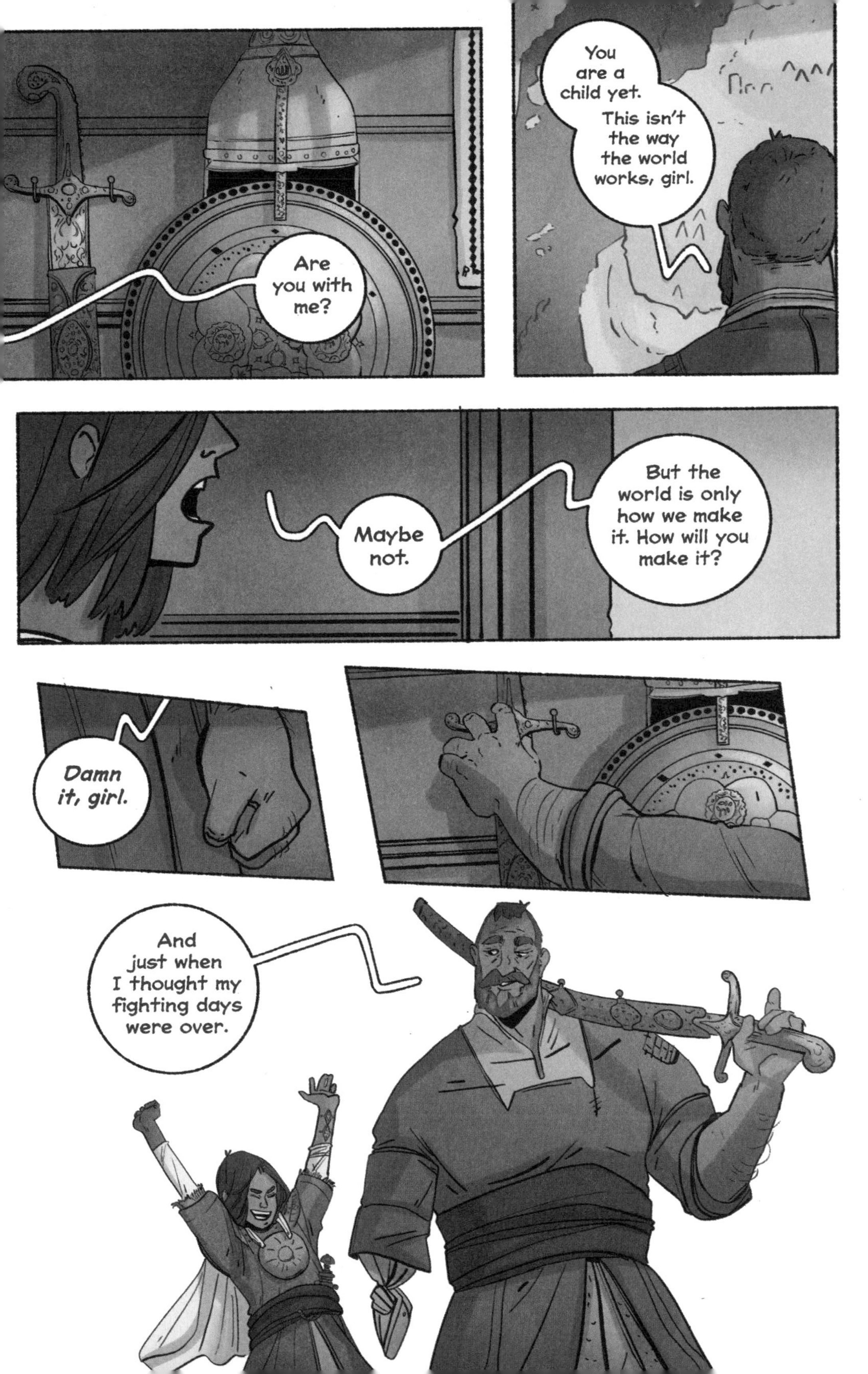
Are you with me?
You are a child yet.
This isn't the way the world works, girl.
Maybe not.
But the world is only how we make it. How will you make it?
Damn it, girl.
And just when I thought my fighting days were over.

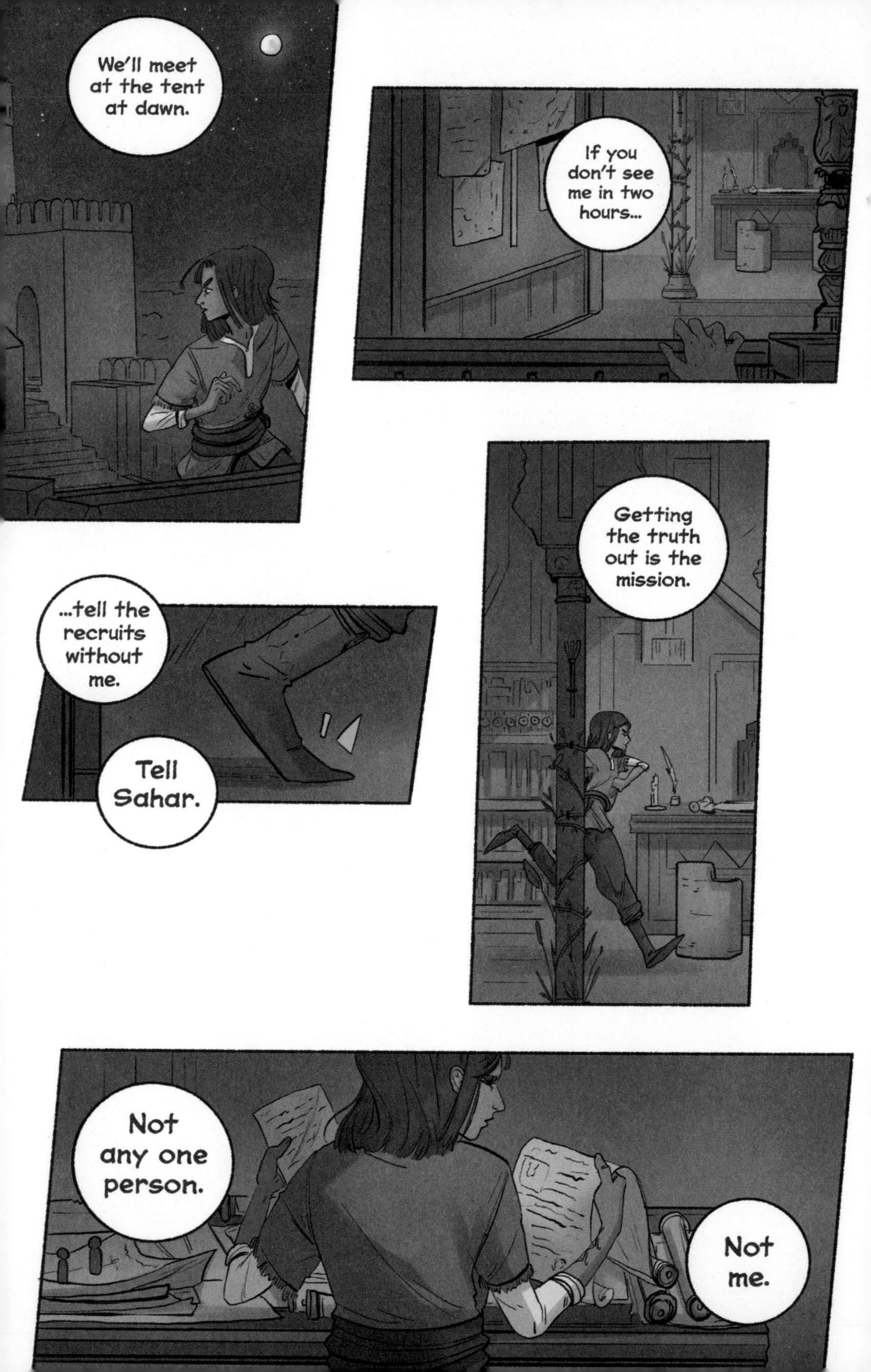
We'll meet at the tent at dawn.
If you don't see me in two hours...
...tell the recruits without me.
Tell Sahar.
Getting the truth out is the mission.
Not any one person.
Not me.

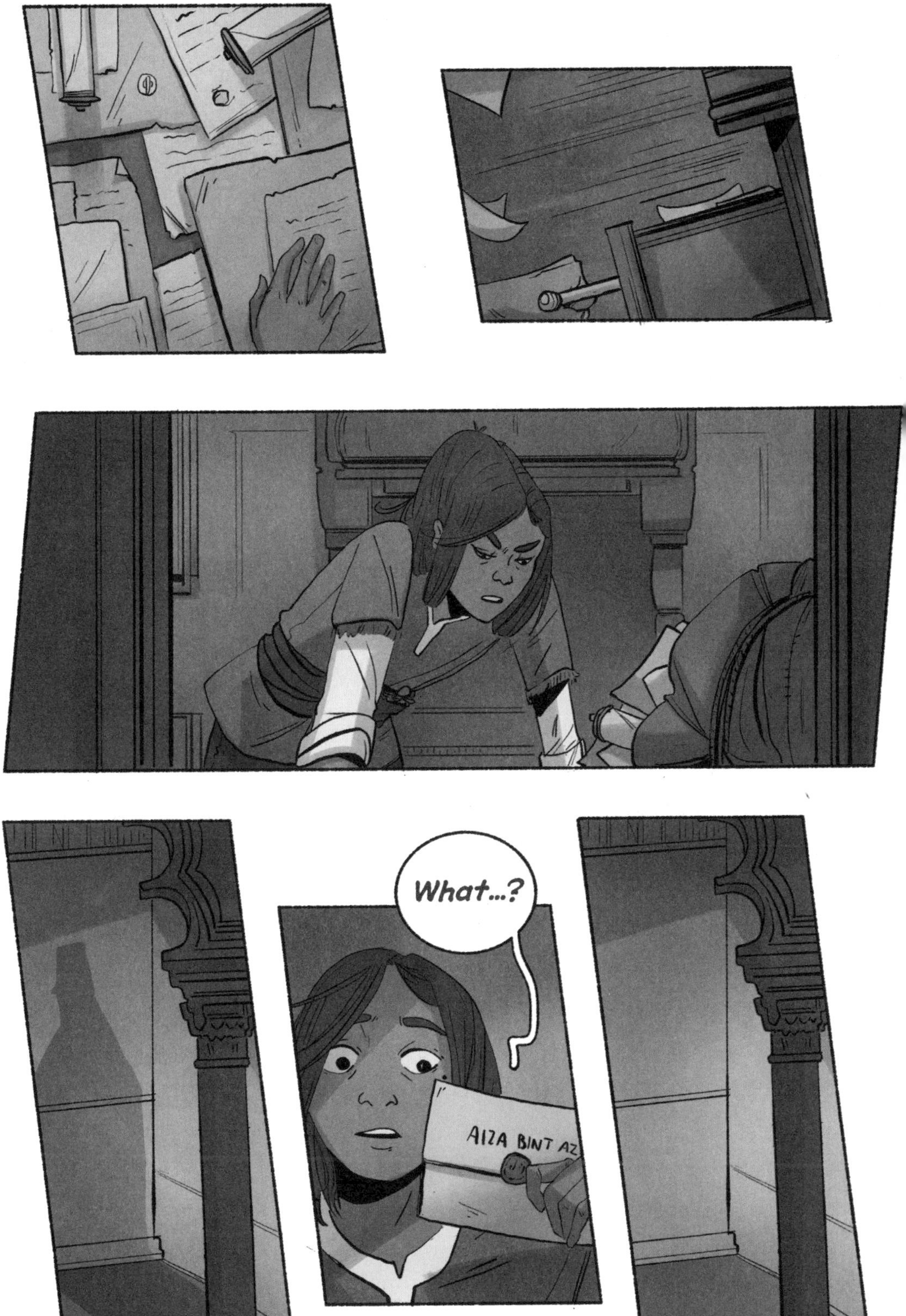
What...?
AIZA BINT AZ

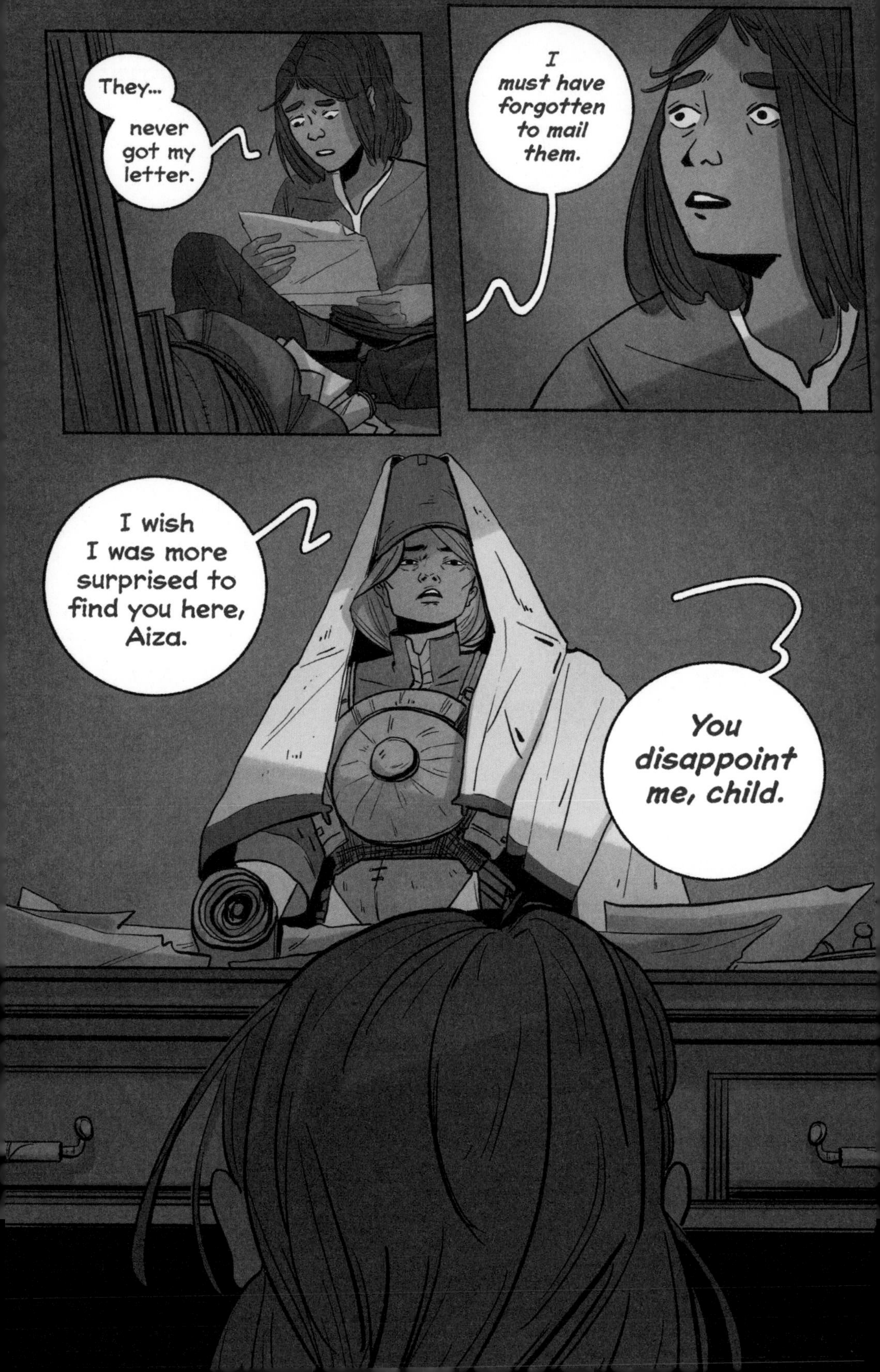
They...
never got my letter.
I must have forgotten to mail them.
I wish I was more surprised to find you here, Aiza.
You disappoint me, child.

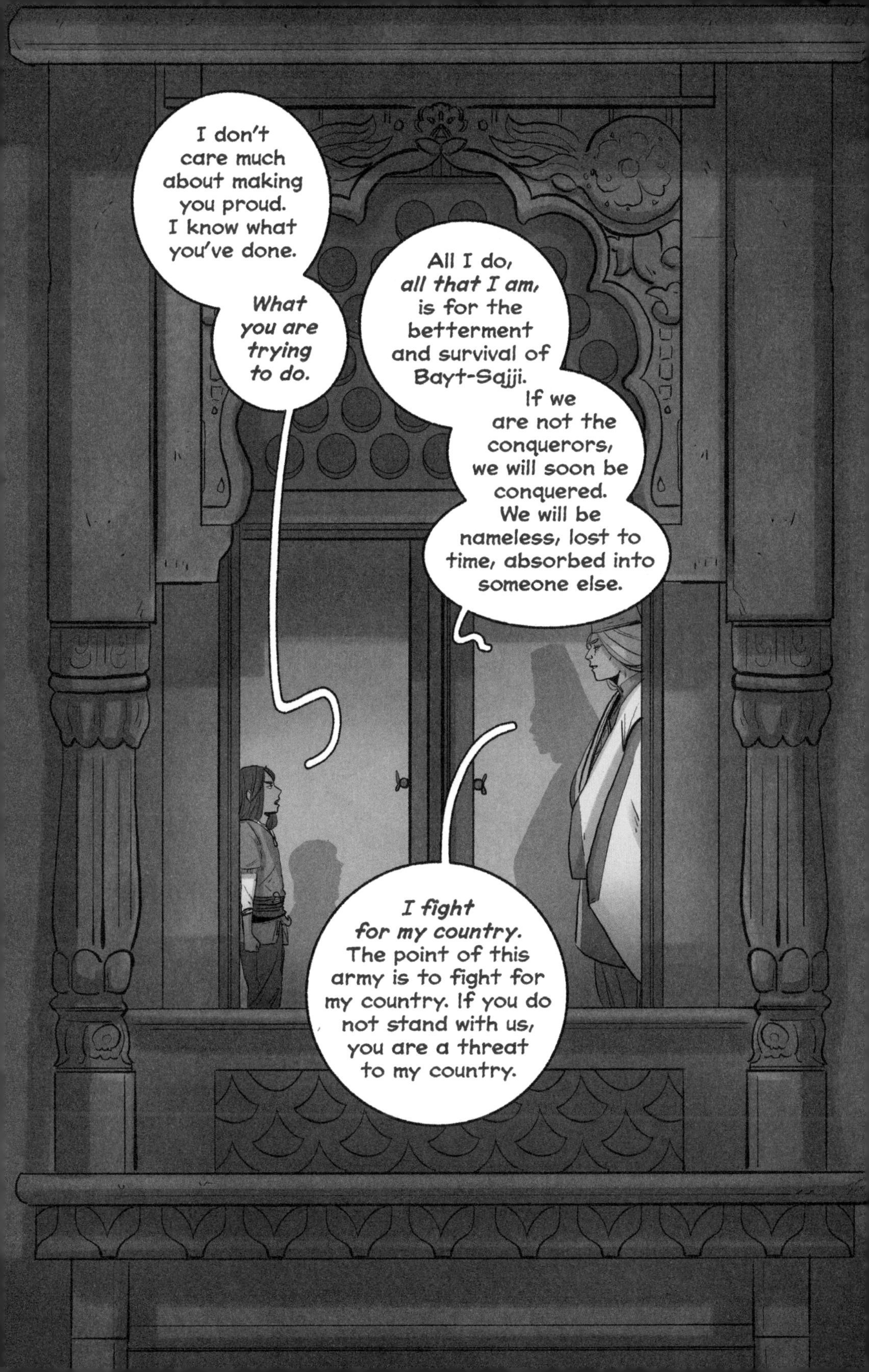
I don't care much about making you proud. I know what you've done.
What you are trying to do.
All I do, *all that I am,* is for the betterment and survival of Bayt-Sajji.
If we are not the conquerors, we will soon be conquered. We will be nameless, lost to time, absorbed into someone else.
I fight for my country. The point of this army is to fight for my country. If you do not stand with us, you are a threat to my country.

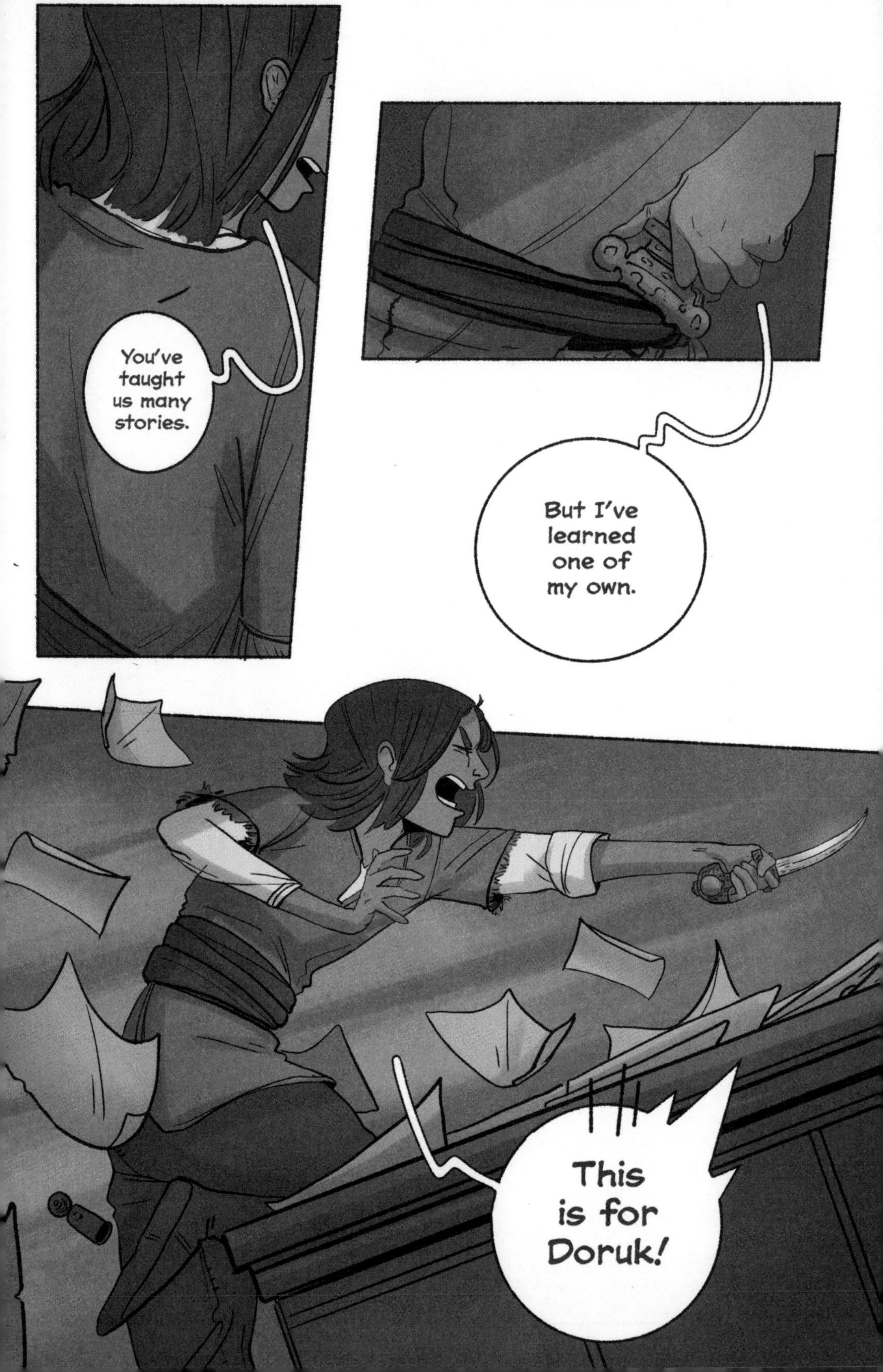
You've taught us many stories.
But I've learned one of my own.
This is for Doruk!

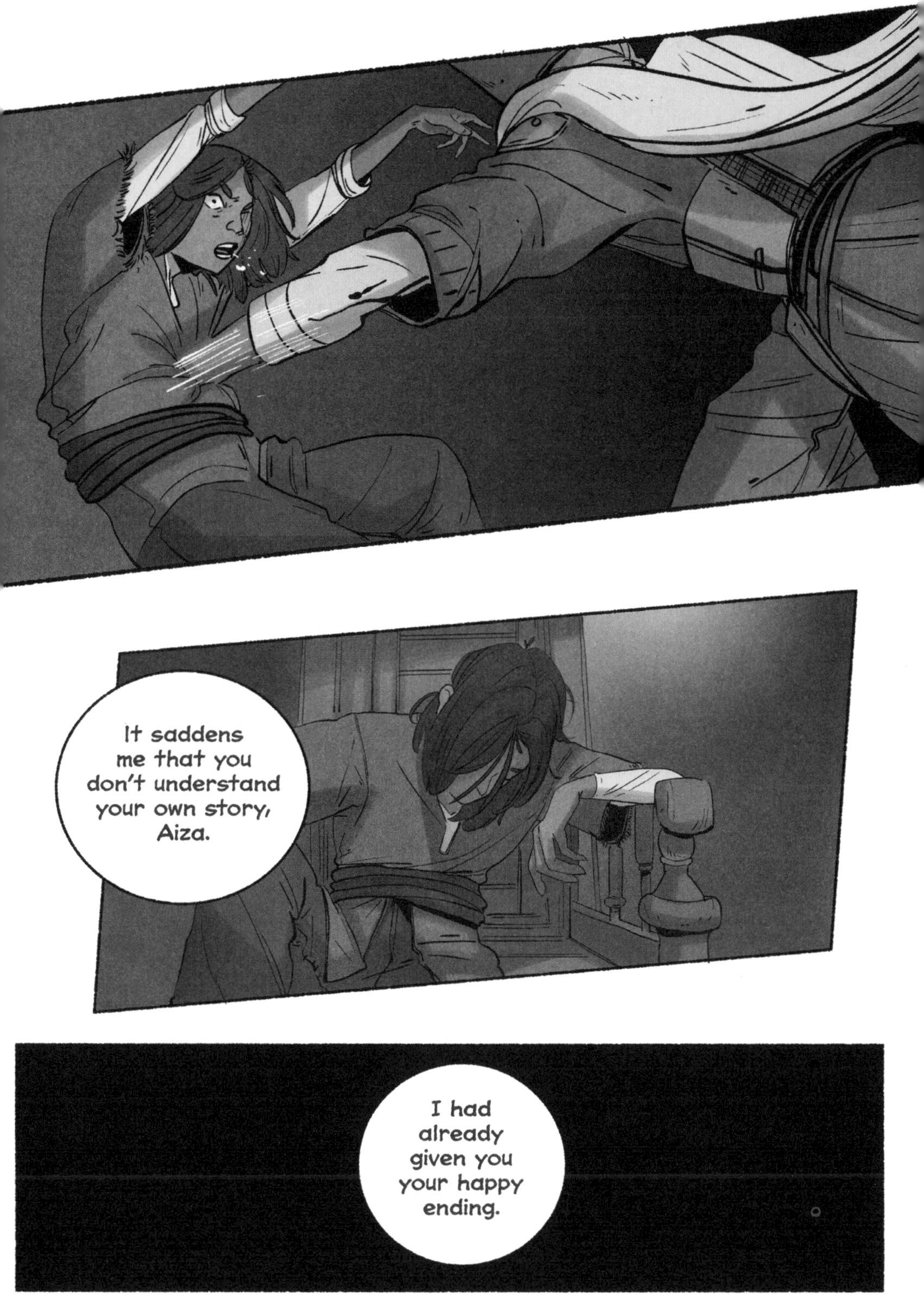
It saddens me that you don't understand your own story, Aiza.
I had already given you your happy ending.

CHAPTER 13

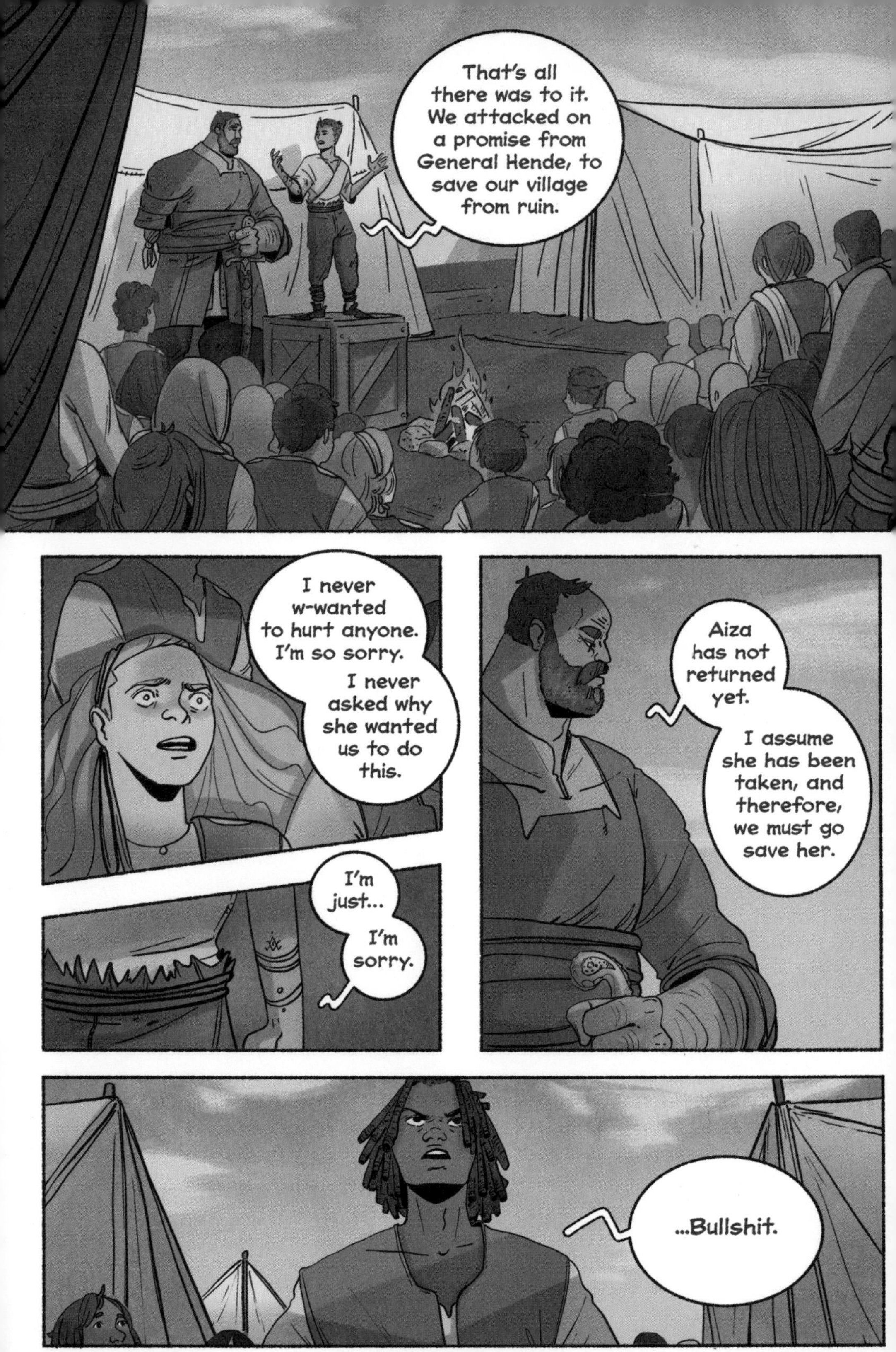

That's all there was to it. We attacked on a promise from General Hende, to save our village from ruin.
I never w-wanted to hurt anyone. I'm so sorry.
I never asked why she wanted us to do this.
I'm just...
I'm sorry.
Aiza has not returned yet.
I assume she has been taken, and therefore, we must go save her.
...Bullshit.

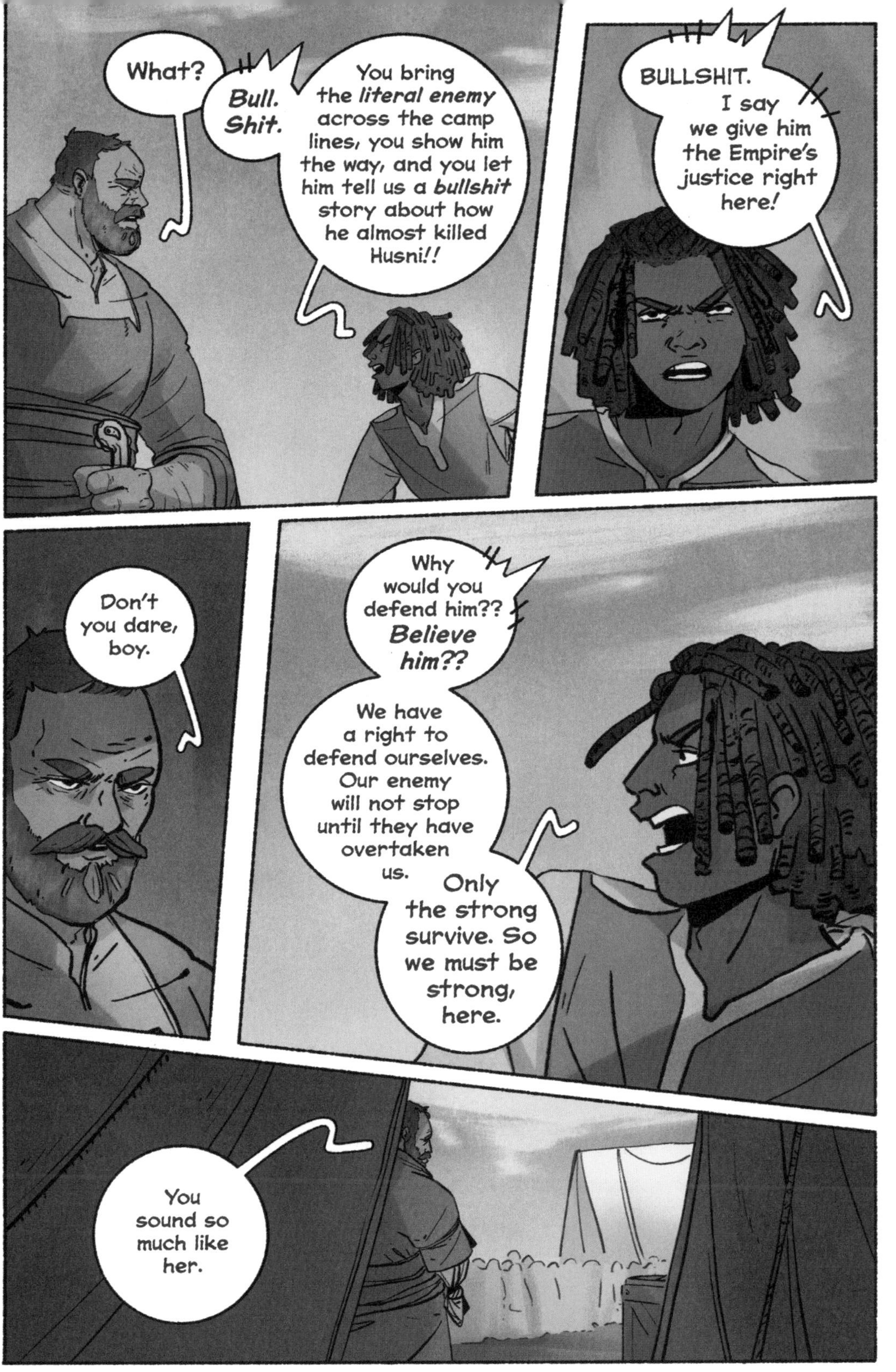
What?
Bull. Shit.
You bring the literal enemy across the camp lines, you show him the way, and you let him tell us a bullshit story about how he almost killed Husni!!
BULLSHIT. I say we give him the Empire's justice right here!
Don't you dare, boy.
Why would you defend him?? Believe him??
We have a right to defend ourselves. Our enemy will not stop until they have overtaken us.
Only the strong survive. So we must be strong, here.
You sound so much like her.

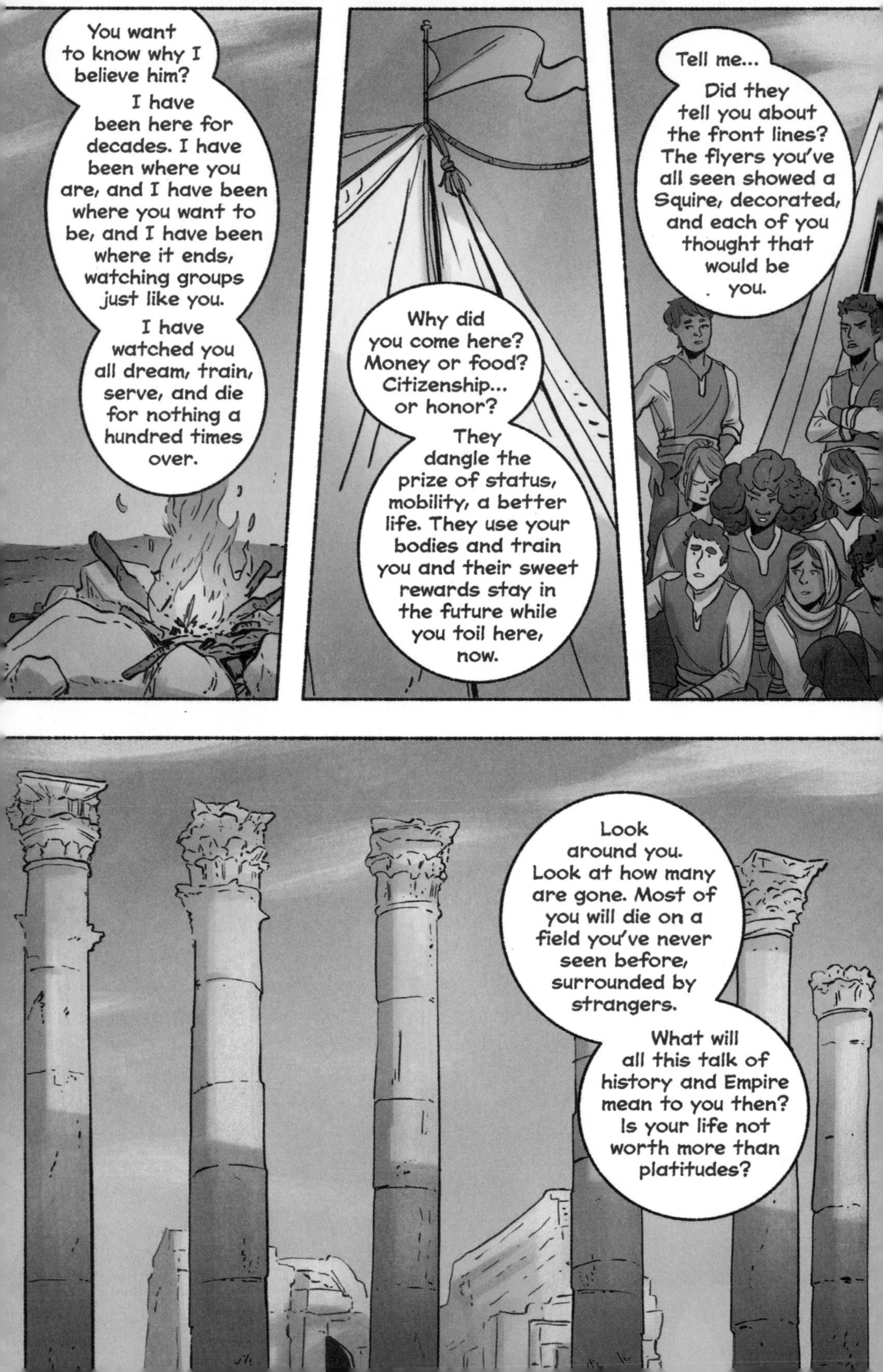
You want to know why I believe him?
I have been here for decades. I have been where you are, and I have been where you want to be, and I have been where it ends, watching groups just like you.
I have watched you all dream, train, serve, and die for nothing a hundred times over.
Why did you come here? Money or food? Citizenship... or honor?
They dangle the prize of status, mobility, a better life. They use your bodies and train you and their sweet rewards stay in the future while you toil here, now.
Tell me...
Did they tell you about the front lines? The flyers you've all seen showed a Squire, decorated, and each of you thought that would be you.
Look around you. Look at how many are gone. Most of you will die on a field you've never seen before, surrounded by strangers.
What will all this talk of history and Empire mean to you then? Is your life not worth more than platitudes?

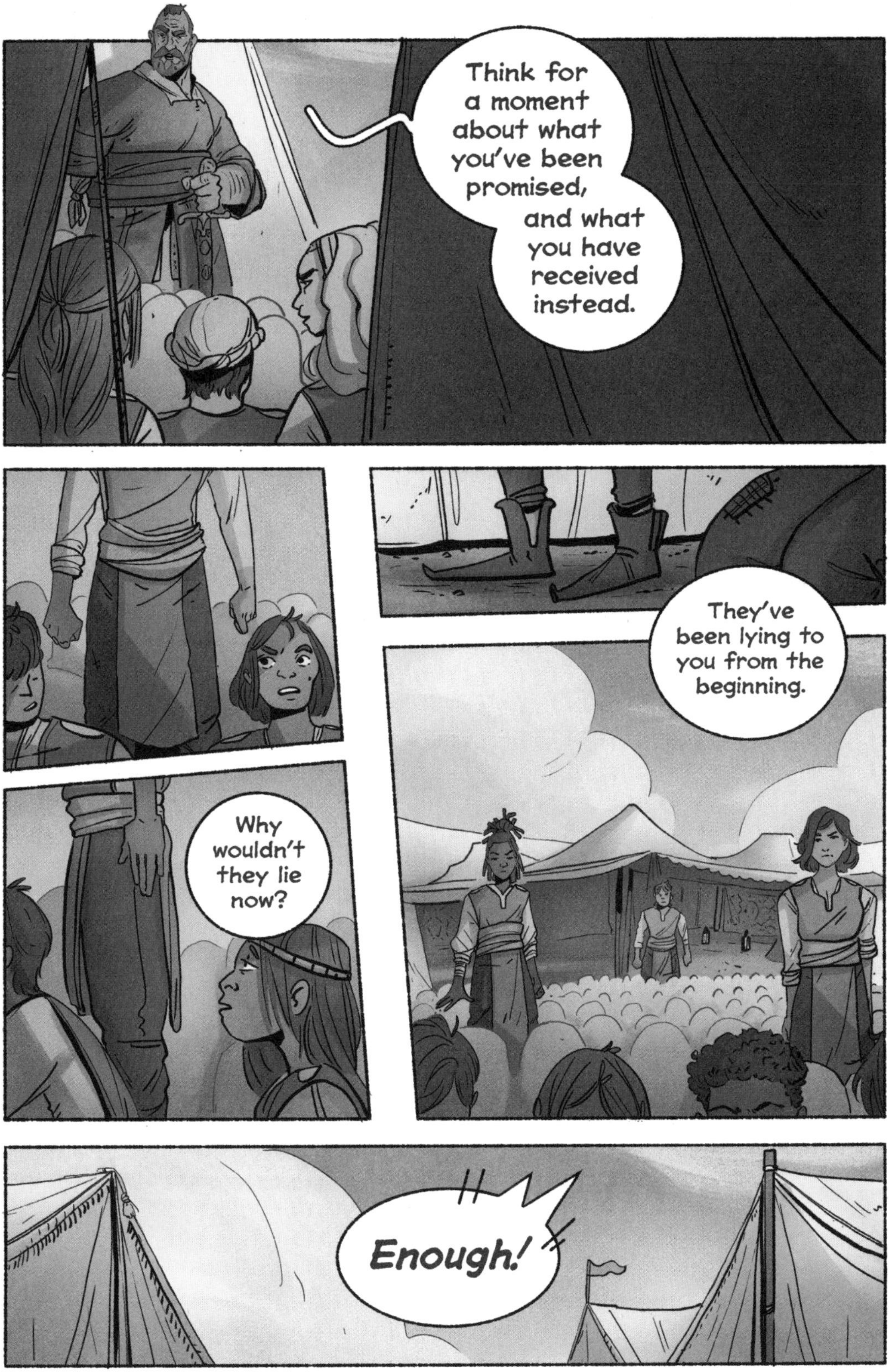
Think for a moment about what you've been promised,
and what you have received instead.
They've been lying to you from the beginning.
Why wouldn't they lie now?
Enough!

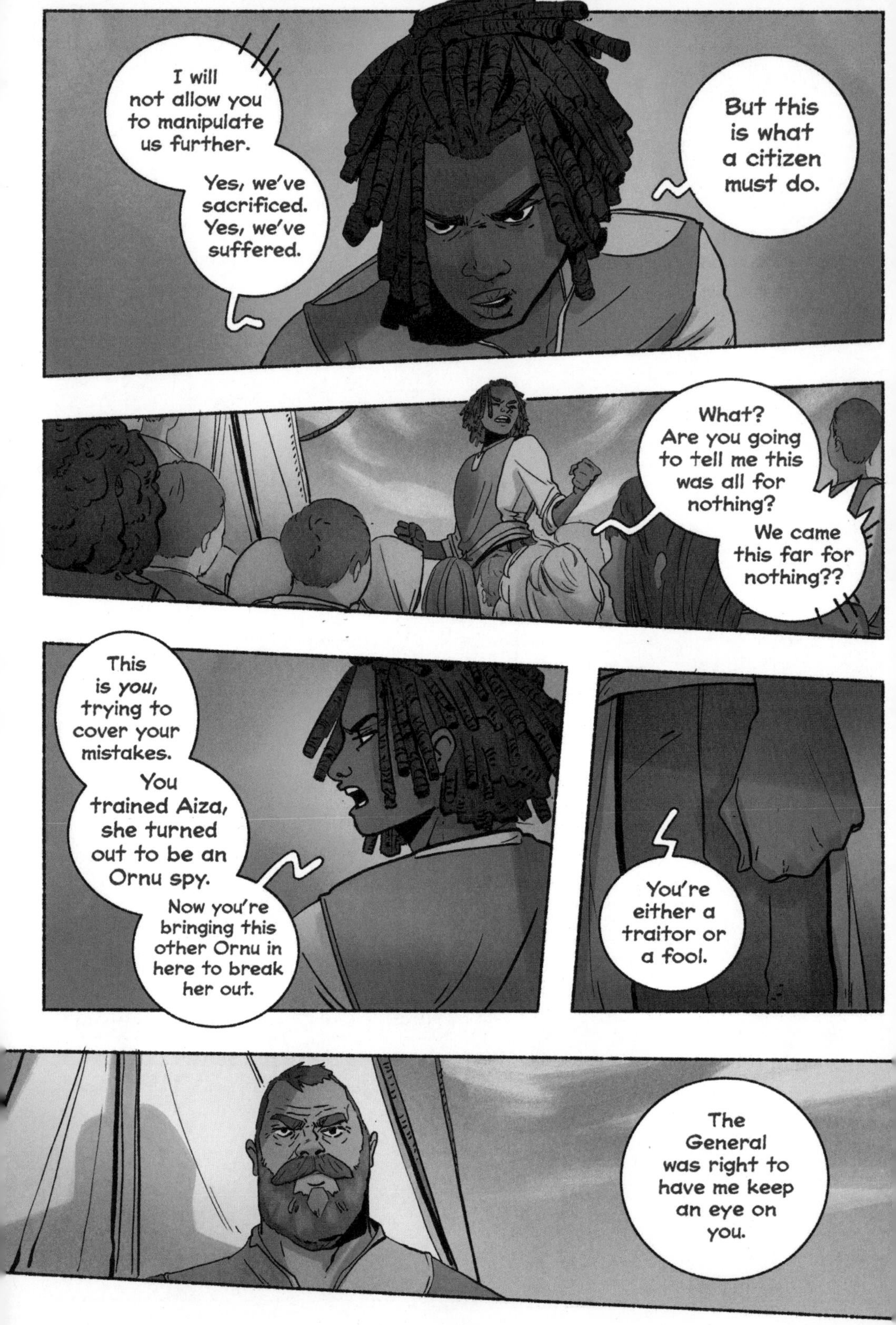

I will not allow you to manipulate us further.
Yes, we've sacrificed. Yes, we've suffered.
But this is what a citizen must do.
What? Are you going to tell me this was all for nothing?
We came this far for nothing??
This is *you,* trying to cover your mistakes.
You trained Aiza, she turned out to be an Ornu spy.
Now you're bringing this other Ornu in here to break her out.
You're either a traitor or a fool.
The General was right to have me keep an eye on you.

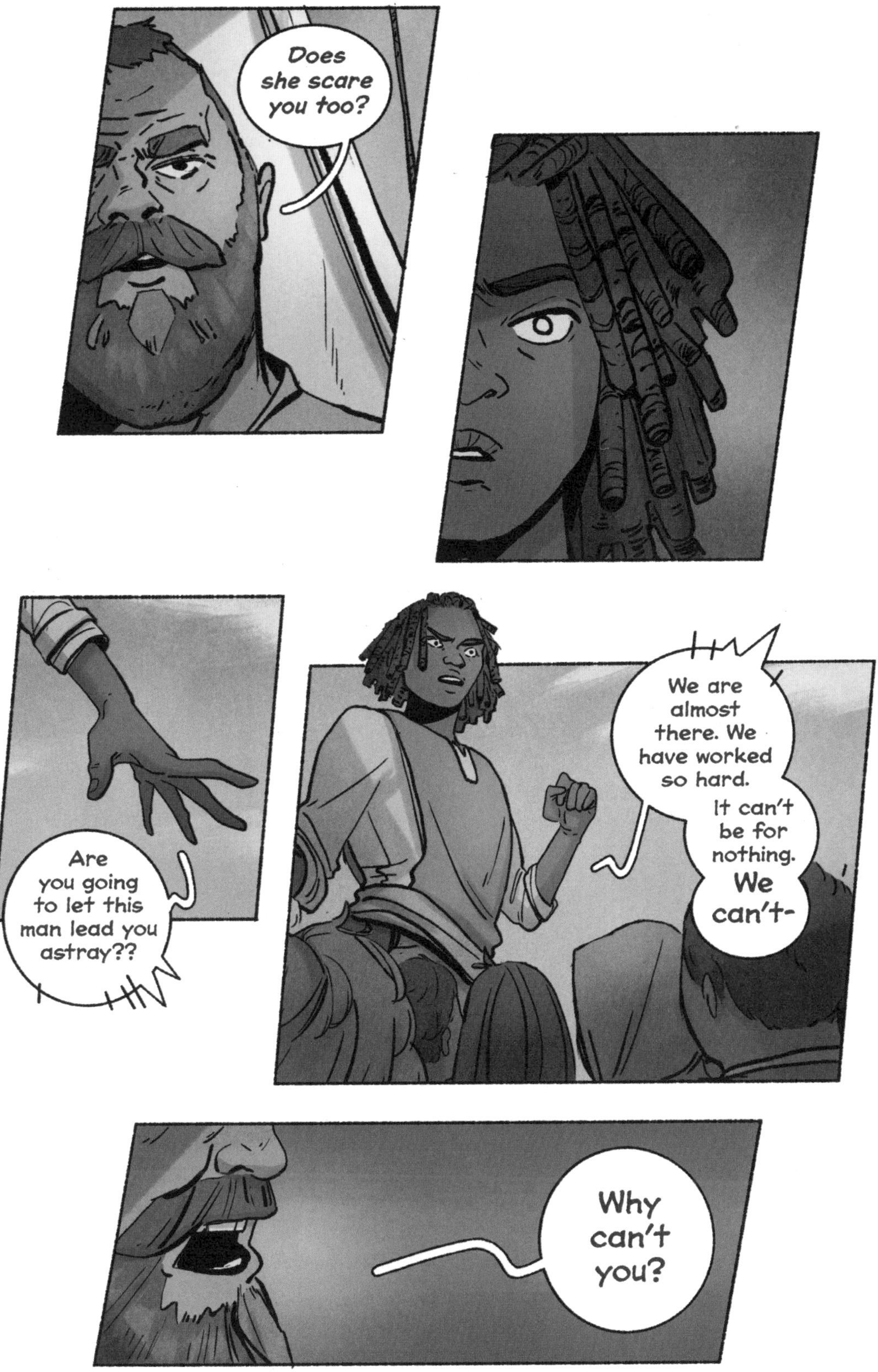
Does she scare you too?
Are you going to let this man lead you astray??
We are almost there. We have worked so hard.
It can't be for nothing.
We can't-
Why can't you?

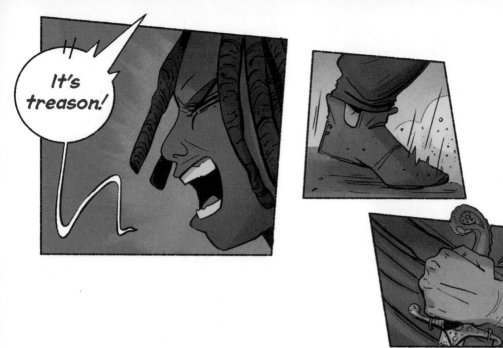

It's treason!

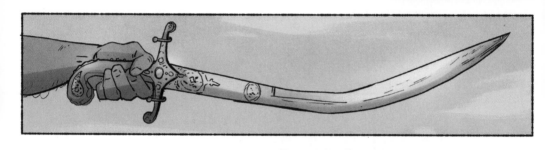

I stand for no Ornu.

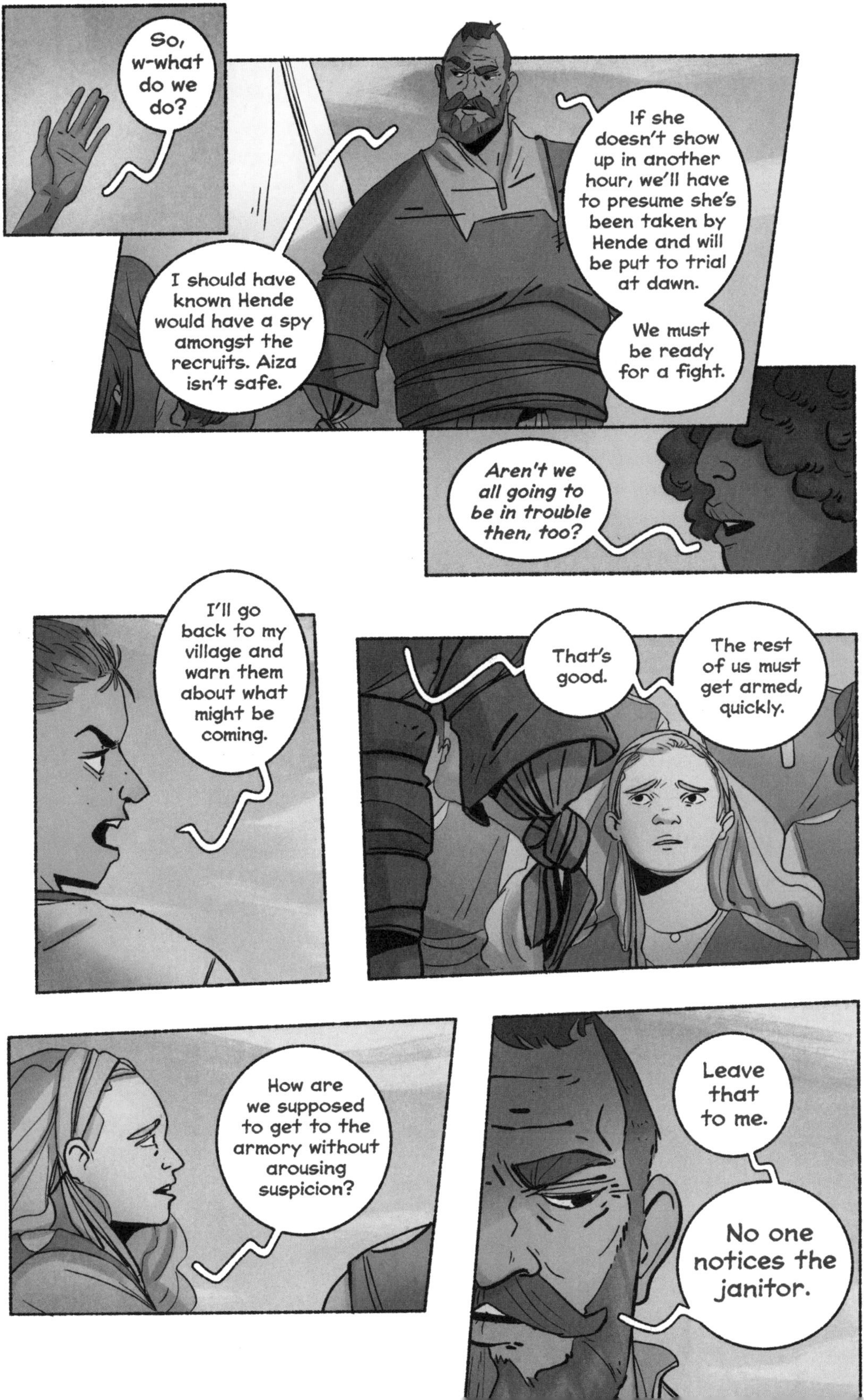
So, w-what do we do?
I should have known Hende would have a spy amongst the recruits. Aiza isn't safe.
If she doesn't show up in another hour, we'll have to presume she's been taken by Hende and will be put to trial at dawn.
We must be ready for a fight.
Aren't we all going to be in trouble then, too?
I'll go back to my village and warn them about what might be coming.
That's good.
The rest of us must get armed, quickly.
How are we supposed to get to the armory without arousing suspicion?
Leave that to me.
No one notices the janitor.

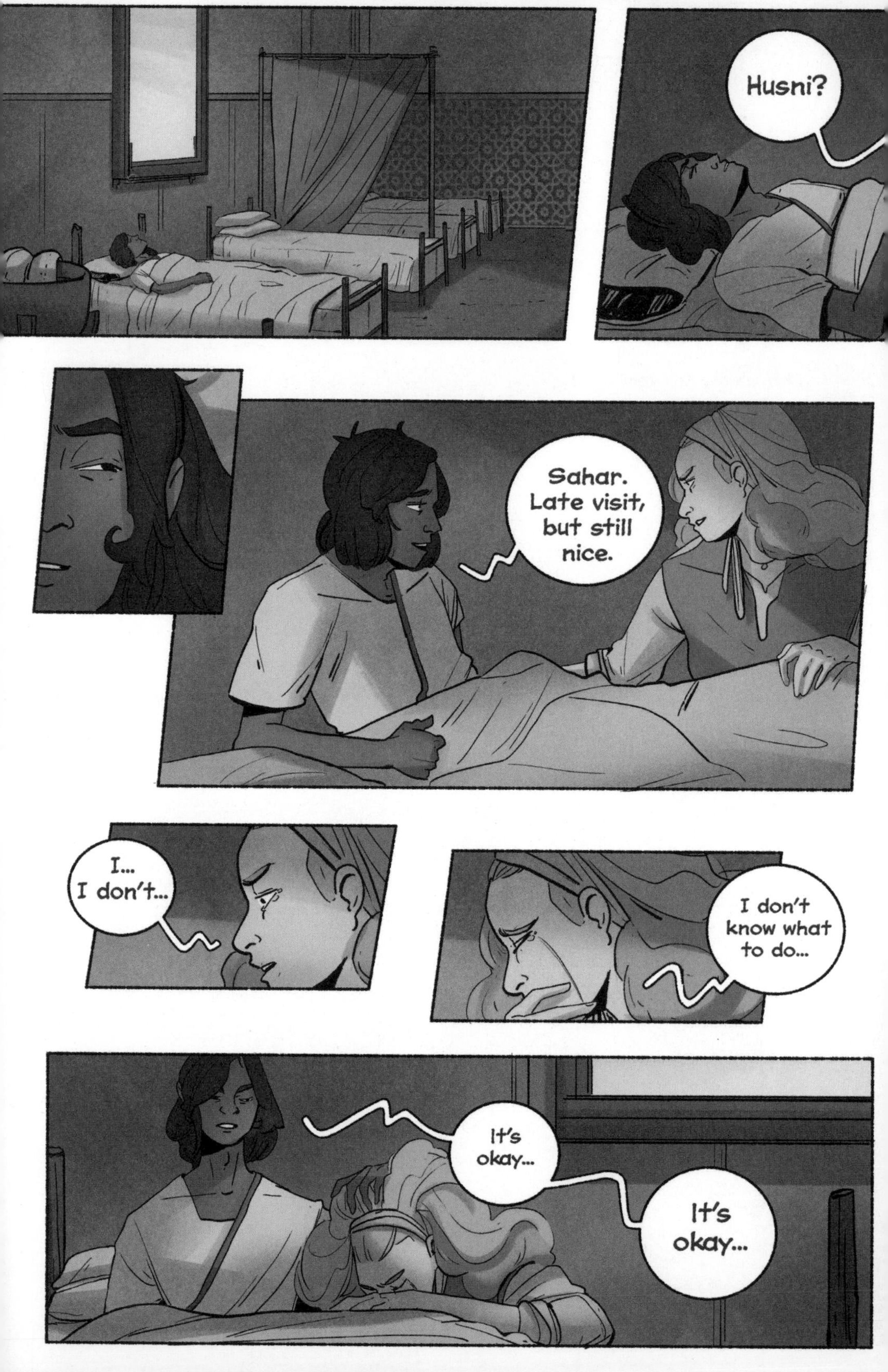
Husni?
Sahar. Late visit, but still nice.
I... I don't...
I don't know what to do...
It's okay...
It's okay...

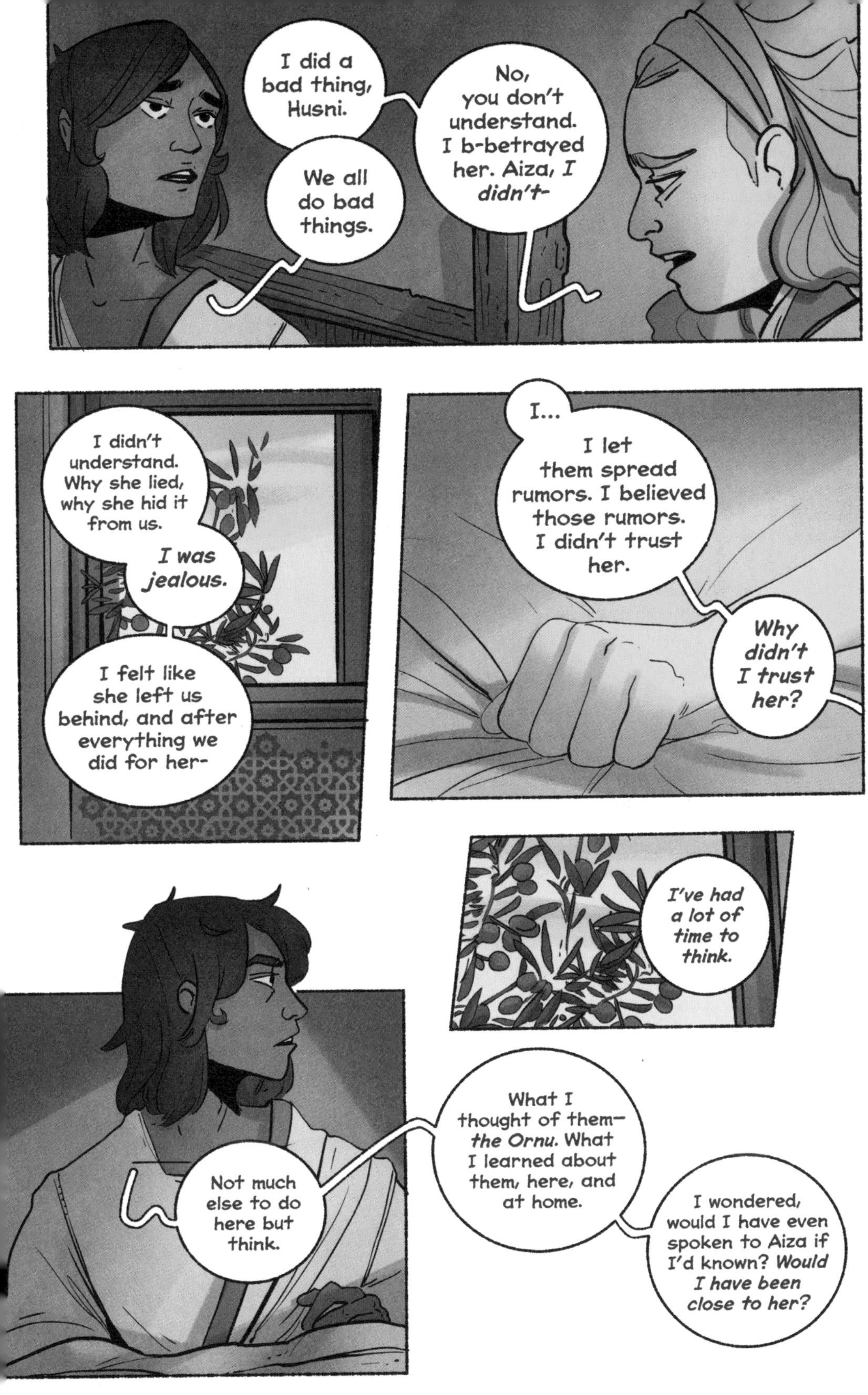
I did a bad thing, Husni.
We all do bad things.
No, you don't understand. I b-betrayed her. Aiza, *I didn't-*
I didn't understand. Why she lied, why she hid it from us.
I was jealous.
I felt like she left us behind, and after everything we did for her-
I...
I let them spread rumors. I believed those rumors. I didn't trust her.
Why didn't I trust her?
I've had a lot of time to think.
Not much else to do here but think.
What I thought of them- *the Ornu*. What I learned about them, here, and at home.
I wondered, would I have even spoken to Aiza if I'd known? *Would I have been close to her?*

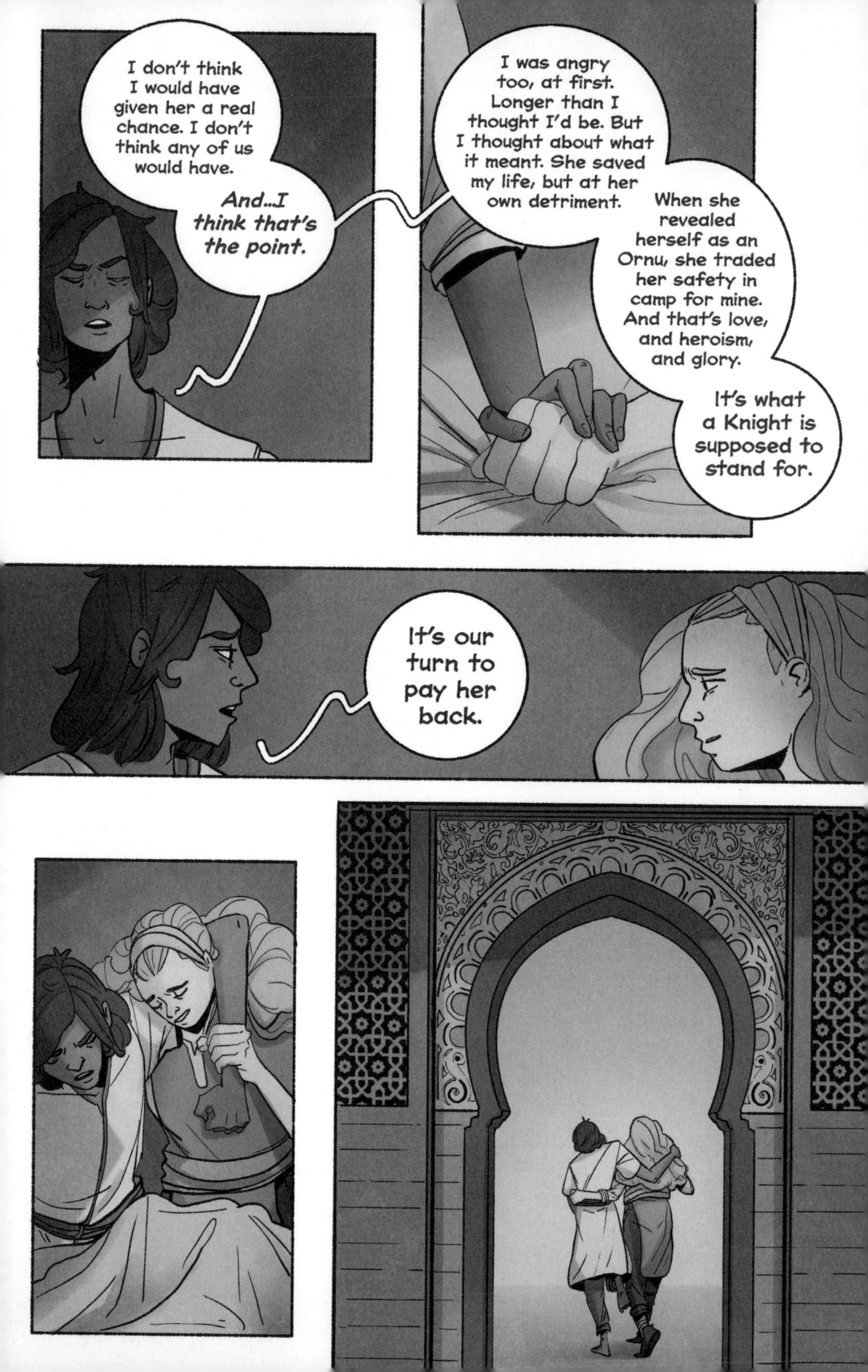
I don't think I would have given her a real chance. I don't think any of us would have.
And...I think that's the point.
I was angry too, at first. Longer than I thought I'd be. But I thought about what it meant. She saved my life, but at her own detriment.
When she revealed herself as an Ornu, she traded her safety in camp for mine. And that's love, and heroism, and glory.
It's what a Knight is supposed to stand for.
It's our turn to pay her back.

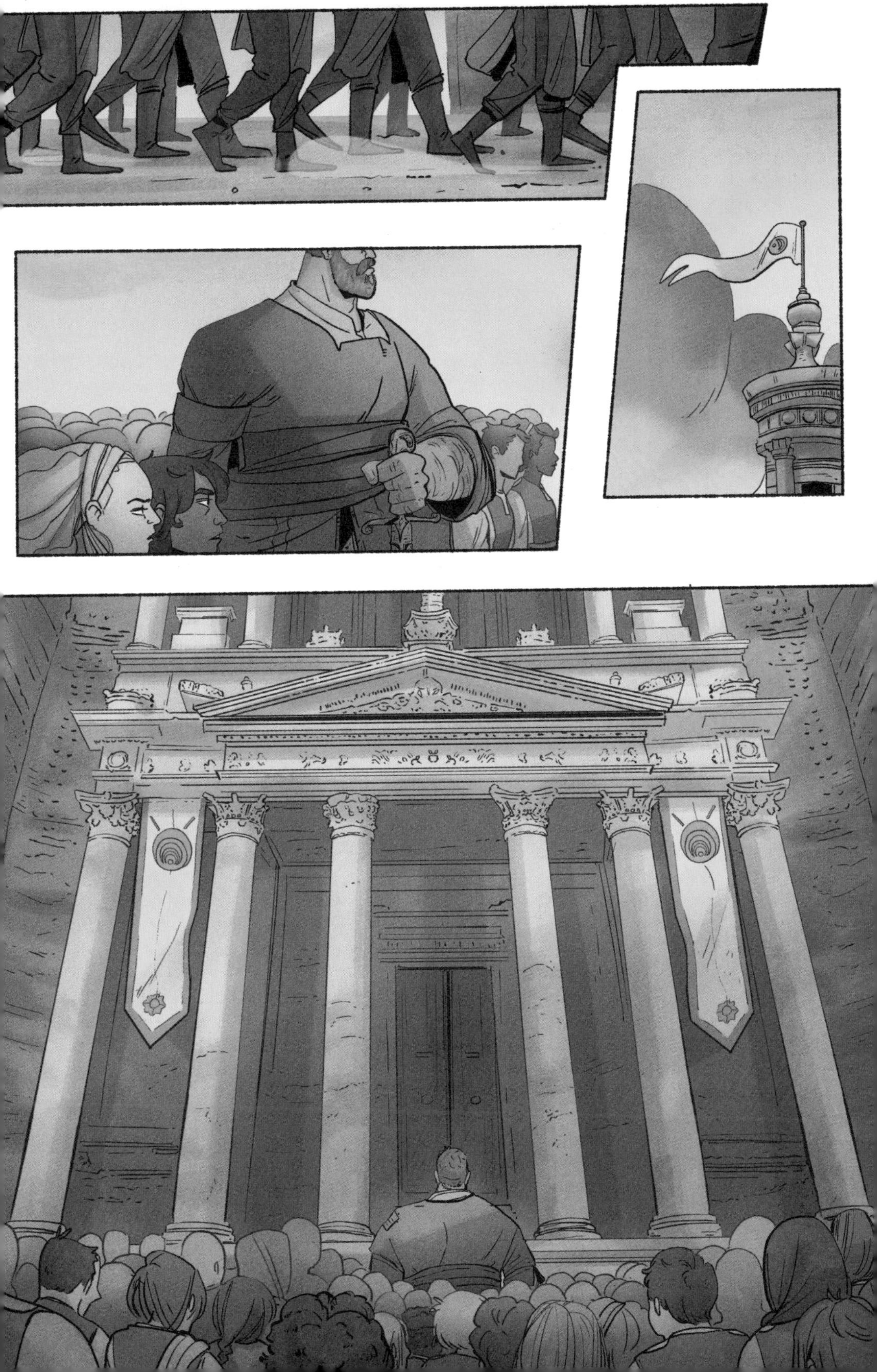

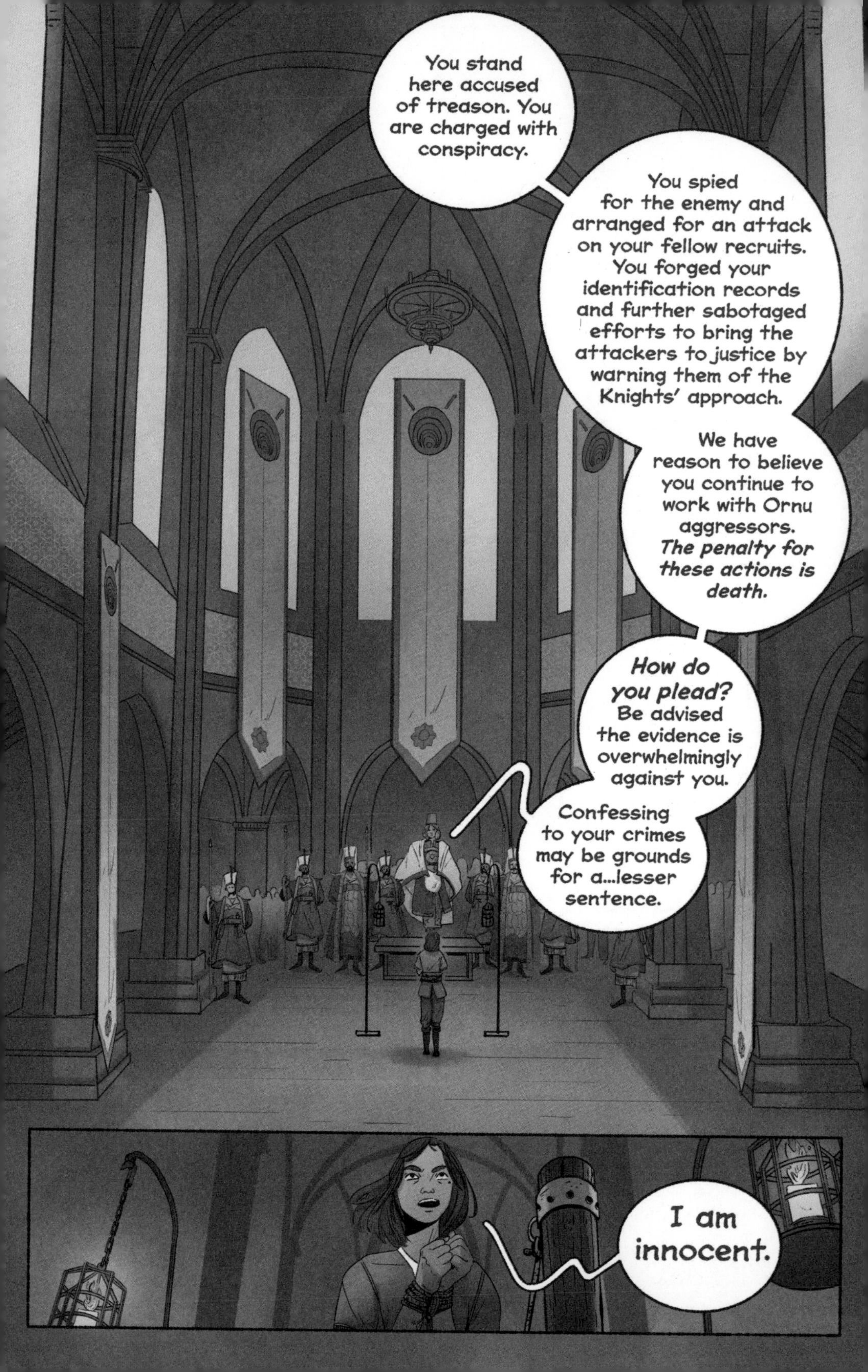
You stand here accused of treason. You are charged with conspiracy.
You spied for the enemy and arranged for an attack on your fellow recruits. You forged your identification records and further sabotaged efforts to bring the attackers to justice by warning them of the Knights' approach.
We have reason to believe you continue to work with Ornu aggressors. *The penalty for these actions is death.*
How do you plead? Be advised the evidence is overwhelmingly against you.
Confessing to your crimes may be grounds for a...lesser sentence.
I am innocent.

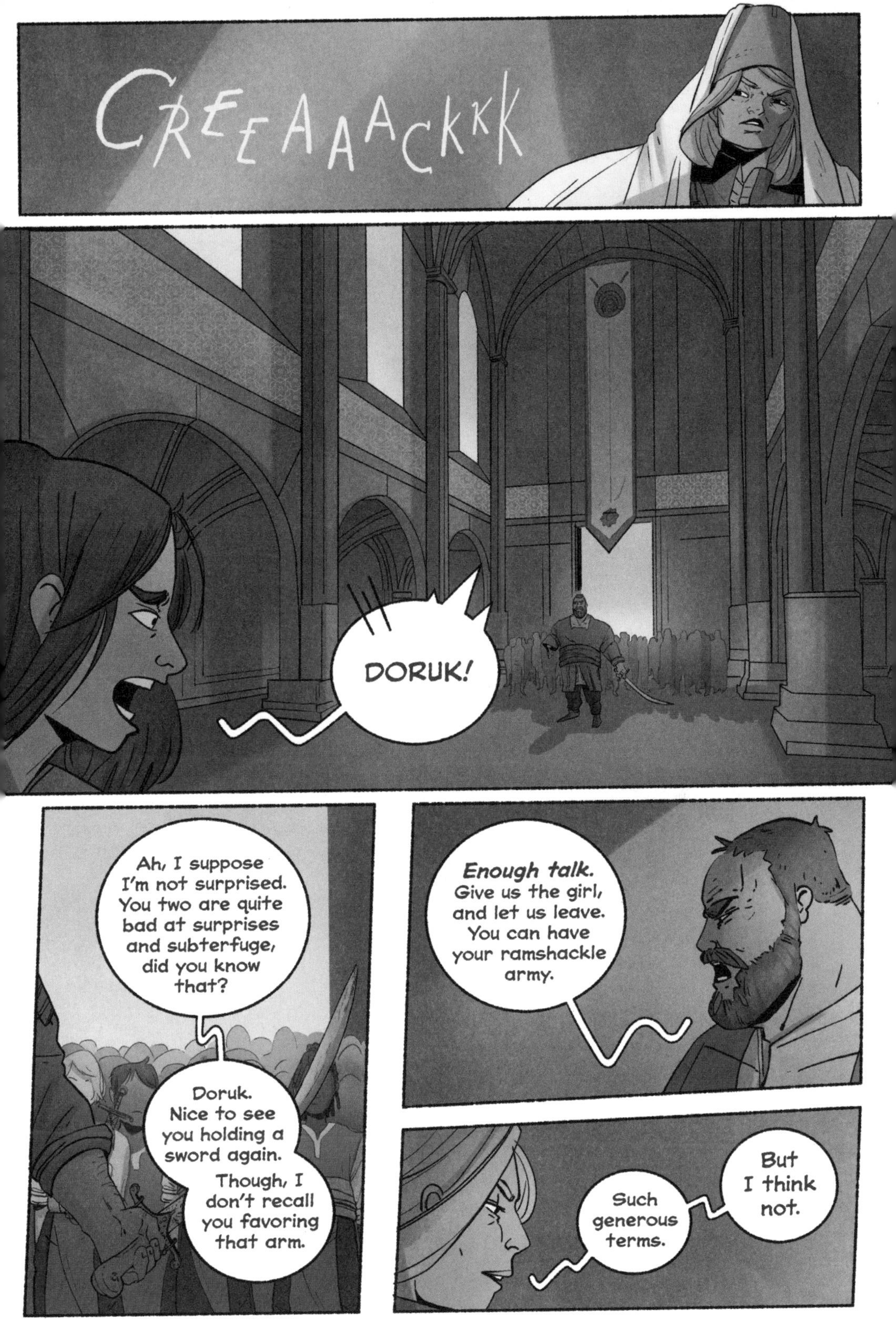

CREEAAACKKK
DORUK!
Ah, I suppose I'm not surprised. You two are quite bad at surprises and subterfuge, did you know that?
Doruk. Nice to see you holding a sword again.
Though, I don't recall you favoring that arm.
Enough talk. Give us the girl, and let us leave. You can have your ramshackle army.
Such generous terms.
But I think not.

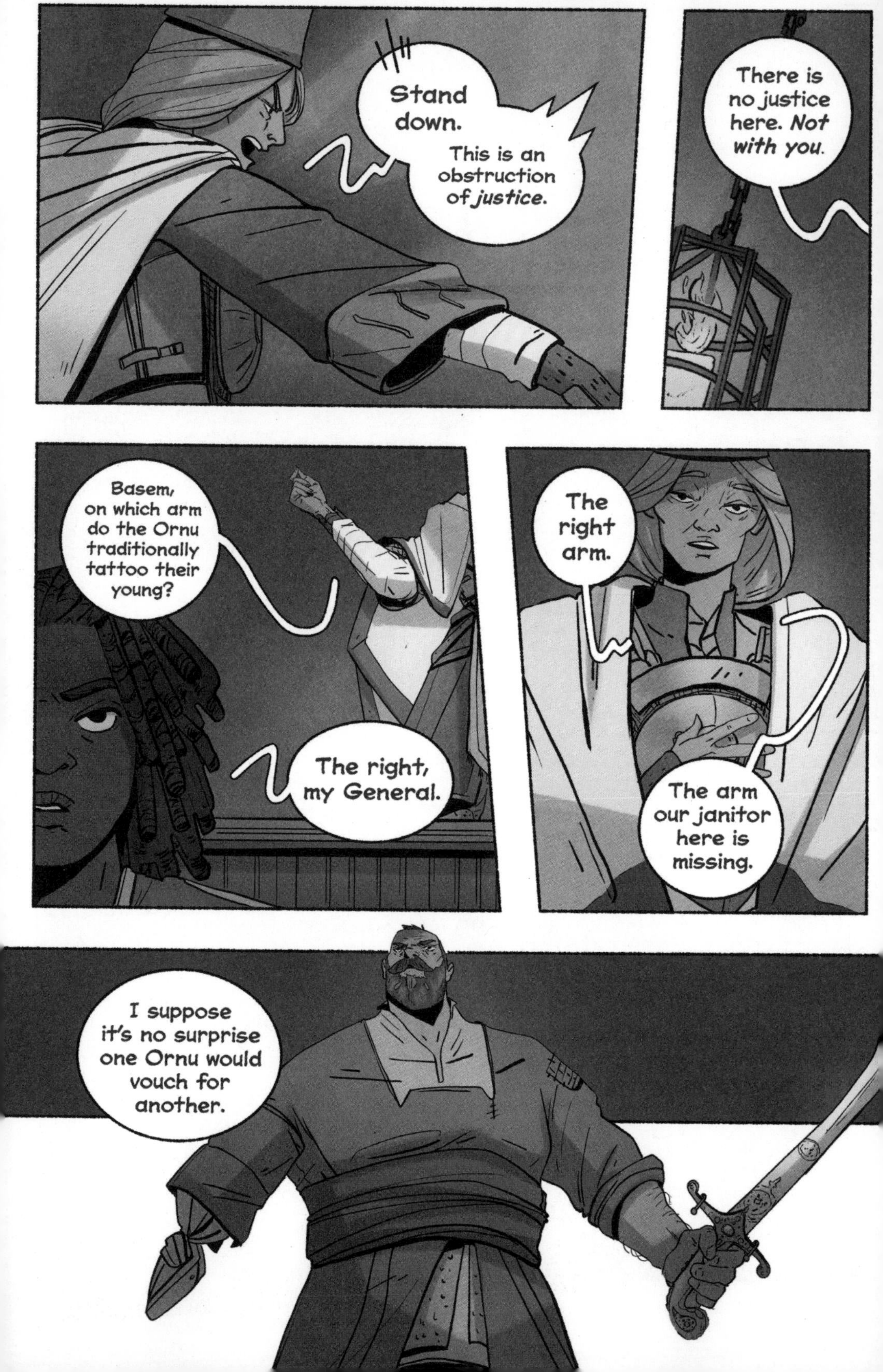
Stand down.
This is an obstruction of *justice*.
There is no justice here. *Not with you*.
Basem, on which arm do the Ornu traditionally tattoo their young?
The right, my General.
The right arm.
The arm our janitor here is missing.
I suppose it's no surprise one Ornu would vouch for another.

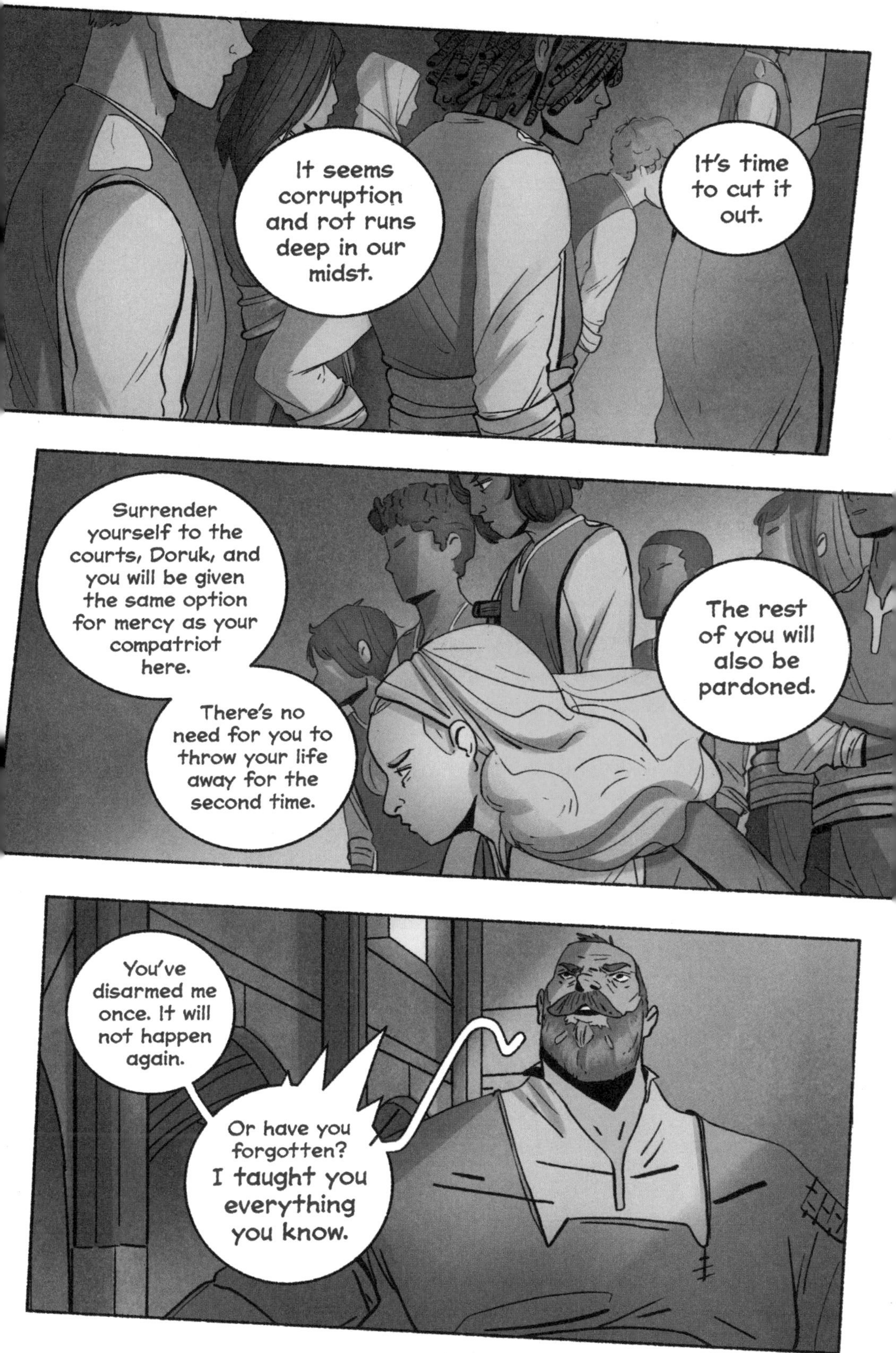
It seems corruption and rot runs deep in our midst.
It's time to cut it out.
Surrender yourself to the courts, Doruk, and you will be given the same option for mercy as your compatriot here.
There's no need for you to throw your life away for the second time.
The rest of you will also be pardoned.
You've disarmed me once. It will not happen again.
Or have you forgotten? I taught you everything you know.

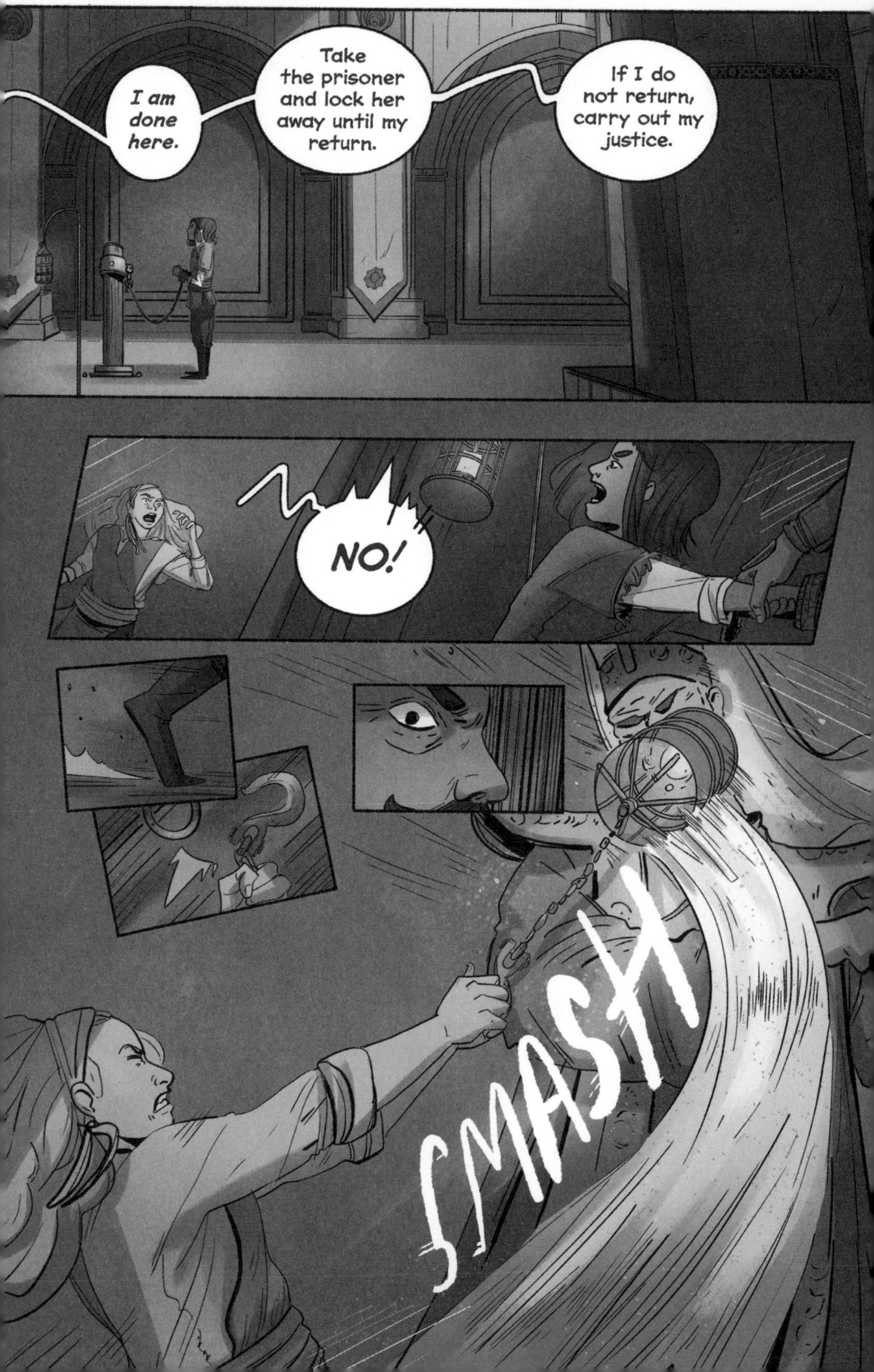
I am done here.
Take the prisoner and lock her away until my return.
If I do not return, carry out my justice.
NO!
SMASH

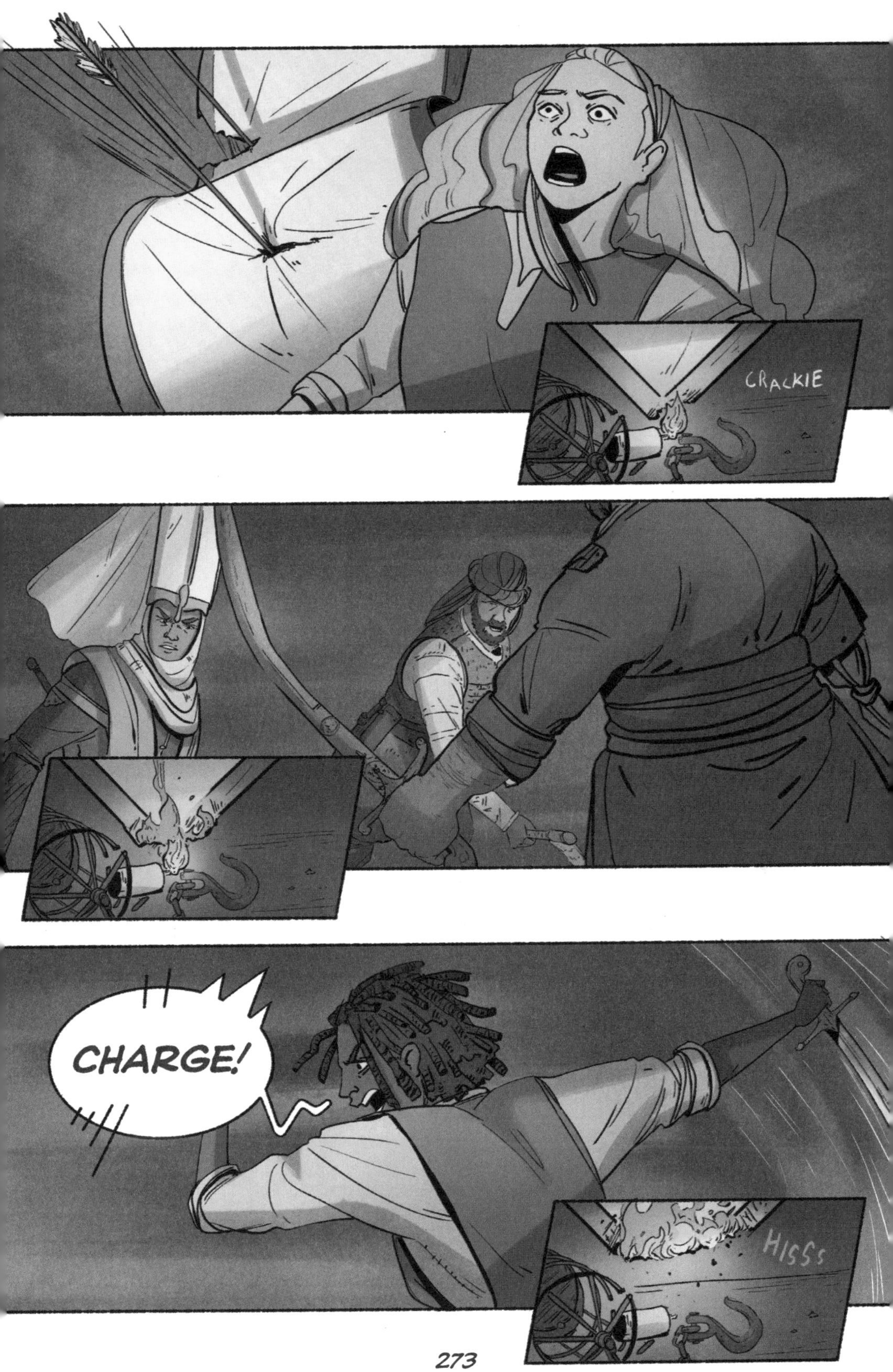
CRACKIE
CHARGE!
HISSS

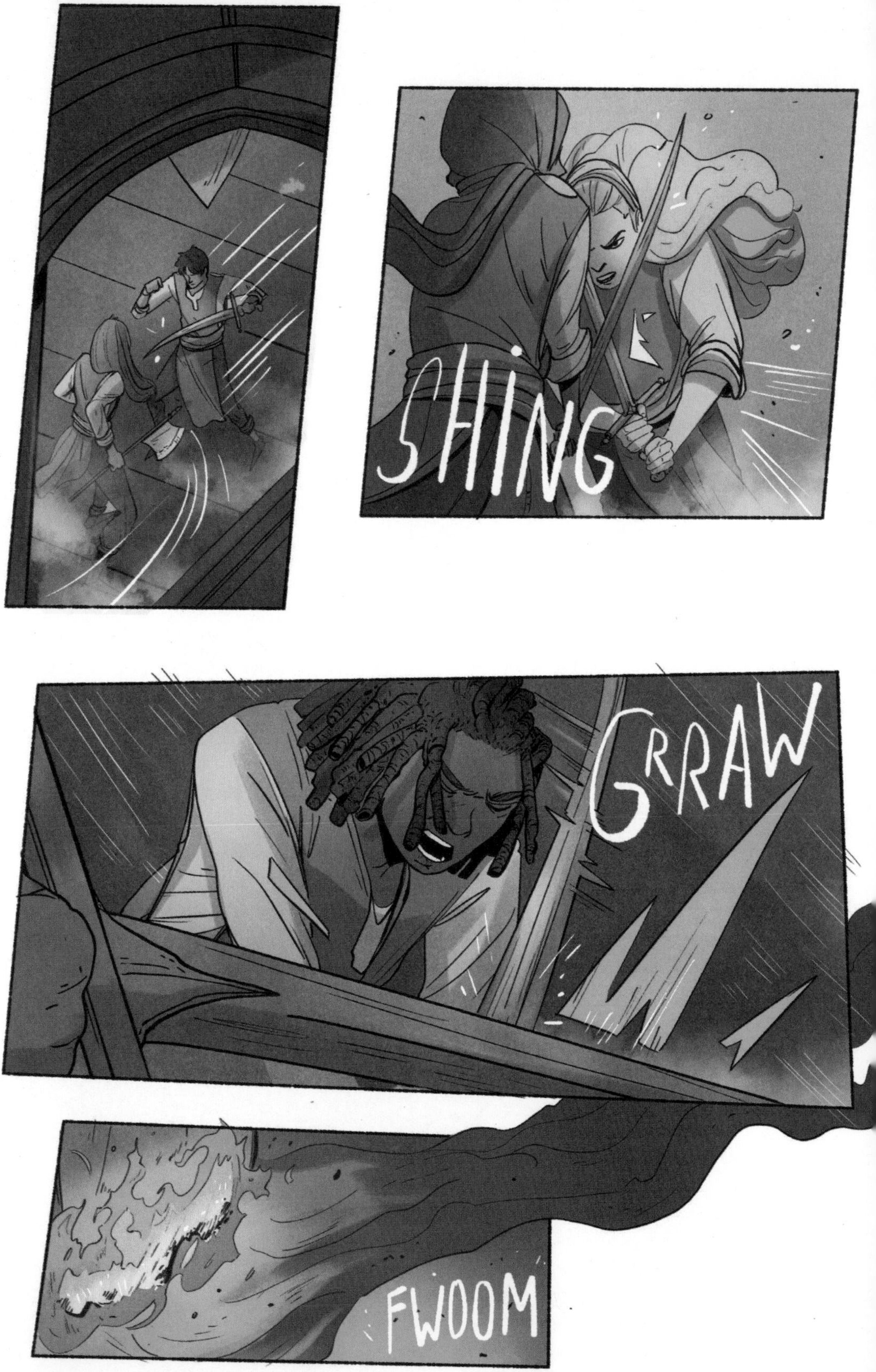
SHING
GRRAW
FWOOM

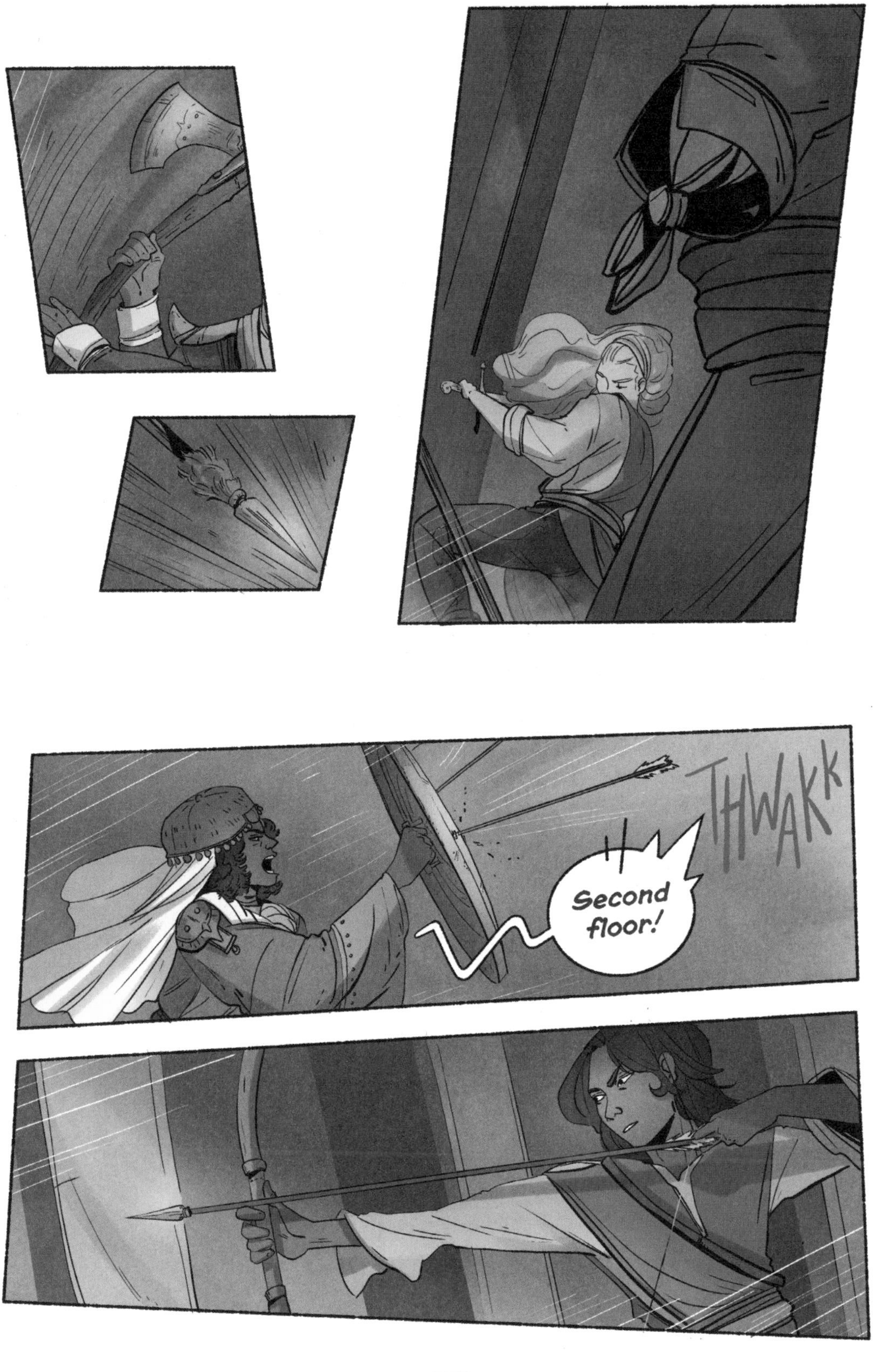
THWAKK
Second floor!

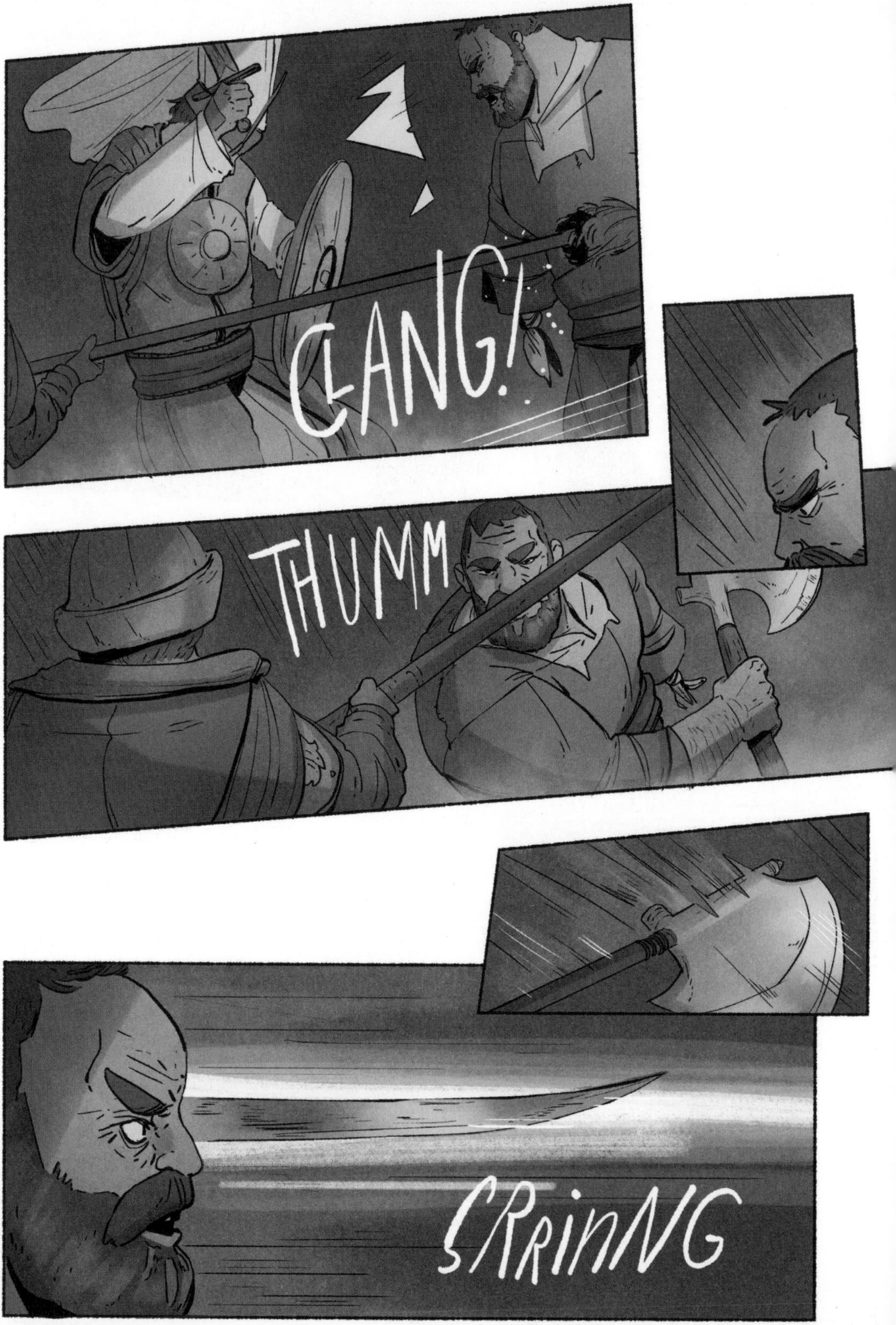
CLANG!
THUMM
SCRRINNG

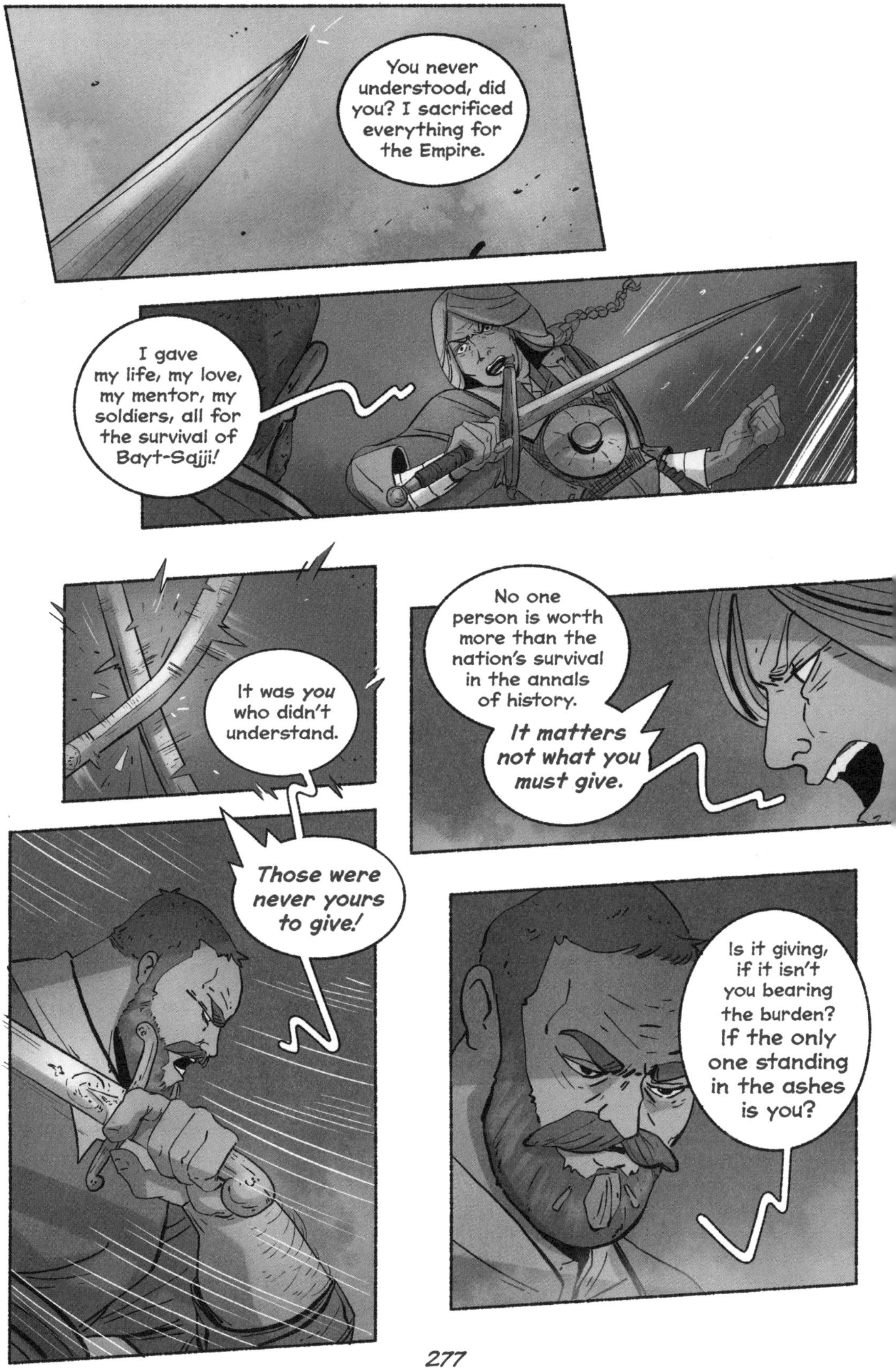
You never understood, did you? I sacrificed everything for the Empire.
I gave my life, my love, my mentor, my soldiers, all for the survival of Bayt-Sajji!
It was *you* who didn't understand.
No one person is worth more than the nation's survival in the annals of history.
It matters not what you must give.
Those were never yours to give!
Is it giving, if it isn't you bearing the burden? If the only one standing in the ashes is you?

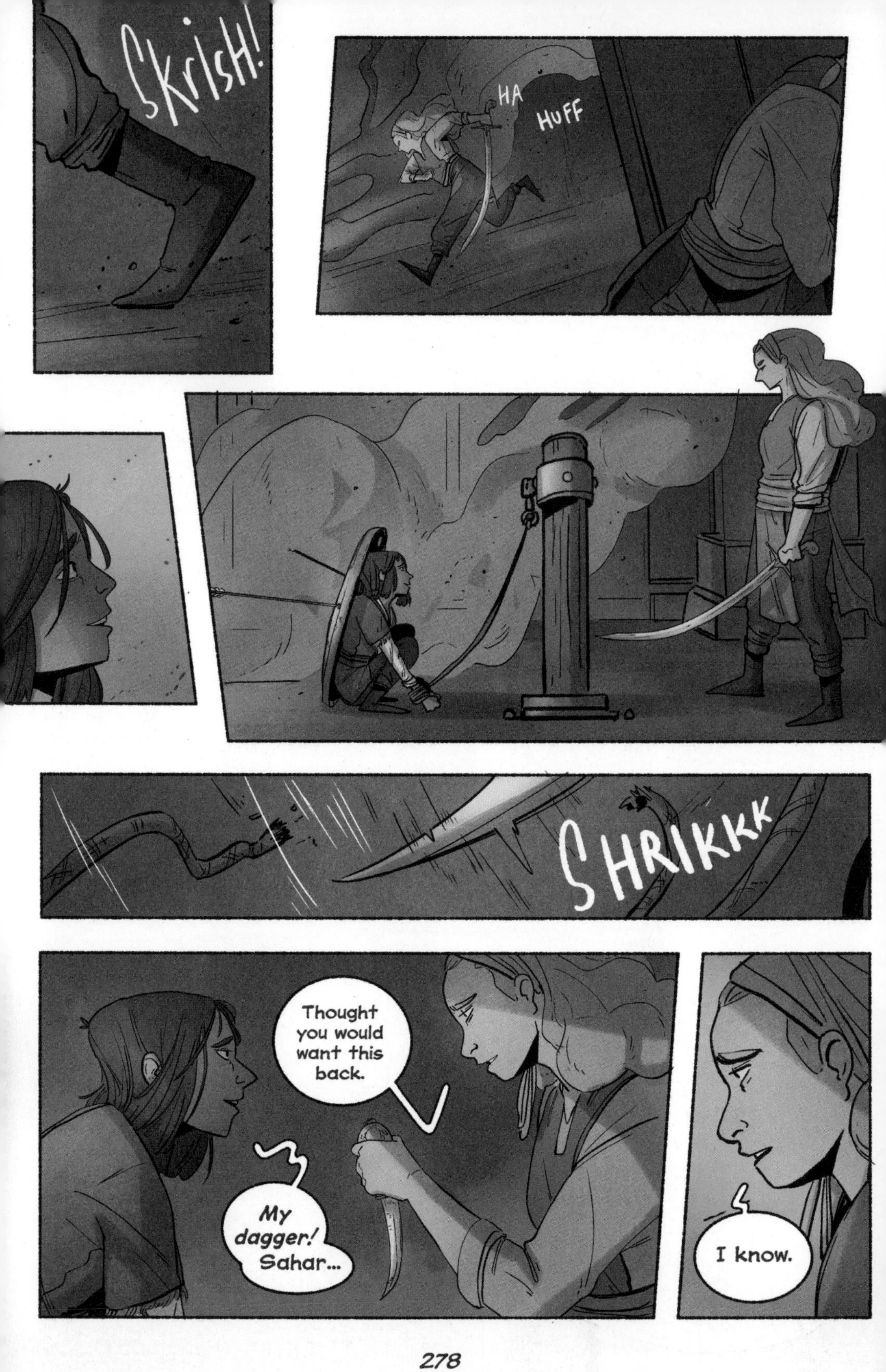
SKRISH!
HA
HUFF
SHRIKKK
Thought you would want this back.
My dagger! Sahar...
I know.

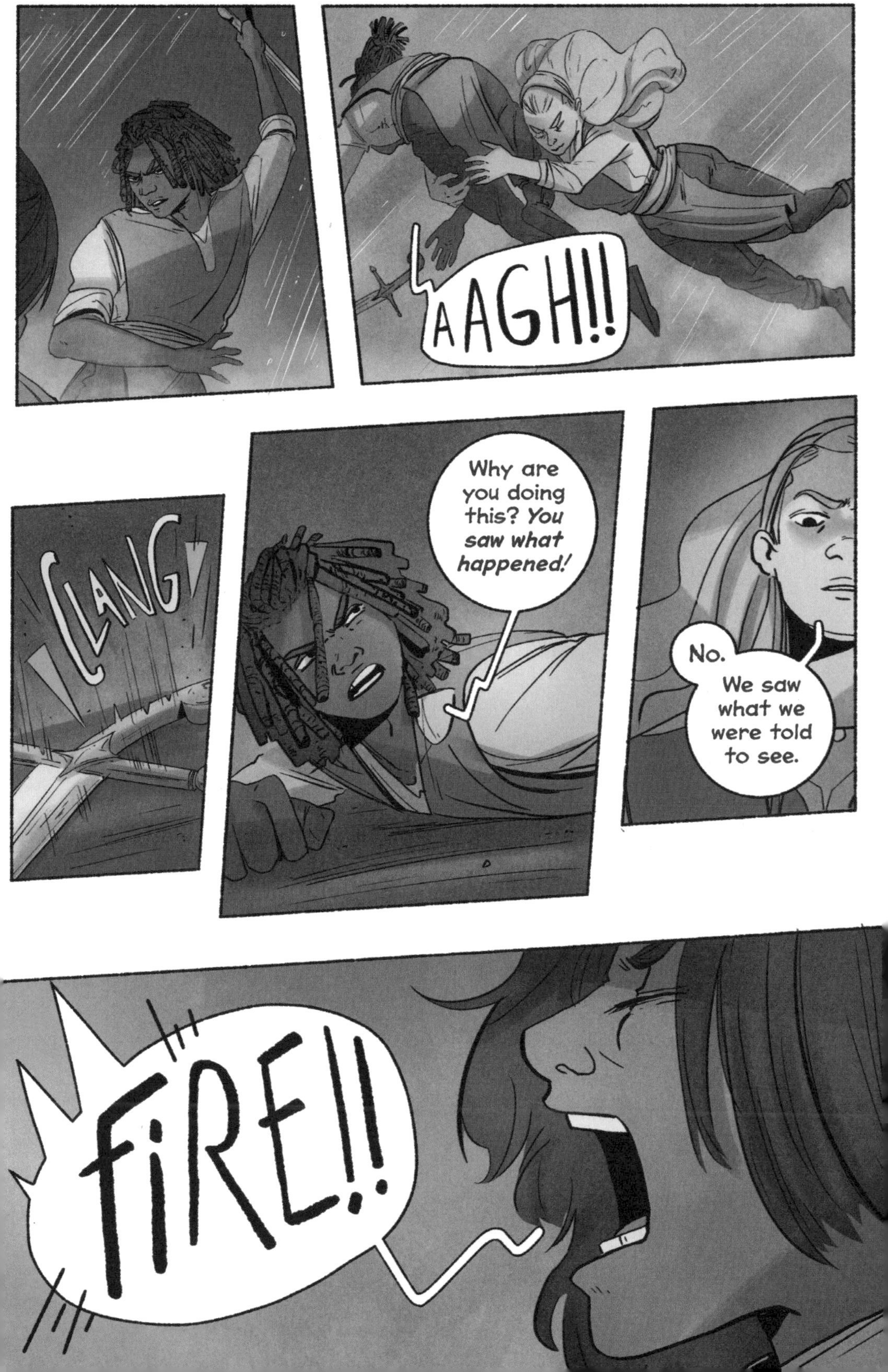
AAGH!!
CLANG
Why are you doing this? *You saw what happened!*
No.
We saw what we were told to see.
FIRE!!

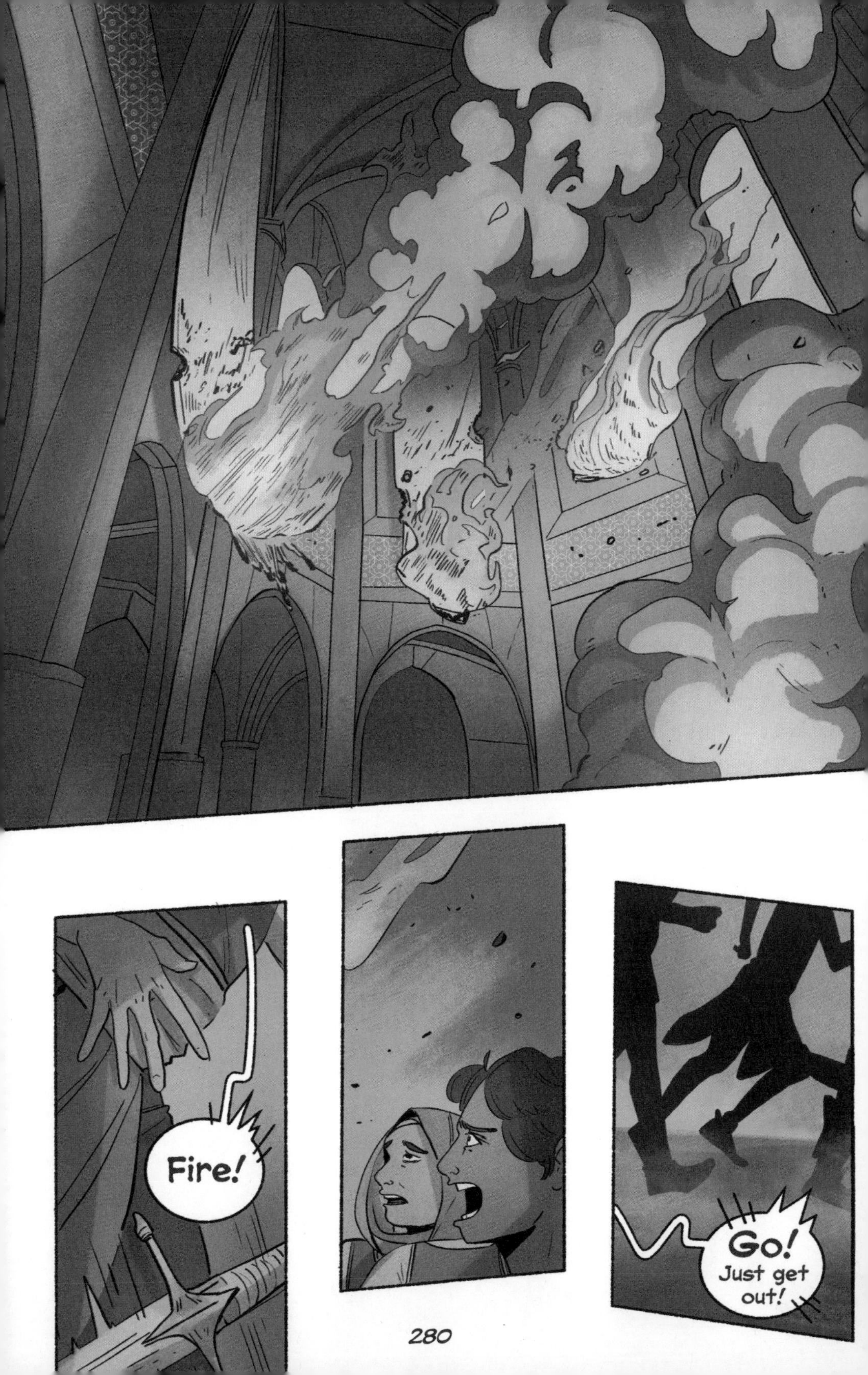
Fire!
Go!
Just get out!

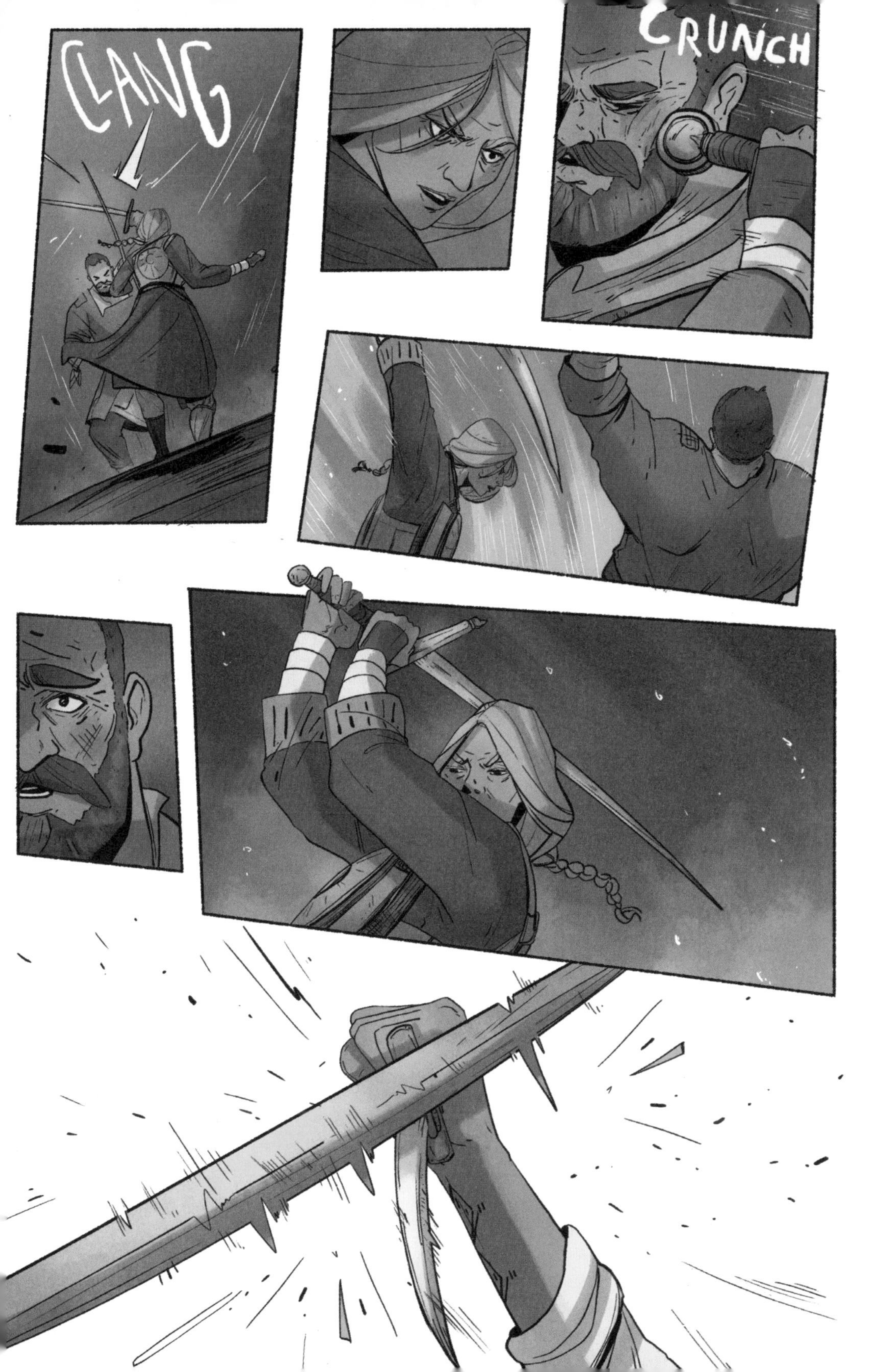
CLANG
CRUNCH

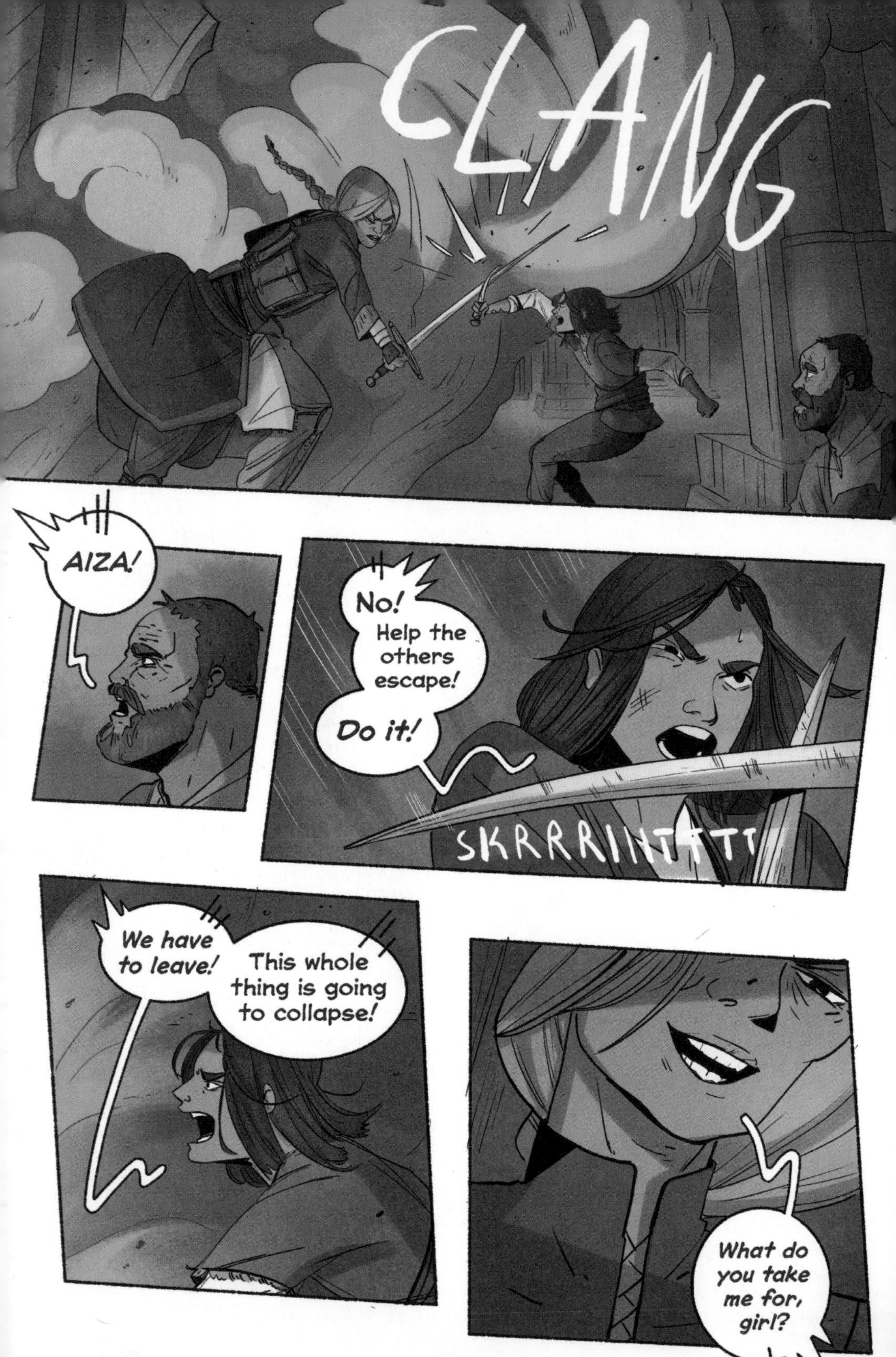
CLANG
AIZA!
No!
Help the others escape!
Do it!
SKRRRIIIIIIIITTTT
We have to leave!
This whole thing is going to collapse!
What do you take me for, girl?

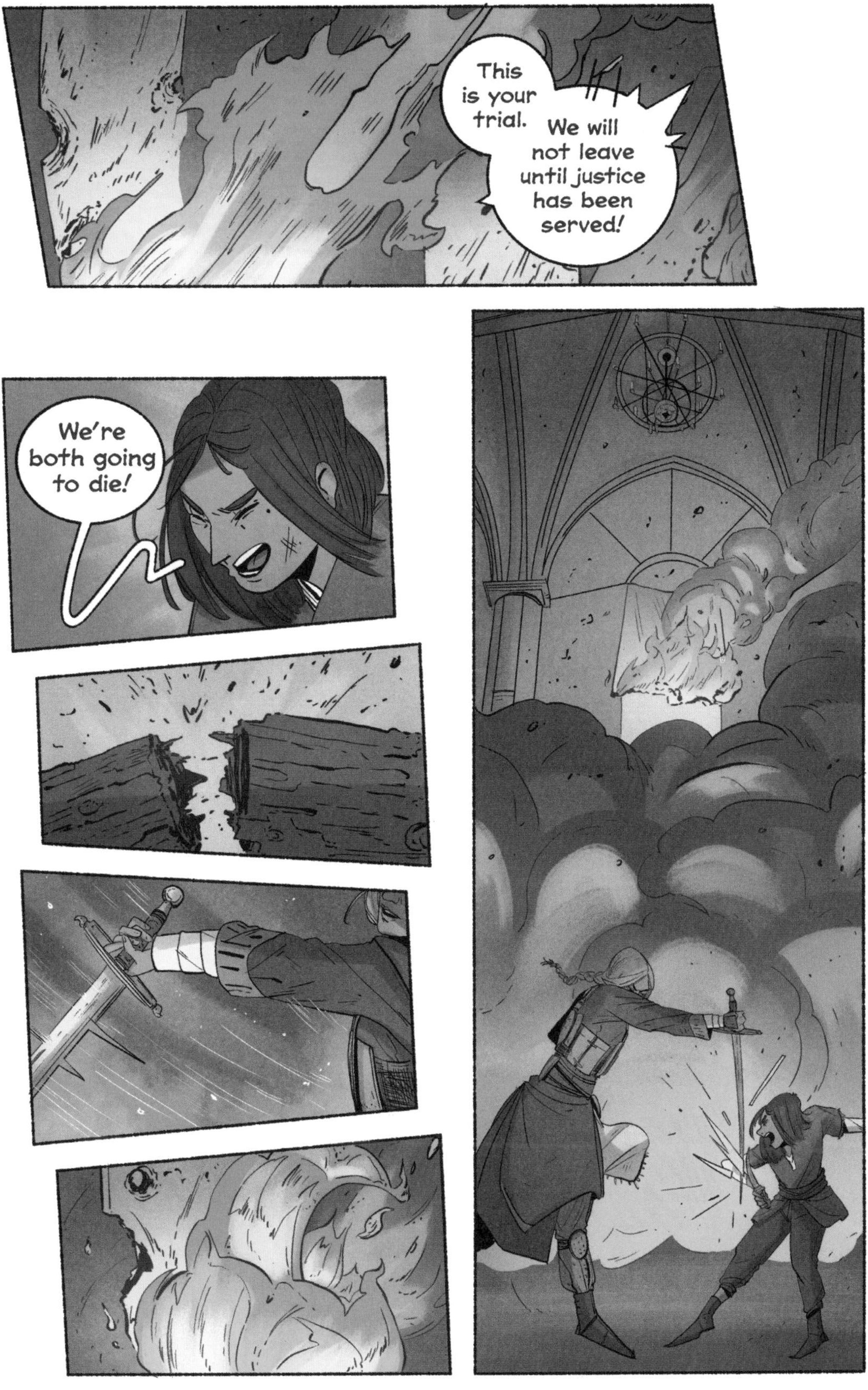
This is your trial.
We will not leave until justice has been served!
We're both going to die!

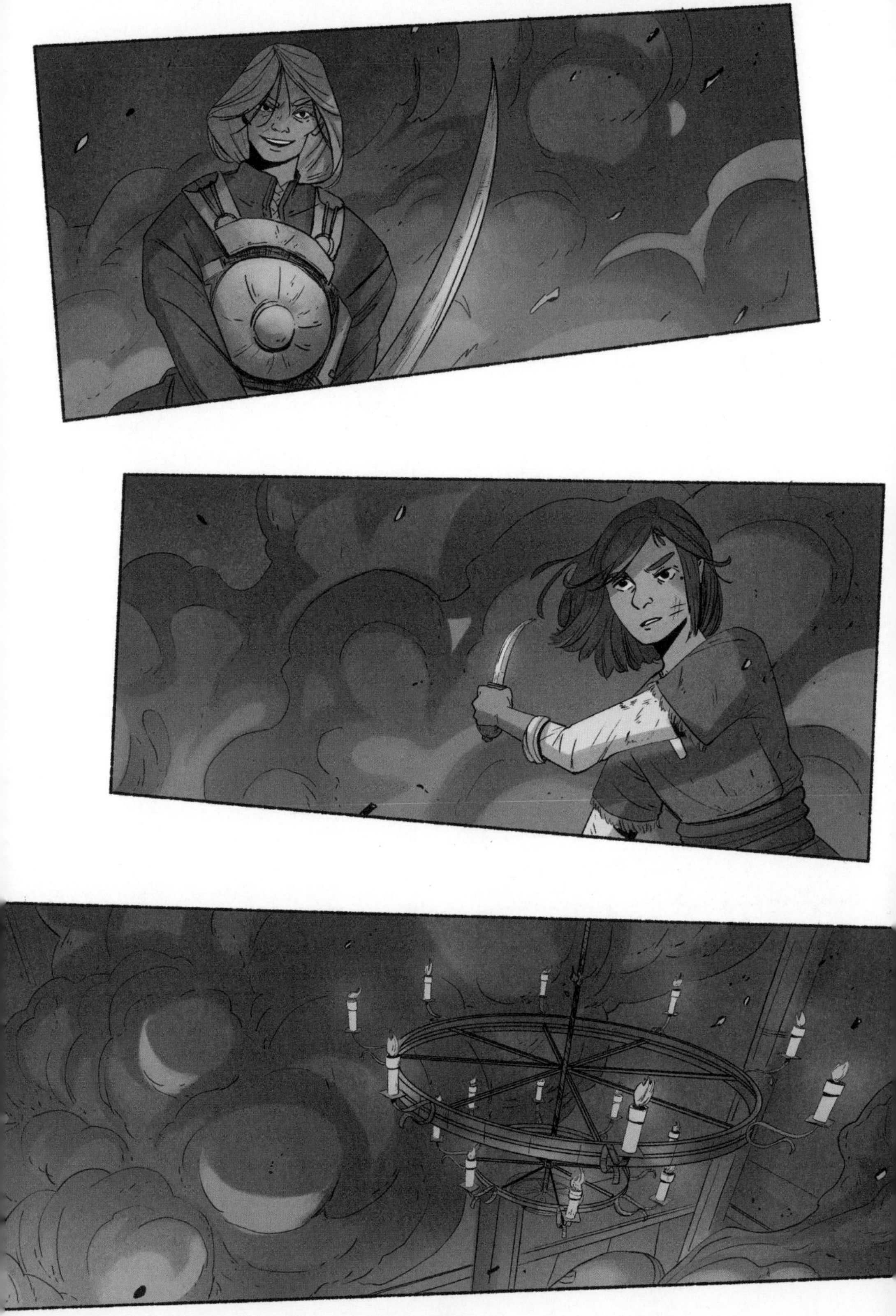

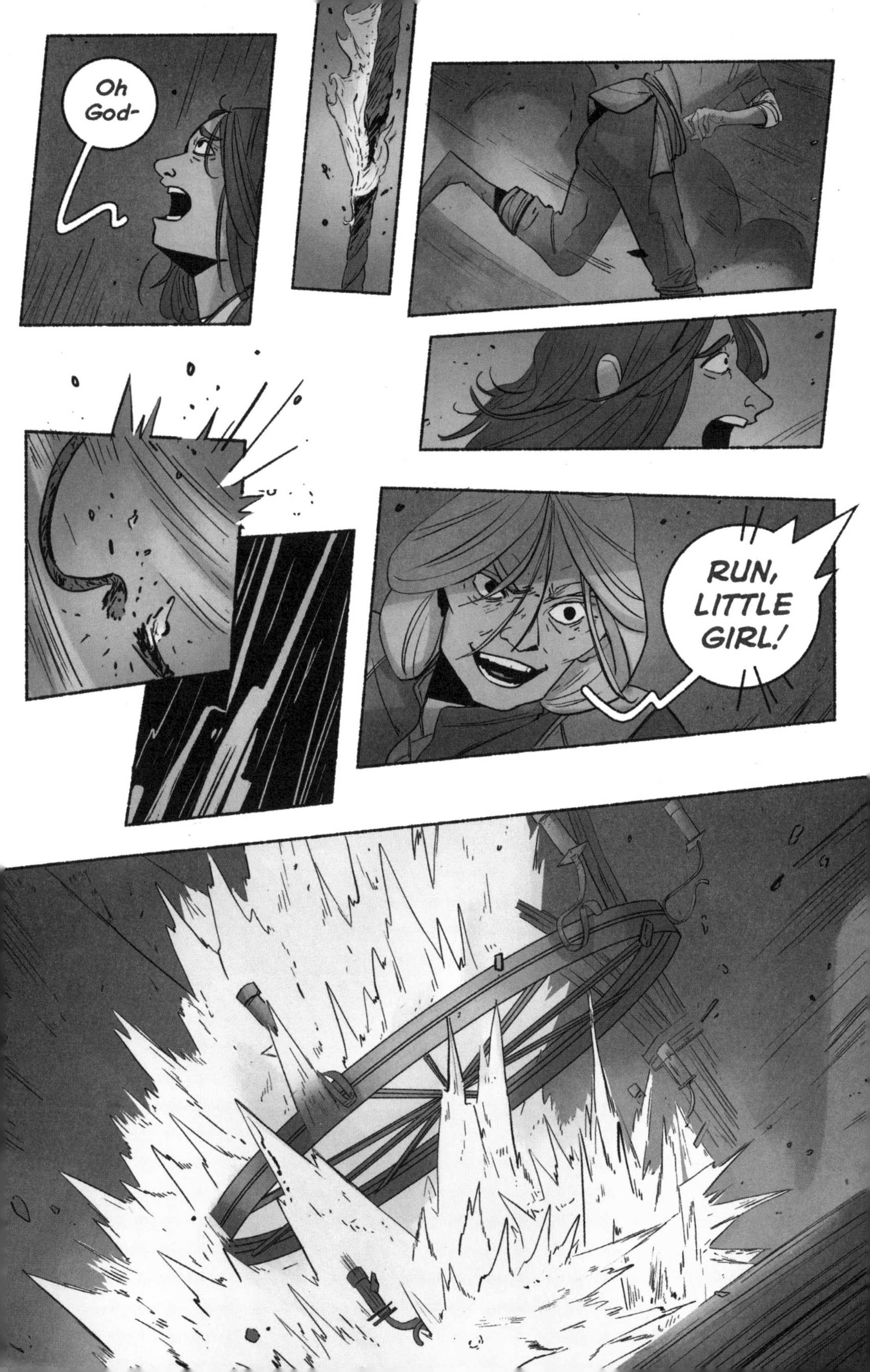
Oh God-
RUN, LITTLE GIRL!

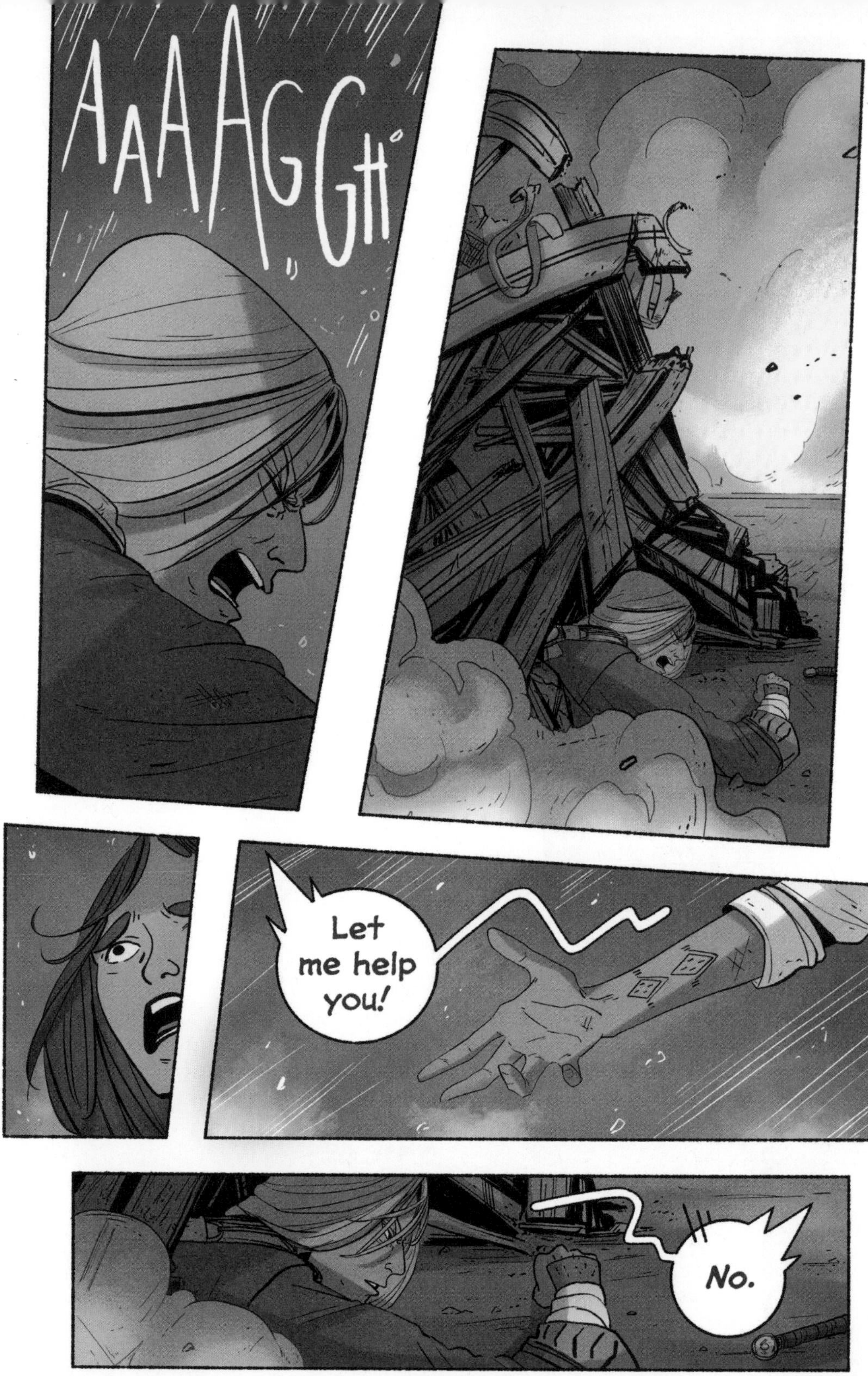
AAAAGGH
Let me help you!
No.

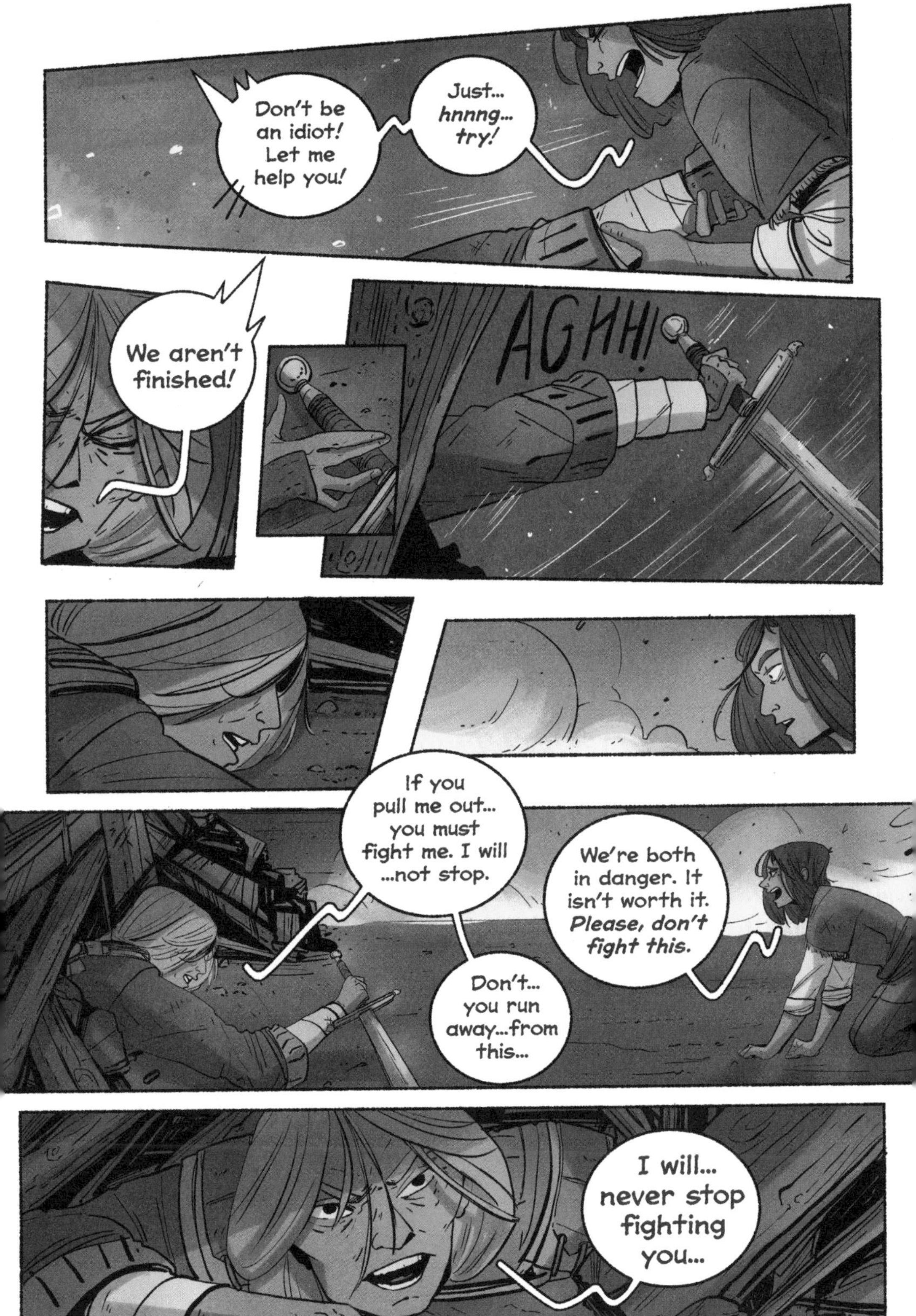

Don't be an idiot! Let me help you!
Just... hnnng... try!
We aren't finished!
AGHH!
If you pull me out... you must fight me. I will ...not stop.
We're both in danger. It isn't worth it. Please, don't fight this.
Don't... you run away...from this...
I will... never stop fighting you...

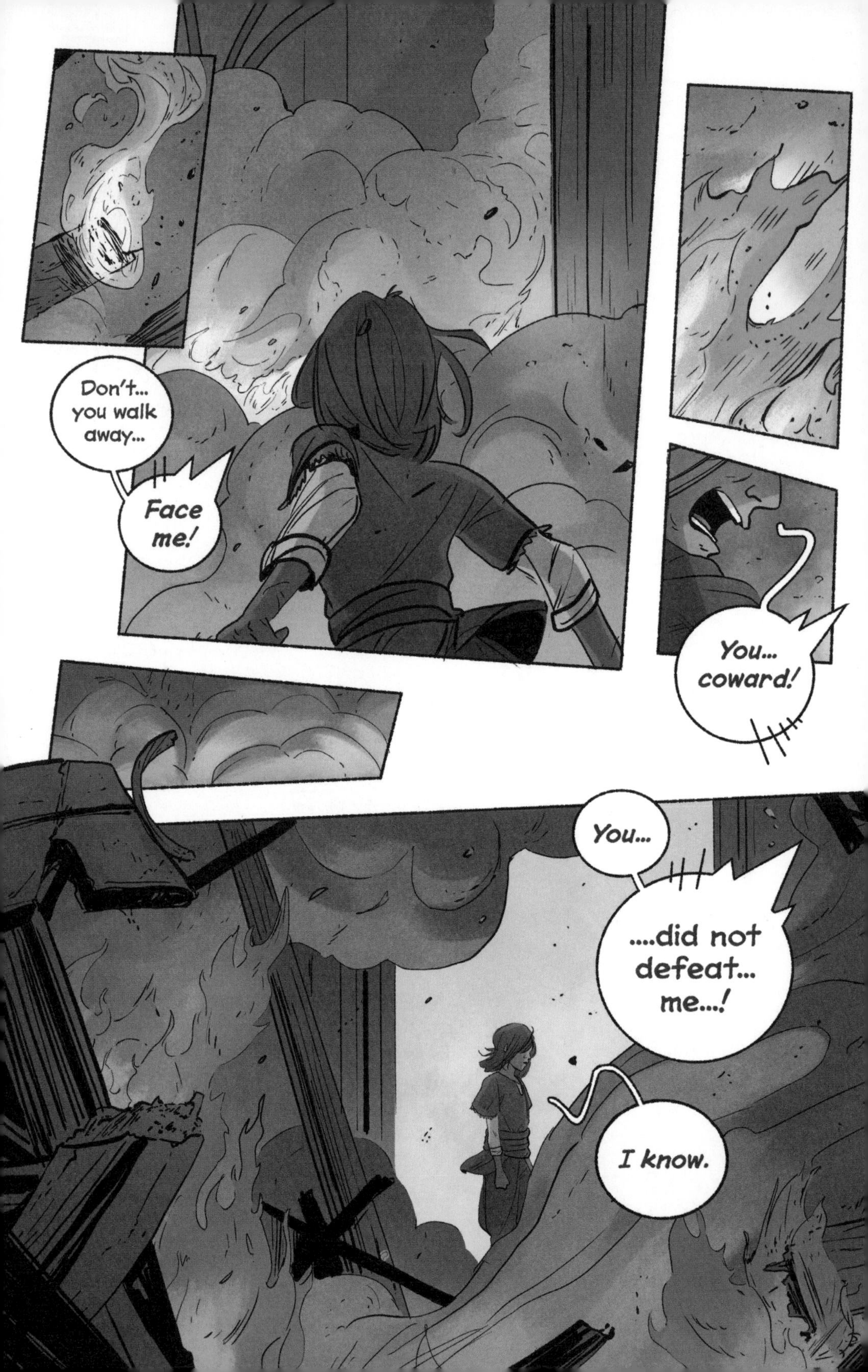
Don't... you walk away...
Face me!
You... coward!
You...
....did not defeat... me...!
I know.

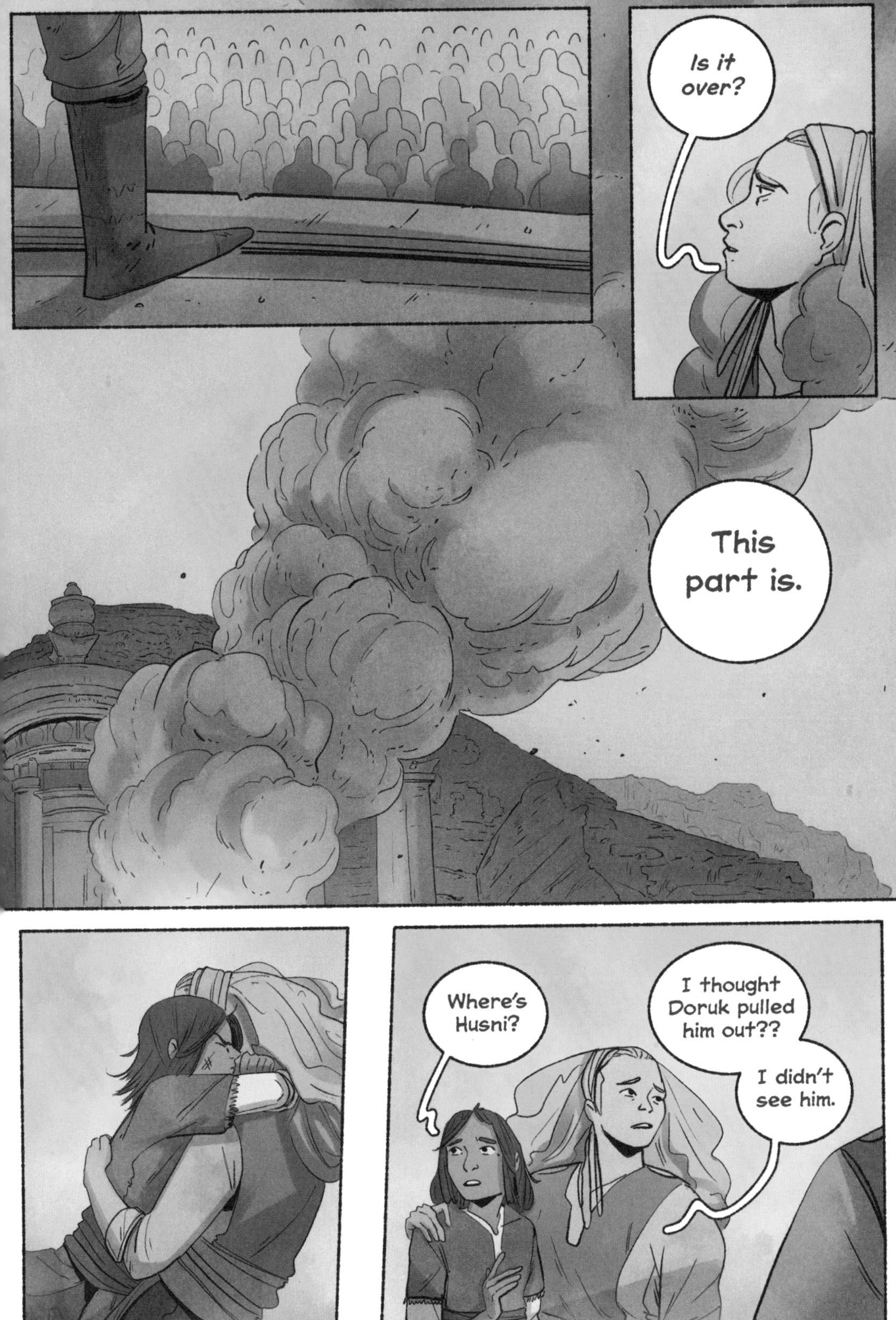
Is it over?
This part is.
Where's Husni?
I thought Doruk pulled him out??
I didn't see him.

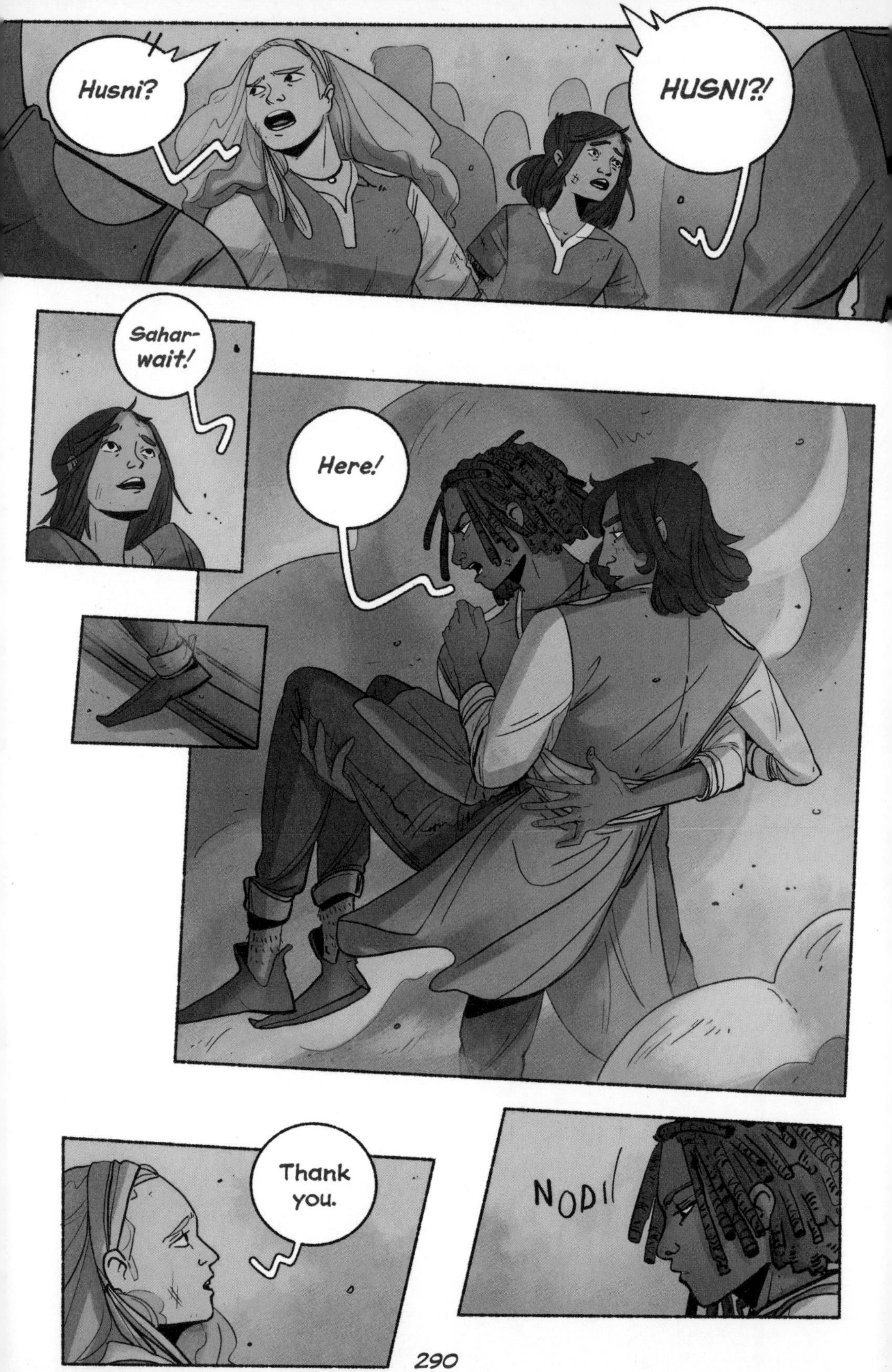
Husni?
HUSNI?!
Sahar-
wait!
Here!
Thank
you.
NOD!

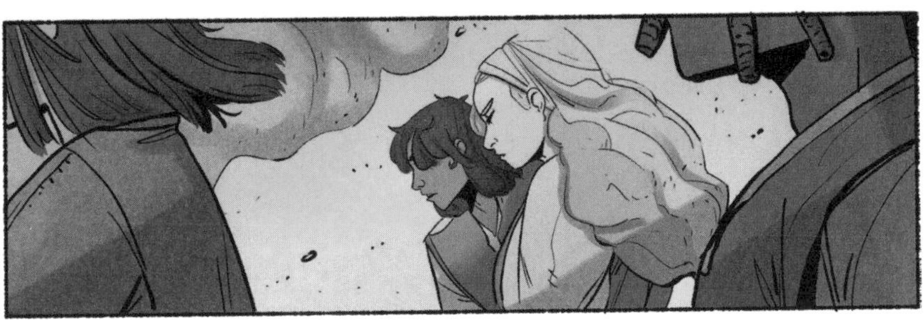

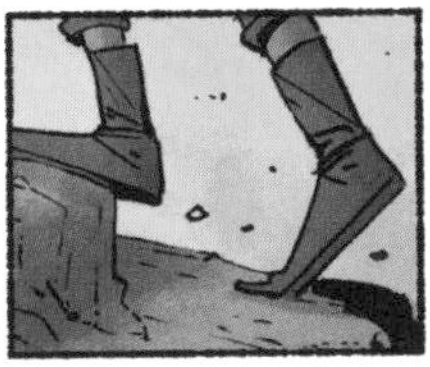

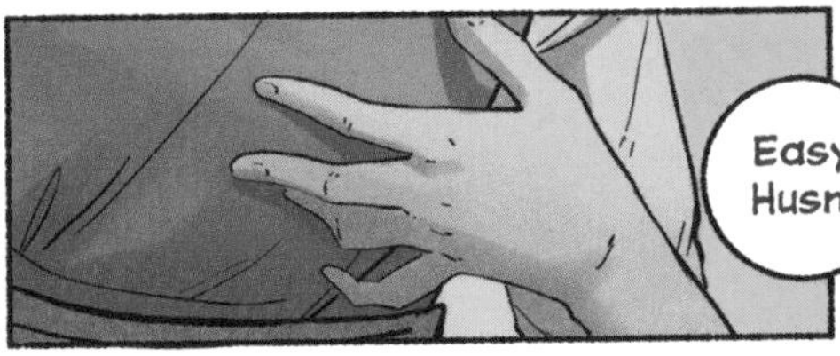
Easy, Husni.

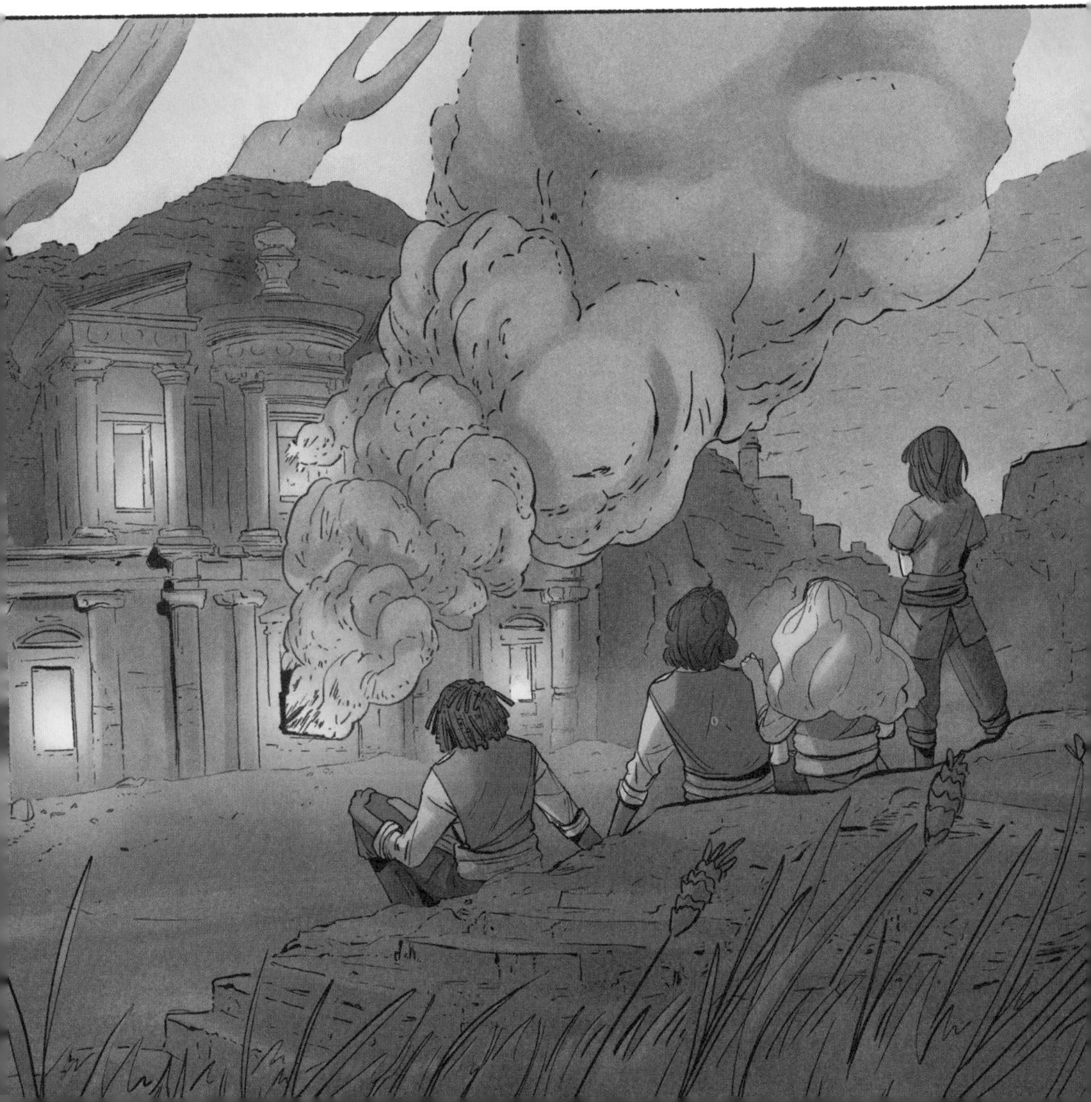

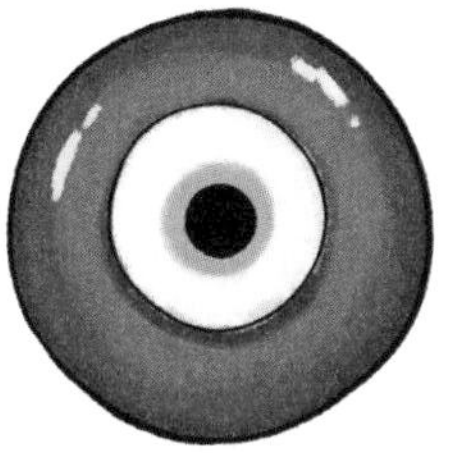

CHAPTER 14

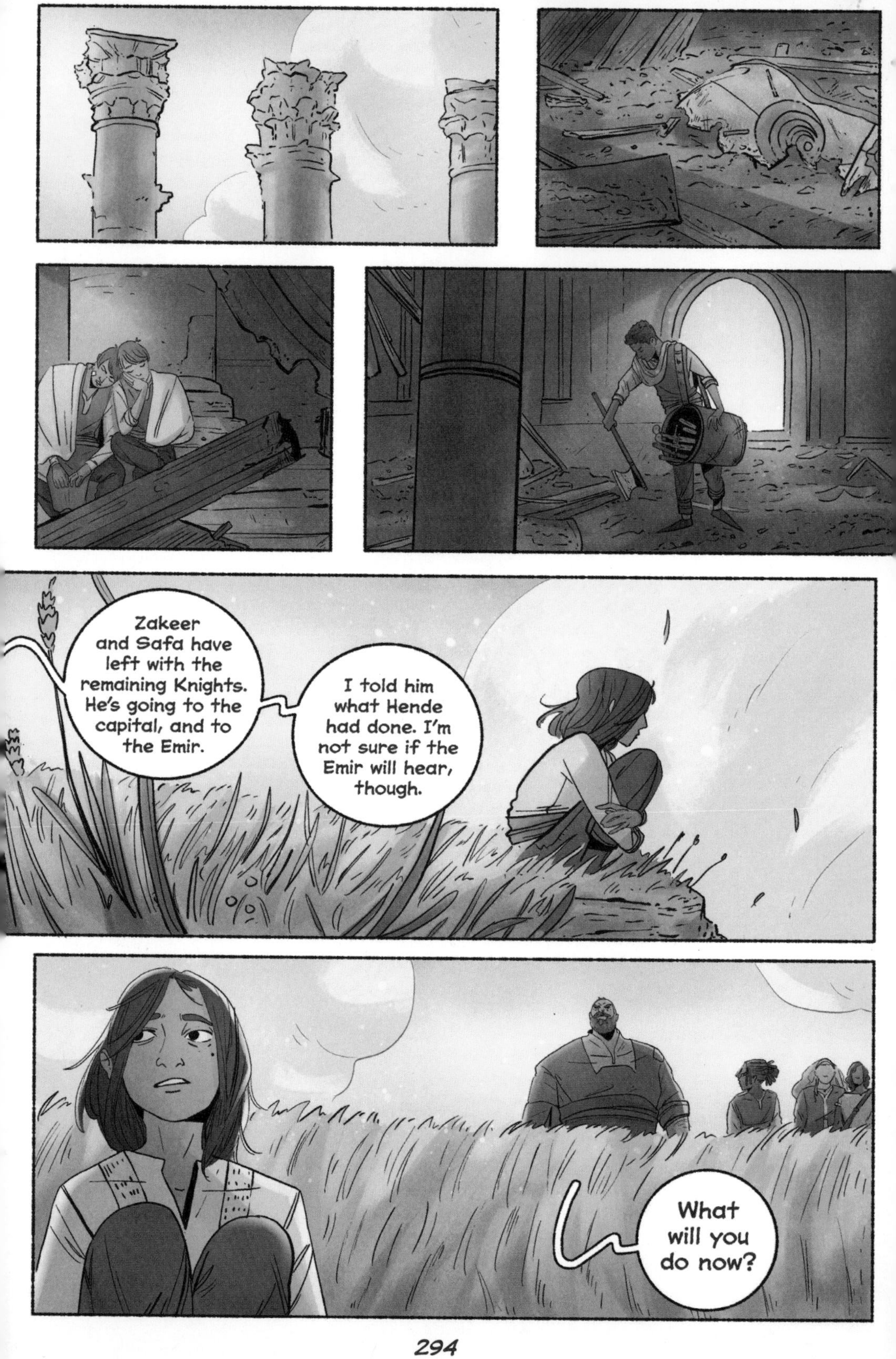
Zakeer and Safa have left with the remaining Knights. He's going to the capital, and to the Emir.
I told him what Hende had done. I'm not sure if the Emir will hear, though.
What will you do now?

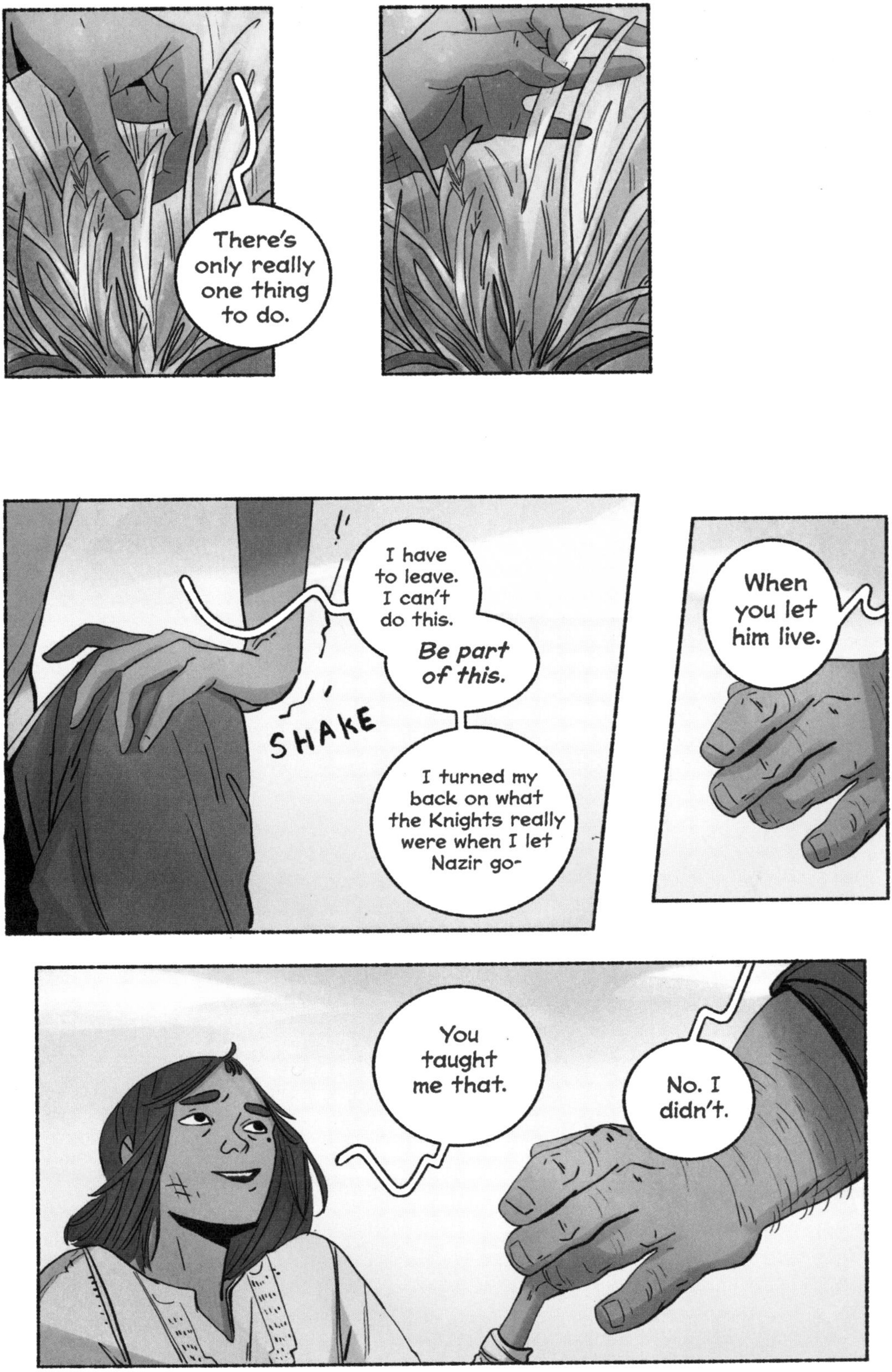
There's only really one thing to do.
I have to leave. I can't do this.
Be part of this.
SHAKE
I turned my back on what the Knights really were when I let Nazir go-
When you let him live.
You taught me that.
No. I didn't.

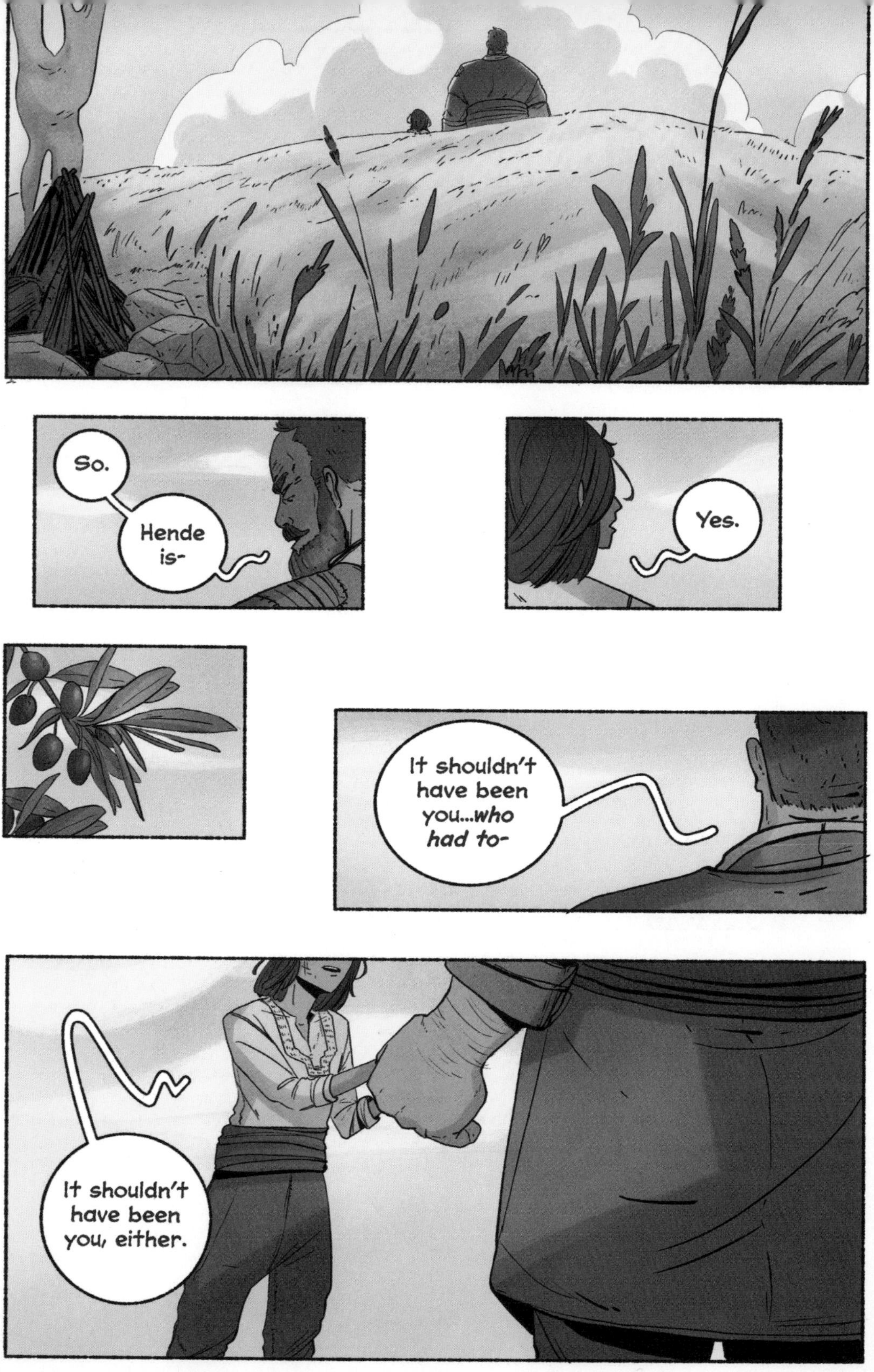
So.
Hende is-
Yes.
It shouldn't have been you...who had to-
It shouldn't have been you, either.

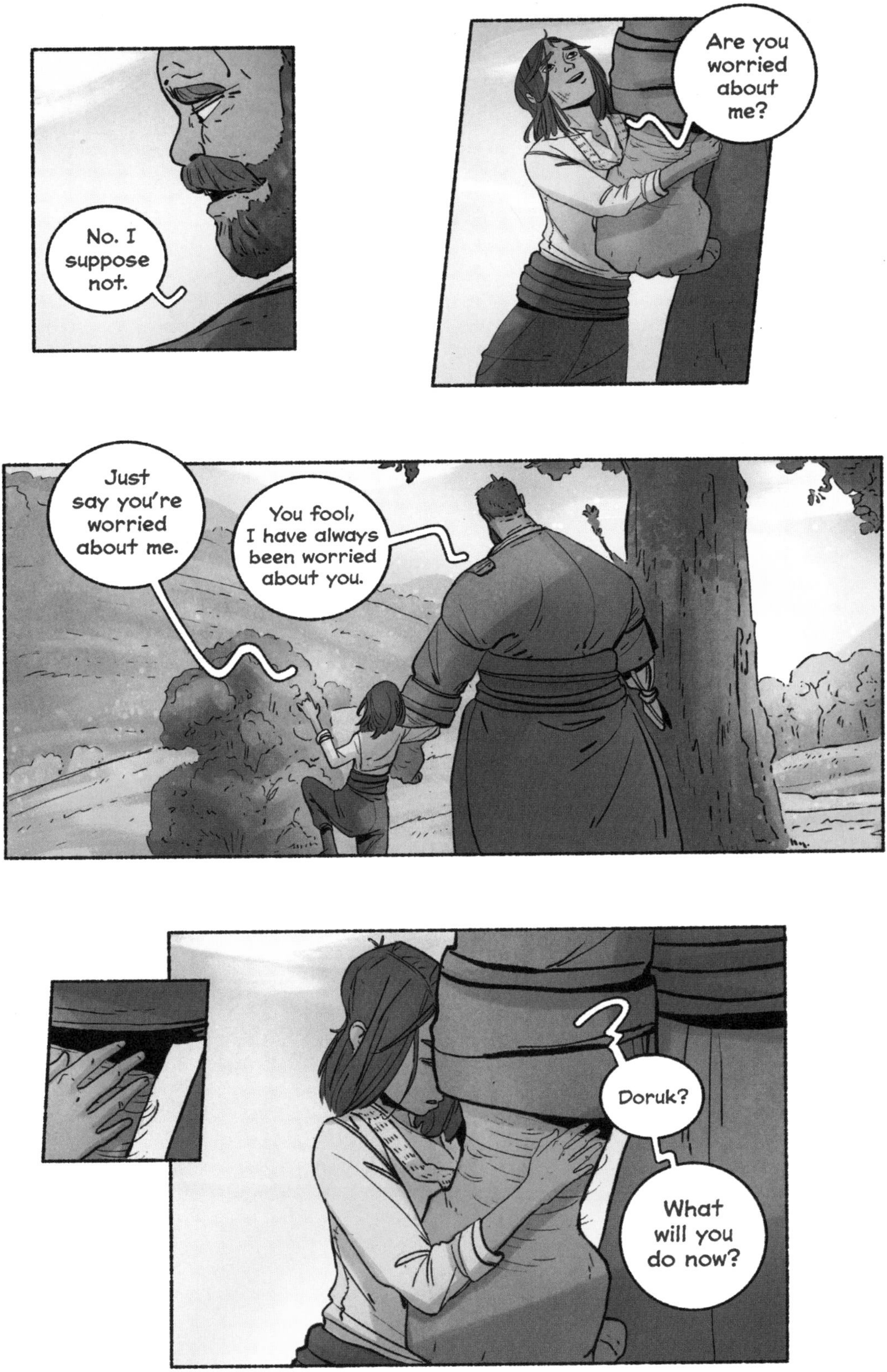
No. I suppose not.
Are you worried about me?
Just say you're worried about me.
You fool, I have always been worried about you.
Doruk?
What will you do now?

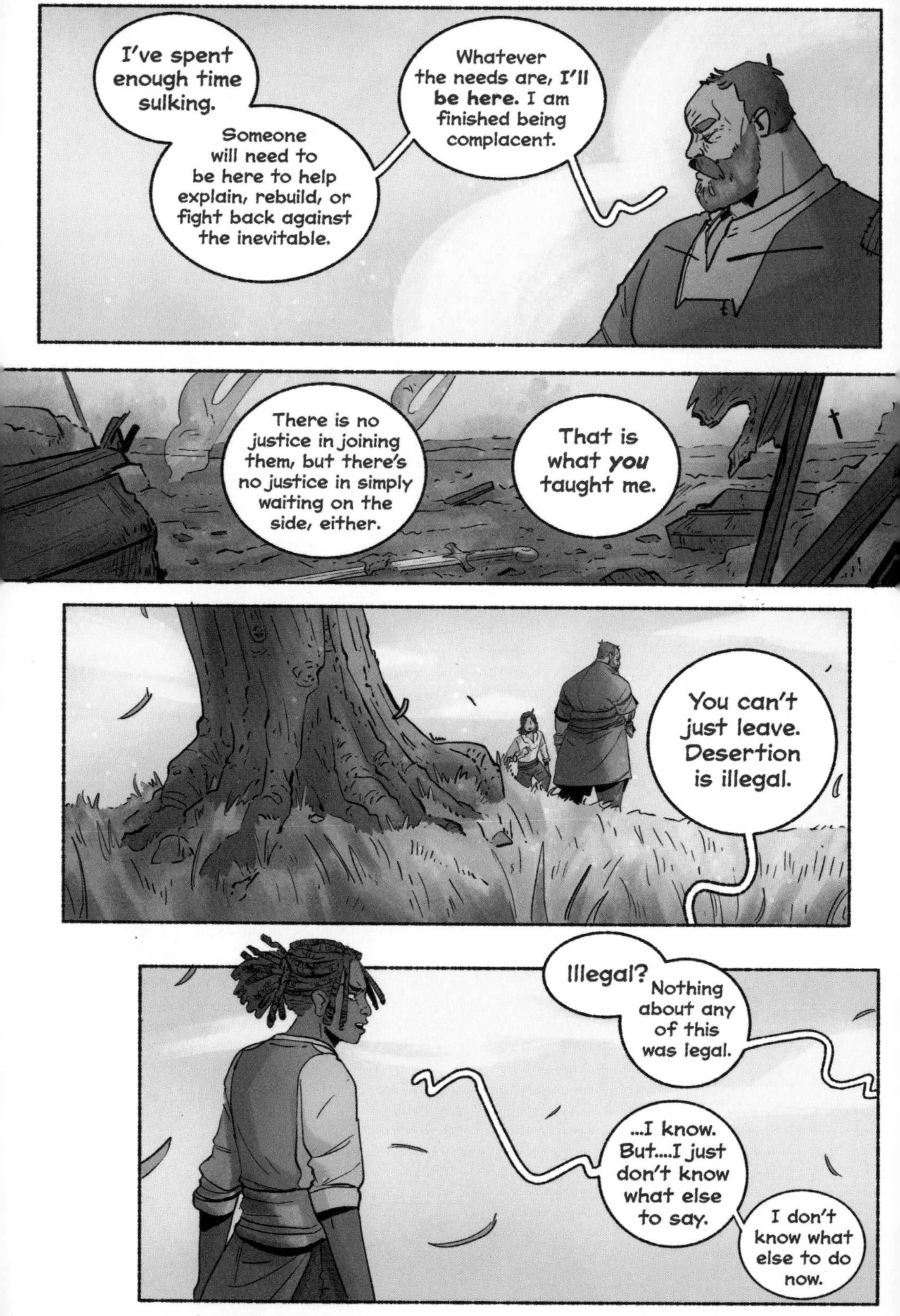
I've spent enough time sulking.
Someone will need to be here to help explain, rebuild, or fight back against the inevitable.
Whatever the needs are, I'll **be here.** I am finished being complacent.
There is no justice in joining them, but there's no justice in simply waiting on the side, either.
That is what *you* taught me.
You can't just leave. Desertion is illegal.
Illegal? Nothing about any of this was legal.
...I know. But....I just don't know what else to say.
I don't know what else to do now.

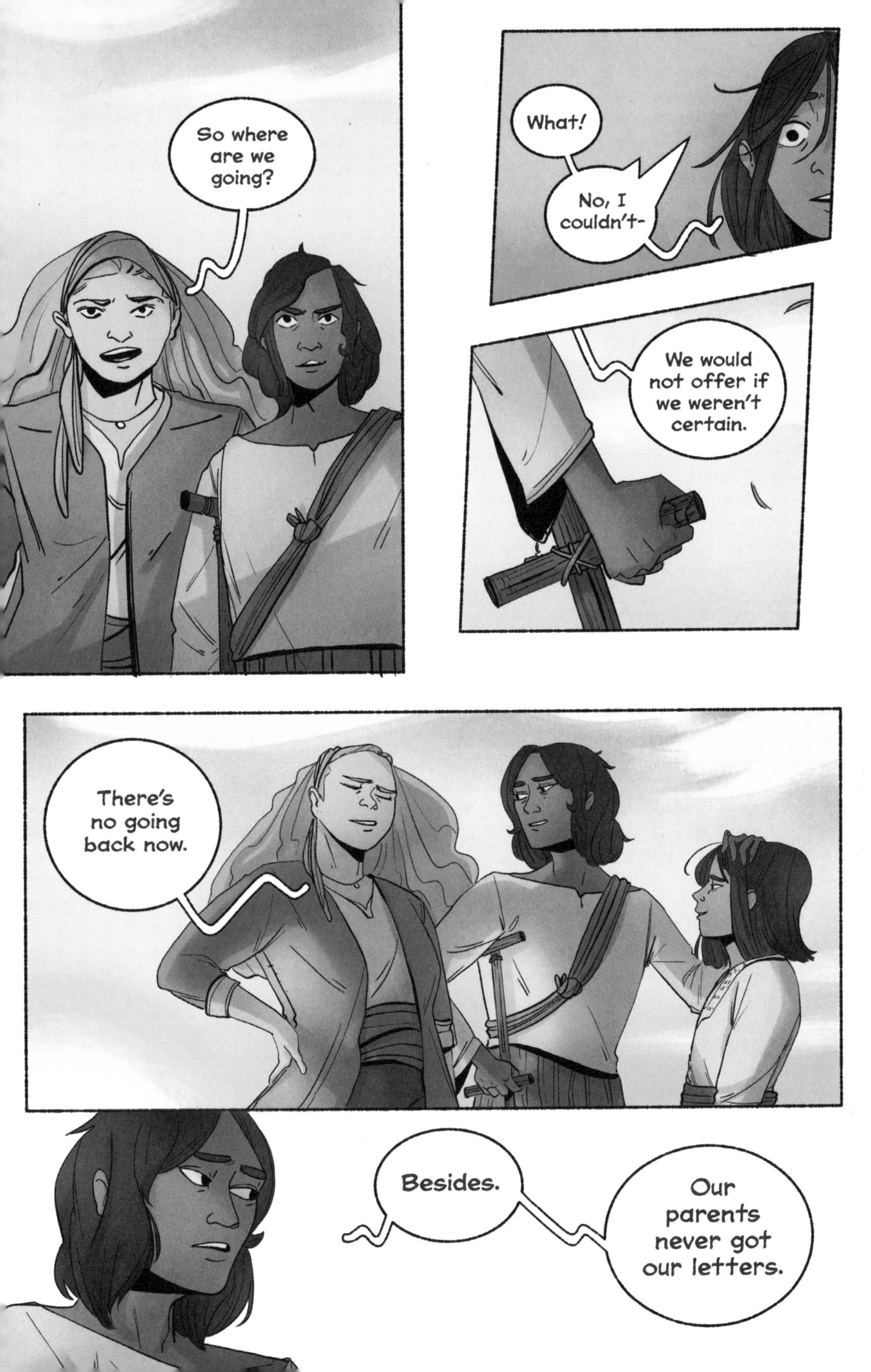
So where are we going?
What!
No, I couldn't-
We would not offer if we weren't certain.
There's no going back now.
Besides.
Our parents never got our letters.

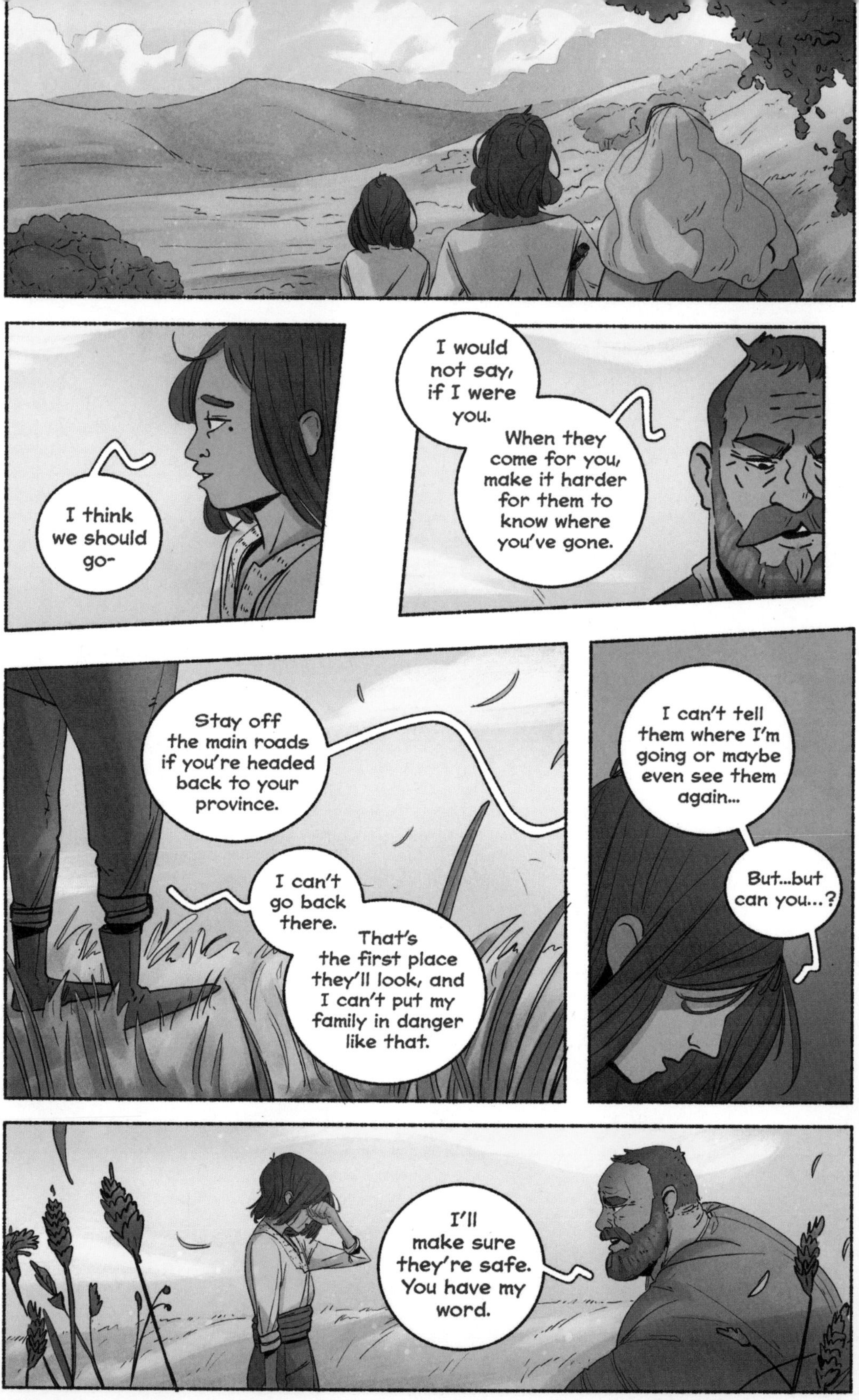
I think we should go-
I would not say, if I were you.
When they come for you, make it harder for them to know where you've gone.
Stay off the main roads if you're headed back to your province.
I can't go back there.
That's the first place they'll look, and I can't put my family in danger like that.
I can't tell them where I'm going or maybe even see them again...
But...but can you...?
I'll make sure they're safe. You have my word.

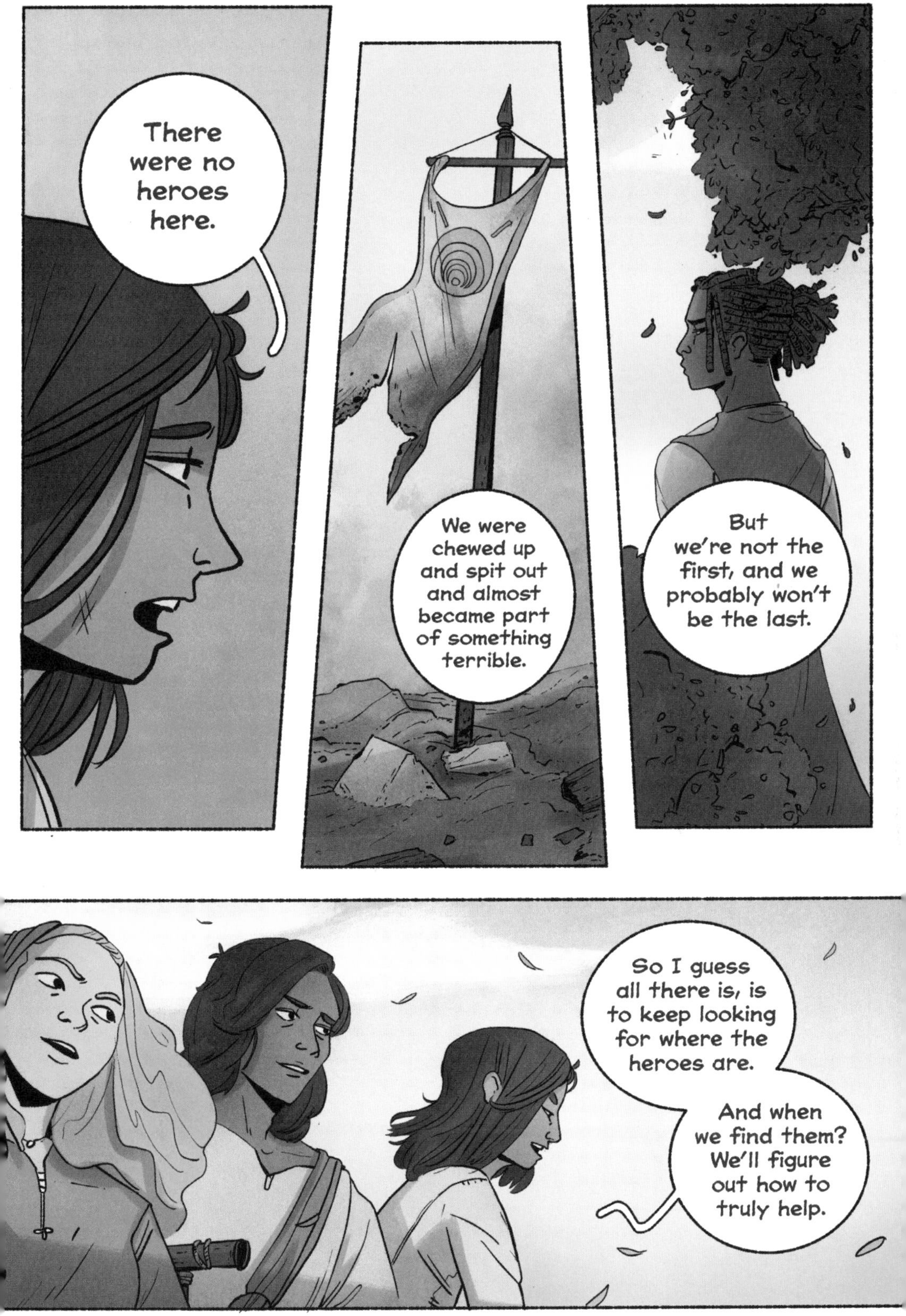
There were no heroes here.
We were chewed up and spit out and almost became part of something terrible.
But we're not the first, and we probably won't be the last.
So I guess all there is, is to keep looking for where the heroes are.
And when we find them? We'll figure out how to truly help.

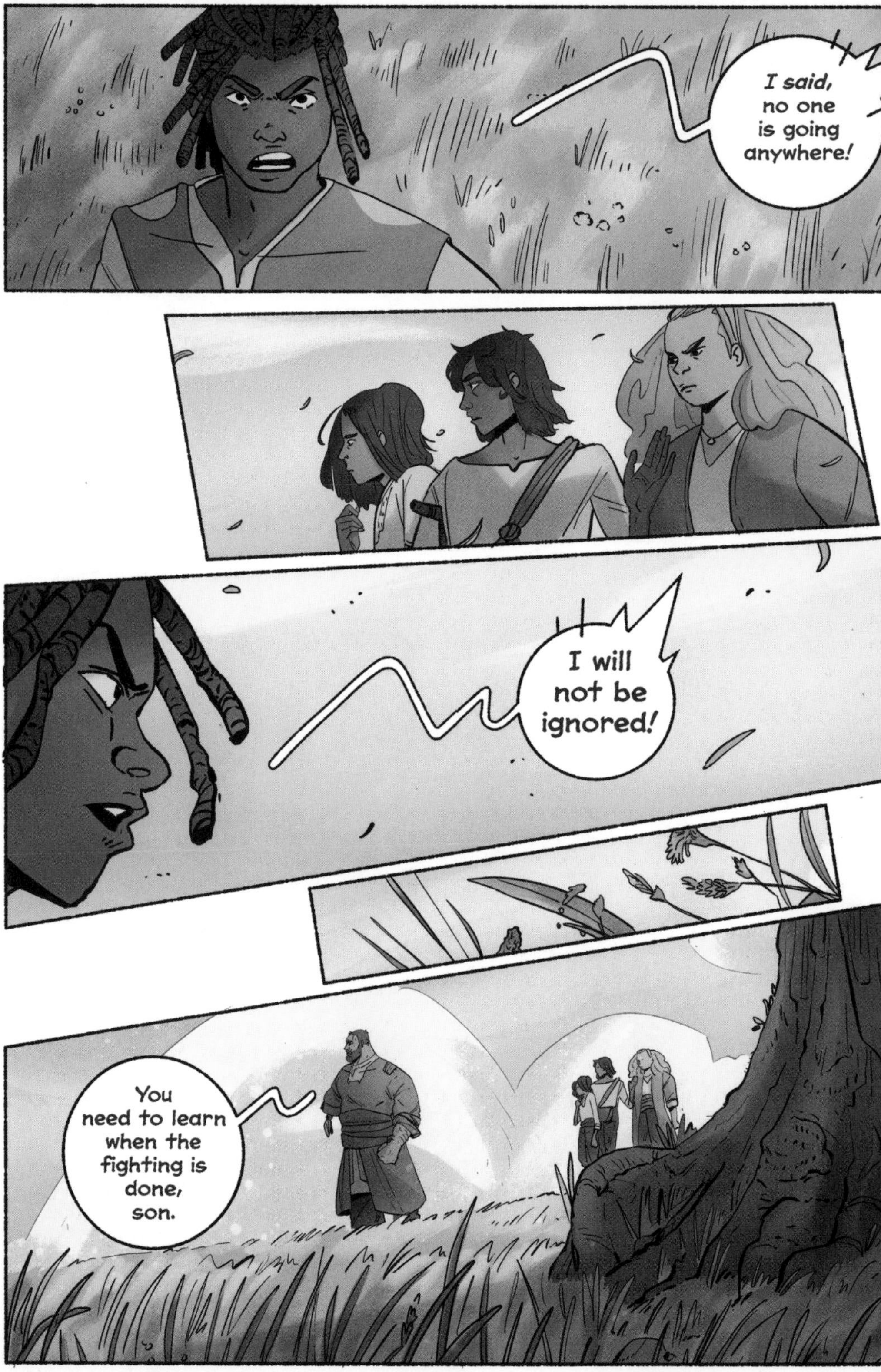
I said, no one is going anywhere!
I will not be ignored!
You need to learn when the fighting is done, son.

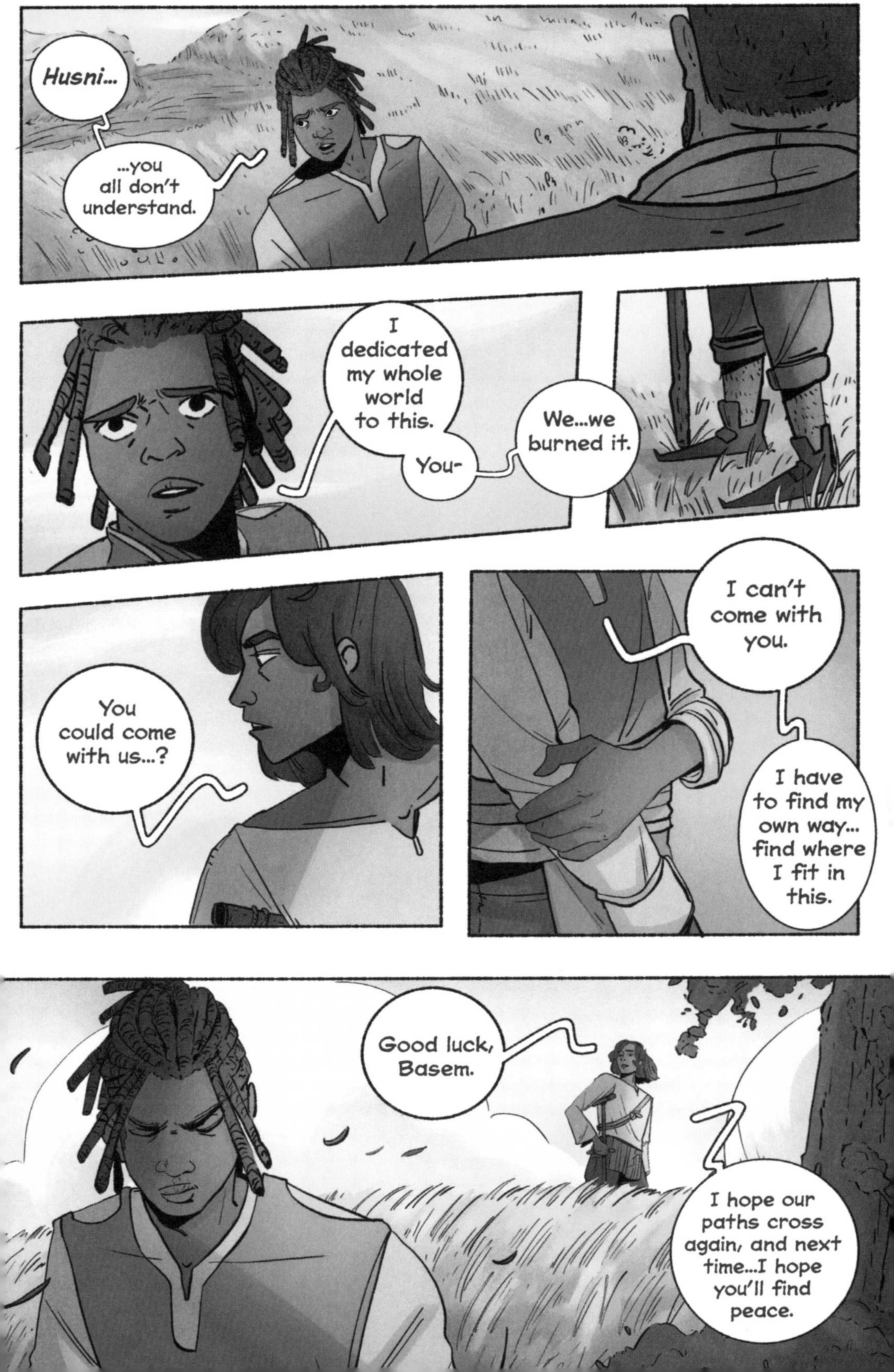
Husni...
...you all don't understand.
I dedicated my whole world to this.
You-
We...we burned it.
You could come with us...?
I can't come with you.
I have to find my own way... find where I fit in this.
Good luck, Basem.
I hope our paths cross again, and next time...I hope you'll find peace.

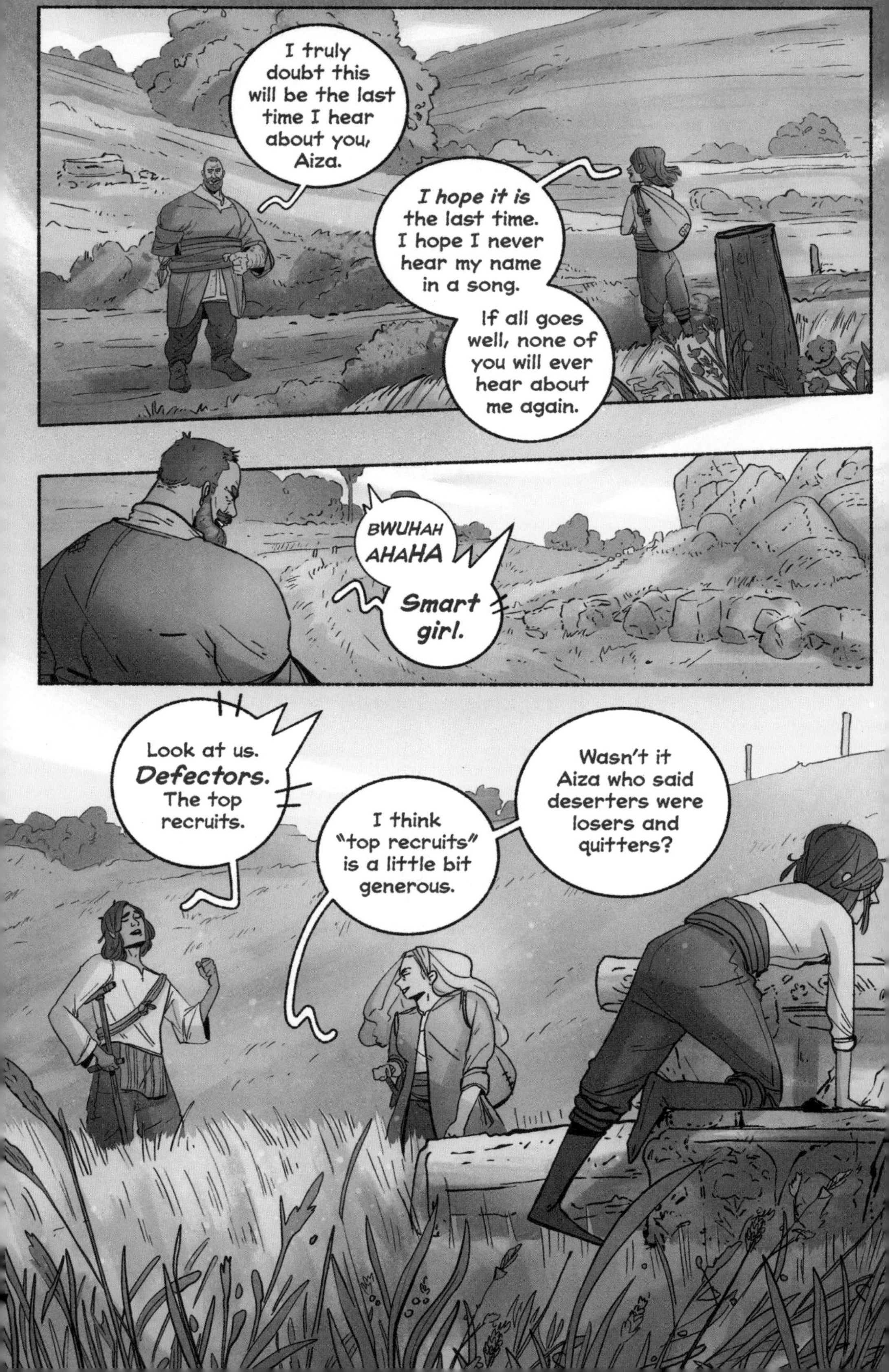
I truly doubt this will be the last time I hear about you, Aiza.
I hope it is the last time. I hope I never hear my name in a song.
If all goes well, none of you will ever hear about me again.
BWUHAH AHAHA
Smart girl.
Look at us. *Defectors.* The top recruits.
I think "top recruits" is a little bit generous.
Wasn't it Aiza who said deserters were losers and quitters?

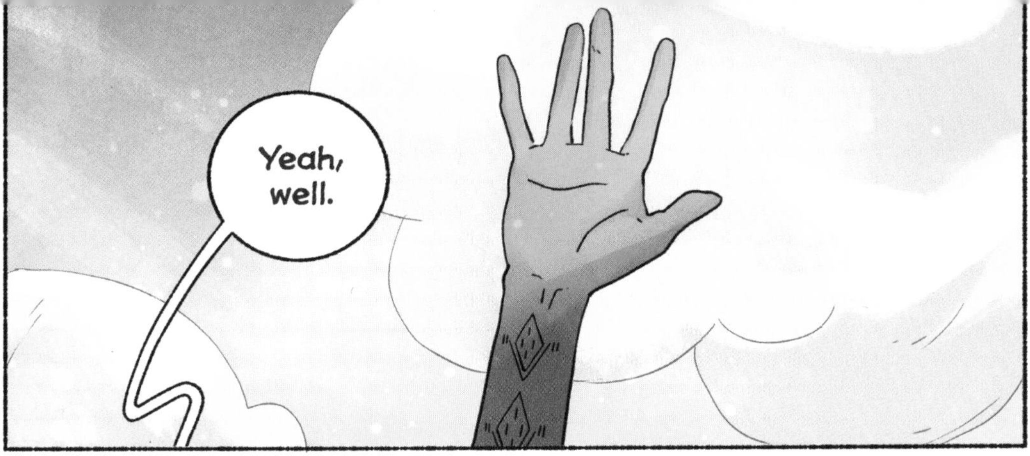
Yeah, well.

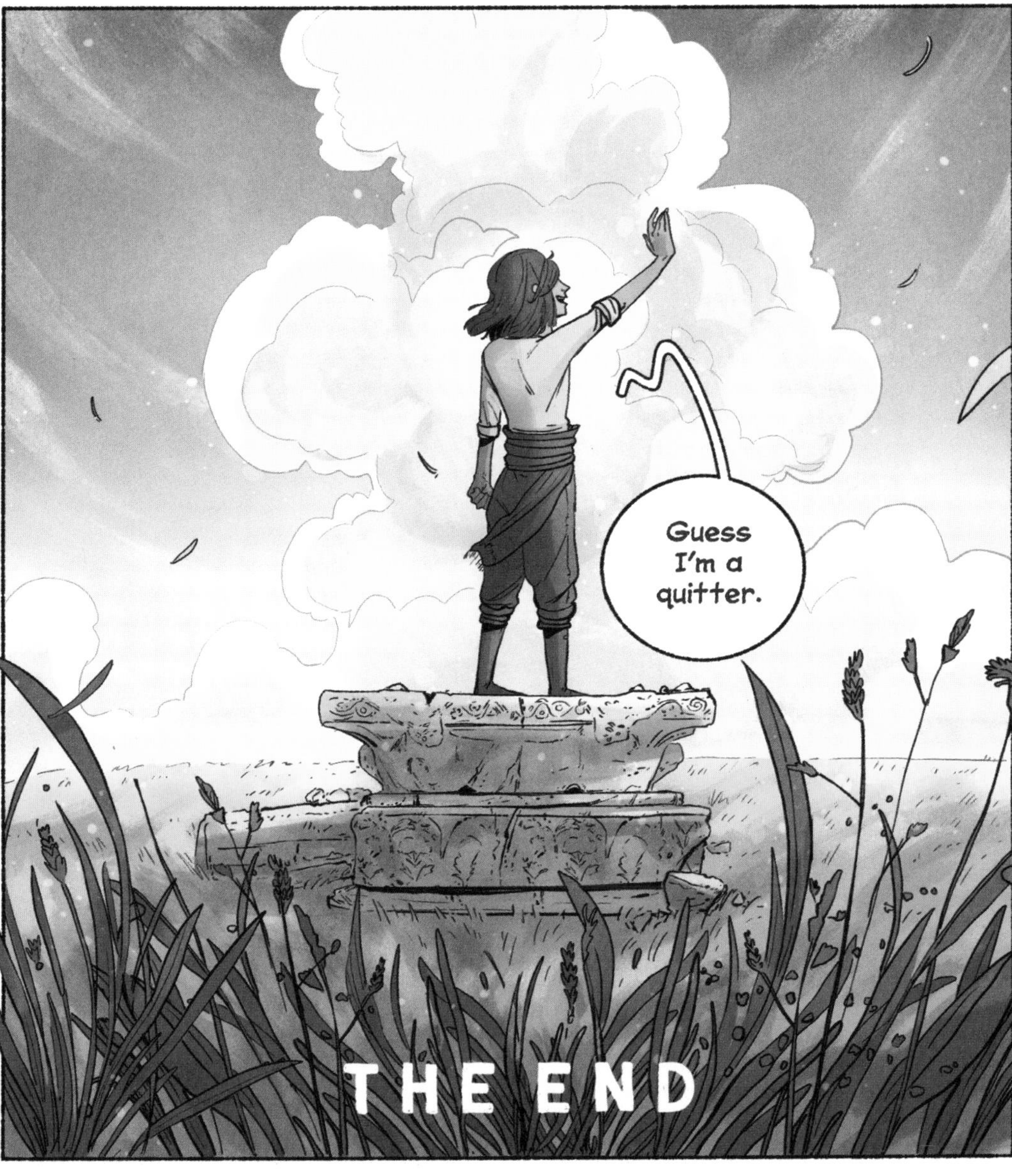
Guess I'm a quitter.
THE END

ABOUT SQUIRE

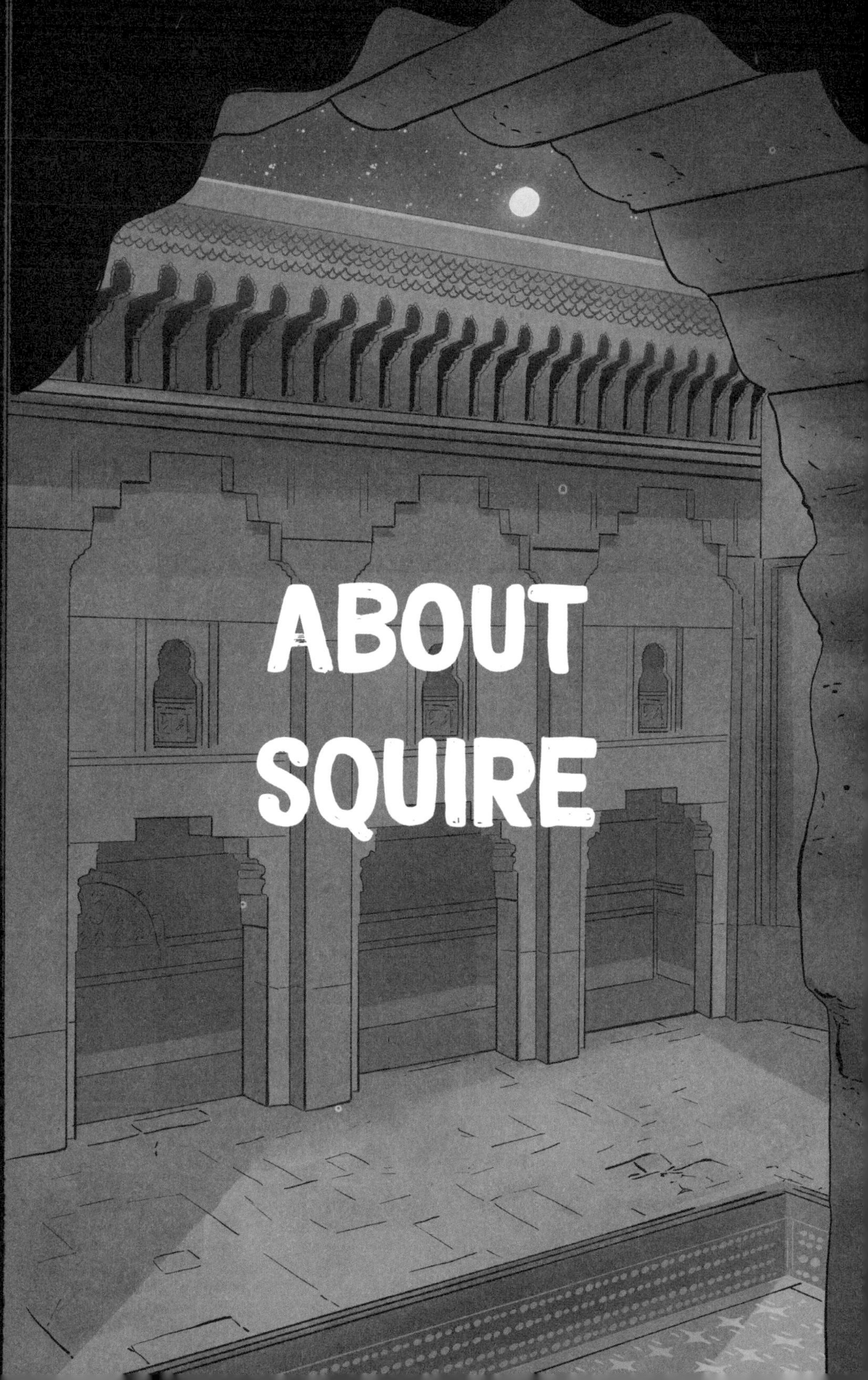

ACKNOWLEDGMENTS

It took a village to make this book. A literal village. I spent summers in my father's hometown of Kafr Abel, Jordan. I'd packed as many fantasy books, comics, and sketchbooks as Heathrow Airport's weight limit would allow.

It was in the shade of olive and fig trees that my mind left to Hogwarts, joined the Knights of the Round Table, and devoured volumes of manga. *Squire* is all the themes I love, in a setting I see myself in. This book is a whole lotta immigrant kid feelings.

I knew Nadia was my partner in this because we quickly found out we had this same stuttered, hyphenated experience growing up Arab-American. We shared the same nerdy connection that started in English, ended in Arabic, and still included a *Fullmetal Alchemist* reference. I just wanted to draw girls with swords, but with Nadia we were able to pull out Aiza's story from each other.

I must thank my editor Andrew Eliopulos, who called me up three years ago and asked me if I wanted to make a book, and I replied "I dunno that sounds like a lot of work" (I was right); and Alexandra Cooper, who pulled *Squire* across the finish line. I owe my everything to my agent, Charlie Olsen, who has helped me navigate the wild waters of publishing this whole time.

Endless love to my family, who would stop the car for every single reference photo I needed in Jordan and Turkey, paid off every library fee I racked up as a kid, and continues supporting this weird art thing I do.

الى ماما وبابا: لا اجد كلمات كافيه تعبر عن حبي وشكري لكما، على ما قدمتم لي من الدعم والدعاء.

All my love to boss man Thariq, Hisham (Squirefan23), Guru, and the whole Tilter crew who have suppored me from the very beginning. Thank you to my first reader, my cat Momo, for keeping me company during late nights of work and always reminding me to take breaks.

Thank you for reading!
- Sara Alfageeh

سارة الفقيه

ACKNOWLEDGMENTS

I've held the themes of what *Squire* would become in my heart for a long time, as long as I've wanted to write. I believed I would have to wait and work for years before making the book of my dreams.
But here we are, at the end of the book, a tangible manifestation of a nerdy childhood, a life's dream, and the support of countless people. Comics gave me community, and I'm thankful for that.

Firstly, I want to thank Sara for doing this with me. This book was created between hours long talk sessions on the phone, going to dinner and plotting directly on the tablecloth instead of eating, and lots of anime fight scene reference hunting. Out of all that, out of my own messy diaspora feelings about growing up where I did, when I did, and out of our friendship, I can say my debut book is, unflinchingly, exactly what I've always dreamed of doing.

I would like to thank my partner, Yuriy, for providing tireless emotional support and whose unwavering faith in me and my voice keeps me afloat on difficult days. I thank my cats, Lilith and Dash, for being wretched little monsters who are excellent at shedding and giving kisses.

I thank our editor, Andrew Eliopulos, and our agent, Charlie Olsen, for holding my hand through this entire experience. I thank every friend kind enough to read drafts and generally listen to me yammer about story. I thank Pantelis for his help in historical research. Thank you Tanoreen in Bay Ridge, Brooklyn, as *Squire* was basically written fueled on your musakhan.

And finally, I thank my dad, Raja, and my mom, Vida, for their support and encouragement as I embarked on this journey even when they weren't really sure what I was doing. You taught me to work hard and to speak up for the things I want and believe in, as in the words of my dad: Squeaky wheels get the oil.

All my gratitude,
Nadia Shammas

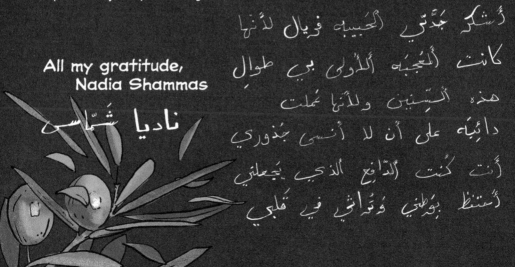

أُشكر جَدَّتي الحَبيبه فريال لأنَّها

كانَت العَجيبه الأُولى بي طوال

هذه السِّنين ولأَنَّها حَمَلَت

دائِيه على أن لا أنسى جُذوري

أَنت كُنت الدَّافِع الذي يَجعَلني

أُحتَفِظ بوَطني وتُراثي في قَلبي

ناديا شَمَّاس

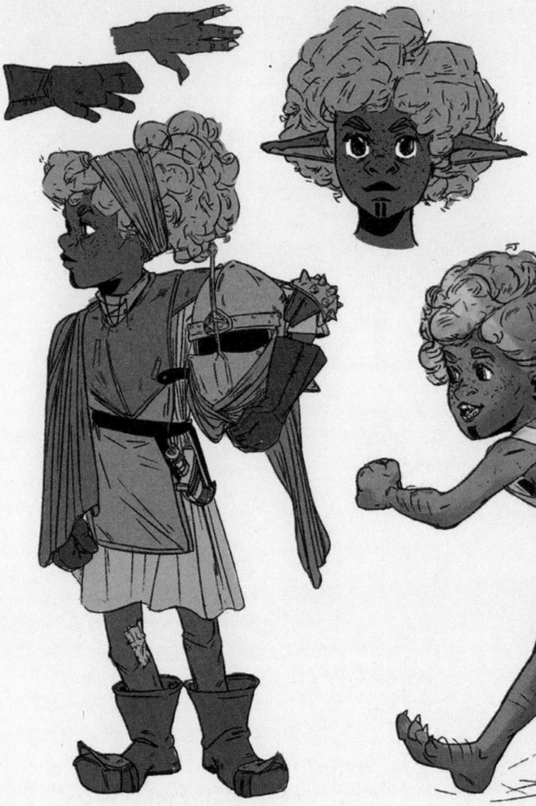

Sara:

When I first came up with *Squire*, it was for a homework assignment in my third year of art school.

I came up with a high-fantasy adventure of a young orc named Flea.

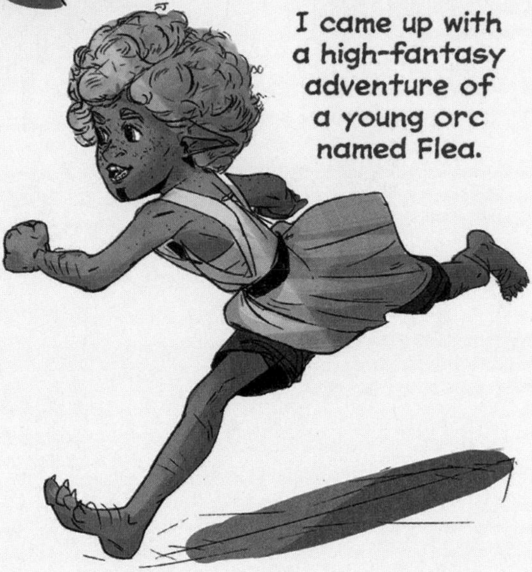

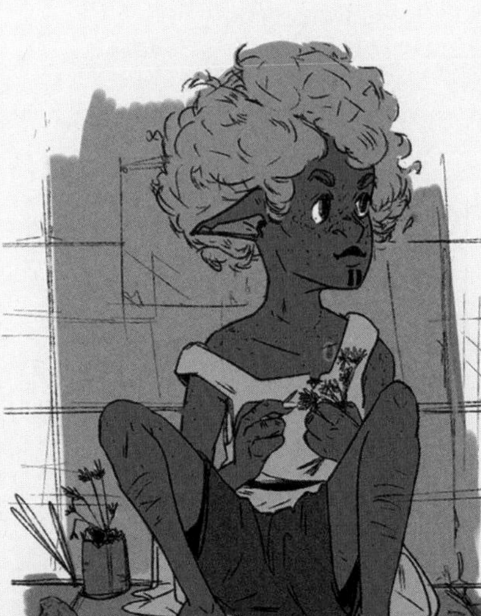

Sara:

I always had a fondness for young, scrappy girls with swords. Much of that same energy transferred to Aiza.

Flea's story was about traveling the land with a disgraced one-armed knight, hiding her identity as they signed up for tourneys.

Flea stayed behind in the sketchbook, as I toned down the magic and fantastical elements of *Squire*, and wanted to age up our main protagonist into more of a teenager.

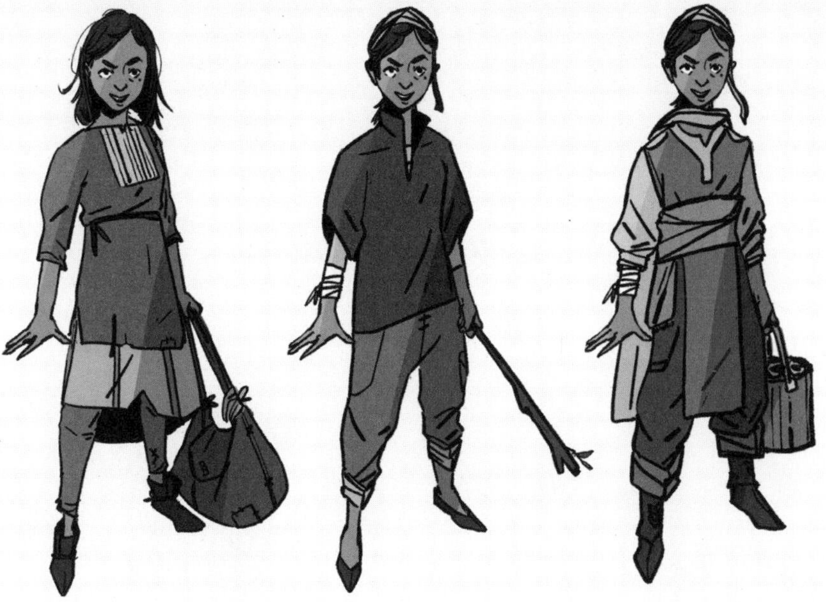

Sara:

Aiza was meant to look like the runt of the litter next to all the others in training. I wanted her to be very expressive in her body language.

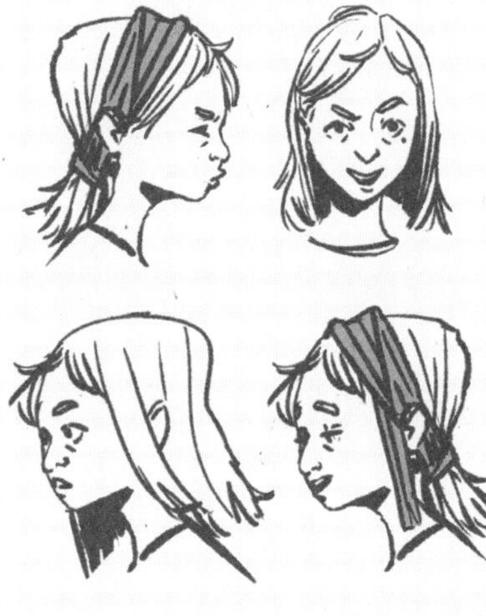

The boot camp uniform was tricky. It had to be practical and look good on many different body types. I took a lot of references from visual archives from Turkey and Syria in particular.

The tattoo was one of the first details I chose, inspired by Bedouin and Berber traditions. My family is Jordanian and these geometric tattoos are part of the Bedouin culture, especially for women. My great aunts had similar designs tattooed on their chins and cheeks.

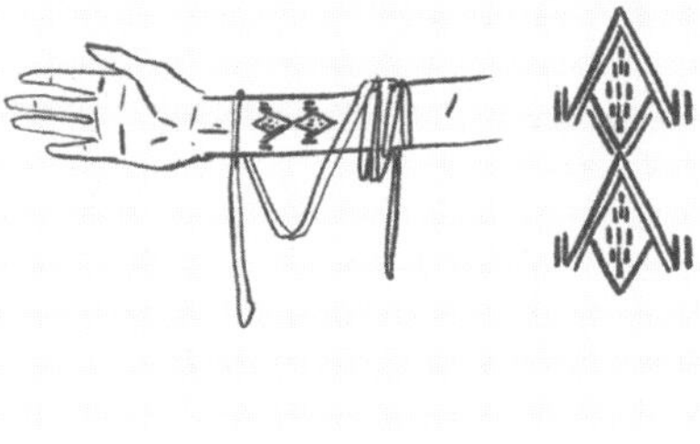

Sara:

Doruk changed the least, from when I first came up with *Squire* until the final page years later.

He and Aiza were drawn as an unlikely pair. Designed as total opposites and yet they are the ones who understand each other best.

I originally wanted him to carry a giant shield, but now my drawing hand is thankful that I scrapped that idea.

So grumpy. So beefy.

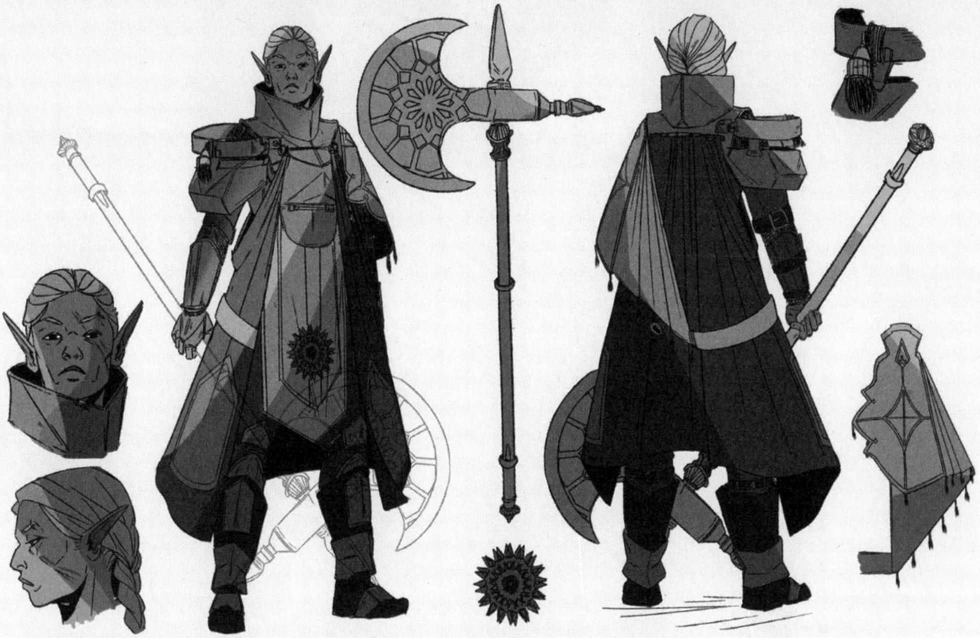

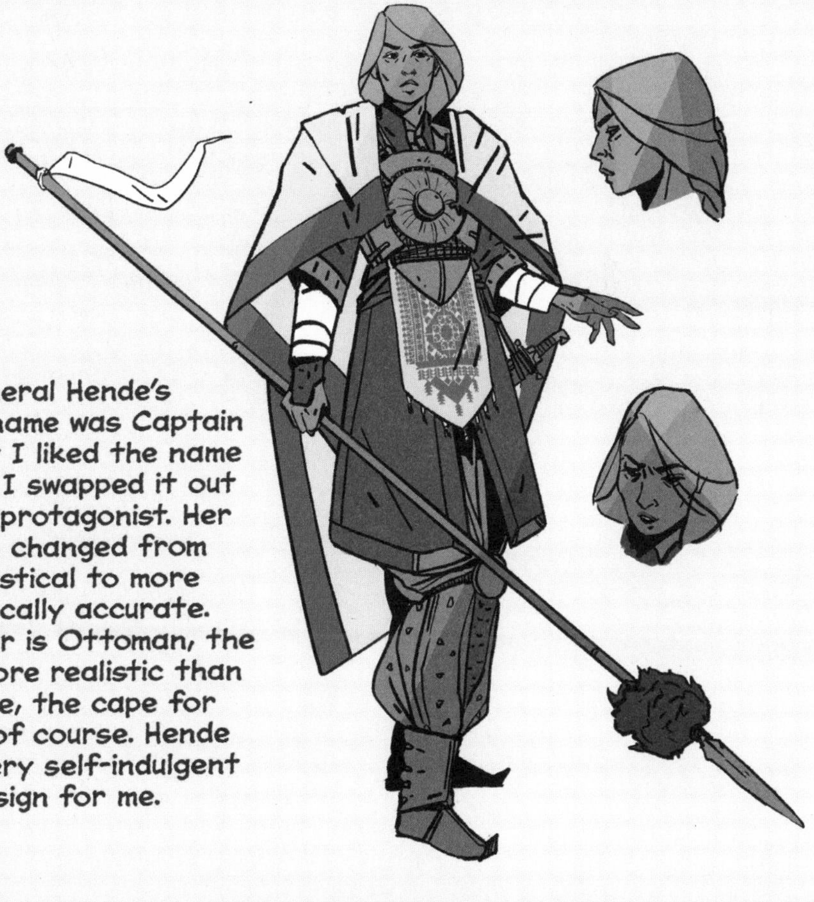

Sara:

General Hende's original name was Captain Aiza, but I liked the name so much I swapped it out for our protagonist. Her design changed from fantastical to more historically accurate. The armor is Ottoman, the spear more realistic than the axe, the cape for drama of course. Hende was a very self-indulgent design for me.

SQUIRE AND HISTORY

I've grown up a lover of fantasy, but fantasy didn't always love me back. Honestly, most of the media I adored didn't. If Arabs were even hinted at in Western fantasy, we were the orcs. The barbarians. The savages with strange customs who needed to be tamed and civilized, usually by an attractive white person. Lots of blood magic, twisted souls, and nefarious sorcerers on our end; a lot of immortal beings of benevolent good on theirs. But, as a young person, you take what you get. Ultimately, the danger is that you start to believe these narratives about yourself. Perhaps the elves are the good to strive for, perhaps the ones who look or sound like you are to be rejected.

The twist of the knife is that this doesn't just appear in our fiction. The way history is told in our classrooms and textbooks is a cut-and-dried timeline of events and names. Tales of empires expanding and falling, tales of heroic figures, tales of how the world came to be are presented in such a way as to suggest that it's natural. This is the way the world is and it's inevitable. In many ways, fantasy and history walk hand in hand, but there's an important thing about the way we view history in comparison: history is, above all else, neutral. If you are on the outskirts of the empire's convenient history, however, you know it's anything but.

Constructing a story, even a story from your own memory, requires knitting together the things that happened in a way that makes sense to someone else, whether or not it happened so cleanly. The way you tell a story is informed by your own perspective and by your own goals in telling it. History exists in the same way. History is made not by the figures who we talk about today but by those who are invested in documenting and shaping it. In their hands, events are a tool. Characters are a tool. History, altogether, is a tool, and tools are neutral until they're wielded. When you listen to a story, think about who is telling it. When you listen to a history, think about who it serves.

In *Squire*, history is as much a weapon as Aiza's blade. The story of a previously illustrious empire, something to aspire to, is used to justify expansion into various neighboring countries. Refugees are second-class citizens who can aspire to integrate by serving the empire. And if you live in the heart of the empire, you serve one way or another, through taxes, through relative safety compared to your relatives back home. If you are Arab-American, you know this. You know what it is to hear about drone strikes and wonder when you might hear about it landing close to your family's ancestral home. You know how it feels to watch the country you were raised in be in constant struggle with the place where you're from. You know what it is to be disconnected both from back home and from where you're sitting right now. But you also know, there's so much to love about being Arab-American. That joy is part of your personal history too.

I wrote *Squire* in the hopes of writing something that not only made sense to me, but reflected me and the people around me. It is a story about someone stuck between conflicting existences realizing that empire never holds place for the conquered. Learning to interrogate history contextualizes the present. History is, in actuality, quite personal. All narratives should be interrogated, including this one. But don't let any one story tell you who you are.

No more orcs. No magical chosen ones. Just people learning how to unlearn the justifications of colonialism and finding their way. Each of us must find our own way there: It's my hope that you found something in this book to help you on your journey.

- Nadia Shammas

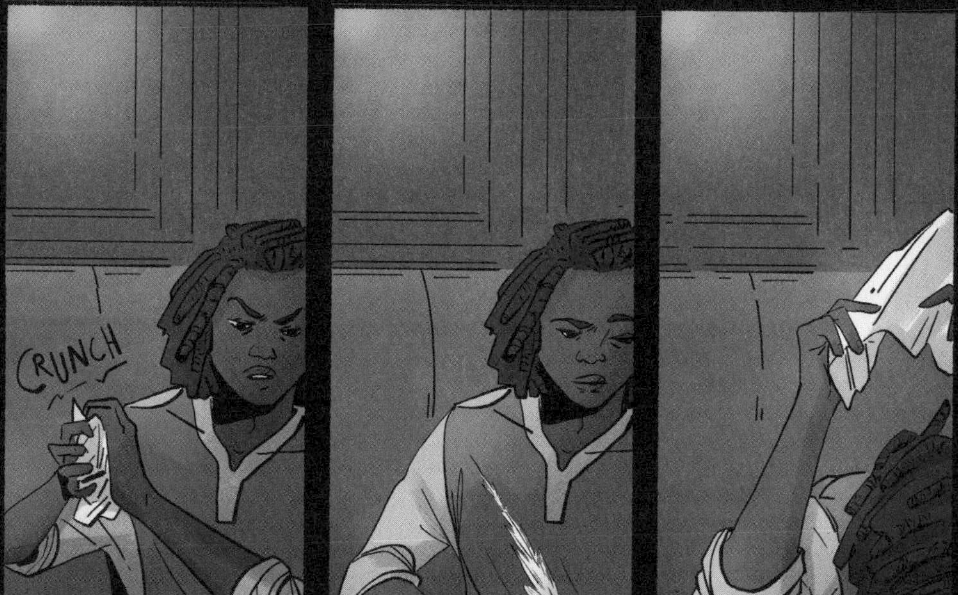
CRUNCH

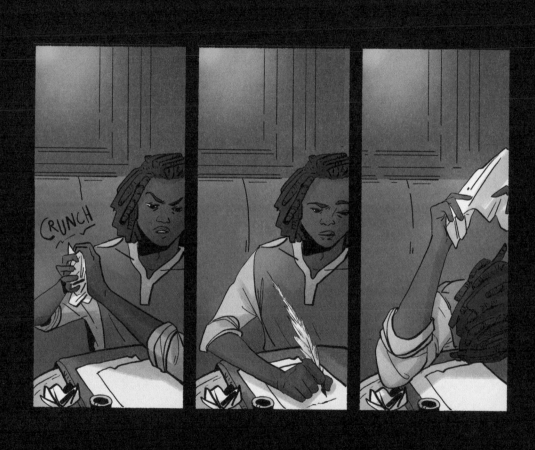

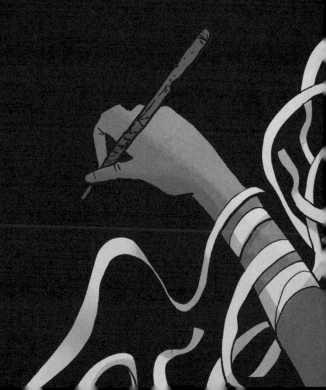

THE MAKING
OF A PAGE

Panel one: We see a shot of AIZA practicing tying a tourniquet to HUSNI's arm. (FORESHADOWING)

1. AIZA (letter): There's just a ton of other stuff too. I'm learning first aid.

Panel two: AIZA is sitting cross-legged on the ground with a plain curved dagger in one hand and a whetstone in the other. She's looking up at an instructor we can't fully see, listening intently.

2. AIZA (letter): Weapon care.

Panel three: Long shot of the kids, including AIZA, running out of the sleeping tent area under the moonlight. AIZA is lagging a bit in the back, rubbing her eyes. A drill instructor carries a torch in one hand and a large bell in the other, which she rings hard.

3. AIZA (letter) : We do drills every day. Sometimes they wake us up in the middle of the night just to do laps.
4. DRILL INSTRUCTOR: Go, go, go! Action can strike at any moment. A Knight is always prepared!
    SFX: *ding, ding, ding*

Panel four: We finally see AIZA in the present, actually letter writing. I imagine she's on the floor in the large sleeping area, writing nearby one of the hanging lanterns. She's writing furiously.

5. AIZA (letter): Which makes no sense to me, I get that we're supposed to be tough and ready for anything, but sleep is important too and this is just—

Panel five: In her vigor, she accidentally gets some wet ink on her bandage and smudges some of the words of the letter. She looks at the damage, wondering whether she should fix it.

NO COPY

Panel six: She decides to ignore it and keep writing.

6. AIZA (letter): It's better than the strategy lessons at least. I'd rather run every night all night than sit through more tactical lectures.

THE SCRIPT

NADIA:

Comics doesn't necessarily have a standard script-writing style, so I do what makes sense to me. I write my scripts for the artists I am working with, so I tend to use references I know they like as best as I can. I focus more on the feeling of a moment than choreographing every action, so that I allow space for my collaborator to interpret the scene. Since the lion's share of work is on the art end, I try to include as many reference materials in the actual script as possible.

SARA:

Nadia and I conceptualized this story together, but Nadia is the one who stopped *Squire* from becoming three hundred pages of jokes I think are funny.

A good script is deceivingly simple. Let the art talk. Trust your collaborators.

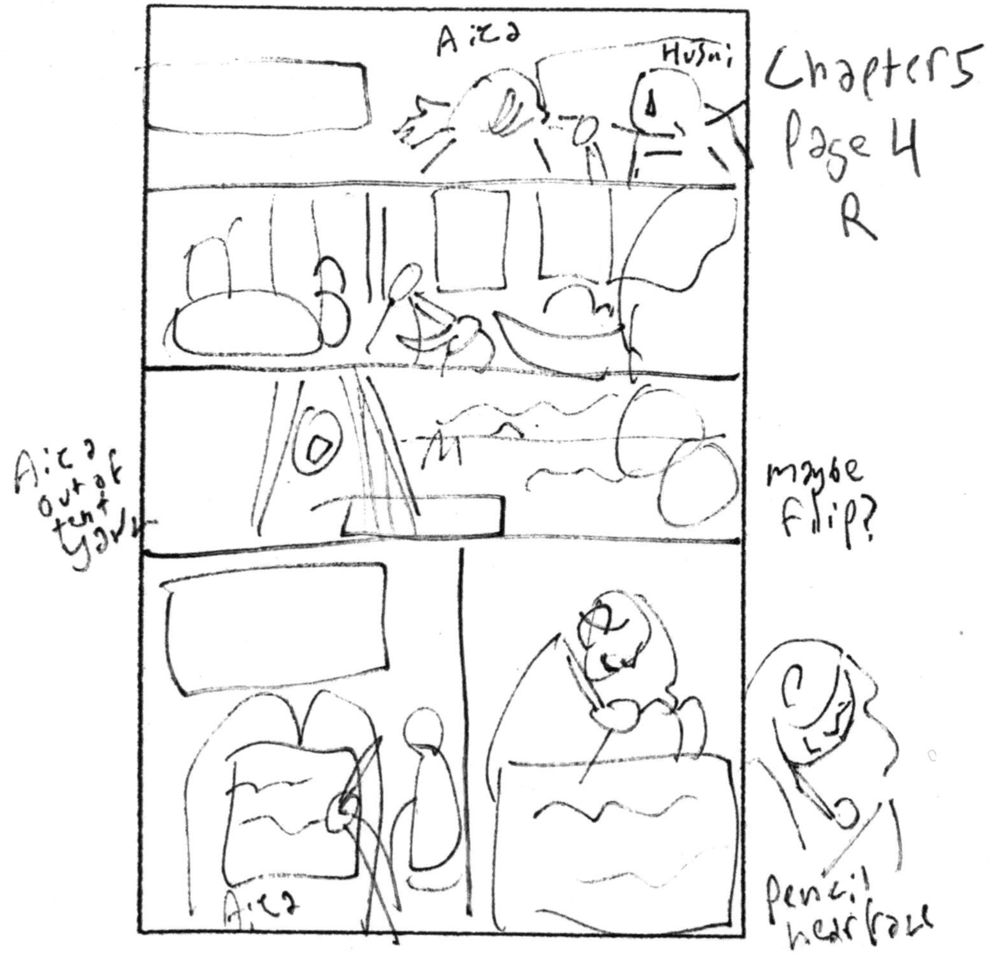
Chapter 5
Page 4
R
Aiza
Husni
Aiza out of tent yard
maybe flip?
Aiza
pencil near face

THUMBNAILS

SARA:

Thumbnails are what I draw as I'm reading the script. It is the only step I do on pen and paper, not digitally. I use super cheap paper and the worst pen I have around so I'm not tempted to make a good drawing. The goal for thumbnails is to make sure that everything fits, and the basic panel structure actually makes sense. These drawings are very small and allow me to test ideas quickly and easily.

No one sees this stage; these scribbles only make sense to me.

PENCILS AND LETTERING

SARA:

Now the real drawing starts. Technically the stage is called "pencils," but I do this stage digitally. I work entirely in Photoshop. I draw on a Wacom Cintiq tablet when I'm at home and on an iPad when I'm traveling.

This stage takes the longest for me. It requires a lot of focus and decision-making. I dig up references, research for specific details, and do all the lettering (placing the dialogue and word balloons).

I have to make it *just* clear enough so my editor can understand what the heck I'm doing, and rough enough so I don't waste too much time perfecting a drawing I might have to change later.

INKING

SARA:

My editor gives me any notes they have, and my assistant, Lynette, cleans up my panels and word balloons. After that I get to do my favorite part: inking!

Here I redraw the page properly, add all the fun details, and decide what parts of the page should be described with line details and what areas should be detailed with color instead.

I have to be careful not to spend too much time on this stage because I could ink forever.

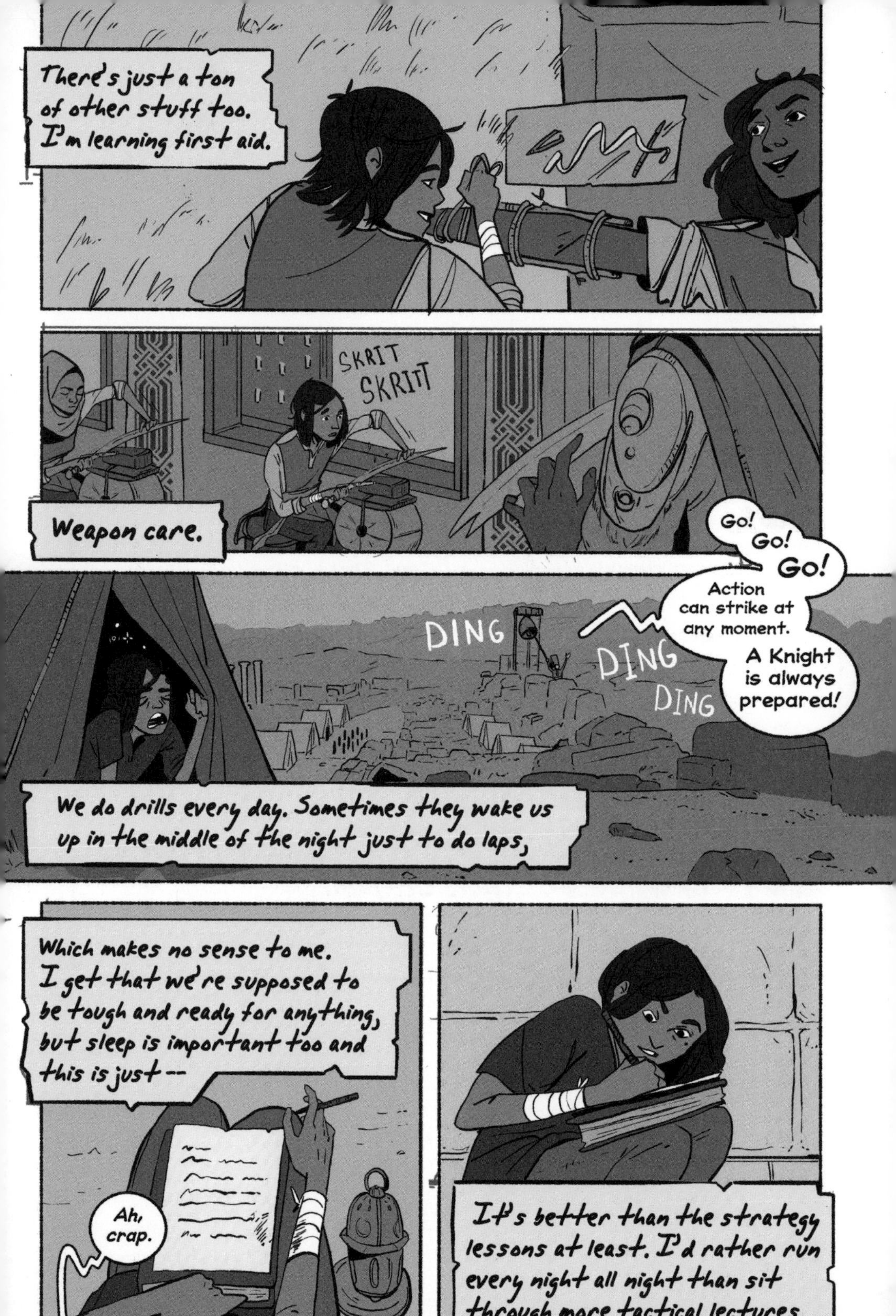
There's just a ton of other stuff too. I'm learning first aid.
SKRIT
SKRITT
Weapon care.
Go!
Go!
Go!
Action can strike at any moment.
A Knight is always prepared!
DING
DING
DING
We do drills every day. Sometimes they wake us up in the middle of the night just to do laps,
Which makes no sense to me. I get that we're supposed to be tough and ready for anything, but sleep is important too and this is just --
Ah, crap.
It's better than the strategy lessons at least. I'd rather run every night all night than sit through more tactical lectures.

FLATS

SARA:

Flats are **placeholder** colors that are put down to make the process of digitally coloring and painting work much easier. It is a time consuming but very important step so changes can be made easily.

The flat colors of Chapter 1 through Chapter 4 are by my assistant, *Lynette Wong.*

The flat colors of Chapter 5 through Chapter 14 are by artist *Mara Jayne Carpenter.*

FINAL COLORS

SARA:

Figuring out how to color *Squire* was one of the hardest creative problems I have faced as an artist. It's this careful balance of what's JUST enough detail to make the art feel alive, but stopping right before the process makes you lose your mind.

Your influences + what you enjoy doing + your specific brand of laziness = Art Style.

Storytelling with light and shadows was very important to me. I took many photos in Jordan and Turkey, and I tried to pull as many colors from the region as I could carry back with me.

Lynette Wong was my color assistant throughout this book, re-creating my style and skillfully working with my wild notes.